Praise for *T*

"*Trial of Intentions* is a sto [...] ing and sacrifice, in an [...] world where characters face difficult and heartbreaking choices. Orullian is doing things I haven't seen in other books, including an original system of magic. This tale will resonate with readers long after the cover is closed."

—Robin Hobb,
New York Times bestselling author

"Peter Orullian is a master of dark-chocolate fantasy; bitter, harsh, and sweet at once. *Trial of Intentions* grabs us firmly by the breastplate and challenges us to face a world of moral contradictions, stunning characters, and harsh choices. An unflinching fantasy."

—Tracy Hickman,
New York Times bestselling author

"*Trial of Intentions* is a book enormous in scope and in intricacy, with a welter of political, cultural, and magical intrigues, behind which lies the role of song in preserving a myriad of cultures, all of which disagree with each other to some extent, even as it becomes apparent to the reader that, without some degree of cooperation, all will suffer, if not perish. A challenging story about challenged cultures, and one well told."

—L. E. Modesitt, Jr.

"Fans of George R. R. Martin or Robert Jordan will enjoy Orullian's intricate but nonetheless immersive story."

—*Booklist*

TOR BOOKS BY PETER ORULLIAN

The Unremembered
Trial of Intentions

TRIAL OF INTENTIONS

BOOK TWO OF

The Vault of Heaven

PETER ORULLIAN

TOR®
fantasy

A TOM DOHERTY ASSOCIATES BOOK
NEW YORK

This is a work of fiction. All of the characters, organizations, and events portrayed in this novel are either products of the author's imagination or are used fictitiously.

TRIAL OF INTENTIONS

Copyright © 2015 by Peter Orullian

A Tor Book
Published by Tom Doherty Associates, LLC
175 Fifth Avenue
New York, NY 10010

www.tor-forge.com

Tor® is a registered trademark of Tom Doherty Associates, LLC.

ISBN 978-0-7653-6470-8

Our books may be purchased in bulk for promotional, educational, or business use. Please contact your local bookseller or the Macmillan Corporate and Premium Sales Department at 1-800-221-7945, extension 5442, or by e-mail at MacmillanSpecialMarkets@macmillan.com.

First Edition: May 2015
First Mass Market Edition: April 2016

Printed in the United States of America

0 9 8 7 6 5 4 3 2 1

To Mom and Dad.
Your example has meant everything.

· ACKNOWLEDGMENTS ·

Something happened on the way to book two. Life, mostly. Upheavals at work. A change of editors. Loved ones passing. A friend taking his own life—more on that later. A writer (me) trying to persist. Trying not to become cynical. Trying to write the best book he could.

To whatever degree I succeeded at any of this, it's owed in large part to others.

First, my wife, Cathy. In this book, there's the notion of a glyph of power. A glyph that represents the pole-star, a fixed point in the heavens by which to navigate. It also represents the continuity of family. Cathy's my pole-star. Also, she has the best laugh. Ever.

Next come my "little ones." If I ever decide to get all "meta" about The Vault of Heaven, I'll probably find that on some level having kids changed the resonances I both seek and feel in fiction. Also, you're never too old for a tickle-fight.

My agent, Nat Sobel, is an extraordinary man. Beyond his superb agenting, he says the exact right thing I need to hear, and does it with an economy of language that's really rather stunning. Also, he knows where to get the best New York bagels.

My editor, Claire Eddy. What a wonderful thing to find trust. Mine for Claire. Hers for me. I didn't start this Vault of Heaven journey with Claire. But I damn sure hope to finish it with her. Also, she taught me the delightful phrase "And that doesn't suck."

I need to mention my beta-readers. Especially those who read the first draft of this book, which topped 450,000 words. Pretty sure there's a sainthood in it for them. Also, collectively, they do the best snark.

Then there's the army that is Tor. Folks like Bess Cozby,

Patty Garcia, Leah Withers, Ardi Alspach, Irene Gallo, the Tor.com crew, the production team (I appreciate your patience), Phyllis Azar and the superb marketing department, and others I've likely forgotten. Thank you. Also, you guys rock!

A special thanks to the Tor sales team. I wasn't in the room when some of the "meetings" took place, but my editor shared them with me. I'm deeply grateful to you for your support and enthusiasm and publishing acumen. Also, you're flat damn creative.

Thanks, this time, too, to Tom Doherty. He graciously accepts my dinner invitations whenever I'm in New York. I learn something new every time. His support on this journey has meant a great deal. Also, the man has stories.

And a very special thanks to Linda Quinton. Linda has been a key decision-maker in how things have evolved for me. I have immense respect for her. And I'm grateful for the support she's shown me and my writing. She also rocks!

Here, again, I'll thank my parents. The most decent people I know. They taught me the ethics of hard work, doing what I say I will do, and fairness. They taught me sacrifice by sacrificing for *me*. Hopefully, I'll be able to adequately express my gratitude to them *someday* (yes, that's a Trans-Siberian Orchestra reference).

Finally, and most of all, to my readers. Thank you for your patience. Like I said, life happened. And since it's been four years since *The Unremembered,* I wrote *Trial of Intentions* so that it could be an entry point to the series. I thought that just made sense. Readers unfamiliar with *The Unremembered* can jump into the series with this book. Of course, there's deeper context if you read book one. But I've peppered in the backstory, so whether or not you've read *The Unremembered,* you're covered.

And as to the story, after finishing *Trial of Intentions* and going back to do some revisions, I saw a few themes that had worked their way into the book. That's how theme happens for me. Organically. And I only see it in hindsight. This time, a person's *intention* as a powerful part of what they say and do was certainly one of them. The study of the sky—astronomy—and the wonder and perspective it inspires was another. And maybe on a deeper level was the topic of suicide.

I mentioned above that a friend of mine chose to leave this life. The harsh world of the Scarred Lands in my series has always been marked by those who do the same. But I feel sure now that the emotional resonance of recently losing a friend to suicide worked its way into Tahn's story here. And looking back, I remembered it all, and it filled my mind again (yes, that's a Disturbed reference). Was a damned hard thing.

And so maybe I do have one more thanks to give. Maudlin as it may sound, I'll go ahead and thank: music. For me, it plays a part in every aspect of life. Sometimes to lift, as good intentions try to do. Sometimes to soothe, like looking up at the stars. Sometimes to prepare for my own battles, when I'm angry or hurt. So it won't surprise anyone to see music move closer to center stage in *Trial of Intentions*. To lift. To soothe. To take to battle.

N

THE BOURNE

QUAROL UICHAR

SHADOW OF THE RAIN

WORLD'S FOUNT

MAI WOOD

NORTH WATCH

DARKLING PLAINS

NALLAN

SEVER ENS

MAL'TARA

MALSETIC

THE RIM

MALVALUT

MAL REEVE LUX

THE DIVIDE

KAMAS THRONE

CON LAVEN FLU

VOHNCE

NOB PLAINS OF SEDAGH

MYRR

THE HOLLOWS

AERETONUS LAKE

EDD FORT

DESTICK MAL

MAERD

ATECHRE

BRIGHT HARBOR

REACHES

KAU-HREN

EBON

SUWNOS

REDAL-TE

SEALD

NDAN

SODEN FEN

THE EAST OF
AESHAU VAAL
IN THE AGE OF
RUMOR

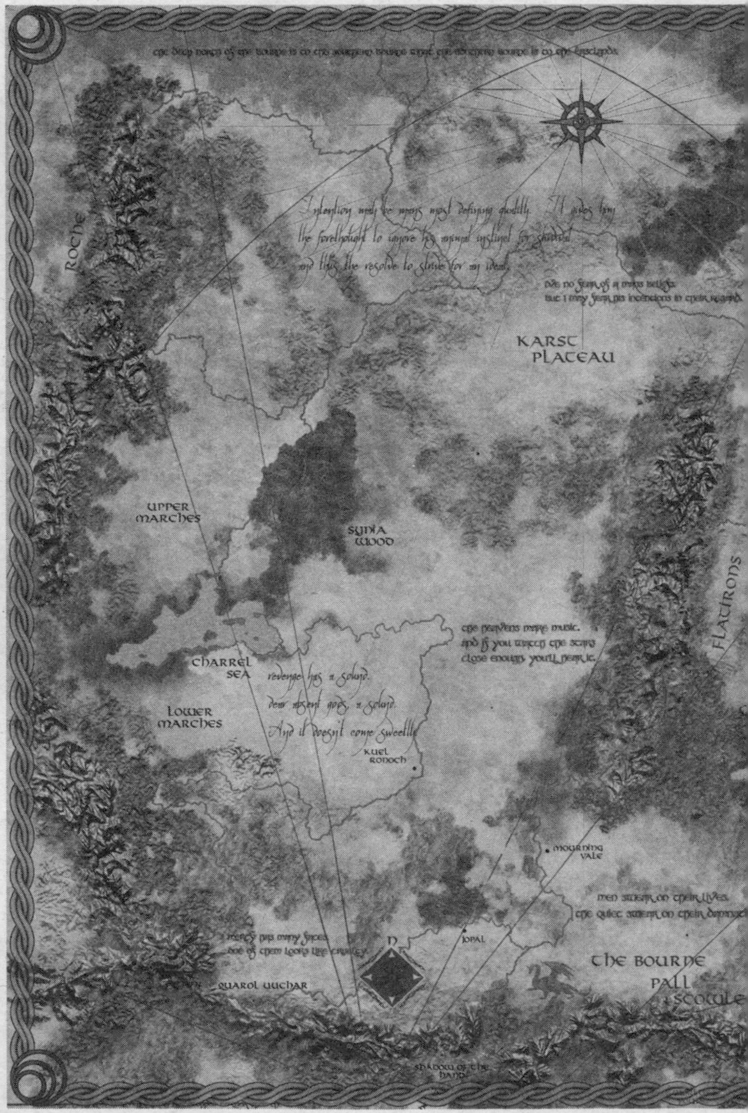

Intention may be man's most defining quality. It gives him
the forethought to ignore his animal instinct for survival
and thus the resolve to strive for an ideal.
no fear of a man's beliefs
but I may fear his intentions in their regard.
KARST PLATEAU
ROCHE
UPPER MARCHES
SYNIA WOOD
FLATIRONS
The heavens make music.
And if you watch the stars
close enough, you'll hear it.
CHARREL SEA
revenge has a sound.
dear absent gods, a sound.
And it doesn't come sweetly.
LOWER MARCHES
KUEL RONOCH
MOURNING VALE
Men swear on their lives.
The quiet swear on their
mercy has many faces
one of them looks like cruelty.
JOPAL
N
QUAROL UUCHAR
THE BOURNE
PALL
SCOWLE
SHADOW OF THE HAND

THE
BOURNE
IN THE AGE OF
RUMOR

LACUS
PLAIN

AEOLIAN COAST

LATEM
FOREST

KASAL
SEA

SALVIA
HAPPARAL

RIDGE
DUNES

WAELAND

LOESS VALLEUS

ARCHOLLEN

LAEN
MOORS

SAECULA FOREST

PALL MOUNTAINS

a song will fill the hole inside a man
better than anything else ever will.
the thing that sends him up upon
he'd rather remain down in a song.

that for which we have no words is infinitely
more powerful than that for which we do.
this is as true of hate as it is of love.

doing things because
that's what friends do
when the heat falls

all things have a resonant signature
and so all things have a song.

I feel it, too.

—Considered by some Aubade Grove philosophers
to be an irreducible proof of Resonance

• BOOK TWO •

Trial of Intentions

• PROLOGUE •

A Third Purpose

Encouragements are drawn from living things—trees, grasses, animals. First and best from family. All are vital. All nourish. Perishment results from the absence of these.

—From *The Effect of Absences,* a correlative war doctrine originating in the Bourne

After long years in the Scarred Lands, Tahn Junell realized their patrols held a third purpose.

First, and most obviously, they were meant to provide early warning when visitors or strangers came into the Scar. Patrol routes held long sight lines of the wide, barren lands. From a distance, newcomers could be easily spotted and reported.

On a second, more practical level, patrols were used to build and maintain stamina for fight sessions. Every ward of the Scar—age three to nineteen—spent no less than six hours a day in ritualized combat training.

It wasn't until later that Tahn finally came to realize a subtle third reason for patrols. They were a way for wards of the Scar to monitor themselves and guard against one of their own wandering from home, alone.

With the purpose of self-slaughter.

Tahn and Alemdra ran fast, arriving at Gutter Ridge well ahead of sunrise. They slowed to a walk, catching their breath and sharing smiles.

"You're starting to slow me down," Alemdra teased. "I think it's because I'm becoming a woman, and you're still a boy."

He laughed. "Well, maybe if we're going to keep running patrols together, I'll just put a saddle on you, then."

She hit him in the arm, and they sat together with their legs dangling from one of the few significant ridges in the Scar.

Alemdra was twelve today, barely older than Tahn. And he intended to kiss her. Seeing the glint in her eye, he wondered if she'd guessed his intention. But if so, the unspoken secret only added to the anticipation.

Casually wagging their toes, they looked east.

"See that?" He pointed at the brightest star in the eastern hemisphere. She nodded. "That's Katia Shonay, the morning star. It's really a planet."

"That so." She squinted as if doing so might bring the distant object into sharper focus.

"Katia Shonay means 'lovelorn' in Dimnian." He liked few things better than talking about the sky. "There's this whole story about how a furrow tender fell in love with a woman of the court."

She made no effort to conceal her suspicion of his timing for sharing the story of this particular planet. "You might make a good furrow tender someday. If you work hard at it, that is."

"Actually," he countered, smiling, "the story's only complete in the conjunction of Rushe Symone—the planet named after the god of plenty and favor. You know, bountiful harvests and autumn bacchanalia." He nearly blushed over the last part, having learned the richness of bacchanal rituals. "Rych is the largest planet—"

She was giving him a look. *The* look. "You seem to think you're smarter than us now."

"What do you mean *now*?" And he started laughing.

She broke down laughing, too. "You really liked it there, didn't you? In Aubade Grove."

"I'd go back tomorrow if it didn't mean leaving you behind." It came out sounding more honest than he'd intended, but he wasn't embarrassed. He stared off at Katia. "It's amazing, Alemdra. No patrols. No fight sessions. Just books. Study. Skyglassing to discover what's up there." He gestured grandly at the eastern sky.

She smiled, sharing his enthusiasm for the few years he'd been away before being called back here. "Do you think you'll ever leave the Scar for good?" There was a small, fatal note in her voice.

He turned to see her expression—the same one she always wore when they talked about Grant. While all the wards were like Grant's adoptive children, Tahn was the man's actual son. He supposed someday he might leave this place, especially if he ever learned who his mother was. If she was still alive.

"Eventually. After my father goes to his earth. I don't think I could leave him here alone." Tahn threw a rock and listened for it to hit far below. In his head he began doing some math to determine the height of the ridge. *Initial velocity, count of six to the rock's impact, acceleration due to gravity—*

"He'll never be alone, Tahn," she said, interrupting his calculations. "Not as long as the *cradle* is here."

Tahn nodded grimly. The Forgotten Cradle. It served as a big damn reminder of abandonment to all the wards of the Scar. And it was how most of them came to this place. Every cycle of the first moon a babe was placed in the hollow of a dead bristlecone pine. Orphans. Foundlings. And sometimes children whose parents just didn't want them anymore. Grant retrieved each child, tried to find it a proper home outside the Scar. Those for whom no arrangements could be made came to live with them *inside* the Scar. Not knowing their actual day of birth, wards celebrated their "cradleday"—the day they were rescued from the tree. Like he and Alembra were doing for her today.

"I don't know why you feel any loyalty to stay, either." She looked away to where the sun would crest the mountains to the east. "Not after what he's done to you."

His father put more pressure on him. Tahn's lessons were less predictable. Harder. One might wonder if, being his son, he bore the brunt of his father's exile here. A sentence he'd earned for defying the regent. And his father could never leave; otherwise who would fetch the babes from the cradle?

Their special morning had struck a somber note. But he couldn't let her comment lie, even though in his heart he agreed. "He just has a different way of teaching."

Alemdra seemed to realize she'd touched too close to private insecurities. "If you go, will you take me with you?"

Tahn smiled, grateful for a change in the direction of their morning chat. "You think you can keep up? I mean, I *have* been off to college and all."

This time she hit him in the shoulder, soft enough to let him know she wasn't offended, hard enough to let him know she was no rube. Then they fell into another companionable silence. The sun was near to rising. They wouldn't speak again until its rays glimmered in their eyes. This was Tahn's favorite time in the Scar. Morning had a kind of wonder in it. As if the day might end differently than the one before it. That moment of sun first lighting the sky was something he made time every day to witness. And he liked these sunrise moments best when Alemdra was with him.

He wanted to kiss her when the sun began to break. Sentimental, maybe, but it felt right anyway. As the time drew closer, his left leg began to shimmy all on its own.

What if he'd misread their growing friendship? What if she rejected his kiss? He'd be ruining future chances to run with her on morning patrol.

When the sun's first rays broke over the horizon, he turned to her, his mind racing to find some words, debating if he should just grasp her by the shoulders and do it.

He neither spoke nor grasped. In the second he turned, Alemdra inclined with a swift grace and put her mouth on his. Her eyes were open, and she left her lips there for a long time before closing them and uttering a sigh of innocent delight.

The sound brought Tahn's heart to a pounding thump, and he knew he loved her. The other wards would tease him; maybe try to convince him he was just a boy and couldn't know such feelings. Let them. Because even if he and Alemdra never knew a more intimate moment than this, he would always remember her kiss, her sigh.

Sometime later, she pulled away, her eyes opening again. She smiled—not with embarrassment, but happily. And together they watched the sun finish its rise into the sky.

Then an urgent rhythm interrupted the morning stillness. Distant footfalls. Someone running. Together they turned toward the sound. A hundred strides to the east, from behind a copse of dead trees, a figure emerged at a dead run toward the cliff. They watched in horror as their friend Devin leapt from the edge. Her arms and legs pinwheeled briefly before she gave in to the fall, her body pulled earthward toward the jag of rocks far below.

Alemdra screamed. The shrill sound echoed across the deep, rocky ravine as their friend fell down. And down. Tahn stood up on impulse, but could only watch as Devin stared skyward, letting the force of attraction do its awful work. *Initial velocity, acceleration due to gravity . . .*

A few moments later, Devin struck the hardpan below with a sharp cry. And lay instantly still.

"Devin!" Tahn wailed, wanting his friend to take it back. Angry, frustrated tears filled his eyes.

Alemdra turned to him. They shared a long, painful look. They'd failed their third purpose. They'd been so caught up in Alemdra's cradleday, in the peace of sunrise, in their first kiss, that they'd missed any signs of Devin. One of their closest friends.

Alemdra sank to her knees, sobs wracking her body. Tahn put his arms around her and together they wept for Devin. At Gutter Ridge, in the first rays of day, with Katia Shonay still rising in the east, they wept for another ward who'd lost her battle with the Scar.

The third purpose. Tahn understood the feeling that got into those who made this choice. Every ward had some kind of defense against it. Or tried. His defense was the sky, morning and sunrise. Those moments gave him something to look forward to, to find hope in.

Sometime later, they started down to gather the body, keeping a griever's silence as they went. The sun had grown hot by the time they got to Devin. They stood a while before Alemdra broke the silence. "She turned fifteen last week."

Wards who found their way out of the Scar often did so soon after their cradleday.

Alemdra sniffed, wiping away tears. There was a familiar worry in her voice when she whispered, "She was strong. Stronger than most."

Tahn knew she meant in spirit. He nodded. "That's what scares me."

They fell silent again, knowing soon enough they'd need

to build a litter to drag the body home. There'd be a note in Devin's pocket. There was always a note. It would speak of apology. Of regret. Of the inability to suffer the Scar another day. There'd be no blame laid on Grant. Actually, he'd be thanked for caring for them, for trying to teach them to survive in the world. But mostly, the note would be about what *wasn't* written on the paper. It would be about how the Scar somehow amplified the abandonment that had brought a ward to the Forgotten Cradle in the first place.

The notes were all the same, and were always addressed to Grant, anyway. Patrols usually didn't bother looking for them.

Alemdra went slowly to Devin's side and knelt. Hunched over the body, she brushed tenderly at Devin's hair, speaking in a soothing tone—the kind one uses with a child, or the very sick. Her shoulders began to rise and fall again with sobs she could no longer hold back.

Tahn stepped forward and put an arm around her, trying this time to be strong.

"It gets inside." Alemdra tapped her chest. "You can't ever really get out of the Scar, can you? Even if you leave." She looked up at Tahn. Her expression said she wanted to be argued with, convinced otherwise.

Tahn could only stare back. He'd gotten out of the Scar—a little bit, anyway—during his time in Aubade Grove. Maybe.

This time, Alemdra *did* look for the note. It wasn't hard to find. But when she unfolded the square of parchment, it *was* different. No words at all. A drawing of a woman, maybe forty or so, beautifully rendered with deep laugh lines around her eyes and mouth, and a biggish nose. Devin had talent that way. Drawing without making everything dreamlike.

The likeness brought fresh sobs from Alemdra. "It's how she imagined her mother."

That tore at Tahn's fragile bravery. He could see in the drawing hints of Devin as an older woman. Simple thing to want to know a parent's face. *Dead gods, Devin, I'm sorry.*

• CHAPTER ONE •

The Right Draw

Mercy has many faces. One of them looks like cruelty.

—Reconciliationist defense of the gods' placement
of the Quiet inside the Bourne

Tahn Junell raced north across the Soliel plain, and
his past raced with him. He ran in the dark and cold of
predawn. A canopy of bright stars shone in clear skies above.
And underfoot, his boots pounded an urgent rhythm against
the shale. In his left hand, he clenched his bow. In his mind,
growing dread pushed away the crush of his recently returned
memory. Ahead, still out of sight, marching on the city of
Naltus Far . . . came the Quiet.

Abandoning gods. The Quiet. Just a few moon cycles ago,
these storied races had been to Tahn just that. Stories. Stories
he'd believed, but only in that distant way that death concerned the living. *Their* story told of being herded and sealed
deep in the far west and north—distant lands known as the
Bourne, a place created by the gods before they'd abandoned
the world as lost.

One of his Far companions tapped his shoulder and
pointed. "Over there." Ahead on the left stood a dolmen risen
from great slabs of shale.

Tahn concentrated, taking care where he put his feet, trying to move without drawing any attention. The three Far
from the city guard ran close, their flight over the stones quiet
as a whisper on the plain. They'd insisted on bearing him
company. There'd been no time to argue.

Through light winds that carried the scent of shale and
sage, they ran. A hundred strides on, they ducked into a shallow depression beside the dolmen. In the lee side of the tomb,
Tahn drew quick breaths, the Far hardly winded.

"I'm Daen," the Far captain said softly. He showed Tahn a wry smile—acquaintances coming here, now—and put out his hand.

"Tahn." He clasped the Far's hand in the grip of friendship.

"I know. This is Jarron and Aelos." Daen gestured toward the two behind him. Each nodded a greeting. "Now, do you want to tell us why we've rushed headlong toward several colloughs of Bar'dyn?" Daen's smile turned inquiring.

Tahn looked in the direction of the advancing army. It was still a long way off. But he pictured it in his head. Just one collough was a thousand strong. So, several of them . . . *deafened gods!* And the Bar'dyn: a Quiet race two heads taller than most men and twice as broad; their hide like elm bark, but tougher, more pliable.

He listened. Only the sound of heavy feet on shale. Distant. The Bar'dyn beat no drum, blew no horn. The absence of sound got inside him like the still of a late-autumn morning before the slaughter of winter stock.

Tahn looked back at Daen. They had a little while to wait, and the Far captain deserved an answer. "Seems reckless, doesn't it." He showed them each a humorless smile. "The truth? I couldn't help myself."

None of the Far replied. It wasn't condescension. More like disarming patience. Which struck Tahn odd, since the Far possessed an almost unnatural speed and grace. A godsgift. And their lives were spent in rehearsal for war. Endless training and vigilance to protect an old language.

"I wouldn't even be in Naltus if it weren't for the Quiet." Tahn looked down at the bow in his lap, suddenly not sure what he meant to do. His bow—any bow—was a very dear, very old friend. He'd been firing one since he could hold a deep draw. But his bow against an army? *I might finally have waded too far into the cesspit.*

"We guessed that much," said Daen.

Tahn locked eyes with the Far captain, who returned a searching stare. "Two cycles ago, I was living a happy, unremarkable life. Small town called the Hollows. Only interesting thing about me was a nagging lack of memory. Had no recollection of anything before my twelfth year. Then, not long before I turned eighteen . . . a Sheason shows up."

The Far Jarron took a quick breath.

Tahn nodded at the response. "First day I met Vendanj, I realized stories about the Sheason are true. I saw him render the Will. Move things . . . kill. With little more than a thought."

"Vendanj is a friend of the king's," Daen said. "Not everyone distrusts him."

Tahn gave a weak smile to that. "Well, he arrived just before the Quiet got to *my* town, too."

He then looked away to the southwest, at Naltus, a magnificent city risen mostly of the black shale that dominated the long plains. In the predawn light, it was still an imposing thing to look at. It never gleamed. It didn't light up with thousands of lights as Recityv or any other large city. It didn't bustle with industry and trade. It didn't build reputation with art and culture. But the city itself was a striking place, drawn with inflexible lines. It had a permanence and stoicism about it. The kind of place you wanted to be when a storm hit, where you wouldn't fear wind and hard light. And where rain lifted the fresh scent of washed rock. Altogether different than the Hollows, with its hardwood forests and loam.

What Tahn wouldn't have given for some hard apple cider and a round of lies in the form of Hollows gossip. "Vendanj convinced me to follow him to Tillinghast."

This time it was Aelos who made a noise, something in his throat, like a warning. It reminded Tahn that even the Far people, with their gift for battle and their stewardship over the Language of the Framers . . . even *they* didn't go to Tillinghast.

"Did you make it to the far ledge?" Daen asked.

Tahn turned and looked in the direction of the Saeculorum Mountains, which rose in dark, jagged lines to the east. Impossibly high. Yes, he'd made it there. He and the few friends who'd come with him out of the Hollows. Though, only *he* had stood near that ledge at the far end of everything. A place where the earth renewed itself. Or used to.

He'd faced a Draethmorte there, one of the old servants of the dissenting god. More than that. He'd faced the awful embrace of the strange clouds that hung beyond the edge of Tillinghast. They'd somehow shown him all the choices of his life—those he'd made, and those he'd failed to make. It was a terrible thing to see the missed opportunity to help a friend. Or stranger. Wrapping around him, those clouds had also shown him the *repercussions* of those choices, possible futures. The heavy burden of that knowledge had nearly killed him.

It ached in him still.

But he'd survived the Draethmorte. And the clouds. And he'd done so by learning that he possessed an ability: to draw an empty bow, and fire a part of himself. He couldn't explain it any better than that. It was like shooting a strange mix of thought and emotion. And it left him chilled to the marrow and feeling incomplete. *Diminished.* At least for a while. Maybe something had happened to him in the wilds of Stonemount. Maybe the ghostly barrow robber he'd encountered there had touched him. Touched his mind. Or soul. Maybe both. Whether the barrow robber or not, something had helped him fire *himself* at Tillinghast. Though he damn sure didn't want to do it again, and had no real idea how to control it, anyhow.

"Yes, we made it to the far ledge," he finally said.

He could tell Daen understood plenty about what lay on the other side of the Saeculorum. But the Far captain had the courtesy not to press.

Tahn, though, found relief in sharing some of what had happened. "Near the top, Vendanj restored my memory. He thought it would help me survive up there."

Jarron glanced at the Saeculorum range. "Did it?"

Tahn didn't have an answer to that, and shrugged.

Daen put a hand on Tahn's shoulder. "The Sheason believed if you survived Tillinghast, you could help turn the Quiet back this time. Meet those who've given themselves to the dissenting god . . . in war." He nodded in the direction of the army marching toward them.

Twice before—the wars of the First and Second Promise—the races of the Eastlands had pushed the Quiet back, avoided the dominion they seemed bent toward. Now, they came again.

"Mostly right," said Tahn, "except all I've been fighting since Tillinghast is a head full of bad memories. For two damn days, I've done nothing but sit around in your king's manor, remembering." His grip tightened on his bow, and he spoke through clenched teeth. "Better to be moving. Better to hold someone . . . or something, accountable for that past."

"Idleness makes memory bitter." Daen spoke it like a rote phrase, like something a mother says to scold a laggard child.

Tahn forced a smile, but the feel of it was manic. "Vendanj was the one who took my memory in the first place. Thought it would protect me . . ."

"From the Quiet," Daen finished. "So you're here with a kind of blind vengeance. Angry at the world. Angry at what you believe are the bad choices of people who care for you."

The wind died then, wrapping them in a sullen silence. A silence broken only by the low drone of thousands of heavy feet crossing the shale plain toward them. Into that silence Tahn said simply, "No."

"No?" Daen cocked his head with skepticism.

"I'm not some angry youth." Tahn's smile softened, and he leveled an earnest look on the Far captain. "If I'm reckless, it's because I'm scared. *And* angry. Do I want to drop a few Quiet with this?" He tapped his bow. "Silent hells, yes. But when I saw them from my window in your king's manor this morning . . . I'll be a dead god's privy hole if I'm going to let the Far meet them without me." He pointed to the Quiet army marching in from the northeast. "An army that's probably here *because* of me."

Daen studied Tahn a long moment. "It's reckless . . . but reasonable." He grinned. "Well, listen to me, will you? I sound as contradictory as a Hollows man." His grin faded to a kind of thankful seriousness. "I'm glad you were awake to see them from your window, Tahn. Somehow our scouts failed to get us word."

He'd been up early, as he always was. To greet the dawn. Or rather, imagine it before it came. Those soft moments were more important to him now than ever. Because images plagued him night and day. Images from Tillinghast. Images from a newly remembered past. Sometimes the images gave him the shakes. Sometimes he broke out in a sweat.

Tahn looked again now into the east, anticipating sunrise. The color of the moon caught his eye. Red cast. *Lunar eclipse.* By the look of it, the eclipse had been full a few hours ago. Secula, the first moon, was passing through the sun's penumbra. He'd seen a full eclipse once in . . . *Aubade Grove!* The memories wouldn't stop. He'd spent several years of his young life in the Grove. A place dedicated to the study of the sky. A community of science. This, at least, was a happy memory.

Does the eclipse have anything to do with this Quiet army?

An interesting thought, but there wasn't time to pursue it. The low drone of thousands of Quiet striding the stony plain was growing louder, closer.

"We'll wait until the First Legion joins us on the shale." Daen spoke with the certainty of one used to giving orders. "Anything we observe, we'll report back to our battle strategists."

They didn't understand Tahn's need to run out to meet this army any more than his friends would have. Sutter and Mira, especially. Sutter because he'd been Tahn's friend since Tahn had arrived in the Hollows. And Mira because—unless he missed his guess—she loved him. So, he'd sent word of the Quiet's approach, and slipped from the king's manor unnoticed.

"I won't do anything foolish," Tahn assured Daen, and began crawling toward the lip of the depression.

The Far captain grabbed Tahn's arm, the smile gone from his face. "What makes you so eager to die?"

Tahn spared a look at the bow in his hand, then stared sharply back at the Far. "I don't want to die. And I don't want *you* to die because of *me*."

The Far captain didn't let go. "I've never understood man's bloodlust, even for the right cause. It makes him foolish."

Tahn sighed, acknowledging the sentiment. "I'm not here for glory." He clenched his teeth again, days of frustration getting the better of him—memories of a forgotten past, images of possible futures. "But I have to do *something*."

The Far continued to hold him, appraising. Finally, he nodded. "Just promise me you won't run in until we see the king emerge from the wall with the First Legion."

Tahn agreed, and the two crawled to the rim of the depression and peeked over the edge onto the rocky plain. What they saw stole Tahn's breath: more Bar'dyn than he could ever have imagined. The line stretched out of sight, and behind it row after row after row . . . "Dear dead gods," Tahn whispered under his breath. Naltus would fall. Even with the great skill of the Far. Even with the help of Vendanj and his Sheason abilities.

We can't win. Despair filled him in a way he'd felt only once before—at Tillinghast.

And on they came. No battle cries. No horns. Just the steady march over dry, dark stone. A hundred strides away, closing, countless feet pounded the shale like a war machine. Tahn's heart began to hammer in his chest.

Beside him, Daen spoke in a tongue Tahn didn't understand. The sound of it like a prayer . . . and a curse.

THEN HE SAW something that he would see in his dreams for a very long time. The Quiet army stopped thirty strides from him. The front line of Bar'dyn parted, and a slow procession emerged from the horde. First came a tall, withered figure wrapped in gauzy robes the color of dried blood. *Velle! Silent hells.* The Velle were like Sheason, renderers of the Will, except they refused to bear the cost of their rendering. They drew it from other sources.

The Velle's garments rustled as the wind kicked up again, brushing across the shale plain. Tahn's throat tightened. Not because of the Velle, or at least not the Velle alone, but because of what it held in its grasp: a couple of black tethers, and at the end of each . . . a child no more than eight years of age.

"No," Tahn whispered. He lowered his face into the shale, needing to look away, wanting to deny the obvious use the Velle had of them.

When he looked again, two more Velle had come forward. One was female in appearance, and stood in a magisterial dress of midnight blue. The gown had broad cuffs and wide lapels, and polished black buttons in a triple column down the front. The broadly padded shoulders of the garment gave her an imposing, regal look. The third Velle might have been any field hand from any working farm in the Hollows. He wore a simple coat that looked comfortable, warm, and well used. His trousers and boots were likewise unremarkable. He didn't appear ill fed. Or angry. He simply stood, looking on at the city as any man might after a long walk.

And in the collective hands of these Velle, tethers to six children. The little ones hunched against their bindings. Ragged makeshift smocks hung from their thin shoulders. Each gust of wind pulled at the loose, soiled garments, revealing skin drawn tight over ribs and knobby legs appearing brittle to the touch.

Worst of all was the look in the children's faces—haunted and scared. And scarred. A look he knew. A look resembling the one worn by many of the children from the Scar. A desolate place he'd only recently remembered. A place where he'd spent a large part of his childhood. Learning to fight. To distrust. Lessons of the abandoned.

Not every memory of the Scar had been bad, though. A name and face flared in his mind: Alemdra. But the bright memory of her quickly changed. Old grief became new at the thought of a ridge where they'd run to watch the sunrise, and seen a friend end her days. *Devin*. Some wounds, he realized, simply couldn't be healed. No atonement was complete enough.

The Velle yanked at the fetters, gathering the small ones close on each side. The children didn't yelp or complain, though grimaces of pain rose in a few faces. Mostly, they fought to keep their balance and avoid falling hard on the shale.

Then the Velle reached down and wrapped their fingers around the wrists of the young ones.

The Far king's legion hadn't emerged from the city wall. The siege on Naltus hadn't yet begun. But Tahn knew the attack these Velle were preparing, fueled by the lives of these six children, would be catastrophic. Naltus might be destroyed before a single sword was raised.

Beside him, the Far captain cursed again and crept down to the dolmen to consult with his fellows. *What do I do?* His grip tightened on his bow. The tales of lone heroes standing against armies were author fancies. Fun to read, but wrong. All wrong. He could get off a few shots at the renderers before any of the Bar'dyn could react. But that wouldn't be enough to stop them, or save the children.

Each Velle raised a hand toward Naltus. Tahn had to do something. Now.

Without thinking further, he climbed onto the shale plain and stood, setting his feet. He pulled his bow up in a smooth, swift motion as he drew an arrow.

Softly he began, "I draw with the strength of my arms, but release as the Will—"

He stopped, not finishing the words he'd spoken all his life when drawing his bow, words taught to him by his father, to seek the rightness of his draw. The rightness of a kill. His father and Vendanj had meant for him to avoid wrongfully killing anything, or anyone, because they'd thought one day they might need him to go to Tillinghast, where his chances of surviving were better if he went untainted by a wrong or selfish draw.

For as long as he could remember, he'd uttered the phrase and sensed the quiet confirmation that what he aimed at should die. Or not. Usually it was only an elk to stock a meat cellar. But not always. In his mind he saw the Bar'dyn that had stood over his sister Wendra, holding the child she'd just given birth to. He saw himself drawing his bow at it, feeling his words tell him *not* to shoot the creature. He'd followed that impression, and it had cankered his relationship with her ever since.

He was done with the old words. The Velle should die. He wanted to kill them. But he also knew he'd never take them all down. Not even with his ability to shoot a part of himself—something he hadn't learned to control. He'd never be able to stop their rendering of the little ones.

More images. Faces he'd forgotten. Faces of older children—thirteen, fourteen—reposed in stillness. Forever still. Still by their own hands. The despair of the Scar had taken all their hope . . . like Devin, and his failure to save her.

And what of the young ones in these Velle's hands? The ravages of *their* childhood? Long nights spent hoping their parents would come and rescue them. The bone-deep despair reserved for those who learn to stop hoping. He also sensed the ends that awaited each of them. The blinding pain that would tear their spirit from their flesh and remake it into a weapon of destruction. And they wouldn't simply die. Their souls would be spent. If there was a next life, if they had family waiting there, these little ones would never find it. They'd have ceased to be.

Sufferings from his past.

This moment of suffering.

A terrible weight of sorrow and discouragement.

Then a voice in his mind whispered the unthinkable. An awful thing. An irredeemable thing. He fought it. Silently cried out against it. But the dark logic wouldn't relent. And the Velle were nearly ready.

He took a deep breath, adjusted his aim only slightly. And let fly his awful mercy.

The arrow sailed against the shadows of morning and the charcoal hues of this valley of shale. And the first child dropped to the ground.

Through hot, silent tears, Tahn drew fast again, and again. It took the Quiet a few moments to understand what was happening. And when they finally saw Tahn standing beside the dolmen in the grey light of predawn, they appeared momentarily confused. Bar'dyn jumped in front of the Velle like shields. *They still don't understand.*

Like scarecrows—light and yielding—each child fell. Tahn did not miss. Not once.

When it was done, he let out a great, loud cry, the scream ascending the morning air—the only vocal sound on the plain.

Bar'dyn began rushing toward him. Tahn sank to his knees, dropped his bow, and waited for them. He watched the Quiet come as he thought about the wretched thing he'd just done.

It didn't matter that he knew he'd offered the children a

greater mercy. Nor that he'd decided this for himself. In those moments, it didn't even matter if what he'd done had saved Naltus.

These small ones, surprise on their faces—*Or was it hope when they saw me? They thought I was going to save them*—before his arrows struck home.

The shale trembled as the Bar'dyn rushed toward him, wearing their calm, reasoning expressions. Already he wondered what he'd do if he had these shots to take again. The bitterness overwhelmed him, and he suddenly yearned for the relief the Bar'dyn would offer him in a swift death. Then strong hands were dragging him backward by the feet, another set of hands retrieving his bow. The Far cast him into the safety of the dolmen. He flipped over and watched Daen Far captain and his squad defend the entrance to the barrow as Bar'dyn rushed in on them.

Jarron fell almost immediately, leaving Daen and Aelos to fight three Quiet.

Tahn couldn't stop trembling. And it had nothing to do with the battle about to darken the Soliel with blood. It was about the way the Quiet would wage their war. About what men would have to do to fight back. Choices like he'd just made.

Abruptly, the Bar'dyn stepped aside. The two Far shared a confused look, their swords still held defensively before them. Then one of the Velle came slowly into view. It stopped and peered past the Far, into the dolmen.

"You're too consumed by your own fear, Quillescent. Rough and untested, despite surviving Tillinghast." Its words floated on the air like a soft, baneful prayer. "Have you learned what you are? What you should do?"

Its mouth pressed into a grim line.

Tahn shook his head in defiance and confusion. Whatever Tillinghast had proven to Vendanj about Tahn being able to stand against the Quiet, the thought of his own future seemed an affliction. He'd rather not know.

"You are a puppet, Quillescent. Or were. But you've cut your strings, haven't you? Killing those children. And for us, you—"

A stream of black bile shot from the creature's mouth,

coating its ravaged lips and running down its chin. A blade ripped through its belly. As it fell, it raised a thin hand toward him, and a burst of energy threw Tahn back against one of the tall dolmen stones. Blood burst from his nose and mouth. Shards of pain shot behind his eyes. In his back, the bruising of muscle and bone was deep and immediate.

He dropped to the ground, darkness swimming in his eyes. But he saw Daen and Aelos and the Bar'dyn all look fast to the left, toward the whispering sound of countless feet racing across the shale to meet the Quiet army—the Far legion come to war.

• CHAPTER TWO •

Losing a Step

The Far people die after their eighteenth year—the age of accountability—before they can transgress. For that, it is said, providence possessed them of physical gifts—speed, grace. The logical test would then be to introduce sin, and measure.

—*Compendium on Extant Eastland Races,*
Ren Solas, scrivener and historian

MIRA FAR WOKE to the sound of rushing wings. She sat in the corner shadows of Tahn's room, where she kept nightly vigil over the young Hollows man. A man she thought she loved.

Absent gods, I fell asleep!

She'd never fallen asleep on watch. But she put it aside for now—Tahn was gone.

She quickly surveyed the bedchamber, assessing everything. At this hour, Tahn usually stood by the window maintaining a vigil of his own, awaiting daybreak. The window was open, but vacant. Even his bow had been taken. *He's gone someplace else to greet the day. Sick of being cooped up.* Then that sound, like many wings, crystallized in her mind: not wings, but boots on faraway stone—lots of them.

Mira rushed to the window. The streets were filled with Far running toward the northeast wall. Beyond it, on the distant shale, came an army like nothing she'd ever seen before. *Fool went out to meet them.* He'd crept out without waking her, knowing she would have tried to stop him.

Never before could *anyone* have crept past her without her waking. That she'd fallen asleep at all . . .

She started for the door, her hands moving over her weapons, taking inventory. The absence of her second sword—the one she usually wore over her left shoulder—was a painful reminder of their days in the Saeculorum. Her broken oath. She hadn't yet replaced the blade—not a thing to be rushed. And there was no time to do so now.

She descended several floors of stairs in quick bounds, and got out through the rear door of Elan's manor. Rather than navigate the thousands of Far moving toward the northern gates, she raced for the northwest wall.

On a dead run, she signaled the tower guard, who got the gate open enough that she passed through without having to slow. Out on the hard plain, she angled north, choosing her path carefully to keep her footfalls quiet in the shadows of predawn. Off to her right, the First Legion would soon emerge from the gates, ready to advance on a great line of Bar'dyn who stood waiting.

But it wasn't only Bar'dyn. As she raced toward the leftmost flank, the shapes of Velle became clear in the morning gloom. *Velle! Gods, no!* And they were close. A hundred strides. The First Legion was still massing as the Quiet renderers began raising arms toward Naltus.

Mira tried to quicken her step, but had nothing more to give.

Fifty strides ahead, someone stood up near one of her people's dolmens. In the weak morning light, the figure began firing a bow at the renderers.

She knew the archer's form. Tahn. *Damn me, he's not*

shooting the Velle. . . . She pushed hard toward the dark moment, knowing it would be tearing Tahn apart inside. It made awful sense. But was he listening only to his *own* feelings? The way he had in the Saeculorum when he shot to save her instead of the trouper boy?

Three Bar'dyn rushed Tahn. Three Far leapt to his defense. They fought near the entrance of the dolmen, one Far dropping fast. Beyond them, the Velle were scrambling for more bodies to fuel their renderings. She cast a glance over her right shoulder. The Far legion now moved at a feverish stride across the shale, their footfalls soft, like a quiet chorus of wings. No war cries. Just silent intent. The morning would erupt soon in a clash of muscle and bone and steel. She couldn't see the end of the Quiet army. The sheer number of them . . .

Her legs began to tire. *Fallen hell, what's happening to me!* But she pressed forward, as one of the Velle closed the distance to the dolmen. And Tahn.

Thirty strides. *I won't get there in time.*

The uttered tones of the dark renderer carried on the wind. The indistinct words sounded of invitation, sounded like the Quiet lies spoken to Tahn at Tillinghast to lull him from his intentions.

Fifteen strides. She bent forward, selecting her path, her boots on the shale louder than the wind. Unlike her kin rushing now to war.

I just need to stop the attack on Tahn.

As she closed the last few strides, someone rushed in silently from the right and put a sword through the Velle's back. Quick and precise, the attacker pulled his blade from the body and thrust again.

Bastard got there before me. She'd wanted to do this, to redeem herself for letting Tahn slip away unnoticed. But her neck and shoulders relaxed now that she wouldn't have to. Doubt had entered her thoughts. Doubt she'd never had before, about things she shouldn't *have* to think about.

The Velle cast Tahn back against the dolmen stone before falling dead. Its killer half-turned toward her: Grant, the former Emerit guard from the courts of Recityv. Grant had been exiled to the Scarred Lands. He possessed the skill to run the shale quickly and quietly. Something it seemed she could no longer do. He looked back at her, a small indictment in his eyes. Maybe some sympathy, too.

In that shared moment, she saw the resemblance. Grant and Tahn. Father and son. Both men spoke with their eyes. Grant, though, had the weathered skin and deeply lined face of a man long in the sun. There was a hardness in him that looked both earned and imposed. Scrutiny. That was the look in his face.

She should have been there. Something had changed. She knew it. So did Grant.

And what had changed wasn't a mystery. Staring at Tahn where he lay, she saw in her mind the moment it had begun.

High in the Saeculorum mountains, they'd been attacked by a squad of Bar'dyn. Both Mira and Penit—the trouper boy who'd accompanied them—had been in danger. Tahn had raised his bow with time to make one shot. A shot he should have used to save the boy. A shot he'd used instead to save Mira.

He'd disregarded his sense of the right draw, his sense of Will, because he hoped for a future with her. But it had been the wrong choice. And his chances of surviving Tillinghast jeopardized by such selfishness.

So she'd asked Vendanj to transfer that stain to her, knowing that she would be forfeiting the Far promise of a life after this one. Because that promise was based on a stainless life. What she *hadn't* known was that her finer abilities of movement and judgment were linked to her own stainlessness.

But Tahn had survived Tillinghast, making her sacrifice worthwhile.

And now? Tahn had just shot down several small ones. Was he simply choosing for himself, as he'd done when he'd shot to save her? Had her sacrifice been well spent, after all?

Don't regret helping someone you love.

And still, losing some of what had made her Far . . . it hurt. It hurt the way a child might feel when she's no longer welcome in the company of her family.

• CHAPTER THREE •

Dark and Bright

*A blade's greatest quality may be its reminder to us of what
we have to lose, of the things we'd trade for life.*

—Colloquial expression used by Alon steel-traders, adopted
by the footmen of the Alon'Itol army

THE DARKNESS ENGULFED Braethen the moment he put
his hand on the Blade of Seasons. With it came the silence of barrow flowers. Fear ripped through him. He gave
out a worried sigh, the sound of it lost in the darkness as
though he'd only *thought* to sigh. He existed outside himself,
outside time and place. Aloneness gripped him. And yet, distantly, he knew he still crossed the plain of shale with the
Sheason, Vendanj, toward the dark line of Quiet.

It was like being in two places at once, like dreaming and
being aware of the dream, yet still caught in its illusion. In
the endless dark, he walked blindly, clenching tight his sword.

Let it go! Drop the blade!

He couldn't do it. The paradox taunted him: The sword was
causing this suffocating blackness, and yet he sensed it
was his only way out. He carried it raised in front of his
eyes, though he could see it no more than he could see the
Quiet ahead.

Then voices came, like the whistling of wind through winter trees, streaming around cold, leafless limbs caught high
against a slate sky. In the sibilant rush, some voices mur-
mured as though carried on those winds for aeons, others
sounded close enough that he might reach out and touch their
owners. But the words themselves escaped him.

Soon even his own steps were vague and dreamlike, as he
slipped further into this strange black. Then he began to lose

the feel of the sword in his hand. A terrifying thought stole over him: *I'm becoming part of it.*

Lost in the emptiness, he admitted he had no idea how to get himself out, nor how he would protect or defend the Sheason. *I'm an imposter. Pretending to be a sodalist.*

For most of his life he'd desired to take the Sodality oath, serve with a Sheason as helpmate and friend. People had called him a fool. Everyone had expected him to follow the Author's Way—*write, study, write, teach, write*—like his father, the Author Posian. Everyone respected A'Posian.

The image of his da rose in the darkness. He could see him clearly; not the way he did in dreams, but as though he were looking at the man, wherever he was, right now. The vertigo of it put Braethen out of sorts. What unsettled him most was how much he looked like his father. Brown-red hair, with a beard more red. A reader's eyes, as if the world itself were narrative. Taller by a hand than most men, but always slumping to look them straight. Braethen saw him sitting in a chair, on their porch, a book in his hand. It was a vision of the life he'd expected to have. It seemed to argue that Braethen *was* a fool, that he should be home, walking his father's path.

But he wasn't an author, and his father's books were to blame. Stories of the Sodality had captured his imagination. So, when Vendanj had come to the Hollows, Braethen had asked to join him. He'd wanted to help his friends, Tahn and the others, but mostly he'd leapt at the chance to become a sodalist. And not long after leaving the Hollows, he'd taken the oath.

That was just a short time ago. His understanding of how to serve came mostly from books, as well as the sword training he'd had from Mira on their way to Naltus. But he had no deep knowledge of *this* sword, this Blade of Seasons. He was lost. He was in the dark.

Even the image of his father faded.

He imagined his body disappearing slowly, until the sword hung upon the air for a moment before falling harmlessly to the shale.

Then, in front of him, the darkness began to jounce and swirl. Twisted lines of black shot across his vision and closed in around him. Soon the heavy iron of a Bar'dyn hammer would crush his chest, and he would see none of it, only feel his flesh ripping before darkness of a different kind encircled him.

No! Braethen pushed back against the assault, trying to command the shadows. But his bluster only stirred the lines of darkness, made them *tighter,* like a fly caught in a web.

Then something new: thrumming in his feet. Like the hooves of a mounted garrison galloping at full speed, the rumbling tingled up through his soles. *The Bar'dyn are charging!*

Braethen struggled frantically for release, to see, to exist in one place and time. His struggle left him breathless, but still the darkness held.

Until . . . a single blade of grass.

In his mind rose the singularly hopeful image of a long, thin blade of greenery placed delicately in a vase. He saw it in sharp contrast to a drab grey hovel that huddled in a hopeless valley of endless rain. *Ja'Nene.* The young widow he'd met on his way to Naltus. Beautiful despite her burned face. Because of it. Her daily ritual of walking a fair distance to pluck a few long stems of grass added life and color to her colorless room.

Determination grew inside him with the remembrance of that simple blade of grass—an emblem he'd taken as his own. With it came the declaration—a battle cry, of sorts—that he'd found along the way from the Hollows: "I am I."

The silence and darkness broke.

When the shadows lifted, Braethen saw the dull gleam of morning's half-light on the edge of his sword. And beyond it, on the sweeping shale plain, came a host of Quiet like nothing he could have imagined. Their swift movement created a slow undulation, like gentle summer winds over a vast field of unharvested wheat.

He caught a quick glance from Vendanj, whose expression asked a question.

Braethen answered with a nod. *I'm ready.* Vendanj, though,

didn't look fit for war. The tall man hunched a bit. His short beard couldn't hide his gaunt, hollow face. The hard eyes were weary. He'd not fully recovered from their days in the Saeculorum.

"No Quiet breaks the line," Elan commanded from Braethen's left. The Far king's words were the only ones spoken, and carried long on the plain.

The First Legion did not slow as the Bar'dyn rushed toward them. Braethen kept moving through the silence—neither army called or yawped, each moving with grim determination, the only sound the grind of shale beneath their feet.

Ten strides from the Quiet, Vendanj thrust up his hands, as though he would take fistfuls of sky. He then drove them at the Bar'dyn in a violent motion. From his palms shot a wave of energy visible only in the grit and stones it gathered as it rushed toward the Quietgiven. Like a powerful river current, it took down a dozen from the first line of Bar'dyn. A few did not get up. The Quiet behind them simply leapt over the bodies, coming at them on a dead run.

To Braethen's left, the Far danced around the attacks, striking vital blows and dropping many in the first wave.

A massive figure surged forward, bearing down on Vendanj. He'd never seen or read about this breed of Quiet before—three strides tall, small spines of bone running like veins across its face, neck, arms, and hands. The creature reared back with a great iron flail, intelligence and intent shining in its eyes.

Vendanj slammed the balls of his fists together. His flesh rent at the force of it, blood spraying from the torn tissue. Time seemed to slow, the spew of blood hanging in the air a moment before whipping into an abrasive red wind that descended on the beast. The haze tore at its face and eyes and skin, dropping it to the ground, before rushing to nearby Bar'dyn.

The bodies consumed by the blood-wind had scarcely hit the ground before more Bar'dyn had filled their places. One heaved a two-tined spear at Braethen, forcing him off balance as it barreled toward him. Braethen managed to get his footing in time to take the brunt of the charge. They went down, the creature's shoulder driving the air from his lungs in a painful gust. Thick hands wrapped around his neck, trying to crush his throat. Braethen swung his sword wildly at the creature's head.

One of the Bar'dyn's arms went up to ward off the blow; several of its fingers fell to the ground. It didn't cry out, only squeezed Braethen's neck tighter with its good hand. Then Elan was there, driving his sword through the Bar'dyn's ear. It fell instantly limp and slumped to the ground.

The Far king pulled Braethen up, and the two turned in time to see the horde part and a smaller figure stroll forward. She wore a dull crimson robe, and had the gaunt face of one who hadn't eaten for a very long time.

Velle.

Braethen rushed to take a stance between Vendanj and the dark renderer. He expected the Sheason to call him back, ask him to find a safe position because of his inexperience. Vendanj did neither.

"Callow youth to defend you, Sheason? Some new sodalist to die for your impertinence." The Velle's tone came low and broken, like the smoke-damaged voice of a nightly tavern singer. "I've a young helpmate of my own."

A Bar'dyn came forward, leading a small figure with a chain around its neck. It may have been the dimness of the morning light, or the dark still in Braethen's eyes after escaping his sword's influence, or perhaps because he didn't want to see this . . . that it took several moments to focus and realize . . .

A child.

The girl was maybe seven. She wore a brown burlap smock over thin shoulders. Her hair stood dirty and clumped. She had the careworn face of a girl who has seen degradation at too young an age. And yet, when she saw Braethen standing there, defiant and holding up his sword, a spark of hope lit her eyes. It reminded him . . . of a blade of grass. And that image lingered an instant before the Bar'dyn roughly yanked her neck collar and pulled her to her knees beside the Velle.

Children, because they can't fight back. Because their spirits are more vibrant.

His anger burned hot. And before any of the others could speak, he stepped closer, his heart pounding. When he spoke, the sound resonated in the weapon in his hands.

"If you harm the child . . ."

The little girl cried silent tears of hope, while Braethen glared into the Velle's stoic eyes.

"Your indignation comes ages too late, Sodalist. Besides, what are you threatening? Death? That is an entirely human frailty." The Velle gave a casual laugh deep in its rough throat.

Without looking back, Braethen held up a hand to Vendanj. He wanted no intervention this time. The Sheason said nothing, honoring his unspoken request. They both knew the time had come for him to stand his own defense.

A strange silence grew, even as farther down the line the battle raged. Nearby Quiet waited on their exchange. Vendanj, and the First Legion, and the king himself waited, watched; he could feel their resolve to stand behind him.

The Velle remained still, staring at Braethen with unsettling apathy.

Finally, with a tone of indifference, she spoke. "I am already in hell, Sodalist. You have no power to save or condemn me. I will cut you down in front of your kings and Sheason, and I will lay bare the sadness of your oath . . . taken by a silly, reading boy who hasn't the manhood to raise the blush to a woman's cheek when she asks, nor the wit to esteem a father who suffered his son's ingratitude."

How does she know all this? About J'Nene? About da?

The words slipped into Braethen's mind, chiding him, undermining his confidence. The sword in his hand grew suddenly very heavy, foreign. Darkness crept in at the edges of his vision, and with it came the feeling of being in two places again, threatening to consume him.

Then, spoken softly, in an unyielding voice, came a single, bracing word: "Courage."

It was Vendanj, uttering, for him alone to hear, the invitation and command.

Braethen refocused on the Velle. "Let the child go." He thought his heart would burst, but he took two steps forward.

The Velle gripped the chain holding the little girl and pulled her around in front, as a master would a mongrel. A strained look of hope and fear shone on the girl's face.

Before Braethen could react, the Velle seized her by the back of the neck and thrust a bony hand at him. In a long, horrific moment the girl's life was drained from her frail, emaciated body to fuel the Velle's dark art. Pain and sadness leapt to her face. She reached for Braethen. A rush of black wind began streaming around him, through him, and he dropped to the hard shale, feeling a burn inside. Others around him fell, too.

He pitched forward onto the rock of the Soliel, his left hand still clenching his blade. *I'm a godsdamned fool!*

He looked ahead to where the little girl had likewise fallen to the shale. Her delicate, dirtied features were lifeless, her eyes open and empty and staring.

The scream began in his heart, where the ache of the child's death churned. That scream erupted from his throat like a clarion come to call all the living to war. It resonated in his hand as the Blade of Seasons thrummed, demanding to be wielded. He pushed himself to his feet and strode toward the Velle with the purpose of an executioner.

Behind him rang the clash of swords. The air itself seemed to rend—the Sheason calling the Will to his aid. But these things sounded distant, unimportant. He focused on the Velle, who stared back with unsettling indifference.

A massive Bar'dyn stepped into his path. Braethen sidestepped a blow and struck the beast in the throat with a single thrust of his blade. The creature fell, trying to stanch the flow of its own blood.

The Velle raised her hands again, forgetting she had no vessel to render. Braethen shook his head and stepped close, raising his weapon for a hammer stroke that he brought down with all the strength he had.

His sword's edge pulled through the flesh of the Velle with satisfying drag. Dark images rose in his mind as the creature gasped. A moment later, she wailed, the sound like the bitter penance of one receding to a lasting prison. The cry faded in long echoes over the silent armies battling across the shale. And the Velle fell.

Braethen took no pleasure in it, staring down instead at the child lying on the hard, cold ground. But he had no time to mourn.

He leapt back to the Sheason's side, swinging his sword at the surrounding Quiet with all the fury inside him. For the first time, he began wielding this burdensome blade with comfort, if not great skill. And as he fought beside Vendanj, thinking of the Sheason's steeling admonition—*Courage*— he also thought about the strange power of the blade.

Two places at once.

• CHAPTER FOUR •

Songs of Retribution

Revenge has a sound. Dear absent gods, a sound. And it doesn't come sweetly.

—From "Suppositions on the Mor Nation Refrains,"
a Divadian conservatory text

WENDRA SAT STARING out her bedchamber window at a garden bathed in the light of a wine-colored moon. Stillness and shadow lay across her room, deeper here on the west side of the Far king's manor. The chamber held the musty smell of a shut-in, the air sour and warm. Her things lay strewn about where she'd thrown or dropped them days ago. She hadn't bothered to change out of her clothes in all that time. And she certainly hadn't brightened any of this with song. Not a single note. Not once.

"Did you ever try to have another child?" Wendra asked. She spoke to the Far woman, Sendera, who kept Wendra company, protected her. The Far sat in the corner, unmoving, as she had for days. Word of the attack on Naltus had come from Vendanj, who'd ordered Wendra to stay put: *You haven't learned to control your song.*

"Yes," Sendera answered, but said no more.

For the last few days it had gone like this. Wendra had learned that Sendera had lost a child during childbirth. But she'd offered little more than direct answers, mostly keeping her sentinel silence. Still, by slow degrees, the two had begun to find common footing.

"Did any of them live?" Wendra pressed, turning to watch the Far's response.

"One." In Sendera's reply Wendra heard a truth most women shared: a great many more children came still, or died soon after birth, than was talked about.

The steady expression never left Sendera's face, and she resumed her silent, protective vigil.

"If you could hold someone responsible . . . if you could do something to settle the guilt and emptiness left when your child was taken from you . . . would you?"

Wendra turned back to the neatly tended garden. This plot of ground, patiently nurtured in the middle of the stark shale city, offended her in a way she couldn't quite name. But for other offenses she had great clarity *and* names: Vendanj for denying her the chance to avenge Penit, swept away by Bar'dyn in the Saeculorum; Tahn, her damn brother, for letting Penit be taken when he might have saved him.

In the shadows, Sendera sat forward—something she'd never done—her chair creaking in the silence. "Revenge won't give you peace." But her voice held no conviction.

Wendra thought it over for a moment. "You're wrong."

Until the Quiet attack on Naltus, Wendra hadn't had any desire to do much more than stare out her window. She wasn't brooding with sadness. She was managing her anger.

It was an anger born in that moment when her own child had come into the world still. Dead, she believed, by the trauma of childbirth forced by a Bar'dyn who'd stolen into her home. That silence in the moments her baby left her womb . . . that awful silence. Followed by the theft of the child's body for some reason she couldn't understand.

So, she'd come with Vendanj and Tahn and the others out of the Hollows because she'd wanted to do something about the Quiet, for the sake of her little one.

Along the way she'd met Penit, a trouper boy. They'd grown close. And after separation from the others, they'd been captured by a highwayman and nearly sold to Bar'dyn as *stock*. And it wasn't just them. She'd learned of a wide human trade that did much the same all across the Eastlands. People—*families*—were being taken from their homes and sold into the Bourne.

Sitting here these last few days, it all fully descended on her: what had happened; what was happening; what would continue to happen, if she did nothing. Thinking about the auction blocks where buyers purchased stock to sell to the Quiet had only caused her anger to deepen.

"You're wrong," Wendra repeated, and finally told her why, relating everything, beginning with the rape that had gotten her with child.

When she finished, she looked out at the garden of cedars and cropped junipers. "Have you found peace or forgiveness for your own lost child?"

It wasn't an idle question. Nor cruel. Nor sarcastic. She wanted to know. She asked with the earnestness of a childless mother. She asked because she wanted to get beyond the city walls, see her betrayers, and take her chances with the songs that played ceaselessly in her mind.

"My first child came early," Sendera said, interrupting the quiet that had fallen between them. "He was so small. . . ."

No further words were offered. The Far woman fell back into her stoic watch. Wendra realized in a way she hadn't before that her attendant—groomed to fight, blessed with the gifts to do so—had also suffered the cheating nature of childbirth. And Wendra had been pressing her to relive it.

I'm a mother's shame.

Then, Sendera spoke again. Softly. "Even if my son had survived, I wouldn't have been his mother long. The Far live only until the age of accountability. I believe you call it your Standing. Eighteen years." She looked at Wendra with some regret. "It leaves us free to defend the Language of the Convenant however we must. But it also means no child of ours will ever remember its mother's face."

For their mutual loss, in a hushed voice, Wendra sang her first song in days. A lullaby. But turned sad. She offered it slowly, with long silences between phrases. She modified a few words, shifting the story into past tense. The tense of children lost. And she lent the sound a part of herself, in the same way she did when screaming out her rough-throat music. It was the power of being Leiholan, giving her music *influence*. She didn't fully understand the ability, and she hadn't learned how to control it. But she'd used it enough to know that her own emotions could give a song weight. Weight that others would feel.

When she finished singing, the room stood heavy with silence. Heavy with remembrance.

After several long moments, Sendera said quietly, "You're Leiholan."

Wendra made no reply.

"Was this the Song of Suffering? I'm told only Leiholan can sing Suffering." She waited for an answer with as much anticipation as Wendra ever remembered seeing in a Far.

Wendra shook her head. "Suffering tells the story of the dissenting god, Quietus, and of all those he created being herded into the Bourne and sealed behind the Veil. Suffering keeps that Veil in place. I don't know its music." Wendra offered a wan smile. "But I wouldn't be surprised to find passages in it like my broken lullaby."

Sendera shared a silent and intent gaze with Wendra. "Come." She stood, and promptly left the room.

Wendra couldn't know if she'd manipulated Sendera with the influence of her Leiholan song, or if the words and melody had been enough. But she didn't wait to find out. She followed at a jog.

The city streets lay empty, a kind of autumn feeling in them. It seemed every Far had either gone to battle or found someplace safe to wait out the fight. She and Sendera hastened through a silent Naltus bathed in the bloody hue of a strange moon. They came quickly to the northeast rampart.

Sendera paused only to say, "I'm going with you."

Her motivation didn't need to be explained. Wendra nodded.

The two passed through a dark corridor, negotiating past several sentries near the outer wall. A moment later, they emerged on the other side. Distantly, the clatter of weapons rose over the shale. Then they were moving, running fast for the eastern flank. Few cries or screams were heard. Occasionally one echoed out ahead of them, lifting into the daybreak above like a death knell. She'd never seen war. The cold reality of it hit her a hundred strides on, when she started navigating rock slickened with blood. And bodies.

Sendera raced to the left, disappearing in the battle fifty strides away. But Wendra stopped. Her stomach churned at the sight of bodies strewn about. And not just dead, but crushed and opened and torn apart. The copper smell of blood and bile overwhelmed her, and she vomited hard over the boots of a fallen Far.

Wiping her mouth, she surveyed the battle, her need for vengeance softening. Then, some hundred strides west, she saw a figure take hold of a child. As she watched, the child fell. Memories and bitterness rushed in on her like a cold floodwater. Wendra whipped around and rushed at the Bar'dyn closest to her. Ten strides from it, she called forth the dark sounds that lived inside her.

Shrill tones roughed from her throat like a shrieking cough. But she gave it a melody of descended halftones, until she struck notes she'd not thought her voice could touch, deep and rasping.

The air shivered with the sound of it, as she quickly found the strength of her song. She screamed it out with angry remembrance.

The dark music came not in words, but syllabic shouts that lent themselves to the sounds her soul needed to make. By turns blunt then sharp, her song cut a path through the battle, dropping everything it touched. Everything.

She had no control. And in her blinding rage, she didn't seek any.

Her eyes filled with a painful contrast of dark and bright, everything becoming a stark mosaic. White was black. Black, white. An unhappy silhouette of reality. She could see no detail, no faces, no suffering. She knew only the certainty of her anger. And she aimed her darkened song toward any movement, where things both white and black dissolved at the sound of her music, scattered like dust before a powerful wind.

But that was not all. Or enough.

She screamed louder and longer. She found new ability to soar beyond the rasping song, and strike a powerful, strident timbre in full-bellied pitches that approached the sound of a raptor. But deeper, more resonant. She began to run headlong into the Quiet, no longer connecting note to note, but barking her song in bursts, directing it with a twist of her head, letting the stabs of song pierce her enemies and usher their souls away.

She wrought destruction of a savage, brutal nature, taking no care for who or what she sang at. She cared only that they fell, as she cut a swath through the living.

And still it wasn't enough. She began to imagine each one being responsible for her loss, each one putting a hand on a child. Her understanding of this song deepened. Her ability moved past any previous attempt to sing this way.

Around her, shale burst, broken stone crumbled to rubble, flesh sloughed, steel melted, and the air shimmered as her song swept about and laid waste to all that heard.

Lost in the furor, she forgot time and place. Sometime later she collapsed to her knees on the dark, rocky stretches, utterly spent. Her body burned hot with fever. Her hair and clothes were drenched from her own exertion. She went facedown, heaving for air, as one held underwater for far too long.

She clung to the cool stone beneath her cheek, seeking relief from the heat inside her. And for a few blessed moments, she thought not of her baby or of Penit, or of those who had failed her in their rescue, or even of all the people being traded as slaves into the Bourne. Lying there, enduring the burn inside, she thought about her song. A sense of wonder filled her. The power in her voice was almost unbelievable. Almost frightening.

She had one fleeting glimpse of a figure draped in white, hair like alabaster, kindly face. *Belamae.* The music teacher, Maesteri at Descant Cathedral. Belamae trained Leiholan like her in the use of their song, and how to control it. He'd asked her not to leave Descant before she could be properly educated. He'd wanted her to stay behind, not come to Naltus, as if he'd known what would happen.

What did *happen?* she thought.

With some returned strength, she got to her knees, and looked around. *Dear dying gods!* So many dead. Thousands. Maybe more. And many who had died . . . because of her . . .

I killed Far with my song. Innocent people.

She blamed the Quiet.

A new kind of anger filled her and she began climbing to her feet, surging with renewed energy. She'd almost gotten up, when a body fell on her. Then another. And another. In the tumble of limbs, her head struck—or was struck by—something, and she fell into the dark of unconsciousness.

· CHAPTER FIVE ·

A Different Aim

Everyone and everything has substance of a kind. What a Sheason must learn is how to manipulate his own. Once he can, permanence means nothing. And everything.

—"On the Nature of Influence,"
a fifth year discourse in Estem Salo

SOMETHING IS WRONG.

The battle raged all around Vendanj. On his right, Braethen fought hard, keeping the Bar'dyn at bay long enough for Vendanj to draw the Will. On his left, Elan marshaled the Far, putting distance between Naltus and the Quiet.

But something was wrong.

The Quiet fought to kill, and yet they hadn't tried to work a flank. They weren't even trying to push through the Far lines.

Why?

Tahn!

He rushed to the dolmen where Grant and Mira were fighting back Bar'dyn who had broken away to try and take them down. He didn't immediately see Tahn. On instinct, he ducked inside the dolmen. Chill air rested heavy over everything, including Tahn, who lay unconscious and bloody.

He quickly sought a tuft of dry grass and pulled it out of the soil. Dividing it into roughly equal parts, he twisted the two clumps together into the vague semblance of a man. He then bent to Tahn and rubbed the grass figure in the boy's blood.

Tahn stirred.

"Lie still. But get your wits about you. You'll need them soon."

Vendanj extended a hand and caused a new kind of stillness in the dolmen air. A complete stillness. To hide Tahn from probing minds.

Then he ducked back into the morning light, searching for a horse. With so many Far already fallen, he quickly spotted a riderless mount and raced southward to catch it. After a gentle whisper on the wind, he quieted the riled beast and soon had hold of its reins.

He closed his eyes and focused his Will on the grass idol. He recalled the many things he'd seen Tahn do, his words, his mannerisms, his anger and laughter. He captured a mental picture of the Hollows boy, forming it in his mind until it seemed to have a separate—if simple—mind of its own. Last, he added fear—not the strongest emotion, but the easiest to track. He imbued as much raw terror and desperation as he could into the grass doll. When he'd transferred the whole of what he'd envisioned to the effigy, he opened his eyes and looked down. The straw had twisted more fitly together, braiding itself, crimping, looping in places, to roughly resemble the persona that gave it a strange bastard intelligence. It twitched in the Vendanj's hand with the distress he'd imparted to it.

Using the reins, he tied the bloodied straw figure to the saddle horn, and slapped the mount on the ass. The horse leapt and ran west, a wild look in its eyes.

The thunder of the mare's hooves clapped over the shale plain, receding fast, as the mount bore away Tahn's effigy.

Vendanj turned his concentration back toward the battle raging to the north. He looked with his eyes, but also extended his connection to the shale and sage and wind. He waited, patient, for the faintest of stirrings.

He didn't wait long.

Moments later, two forms at the far edge of his senses moved subtly, looking west and judging. He could feel them assessing the escaping rider, considering their response. The movements and assessments touched Vendanj the way a ripple at one end of a pond will reach the far shore.

Then stillness again. Vendanj had his answer.

He ran back far enough that his companions could hear him. "With me!"

Then he spun, and bolted toward the city wall. He glimpsed Mira and Grant and Tahn as they began to follow. Over the scree and shale he raced, dread filling him with each running stride. *How could I have been so blind!*

He waved a hand twenty strides from the ramparts, signaling the guard to open a way for them. They passed through on a dead run. The clap of their boots on cobbled stone echoed through the vacant streets. Far children had been hidden. Far warriors were embroiled in battle. But a Far contingent would be standing guard at the vault library. *Grant a fool a prayer.*

Vendanj mounted the steps to the Naltus Forum, and crashed through the main doors into the forum proper. Oil lamps burned about the room, but there was no sign of Quietgiven. The chairs still stood upright, undisturbed, and the air remained settled, unmoved by the eddies of recent motion. But his skin prickled with anticipation. Something was close.

He dashed through the center of the room toward the stone

stairway, which descended into blackness. Lying on the top few steps, their blood pooling beneath them, were two Far and two Bar'dyn. *They're here.* He grabbed a nearby lamp and started down, Braethen and the others close behind. At the base of the first set of stairs they came to a massive stone portal where a door should have stood. The short landing lay strewn with the rubble of what had been the door. And more bodies—four Far, two more Bar'dyn.

These doors were ward-locked. No battering ram would have crumbled them. . . . Velle.

He stepped over the dead, through the piles of broken stone, and down a second set of stairs. Through two more ruined doorways they went, the dead count rising—a handful of Bar'dyn, a Velle . . . over twenty Far. But he heard no moan or clatter from the dark corridors ahead. There was only the labored breathing of the sodalist behind him, and their own hurried movements. They descended deeper beneath Naltus, navigating the labyrinth that protected the Language of the Covenant.

The Covenant Tongue was the language of the Framers— those gods who'd formed the world of Aeshau Vaal before abandoning it. The smallest parts of its speech could be perfectly understood and used and combined. One could speak something into existence. Or *unmake* it. With this language, the Quiet could end the Veil that held them, walk into the Eastlands. What had been harbored as an instrument against the possibility of such an invasion would become the tool of its success.

Vendanj shivered. This was why the Quiet hadn't tried to flank the First Legion, or press on the city as a whole. The war on the shale was a diversion, while a small band stole its way into the heart of Naltus to seize the Covenant Tongue.

If that happened, everything he'd done and sacrificed would be for nothing. He thought of his wife and unborn child; both had died years ago in the aftermath of a Quiet attack. Though blame for that belonged to the League of Civility, too. On the authority of a law known as the Civilization Order, the League had prevented Vendanj from helping his injured wife.

The Quiet and the League. Two godsdamned sides of the same coin.

Down several sets of stairs they passed, weaving inward and earthward. He could only hope that the protections of darkness, silence, and the labyrinth itself would safeguard what lay below until they could get there.

They passed another doorway. More dead Far.

Soon, he glimpsed a flicker of light ahead. A few moments later they stepped out onto a landing overlooking a great hollow in the earth. A vaulted ceiling arced two hundred strides above; a floor lost in shadow below. The cavernous grotto measured easily three hundred strides across. And at its center, rising up like an island, stood the Naltus library.

Countless sconces on the grotto walls offered light to the great hollow. More burned along the perimeter of the library, brightly lighting an encircling catwalk. Three narrow bridges spanned the emptiness between the outer wall and the library. Across those bridges moved no less than twenty Bar'dyn in charcoal-hued vestments. They didn't rush, their attention fixed on several Far standing ready to meet them on the other side.

But it wasn't the Bar'dyn Vendanj searched for. He scanned the hollow again, peering through the dim light until he caught sight of movement on the flat library roof.

No. Not today.

He set down his lamp and stepped to the lip of the landing. Uttering a single word, *"Suuthor,"* he raised both his palms, summoning a wind. From the grotto depths, the air began to stir and whip. Soon it rushed like a sea storm. Vendanj threw his hands to the left. The storm whirled around the chamber, creating a crosswind over the several bridgeways.

Caught off guard, a few Bar'dyn tumbled from the bridges into darkness. A few Bar'dyn crouched low, and pushed forward. Those closest to the other side leapt for the library catwalk, flattening themselves against walls to avoid the churning winds.

Vendanj raised his arms again, higher this time, conducting the wind to furious speeds. It whistled over the walks and howled against the walls of the grotto. The last few Quiet still crossing to the library were pulled from the bridge and sent tumbling into the air. This time, the rushing wind muted the sound of them hitting the stone floor far below.

"Now!" Vendanj yelled, and lowered his hands to still the wind.

Bar'dyn already on the other side engaged the Far, as Grant and Mira raced across the middle bridge. Tahn began firing at Quiet. The sodalist leapt forward, crossing the nearest foot-path on a dead run. Vendanj followed close, and had nearly reached the far side when two things happened: Mira went down, and he caught sight again of the dark shape on the roof of the library.

"Braethen, get to Mira!" Vendanj called. Then, at full stride, he placed a foot on the downed body of a Bar'dyn and launched himself toward the top of the library wall. He crashed hard against it, slamming his forehead and tearing a gash that began to bleed.

He ignored it—the blood thankfully not running into his eyes—and pulled himself up to the roof. Ahead twenty paces stood a Velle with its back to him. It concentrated on the shale roof underfoot as it gestured with its left hand. *It's rendering.* But shale held little Forda—little energy—of its own. *And this Velle has no vessel . . . is it willing . . .*

"Hold!" Vendanj cried.

The Velle turned, looking like an average physic blackcoat—someone a parent takes a sick child to see. It wore a wool coat over a threadbare vest. Familiarity flared for Vendanj, then was gone.

The Velle strode casually to one side of the roof and looked down on the battle encircling the library. "You're too late." Its melodious voice carried above the din of swords and scuffling feet. "But the wind was clever." Then it fixed him with a gaze. "You're Vendanj. The skeptic . . . the heretic.' Not exactly the kind of Sheason that commends your order to others, are you?"

Vendanj ignored the rhetoric.

The other smiled, and sauntered back to the center of the library roof. Vendanj caught a closer look at the face, pale and seamed. *Do I know him?* The Velle turned a circle, surveying the great hollow deep beneath Naltus. Smug satisfaction rose on its countenance as it slowly nodded to itself.

"Now we come to it. The voice of the gods lay beneath my feet, and with it, the injustice of the Abandonment will be made right." It stopped again, facing Vendanj. "This should have been the work of the Sheason. It's what Palamon would have wanted."

Vendanj shook his head. "Palamon helped send your kind away."

"You're misguided." The Velle pointed at Vendanj. "Of all the Sheason, *you* should understand. Rejected races, creations of the Framers . . . *dissenters*"—the Velle gave a cruel smile—"all imprisoned in a fallow land. The Bourne, you call it. How do you know the ages haven't refined us there? Cultivated in us the *humanity* that men hope to achieve?"

There was only one honest question in the Velle's words, and it made Vendanj think before answering. Yes, he was a dissenter. But was he like the Quiet?

When the council of gods had framed the world, one among them had gone loose. Mad, some stories said. Maldea was his name. He'd been tasked with forming those things, those creatures, that would test men. Refine them. But he'd gone too far, and had been brought before the council and Whited—stripped of his place among them—given the name Quietus, and banished with all that had proceeded from his overeager hands.

Vendanj might hold a separate view from most other Sheason, but "dissent" wasn't the core of being Quiet. Something had long ago gone wrong with those who lived inside the Bourne. Their intention no longer had anything to do with refining men.

"When the Quiet pierce the Veil, they don't come with entreaties," Vendanj said, speaking sharply. "They come with the stripping of earth." He took a defiant step closer, galled at the suggestion of Quiet empathy. "And *you*. You stand there, ready to steal or destroy one of the few defenses given to us." He shook his head again. "You don't seek to test us. You want dominion."

"You're misguided," the Velle repeated. It lowered its chin, setting itself for conflict.

"I am not the misguided one." Vendanj started toward the Velle, his patience gone, Will bristling in his arms and fingers.

The Velle's hands shot toward him, thrusting an unseen force that knocked Vendanj off his feet and hard on his back. His head slammed against the shale roof, opening another gash. He rose quickly to his feet, his vision swimming with black spots. Before he could summon a defense, another burst of energy encircled his head and began to press inward. The pressure mounted fast. Stabs of pain shot behind his eyes, until something burst far down the canal of his ear. He began to sway. Unable to keep his balance, he dropped to his knees.

He took his head in his hands and invoked his Will to try to curb the immense pressure. But he couldn't concentrate behind the pain.

Distantly he heard Tahn cry out for Grant—something about Mira. The clangor of weapons and the grunts of those wielding them faded as though Vendanj were sinking into the darkness of a cold sea. He pitched forward, his face striking the stone. This time his chin took the brunt of it.

The Language of the Covenant rested below him, on the other side of this shale roof. But he was weakening by the moment. It was all he could do to fight the pressure that threatened to shatter his skull and send bone fragments into his brain.

Boots swam into his vision, the dark renderer coming close. It hunkered down, looming over Vendanj, its boot leather creaking, its coat gamy with rotting mud and sour sweat and old straw.

Through his pain, Vendanj rasped a single curse: "Velle," a covenant word meaning "mine."

"Brother," the other gently corrected. "Join me. There is beauty to be shared in reunification. It's not so difficult to see, is it? The lives you would keep hidden and captive inside the Bourne . . . they are the ones who are truly abandoned."

Vendanj could feel his skull beginning to give, the bone yielding. *Divert its attention.* "Brother . . ."

Addressed with the honor of fraternity, the Velle lost a small measure of concentration. Only for a moment. But in that moment, Vendanj saw regret, like humanity lit briefly on the Velle's face. He saw it just before he shot a burst of Will, driving the creature off its feet and down hard on the roof.

The pressure on his head immediately lifted.

When he heard scraping across the stone, he turned and saw the other trace a circle around itself. The next moment, the Velle dropped through the shale roof as readily as a ghost.

The Language of the Covenant was moments from being taken or destroyed. He summoned all he had left inside him and did as his enemy had done, falling through the roof like a stone passing through the surface of a lake.

• CHAPTER SIX •

Hope Burns

If it's true that the world was made with words, then it must also be true that it can be remade. Or unmade.

—First lines written by Denolan SeFeery
in his heretical new Charter

M IRA'S DOWN!"
Grant put his sword through the wrist of the Bar'dyn in front of him, and used it like a handle to spin the beast off the catwalk. He turned to see Tahn rushing toward Mira, who lay on her back, parrying blows from another Bar'dyn. She held just one sword, and was slowly being driven backward toward the lip of the walkway.

Scanning the dead Far around him, he spied what he needed. In a single motion, he picked up a blade and hurled it, end over end, at the back of the Bar'dyn beating down on Mira. The weapon bounded off the beast's thick, rough hide,

but caused it to turn toward him. That gave Tahn enough time
to set his feet and fire an arrow into one of the creature's eyes,
dropping it almost on top of Mira.

Momentarily distracted, Grant nearly took a hammer in
the side of the head. But Braethen was there, deflecting the
blow and countering. He and the sodalist doubled up on the
Quiet, driving it back until Grant leapt and kicked it over
the edge.

From above, he heard voices, one of them belonging to
Vendanj. But he didn't have time to help the renderer, as two
more Bar'dyn rushed him and Braethen. Arrows whistled
through the air, striking these Quiet from behind. Their faces
showed no signs of pain as arrows lodged in their skin. And
they did not slow.

Grant grabbed Braethen and shoved him back around the
corner of the library. He then dove at the charging Bar'dyn's
knees. Extending his arms, he tripped them both and sent
them sprawling.

One went over the lip of the landing, falling into darkness.
The other rolled and came up with its hammer in hand. As it
reared, an arrow took it square in the throat. When the
Bar'dyn fell, a sudden silence fell with it.

Battle almost always ended without fanfare. And those still
standing fidgeted, at a loss for what to do with themselves.
The need to defend, to fight, didn't end so abruptly, leaving
men restless, unsatisfied. After a few long, unsettled moments, the door to the library opened.

Grant jumped to his feet and was the first inside. On his
left was Vendanj, who'd obviously opened the door. Seeing
them, the Sheason settled his head down on the stone where
he lay. Tahn and the others came up beside Grant.

For a moment, no one moved, as he surveyed the dimly lit
room. Years of exile in the Scarred Lands hadn't burned away
his sense of wonder. Or hope. The Covenant Tongue. The
power by which the gods had put the world in place. If it was
real, and if it was still in this library . . . then all was not lost.
In spite of those abandoning gods, perhaps man could learn
to use this power for himself.

That was the secret of his heart. The heresy, some might

say. Back home in the Scar, that small hope had started him writing during the evening hours. Writing—or maybe *rewriting* was more accurate—the Charter. The original Charter may never have actually been a document. But it was said that the Framers had established the purpose and values for this world during the Age of Creation. If followed, those values would lead to fairness, refinement, peace. But the gods left. People lost sight of the Charter. And disregarding its purpose seemed to bring no consequence.

So, he'd begun writing the Charter down. What he understood of it. But adding to it, too. A new tract, for how things ought to be. Principles to guide actions and choices. *Ethics, by every absent god!* And real consequences. Consequences one could see and feel personally, without reliance on laws or soldiers . . . or even vengeance. But to give it weight, make it real, he knew he'd need to find the authority to breathe life into his ideas. Something like the Covenant Tongue. To make his ideas binding. To change the fabric of things. Change the way people thought. Change the way they regarded one another.

It was a preposterously large idea.

It was the secret of his heart.

And his little document had become like a primrose in his Scar desert, reminding him in the smallest, most delicate way . . . of something beautiful.

My primrose . . .

It was an ideal. He knew that. But he hadn't been able to give it up.

Inside the library, small pedestals lined the walls. Atop each, a wide basin filled with oil fueled a lit wick. In the stillness, their flames didn't flutter or wave. Their soft light caught the edges of a single, unending line of text chiseled into the shale walls at eye level. He assumed the foreign letters to be the Covenant Tongue.

The candles also illuminated a few shelves of books set against the walls. Beside each of these sat a padded chair, as though a place to read those same volumes. At the center of the room, another pedestal stood, ringed by more oil-basin candles. On it, a single book.

He'd imagined a great archive, endless shelves, stacks of parchment and bins of scrolls. He'd envisioned layers of maps and paintings and tomes of math and equations and philosophy. He'd been sure he'd see star charts, and histories written in hundreds of derivations, all in different tongues. There'd be countless copy desks, where inkwells served scriveners rerecording the thoughts and translations of generations, sometimes expounding on the work, interpreting, distilling, illuminating . . .

None of this.

Beyond the modest number of books and the attendant chairs in which to peruse them, there was only the one book. And no great tome was this. Rather, on the pedestal rested a small, thin volume with a dark leather binding. Several small candles placed around the lip of the pedestal washed the book in warm light.

There could be no more than five pages in it. How could such a volume contain the whole of the Covenant Tongue? And yet, after regarding the book a moment, he became convinced. Great power didn't draw attention to itself. Real strength came in simple forms, subtle movements. New confidence filled him, until a figure stood up in the shadows beyond the pedestal, reached down, and picked up the small book. *Velle!*

"Put it back," Grant commanded evenly, though his heart thrummed.

The Velle caressed the leather binding and casually thumbed through a few pages before looking up at him. "You're too late."

Keeping his eyes trained on the Quiet, Grant told Mira to close the door. "You have no way out."

Its laugh was soft, unconcerned. "I will leave the way I came." Then it turned to look at Mira. "You, at least, should find some peace in this. *All* Far have now failed their oath."

Mira didn't reply, and moved into the light of one of the oil basins.

"The book won't do you any good." Braethen stepped to Grant's left, his sword in hand. "You've no codex to decipher it."

"And how do you know this?" the Velle asked with patient amusement.

"Because you watched the library at Qum'rahm'se burn. If you had a way to translate that book," Braethen pointed at the volume in its hands, "you wouldn't have gone there in the first place. The scriveners at Qum'rahm'se had been trying to assemble a way to decode the Language for centuries. They burned their work rather than see it fall into your hands."

The Velle's face slackened, its amusement gone. "We are not idle in the Bourne, Sodalist. You'll want to remember that when we return to the Eastlands." It raised a hand toward them.

In the stillness came the sound of bow wood flexing. The Velle's eyes widened in surprise, its gesture frozen as Tahn stepped in front of them all.

"Put the book down," Grant's son said.

The Velle stared back with an appraising look. "You know by now that you're not like them."

Tahn deepened his draw.

Grant moved left, trying to get behind the Velle. "We can make it quick for you. Just put the book back."

The Velle paid Grant no mind, focusing on Tahn. "Your little sticks are meaningless, Quillescent."

Tahn seemed to consider this a moment, reluctance touching his features. Then he dropped the arrow nocked in his bow. It fell harmlessly and clattered on the floor. Next he let go the string. But the bow didn't relax. He curled his fingers in the empty air, as though drawing again.

This is what he did at Tillinghast.

Concern passed across the Velle's face. It made a quick circular motion with its fingers and thrust its free hand at Grant, who'd gotten within a few strides. Grant flew backward as though struck hard in the chest. A sudden sound like shattering glass filled the library. His sword, his knives, Mira's blade, they all broke into a hundred pieces like ice cast against stone. Only Braethen's blade and Tahn's bow seemed unaffected.

Tahn pulled deeper still. A brief look of uncertainty crossed his face, as if he wasn't sure he could control what he was about to do. Then his expression hardened, and he let go his draw. Candles guttered. Pages in open books flapped. A wave of distorted light shot across the library, as though the light was bending around something Grant couldn't see. It struck the Velle, sank into it, and dropped it to the floor. Tahn collapsed near Vendanj.

No one moved. Not even the Velle. Moments stretched. Was it over so fast? Breaking the silence, the Quiet muttered something from where it lay on the other side of the library. Then it began rising toward the ceiling.

"It's trying to escape!" Vendanj called out.

Mira swept up a document laying atop a nearby reading table, crumpled it lengthwise, and set it alight with the flame of a candle. She then scooped up an oil basin and rushed the Quiet. Half a moment later, she splashed the rising Velle with oil and leapt, catching hold of its feet before it reached the ceiling. She lit its oil-soaked robe, then dropped, landing hard and ripping off her own burning tunic before she was engulfed in flames.

The oil flared and in the space of a few breaths the Velle looked like a living torch. Its flesh seared, its hair sizzled. Yawps of pain puffed the flames licking over its mouth.

The fire spread up its arms toward the book it held aloft.

The Velle writhed in the air as it neared the ceiling. Grant stood up as the creature cried out a final time and fell to the floor, engulfed in flames.

My primrose!

He rushed past the pedestal, toward the Velle, hoping to save the book before fire consumed it.

• CHAPTER SEVEN •

Imparting

It is thought that memories leave a residue that alters the corporeal and incorporeal self. If true, then memories have an energy of their own.

—From "Behaviorial Postulates," a Sheason reader
on the topic of consequence

As GRANT RUSHED toward the burning Velle, Braethen turned and dropped to his knees beside Vendanj. The Sheason's breath rasped in his throat, his face gaunt and wet and red, as with winter fever. Braethen placed his ear on Vendanj's chest and heard a weak, irregular beat.

This needs more than a sprig of herb. He closed his eyes and concentrated, recalling a particular tale from an old volume. A passage about a healing ritual. Something a *practiced* sodalist could do. It involved more than applying a salve or drinking a nostrum remedy. *Damn me, he needs a* blackcoat, *someone acquainted with prayer.*

He'd never even seen this old rite done. For pity's sake, he could count the number of days he'd actually been a sodalist.

And what if I do it wrong?

Mira startled him. "Sodalist! Do something!"

He placed one trembling hand on Vendanj's forehead and the other on his own chest. He then closed his eyes . . . breathed. In, out. In, out. He pushed everything else out of his mind, finding a place of inner calm where only he and the Sheason seemed to exist. Then, as best he could remember them, he spoke the words to this old sodalist custom:

"Isala, els uretae. As I have, so may you."

He repeated it. Again and again. And filled his mind with images of himself, images of the Sheason, back and forth. He had no idea how long he'd been concentrating on the simple phrase, when his hands began to feel warm on Vendanj's skin. And moments later, his entire body began to sweat as Vendanj's did. Weakness flooded him.

He was feeling the effects of passing through the shale ceiling. Vendanj had aligned the matter of his body with that of the stone so that he could slip through. It had been an immense act of rendering. It felt like water passing through scouring sand, abrasive to every part of him.

Then vague forms and shadows danced past, too quick to be seen or understood. With them came smell and color and sound, all whisked away like a breath on the wind before he could name them. Suddenly, he found himself looking out on a small town. It was well after dark hour. *One of Vendanj's memories.*

FAR AWAY, LANTERN light flickered in windows like lightflies against the dusk. A few open fires burned here and there, touching the nearest surfaces with light and giving shape to the outbuildings of Maelar. The river town nestled beside the banks of the Tolin River some fifty leagues north of the fork where the Tolin and Cantle Rivers converged.

Vendanj had come into the far north of Alon'Itol to see for himself, to confirm the infestation. He'd not even had to enter Maelar to know: The Quiet had taken root here. He felt it as surely as the wind on his skin.

Beside him, waiting patiently in the dark, stood his wife, Illenia. "What do you see?"

"Quietgiven," he said. "More than I can count. And the people there are helping them." He paused, staring across at the unassuming river town. "It's not a launch point for invasion, though. It serves a different purpose."

She put a hand on his shoulder. "What are you talking about?"

He shook his head, not wanting to say it out loud.

Illenia's next words anticipated his purpose. "Surely there are some here who don't serve the Quiet's cause."

He didn't answer this either. Instead, he turned and watched as the shadows thrown by firelight grew weaker against the river's dark edge.

With gentle insistence, Illenia repeated her question.

He took her hand. "Maybe. And if there are, they unknowingly provide cover and protection for Quiet plans."

"We'll get them out." She began walking toward Maelar.

Vendanj pulled her back. "Even if some are untouched, trying to warn them will cause panic. And panic will alert the Quiet."

"Then we'll drive them out of Maelar. Send them back across the Pall." She looked into his eyes with a quizzical expression. She clearly wanted to understand his hesitation.

"Chasing them out doesn't solve the problem. They would find another place to do their work. We need to put an end to them here, tonight." He hated his own implication.

Illenia stared him in the eye. "Then tell me, what is their work?"

With little more than a look, she was offering to help shoulder his burden. So, he told her, explaining that this port town so near the Pall was trafficking men, women, and children into the Bourne. The river provided easy movement, and along its edge were towns with willing conspirators.

"Why?" she asked in her unique way. Illenia believed that with enough information, every problem had a solution.

Vendanj shook his head again. He didn't truly know. He had his suspicions, but no proof. And it wasn't something he would speculate about. He only repeated, "We must put an end to them here, tonight."

Understanding slowly spread on her beautiful face. Then came horror and disbelief. "No, Vendanj, you mustn't. Say you won't."

He showed his beloved sympathetic but unyielding eyes.

"You can't," she persisted. "They don't know. They deserve a chance to—"

Vendanj put his palm against her cheek to gently silence her. "I'm sorry, Illenia. If you must hate me for it . . ." Then, softer, he added, "There is no other way."

He turned, and in those small hours of early evening, faced

the town at the river's edge. *Forgive me.* He hunkered down and traced an emblem in the dirt at his feet. The same emblem that he had, over the last few days, traced on every shutter, every door, every gate in the town of Maelar. He spoke a few words, drawing the Will within him. Then he settled his hands on the inscribed soil. The air shimmered in the shadows, undulating like the surface of a lake rippled by wind. The force of Will raced through the night, catching in the symbols far away in the town, setting them alight. The flames leapt instantly, uncontrollable and raging.

In moments, the fire blazed out of control, becoming an inferno that consumed everything, everyone.

Vendanj sat back, spent from his rendering, listening to the frightened cries of women and children carried on the night air. He heard them over the distant roar of fire and the soft weeping of his beloved kneeling at his side.

"We will hope to have a better mercy if the life of our own child is ever in jeopardy," Illenia whispered, mostly to herself.

The revelation of their unborn child struck Vendanj speechless, as he sat aching from what he'd just done. Now, that ache burned more bitterly. And though he remained convinced it had been right—that the struggle against the Quiet required awful choices—he began to know self-hatred. He rolled over and pushed his mouth into the loam beneath him, thinking to muffle a scream. In the end, even that seemed too much like a pardon. So, he laid his cheek on the cool soil and listened to himself breathe.

BRAETHEN COULD BEAR it no more, and opened his eyes to find Vendanj staring up at him. Surprise and concern rested in the Sheason's face. There was also gratitude.

"Thank you," Vendanj said with a weak whisper. "I didn't know you'd learned to *impart.*"

Braethen removed his hand, and took a long, steadying breath. Any sense of accomplishment was swept away in the wake of what he'd just seen.

"You didn't know it moves both ways." Vendanj waved a hand back and forth between them. "Not a fair bargain,

Braethen. If I could undo it, I would. But now the memory is yours, as well."

Braethen stared back at Vendanj. "You were an advisor to the smith king of Alon'Itol. And you burned an entire town there before telling him. . . ."

"We'll talk more of the smith king soon enough." Vendanj struggled to sit up, and weakly pushed Braethen aside. "The Velle? The book?"

From the smoke and shadows Grant emerged. In his hands he held only so much ash. "The flames took them both."

• CHAPTER EIGHT •

Causing Death

'Kids are resilient' is the lie a horse's ass tells for treating little ones poorly.

—From an interview conducted by League recorders
on the ill effects of pageants and poverty

SUTTER TE POLIS knelt in the shale, exhausted, as the Quiet trudged away to the northwest. The siege on Naltus had failed. "Go, you piles of horseshit." They should be pursued. But the Far were as weary as he was. *Hells, most of them are dead.* Far littered the plain.

Survivors slowly walked the shale, searching for other survivors. Their boots shuffled through the loose rock—an unnerving sound. But he remained kneeling, holding his Sedagin blade across his lap.

The sword, as well as the Sedagin glove, had been gifts from the leader of the Sedagin people. They had come with that man's belief that Sutter had earned them.

He fingered the glove with his other hand, and spoke to no one. "All I did to deserve these was remind a man that a lady decides who she dances with." He blew a burst of air from his nose. "Hardly helps when the battle starts."

The Sedagin were celebrated for their swordwork with their longblades, celebrated for their valor, too. They'd been the first to march against the Quiet in the wars of the First and Second Promise. *They keep their honor, damn me.* Sedagin honor meant holding one's own in battle. Sutter hadn't lived up to that today.

"I should go back to my roots," he said to the glove. He longed for a day back in the Hollows on his father's root farm. *Damn me twice. Never would have imagined that.*

But he couldn't stand up. Not to return to his father's farm. Not to find a place to hide his shame. He could only stare at the dead Far lying in front of him. That's why he was kneeling here. That's why he hadn't moved. Because from his window in the deeps of night, he'd seen this Far's spirit. Like he'd seen so many spirits over the last moon cycle.

The first time had come a day or two after his and Tahn's encounter with the barrow robber in the wilds of Stonemount. That ghostly creature had put its filthy hand in Sutter's chest. Changed him somehow. Given him this damned *sight*. He'd realized it when he'd seen the soul of a Sheason woman scheduled to burn the next day. Her spirit had found the guest room window where he'd been laid up, healing.

Last night had been much the same. Except he'd seen thousands . . .

Then this morning, he'd gotten separated from Vendanj and the others. He'd been in trouble. This Far in front of him had come to his defense, and gotten killed for it.

I saw the spirit of a man who would later die saving my life.

And this Far was not the only one. Sutter had insisted on going into the fray. Several had died rallying to save him as he made a poor job of his own defense. He eyed his Sedagin blade again with disgust.

Did I kill them? Because I'm no damn good with a blade, did I kill them?

The bodies of the Far whose spirits he'd seen from his window in the small hours of night now lay dead across the rocky plain. They'd sought him out. He had no damn clue what they'd wanted, and it gnawed at him.

He reached out and gently closed the Far's eyes. He had no elegy to offer. But he knew a simple farmer's poem, and whispered it, the sound lost beneath the scrape of boots over shale: "The earth is warm and will provide. She'll give you meat and later become the best, last bed to your weary hands." It was something his father said every morning when he led them to another day's labor in the field. That's what Sutter was, even still: a rootdigger. Yes, he might be better with a blade now than when he'd left his father's farm, but ask him to root out some potatoes and you'd see his true talent.

Da's farm. He missed that place an awful lot. Missed hearing his father's daily poem.

Wanting to find his friends, he finally pushed himself up. A sickening dread opened in the pit of his stomach. He'd never scoured a battlefield before. He clenched his blade until his fingers ached, unable to loosen his grip, which was sticky with blood. There was blood all over his clothes, too. The remnants of death had soaked his shirt and trousers just as they'd soaked the soil around him. He felt like a blood rag, the kind used to prepare the dead for burial.

He moved from body to body, recognizing more Far whose spirits he'd seen the night before. More who'd died defending him. He turned fast, dropped to his knees in an open area, and retched. His gut continued to heave long after it was empty.

Staring down at the sour spillage, he vowed to become decent with his sword. It might not be enough to ease his guilt. But it was part of the answer. A part he could do something about, by damn.

He struggled to stand again, then continued his search through the bodies of the fallen. He placed his feet carefully on shale that was slick with blood. Many of the surviving Far had begun to wend their way back toward the city. The few who remained stood talking in reverent tones, looking north and west.

A moan.

At first it sounded like just another Far conferring over the dead. But it became distinct the farther east he moved. *That's someone in pain*. Sutter hurried, following the sound to a heap of dead Far. But none in the heap seemed alive. Then he realized what he was seeing. He grabbed one of the Far by the arm, and gently pulled him off the pile. Then another. Three bodies later, Sutter stared down at one of the living.

"Wendra!" He smiled wide, glad to see her. "You're a wreck."

She clearly hadn't eaten in days. The dusky brown hair he'd only touched once lay matted and tangled. Her eyes were badly bloodshot, and darkly ringed from lack of sleep. And blood covered her cheeks and chin. He dropped to his knees and wiped it away with his hands.

"Where are you hurt?"

She moaned again, sucking air like one who's been too long underwater, and shook her head.

"Show me," he insisted.

Wendra drew more ragged lungfuls of air, as though learning to breathe. "I'm not hurt," she rasped.

He pulled a bit of balsa root from his pouch and broke off a small piece, pushing it gently into her mouth. "Eat this anyway."

She gulped it down whole and turned to look at the dead Far that Sutter had pulled off her. "They piled on top of me." She took another deep, stuttering breath. Her next words were hard to hear. "Why would they . . . ?"

A look of understanding spread on her face. Her mouth opened wide in a silent cry. In that moment, Sutter knew the battlefield rumor was true: Wendra's song had torn at Quiet and Far alike.

She gasped, filling her lungs as if she might sob or wail. She did neither, but stared at him with pleading eyes. He pulled her close, and began to rock forward and back, the way his mother had when he was sick.

He wanted to say something that would help. But he had no words for any of this. Best he could do was hold her while she suffered it out.

They sat that way for an hour. A mild breeze tugged at their hair as he held her and they stared away south.

Wendra spoke first, her voice soft when she asked, "How are you?"

Not wanting to share the curse of seeing the dead before they fell, Sutter just shook his head. "I'm a fool." He swallowed hard. "A lot of them died saving me. I don't know how I'm going to live with that. . . ."

Wendra nodded and sat up. "These Far . . ." She motioned to the dead bodies Sutter had dragged off her.

"I know." He took a long look around. "And I understand they honor an oath and all that. But does it make you feel like they think we're something we're not? Like they've placed some faith in us that we just don't deserve? I'm a godsdamned rootdigger."

Wendra looked back at him with understanding eyes. And he decided to tell her. Like he'd told Tahn.

"I wouldn't be here at all if it weren't for my da," he began. Her brow furrowed with question.

A wan smile touched his face. "I'm not truly a Te Polis. My father was walking his fields when he saw a couple of pageant wagon folk out in his hay. They were birthing their baby. And when that child came out, they started to put it down in a water bucket. Drown the boy." He looked into her eyes. "That was me."

"Dear gods, Sutter . . ." Wendra put a hand in his.

"Don't know who they are. But I have a good righteous hate for them." He clenched his teeth a moment. "Part of leaving the Hollows was wanting to find them. No idea what I'd say. But I'd probably start with something about that bucket." He laughed to keep from crying, his emotions raw from the sight of so much death. "I'd beat the last hell out of them. That's what I'd do. A day doesn't go by that I don't think about that bucket." His smile came more warmly. "Or about my real da—the one who *saved* me from that bucket."

"You're like him, Sutter." She shook his hand gently. "You showed *me* kindness when no one else would."

He returned her thoughtful look, remembering hard days in the Hollows. Then he pointed at the Far, thinking of those who'd died defending him. "I've been saved too many times by others. I should try and return the favor for someone else."

New firmness settled his nerves. "At the least, no one else will die because of me."

Wendra nodded understanding and got to her feet. "Where are Tahn and the others?"

Sutter stood, too. "I haven't seen them."

"They're probably fine," she said. "We won't find them in the dark anyway. Help me back to the city."

He hoped she was right.

He pulled one of her arms around his neck and put his other arm around her waist. Together, they started back. It was only then that he relaxed, realizing for the first time that he hadn't seen any of his friends' spirits. They weren't dead. Not yet.

• CHAPTER NINE •

Lamentations: The Past

I don't think we have any idea what might result from orbital dissonance. And by the time we do, it may be too late.

—From the end papers of *Scant Evidence of Eternal Truths,* a cosmologer's philosophy text

IN THE LATE-AFTERNOON sun, Tahn gently removed his arrows from the bodies of the six children he'd shot down. He looked a long moment at the peaceful face of each child before covering them with heavy wool blankets he'd brought from the city. He then laid them side by side. And wept. He wept for young lives ended so early. And he wept for himself.

"I wish I could have found another way," he whispered. "Please rest well."

He wiped his eyes, tied back his hair, and began to dig their graves. He hadn't been at it long when someone interrupted him.

"Can I help?" The weathered voice of Grant. His father.

"We've had plenty of practice, haven't we?" Tahn continued to dig without looking up.

Devin. A friend from Tahn's time in the Scar. The memory of her had flared that morning when he'd shot to spare these little ones. She'd been one of many that his father had cared for in that hellish place.

"I guess we have." Grant had brought his own pick and shovel, like hundreds of Far who were burying their countrymen across the Soliel plain.

Without further discussion, the two worked the hard soil together. Only the sound of iron striking dirt and shale accompanied them for most of an hour. Their shadows, often moving in unison, reminded Tahn how much he looked like the man. Grant's hair was close-cropped and a paler shade of black due to his years beneath a Scar sun. His skin darker. But a considering, sometimes broody brow over sky-colored eyes might have been Tahn's own.

They managed to carve out several short pits—the graves for these little ones needn't be long.

After the digging, they stood back, resting their arms. The stillness of dusk had settled in around them. Grant broke the silence. "We haven't really spoken since Vendanj restored your memory. How are you?" There was a moment's hesitation before he added, "You probably have questions. Maybe I can help."

Tahn looked out over the shale where the Velle had almost rendered the lives of these children. "The Scarred Lands were formed by Velle. Did they do it this way?" He pointed at the six wrapped bodies.

Grant leaned in on his shovel. "No, they drew energy from the earth during the Battle of the Round. That's what left everything barren."

Tahn could see it in his mind. A wide place of dryness, of black dust, of red stone, of bleached wood, of hard sun.

"You had to live there because you tried to stop the regent's child from being revived by a Sheason." Tahn looked at his father, wondering how anyone could do such a thing.

Grant sighed with understanding. "Reviving a child violates the most basic principles of the Charter, Tahn: Men are not gods; the dead should be allowed to rest. . . ."

Tahn looked down at the little ones laid across the hard shale. If he had the power to revive them, he'd do it in an instant. *Let the Charter burn.* Then he looked up at Grant, whose eyes were locked on the same blanket-wrapped bodies. There was a weariness in his father's face that Tahn couldn't remember seeing before, as if the man had been caring for children in a dry, rough place for a long time . . . and failing.

"I was seven when you sent me to Aubade Grove." Tahn turned his gaze to the southwest, where nations away the Grove stood. "I was happy there. Studied the stars. Other sciences, too. For a while."

Tahn had been torn away from the Grove after four short years, and sent back into the company of his father. Into the Scar. Half a year later, Alemdra and Tahn had been out on patrol. They'd shared a first kiss. And they'd witnessed Devin's jump. . . .

He found he did have a question for his father. "How many have taken their own lives?"

There was no surprise in Grant's face. He knew what Tahn meant.

"Thirty-seven."

And from the way he said it—with such sad certainty—Tahn guessed Grant knew every name, too. They kept a mutual silence for those dead wards of the Scar.

After a time, Grant interrupted their quiet moment. "Tahn, you'll learn this sooner or later. And I should be the one to tell you. One of the thirty-seven . . . was Alemdra . . ."

Tahn grew weak in the legs. He dropped to one knee, his eyes suddenly hot with tears. He shook his head. *No, Alemdra.*

Grant put a hand on Tahn's back. "I don't think she was the same after Devin. Blamed herself. It was a few years. . . ."

Tahn understood. Since remembering Devin, he'd felt the

same guilt. *Damn me*. All because he'd wanted his morning sunrise. And a kiss.

Grant removed his hand from Tahn's back and took a deep breath of the cooling air. "People will disappoint you. It's not usually malicious on their part. And it's not usually done with good intentions, either . . . as I tried to do with you. But motivations won't matter when someone fails you."

He looked over at his father. "You mean the way thirty-seven wards failed *you* by giving in to the Scar."

Grant shook his head, his voice raw with grief when he said, "I mean the way I failed my wards. Especially those thirty-seven . . . Especially you."

It was the first time Tahn had seen the man hurting. Grant swallowed hard. "That's the wisdom of an exile. Others will have brighter things to tell you. But they won't make what I've said untrue. And at some point, Tahn, you'll have to decide that you do all this," he gestured around them, "because *you* want to. Not because the Sheason asks it."

Tahn turned his sight skyward. The moon and stars shone brittle and bright, casting silvery light on the edges of stones and dolmens and patchy grasses. As it always had, it comforted him to simply gaze up and lose himself in the vastness of the heavens.

But the comfort was brief. At his feet were six dead children. As dead as Devin. As dead as Alemdra, who'd kissed him and spoken of leaving the Scarred Lands. As dead as the thirty-seven.

He hated the Scar. He hated the Quiet for creating the Scar—a desolate land that grew each year, as if the effects of the Quiet weren't done. More barren terrain. More wards. Every cycle of the moon.

And every *few* cycles, a ward chose to leave, using death as an escape.

"That's one of the reasons we took your memory," Grant said, sounding confident of the decision, but still tired. "It started to get to you. It gets to all of us in one way or another, I guess. But in you, it was taking a toll." Grant looked him straight, hesitating a moment. "I'm not sure you'd have made it, otherwise." The thought chilled Tahn. He might have joined Devin, Alemdra. "We thought it would be easier for you to deal with when you got older. So, we veiled your memory and sent you to the Hollows. Safer there, too." His father sounded less sure of the last part. "Fewer friends to watch die, anyway."

He remembered many of their faces and names. Terrible thing to lose a friend as a child. Hard to make sense of it. No one to blame. Nothing to be done about it. And saying good-bye to a friend—good-bye, Alemdra—who had already gone to her earth . . . was a hollow good-bye.

That's what the Scar meant to him. That's what the Quiet meant. In that moment, he decided which side of things he was on.

"I didn't use the old words today." Tahn paused a long, painful moment. "It was my choice. I imagined their lives. Imagined how they'd die. I couldn't save them. But I couldn't watch them suffer either. And if there's a next life, I sure as every hell wasn't going to let the Velle steal their chance to be family there." He stopped, breathed. "So, I killed them."

Grant squeezed Tahn's shoulder in a comforting way. Then offered another sad smile when he said, "Much as you'll hate to hear it, you sound like me." He then spared a long look at the graves they were digging. "You showed them mercy. A tough mercy. But mercy just the same. You may need to live with your guilt for a while, which isn't a bad thing. Guilt tempers a man the way forge coals do a good steel. But not for long, Tahn. For a while, then let it go."

"The way you've let go of *your* guilt." Tahn smiled weakly.

"Ah, but I'm a bastard, Tahn. Or didn't you know."

They both laughed. The sound of it was the best eulogy they might have offered over the six small ones.

Tahn gazed upward again.

Grant looked in the direction he saw Tahn staring. "What is it?"

"We had a lunar eclipse last night," Tahn said. "Did you see it? Red moon."

"I'm no good with moons and such. I'm better with people."

They laughed again. Easier this time.

"Stars are as clear here as they are in the Scar," Tahn observed. "But not nearly as bright as they are in the Grove."

The Grove. Those had been good years. Kind years. Spent in a place where his natural affinity for the heavens could be fostered, pushed.

"I never visited you there. But I'm told you made a name for yourself."

Tahn then pointed into the northwest at a planet he knew all too well. "Pliny Soray. See her?"

Grant scanned the sky and fixed on Soray. "I do. I wouldn't have if you hadn't pointed her out."

"She's off her course," Tahn replied with the distraction of memories that were fitting together like puzzle pieces in his head. Memories of the Grove. Of Pliny Soray. And one memory in particular.

"A GOOD ASTRONOMER can learn as much observing a vacant stretch of sky as he ever will measuring out the procession of a great starry field." Scalinou Dechaup huffed the words out as he led Tahn up the tower steps. All 998 of them. The same as the other four towers.

"So, we're going to look at empty sky tonight?" Tahn asked, a wry grin on his face.

Scalinou, savant of the College of Cosmology, paused in his ascent, and gave Tahn a sidelong look. "You up to the challenge?"

"Of staring at nothing?" Tahn teased again. He was as comfortable with Scalinou as he was with the savant of his own College of Astronomy. "I'll manage somehow."

Scalinou reached the glass dome, pausing at the top step, out of breath. "When my heart stops pounding in my ears, we'll begin."

"We should have just taken the pulley-lift." Tahn said it to goad Scalinou a little.

"Nonsense. Against the rules. And hells, stairs keep me young!" The old man's voice echoed songlike in the wide observation dome.

Tahn stood beside his older friend and mentor, scanning the glass panes that made up the great dome. Each was a full stride high and wide, and held in place by an impossibly thin strip of ironwood. From the dome floor, it was like there were no panes at all, leaving an unobstructed view of the sky in every direction.

Some of the towers had alchemical lamps, or light-stones activated by motion or heat. Scalinou forbade such nonsense in his dome, where oil lamps were the high technology. The man actually preferred candles. *Give me a good chandler,* he was fond of saying.

Here and there tables stood in the dark. On them: armillaries, orreries, quadrant maps, water-clock gears that turned the dials on timepieces set to different rotations of the planets. They all worked in silence, but a good astronomer walking the dome would see a hundred calculations laid in and being tracked. There were a few low bookshelves. Scalinou's books. And of course, at the center of the dome, on an inset rotating floor, was the second-most impressive skyglass in Aubade Grove—the *most* impressive stood in the College of Astronomy's dome. Tahn thrilled just looking at it.

The whole affair resided in a hemisphere fifty strides in diameter. The domes were Tahn's favorite place in Aubade Grove. He never tired of visiting them.

When Scalinou had steadied himself, he shuffled over to the long skyglass pointed at an open shutter. With the same warmth another man might show when patting a favored pet, Tahn gently tapped the brass tubing of the skyglass. A tuneless *tep tep tep* sounded in its broad hollow. Then he stared up past its gathering lens, some nine strides away.

Scalinou got himself into his armless chair—he didn't like having his elbows encumbered in any way. Then he bent forward over his workbench and a quadrant map laid out atop it. The map was held flat by sand weights at each corner. He made a satisfied noise in his throat—part surprise, part relief. "Young fusspot cosmologers left it the hell alone for once."

Then, by the light of a thin crescent moon and countless stars, he bent close to his armillary sphere and dialed in a slightly modified direction.

"Finding our empty stretches?" Tahn inquired.

Scalinou harrumphed, then cross-checked his armillary

with his map. Last, he pulled a ledger out and read over entries with notation dates that ran back more than a year.

Once all this was done, he sat up and rolled his shoulders like an athlete preparing for a contest. For Scalinou, it would be a wrestling match with his bit of sky.

Tahn held up a hand, as one set to referee the bout. "Isn't this why you invited me?"

Scalinou seemed momentarily bothered. But a grin soon spread on his wrinkled face. He stood up with flair, and gestured extravagantly for Tahn to assume the armless chair—a cosmologer's throne.

Tahn laced his fingers and turned them outward—as he'd seen musicians do—adding some pomp to it all. Then he swiveled on Scalinou's throne and began slowly to turn two hand cranks on the skyglass catapult stand. He carefully matched the degree and minute, as well as longitudinal mark, of the armillary.

That done, he took a long, slow breath, exhaled, and gently leaned in to stare through the eyepiece. *Empty stretches.* Then he settled in for a long, patient looking.

For a few hours he rarely left that position, fidgeting less than other observers his age. Far less. Patient looking suited him fine.

"There's quite a bounty of peace to be found looking at an empty spot in the heavens." Scalinou sat nearby, having put his nose in a first-edition copy of *Scant Evidences of Eternal Truths*—a philosophical tract one couldn't find even in the college annals.

"Damn pretty thing to see," Tahn said, not realizing he'd just cussed in front of a savant.

"Haha! Yes! This is my cosmology." Scalinou grinned with satisfaction. "This is why you're the only astronomer whose company I can stomach for more than an hour's time. Now, back to the show."

It was Scalinou's way of telling Tahn to attend his skyglass eyepiece. And the *show.* Scalinou's name for the dance of stars.

It was Pliny Soray they were watching—a wandering star. Soray was actually a planet, but Scalinou—like Tahn—found the old term more poetic, so here they referred to Soray as a "wandering star."

He watched closely, time passing, as the familiar ache crept into his neck and shoulders, cramping his muscles. He wanted to take a break, stretch, but he was glad he'd remained watchful, since a moment later . . . it happened.

He let out a weak sigh when Soray completed her retrograde. No loud slapstick, no stomping of feet on wagon boards, no show-ending tune. Just the silent, immeasurably distant completion of the wandering star's loop. And she was off. This was not the ellipse she usually made. The length of the loop had changed. *She's farther away . . .*

He sat back, dumbstruck.

Seeing Tahn's expression, Scalinou nearly squealed with glee. The old cosmologer poured himself a tall glass of pomace brandy. While Tahn thought through what he'd just seen, Scalinou drank, waiting on Tahn's thoughts.

"Perhaps your skyglass is out of true," he suggested. "Let's check her bearings."

Scalinou blew air through pressed lips, making them flap in a mocking sound. "That's a doubter's trap. A sky coward's way. You know what you saw. Write it down."

Tahn picked up a short knife and sharpened a piece of graphite. No star man committed a fresh find to paper in ink. But when he did make his notation in Scalinou's journal, the math wasn't hard. They'd be lending it ink permanence soon enough.

Once he'd jotted it down, he stood up and rolled his shoulders several times, trying to loosen his neck and back. A little more relaxed, he poured a room-temperature glass of water and stared at Scalinou through the shadows. The man's grin threatened to break his face.

"What do you think of my empty stretches now, Gnomon?" The appellation was a reference to a sundial stylus, the part that casts a shadow, as Tahn did every morning when he watched the sun rise.

"What does it mean?" Tahn asked.

"I don't know yet," Scalinou replied. "But isn't it wonderful?"

Then the older man gimped over to the edge of the dome. Tahn followed. There, Scalinou stared up "unassisted," as the young astronomers called it—no sky tools.

The man put one hand against the dome glass, breaking another of his dome rules. Tahn did the same. The glass was cool to the touch.

"That's our city, Tahn. Aubade Grove." He stared down at the rooftops and streets and out at the other four towers.

Scalinou's voice then took on a different sincerity. Simpler. "You love it, too, don't you? The inquiries and arguments. The study of the sky."

He did. He loved the old man, as well. They had these kind of talks every time they were together. Saying out loud the stuff that mattered. No clever language about it.

Except tonight was a little different. He thought he heard a subtext in the man's words. It didn't change Tahn's answer, though. "I don't ever want to leave."

Scalinou's smile tapered.

"You didn't really need my help with the empty stretches tonight, did you?" Tahn deduced.

"Nonsense. I can always use your help," Scalinou scolded mildly.

Tahn gave the man a forgiving smile. "But it's not the only reason you brought me here, is it?"

The Grove had been through a Succession of Arguments recently—a ritualized discourse and debate where one scientist sought to prove a hypothesis by successively arguing and defending it against each Grove college. Tahn and his best friend, Rithy, had helped her mother bring the Succession this time. She'd argued for a unification of celestial mechanics, calling it Continuity.

"Your life's stars are turning rather fast," Scalinou noted.

"You're sending me away, aren't you?"

Scalinou closed his mouth tightly, chewing on words that sought to escape his lips.

Tahn was quiet for a few moments before saying, "It's my fault."

"What's your fault?" Scalinou asked carefully.

"That Rithy's ma . . . did that to herself. I should have been more help to her in her astronomy argument in the discourse theater."

The comment visibly shook Scalinou. Rithy's mother, Nanjesho, had been a brilliant mathematician. But her argument had failed when she got to the College of Astronomy. Tahn and Rithy had shared their budding skills with Nanjesho throughout her Succession. Ordinarily such help would have been viewed as an amusement. But not from Tahn. And not from Rithy.

Regardless, a few days after the woman's failure to prove Continuity, she'd taken her own life.

Like a ward of the Scar.

"It's an unfortunate thing," Scalinou said. "Unfortunate for her. For her daughter. For all of us. But"—he gently shook Tahn's shoulder—"not unheard of. It was a large argument she was making. Large arguments—the kind that reshape our understanding of the sky—well, they consume a person. Become everything to her."

"But I—"

"And no matter how bright a young astronomer you are, Gnomon, the blame for what happened doesn't belong to you." Scalinou looked down at him with serious eyes. "Nor is it why you're going away."

Tahn fell quiet, and looked up to where Soray was wandering. Now *truly* wandering. Then in a small voice he said, "Don't make me go. Not back to the Scar. All the kids there, they're like scarecrows. Waiting in dry fields. But no parent ever comes to claim them. . . ."

Scalinou's face filled with sympathy. "But *your* father is there."

This fetched a heavy sigh. "He cares more for the other children he takes in than he ever did for me. And we don't study the sky there. We just train. Patrol." He looked up with a new worry. "And Rithy will think I'm abandoning her."

"Rithy will be fine. Not right away. But eventually. And you, you're always welcome here," Scalinou offered, his face full of sincerity. "I think right now your father and his friends just believe you'll be safer with them."

"Safe from what?"

Scalinou looked like he might actually lie to Tahn for the first time. But whatever touched his face left as quickly as it came. "The Continuity argument drew a lot of the wrong kind of attention, Gnomon. I think your father is right to want you out of Aubade Grove."

He pulled Tahn closer, and together they stared up past the skyglass to where Soray defied her regular rhythm and pattern.

"If Nanjesho had succeeded," Tahn observed, "you might have had a way to explain Soray."

THE MEMORY OF Scalinou and Rithy and Nanjesho slowly faded as Tahn continued to look up into the night sky. Memories of the Grove and his studies there flowed as through a burst dam.

"I can't believe how much of the sky I'd forgotten." Tahn shook his head.

"I take a spoonful of credit for that. The amount of knowledge, I mean," Grant clarified. "I taught you—teach all my wards—Dimnian study techniques. Children in Masson Dimn know more than two handfuls of adults anywhere else. And with you . . . you've been looking at the stars since you could lift your head on your own. One doesn't squander an interest that strong. That's why we sent you to the Grove."

"I have friends there." Gods, did he miss that place. "I could find them again." He pointed up. "Use the boreal star. Make my way."

Grant nodded, seeming to like the idea. "Maybe you should, at that."

"I have friends in the Scar, too, though," Tahn added with soberness. "Let's finish." He began to clear out the loose dirt and rocks from the graves.

Grant joined him. And in short order they'd cleaned the barrows, laid the children inside, and gently covered them over. Grant spoke an old prayer.

When his father had finished, Tahn hunkered down, as though by being closer to the dead they might hear his whisper. "I won't let the Scar widen. It won't have one more of us."

He was thinking of these six, certainly, but also of the thirty-seven. Of Devin. Of Alemdra.

By every absent god, this time he meant to stop the *intruder* from strolling where he shouldn't. Whether one man . . . or a whole damn army of Quiet.

No more asking whether he should release his arrow.

No more choices about which friend to save.

No more rescuing a little one by ending her life before the Quiet could.

And no more orphans and foundlings sent into the Scar.

No more!

The Quiet must be stopped.

He gave a last look at the sky above, feeling a small measure of peace. It was a peace he'd learned to appreciate so much more during his time in the Grove, where his father had sent him to escape the Scar.

"Thanks, Da," Tahn said, and started toward Naltus.

"Where are *you* going?"

"To have a long-overdue conversation."

THANKS, DA, TAHN had said. Grant had never thought he'd hear the boy call him that again. *Da.* It was the first time Tahn had said it in more than twelve years. And it left him feeling like a father for the first time in just as long.

He wasn't naïve enough to believe all was right between them. But he'd stopped pretending that it didn't hurt him to think that after tomorrow he might never see his son again. He'd decided that even if Tahn couldn't forgive him, he could at least offer the boy some clarity about things. And he'd done that. Mostly.

When he'd come out to help bury the dead, he'd meant to share with Tahn an even fuller truth. Something he believed might forever drive a wedge between them: who Tahn's mother was.

His son knew Grant had been sent to the Scar because he'd tried to stop a Sheason from reviving the regent's stillborn child. What he didn't know was that Grant had been married to the regent, Helaina. She was Tahn's mother. And the child Grant had tried to prevent from being revived . . . was Tahn.

He loved his son. But men had no right to disregard the Charter that framed their world. The conflict of those two things was a godsdamned briar.

But he'd not shared any of it with Tahn, because then the boy would have known that Grant being exiled to the Scar had everything to do with him. And Tahn would then have blamed himself for *all* the wards of the Scar. Including those they'd buried too young. The thirty-seven. And the moment Grant had seen the light in his son's eyes—when Tahn had remembered the Grove—he'd decided this wasn't the time to share it. Some secrets were right to keep.

Soon, the scrape of iron through soil—the digging of barrows—seemed to fade. There was only the low whisper of grass stalks brushed together by wind.

• CHAPTER TEN •

Lamentations: The Present

The severity of one's suffering after breaking an oath reveals their true nature. Anyone who feels nothing when breaking their word isn't worth the spit to shine a boot. Garbage, really.

—From the published journal of Isabelle Rycher, member of the Circle of Poets

UNDER A CLEAR night sky, Mira walked the field of battle. Across the wide, rocky plain, barrows were being dug for the fallen. The tradition of erecting dolmens for Far who'd gone to their final earth would be broken tonight; there were too many dead. Instead, simple graves.

The sound of heavy iron tearing at the earth created a steady, calming music. Around her, she took in the smell of old earth newly turned, and thought about losing a step.

The reality of what was happening to her returned with its suffocating consequence: She was no longer Far. Not completely. She was slowly losing the traits that were naturally given to her people. *I'm an oathbreaker.*

All her years, she'd looked forward to what followed this life, that moment when she'd be reunited with her mother. A mother she'd never known. Her girlhood had been spent with so many *caregivers*. She'd never felt the warmth of a mother's embrace. She'd never fought beside her mother. No quiet conversations as mothers and daughters should have. No laughter of the kind that only they would understand. Nothing.

But the Far promise had made it bearable. She'd see her mother when this life was through. Except that she wouldn't. In bearing Tahn's stain, the promise was no longer hers. She would never know her mother's embrace. As simple a thing as that might be, she ached with the loss of it.

She breathed deep, taking in the stench of coagulated blood. She might later grieve what she had lost, but for the moment, she put it aside. It just didn't seem to matter in the face of such overwhelming loss.

A few Far came near, pulling a cart. They knelt in turn beside each dead kinsman, respectfully collecting personal effects and lashing them together in large squares of leather. A name was written with care in dark ink on the outside of the bundle, and placed in the cart.

Behind them came more Far, who kicked rocks out of the way and began to dig in open patches on the shale plain. Mira asked for a pick and shovel. Wordlessly, a stoic Far handed her his own and went to retrieve a new set for himself.

She wandered the battlefield another half hour before she found Elan, as she knew she would, digging a grave. She cleared an area next to him and began to strike at the earth. The heat of her labor rose in her arms and neck and face. She worked faster, breaking caked soil for the resting place of someone whose name she didn't know.

Her breath soon rasped over dry lips, but she didn't stop. Stroke after stroke she pounded at the hard dirt, remembering faces from her own girlhood, then the face of her sister, even the face of the boy Penit. All gone. She thought of Tahn, which brought a fury of pick strikes—she had genuine feelings for him.

Perhaps we could have a few years. . . .

It was an irresponsible thought—the Far still needed her to produce an heir—and it faded as she recalled Far after Far after Far, each playing the part of her mother until the time came for their own final earth. *The blessing of shortened lives . . .*

As if waking from a dream, Mira realized she'd stopped digging. Slick with sweat, she turned to look at Elan. He stood waist-deep in the barrow he dug, staring back. Her king.

"You look like her." Fondness and sorrow vied in his face. "Same skin, like snow. Same eyes, clouds after a storm. Hair like tilled earth . . . I miss her."

Lyra. Mira's older sister and Elan's wife, gone to her earth not two cycles ago.

She nodded. "You should rest."

"There's much to be done." He gestured to the grave she dug. "For someone you know?"

She shook her head, and worked in silence for a time. Exhausted, she finally had to stop. Her king kept at the hard soil.

"I want you to stay," he said, glancing her way between shovelfuls of earth. "I know the importance of what the Sheason asks, but you're needed here. Another Far can accompany Tahn and Sutter. It's the guardianship that's important, not the guard."

Mira leaned back against the lip of the grave. "I can't stay, Elan, and neither can you."

He gave her a reserved expression. "You mean Convocation."

"You have to go. I promised to claim that seat myself if you would not."

"The Far have never attended Convocation," he said.

"The regent needs your support this time. Without it, I don't think we'll push the Quiet back again." She surveyed the plain of Far dead.

Elan followed her gaze, and let out a long sigh.

The Veil that held the Quiet inside the Bourne was

weakening. This field of dead was proof of that. And if the Veil fell, the tide of Quiet that would flood the Eastlands would be immense. The regent of Recityv had called a Convocation of Seats—all the kings and rulers of the east—to form an alliance to meet that tide.

"Our people need an heir, Mira. We're the end of the bloodlines, you and I."

"Does that matter anymore?" She stared into the shadows of the grave around her. "I saw the book burned to ashes."

When she looked up again, surprise and disappointment hung in her king's eyes.

"The responsibility to lead is still ours," he said with firmness. "The lives of these people . . ." He looked around at those burying the dead. ". . . they still matter. It will be hard to rebuild. Harder still to give them purpose. But that begins with me, and you, and the child we must give them."

Elan's young face showed a different kind of concern. There had been many Far kings; their names graced the walls of the Forum, forever etched upon the dark stone. Like them, Elan was a great warlord. But he was unique. He'd also found a way to make their lives feel individual, significant beyond the commission of guarding the Language.

"And there is still hope," he added, a light in his eyes. "The scholars are scouring the histories now. Some suggest that a child born to us could have the Aloin gift, could be a native speaker of the Covenant. That's the gift that lives in your blood. The gift that only you can give a child." Elan paused. Around them echoed the sound of graves being dug.

"We've never seen this, Elan—"

"Because we've never needed to. We've only taught our daily speech, routine words, the training figures. Perhaps if we—"

"Elan, I can't bear you a child . . . because I've broken my oath."

His brow tightened.

She told him of the battle in the Saeculorum, of Tahn's shot to save her instead of the boy, Penit. She explained that she'd taken on herself the cost of that selfish choice, to help Tahn succeed at Tillinghast.

"Oathbreaker," Elan whispered, his gaze distant.

She hadn't heard the word since Tillinghast. Hearing it now, spoken by her king, struck her more painfully than she would have thought.

She'd known him a long time. They'd been friends who could share secrets, so she knew the expressions of his heart. What she saw now chilled her, if for no other reason than she'd never seen it in his eyes. Uncertainty. It touched his face briefly, replaced by the grit of a king who'd faced annihilation before.

"There may be a way for you." He let a couple of Far move past them before continuing. "West across the Soliel there's a people with a gift of their own. The Laeodalin. You probably know them as the handsingers. They're reclusive, but they're old cousins of the Far. If you can find them, their handsong may be able to help you. Help *us.*"

Fresh hope flared inside her. She remembered the stories of the handsingers. They possessed a song known as the Soriah, said to be the gentlest song that ever changed a heart. They wove their music with movement and touched the quietest part of those who heard it. Elan was right. The Laeodalin handsong might be able to remove the stain. She could be whole again. She could bear her people an heir. And the Far might even reclaim the Language they'd lost.

But there was a private, more selfish hope to go with the rest. If she were whole again, she'd reclaim her inheritance . . . and meet her mother in the next life. Mira would get to hold the woman who'd cradled her in those first few years before dying at her own Change.

"Go to Recityv," Mira said. "Answer the call of the regent. Help the Sheason convince the others to pledge their support to Convocation. I'll find the Laeodalin, and hope that they can heal me." She paused. "Thank you, Elan."

He nodded, still waiting on her answer.

"And as soon as I can, I'll return to bear you an heir."

Elan didn't seem relieved. "Such journeys have a way of taking more time than we believe they will."

"I know," she said. "But a child born now won't have much of a future if this Convocation fails. You saw what happened today." She nodded out at the plain, where thousands of Quiet lay on the shale. "If we can't push the Quiet back, any heir I give the Far will meet the same fate as human children will. Your presence at the regent's table will convince the doubtful. And your army alongside theirs will make a difference." She crawled out of the grave she'd been digging and went to take his hand; not in affection, but in reassurance. "I'll hurry."

Elan finally nodded. He reached to the side of the grave he was digging and picked up a long bundle wrapped in heavy, dark leather. He regarded it a moment, then handed it up to her.

"What's this?" She began to untie it.

He said nothing, only watched, as she unbundled a new set of swords. Or rather, an old set . . . her father's. "It isn't allowed," she said first. Then she looked up. "You knew."

"I'm glad you told me yourself, but yes, I knew. We've been friends too long for me not to notice. But oath or not, you need a matched set. And your father would have wanted you to have them. The quality is splendid."

She then noticed a smaller rolled piece of leather beneath the handles. She unrolled it, and held it up to the moonlight.

"A map," he explained. "It'll help you find the Laeodalin. If there's danger or threat of losing that," he pointed to the map, "destroy it. They guard their privacy, and so should we."

Her esteem for him grew double in those moments. But he waited for no gratitude. Taking up his pick, he started again to dig at the hard soil.

• CHAPTER ELEVEN •

Lamentations: The Future

*Let us not forget that beside absolute sound is related sound.
The very real power of the latter belongs to anyone willing
to offer song as a comfort.*

—First tenet in the instruction of absolute sound, taught to
  Lyren and Souden alike in the cathedral of Descant

A SOUND OF GREAT languor woke her. Wendra sat up, chill
and fever still rippling across her skin. Her bedchamber
lay in darkness, a lighter charcoal color where her window
stood. It was music she heard. A hymn sung in a tongue she
didn't know. The language didn't matter, though. She knew
this hymn rang out for the dead.

It was beautiful. The song didn't rush, didn't swell. The
wailing so often associated with songs for the fallen wasn't
present in this lament. It wafted with a steady, unending expression of loss. It had been composed with what her father
had called "the sad notes." Belamae called them halftones,
notes between notes often used to compose dirges.

She stared out through her window at the Far king's
garden, and lost herself in the sweet anguish of the song
itself, which—to her ear—bore an undertone of hope.

"Tell me about the song," she said to Sendera, who occupied her shadow in the corner.

"A great many fell today," Sendera answered.

"I want to go," Wendra said. "Can you take me?"

"You're not welcome there." Sendera spoke without any
particular prejudice.

Wendra turned to her. "I should go. Please. Many of those
they sing for . . . I'm to blame."

"That's why you cannot."

If not for the guilt running through her over the deaths of

the Far, she'd have marveled more at this ability awakened in her. As she sat, thinking back, she could remember only one time she'd invoked its power to do anything other than tear down. The first time. She'd sung her song box tune, and healed the fever that had gotten inside her after being wounded by a Bar'dyn.

"I'd like to mourn with them. I owe them that."

Sendera kept a long, taut silence, before saying simply, "No."

"Then take me closer? I'd like to hear the music better."

The Far hesitated a moment, then stood. Wendra dressed quickly, and together they passed into the Naltus streets, following the sound of the lament through the city of black shale. The streets were empty, windows mostly dark. Everything smelled of dusty stone and timber thirsting for rain.

After a time, they came to a great building raised in shale, like the rest of the city, but whose exterior had been scored in tight script—names. Rendered small, the names began at the doors and ran in columns to the roof some thirty strides high. And on each side of the hall, long lines of Far waited patiently, silently, to file through side doors.

Sendera pulled Wendra's cowl up and forward, obscuring her face. "Leave this on."

They stood across a wide street from the great house of song, listening. For most of an hour neither of them moved. It helped to be closer, but Wendra wanted to join them. Knowing that she couldn't, she soon found the song too painful to listen to.

She turned to Sendera. "I need to walk."

The Far woman started away. When Wendra didn't follow, Sendera looked back.

"Alone," Wendra said.

The Far woman wasn't her jailor. Her duty was only to watch while she slept. "Keep the hood up," she advised, and returned in the direction of Elan's manor.

As Wendra walked the cool evening streets of Naltus, heading as far away from the funeral hymn as she could, she thought about how easily she'd lost control that day. How the song seemed to take over. But mostly she thought about the Far who slept alone tonight, and the beds left empty. Many of those emptinesses were because of her.

She hadn't meant to do it, of course. She'd wanted only to sing an end to the Quiet. For all the damage they were doing to the lives of so many, she'd sung to end them.

Sometime later, she realized the streets were silent. No funeral dirge. She kept walking, and soon heard another lament. Not a chorus of voices. A single voice. And not a song. A fragile sound. A quiet sobbing. Wendra followed it, and found herself outside the window of a Far home. She peered through a small opening between the curtains to see a child curled on his bed. He might have been five.

She heard it in his voice—he'd lost loved ones in the day's battle. And when a child wept so, it meant a parent. Maybe both parents.

Wendra leaned against the wall of the house to brace herself. *Is this my fault?*

She needed to make it right. But it was a foolish thought. There was no answer for the loss the little boy was feeling. But she *could* do something.

With a softness such that one hearing it might think it a dream, she began to hum. Not a bold sound. Not a song to cheer. She hummed a lullaby. One she would have sung for her own child, had he lived.

She gave it all the empathy she knew how to sing. She wove it beyond what she had originally written, making it new, making it for this boy. It carried apology in it. It held tones of reminder for memories he could cling to. Mostly, it soothed. It said to know that he would be all right. That his parents loved him. And to know that the feeling of their love never needed to go away.

She didn't lend it the influence of her Leiholan gift. She was afraid what might happen. This time, she simply sang with what tenderness she could. There was a common place she shared with the boy, a place of loss. She sang the sound of that, and shared the sense of healing she'd hoped for after her own losses. After losing her own parents. She could still see the fresh earth being shoveled over their bodies laid down in the ground. She could still feel the sense of permanent separation that followed each shovelful of dirt. No more songs together. Not even a chance to say good-bye. Her song grew thick in her throat with emotion.

She continued to sing long after the boy had ceased to weep and fallen asleep. She sang for herself. And the pull toward Descant was stronger than before, to learn more about her song. How to control it. Strengthen it. For the next time.

• CHAPTER TWELVE •

An Overdue Conversation

A good astronomer—hell, any good scientist—finds little value in the notion of destiny. That's an entirely different matter from predictive ends that follow from close observation.

—From *On the Reconciliation of Poetry and Science,* an examination of providence, astronomy annals, Aubade Grove

MOST DOORS IN Naltus, including those in Elan's manor, didn't lock. Such would violate Far hospitality. And locks were largely unnecessary, anyway—the Far didn't bother with valuable personal items, and were well-mannered besides. So, Tahn quietly pushed the door open. He wouldn't wait another hour to have this conversation.

He stepped inside the bedchamber and gently nudged the door shut. Then he turned, allowing his eyes to adjust to the dark. In the opposite corner, a bed squatted in the shadows, where he could hear the long pull of a sleeper's breath.

He was nearly ready to wake Vendanj, when the Sheason asked, "Things to discuss in private?"

"Why did you take me away from the Grove?" Tahn took one step into the room.

Vendanj rolled over to face him. "More memories?"

Tahn pressed. "You must have known I was happy there."

"Why do you ask questions you know the answers to?" Vendanj made no effort to get up. He squeezed the bridge of his nose, as one with a lingering headache. His movements, even his words, were slow.

"To protect me. Protect the Grove." Tahn took another step into the room.

Vendanj spoke with a slow sigh. "You were fond of the Grove. More than fond. And of the many reasons to veil your past, one was to keep you from leaving the Hollows—where you were safe—and returning there." Vendanj motioned to a chair near his bed. "Please, sit down."

In the man's words Tahn heard an invitation to learn more about his own past. He quickly sat.

Vendanj leveled a thoughtful look at him and pointed at his bow. "You have certain aptitudes, Tahn. Certain abilities. Everyone does. Things that set them apart. And because of it, there's a role for everyone to play in what we're doing."

"You mean Braethen and Wendra."

"I mean everyone," he replied without any pointed correction. "Most of this help will never be seen or heard. Small sacrifices. Endings without clamor . . ." Those last words sounded like Vendanj was quoting a favorite line of poetry, and his voice trailed off for a moment. "For you there was Tillinghast because of the way you draw your bow."

How I used *to draw my bow.*

"We haven't had time to talk about the children." A look of understanding touched his face. "I'm sorry. It was a difficult thing you did. But it was the right thing. For us, but also for the small ones. Don't let it unsettle you for too long."

Vendanj then told Tahn about his own child. An unborn child. A child that perished when his wife died under the poor physic ministrations of the League. A small smile touched the Sheason's lips as he spoke of the future his child might have had. It was as fanciful as Tahn had ever seen or heard Vendanj.

"She would have been ten come spring." Vendanj made a circular motion with his hand, as though rolling time forward.

"I like to think of her making me drawings. We would have wrestled together, and she would have laughed when I let her pin me down. And in the early morning we would have walked the markets looking for the perfect apple. Except she would have made us buy one badly bruised, because she would have hated to think that no one else would buy the poor thing."

He went on like that for a while. Sometime later, and without pause, he transitioned to imagining the futures of the children Tahn had mercifully killed that day. He gave them life, conceiving specific moments that felt as though they'd actually been lived, and lived fully. Vendanj never rushed, never sounded as though there was anything more important to be saying.

And when he did pause, he invited Tahn to imagine with him.

So Tahn began, fighting through regret that burned in his eyes. "The first boy . . . I think he was a prankster. He liked to sneak up on his friends and shriek like a demon and watch them jump."

Vendanj laughed, his eyes looking like a man who saw it clearly. "He'll grow to be another Sutter."

Tahn laughed, too. "But he was also the first one to step into a fight to defend a friend," Tahn added. "And at night, when the other children started to weep with fear because another day had passed without their parents coming to save them . . . he sat by them with an arm around their shoulders and explained how it took a long time to climb the Pall, and that their parents were coming. Telling them to be patient."

Vendanj nodded appreciation at this imagining.

"The tall girl was his sister," Tahn went on. "The strongest among them. A peacemaker. She would have been a trusted counselor. One day the king of Nallan would have been planning to raise taxes so high that families would starve. And she would have convinced him to walk with her in the slums, where soup is brewed from rotten potatoes. She would have showed him what comes after he collected his taxes. And the king would have become known as 'the feeding king,' because during his time, not one of his people would have known hunger."

The two of them sat for a good while giving life to those small ones, honoring them in this way. He'd never forget their faces, and somehow now believed more deeply that he'd rescued them from something worse than death.

A companionable silence fell across the room when their imaginings for the six children came to an end. Tahn, though, went on in his head, doing the same for friends he'd known in the Scar. And a little for himself. But it was their memory— those thirty-seven—that helped him finally tell Vendanj. "When I saved them from the Velle . . . I didn't use the words."

I draw with the strength of my arms, but release as the Will allows.

He could barely stand to think them anymore.

Out of the darkness came the Sheason's tired voice, edged with a note of despair: "Oh, Tahn, you've let it go. My dying gods . . ."

The words were chilling to hear, filled with a serious sound. Vendanj slowly sat forward, his face catching a hint of moonlight from the window. Tahn was grateful for the darkness that softened the look of disappointment he saw in the man's face. The Sheason stared at him through the dark for a long time, his shoulders sagging.

Vendanj finally hung his head down, making it hard to understand the words he muttered. "It wasn't just their focus on the library. The Quiet didn't follow the effigy because they've lost regard for you. They knew you had let it go. In the Saeculorum, you ignored the guidance of the Will. Now . . . you reject it."

Tahn didn't want to talk about that, and turned to his other question before sharing his plans. "Tell me what 'Quillescent' means."

Vendanj lit the bed table lamp and turned up the wick, lending the room a warm light. The flame revealed the depth of loss in the Sheason's expression. It was the look of discouragement and wasted years. The man appeared unnaturally older.

He'd been lying, fully clothed, atop a made bed. He leaned forward with his elbows on his knees and rubbed at his face for a moment. Tahn thought Vendanj was preparing to scold him, that he'd try and persuade him to embrace those words again. But after a good while, and to his credit, he simply looked up, showed Tahn a sad smile, and asked, "Say it again?"

"Quillescent," Tahn repeated.

Vendanj looked back at him with reddened eyes rimmed by dark circles. "You've asked about this before. I don't know the word. I'd thought I could find it here, in the Naltus library."

Tahn regarded him with suspicion. "You don't even have an idea?"

"Lots of ideas." Vendanj's eyes glazed a bit. "It's likely a curse. Maybe a name they use for someone they seek."

Tahn shook his head again. "I think it's more specific than that, specific to me."

The Sheason stared at him, unspeaking.

"That give you any more ideas?" he asked earnestly.

It was Vendanj's turn to shake his head. His eyes still seemed to weigh earlier revelations.

Tahn began to wonder if his two questions could be related, if being called Quillescent had anything to do with the Grove. "Why did you send me to Aubade Grove in the first place?"

Vendanj scrubbed his face again, looking like a man trying to freshen his wits. As he did, Tahn focused his own thoughts on the Grove. It was a place of science, a place to learn, too, but that wasn't the main thing—it wasn't a school. His memories were more of debate and inquiry, research and hypothesis. No classrooms or exams. And it all revolved around several disciplines that focused their efforts on the vault of heaven.

Vendanj succeeded in regaining some vigor. "One of the great towers there is devoted to astronomy. Do you remember it?"

"One of five towers, actually," Tahn added. "Each with a different scientific focus."

Vendanj nodded. "We weren't sure we'd ever ask you to

go to Tillinghast. There were others before you, and more we could have asked." The Sheason seemed to look into the past then. "The sky, though. You were drawn there from the beginning. Seemed right to cultivate that interest. And to your question, I suppose we thought sending you to the Grove might help if we ever did ask you to go to Tillinghast. Knowledge of the sky is a good way to keep a man grounded."

Tahn suddenly yearned to be holding an astrolabe and quadrant map and looking up through a skyglass.

Vendanj might have seen the yearning in Tahn's eyes. "You learn more about yourself watching the long turn of a night star than you ever will in the company of philosophers and priests." He pointed at Tahn. "That's a kind of wisdom you seemed to have right from the start. Made the Grove a good place for you. At least for a while."

Tahn sat there, staring into his own past, where years of his life had emerged, fully clothed and ready to dance. Sometime later, his eyes focused again. The notion he'd had out on the shale became a conviction. "I'm going to Aubade Grove."

"Tahn—"

"I can do more good there than anywhere else." It seemed so clear and obvious to him now. "You'll want to send Wendra to Recityv to sing Suffering, but there may be other ways to keep the Quiet at bay. I think I know one. But I'll know for sure if I go to Aubade Grove." He gave Vendanj a long look. "You're preparing to fight a war, when you should be trying to *prevent* a war."

"Tahn," Vendanj's voice held an awful tone of certainty, "the war has already begun. And it's not only a Quiet war." The Sheason breathed a heavy sigh. "Oh, the Quiet will come. But while they do, we bicker with the League of Civility over immoral laws . . . and we try to reconcile a brotherhood that has become divided."

"The Sheason," Tahn said.

Vendanj nodded again. "Many believe as I do, that the threat of the Bourne is real, and that we can't afford half measures. But others . . . they believe my personal losses have driven me mad." He gave a wan smile. "The order is at odds

with itself. And I'm hoping that you can help me make them
see more clearly."

"See what?" Tahn asked.

The Sheason took a long breath, giving Tahn the feeling
that he'd come to the crux of it. "Do you remember the story
young Penit told us around the fire? About Grant trying to
stop the Sheason Artixan from reviving the regent's child
who came still?"

Tahn remembered. Chill bumps had risen on his skin. The
story had rung with hard truths.

"Grant and I disagree about this," Vendanj explained. "Just
as Thaelon and I disagree. Thaelon is the Randeur of the
Sheason; he leads our order. And he believes there are bounds
on how we should use the Will. He would have helped
Grant try to stop Artixan from reviving Helaina's stillborn
child. He would have told me that trying to give life back to
the babe was arrogating to godhood. Not our place, as men,
he'd say."

Weakly, Vendanj tapped his own chest. "I, on the other
hand, will die believing that the Will should be used in any
way necessary to alleviate suffering. Any way necessary to
stop the Quiet." He smiled, seeming to want to lighten the
mood. "The abandoning gods didn't leave us much. Let's
make the most of what we *do* have."

Tahn began to understand the weight Vendanj carried.
Sympathy got inside him for the man. With slight humor, he
asked, "And you think *I* can change his mind?"

"You've seen the Quiet, spoken to them." Vendanj looked
out the window at the night. "You've heard the stories of the
League poisoning its own. Your time in the Scar, and even
in Aubade Grove, gives you insight Thaelon will respect. You
stood at Tillinghast, Tahn . . . and lived." He took a long, slow
breath. "If we don't unite the order, the next Suffering will
be our own."

Vendanj looked back and patted the side of Tahn's leg with
warm familiarity. "The time for politics is over. And the only
way through this mess is together, and unified. I think you
could help the Randeur see this. And I'll tell you something
else, even if Convocation is successful and Helaina unites the

Eastlands . . . I don't believe we can survive the Quiet if the Sheason remain divided. We need Thaelon to understand. We need the Sheason Order to be whole again."

Everything Vendanj had said convinced Tahn even more that the best thing he could do was find a way to stop the war before it started.

"I'll get to Estem Salo. And I'll do everything I can to convince your Randeur," Tahn promised. "But by every hell, I'm going to the Grove first. To try to stop this war before it comes."

"Tahn—"

"Look what happened out there today. How did so many Quiet cross the Pall?" *A lunar eclipse. Pliny Soray slipping her orbit.* "There's something wrong with the Veil. We're running out of time."

There's a better way.

And he thought he could find it in Aubade Grove. He could build on what had happened in those last few cycles before he'd had to leave there.

"What is it in the Grove that you think can help us?" Vendanj's eyebrows rose with interest.

"A hypothesis," Tahn answered. *He* now looked out Vendanj's window, gathering a look at the stars. He could see Reliquas, the third planet, and thought suddenly about orbital resonance. "If we knew how the Veil works, the principles that underlie it, we might be able to strengthen it. Keep the Quiet where they are."

"More than the resonance of the Song of Suffering, you're saying." Vendanj seemed intrigued.

"It's about the connection between things. Even across great distances. Even when you can't see the connection." He looked back at Vendanj, and began talking faster and faster, his excitement mounting. "It's just a hypothesis. And a complex one, at that." He smiled, unable to hold back anymore. "But yes. A good godsdamn yes!"

"Not a new hypothesis, though, is it?" The Sheason offered Tahn a knowing look.

"No, and not easily proved. But I think I have a new approach." He smiled wide, thinking about Suffering, and the

Sheason power over Will, and his own ability to fire a part of himself. *They've got to be related.*

"Actually, what you're saying is sensible." Vendanj nodded and rubbed at his eyes again. "I didn't want to take you away from Aubade Grove. But things didn't go well the last time you were part of trying to prove this hypothesis." Vendanj showed him concerned eyes.

"Last time it wasn't my argument to make," Tahn countered. "This time . . . it is."

· CHAPTER THIRTEEN ·

Call for Intent

I've no fear of a man's beliefs. But I may fear his intentions in their regard.

—From the journal of Palamon on the eve
of the first Trial of Intentions

IT WAS NIGHT, deep in the small hours. A light rain fell on the rooftops and cobblestone streets of Estem Salo, the Sheason city high in the Divide. The storm came without wind or anger, the slow, straight fall of drops engulfing the sleeping city in a greater silence. Thaelon Solas, Randeur of the Sheason, stood in his study, watching the rain.

The private chamber was situated at the rear of the Vault halls. Its view from the first story looked out at a tall grove of aspen, interwoven with high mountain spruce, though none of their color or cheer was evident in the darkness. In recent days, he'd found himself here often, well after dark hour, keeping his own company.

The rear wall had been bisected and framed on stone rollers that were set in channeled grooves in the floor and ceiling. From inside, and with little effort, one could unfasten three iron latches and roll aside the two halves of the wall. It gave his study the feeling of being set among the trees, and he was glad of it.

Behind him, littering his desk, were letters. Some bore the seals of kings or councils. In looping formal script, these rulers and nations were informing him of the changing social and political landscape in their countries. The Sheason weren't yet being asked to leave, but the spread of the League of Civility's creed was reshaping the perceptions about Thaelon's kind. The League's Civilization Order, which made rendering a crime, was spreading. Sheason caught violating the law were being put to death.

Ignorant politicians.

He bridled his anger before it got away from him. "Emotion is no bedfellow to reason," his father had taught him. It helped to consider the other letters on his desk, the ones that came scrawled in the unpracticed hands of those who might make better use of a hammer than a pen. They were the pleas of parents whose children had fallen ill to unknown disease or carried a blade to some vague purpose. Armies were swelling. The League grew more militant.

In different ways, all the letters asked the same question: *How* should the Sheason serve?

Vendanj. The hard, outspoken Sheason didn't give a damn for anything but his own purpose and philosophy. That was the difference between them, and likely what lay at the heart of the League's condemnation of Thaelon's kind. Rendering the Will as a means to an end was wrong, and a short step from becoming Velle. Some renderings should never be made. Some uses went too far.

Vendanj's intentions weren't heartless. Just reckless. He was a problem.

Thaelon breathed deep the calming scent of rain, trying to focus on finding an answer. A moment later the quiet sound of footsteps through sodden soil rose in the night. Out of the dark and rain emerged Raalena Solem, his closest friend, and leader of the Sodality. Her hair lay flat against her head, drenched. She refused to wear her hood up. *Too much mystery,* she was fond of saying. Thaelon knew there was another reason tonight: She wore it down because she liked the feel of rain on her skin.

A pleasant musk arrived with her, a mix of wet wool and sweat—Raalena had been on the road for weeks. A small smile of appreciation touched his lips that she'd known where to find him.

She returned the smile. "You look like living rot. When was the last time you shaved your head?"

He ran a hand over his scalp. Several days of stubble. For good measure, he felt his cheeks and found the same. Deafened gods, he was tired.

She moved past him and dropped a waterproof satchel atop the letters. "One guess what's inside." She fingered a raindrop off the end of her nose.

More letters. Thaelon said nothing.

"It's accelerating. Regard for us wanes fast." She came up beside him, and together they watched the rain. "Some say we're too secret. The pragmatists simply feel we've outlived our usefulness."

He drew a heavy breath. "What of the sick and fearful? What protection is sought against the Bourne?"

She offered a sad laugh. "Many suggest the Bourne is an author's fiction, meant to urge children back to their chores." Her tone grew quickly serious. "Those who know there's life beyond the Pall see those races as distant neighbors. Perhaps neighbors with expansionist ambitions, but not the malefactors of a child's rhyme."

"But *you* still believe, eh?" he said, smiling.

"I don't get involved in politics. I prefer my wine have dregs." One of her standard replies; Raalena didn't suffer fools, who she readily identified by their taste in wine.

They fell silent for a time, observing the rain in its unhurried fall. "But there *is* something that you need to be watchful of," she finally said. "Vendanj has gathered dissenters around him."

At the news, he nodded. "That was inevitable, I suppose. But don't judge him too harshly, yet. He's rash, but we're not sure of his intentions."

"I don't give an tinker's damn for his intentions," Raalena

shot back. "Others will throw in with that one on reputation alone." She then gave him a thoughtful look. "I have news of those who travel with him."

"It must be gnawing at you to share it, too." He laughed tiredly.

"Don't play as though you aren't itching to know. It's half the reason you sent *me,* when a hundred others could have gathered up these cowardly documents." She waved dismissively with her free hand at the satchel she'd set on his desk.

He grinned at her ability to clearly read a man, and *inability* to sometimes keep those insights to herself. Men, as a rule, needed some thoughts to remain private. Raalena hadn't yet mastered the related skill of *not* sharing everything she observed.

"Where to start." She tapped her lip, playfully drawing out her revelations.

Then she described each of Vendanj's traveling companions, after which a silence fell between them. She seemed unwilling to share any more. Perhaps she'd learned something, after all, about how much truth a man can—

"Vendanj is leading a boy to Tillinghast," she said. "Hells, they're probably back by now. I suspect he'll also try to make it to Convocation, spread his unique brand of goodwill there, too."

Thaelon smiled patiently. "I've already asked Artixan and E'Sau to sit proxy for us at Convocation. Had a feeling we'd be needed *here.*"

She pointed back again toward his desk, her satchel, and the official declarations of kings. "While the rest of the world goes one way, Vendanj goes another and damns the costs." She gently put an arm on his shoulder. "You must choose a side."

"Is this the insight I sent you to find?" It came out a bit more tersely than he'd intended. She'd only *brought* him the news, not created it. Less sharply, he added, "I knew this before you left."

"And it's just half the story." She showed him no wicked grin, as she usually did when doling out information in her successively shocking way.

"Oh?" And where a moment ago he might have braced again for the worst of the news, he found—or perhaps reclaimed—his ire. It wasn't an anger of retribution. It was the fire of his own decisiveness—the mantle of being Randeur.

As though sensing it in him, Raalena related the rest with caution. "I've been back five days already. I kept my return secret, to verify in Estem Salo what I've heard and seen beyond her borders."

"Spying on your own? That's a bit coarse, even for you, Raalena."

The silence that followed seemed to drown out even the mild storm.

Raalena bore the criticism well, saying only, "They've begun to choose sides, Thaelon. Here in Estem Salo. Some wait upon the path you would lay before them. Others believe in what Vendanj has been teaching since the death of his wife. Dissent mounts. Schism in the order has formed."

Her words still lingered in the air of his private study, attended by the hush of the gentle rain, when he commanded in a soft, certain voice, "Call for the Trial of Intentions." He paused. "We have to know who would render without regard to their oath."

"You mean we have to know who sympathizes with Vendanj," Raalena said.

He didn't look at her. "They are the same."

CHAPTER FOURTEEN

Asterism

If the distance between two bodies is halved, the attraction between them increases by a factor of four. And so on.

—From *Gravity and Attraction,* a bawdy rhea-fol penned by
Martin Tye, former trouper turned astronomer

MIRA STEPPED INTO Tahn's room, glad to find him there. Wearing her father's swords, she felt almost normal. And the Laeodalin map she'd tucked into her shirt felt like a small bundle of hope. But Tahn brought more ease to her heart than any of these things.

She drew a chair close to where he lay on the bed. After sitting, she settled a regretful look on him. "I'm an oath-breaker, Tahn. My life has always been about one thing: keeping the Language safe. I gave that away."

Tahn's expression tightened with guilt. "I'm sorry, Mira."

"It was my choice. And now I'm losing my ability to react and anticipate the way Far do." She smiled, feeling the map in her shirt. "But I've got a chance to restore what I've lost. Even bear the Far an heir. I'm going to find the Laeodalin handsingers west across the Soliel. I leave in the morning."

Tahn sighed. "I'd go with you, Mira. I would. But I can't. I need to go to Aubade Grove. There are things I can do there." He shared the conversation he'd had with Vendanj.

She listened as his words came in an excited rush. "You should go," she said. "But I need to find the Laeodalin."

"So you can become Elan's queen." Tahn's words carried an undertone of resentment.

She smiled. "I'm essentially queen now. But it's more about having a child than a title. Elan isn't asking for my affection. That belongs to you."

The look on his face pleased her, until it soured in a way that made her worry. "What's wrong?"

He didn't answer, but shook his head as if vying with himself. She could see the conflict in his eyes. "I may not see you again after tomorrow," he finally said.

"That's been a danger since we met."

"No . . ." Tahn's brow furrowed more deeply with concern. "I love you. And I can't . . ."

Then she understood. She might not officially be Elan's queen yet, but Tahn struggled with the ethics of loving her when she would be wed to Elan eventually. She smiled again. He truly was Grant's son.

She then showed Tahn a thoughtful look. She could make this easy for him. She could leave the room, perhaps even find someone else to watch over him tonight. But she didn't want to leave. In fact, she wanted to be closer still. But it would put him in a difficult position. And she didn't want to do that.

She smiled sadly at Tahn and began to stand, when he grabbed her firmly and pulled her into a hard kiss. He drew back once to look at her, then tugged her onto the bed. He rolled atop her and kissed her again, deeply, more gently. His hair fell down around his face, brushing her ears and neck. She shouldn't let him do this. But even as she thought it, she wrapped her legs around his hips.

Tahn smiled through his next kiss. Not a smile of self-congratulation, or even of lust. It was a comfortable smile that felt good to press her lips against, more so for the small urgency in it.

He whispered something to her then, something that meant more to her than any proclamation of love. "I won't let an oath come between us again. Not yours. Not mine. Not ever."

She smiled. "That was rather poetic."

He gave a small laugh. "You're a kind critic."

Then, maybe because the Far needed an heir, she found herself wondering: If she and Tahn were ever to have a child, would it have her fair skin and grey eyes and narrow frame; or would it be more like Tahn, broader in shoulder, and more constantly wearing concern in its face? It would have their straight dark hair, and stand tall as they both did. And she'd teach it . . .

She felt his breath against her neck, warm, traveling in small exhalations. And her hesitation faded. She ran her hand over his brow and down his cheek, feeling the face that carried such weight now. And yet, there was newness in him, too. A kind of confidence that made her smile. They shared a different, silent oath.

Then they made love for hours, without regret, without self-consciousness. They were changed, each of them. And she reveled in that change for now, forgetting death, and the Quiet, and motherlessness. Those things waited for her on the other side of this night. But in these moments, she abandoned herself to Tahn, as he did to her. Their bodies wove a kind of dance and musical motion that she would remember warmly even if she never reclaimed the singular rhythm of being truly Far.

THEIR LOVEMAKING PUSHED everything out of Tahn's mind. He'd thought for a moment that perhaps he'd sought refuge in Mira's arms from so many anguishes. That maybe some part of him wanted to feel pleasure as intensely as he'd been feeling pain. That maybe he needed to affirm life. That perhaps her love would be enough to mend the wounds that had opened inside him, because he could only imagine love having the power to do it. And he did love her.

But it wasn't any of that. What he found instead was simple and wonderful. What he found instead was that love made the rest bearable.

Finally admitting those feelings, he realized they weren't filled with romance or poetry. His love had been tempered by real loss, the kind that helped you know you could live without someone, but also that you didn't want to. He spent his last night in Naltus embracing that simple truth.

Afterward, they sat at the window, looking up.

"Do you see that?" Tahn asked, pointing.

She followed his arm. "Where?"

"Those three stars." He twirled a tight circle with his finger.

She nodded.

"It's called the Chapel asterism—a unique triple star." He smiled, happy to be sharing something he enjoyed so much. "Two of the stars are fixed. They track across the vault of heaven as the world spins its course. The third, though," he indicated the top star, "that's Reliquas."

"A planet," Mira observed.

"A wandering star," Tahn said. "That's what I like to call them. The Chapel asterism only occurs when Reliquas's path crosses the dual Chapel stars. Happens a few times each year."

She grinned. "You're making a bad metaphor about us, for tonight."

"Reliquas joins the Chapel stars for a brief time, then wanders on." He laughed. "It's not an amazing coincidence. Just a sky pattern. Reliquas will cross the Chapel path again."

"I see," she said, and got up to undertake a pattern of her own—oiling her blades.

A knock came at their door, then a voice. "Elan would see you in the kingchamber." Footfalls receded down the hall, followed by knocking on other doors.

• CHAPTER FIFTEEN •

Nothing More, Nothing Less

*Some say the language of the gods—the language they used
to make the world—held power because of sound pairings
and particular emphasis and intention. Are these things not
learnable?*

—Extract from "On the Nature of Diety," a principles
of preparation text use by Emerit

LIGHT SHONE BRIGHTLY in Elan's kingchamber. Lamps
in each corner. Lamps on ashwood pedestals set around
the room. And more lamps across his long table of a desk.
Vendanj paused to let himself feel the warmth and brightness
of this place, set at the dark heart of the shale plains.

Bookcases had been chiseled directly into the shale walls.
Likewise, words had been hewn into the rock above and behind the king's desk: *Deleadem solet a rahmen caleendra
ruel.* They were words every Far child learned as soon as he
or she could speak: *We will keep our trust to serve your last,
most desperate need.*

They were all waiting on him. Tahn, Grant, Wendra, Sutter, Braethen, Mira, and, of course, Elan. Vendanj went in and
stopped in front of Elan's great table, facing them for a long
moment.

"The book of the Language of the Covenant is no more."
He shared a regretful look with Elan, for whom the news
would come hardest. "I tried to restore it. But what remained
was little more than ash."

Braethen turned to the Far king. "Surely you keep copies."

Elan spoke with the weariness of a man well beyond his
years. "Two copies, kept in separate vaults elsewhere in
Naltus. Velle found both. The standing order is to destroy the
book before letting it be taken. . . ."

Vendanj had tried restoring what remained of each volume. But no amount of rendering could undo the work of the flames.

The silence of failure deepened in the kingchamber.

Until, with the slow cadence of confession, Elan spoke. "We failed to keep the Language of the Framers . . . even if we had saved the book."

The Far king crossed the room and took down one of many volumes from a bookshelf there. He caressed its cracked cover for a moment, then opened it and read a few lines to himself. He shook his head at something and crossed back to Mira, handing her the book. Pointing to a spot on the page, he invited, "Read this." Vendanj joined them.

They looked down at a passage set apart by a lined border. Though it was unfamiliar, he could tell it was written in the Language of the Covenant.

She shook her head. "I can't. What does it say?"

"What it says isn't the point," Elan said. "That we cannot read it *is*."

Mira looked up from the page into the sullen face of her king. Elan said nothing more for a long time, letting the revelation settle on them. Mira shook her head in denial. "You're mistaken."

Elan returned a sad smile. "When you left for the Saeculorum, I spent several days trying to convince myself that the preservation of our stewardship over the Covenant Tongue rested with you. But I've been piecing together this passage from fragments of the Language we still memorize in our schools. . . ."

Mira took his hand. "What does it say?"

With an unsettling monotone, Elan answered, "It says that the commission of the Far is to protect the Language."

She shook her head. "We know this."

Elan pointed to a specific place in the text. "The word *silaetum* means 'to protect.' It also means 'to possess.' Somewhere along the way, we grew too enamored of our physical gifts. We developed our regiments to train and study the art of movement. We mapped them with efficiency and anticipation. We kept the Language as part of our instruction, but only a few poems and quotes—things that lent vigor to the Latae dances." He turned to look at the inscription on the wall of his chamber. "But over time, we simply memorized the translation, without being able to translate it ourselves."

"What of the invocations we use in battle? They're from the Tongue," Mira argued.

"But do you know what the words actually mean? Or just what they do?" Elan paused, looking back at Vendanj. "We've made a trifle of our commission. Not because we're slothful or irreverent, but because we focused on the wrong thing. We were supposed to keep the Language alive, and we've let it die. We stored the texts like treasure, instead of carrying them inside ourselves as we were supposed to."

Vendanj kept hold of his anger for the moment. "Is there no one who can speak it?"

"Only fragments." Elan looked up, as if he might petition gods for an epiphany. "And it was more than the words. It was how to couple the sounds, the various inflections when they are voiced, proper intention. That knowledge . . . is gone."

"Fools." Vendanj's effort to restrain his anger made the declaration more savage. "Generations have lived and died fighting the Quiet. Never in all that time have men called on the Far to make good on their stewardship. And at the hour of our need, when we could use the Language as a weapon against the Quiet, you find yourselves incapable." He paused, spoke through gritted teeth. "It's shameful. By every dead god, Elan, what choices have you left us?"

Elan accepted Vendanj's contempt without a word.

A long silence fell between them. Slowly, Vendanj put his anger away and began to reason it through. "The library at Qum'rahm'se is gone. The Naltus library is gone. We no longer have the Language of the Framers, but we've also kept it from the Quiet."

His thoughts turned south, to the Convocation of Seats called by the regent at Recityv. They could still succeed in uniting the nations of the east. That was now more important than ever. But it wasn't the *only* important thing. The Sheason were divided. They needed to be one again. One in purpose. Without the Covenant Tongue, Sheason support would mean everything when the Quiet came.

Vendanj let out a slow sigh. "We need to get to Estem Salo. But the third Convocation of Seats is about to commence. That must come first."

Grant rubbed his chin like a man with a suggestion. "The Sheason Artixan is in Recityv. He sits on Helaina's High Council. Let *him* speak for the Sheason."

"I have great respect for Artixan. Spent many years learning from him. He's a good friend. But he's not young anymore." Vendanj reflected a moment. "Besides, I've personally seen the threat Convocation is convened to address."

Grant raised a finger to make a point. "Not all nations are going to answer the regent's call. Some will view Helaina's invitation as political maneuvering. Others will refuse because they see no personal advantage." He gave a cynical laugh. "Some will dispute the need of a Convocation at all. Our time would be better spent persuading these holdout nations. We both know who they're going to be."

Vendanj agreed, and turned to Elan. "My friend, the Far have never claimed their seat at Convocation. Yours has been a unique commission. It's existed outside the governments of men. But that time has passed. You must now—"

Elan held up a hand. "I'll consider it." He looked at Mira.

"Strong as the Far presence would be at Convocation, it wouldn't be enough," Grant pressed.

Vendanj knew who Grant had in mind: Jaales Relothian, the smith king of Alon'Itol. Vendanj had been thinking the same thing for several days now. Manufacture and trade into and out of Alon'Itol—all warcraft. Like a rank chore, it had eventually become routine. When Jaales Relothian had ascended the Throne of Bones, he'd been a smith—a gifted smith, who'd taken that rank chore and made of it a real craft. Their war engines, their . . . gearworks, had become modern legends.

But ties with the smith king had been badly damaged. Much of that was Vendanj's fault. "Years ago I was assigned to King Relothian as an emissary of the Sheason. I counseled with him, hoping to broker peace between his court and those he fought. I was less successful than I might have hoped."

"Deaf gods," Braethen said, recalling the memory he'd shared with Vendanj. "You burned one of the king's towns."

"Nevertheless," said Vendanj, "we need their help. And no army is better trained than Relothian's. But Jaales won't lend his strength to us out of goodwill or common interest. We need him bound to Convocation some other way."

Sutter straightened. "I'll go."

Vendanj turned to look directly at the young Hollows man, surprised and pleased.

Sutter offered a soft laugh. "Silent hells, after everything that's happened, if I can't convince a blacksmith to fight with me, I may as well go home."

Grant's eyebrows rose. "That's not a half-bad idea, actually." He looked at Vendanj. "We're forgetting Sutter wears the Sedagin glove and carries their blade. The smith king respects the Sedagin like he doesn't anyone else."

"It gives him a chance, doesn't it?" Vendanj said. He fixed Sutter in a stern gaze. "Try not to offend the king in the process."

"Don't worry. Tahn and I are a good pair to—"

"Tahn goes to Aubade Grove. Alone," Vendanj quickly added. "There may be knowledge in the Grove that can help us against the Quiet. He'll go and do what he can to uncover it. None of you will repeat that. Don't even discuss it among yourselves."

Sutter rounded on Tahn in honest surprise. "Woodchuck?"

"We'll have no need of a rootdigger, Nails," Tahn said with a smile.

Vendanj smiled, too, if only for the normalcy of something as simple as nicknames: one for Tahn's time spent in the woods, the other for Sutter's farm-dirty fingernails.

"Your glove will serve us best in the Relothian court, Sutter." Vendanj pointed to the Sedagin glove he wore. "And Mira would like your company."

Sutter laughed at Vendanj's mild attempt at humor, filling the kingchamber with its first real life of the evening.

"For double pay," Mira said, her own smile a crook at one

corner of her mouth. She shared a look with Elan, who returned a reluctant nod of agreement.

Vendanj then looked back at the brash lad. "Just remember that carrying Sedagin emblems doesn't make you fully Sedagin."

"Appreciate your confidence in me," Sutter quipped.

That business taken care of, Vendanj shifted focus to Wendra. She sat somewhat apart from the others. "Wendra, I'll ask you to accompany me to Recityv. Return to Descant Cathedral. You can train with Maesteri Belamae. I know he'd be glad to see you." He offered her a confident look. "Once you gain control of your song, my guess is you'll sing Suffering like no other."

Her expression was one of tentative thanks. She looked around the kingchamber at all her friends. Then, just above a whisper, said, "I killed so many Far." She paused a long moment, holding a distant, mournful stare. "And I could have killed any . . . all of you. I wouldn't even have known." Her voice thickened with regret. "I'm sorry."

It was Elan who went to her. The Far king gave her arm a reassuring squeeze. "It was war. Nothing more. Nothing less."

Wendra shut her eyes and took a steadying breath, obviously holding back tears.

Vendanj let them linger in that moment only briefly. He needed to keep them focused, their spirits high. "Grant, you'll come with Wendra, Braethen, and me. I'll need your experience in Recityv."

Grant laughed, the sound rough in the man's throat. "I'm not terribly popular there."

"I don't need your popularity. I need your dissenter's skill in the Hall of Convocation." Vendanj gave his old friend a wry look. "You have a flair for convincing shiny-button procedure hounds that they squat over privy holes the same way the rest of us do."

Grant returned a devious smile, seeming to take a certain delight at the notion.

Vendanj decided to add, "And you don't seem to get caught in logic games. Your rhetoric is impenetrable—which is a puzzle to me—but undoubtedly something we'll need when we address the Convocation."

A few of them realized he'd attempted another small joke, and looked at one another as they laughed.

Vendanj then took six strides to the door, stopped, half-turned. He thoughtfully appraised the young king and then the rest, each of them, a last time. For a reason he couldn't explain, he simply wanted to mark the moment.

"We leave at first light. Sleep well." He then left the room with hope and doubt vying inside him.

We must unify the Sheason. But first we must unify men. Beyond that, the rest is just wind in dry grass.

• CHAPTER SIXTEEN •

Gardens of Song

A Telling is a sort of way-finding. It's words that bring a distant place into such sharp focus, that you can reach out and touch it. Those words need to be given voice, though. And most authors can't sing worth a tinker's damn.

—The *Twelfth Example of Clarity,* an author's study aid, by A'Garlen

SUTTER FOUND WENDRA at the far end of Elan's neatly tended garden. Small juniper shrubs and berry-producing pyracantha bushes nestled low to the ground between stretches of thick, closely shorn grass. The garden seemed an oddity in the city of shale, but a welcome one. He veered to the left, stopping near the low bench where the woman he'd always thought he'd one day marry sat staring blankly into the dark of pre-dawn.

"Good morning," he said with a cheerful tone.

Her face hung with the fatigue of sleeplessness, her eyes

drooping and ringed with dark circles. More than that, her shoulders slumped the way a man's will at day's end, when he plows without a horse. This wasn't like Wendra. She had a straight back. Even in the face of the rumors and innuendo following her rape, she'd not lost her confidence.

Looking at her this way, he remembered something he hadn't thought about in a long time. "Did I ever tell you my da had a song?"

She looked at him with mild surprise. He'd never spoken of this with her. With anyone, really. But it seemed right to share now. She motioned to the other side of her stone bench. Not a great invitation, but good enough.

He sat down, sharing her view of the rows of neatly manicured juniper. "It's not something you would've heard," he began. "I'm pretty sure Da wrote it himself. It was the only song he ever sang. And he didn't do it often. But when he did, I knew he meant it. Kind of like he needed to sing it. To hear it. You know what I mean?"

She nodded.

"It helped me," Sutter added. "Now, don't laugh at me. I'm no talent at this." He didn't wait for her to deny or encourage him. He wanted her to hear it, no matter how bad a job he made of it. He swallowed to clear his throat, and sang it as much like his da as he could.

> So now the chance to fall
> Too great for simple plans.
> Should I fail, others' lives
> Will suffer with this man.
> I don't belong to those
> Who lift the brighter veil.
> I'm confined to the ground
> With dirt beneath my nails.
>
> So, when north winds blow
> And call the autumn wind.
> I will hope I have saved
> Enough to fight the cold.
> Won't let him in.

Reconciled to all the pain I've ever known.
It is just the way this world
Dispenses of its own.
Can I live beyond
The name they make me wear?
I will try to be strong,
To stand again I swear.

Standing has a subtle way
Of giving men the trust
In their only strength,
The will to leave the dust.
So, when I've grown old,
I'll find my way back home.
And I'll fly in that sky
Where summer light has shone.
Don't mourn for me;
It's not a labor's wage
That I sought
When I fought
To find my way back home.
I'll find my way back home.
To find my way.

When he finished, he found her looking at him with a soft expression of thanks. "I guess it's rather simple. Small, maybe," he said. "But I think the feeling inside it is big."

She reached out a hand and placed it gently over his. In the chill morning, her hands were warm. He showed her a smile. "Can we talk a moment?" he asked. He hadn't planned the song, and what he'd actually come to share this morning would brighten her mood further.

"It's not my place to tell you to 'get on with it,'" he said. "But what I have to say may make you smile."

Wendra showed no look of eagerness or expectation. She seemed, at the moment, rather content. Watching her, he glimpsed the power of a song to provide perspective. But he did have good news.

"First, I have to tell you something about me. And you have

to promise not to share it with anyone, not even our hilarious Sheason. But Tahn knows."

Wendra remained silent, though her lips twisted in a thin zag of distaste at Tahn's name.

Sutter let that go by, and began. He explained about the faces of the dead that came to him. He told of the woman in Ulayla, burned alive; he told of the spirits he'd seen in the catacomb prison cells under the Halls of Solath Mahnus. And last, he told her about the host of Far souls he'd seen before the battle on the shale had started.

This woman that he thought he might love turned searching eyes on him.

He squeezed her hand. "Wendra, I haven't seen Penit's spirit."

The darkness of predawn still held in the skies above the Far king's garden, deeper still in the shadows of tall junipers shaped like inverted teardrops. But through the black, Sutter saw the light of hope dawn in Wendra's face. It grew there slowly—confusion, doubt, tentative belief, then real hope.

Her fingers tightened on his, and her smile lit his heart.

The sound of footsteps on the crushed-shale path rose up in the morning stillness. They turned to see Vendanj approaching.

He came and stood in front of them. "Sutter, I need to speak with Wendra alone."

He nodded. "All right. But she's feeling a bit better. Let's try and keep it that way." Sutter squeezed her hand with encouragement and stood.

Vendanj didn't acknowledge Sutter's jest. "Wake the others. Tell them we'll leave soon."

WENDRA LISTENED AS Sutter's steps through the crushed shale faded to nothing. He'd brought her some hope, and a smile besides. When they got past all this—*if* they got past it—she'd marry him if he asked her.

The hope he'd brought her, though, wasn't solely about Penit. She'd realized in that moment that if Penit was still alive, there might be thousands of people alive and held captive inside the Bourne. Taken there by highwaymen. Just as she nearly had been. The inkling of a new purpose took root inside her. A new anger. But that anger didn't feel wrong. In quiet moments like this, sitting in the Far king's garden, her anger felt *true*.

And with that thought, she left behind much of her resentment about her own child—taken by a Bar'dyn—and Penit, and even Tahn. Her thoughts were filled with the idea that fathers and mothers and sons and daughters had been seized and sold into the Bourne. A tremor of song stirred deep inside her.

She then looked up into the Sheason's calm face. He nodded and took the seat where Sutter had been. "It's good to take some solace in simple things." Vendanj's voice rang low and calm across the garden.

"At home, we'd sit on the porch at night. Light-flies would wink against the trees across the field. Da played a fiddle. Ma sang. That was before they both went to their earth. . . ." She let the remembering go.

Vendanj didn't speak for a long moment, seeming to let the memory have its due. "I know you grieve for the Far who fell to your song. Just as I know the anger in you seeks its release through these dark sounds. Trust me, I understand the conflict in a soul that aches for justice, has the power to do it, but must wait for the right time."

She stared back into the Sheason's dark eyes, and said nothing.

Vendanj's face softened. He put his large hands on her shoulders. "But as strong as your song may be in blind anger, it can be more powerful if sung with the right intent. I'm not the one to teach you this. But Belamae is."

She did want to return to Descant Cathedral. Learn more about her song. Learn to sing Suffering.

"Right now, though," Vendanj pushed on, "we need your help. I have something for you to try."

He let go her shoulders, reached into an inner pocket of his coat, and pulled out two folded parchments. He handed them to her.

"What are these?" A kind of dread filled her belly.

"Open them," he invited, and waited.

She unfolded the sheets and turned them to catch a bit of light from the eastern sky. On the first one, in a carefully rendered script, was a beautiful description of Recityv. The words brought vivid images to mind, capturing the grandeur and sense of promise in that great city. Reading it, Wendra had the feeling of being there, and a sudden longing for that place.

When she'd finished, she looked up at Vendanj, feeling slightly spent, as though part of her had traveled to Recityv and back in those few moments. Vendanj gave her a knowing nod.

"It's a Telling. Like the one Belamae sang for us when we came to Naltus. There are authors with the skill to write the essence of a place." He tapped the sheet in her hand. "If sung by Leiholan, it can open a passage to Recityv that will save us valuable time." Vendanj looked the question at her.

She'd used her song mostly to fight. And even then made a mess of it. He needed someone trained. Someone from Descant. "I don't think I can."

"You can," he said simply. "The second parchment is of Aubade Grove, somewhere you've not been. But its words are equally vivid."

"What if I can't?"

The Sheason's brows rose, as if he was honestly considering the question. "The truth is, we may already be too late. But if you can't do this, the Convocation will almost certainly fail. You have to try." He paused a moment, then added genuinely, "Please. We need you."

It was the first time she'd heard him ask so. *Please*. She looked again at the parchment in her hand. "I don't even know how to begin."

"Read them," he said. "Over and over until the words flow. I'll return with the others in an hour's time. We'll try then."

Wendra stared down at the parchments as the sound of Vendanj's footsteps passed over crushed stone and faded into the distance. In the silence of the garden, the thought she'd begun—the center of her anger—returned as if it had been waiting for her attention: *highwaymen trafficking men, women, and children into the Bourne, into the hands of Quiet.* Highwaymen like the one who'd nearly sold Wendra and Penit to Bar'dyn.

There was a piece of the puzzle missing, though: Why did the Quiet pay slavers to move human stock beyond the Pall? That was the part she wanted to understand. The part she thought her songs might help answer. One way or another.

Does that mean singing Suffering at Descant Cathedral for Maesteri Belamae?

She didn't know. What she *did* know was that she had to do something to help those who'd been taken into the Bourne, and do something to try to stop any more from having to go there. But *her* way was reckless. Her way wouldn't help answer the center of her anger. She needed to go to Descant and train.

Just now, she wished she'd learned more when she'd been to Descant the first time. If she had, she wouldn't be worrying so much about these Tellings.

THE LIGHT HAD slowly strengthened out of the east. Wendra had read each parchment ten times, poring over the words, before she heard the sound of many feet approaching. When she looked up, she saw them: Vendanj, Braethen, Grant, Sutter, Mira, and Tahn. They came with a few of their mounts.

When they'd all gathered close, Vendanj explained why they were meeting in the garden. "I've asked Wendra to sing two Tellings. One to send Tahn his way. Another to Recityv."

Everyone looked at her. She saw surprise, reticence, and even—she thought—some admiration.

"There's risk," he added. "But I have confidence in Wendra. And so should you."

"What about Sutter and Mira?" Wendra asked.

"They'll head west on horseback. Mira has a call to make on the Laeodalin. We've no Telling for that place." Vendanj gave Sutter and Mira a look of caution, and directed his next words at them. "After you're done there, move fast toward King Relothian. Tell him what you must to convince him. If the Quiet come, we don't stand much chance without his support."

"You'll need to be firm with him," Grant chimed in.

Vendanj nodded agreement. "Then get to Estem Salo. Mira knows the way. We'll do all we can to succeed at Convocation." He paused, choosing the right words. "But none of that will be enough to stand against the Quiet if the order of Sheason falls. . . . And we're on the brink of collapse."

A shocked silence followed.

"Some blame me for the schism in the order. There's some truth to that." Vendanj nodded with regret. "But we can mend the dissent. We *must*."

He took a few steps forward and gave Tahn a reassuring pat on the shoulder. "Once you're done in Aubade Grove, we'll get you to Estem Salo, too. If you arrive there before us, find Randeur Thaelon Solas. He leads the order. Tell him the library at Qum'rahm'se is burned. Tell him what has happened here at Naltus. And the sigil you took from the Draethmorte at Tillinghast . . . be sure he sees it."

Tahn pulled out the pendant and they all looked.

Formed of simple iron, the sigil resembled a smooth, thick handcoin with a hollowed middle, save for a small center disk. That inner disk, despite having no physical tie to the outer ring, did not shift from the sigil's center. There was continuity across the gap that made the inner circle immovable, even though one could run the tip of a knife around the inner hollow and feel nothing.

"The sigil is more than a marvel of physical law," Vendanj explained. "It's a glyph. A symbol from the time of the Framers. Unique because in addition to height and width, it has depth. It stands for fraternity. Family. It also signifies an inner resonance with outer things—connection and familial bonds that cannot be undone or unwritten.

"Thaelon needs to see the Draethmorte pendant, and understand these Quiet leaders still wear the glyph. It says much about what they believe. It says that aside from whatever bitterness or anger the Quiet bear, they still hold to a simple idea about their relationship with the races of the east."

"What relationship?" Tahn asked.

Vendanj looked away at the Saeculorum. "Their arrival will be more than maddened revenge. They'd come with a sense of purpose. The same purpose with which they began: an ordination to *refine* man. They'll come believing they belong. Perhaps are even kin. With men. With Sheason."

Vendanj then faced Tahn, and raised a finger of warning. "Be careful, though. The Quiet came to Naltus for the Language. But others may still hunt you. If so, traveling to the Grove by Telling won't throw them off for long. The glyph will draw more Quiet to you—"

"Give it to me," Sutter broke in. "I don't know anything about this Aubade Grove, or what you think you can do there without *my* help." He paused to offer a winning smile. "But if I take it, any tracker will think you're lighting out from Naltus, and they'll follow me and giggles here." He stuck a thumb at Mira.

Tahn shook his head. "I can't let you—"

"Don't start that. We'll just argue and argue and delay all this fun we're about to have." Sutter looked sideways at Vendanj. "Makes sense, right?"

The Sheason nodded appreciatively. "If you hadn't volunteered, I was going to suggest just that. It's half the reason you're going by horse." Vendanj looked to the Far. "Mira?"

She hesitated so slightly that most might not have seen the worry in her eyes. But she nodded, too.

"And before you say it, yes, I'll be careful. I'm with Mira; we'll be moving too fast for the Quiet to keep up." Sutter stopped smiling, and spoke to Tahn the way only a friend can when he wants to get to the heart of something. "You'd do this for me. Let me do it for you."

Tahn said nothing for a long while, staring back. Then he handed the pendant to Sutter with one hand, and with the other took him in the Hollows grip of friendship.

"It's a good deal, Woodchuck," Sutter said, and clapped Tahn on the shoulder.

Vendanj looked pleased, but his expression quickly returned to his familiar look of hard caution. "We should make the deception complete." He came and took Sutter's right hand between his palms. Almost instantly the back of

Sutter's hand began to burn, though he didn't seem to be in any pain. When Vendanj pulled away, Sutter's skin bore the same hammer brand as Tahn's did.

"What do I tell people this means?" Sutter asked. "It's hardly a random mark. Is it a sign that I'm meant to be a savior?"

Grant laughed with his rough voice. "It's a reminder that life is toil. And that tools are your best friend. Trust tools." Grant then stepped forward and hung his bow on Sutter's shoulder. "Carry this. Put your Sedagin glove away, and play the part of Tahn until you get to Ir-Caul—"

"And then show them the glove," Sutter finished. "I know."

Mira eyed Sutter's sword and glove. "The Sedagin emblems may not be enough."

"Perhaps not," Vendanj agreed. "But the people there have forgotten who they are. Make them remember. The glyph will help."

"Would you mind explaining that?" Sutter asked.

"I'll put it in simple words for you along the way," Mira offered.

Sutter laughed, hung the pendant around his neck, and that was the end of it.

Vendanj then addressed them all. "The Quiet don't always fight in open battle. They'll use our own kind against us, spread rumors." He gave Sutter a thoughtful look. "This will make your disguise more useful to us, and more dangerous for you."

The Sheason then turned and cupped Wendra's chin with one hand, his touch fatherly. "Now, clear your mind. Concentrate on the words, their meanings. Envision what is described as crisply as you can. Let it take shape before you." He squeezed her chin gently. "Melody, Wendra. Strong if your heart tells you to sing it so. Do you understand?"

Wendra nodded.

"Tahn will go first." Vendanj turned to Tahn, and spoke rather cryptically. "Don't let go of the words that have helped define you. It's a mistake." Then the Sheason stepped back with the others.

Before starting, Wendra stepped close to Tahn, took gentle

hold of his arm, and pulled him a few strides away. "I'm still angry. But it's not as much about you anymore. Or Penit." She glanced at the Tellings in her left hand. "There's hardly been time to talk since we left home. Still, I should have found you, so we could argue it out the way Balatin used to make us." She gave a weak but sincere smile.

He took her hand. "There'll be time for that later on." He offered a conciliatory laugh. "But I won't be adding any more reasons for you to hate me."

She studied his face a moment, questioning.

"I just mean that from now on you can count on me with this." He tapped his bow. "And the reason I'm going to Aubade Grove is because I think there's a way to stop this whole thing before it starts."

"The Quiet?" she asked.

He nodded. "You go learn to sing Suffering," Tahn said. "And I'll do what I can to help you from the Grove."

She saw earnest passion in Tahn when he spoke about this Grove and what he meant to do there. He looked determined and excited.

"But I don't want any of that to change us so much that we forget the Hollows," he added. "Fresh rhubarb in the spring. Remember? Your anger is sweet and bitter."

She smiled at that. "When this is all done, I'll make us a rhubarb pie. We'll eat it on the porch with a pitcher of chilled cucumber water. I should be cooled off by then. Belamae will help me with that." The thought of the Maesteri widened her smile. He had a calming influence. And he'd teach her how to use her song. Something she wanted now more than ever.

Grant stepped close. "Both of you, take care."

Tahn extended his other hand to Grant, who held it long enough to be more than a simple farewell. It looked like Grant wanted to say something to Tahn, but finally just nodded.

Wendra then squeezed Tahn's hand and let it drop. She turned toward an open area beside a row of high pyracantha bushes. She breathed deeply, and started to read. Slowly, softly, she began to hum the *feel* of the words, giving rise to a melody that sounded to her like the place described in the Telling.

A very low sound resonated over her teeth as she read and saw the images of Aubade Grove in her mind. Soon, she sang a few lines of spontaneous melody inspired by the beauty of the words and the images they conjured. A few moments later, she was singing without pause, in a fuller voice, raising the words into a song that expressed the feeling of the place and gave it shape and substance.

As she sang, two things happened.

In the space before her, the air began to ripple. It appeared as if a thousand threads danced in vertical and horizontal lines, weaving in and out of each other, tightening. It reminded her of looking through summer heat rising from sunbaked earth, blurring whatever lay beyond it. Except that this had a pattern, as though a fabric or rug was being woven.

At the same time, something inside her screamed for her attention—the song that gave her relief from the memories of childbirth and slave auctions and children whisked away by Quiet hands.

Her voice warbled. The passage taking form in front of her undulated as if unstable. She tried to focus on the words, force her voice to follow the lines of melody she'd found. But the harder she tried, the less cohesive the strands of air seemed to become.

"Focus, Wendra," she heard the Sheason say somewhere behind her.

She closed her eyes and found the image of Penit, remembered the pageant wagon plays he'd perform for them, his vibrant wit and trust. Then she saw Jastail, the highwayman who'd taken her and Penit and tried to sell them into the Bourne. That was enough. She opened her eyes and focused on the words, reading and singing until the two things felt like the same action.

Over the top of the parchment, the air shimmered brightly before her. It drew itself in long threads, as if on an invisible loom. She stared at the image taking shape, like a mirage on a desert plain. Her voice grew stronger, declaring the grandeur of this place called Aubade Grove.

She wove her melody into a higher register, the sound of it

coming more naturally now. The clear tones rose high on the morning air, reaching out over the garden. And in front of her, the fabric of the world crystallized into a large portal, through which the image of five great towers appeared.

She didn't see the last good-byes. She only saw Tahn walk past her and through the Telling she'd sung. She saw him double over as if in great pain just before he dropped out of sight. She let go her song, and the threads of the Telling unraveled until she was looking only at Elan's pyracantha hedge.

"Again," Vendanj prompted her, not commenting on what they must all surely have seen when Tahn hit the Telling window.

Wendra opened the second parchment—Recityv—and repeated what she'd done.

After several moments, another opening wove itself together, showing them the capital of Vohnce.

"You'll come last," Vendanj told her. "Don't stop singing until you're standing on the other side."

Her pulse quickened. She could see Recityv as through a dull haze. She hadn't noticed the skim layer when she'd sung for Tahn, but then she wasn't familiar with Aubade Grove. Before she could stop or warn them, her companions were moving through the opening.

"Keep singing," Vendanj said, as he led his horse through.

The Sheason's confidence in her bolstered Wendra's song, and she gave everything she could to it. A few moments later, she went in.

The movement was like trying to run through chest-deep water. The mounts all lurched, and fell. Sound traveled slowly, the tones bending, deepening.

Around her, Braethen and Grant tumbled to soft, wet earth. With great difficulty, she rolled to her back and ceased to sing. The window through space began to fragment, dissipate, and then was gone.

Wendra dropped her head back into mud, but quickly rolled and retched. She could hear others doing the same, even as her own stomach heaved from sickness and nausea. Some kind of filmy residue had gotten on her, in her.

She flopped onto her back and drew deep, ragged breaths.

Dark clouds rolled in the sky above, and she tried to concentrate on their gentle movement to ease her senses. Sometime later—she didn't know how long—the Sheason crawled to her side.

"Are you all right?" he asked.

Wendra nodded. "I told you it was too soon."

She could feel the wet, brackish mud on her fingers and face. From the smell of rotting plants, and the awful feeling that still roiled in her belly, she was afraid to know where they had ended up. Her mind raced to dark conclusions.

"It wasn't perfect," Vendanj admitted, "but look."

He helped her to sit up, and pointed. In the far distance, looking like another mirage, were the walls of Recityv. The sight of it brought relief, and tears of gratitude.

"We owe you much, Anais," he said, using the old term of respect.

She looked over at Braethen, stretched out on the bank of what she could now see was a wide, stagnant pond. He shared a look of thanks with her and nodded, not yet ready, she assumed, to test getting up or speaking. He didn't look well.

Grant was trying to stand, his face tightly pinched with pain.

She laid her head back into Vendanj's lap and closed her eyes, fighting another wave of nausea. Beneath it, though, rose a hint of small victory. She'd done it. She marveled again that her song had any power beyond mere melody. And her excitement grew at being so near Descant, near a chance to learn Suffering. For the moment, though, she allowed herself to enjoy the accomplishment of having brought them so far.

• CHAPTER SEVENTEEN •

The Bourne: Prelude

If you learn that a prisoner is innocent, do you not set him free? How is our conscience, then, if the creation stories are true and the Inveterae races' only sin—which committed them forever to the Bourne—was being undesirable.

—"The Condemantion of Gods and Man," a new abstract set forth by Darius Franck, College of Philosophy, Aubade Grove

KETT VALAN DROPPED to his knees in a puddle of his own blood. His arms were yanked hard in opposite directions by thick leather bands tied to his wrists and anchored to dead trees on either side. He howled in pain. The sound rose past the tribunal, beyond basalt crags, toward a lowering Bourne sky. A deep autumn chill hung in the air. Morning frost covered the ground, save where it had melted in the warmth of his blood. His lips trembled. But not from cold, or even pain. They trembled with confession. He would confess, not to stop the whip and its barbs of rusty steel—the pain he could bear. He would confess, and betray the Inveterae races who secretly sought escape from the Bourne, because he hadn't the will to watch his family suffer.

The Inveterae were his people, too. Which made the confession more bitter still. The First Fathers had herded Inveterae races into the Bourne with Quietgiven when they'd abandoned this world. Or so the old stories told. The Fathers hadn't found enough value in his kin to let them remain in the lands of men. Kett believed the gods were wrong. That they'd been hasty.

He was Gotun. Not a beautiful race. Not like men. Denser of muscle and bone. Thicker of nose and waist. More like Bar'dyn, but boasting smoother skin—easier to brand. But a father doesn't see those things when he looks at his children or mate.

His little ones, Marckol and Neliera, stood in the firm grip of Quiet guards. Filthy Bar'dyn hands on them brought fresh anger. He might defy the tribunal even now, were it not for the fear in his son's eyes, and the tears on his daughter's cheeks. Their worry and dread was for him; they didn't understand that their own lives hung in the balance of his choices here today.

His companion, Saleema, tried to show him a brave face. But the haggard lines on her brow told a different story. He pushed back his pain and shame, and offered her a look of strength to set her heart at ease.

"Stand," Balroath commanded. The Jinaal officer's voice rang with deep clarity—the hallmark of the Jinaal House. "Have the strength to meet your judgment on your feet, Kett Valan. Or else confirm the rumors of your treachery. Admit that you lead this separatist movement with fellow Inveterae conspirators."

Kett drew one foot forward and pushed himself to his feet. A wave of nausea and dizziness threatened to tumble him again to his knees, but he fought the sensation, using the lashes bound to his wrists to steady himself.

Balroath nodded. "Good. Traitors should have the same courage in the face of those they betray as when they plot in the dark. Now, let's speak plainly, you and I, so that we don't misunderstand one another."

Balroath drew back his whip and brought it down savagely across Kett's neck. The force and bite of the blow almost dropped Kett again. But he locked his knees and squeezed his arms as close together as he could, using the leathers to keep himself upright.

This time, he bit back his cries, trying to spare his little ones. He couldn't let them watch this any longer. He had to tell Balroath. But how could he condemn all the Inveterae races, give up their search for escaping the hopelessness of the Bourne. As he convulsed from the strain of torture, he cast his eyes heavenward.

We should never have been sent here.

When the pain receded, he lowered his stare to his torturer and judge. "No misunderstanding." He tried to sound dignified, but struggled to talk through his own shuddering breath. "You force my confession with the rough end of your whip and by threatening my family. Your tribunal is a mockery. We are not like you—" He gasped a breath. ". . . never have been."

Again the whip lashed out, this time tearing deeply at his cheek.

"If you mean that you're ungrateful, then we agree." Balroath gathered the lash. "You plan to lead Inveterae away from the only advocates they've ever had. You may have descended from the hands of different gods than we did, but those gods caged you here with us. So what is it, Kett Valan? How are you different? Is it that you think only Inveterae deserve to escape the Bourne?"

Kett smiled, the rip in his face sending new shivers of pain down his neck. "You don't want liberation, Balroath. You want dominion." He laughed. "And advocates? Inveterae are your footstools. Always have been. We raise your crops, tend your prisoner camps. You shove us ahead of you when you try to push through the Veil, then walk over our backs when we fall dead in the breach."

Balroath let the flail fly again. And again. And kept on until Kett dropped. This time his shoulders popped as his arms separated from his shoulder joints. He hung down, his face near enough to the ground that he could smell coppery blood and fallow earth.

He whispered, mostly for himself, "We want what was taken from us, but not through war. We just wish to go south. And live."

A long silence settled among them. Balroath interrupted the stillness with a subtle threat: He put down the whip. The next assault would be on someone he loved.

"I will not ask again."

Kett's chest and gut tightened. Could he reveal the names and plans and hopes of countless families?

I have to get us out!

One last time he turned to Saleema. He needed her look

of faith and courage. There was none. Only an aimless plea. Her heart had been pushed too far. He was alone.

He wanted to cry out to his gods, then. Seek rescue, or strength, or just relief. Their Abandonment had never struck him as deeply as now. He was not alone merely in this remote tribunal. He was alone under all the skies of heaven.

In his mind rose the story of Tanelius, an Inveterae of the Fennsalar race herded into the Bourne after the Whiting of Quietus. Tanelius, who, though abandoned by his makers, would not abandon them. Tanelius, who had believed that his own decency would qualify him one day to return to the lands south of the Pall. Tanelius, who had earned the trust of the Quiet through labor. . . .

A new thought lit in Kett's mind. A dangerous one.

There were rumors that the Quiet had discovered a way out of the Bourne, or at least knew a way of disrupting the Veil while they crossed. It was only a rumor, but one Kett had heard enough times to lend it some weight.

So, there was a way.

Coughing up more blood, he gathered all his strength and stood, his shoulders throbbing with pain. "Place me in service. Give me a rank."

Balroath's eyebrows rose. "What do you mean?"

"If I betray my cousins, I'll be dead in a few hours—my people won't suffer a double tongue. But if you pardon me, give me a brand and rank, I am more valuable to you."

"I'm listening," Balroath said with neither interest or skepticism.

Kett composed himself, drew a lungful of air, and looked around at the other tribunal members. "If there *is* an Inveterae exodus planned, it will take much for *you* to stop it. Not to mention the distraction from your own plans. But Inveterae races will listen to me. I can be an example. I can lead them in a new direction."

Balroath studied him. "Why would you do this?"

"You know the answer to that." Kett glanced at Saleema and his children. "But I must be raised in the estimation of your leaders, the Sedgel. I must have a place among you."

Balroath stared at him with questioning eyes.

"Otherwise," Kett continued, "Inveterae won't believe what I tell them."

"And what would you tell them?"

Kett formed the words carefully. "That you will lead us *all* into the world beyond the Pall. That you don't want war. That you will return us to the first intentions of the Framers."

Balroath laughed—an awful, basso sound that got into the very soil. "You think you can convince Inveterae of this?"

Kett stared back with as much challenge as he dared. "If they see me seated in the halls of your leadership . . . yes."

The sour mirth on Balroath's face fell away. He stepped forward, brandishing his whip. "You don't understand the bargain you strike, Kett Valan. The south of the Bourne is a good place for you. North and west . . . it has a different occupation. And if we agree, you will be changed. You might prefer to die as you are."

Balroath paused, his eyes searching. Kett stood firm. Chuffing warm, billowing breaths into the chill air, the Jinaal looked at each of his fellows. Nods followed from the others.

"You have your bargain."

Kett let out a held breath, steaming the air around his face so that he didn't at first see Balroath's movement.

When the air cleared, his heart slammed painfully in his chest.

Balroath had taken three commanding strides toward Saleema, and turned her to face him. He stared into her eyes for a long moment, the look nearly tender, nearly intimate. Then he inclined toward her as if to steal a kiss. But he stopped just short of her lips, and drew a slow breath through his nose, filling his lungs. Thin vapors streamed from Saleema's nose and mouth into him. She began to slump. Her shoulders rolled forward; her knees and hips flexed, threatening to drop her down. Balroath put a hand around her waist to hold her up.

He's drawing in her spirit.

"Please, stop!" Kett cried.

Balroath turned a hard eye on him. When he spun Saleema around to face him, she was gone. The part that made her

Saleema was gone. The shell that remained looked back at Kett with vacant eyes.

Balroath lifted his knife from an iron-studded belt. In one easy motion he grabbed her head by the hair and drew his blade across her throat. It happened so fast she didn't have time to fight or scream. She hardly tried.

But shock rose on her face, distant eyes imploring. She dropped to her knees, clutching at her throat to stop the bleeding, as if momentarily herself again. She pitched forward, turning to look up at Kett, reaching out to him.

"You understand the consequences of betraying our trust." Balroath started to lead Kett's small ones away.

A last wretched cry shot from Kett's throat as he cursed the Quiet and the god that made them. The sound mounted the crags and raced heavenward.

MORNING WAS A good time to lay the dead to rest.

Kett emerged from the mouth of a narrow canyon, pulling a handcart laden with the body of his companion. The wheels creaked in the morning stillness, echoing out over a long, narrow lake at the bottom of a deep valley. He paused there, at the end of a three-day journey to reach Mourning Vale, where Inveterae had, for ages, brought their dead to say good-bye.

Anymore, few Inveterae observed the traditions of their ancestors, many having forgotten the Vale existed at all. Most Inveterae simply focused on harvesting thin wheat and dredge roots for the Quiet, or they worked the camps, shepherding prisoners from both sides of the Veil.

And they'd all but given up the idea of escaping the Bourne. Even the old stories of the Mor peoples—Inveterae races said to have a powerful song, a song that had helped them tear through the Veil and cross into the Eastlands—even those stories were fading.

Kett walked to the water's edge, and watched as littoral mists eddied languidly across the glassy surface, touching the shore and the tips of his feet. He saw his own pale reflection, and thought, as he had so often before, that his kind had a touch of the grotesque.

At a fair distance, it would be hard to discern the difference between his own Gotun race and a Bar'dyn. Nearer, one would see deeper-set eyes, thinner lips, and smoother skin.

But the real difference was their intentions. Gotun—silent hell, all Inveterae races—held no real malice toward men, as Quietgiven did. They owed that to a different set of Framer hands: the Quiet's first and only father was Maldea, the dissenting god; Inveterae were the get of the absent gods.

He looked out over the lake, surveying its eerie calm. No fish broke the water's plane, no insect buzzed, no bird let out its cries. A few trees clung to life, their leaves and needles grey-green under the cloudy sky; most were dead, and appeared like bony hands reaching heavenward with their bare white limbs—perfect companions to the bones that lay beneath them.

The Inveterae didn't bury their dead. Instead they were laid faceup to wait on the grace of the Fathers who might reunite them with the already departed. Like cordwood, the bones of generations lie stacked at the shoreline around the lake, weapons and armor and raiment of their funeral rites hanging from their skeletal remains. Up the sides of the hills around the lake, Inveterae had been laid as far as the eye could see—dark waters framed by endless white mounds of bone.

Kett returned to the handcart, gently picked up Saleema's body, and walked her to the shore. He cupped his hands and drew water from the lake, gently anointing Saleema's face and neck.

He touched the gouge in his cheek that he'd received during his interrogation. He liked the reminder its scar would become once the scab was gone. He would remember Saleema, and he would not give up.

Then he was ready, and began to recite the old words:

Remember us as we remember you
Give to us as we give to you
Follow us as we follow you
Despair for us only that your escape comes too soon
And leaves us here to bide as best we can
Until all is done that we may do

Or else abandonment is ended and we with you
Are reunited on a happier shore

He said it again. And when he'd finished, he remained silent for several moments, saying a more personal, silent goodbye. Then he raised his chin toward the far end of the lake and wailed. The tormented cry raced across the water's dark surface, across the bones of countless forebears, and seemed to fill all the space of Mourning Vale.

His cry was joined by voices from the lip of the canyon behind him, sending awful harmonies into the grey light of morning.

He jumped up and whirled toward the intrusion. As his howl still echoed down the lake, several large shapes ended their own cries and stared at him. When silence returned, six Inveterae, each a different race, slowly approached.

They gathered around his wife's body, looking down with expressions of regret and appreciation. Then each knelt, laid a hand on Saleema, and kept their own private reverence for her. Some time later, they looked up, focusing on Kett.

It was a Raolyn Ela woman who spoke first. The Raolyn had removed themselves from the company of other Inveterae six generations ago. They were easy to spot, with their perfectly white skin and dark, pupil-less eyes.

"You are Kett Valan. I am Sool." The Raolyn woman spared a look at Saleema. "And this is your companion, Saleema."

Kett nodded.

"You plan to lead the Inveterae races beyond the Pall." Sool stared at him with her large black eyes. She gestured at the others kneeling around Saleema, and said simply, "We are with you."

Kett's heart thrummed in his chest. For many bitter years he had taken every possible—and secretive—occasion to share his hope of liberation from the Bourne. But for every hundred who would even listen to him, maybe five believed anything could be done, and only one was willing to help.

Still, over the years, a small faction had grown—a *move-*

ment Balroath had called it when he'd taken the whip to Kett at his tribunal.

But here, now, on the shores of Mourning Vale, leaders of the central houses had pledged themselves to him. It quickened his blood. Gave him a new sense of urgency. He looked into the faces of these representatives of each house—the Thealote, Simsi, Dystontal, Uren, Waelon Sol, and House Raolyn Ela—and thought for the first time that just maybe . . .

"I am to be initiated by the Jinaal," Kett explained. "I'll come into your towns and villages spreading a message of unification and allegiance to the Quiet." He paused. "They're expecting a count of separatists."

"A careful ruse." Sool smiled. "You will gain insight into their plans. And we will have warning when they come to raid."

Kett looked at Saleema and thought about sacrifice. "I think it will mean more than that. I've heard rumors. The Jinaal believe they've found a way to cross the Veil. And not just a few at a time. A way to part it completely. Or at least for as long as is needed to send an army through."

Amazed murmurs from his new friends.

"I mean to find out how," he said. "Use it to *our* advantage. To get *Inveterae* out."

Each of them nodded appreciation and agreement to the plan.

"But I must be seen as part of them." Already he would be testing their pledge to him. "If there's no resistance when I come to you, it will seem suspicious. Some of you will need to defy me. . . ."

The leader of the Uren House put a hand on Kett's shoulder. The slick feel of his pitch-black skin reassured him. He spoke with a mouth full of teeth. "I am Rorgard. It won't be hard to find Uren willing to sacrifice themselves."

"And I am Fedema," said the Simsi woman. She arched her back and stood to her full sinuous height, two heads taller than Kett. Something like a shiver coursed over her body, lifting arrow-sharp hairs in a wave across her skin before they settled back with a whisper sound. "You have already given much," she said, looking into Saleema's peaceful face, "but you may have more sacrifices to make."

Kett thought of his little ones. For now, they were alive.

Two of the other Inveterae he knew by reputation. Lorin, the Thealote, sat thoughtfully and quiet, his massive shoulders and long arms giving him the option of a four-appendaged gallop when he was in a hurry. Malat, the Waelon Sol, fidgeted a bit, with shoulders as narrow as Lorin's were thick. The Waelon were the smallest Inveterae race, but by far the quickest. Physical laws seemed to have less hold on them. Neither Lorin or Malat spoke, their expressions showing peaceful agreement with what they'd heard.

The last Inveterae house, Dystontal, had sent a young female in the midst of her speechless cruciation—her mouth had been sewn shut. She wore no clothes, but hardly seemed naked. Her skin below the neck read like text of symbols and images. She nodded. The Dystontal were with him.

Kett gazed down the long length of Mourning Vale, taking in the sight of dark waters and thickets of bone that filled the valley hills right up to the slate-colored sky. The wind stirred the lake, causing ripples that lapped the shore softly in front of him.

He began the last part of the exequy, raising his voice in strident petition of the gods to protect Saleema's departed spirit. It was the oldest prayer he knew, and his conspirators joined him.

The customs aren't dead.

Generations had pled for the aid of the gods that sent them into this far Bourne. The requiem asked the First Fathers to receive the Inveterae spirits they'd found unworthy to live alongside men.

Kett offered the elegy, his mourning song racing across the surface of the lake and fields of bone.

• CHAPTER EIGHTEEN •

Death of a Song

*Leiholan song has implications for both the listener and the
vocalist. So, then, consider the Song of Suffering.*

—From a dissertation given at the Second
Assembly of Conservatories

DESCANT CATHEDRAL, FOR all its music halls and spires
reaching skyward, huddled against the night like a forgotten child. Except for a few dim lights behind boarded
windows, it might have gone unnoticed in the dark, just one
more shadow at the end of a tired street. Once the crown jewel
of Recityv, it stood now at the center of the quarter that bore
its name, the Cathedral Quarter—Recityv's slum.

Its patrons came in two stripes. The first were musicians
who still studied inside its vaulted halls. The second were
derelicts, whose only need of it was a place to urinate against
when they'd gotten too deep in their cups. Helaina Storalaith,
regent of Recityv, was neither, but sought Descant for the second time in as many weeks. Though, this time she'd been
summoned.

Along the quarter streets, fires burned in open pits, around
which men and women warmed their hands through gloves
more hole than fabric. Jangly music drifted from taverns—
after dark hour, stages were taken by those who needed the
practice. And prostitutes, loaded on laudanum, turned their
paint-caked, half-lidded eyes on men and women alike, bray-
ing laughter when passersby tried to scuttle past untroubled.

The streets reeked of feces, men's and animals'. Helaina
tried breathing through her mouth to avoid the smell. With
her hood drawn forward, she passed through the slums un-
hindered and reached the cathedral's front entrance. She

arrived with joints aching from arthritis and feeling more tired than she would have thought.

The lignum wood of the door didn't catch or reflect the vagrant fires behind her. Dull and massive, it had withstood more than one assault in its many years, and had the nicks to show for it. Up close, she could also see the barest of carvings in its ironlike surface—musical notation of a type she hadn't seen before.

She knocked and stepped back to wait. Standing at the foot of the once-great sanctuary, she cast her gaze up its stone face. The immense shape of it carved a figure from the starry sky above. *Implacable,* she thought. The grandeur of Descant had changed, but it was still there to those who looked. Once a feat of architectural achievement and a center of thought, the cathedral still showed its strength, but now more as a testimony of endurance.

Music students came and ushered Helaina inside. They bowed in deference to her office, and led her to her summoner.

All around her, the Song of Suffering seemed to run through the very stone. Sung somewhere at the cathedral's heart, the Song seeped into the foundation, spreading out and up. Though her people knew Descant's work and purpose generally, few had any idea about the true nature of her song.

She followed the stately pair of young students—Lyren, they were called. Together they passed Maesteri portraits and braziers of coal that lit and heated the cathedral passageways. They passed music instruction rooms where instruments lay dormant for the evening. They passed great recital halls and atriums set with rows of empty chairs. The entire place gave her the feeling of latent song.

Finally, the Lyren parted at a door, nodding for her to enter. Alone, she followed a short corridor into a great round chamber that rose a hundred strides or more to one of the grand Descant cupolas. She could never have imagined the immensity of the room from outside; a space so big even the silence hummed a soft note.

Five more corridors receded from the hall at equidistant points around its circumference. As she stepped farther inside, the Lyren entered, closed the door behind them, and took position in front of it like gatesmen.

Standing basins of water stood at even intervals along the wall. On either side of each basin, large marble statues rose in the attitude of song. The floor, like the domed ceiling above, had been carefully crafted with variant colors of stone to create a mosaic of the sky. At times it seemed as if she drifted in the great expanse of space, surrounded by nothing but the heavens.

In the center of the room stood a round stone dais, and on it a lone Leiholan . . . singing. The entire chamber resonated quietly with her song. The smallest sound made from the dais carried perfectly to every surface of the chamber.

As she listened, rapt by the lament, the walls seemed to disappear. It was as if she stood in the place the song described. By turns, the scene shifted, even as the song shifted, in tone and tempo. She witnessed atrocities great and small, some from the annals of their histories, others she'd never heard of or read. After a few moments of the song, the heartache overwhelmed her and she began to feel faint.

She staggered. The Lyren rushed forward, hooking arms with her on each side. Only when the refrain of the melodist lightened did the walls of the chamber return to stone, and she could see Maesteri Belamae rushing toward them.

He smiled warmly and took her arm, nodding to his students, who retired to their posts.

He spoke quietly—so as not to disturb the music. "You looked peaked; would you like some water?" He didn't wait for a reply, and led her to the closest basin, where he fetched her a small cup.

The coolness on her lips refreshed her a bit. "Thank you," she whispered.

"And now you look better than ever." He smiled.

She wished her appointment with Belamae hadn't come in the company of others, so she could let down her façade of strength a little. All hells, her joints ached. And she was sweating now the way she often did at night—though, usually, it was for no damn reason. Tonight, at least, she'd taken a brisk walk.

She pushed her hair back. "You're a bad liar. I'm old."

Belamae pinched a tuft of his own hair, as snowy silver as her own. "Leave me with my delusions."

She gestured to the wide hall. "It's remarkable, Belamae."

"And this is only the rehearsal hall." He looked around with satisfaction.

"For the Song of Suffering?"

He nodded, blinking slowly as one who had not slept.

"Well then, I can't imagine what it must be like . . ." She stopped. She'd never been in these inner sanctums, either as Belamae's friend or Recityv's regent. The inner workings of Suffering were available only to those who sang its song. This wasn't a time for banter. "What's wrong?"

His familiar smile faded, replaced by heavy concern. He didn't speak, but took her hand again and led her halfway around the chamber to one of the corridors, where two more Lyren crouched over a form lying on a low bench.

The song behind them modulated to a sound of requiem.

As they approached, the two attendants drew back. One looked at Belamae and shook her head. "Even the healing acoustics here haven't helped," she said.

Belamae nodded and knelt at the side of a dead Leiholan. He gestured for Helaina to kneel beside him. "This is Soluna. She sang Suffering for eight years. She came to study with us from Masson Dimn at the age of sixteen. And tonight, the Song demanded too much of her. . . ."

Helaina stared down, astonished . . . and frightened. "How could it bring her to death?"

He looked up, still holding the young woman's hand. "It's an exacting thing to voice Suffering. The words and music are always the same, but the cadence and intonation are unique every time it's sung."

"I don't understand."

"The Veil is not unchanging," he explained. "It waxes and wanes like a moon. But unlike a moon, its change isn't a set pattern. It ebbs and flows with the encumbrances placed on it . . . from either side." Her old friend looked at her straight. "The Bourne surges against the Veil, Helaina, and when it does, the Song demands more from us."

The waste of life lost so young darkened Helaina's mood.

"The Leiholan gift comes less frequently than it once did. Or is less often recognized." Belamae shrugged a slow shrug. "Either way, our conservatory suffers from too few students. And as a result, the Song suffers. It's not hopeless." He smiled wanly. "But I worry, Helaina. I worry. . . ."

"What are you telling me, Belamae? Why did you bring me to see a dead Leiholan?"

Against the low hum of Suffering, which now sounded like a prayer, Belamae stared regretfully, seriously. "Time is short. Get on with your Convocation. But unless something changes . . . we may be unable to keep the Song going every hour. There could be silences. And if there are, deaf gods help us."

The implications shook her. The Quiet were already pushing through the Veil in small numbers. It was why she had called for a Convocation of Seats in the first place. No single nation or realm, no two or three together, would be enough to stand against the Quiet if they came in force. As with the first and second Convocations ages ago, to succeed, they would need many banners to fly together.

But what Belamae was suggesting was more than war—should it come to that. It was stretches of time without the protection of Suffering. The Quiet could come . . . all at once. A new kind of worry entered her heart.

Belamae broke her stream of thoughts. "We spoke not long ago about soliciting my people for use of the Mor Nation Refrains. That time has come."

She knew little about the Refrains. Histories revealed next to nothing. And though Belamae had spoken of them, he'd always done so guardedly. The Mor nations had gathered themselves into a kind of confederacy known as Y'Tilat Mor. The annals suggested they were races that had escaped the Bourne using a collection of refrains. Songs of power. Similar to Suffering, but used in battle. The Mor nations were reclusive, though. Extremely so.

She nodded. "We'll prepare a formal request."

"Do you remember the language?" he asked.

"I remember." It was one of her fondest recollections of their early friendship. "You were the perfect tutor."

His managed a small smile. "You southern races and your single-cant speech. You miss the beauty and complexity of language to be found in the rhythmic and intonational layers. But you had a good handle on it by the time we were through, as I recall."

She hadn't spoken or read the Mor tongue in years. There was work ahead to refresh herself on its many complex levels of meaning. She held another moment of silence for Soluna, then stood. Kings and queens and ambassadors from across the Eastlands had begun to arrive for Convocation, and they expected to find "the fist in the glove"—the appellation she'd become known by. She still had days of preparations for that little affair.

Belamae bent and placed a kiss on Soluna's cheek. Then he rose and faced Helaina. "I hadn't planned on rejoining your High Council. I've no stomach for politics and its duplicities." There was now fire in his eyes. "But I will. And be damned those that come against us."

His voice sounded like a quiet roar, mingling with Suffering in soft dissonance. And while Helaina was glad of his support, their immediate threat came not from beyond Recityv walls, but from within.

CHAPTER NINETEEN

Some Must Lead

They fight us. I wonder if they know that we don't seek to convince the gods of anything, but only to reconcile ourselves.

—From The Irony of Hate, an unpublished letter penned by
Marta Solemy, Reconciliation prioress, in response
to the beheadings of several members of her faith

ROTH STANED, LEADER and Ascendant of the League of Civility, strode confidently up the center aisle of Bastulan Cathedral. When Recityv was still young, Bastulan had rivaled Descant for consideration as the grand jewel of the city. Its magnificent columns and intricate vaults rose so high that the ceiling hung in a haze of sunlight admitted by dormers a hundred strides above. Underfoot, alternating squares of polished granite and obsidian made a checkered mirror of the floor. The hallowed place had been consecrated to worship by the Church of Reconciliation. Its very name—*reconciliation*—made Roth smile. Adherents to this archaic doctrine still believed in the plausibility not just of the Framers, but that through devotion the abandonment of the gods might be brought to an end. *Fools.*

Long green and violet banners hung from the rafters against the walls. Statuary stood in alcoves here and there. Incense burned at altars before tracts carved directly into the rock. Braziers glowed with embers in the shadowed halls receding from the main axis. No less than a dozen smaller chapels lined the great interior—each wrought in the wood of its patron's homeland. It reminded Roth just how wide the nation of Vohnce itself actually was. And how old and burdened with myth.

The cathedral was mostly empty today, as he'd expected.

His appointment was here. And over on the right, several pews up, a few cripples prayed for healing.

At the far end of Bastulan, long steps rose off the main floor, climbing to a grand pulpit, atop which a scroll lay open. Behind it, facing the pews in exquisite relief, the immense granite wall had been carved to depict the Tabernacle of the Sky, where more myth told of gods making the world.

Roth smiled again.

He found the belief to be little more than a balm for simple minds. And to be perfectly honest, it had less to do with the gods themselves, and more to do with the idea of reconciliation. It seemed a desperate notion—too little within one's own control or influence. As he made his way forward to the pew where his appointment waited, he felt a pang of sympathy, though, as well. Because those who came here seeking hope were sure to be disappointed, where *he* could show them a better way to take comfort from their woes. Remake themselves, even. And the encouraging part was that it was simple. Not easy, but straightforward. As plain as staring at one's reflection in a still pond.

He would offer as much to this one, his appointment, if he could first convince her to see things a bit more clearly.

"Thank you for meeting me," Roth said, coming around to look down into the woman's haunted eyes. She was beautiful; he had always thought so. "May I sit?"

She motioned to the pew beside her. As he took a seat, he could feel her anxiety. He needed to first put her at ease if he meant to convince her of what he'd come to ask.

"Leona, I'm sorry about what happened to your husband. I would never put you or your family in harm's path. It must have been one of our more zealous leaguemen." He smiled reassuringly. "I hope you know me better than that."

Leona's little girl had been poisoned as a way of testing her father, a leagueman, to see if he would resort to calling on the craft of a Sheason to heal her. Roth had known the man would do so; the fellow wasn't a particularly stalwart member of the League. And once he'd violated the law, he was sentenced to hang. He'd been saved by a stranger—an archer named Tahn—who'd cut him down from the gallows before the rope snapped his neck.

What he couldn't tell Leona was that he'd ordered the ruse. And that his men had had the poison's antidote, and would have rescued the child before she went to her earth. It was only a test of allegiance, after all. One that should have cleared the way for Roth and Leona.

She looked at him and tried a smile that trembled on her lips. "We just want out, Roth. Please."

"This isn't a time for families if they don't have proper affiliation. You must think of your daughters. What are you teaching them if you turn your back on those who've supported you for so long?" He put a hand on her cheek. "It's a frightening time. And you've been through some frightening moments. But if you'll let me, I can protect you from these things."

She looked down into her lap, where her hands worried a kerchief she now used to dab her eyes. "What did you want to see me about?"

Roth nodded. "I've always admired your directness. But some forbearance, just a moment's worth. Your husband, is he well?"

Her haunted eyes rose to meet his own. "Released by the regent with assurances of protection from . . . League retribution."

Roth held his smile. It was true, then. His League of Civility shamed not only by the release of her husband, Duugael—whom they had accused of conspiring with Sheason—but by the regent's extension of protection—a gesture that cast aspersions on the character of the League.

"We asked for neither," Leona continued. "Of course we wanted Duugael home. But it was a stranger who managed it with the regent."

Roth found fresh interest. "And who was this? I owe them a debt of gratitude, and I'd like to offer it in person. Since they did for you what I could not."

Leona's eyes showed suspicion, but not defiance. "I don't know her. Young. Pretty. Dressed like a guardian—two swords. She sat with those that brought the Dissent in the Court of Judicature to free Duugael's rescuer."

Roth pictured her. The quick young woman that had come with the Sheason, Vendanj. She was Far. Strangers meddling in affairs they should have left alone. But it didn't surprise him that someone accompanying a renderer would defy the League. Their arcane arts had ways of manipulating the wills of the weak-minded.

"Where is your husband now? Resting, I hope." Roth patted Leona's hands.

She shook her head, beginning silently to weep. "Please, Roth. He's a good man. We only want to live a simple life and be happy. Can you just let us be? We won't make trouble . . . for anyone."

"Shhhh," he consoled, drawing her head to his chest. "If it upsets you, I won't call on your husband to pay my respects."

He rocked slowly for several moments—as a parent might to comfort an ailing child—until her sniffling came to an end. It rankled him that when he'd requested to see her, she'd asked that it be here. It smacked of distrust. But he'd quickly seen the fortune in this location. That would come later.

"Leona," he started again, adopting a softer tone, "what is it about this place? Why do you come here?"

She sat up, removing her blessedly warm cheek from his chest. "Peace." After a few moments of looking about the cathedral, she brought her gaze round to his. "I know you think Reconciliation and other faiths are at odds with the purpose of the League. But we've felt a sense of comfort inside these walls."

"And do you think the gods hear your prayers?" He made sure to sound the earnest inquirer.

She paused before answering this time. "I don't think that matters. The value is in offering the prayer to begin with. I'll tell you something else"—she paused a moment—"I prayed for Duugael to come home to us."

Roth nodded, maintaining a thoughtful expression. Inside, his resentment and anger roiled. The regent and her cronies were promoting superstition by allowing places like Bastulan to continue unchecked. The result: outmoded and destruc-

tive beliefs. It had to stop. Even if Leona wouldn't acquiesce
to his entreaties. Even if he didn't win the right to look daily
at her beautiful face.

He'd seen her for the first time many years ago. She'd come
to the door of his boyhood home—a shanty in the portside
city of Wanship—peddling herself. A "waif of the wharf,"
as they were called. She'd been maybe thirteen. The sun had
caught her bright blond hair as she searched his father's eyes,
hoping he would pay her a thin plug for a turn in bed. So far
away, in time, in place, in circumstance.

Here and now, her cheeks were drawn earthward with care
and worry of a different kind. Her beautiful green eyes stood
ringed with dark circles. He ached in his chest to hold her,
comfort her, as only a husband could. It'd been a happy coincidence, after the long journey from childhood, to find her
a few years ago in Recityv. And since their fortuitous reunion,
the many meetings, always at his request, had taught him
much about the woman she'd become. The patient strength
inside her. She possessed a healing heart: compassion, forgiveness, perseverance, and obvious hope—remarkable qualities for a woman with her past.

But he had no more time for false pretenses. No doubt she
cared for her husband. But he thought her feelings for him
had grown over the last many visits they'd shared. And Roth
loved her. He'd known it for a long time.

"Leona, do you care for me?" His words echoed softly in
the near-empty cathedral.

Without surprise she looked at him. "Yes, Roth. You
are uncompromising, but you believe your work will help
people. That's why my husband and I serve the League."
Then her lips began to tremble again. "But if you're asking
more of me than that . . . mine is not a marriage of conve-
nience. I love Duugael."

"Of course you do." Roth nodded once. "But let me ask
you, could you do more good in this world if you stood
beside a man with the authority to change things? If your
encouragement could help a city or nation or all the Eastlands? You must know of the Convocation that starts soon.
I will make my appeals there. You could be part of that. You

could help me with it." He paused, ready to ask. "If your feelings for me are genuine, maybe you have a choice to make."

Leona began to worry her kerchief again, clenching and unclenching, staring into her lap. She didn't look up when she said, "You misunderstand me. I care for you . . . but it's not love."

Roth shared a gentle, understanding laugh, the sound carrying through the shafts of light high in the vaults above. The intrusion of his amusement echoed about Bastulan with subtle irreverence.

He looked back at Leona with softer eyes. "My lady, I wouldn't expect your love immediately. Love would grow, as you worked with me to reform the vulgar ways of men and those who lead them. We will restructure government. We will create schools accessible to every child. The carpenter's wage will seem fair beside the jurist's. We can do this, Leona. It's a glorious future we could build. A lot of work, to be sure, but worth the effort. And achievable with you at my side."

She sat silent. And so Roth added, "Your daughters would be welcome, too."

Her expression reset into something more decided. "Is this why you asked to see me?" Her eyes widened as if in new realization. "Is this why my daughter was poisoned? Why Duugael was arrested? Roth," her glare spoke volumes, "did you do all this to make me available to you?"

So much would hang on what he said next. He might deny these *allegations,* repair her trust, continue the secretive meetings taken under pretense. Or perhaps it was already over, and he simply hadn't the heart to accept it yet. He sat, undecided, reveling in her beauty, reveling even in her anger.

He would have liked if their relationship had come more honestly. He would have liked if together they could have given others a way out of the shanty lives they were living. He'd thought that idea would rise above all the obstacles between them.

But looking at her, he knew it was already over. He sat several moments, mourning the idea he'd held for so long.

Mourning her. Then, after a time, his indignation warmed, and he slowly stood.

"You've few flaws, but lack of vision is one of them." He stepped into the aisle and faced the cathedral altar. "Your childish affiliation with this institution is another."

He looked up into the vaults above and whispered, "No more."

Then, he turned and stared down at her. "You disappoint me. Not only because you reject the life I offer you, but because the alternative you choose is *this*." He raised his arms, his palms up, indicating the whole preposterous concept of Reconciliation. "Tell me you hate me. Tell me you hate the League. These things I can respect, if not understand. But this, Leona? These walls were built on false hope, in honor of myths that make men foolish and unable to embrace their own potential."

She trembled before him like a trapped animal. But when his words had rung their last, she said softly, "There are many paths to greatness."

"What?"

She flinched, but continued. "What happened to you, Roth? Why can't you let others find their own path to distinction? Why must hope be found only in the brand of civility *you* offer?"

A bitter smile turned up his lips. This was the boldness—soft and sure, present even now—that he'd sought to have at his side. He would miss it.

"*Leadership* is what I offer, Leona," he explained. "Structure and advocacy for those who have no voice or wit to do it for themselves. Defense against charlatans with tricks and hollow promises. There's hope in a commonwealth that directs itself. Earnest change and growth. Not the backward stagnation of this place." He swept one arm high, pointing into the vaults above.

"Your civility mocks what others hold dear." She trembled still, but finished. "Which is why we want out, Roth."

She was scared. And for a moment, he saw her the way he had that day she'd come to his father's door. He'd fallen in love then. Not with her beauty, but with her strength. With her willingness to do what was necessary to survive. He'd not been able to do anything for her then. But he could now. For all those who today were as she had been, he could. He'd wanted badly for her to see that, and to help him. It seemed right. He still loved her. But he knew now, finally, that she would never love him in return.

He gave her a regretful smile. "Some must lead."

He left her there and strode to the front of Bastulan. There he mounted the altar, took up one of the braziers of coals, and turned to look down the grand hall. She looked small and insignificant from here. He missed her already.

He understood the idealism of his plans. But he would not flinch. To keep his focus, he had only to recall the wharfside shanty where he and his father had struggled from meal to meal.

He grabbed the open scroll that lay upon the granite pulpit and set it across the brazier. In moments it blazed. He then took the brazier and went to one of the great hanging tapestries and set it aflame. Then another. And another. Until the front of the cathedral crackled and seared with fire. He dropped the brazier to the floor, spilling coals and the flaming scroll across lush carpet, which soon began to burn, as well.

He descended the stair and turned to watch the blaze. *I should have done this long ago.* This pyre to dead gods was a declaration that would steel his movement.

Behind him he heard the tattoo of retreating steps—Leona rushing for safety. Maybe she'd go to the regent for protection. More foolishness. Helaina could promise Leona protection, but he would find her if he needed to. Maybe she'd name him the arsonist of Bastulan. He didn't care. The time had come to begin drawing lines. He nodded to himself and started to exit the cathedral to the sound of flames.

He didn't get far. On a pew far to one side, Bastulan still had petitioners: one an old man, the other a young girl. It was custom that invalids were helped to their seats, where they often sat all day, praying, beseeching the deafened gods for healing. Only these two, unable to walk, remained. This man and girl would die in the fire. Their ruined limbs were no use to them. They huddled together in fear.

As the flames licked higher, Roth went to them, hoisting each over a shoulder, and carried them on his way out of the damned place.

• CHAPTER TWENTY •

Doubts

Metaphor is a "meaning hammer." Sometimes you must cease with subtlety, and hit the reader over the godsdamned head with metaphor.

—From the pages of humorist Stephen Wright's glossary on the Author's Way

BRAETHEN HADN'T DONE much more than drag himself to the fire. He'd been lying near it for hours, trying to warm himself. Passing through the Telling had played havoc on his stomach, too. But it wasn't only the Telling that was bothering him.

When he caught Vendanj's eye across the flames, the Sheason nodded. "Something on your mind, Sodalist?"

Braethen had many questions—about what had happened between them in the Naltus library, about the Sodality itself. But just now, he tapped the Blade of Seasons he wore at his hip.

"Every time I raise this, I'm caught in darkness." He struggled to explain without sounding childish. "I understand the blade is more than steel. But I'm not using it well, whatever it is."

Vendanj offered a smile. "It's just doubt, my friend."

"Doubt?"

Vendanj remained sitting on the ground, but rocked forward and raised a finger toward him. "You don't trust yourself with the blade's uses."

He stared across at the man, more uncertain than ever. "You said the blade was about remembering."

Vendanj stared back several long moments, then looked around. Grant and Wendra slept nearby. "There's a great deal of power in that. In helping us see . . . even *be* in another place so that we *can* remember."

Braethen recalled raising the weapon. The darkness taking shape. The feeling of being in two places at once. The image of his father on their front porch.

Vendanj sat back against his rock. "You'd better resolve whatever questions of self-confidence you have. Until you do, the sword is a danger to you."

Braethen looked down at the blade. "That should be easy enough," he said, smiling some.

The Sheason returned another rare smile of his own. "Maybe I can recommend a good book to help."

Braethen laughed. "You sound like my father. He had a book for every occasion, every malady. Whenever I was sad, Da showed up with an Owan Crabtree tale—some bumble-fool usually winds up marrying the prettiest girl in town. Or when the mockery for wanting to become a sodalist got too much, there was Da with a Luie Sonestev book—tales of bravery on the high seas." He laughed, shook his head. "And when I was sick, a stack of stories found their way onto my bed table. Tragedies. Things far worse than my fever. Made me feel less pitiable."

Vendanj smiled at A'Posian's good use of story. "Your father was a wise man, and a gifted author. I suspect your doubt comes mostly from your feeling that you disappointed him by not following in his footsteps."

The words cut deep. Braethen loved his father, respected him; and yet long before joining Vendanj, he'd rejected the idea of becoming an author himself. Doing so had been like rejecting his da. He hung his head, hoping again that his father hadn't felt unappreciated or unloved.

But the Author's Way wasn't a light commitment. It meant

a lifetime of reading. Of writing. Of studying written art forms. Of telling story to instruct and entertain and edify. It meant being a consoler, a philosopher, a sage ear and voice when men's blood ran faster than their wits. Much of that Braethen *had* loved and pursued. But not all of it. And not for a lifetime.

Ironically, it was in all that reading and study where he'd discovered the Sodality. He'd learned about it. Read stories about it. And it had taken root in him until he could think of little else. Then came the chance to accompany Vendanj when he'd arrived in the Hollows, and to later take the oath.

"You're right. My father was a wise man, and a gifted author," Braethen agreed. "And I did disappoint him."

"Did you?" Vendanj asked, somewhat incredulous.

"All he ever wanted was for me to follow him as an author. He spent years teaching me how to read beyond the words on the page, to find meaning, and then apply the things I'd learned. Every eight days of my life my chores included writing a parable or poem that could be shared at Endnigh supper. He wanted me to benefit from the path he'd forged."

Vendanj pointed a finger thoughtfully at him. "And these skills your father taught you, would you say you can apply them with some expertise?"

Braethen stared back, puzzled by the question. "For the most part, yes."

"I see." Vendanj reached back and retrieved his satchel. After placing it in his lap, he caught Braethen's eye again. "Did I ever tell you I was one of your father's faithful readers?"

Braethen's jaw gaped open more than a little. "You knew my father?"

"That's not what I said. I knew his work." He then reached inside his satchel and pulled out a book with a well-worn binding. Holding it reverently in both hands, he studied its cover. Without looking up, he said, "There are few things a Sheason prizes more than the work of a good author. The right tale has a way of looking back while looking forward, of inspiring humility while lending confidence. Your father"—he finally looked up at Braethen—"was particularly good at this. I've made a habit of acquiring his most recent work. But this"—he tapped the book in his hands—"isn't so recent. This was written some fifteen years ago."

Braethen craned his neck to try to see the title. "Which one is it?"

"*The Seamster's Needle.* Do you remember it?" Vendanj stood and brought it to him.

Braethen took the book gently from the Sheason's hands. "I read it, but it's been a long time."

"I think the book will make more sense to you now," Vendanj suggested, a tired smile on his face. He returned to his blanket on the other side of the fire. "It's about a tailor who winds up having to choose between sewing garments for nobility with his seamster father, or leaving the comfort of the palace to patch groundcloth for field laborers."

Braethen looked up at the Sheason, the story's meaning becoming rather obvious. Fifteen years ago, it had seemed a silly conceit for a book.

"Look at the first page," Vendanj invited.

He turned back the cover. There, like a personal inscription, was a dedication: *To my son. Lend your needle where you find it does the most good.* A weight lifted from his shoulders. He drew a deep breath, and his sight blurred with tears. He wanted badly to see his father just now. Tell him how much he loved him.

"That seamster reads a lot like a boy with the notion of serving the Sodality. In case that wasn't clear." Vendanj smiled. "You could say I had a sense of you before we ever met. You have your father to thank for that."

Vendanj then held up an inviting hand. "Read it. The tale is short."

Braethen carefully turned back the first page, and lost himself to the story. Subtle details of how his father had seen their relationship revealed themselves. In many ways, it was like having his da with him. It gave Braethen a vaguely happy feeling, even though the story left him somewhat unsettled.

The seamster in the tale had left the sure and safe path of his father's royal appointment. The son meant to apply his needle to the clothes of fieldworkers and those unable to pay.

With time, he'd lost or worn out the simple tools of his trade, thimbles and fabric scissors and the like. The meager pay from his rustic clientele didn't allow him to replace much—often he took food in trade for his work.

Eventually, the seamster's fingers had grown leathery from the prick of countless needles, calluses forming from the constant use of his hands.

And while the selfless seamster seemed the obvious metaphor for Braethen, the man's hands bothered him. To Braethen's mind, the metaphor indicated not just selflessness, but a loss of feeling. In fact, if the seamster's hands and fingers were the way he experienced and added to the world around him—and Braethen thought they were—then they suggested the seamster himself might be, at least figuratively, dead. Or expendable, anyway.

When Braethen turned the last page, he shut the book and looked up. Staring at him across the fire was Vendanj, his face uncustomarily serene. It seemed as if the Sheason had been waiting for Braethen to finish, knowing he'd have questions. Braethen did.

With the crackle of the fire in accompaniment, Braethen asked, "The seamster's hands, what do you think they represent?"

Vendanj didn't immediately answer, taking a deep breath. "I'm not sure what *I* think matters."

Braethen blinked, considered. "Maybe the question should be: What did my *father* think they represented?"

Vendanj said nothing, waiting.

"The seamster's hardened hands seem to say that giving your life to the service of someone else means you lose the feeling for what you value most."

The Sheason's eyebrows went up. "That's your interpretation?"

Braethen thought, and nodded. "It changes you. Maybe not for the worse. But the seamster's hands were his life, his livelihood . . . his soul, if you want to go that far. Losing feeling in them . . ." Braethen had a new epiphany about the story. He shifted his legs and refocused on Vendanj. "If the seamster is me, about me giving my life to the Sodality, then something about the order—at least as my father understood it—requires that I lose or give up what matters most to me."

"And what is that?" Vendanj asked.

Braethen didn't have to think. "The idealism I hold about the Sodality itself." He stared across the fire at Vendanj, beginning to understand the reality behind the oath he'd taken.

Vendanj looked back at him for a long moment, then asked him a troubling question—troubling in its simplicity. "Do you know how the Sodality began?"

The excitement of imminent academic discovery hit him. For all his searching, a record of the Sodality's formation was something he'd never been able to find. There were author accounts of it, but they were so different as to make it clear they had no idea.

Vendanj settled back against his large rock. "You've heard the story of the first Sheason, Palamon, wrestling Jo'ha'nel, who followed the dissenting god." Vendanj did not rush. "To say they *wrestled* is an author's way of adding poetry to their fight. It was a struggle of wills. A struggle that took place over many days and many bloody fights. But it was *this* contest where lines were drawn, *this* contest where the intentions of those loyal to Quietus were made known. It's also when the need for the Sodality became clear."

"Why is there no record of the formation of the Sodality?" Braethen asked.

Vendanj held up his hand. "Patience." He held a long silence, then began to tell a story.

• CHAPTER TWENTY-ONE •

Two Sides of the Same

Things that matter are born from pain. It's a special kind of madness.

—Expression Eight from the *Faces of Madness,* author
unknown though often attributed to Hargrove

VENDANJ GREW SILENT for many long moments, his eyes fixed in thought. Then he began to tell the story of the Sodality's creation.

EFRAM CLOSED THE bedroom door, leaving his two small ones at the kitchen table, eating their supper. He turned to his wife, Volleia, who lay on their bed. "Jo'ha'nel is returning," he said.

Volleia stood up immediately, fear rising on her face. "We must leave. I'll get what we can carry." She started past him to the door.

Efram reached out and put an arm across her chest, gently grasping her shoulder. "It's too late," he said softly. "He doesn't come alone this time."

His wife's face slackened with horror. She stared, unable to speak.

Efram nodded, feeling helpless to reassure her. "Palamon isn't sure how many, but they come up from the south and down from the north. We're surrounded."

"We'll go up the bluff face," Volleia desperately suggested.

"With the children?" Efram shook his head. "And there's no time, anyway."

She put her arms around his waist and hugged him close. "What are we going to do?"

Efram held her for a long time, noting the smooth feel of her arms and the lilac smell of her hair. He would want to remember those things later. Then he drew gently back, taking hold of her hands. "Palamon is alone. A few of the people are trying to flee. Others are hiding in their cellars. Most are still away in the south, looking for warmer, more fertile lands to till."

He watched as realization dawned in her eyes, without him needing to say what was in his heart. "Efram, no. What can you possibly do? You don't render. You've got only a hayfork—"

He squeezed her hands. "I may be little more than a diversion, but if I can give Palamon some time . . ."

"You would throw away your life to buy the Sheason a few seconds?" Ire lined her tone.

"I will be more trouble than that," he said. It was not idle talk. He didn't go lightly to the Sheason's side to stand against Jo'ha'nel. But he also knew there was little hope of returning to this home, this room . . . to Volleia and his children.

"And what of us?" Her question came as if she knew his mind.

His silence was the only answer he felt strong enough to give.

The sadness and disappointment in her face would surely damn him. "You would choose to stand with him, rather than stay here with your family? We will die, and you will not be here to fight or fall with us," she said, an awful resignation in her voice.

Efram tried to think of what to say. There really wasn't much more to it. But he hoped he could help her understand. "Volleia . . . the only chance we have is for me to help Palamon. It's not a hope for those of us caught here, not for you or me . . . not for Tula or Ridel." His throat grew tight as he spoke his children's names. "It's for those who may come after us."

As she always did, she reasoned it through and found the most right way. This time, Efram—after great struggle—had simply realized it first. Tears rolled down her cheeks. "I know," she said.

"And we may defeat him, Volleia. All may not be lost." He tried to smile.

"How soon?" she asked.

He fought his own grief. "I need to say good-bye to the little ones."

The immediacy of his departure brought fresh tears to her eyes. He kissed her, tasting the salt of them on her lips. Then he led her by the hand out of the bedroom to the kitchen table. He walked to Ridel's chair and hunkered down to his son's eye level.

"How's that turned duck?" he asked.

"Good," his boy said.

"I'm going away for a while, son."

Ridel nodded, still eating.

Efram pulled his son around and took him in his arms. "Be helpful to your mother while I'm gone."

When Ridel finally looked into his father's eyes, something registered in the boy's face. But at three years of age, the lad hadn't the words to express it. So he wrapped his arms around Efram's neck and squeezed his hardest—what he always did to say good-bye when Efram went away. But this time he didn't let go. Efram hugged his son back, fighting the emotion so he wouldn't worry the boy. "I love you, son."

"Love you," the boy repeated.

When Ridel released him, Efram turned to Tula, and his tears finally came.

Without a word, she leapt into his arms and hugged him with all her strength. "Take me with you," she whispered in his ear.

"I cannot," he whispered back, his voice catching with emotion.

"When will you be back?" she asked.

In all his life he'd never lied to his little girl. "Not long, Tula. Not long. You be a help to your mother, too. . . . I love you."

Tula's eyes were still slightly skeptical, but perhaps that was only Efram's own worry. "I love you, too, Papa." His little girl reluctantly let him go.

Efram gave them each a last look, smiling at them, and hoping it didn't look too fateful. Then he led Volleia to the door and kissed her one last time with the cool night air on their wet cheeks. "I love you, Volleia."

"And I you." She gave him a tortured, earnest look, one few women will—or should—ever know. It was the look of a wife and mother encouraging the man she loves as he goes to die. "Give Palamon your best."

Efram's heart surged with loss and pride and the desire to prove he deserved her love. He brushed the tears from her cheek and started out into the night, allowing himself to wonder if he would return. And if he did, would his family . . . He couldn't finish that thought.

All night he walked, arriving at Palamon's house in the small hours of morning. He'd hoped others would have gathered to stand with the Sheason. But it was as he'd feared. It was only the two of them. Under a starry sky they walked to the high ground, where they could survey the valley below and stand to defend it against Jo'ha'nel, who marched out of the canyon to the northwest.

As the first inklings of light lit the eastern sky, the other emerged, four hulking figures at his back. And the battle began.

Efram proved more than a distraction, keeping these Bar'dyn from getting to Palamon, while the Sheason fought the nightmare out of the Bourne.

The sun had not yet touched the sky when screams from the valley began to echo up to them. Tears flowed from Efram's eyes as he fought. He wondered if each new agonized cry rising up on the morning sky came from one of his family found by the Quiet.

Until one particular scream.

After that he fought with abandon, his wrath and anguish fueling a furious attack. And still, they were losing. The Quiet-given that swept in from behind them were drawing nearer. Efram glanced over at Palamon, who looked like he might drop at any moment from exhaustion.

In a blinding moment of realization, he screamed to the Sheason, "Use *me*!" and bolted at a dead run toward Palamon.

Efram saw a look of dread acknowledgment in the renderer's face as he neared. But it softened fast to acceptance and gratitude. Then hardened as new determination lit Palamon's eyes. A moment later, Efram stepped into the iron grip of the Sheason, and a warmth spread immediately throughout his body.

He had time to utter, "I'm coming," and think of lilacs before his spirit entered Palamon and gave life to a thought so devastating that he had no word for it. Then his spirit rushed outward, dispersing with awful power and disregard, like a firewind.

He passed through the bodies of the Bar'dyn that still stood as well as those climbing to the high ground, and through the bitter form of the Draethmorte, too. His consciousness faded as all those he touched fell dead, leaving Palamon alone in the desolation when the sun came fully into the sky.

WHEN VENDANJ FINISHED the story, he found an unsettled expression on Braethen's face. "In the season that followed," he added, "Palamon realized that if he meant to build an order of Sheason to stand against the Quiet, he would need help. Perhaps not always the same kind of sacrifice as Efram's, but more than a Sheason could do alone. Efram had shown him the way."

Vendanj stopped, the story lingering heavily in the air around them.

Braethen stared across the fire at him.

"The use of another to render wouldn't happen again for a long time," Vendanj said. "Even the name 'Sodality' came much later. But that's where it started."

Braethen shook his head in disbelief. "I thought only the Velle used others to fuel rendering."

He feels betrayed. Vendanj couldn't begrudge Braethen the feeling. "You want to know if you'll be required to do the same as Efram."

Braethen said nothing.

Vendanj offered a tired, reassuring smile. "I won't ask it of you. No Sheason ever does. It must be offered."

"Like when I helped you in the Naltus library," Braethen said with calm certainty.

Vendanj nodded. "You revived me. Lent me a portion of

yourself. You did it naturally, never having done so before. That told me you were ready to learn what it could mean to give more. Which brings me to an important question." Vendanj sat forward, so that his face could be clearly seen.

The sodalist did likewise.

"If you wish," Vendanj said evenly, "I'll relieve you of your oath. There's no shame in leaving it behind. Whatever you decide, you have my respect and thanks for all you've done." He paused a moment. "You're one hell of a seamster."

Braethen showed him a blank look of surprise. But Vendanj meant every word. He hoped Braethen would embrace the fullness of the Sodalist call. But the young man had doubts. And it would tear him apart in more ways than one if he didn't give all of himself. It was that, or quit. Vendanj owed him the choice.

"Don't answer now." He stood, rubbing his fire-warmed knees. "You should ponder what I've shared with you, consider your feelings carefully. And not while I watch and wait for your answer. We'll stay together until we go in to Recityv. Then, if we part ways, at least you'll be in a safe place to decide what's next for you."

Before Braethen could respond or ask another question, Vendanj turned and strode out into the cool evening air. He needed some time of his own to think. About his friends. About his own doubts.

As he walked in the shades of evening, he looked up at the stars and thought of his wife, Illenia, and their unborn child. He thought of the Quiet attack she'd defended without him. He thought of the League blackcoat who'd forced him out of the room while she died trying to give their child life.

"I miss you," he whispered.

After several moments, he dropped his gaze to Recityv, which stood proud against the horizon. And his mind turned to Convocation.

Most of his companions were too weak to go into the city. It had taken some rendering to restore his own strength. But earlier he'd seen a Wynstout Dominion wagon parade moving south toward Recityv. He'd gone to meet it and learned that Convocation wasn't set to convene for a few days yet.

He finally stopped walking, far enough now from their campfire that he could hardly see it. He hunkered down and dragged his fingers across the hardened earth, if only to remind himself that some things had a sense of permanence about them. It was an important thing to remember.

Vendanj clenched a fistful of soil. All the insecurities of those around him, piled on top of his own losses, led to a manic grin that felt strangely good on his face. It should have been the Sheason who did this, who stood in the gap. But somewhere along the way, they'd begun to interpret service as servility. The League had used this to its advantage, twisting the use of the Will into a crime, imprisoning Sheason like Rolen for doing nothing more than healing a sick child.

The way of things was backward. And it led to his dissent with his own order, a schism that made him an enemy to his own kind. His smile tightened, and he slowly let go the earth from his clenched fist. He would make them see. Those at Convocation. And those in Estem Salo. By the name of every last absent god, he would make them see. Or die in the attempt.

Vendanj looked one last time into the starry night, then stood and strode back to camp, wrapping his determination about him like a suit of iron.

• CHAPTER TWENTY-TWO •

Given or Taken

What can be given, can be taken away.

> —The Parity Principle, considered part of the Charter,
> and one of many ethics rumored to be expounded upon
> in the very stone deep inside the Tabernacle of the Sky

IN THE LIGHT of morning, Thaelon paced the gardens south of the Tabernacle of the Sky. He'd gotten there early, before his trusted friends arrived, to ponder the gathering he'd called. Behind him, the Tabernacle rose in failing majesty. Time had worn at her, dulling the stone, crumbling its ceilings, the forest creeping in. And still, the pillars cut deep into the sky, appearing to support the firmament above and connect it to the earth below.

A gentle feeling of safety resided here. Perhaps something of the authority of the Tabernacle yet remained, from when gods had trod this place, framing the world. Ages ago. He had never entered the ruins to investigate. By unspoken assent, no one did.

His friends began to arrive, emerging from between towering hemlock and aspen. Each nodded a silent greeting, keeping the reverence of the morning and Tabernacle for now. Thaelon sat on some lower steps that were cracked and overgrown by ivy. He settled himself, breathing the fresh scent of dew nestled over the holly scrub brush.

The others sat or stood in a rough semicircle in front of him, waiting. These were men and women of powerful understanding and ability. They led entire disciplines of study for the Sheason Order. They were his closest friends. Part of his full council. And they didn't hide their concern as they waited for him to explain this meeting leagues from Estem Salo, at the foot of the Tabernacle.

He didn't waste words. "I'm calling for a Trial of Intentions."

The four looked around at one another without speaking, then back at him.

"Because of Vendanj," Jak finally said, matter-of-factly. Jak Obsen was Exemplar of Discernment. His brow was perpetually smooth, as though discernment earned him continual peace.

"Not only him." Thaelon clasped his hands between his knees. "There's dissent in the order. I can't ignore it any longer. Thought differs on the right way to serve and how we should use the Will."

"You might want to be slightly more accurate," Warrin suggested. Warrin Cochellas was Exemplar of Argument, and his brow was the opposite of Jak's, always in a pinch—concentration and objection ever present. "Isn't it whether or not to *use* the Will that is dividing us? And the *League* is responsible there."

Odea Ren, Exemplar of Battle, cut in sharply. "We can remedy that. The surest way to solidarity is to define a common enemy."

Odea let her comment linger a moment before adding the wry grin that always followed her invocation of combat strategy to solve any problem. The rest of them laughed softly in the weak morning light. Still, her eyes had a unique glimmer whenever she suggested it.

"You actually have two dilemmas, don't you," Jak offered, again with his calm certainty.

Thaelon nodded at his discerning friend. "I do. And maybe three, depending on how you look at it. First, there's the League. Their Civilization Order tightens." He sighed. "I have reports of the sick and weak, who go uncared for because it's unlawful to call the Will."

"Like Rolen," Lorra pointed out—Lorra Fonn was Exemplar of Imparting. "Rolen is one of the Sheason appointed to Recityv. Imprisoned for rendering to help a sick child."

"What to do about the League is one thing. Second," Thaelon said, "*some* Sheason are finding hope in a man like Vendanj, who counts costs later."

"It's the thinking of an outlaw," Warren commented. "I respect Vendanj. But I don't think he's been the same since Illenia died. He blames the League for that."

"That may all be true," Thaelon conceded. "But it doesn't change the mounting support Vendanj is finding within the order. Many believe in his fearless use of his gifts to do what he thinks best."

Warren stared back at him, his brow deeply pinched. "To my mind, Vendanj has crossed into aggrandizement."

"And yet he takes the fight to the Quiet. Who among us has been so bold?" Odea didn't follow with her wry grin this time.

Thaelon nodded again. "That's the third question that I've asked you here to help me work through. Regardless of what the League does or believes, we know the Quiet press at their bonds. Whether or not we agree with how Vendanj chooses to meet this threat, the threat is real. The nations of the east are unprepared. And their warcraft is insufficient, in any case. We must decide how to stand against the Bourne."

Odea picked up a stone and tossed it away with some irritation. "The Sheason aren't ready for war, either."

"I know," Thaelon agreed. "Though I suspect you could fix that."

Odea found her grin again.

"What do you plan to do with a Sheason who declares sympathy or support for Vendanj?" It was Jak, cutting to the heart of the matter, as he always did.

Lorra, who had been mostly quiet, looked up into the heights of the Tabernacle. "Thaelon, you could have held a private meeting anywhere. You chose this place to remind us of who we are." She lowered her gaze to him. "On the first question, about the League, ours is the authority to render. No law will change that. And it's foolishness for the League to preach that our gifts threaten the self-determination of men. The time has come to meet the Ascendant and make him see this for himself."

"I'll go," Odea offered. Her grin this time showed eagerness.

Thaelon smiled briefly. An envoy, then. To try and reverse

this damned Civilization Order. "Someone will go, but not you."

Jak laughed out loud. "As I see it, your real dilemma is what to do about the Bourne, since we all know that any answer there will require Sheason to fight. The question then becomes: Will it be your way, or Vendanj's?"

Warrin nodded to himself as though he'd found his own clarity of thought. "On your second question, about Vendanj and the right use of the Will: You should still conduct your Trial of Intentions."

Both Odea and Lorra turned scrutinizing eyes on their Exemplar of Argument. He seemed not to notice.

"We can all agree not to submit to immoral League laws any longer." Warrin pointed at each of them one by one. "But we should *also* agree that Vendanj's use of the Will is a perversion of our oath. Yes, he's trying to meet the threat of the Bourne. But he does so in rogue fashion, and his methods are irresponsible—"

Thaelon held up his hands to stop Warrin. He'd deal with the third question, the Quiet question, later. "Thank you, my friends." He looked at Odea. "Escalate battle training. Double the practice time on defense and attack strategies, as well as personal fighting techniques."

Thaelon didn't like having to give the next directive, but he'd found no alternative. Looking both Warrin and Jak in the eyes, he commanded, "Proceed with the Trial of Intentions."

They each nodded, and Jak repeated the question he'd begun with. "What do you plan to do with a Sheason who declares sympathy or support for Vendanj?"

Thaelon turned then to face the Tabernacle. "You were right, Lorra. I chose this place because it's a reminder of who we are. But much of what we are is *given* to us." He paused, being certain he wanted to relate what was in his heart. Moments later, with the certainty he'd come here to find, he added, "And what is given can be taken away."

Morning birdsong at the foot of the Tabernacle of the Sky became loud in the silence that followed. The scent of dew on ivy and old stone warming in the sun usually gave Thaelon some peace. Not today. Their discussion had seeded in his mind dangerous thoughts about the oldest of schisms. About the Quiet. But that was for later.

He watched his friends begin their descent back to Estem Salo. Once they were out of sight, Raalena emerged from a copse of aspen seedlings. Together, they mounted the southern steps to the Tabernacle. Deep within its vaults, he hoped to find, graven in the stone, inscriptions that held the answer to the one thing not recorded in the Vaults at Estem Salo: how to divest a Sheason of the authority to render the Will.

• CHAPTER TWENTY-THREE •

The Poison of Politics

When the Mors escaped the Bourne and came into the East-lands, they were welcomed with steel. Even the chroniclers died in what is referred to as the Retribution of the Mors. We can be glad they now keep to themselves.

—Drawn from chapter "The Mor Nation Refrains,"
belonging to The Unmusical Historian,
a consideration of song in history

HELAINA LOOKED EAST over Recityv from the aerie of her High Office atop Solath Mahnus. Tendrils of smoke still worked their way into the sky from the recent burning of Bastulan Cathedral. Roth was on his way to see her. Word had been passed ahead of his approach. She'd been having him followed for several cycles now. Not perfectly. Sometimes he slipped her spies, which made her only more sure he had something to do with Bastulan.

Through the crisp autumn air, Helaina gazed northeast. Far distant, the plains disappeared from sight. Beyond them lay the dry, lifeless span of the Scar, home to Grant's wards.

Her own son had gone there days after she'd pushed him from her womb. She'd had reports of him, of his training and education. But they were vague at best. She knew him no better than prisoners she sent to her pits. But she did remember his birth. That night pulsed in her memory more than any other—the night Tahn came into the world, ending many sad years of barrenness.

She'd seen him only once since he'd gone away, when he'd returned to Recityv with the Sheason Vendanj and others. Tahn had freed a convicted Leagueman and gotten thrown into the pits. A Dissent brought by his friends to release him had failed. But he and the others had escaped the city. In the time since, she'd had the ruling against him reversed, hoping he'd find his way back. From Tillinghast. From the long years away from her.

"This is what aching bones do to the aged," she complained mildly to herself, "force us to remember." Helaina rubbed her hands together, massaging the ache and stiffness that had beset her joints in her elder years.

Lately, she could scarcely hold her pen to write more than a few words before needing to relax her hand. The message she'd been composing this morning had required ten long pauses to rest—and that was just *her* portion. Belamae had begun the letter, leaving the rest for her to finish. It had taken her a long time to decide how to conclude it.

But this morning, watching the smoke from her east window, it had come to her. She'd been standing here ever since, slowly committing her thoughts—and plea—to paper for the third time. To her right sat the cage of three falcons. It was a precautionary redundancy to send three. And for this particular letter, she'd called her falconer—this time, the shrikes would not do. Three grey falcons taken from the cliffs of Masson Dimn perched hooded, waiting.

As she prepared to finish the last of the three copies, a light rap came at her High Office door. "Come," she said. She turned and straightened herself, so as not to show her caller the least weakness.

Roth Staned, Ascendant of the League of Civility, strode with his particular self-assured gait into her chamber. "Your

Grace," he said, bowing slightly at the waist, though he never dropped his gaze from her own. *Using the appellation, bowing—he's already setting the tone for our exchange.*

A tall man, Roth carried himself as one ready at any moment to lend a hand. His expressions and mannerisms were those of a *pleaser.* And because everything about him seemed so *considered,* she found him particularly unsettling.

"Ascendant Staned," she replied formally, using the leagueman's title. She bowed, but not as deeply.

Roth smiled. "You've no doubt had news of the fire."

"And seen it from my window." She gestured to her right. "Who would benefit from the destruction of such a holy place . . ."

"You assume it was arson, then." Roth looked across her High Office at her, betraying no guilt.

"I assume only that there are precious few who gain from its ruin." She took her seat behind the black marble table she used for a desk, and folded her shaky hands in her lap to avoid the appearance of age or fear.

"The League, you're thinking." Roth went to the window and looked out at the smoke, now thinner, whiter.

"What is the tradition of Bastulan?" she said, answering Roth circuitously. "It's said that hidden somewhere inside—in its crypt or many towers—is the Lens of Samalnae, the Pauper's Drum, and other relics that appear only in the oldest stories."

"Which the League would like to see destroyed, you think." Roth's voice carried a hint of amusement now.

"The idea of a relic is to place importance on a physical thing to answer some human need. Last I knew, the League preferred personal endeavor to meet the trials of life. Thus, I don't think relics have a place in your doctrine." Helaina sighed quietly, already weary of the effort to trade exchanges with His Leadership.

"I don't suppose any of us will mourn its loss," Roth conceded. "But that's not the same as causing its destruction."

"I wouldn't want to have the Dannire looking for me," Helaina replied, a wicked, thin grin on her face.

Roth looked truly surprised. "What? The old story about

holy assassins? A few heedless sword-bearers, fighting in the name of dead gods? Those Dannire?" He smiled.

"If I was the arsonist of Bastulan, I would fear even the idea of the Dannire. Let alone the stories that make children believe the gods sanction murder." Helaina nodded toward the smoke. She was goading him with the very myths he hated. "I'm not sure the arsonist who got that blaze going was thinking too far ahead." She then changed the subject. "Why have you come?"

"Ah, the patience of old age, I see . . ." He turned from the window.

So now you'll seek my office. It was a long time coming, intimations here and there over the last three years. But the timing couldn't be worse. And yet it made perfect sense that he would choose this time to make his play.

"The regency is an appointment of lifetime tenure. I'm still alive. These facts were obvious to you before you called on me today," she pointedly reminded him.

"Indeed, Your Grace, but I come with genuine intent. Please forgive my remarks. They're nothing more than my awkward attempt to seem less . . . forward. Perhaps neither of us has been a good ally to the other since our service together began."

Helaina laughed inside. His politics were truly exceptional. Though, she paused long enough to consider that perhaps her cynicism had gotten the better of her. After all, she herself had thought lately that her office rightly belonged to a younger leader. *One who doesn't have to rest from the composition of a simple letter.*

"Fair enough," the regent offered. "Why have you come?" This time, she spoke with her own earnestness.

"It's not easy for me to say, because I know how it might be perceived, Your Grace . . . Helaina. We have stood on opposite sides of many issues. Even now, this Convocation that floods our city with ne'er-do-well leaders from distant principalities . . . I think it's a mistake. Whether the threat from the Bourne is real or not, I would not have recalled these ineffective kings and queens and warmongers to a Convocation."

"And why not," Helaina challenged civilly. "Federating as many of the kingdoms as we can will have benefits beyond military strength and coordination. Think of the good that can be done with the institution of more academies and colleges to advance learning, of the safe trade for goods that might feed the hungry." She laughed again inside—not because these things weren't true, but at her own anticipation of Roth's response to her embracing his political agenda.

"If I may speak plainly, Helaina, I would say it's shameful that it takes the threat of a myth like the Bourne to prompt you to look after your people's welfare." Roth said it with all humility and tact and sincerity. If not for years debating the man, she might have believed he had no ulterior motive.

But if her age made her hands cramp and ache, it also made her twice as shrewd. "A fair criticism, Roth. That is precisely the kind of wisdom I expect and appreciate from a member of my High Council." She shifted in her chair to face him more directly. "But I can't change the past. And if present threats bring civic benefits, then those are happy consequences. They'll become matters of government that I'll need your help to define and make useful to our people."

Roth stood near the eastern window, staring at Helaina for several moments. She imagined him calculating how next to criticize her, where he could find chinks in her political armor to illuminate her unfitness to rule, to lead.

It was a dance they'd had with increasing frequency in recent years. But his visit today held a different poignancy. And the prevarication between them began to collapse before the next words were uttered. His face hardened, losing its façade of comportment and concern. Helaina likewise put away her genteel manner, letting the distress of her rheumatic hands and all the other pains of age lend her their acerbic gifts.

"I will ask you in private, this once, to step down. You are not fit to lead."

"Because of my age?"

"In part, yes," Roth said. "But *not* because you sometimes walk with the assistance of a cane. It's the aging of your mind that compromises the welfare of your people. Yes, we've disagreed, vehemently at times. But I'm not here to assert that I should replace you. Only that you need to take a close look at your ability to conduct the matters of state. Ask yourself if you're still truly in a frame of mind to do so."

Helaina stood, biting back the pain that shot up her legs at the effort. She kept her hands flat on her desk for support and to keep them from clenching shut, as often happened after their overuse.

"Ascendant Staned, these are valid concerns. And not, you should know, something I trifle with. Officially, my health, while not what it was ten years ago, is fine. And my *frame of mind* . . . I have never seen the needs of this nation more clearly than I see them now, nor—"

"What do you see—"

"Nor," she said more loudly, "what must be done to answer those needs."

Roth then dropped all pretense. His face showed his dislike, skepticism, and ambition, all at once. "Officially, you say?"

Helaina likewise dropped all pretense. "Unofficially," she said with a sharp tone, "I am old! My body aches, and I have the experience to worry if my decisions are right enough to direct a nation."

Roth smiled.

"But these are the *virtues* of age, civil man." She uttered those last words—*civil man*—with extreme disparagement.

"What about all these *other* nations?" Roth asked. "You called for Convocation. Do you really think they'll be persuaded by a woman grown slaphappy in her old age?"

Helaina showed him a smile of forbearance born of experience. "You forget that some of these kings are my own age. And many of the younger ones grew up respecting the stories of the First and Second Promise, not to mention the men and women who gave them life. They'll vote to reestablish the promise of Convocation."

Roth laughed again, sarcasm clear in a single arching eyebrow. "You're a product of your own propaganda. This is precisely one of the reasons you should step down. You seek to elevate the stature of your rule by calling the Convocation

a third time. It's political posturing. You know it as well as I
do. But it's an abuse of power."

"That," she shouted, "is what you object to, isn't it, leagueman? You want my seat so *you* can be the one to direct Convocation. Our feud was . . . *civil* until I sent the call for
Convocation. It's opportunism that brings you here to insist
on my resignation. You see the chance to extend your influence by exploiting their fear of the very threats you decry as
myth." She pointed another savage finger at him. "You're a
hypocrite!"

"What about you, Helaina?" Roth shot back. "You stood
in the Court of Judicature and upheld the law and sentencing
of a leagueman and his rescuers, then turned around and
freed them in secret. *You* are the hypocrite! You abuse your
power for your own private interests, whether it's your political legacy or the petition of a friend. I will publish your
crime, and then we'll see if Convocation will follow a woman
who speaks with a double tongue."

Helaina leveled him a glare with all the power of her office, and spoke in a grave, even tone. "What I have done, I
have only done with the hope of avoiding open war with the
Quiet, and the loss of another generation of our children.
These are the choices of a regent, and you will neither question nor announce them. To do so . . . is treason."

Roth came near, his physical form dwarfing her. "You
are gone in the mind to think that you can act without
consequence, without accountability to the Council and the
people they represent. You can't take action in a closet and
be allowed to keep it hidden there. You owe us all a full accounting."

It was Helaina's turn to smile. "Beware, Roth. Everyone,
even the lowly whoreboys on the street, have secrets they
wish to keep. Their brand of *civility* is not what you would
have it be. But take care that you don't push so far so fast that
instead of taking my seat you wind up losing your own . . .
and killing the League in the process." She spoke the last as
an overt threat. It was time to take the offensive.

Then she returned them to where they'd begun, to remind

him of common ground. "Roth, I've recalled Convocation not just to answer the Quiet threat. We are finally at a place where we may forge a lasting alliance. Unify the kingdoms and nations of the east. This is my political agenda, my highest objective. It will fortify us against . . . against any enemy." She paused, considering. "And if you're right, and no enemy comes at us from the Bourne, then we'll have established a confederation that will better address our shared goals." She softened her voice, to strike the right amount of cynicism. "If your goals are truly what you say they are."

Roth glared a threat back at her. "If you make war on the League, you will regret it." He seemed to consider. "It's too late. Remember that you brought this on yourself . . . on others . . . for your unwillingness to see the need for change."

Fear struck Helaina's heart. *It's too late.* Her mind raced to understand what he meant. But she couldn't show him weakness, and instead gave him an impassive look when she said, "I've held your crime in abeyance for too long. But no longer. The League will stand trial for the poisoning of Leagueman Duugael. If convicted, Ascendant Staned, the rights and privileges of the League of Civility will be revoked in the nation of Vohnce. And I will see *that* published in every court and hall in the known world."

Roth seemed on the brink of true violence, but remained collected. Helaina held her head up, her body still, until he turned and strode angrily from her High Office.

Helaina collapsed back into her chair, unable to stop her legs from shaking—some bit of fear and of rheumatism besides.

When she thought she could manage it, she pushed herself to her feet and struggled to the window. There, she picked up her pen, dipped it in her vial of ink, and without stopping—despite the great pain—finished the last of the three letters. Then she promptly rolled them into their tiny tubes, and one by one tied them to the falcons' feet.

With only the briefest hesitation, she spoke the words given her by her falconer to direct the birds, then shooed them into the air. The falcons banked hard right, passing across the

vistas of her eastern windows. Soon, their grey feathers
were lost in the sky hues of midmorning, as they raced to
take her entreaty to the Mor nations. *Pray gods the Mors
don't still harbor their old grievances.*

• CHAPTER TWENTY-FOUR •

Old Friends

*We left Estem Salo not to reject our Sheason oath, but be-
cause we wanted to focus on scientific knowledge of the sky,
and our place in these vaulted heavens.*

—Portion of the first correspondence from Pealy Omendal,
to Estem Salo astronomet, after its establishment
from Aubade Grove

TAHN WAS FALLING. Debris swirled about him as
though he'd been caught in a violent whirlwind. Stones
struck his arms, back, and face. A great rushing noise filled
his ears, drowning out his own cries. A moment later he
landed heavily on hard soil, where the storm of rocks and
small branches continued to pelt his back, the wind pressing
him down. He lay helpless, his entire body bearing a great
pressure. Then, unexpectedly, the winds died, the debris fell
harmless on and around him, and he gasped a dust-filled
breath.

He coughed, and fought to take another lungful of air. The
smell of a storm lingered in his nose, but more acrid, like
alderwood singed by a firebrand. His ears were ringing, an
incredibly high pitch in his head. Finally, he opened his eyes
to find the world cloaked in the dark of night under a cloud-
less, starry sky. It appeared he'd fallen onto a long sagebrush
plain, giving him an expansive view to the horizon. With
some pain, he turned his head to look in the other direction.

A few hundred strides away, several towers rose up off the plain like silent sentinels, carving dark silhouettes from the star-filled sky.

Aubade Grove.

The columns were familiar, but his mind was clouded, and the towers offered no comfort from the sharp pain in his body or the ache in his head. He shut his eyes again and focused on his breathing, trying to calm himself. Only after he'd gotten the rhythms of his body under control did he relax enough to think through what had just happened.

He'd passed through the Telling Wendra had sung for him. But pushing through it had been like walking against a stern wind, one which left his skin stinging—even beneath his clothes—as though that wind had been filled with sand.

He tried to get up, and quickly abandoned the effort. Every movement was agony, and he had little strength left, besides. So, he turned his head east again, and became still. He lay where he'd fallen, watching the slow procession of stars rising in the east, and fell asleep waiting for dawn.

THE PAIN WOKE him. He'd only been asleep maybe an hour, but his body stiffened, and he could feel the ache of it down where muscle met bone. He lay in a ball on the cold ground, curled up against the chill. When he opened his eyes, he thought of daybreak.

It's no small miracle to have just one thing you can rely on. It was something they said in the Grove when their hypotheses crumbled beneath them.

Lying there, aching and cold, far now from his companions, he thought of newly tilled fields steaming in the first light of day. He thought of morning dew sweetening the scent of hay. He thought of sunrise through pine boughs, its rays shining between needles and falling in hazy shafts on a forest floor. It was his predawn ritual—imagining the coming sun.

A moment later, he heard the familiar sound of footsteps grinding dirt and pebbles. He remained still, knowing he would be of no use in his own defense, and hoping whoever it was was friendly.

The footfalls grew louder, but didn't come directly at him. He waited. His heart raced. And then the unseen stranger stopped. He heard a sigh when the first hints of color rose in the eastern sky. With each passing moment, he began to believe something that hardly seemed possible: Whoever this person was . . . had also come to watch the sunrise. With that thought, his anxiety eased.

For half an hour he lay unmoving, as daylight lit the east, brightening it with hues of fire orange and autumn yellow. And above it all the darkened heavens faded to skylark blue. He breathed easier, just as he always did when the sun peeked over the line of earthsky. But the moment of peace shattered when a voice called out over the sage plain.

"Gnomon? Is that you? By all my integers, it's not possible!"

Running steps came at him, and Tahn struggled onto his back. His muscles were so tight he worried they might snap. But he reached out against the pain, flailing to find his bow. He did little more than stir a small dirt cloud and send shards of pain through his bruised body. He was at this stranger's mercy.

Until he remembered his knife. He'd just taken it in hand when the face of a woman came into view.

A wry smile gradually swept the shock from her face.

"Rithy?" he asked tentatively.

Tahn turned to look west, and saw the towers again, now basked in the light of the morning sun. Five towers, like great limbless stone trees, set in a wide pentagon on the western plains of the Kamas Throne. Then he looked back at Rithy.

The young woman screwed up her face and said, "I want to know why you left. And I want to know now."

He struggled for a moment to recall her real name . . . Gwen. They'd been close friends in his years here, giving each other nicknames as close friends do: Rithy, because she studied mathematics, and was wickedly brilliant at it, too; she called him Gnomon because—

"Gnomon's the part of the sundial that casts a shadow," he said, smiling.

"It also suggests 'one who discerns' or 'that which reveals,' but enough of that. I'm waiting." She comically tapped her toe.

Tahn's smile widened.

"You don't want to be wearing a mocking grin after disappearing for almost eight years." Rithy pointed a finger at him. "Now, out with it. Where'd you go?"

Before he could think better of it, he heard himself say, "It wasn't safe for me to stay. I was sent back to the Scar and then to the Hollows, which was supposed to be protected from the Quiet. . . ."

Rithy's eyes seemed to calculate the truth in his words. He couldn't wait on her assessment; the pain of holding himself up became too great. He eased himself back to the ground with an audible sigh of relief.

"Really, Gnomon? You're going to stick with that excuse? And probably you'll say that's what did this to you." She gestured at his entire aching body.

"No," he replied. "Not directly, anyway." He took several deep breaths, before observing, "You still come to watch the sunrise." This was where they'd always come together, once she'd learned of his little ritual.

"Helps me remember." But that was all she said about it. "We need to get you to a bed, and fill you with warm willow tea."

Sounded good to Tahn. He nodded. The operation took the better part of an hour. She ran back to Aubade Grove and returned with a small flatbed wagon. She'd chosen to fetch him alone, keeping his return quiet for now. Climbing into the back of the wagon proved a minor miracle; the pain was excruciating and he had a hard time not vocalizing it. Which probably accounted for the glacial pace at which she drove them back to the Grove and up behind her modest home. And even at that, every small rock or rut they hit felt like a kidney jab made with bare knuckles. She carried him into her bedroom and gently laid him on her bed, returning promptly with warm, bitter-tasting tea.

Tahn downed the mug of bark broth without complaint, and had just eased back into the soft feather mattress when he heard the door in the outer room open again. The shuffle of feet came at a hurried pace. And for the second time in as many hours, he was staring up into the unbelieving face of a woman from his past.

"Gnomon," said Savant Polaema. The creases of time and good humor tracked more deeply through the skin around her eyes and mouth than he remembered. But they still gave her the look of the mother he'd taken her for in his years here. "It's good to see you again, my boy."

Her voice washed over him, every bit the balm that the willow tea might be. Tahn smiled. "It's good to be back," he said. "It's good to be anywhere, actually."

"That's a statement I'll ask you to explain at some point," Mother Polaema replied.

The savant of astronomy seemed to have her suspicions about him, even though she knew why he'd left the Grove. He caught sight of the subtle symbol woven into her overcloak over her left breast. Black thread on black wool, two convex lines, touching at the center, one bowing slightly up, the other slightly down. The lower one represented the horizon, the upper one suggested the vastness of the sky above. He'd earned the right to wear that symbol when he'd been here. Polaema sat at the side of his bed, Rithy looking over her shoulder.

Catching sight of the insignia of the College of Astronomy, Tahn looked up at Rithy, and noted for the first time the equally subtle insignia she wore for the College of Mathematics. Two gently curving lines standing vertically close together. At their tops, they bowed slightly away from one another; at their bottoms, they curled gently toward each other. Some said these lines represented letters from the Kamasal root, the left a flowing I to signify imaginary numbers, the right a delicately sweeping S to stand for summation. Theorists liked to say they were both I's and that dually they suggested concrete numbers; that math could arrive at full proofs for any question.

"I can see you're in pain," said Mother Polaema. "But you look capable enough of fielding a few questions. Have I misjudged?"

"No," Tahn answered. "I'm well enough to talk."

"Good. Because your sudden appearance, in this condition

no less, suggests many things. And before we share the news of your return with the other college savants, I'd like to have a sense of why you're here. If only to control our general anxiety, you understand." She showed a tentative smile.

"So, you're asking me to explain my 'anywhere' remark already," Tahn said, returning her smile. Pain still rippled through him, but damn, was he glad to be here. He felt surprisingly at peace, at home even.

"I suppose we are." It was Rithy speaking. "Mind the truth, too. There were no footprints in the soil where I found you. It's like you fell out of the sky."

Tahn laughed aloud at that, and instantly regretted it, clutching at his chest and gut. He moaned for a few moments and finally relaxed. When he looked up again, the two women who'd been his closest friends were watching him with expectant concern.

He hadn't known how he might answer until he opened his mouth to speak. Not really. And when he did, he told them most of it. About his years in the Hollows, and everything since being chased from there by the Quiet. He didn't speak of his bowshot in the Saeculorum, or the details of what he saw at Tillinghast. And he didn't go into his relationship with Mira. Beyond that, he trusted both Polaema and Rithy as he would Sutter. Talking to them came every bit as easily.

When he'd finished speaking, he could see the amazement in their eyes. That, and a hundred more questions.

"But why here, why now?" his old mentor pressed.

"Over the past several days I've begun to remember my astronomy training. I remembered the focus here on inquiry and exploration, and the rigor of thought to solve problems."

"And?" Mother Polaema questioned politely.

Tahn stared back at her, and finally gave her a lopsided grin. "Yes, there's more," he said. "But first a question. Rithy, did you ever make it into those sealed halls in the mathematics college?"

"Tahn?" Rithy said, impatient.

He was about to ask a hell of a thing. "I want to call for a Succession of Arguments."

A look of deep concern stole over Mother Polaema and

Rithy's faces. But they didn't say no. They stood, waiting to hear more. He began to feel the nausea rolling back in like a flash flood. He needed to get it out before he puked.

"If we can find a unifying principle for how the Veil works," Tahn said, wincing a bit, "then we'll understand how to strengthen it."

He could see a question still in their eyes. An apprehension. Fear. He knew they were waiting for him to say he meant to make the same argument they'd made together just before he'd left Aubade Grove before. Which wasn't the case. Not exactly. And they needed to understand *why* he'd ask for Succession.

Wincing again as his gut tightened, he hurried to finish, "Which will prevent the war that's coming if we don't . . . because the Veil is failing. And there's not much time."

Before he could explain further, the sickness from passing through Wendra's Telling circled back on him with a vengeance.

· CHAPTER TWENTY-FIVE ·

The Bourne: Nocturne

The deep north of the Bourne is to the southern Bourne what the southern Bourne is to the Eastlands.

—Remark of a highwayman who'd given up trading human stock in favor of brewing

A GIBBOUS MOON SHONE bright on the frozen ground. Kett walked slowly, rehearsing what he would say to the praefect. Each exhaled breath plumed before him, illuminated briefly by moonlight before it dissipated to nothing. The scent of dead, winter-frozen grass hung in the air, and he could hear nothing save the crunch of his own steps over brittle twigs and small rocks.

In his many years, he'd made but a few friends. The idea of friendship simply held little value inside the Bourne. Expectations were simple, punishments severe. It required dogged determination and almost all of one's time simply to survive.

And while he now had some allegiance among Inveterae houses, it was one of his few friendships that had him braving a walk in the deeps of evening.

Lost in his own thoughts, he vaguely noted a bare tree passing across the face of a low moon to his left. So few branches . . .

He stopped. Giving the tree his full attention, he saw it for what it was: a crucified Inveterae. A friend. Not the one he was on his way to see, but still a friend. Rough poles had been lashed together, and Taolen inexpertly nailed up.

Around Taolen's neck hung a sign with a single word written in the Bar'dyn tongue: EXAMPLE.

The moon lent his friend's bloody face a soft peace. He hoped those who crossed this way saw the admonition— *Example*—another way: as a rally cry for Inveterae to stand up against their persecutors, rather than the deterrent Quietgiven hoped it would be.

He offered a quick, silent appeal for Taolen's conveyance to the gods, and started to go, when he heard a soft moan. His head snapped in the direction of the crucified.

"Taolen?" He took three quick strides to the base of the pole. "You're alive."

The other's head rose slightly, then lolled forward again. In his arms were several cuts made with precision, following the blood veins under the skin. Most of these had been bandaged to stop the bleeding; it seemed the crucifier was slowly bleeding him out. One of Taolen's eyes had been completely ruined. And little of the left side of his face remained. But with his one remaining eye, his friend looked down at him wearily. In a hoarse whisper, Taolen managed three words: "I said nothing."

Then his eye closed, and he fell unconscious again. He'd be dead by morning.

Kett didn't linger to ponder or mourn. The only right honor for Taolen, for Saleema, for the countless others who would fall, was resolve.

Up the path he continued, slow but confident, toward the distant light of the praefect's tent. The wind stirred the fallow-smelling air—old earth, unseeded, unused—and rippled the tent flaps as Kett stopped before two sentries standing stock-still in the cold.

He paused long enough for them to raise an objection. None came. They knew him. It wasn't his first visit to the praefect. He ducked through the tent flaps into the yellow glow of oil lamps that hadn't warmed the air a bit.

"Why did I think you'd come tonight?" Lliothan asked. His words pushed plumes of breath into the lamplight.

Kett didn't step into the tent proper—he hadn't yet been invited. "Because you crucified Taolen."

"Maybe." Lliothan poured a viscous-looking drink from a bronze decanter. "Or maybe because the rumor is you're to be initiated and given your own command, doing . . . very much what I do."

"I'm no threat to you," he replied immediately. "And I'm no martyr. They killed Saleema."

Lliothan offered no consolation, but drank two draughts in quick succession, which Kett recognized as a salute of respect in the Bar'dyn ranks—one for body, one for spirit.

"You aren't planning your own justice?" Lliothan's question was rhetorical.

"Gotun women die every day," Kett said. The words were hard to speak, but he could have no suspicion.

"They do," Lliothan agreed. "So why do you come?"

The praefect still hadn't offered full entry. Kett needed to get closer to make his appeal. Lliothan must see Kett's eyes when he asked what he came here to ask. "May I come in?"

The Bar'dyn turned his back to him. "Come."

He went in, passing the thick wool blanket laid over a mat of straw that served as a bed; a single three-leg stool; a lap desk that held a ledger for recording Inveterae movements, executions, events of interest; and a black oilcloth laid out with weapons and whetstones—a simple command tent, but efficient and mobile.

Kett passed all these things, and one more besides—a corner of the tent where the thick canvas walls showed splatters of blood, and the cold ground shone crimson in the sallow light of two small lamps.

He got around beside Lliothan, where he could be seen. He stood a moment, watching his old friend drink from his iron mug, his nostrils pushing more plumes of hot breath over the rim of his cup.

Finally, he asked the simple question. "Can I trust you?"

Lliothan didn't turn to face him square on. "You'll soon sit in command. I follow orders."

"That's not what I asked," Kett replied. "In our youth, before we understood what it meant to be Gotun or Bar'dyn, we were friends. Do you remember?"

Lliothan drank again, and this time Kett could smell the copper scent of whatever the Bar'dyn had in his mug. The praefect still didn't turn, still faced the rear of his tent, his countenance partly obscured in half shadows.

"Kett Valan, you are unique. But you're also naïve. You, and all the Inveterae, live here in the south, wallowing in your abandonment. You curse the coarse ground which yields you little for your labor, and you distrust us." He tapped his barrel chest. "But your understanding is narrow. The secrets of the Bourne, its afflictions and cruelty . . . and abominations, are far from you. Your discontent is not suffered well by those who live farther north."

"Then tell me." He came around to face Lliothan straight. "Teach me to be thankful for crucifixion and ignorance and laughable tribunals that leave only the option for treachery against my own kind."

Lliothan glared back. "We are each of us in the Bourne," the Bar'dyn said impassively. "We should not seek to leave unless we *all* go."

"Does that include the men and women and children you make us tend in the camps?" He carefully meted out his ire—their old friendship would offer him only so much latitude.

"Inveterae tend the captives in the south because none of you would survive farther north or west." Lliothan finished his drink, dropping the cup unceremoniously beside his feet.

Kett pushed gently. "What good are they to you? Especially the women and children. They can't fight. And they know little about the politics or armies south of the Pall."

Lliothan gave Kett the most piteous look he seemed capable of. "These are things you don't want to know. Trust me. Soon enough, your eyes will be opened. Until then, let it alone."

"Very well," he said, nodding. "I will *trust* you."

Lliothan's pity changed to a grimace Kett recognized as mild mirth. "And in trusting me, you'd have my trust in return. You are, indeed, a politician, Kett Valan. I'm surprised you didn't talk the flail right out of the Jinaal's hand."

Kett then did something that in the presence of any other Bar'dyn would have meant instant death: He laughed. The sound of it fell coldly in the praefect's tent. And Kett realized with horror—in his friend's own grimacing smile—that Lliothan's teeth were slick with blood. In that moment, he also knew what the cuts on Taolen's arms were for.

When the mirth faded between them, Lliothan turned back into the lamplight. "What brings you to me in the dark? A request, no doubt."

Kett had a moment to consider just how much to share. Lliothan's guardianship extended across several mountain ranges and broad valleys, and east to the Mourning Vale. He held considerable influence. Kett must guard what he told him.

"I came tonight—before I'm given to the Quiet—because I want to ask two favors. And I want your answers to me as your friend, not your commander." He looked around the tent again, reassuring himself they were alone.

Lliothan said nothing, waiting.

"First, there may come a day when I ask you to help me—if

only in looking another direction." Kett lent as much gravity as he could to what he said next. "Should that day come . . . I ask for your devotion."

Lliothan's expression didn't change. If anything, he seemed that much more indifferent. "What is your second favor?"

Kett looked down at the praefect's dropped mug. He hated having to ask this. But the path ahead had many turns. And in one possible future, he would need a friend inside the Quietgiven ranks.

He stepped even closer. So close, he caught the scent of carrion on Lliothan's breath. But he didn't step away. "The Jinaal killed Saleema so that I would know the price of betrayal. All I have left are Marckol and Neliera. . . ."

The praefect's eyes narrowed, as though he guessed what Kett would have of him.

He steeled himself to say it. "If they're seized, Lliothan, I want you to be their executioner. They've seen you; I've spoken of you; and they will be less afraid when death comes if it's by your hand. I ask you to make it quick and painless. And by the gods, take them in the flesh; don't allow the Jinaal to render their spirits." Anger and sadness mixed in his words. "Will you swear it?"

The Bar'dyn's heavy features moved in a way he hadn't seen before. The thick, fibrous skin stretched over the great bones of Lliothan's face as he held Kett's questioning gaze.

The silent tent, reeking of blood and spent oil and cold earth, seemed to lock them together in a pact that chilled Kett's heart.

The praefect bent, bringing his massive face in line with Kett's. "Kett Valan, you live this side of the Veil, but you are not in the Bourne. Nor has the Bourne gotten inside you."

Kett shook his head. "You're wrong. What I do . . . what I have done . . . We're not so different, you and I."

The Bar'dyn's grimacing smile came again. "Tell me about this."

"I won't have to. You'll see it for yourself. I intend to take you into my service after I'm given."

The praefect picked up his mug, poured another cup of the viscous, copper-smelling fluid, and gave it to Kett to drink. "We are sworn."

He drank of Taolen's blood, securing the help he might later need, and slid further into the taint he hoped to escape.

• CHAPTER TWENTY-SIX •

Chilled Milk

Information trumps all.

> —Pulled from an informal survey conducted of street-
> sellers by the Chair of Commerce, Recityv, regarding
> the types of goods being sold by Merchant Houses

THE MERCHANT DISTRICT had a scent of its own, one Helaina had missed more than she realized. It was the musky smell of sheer fabric used for provocative garments; it was the papery aroma of books considered apocryphal but not scandalous; it was the alchemical smell of brass molded into survey instruments and given a polish that gleamed by lamplight.

She'd grown up on these streets, learning the difference between a pressed coin and metal plug, between alloys and single-metal currencies. Much of this she'd learned from her father, before she broke his heart.

But she let that memory alone for now, and reveled in the excitement of night commerce. It had a particular flavor distinct from the other classes of merchant activity. Lowest of these was the handstalls drawn up in makeshift fashion alongside the roads beyond the city wall. Those overland merchants often traded in "double goods"—meaning you were the second owner of something stolen. And if not stolen, then the items you were browsing were banned by law or crudely made, and able to be had for a few thin plugs.

Near cousin to the overland merchants were those inside the Recityv walls who set up handcarts in alley-fronts all across the city. Things they sold were a half step up from goods had on the road. That included the flesh trade. When a man or woman wanted practiced love, it could be bought. Some whores went it alone. Their services were cheap and fast and often had for a drink or drab of laudanum. The savvy ones, though, attached themselves to the Geneese family, who plied that particular trade with great aplomb.

And at the top of the commerce ladder: the Merchant District. Here, there were three levels of commerce. The night market, which buzzed all around her now. Then, in the day, a different set of merchants would line up in chalked stalls. These usually stocked discounted items cleared from the shelves of the merchant buildings. And highest in the pecking order were the merchant family warehouses. The district had as many as forty-seven families.

Helaina moved casually through the night market, feeling at home in a way she never quite did at Solath Mahnus. She loved the immediacy and urgency of chalked slate announcing goods and prices. It left the buyer with the sense that items written there might soon be gone, that prices weren't fixed.

Eager chatter filled the air. The sweet smell of honeyed barley-bread. The sharp tang of roasted sausages. More than a few musicians played on street corners—not carnival tunes, and not the airs of operettas. No, they played accompaniment to stroll and purchase by; they played songs like "Coins to Rub Together," "Jubilee Is a Bargain Made," and "Give It Here, It's Mine." Gods, how she missed all this.

Before she knew it, and before she was ready, she stopped in the middle of the central merchant road and turned to face her family's warehouse. The bright, warm light of night commerce lit the granite facings, giving it a stout, lasting appearance.

In heavily serifed letters, chiseled into the stone above the high entryway, was a single word: STORALAITH. Her family name. One of the most influential merchant houses in Recityv. One she'd have been asked to run if she'd remained in the business. One that believed she'd betrayed their interest in her very first year as regent.

Dear absent gods, I'm going in.

She was too old to be afraid of the ghosts of her youth. Besides, she'd been right to pass sanctions on trade. *And it was thirty years ago.* She didn't even bother to knock. Knocking would suggest that she didn't feel she was still permitted to enter the home of her family. She signaled to her Emerit guard, who would be close by and hidden, that she was going in alone. Then she opened the front lock with the key she still carried—a key fashioned by a Dimnian craftsman, nearly impossible to replicate.

The buzz of night commerce muted as she closed the door. Inside, a few oil lamps had their wicks turned down low. Her father preferred oil light to alchemical lamps. Flickering flames outlined furniture in the front sitting room. Closed doors to offices on the right. A lacquered banister ascending the stairs to the bedchambers above. And more light on her left—the kitchen, where the real business always took place.

Helaina put her key away and took a long breath, steadying herself. Then she went in. It wasn't a surprise to see her parents bent over glasses of chilled milk, scratching at numbers on a ledger, and conversing in hushed tones as they'd always done. They sat at a thick butcher-block-type table—sturdy enough for family meals and the occasional side of beef they portioned themselves. She missed that, too. In a family tradition, everyone wielded a knife of Alon'Itol steel and helped carve up the meat. Throwing slices of parted beef fat at one another had been good sport; laughter had kept them company during the task. Her father told all his old jokes about how if the family failed at its "business of knowledge" they could all become butchers.

As far as she could remember, this was the pose she'd last seen them in, too. If she squinted, it looked like they were bent in prayer, their words having a similar kind of reverence.

They didn't notice her right away, so she stood and watched for a while. She could count on one hand the number of times she'd seen them since she'd been made regent. And most of those had come before the trade sanctions she'd invoked.

She'd run into her father twice since, and both times he'd skirted her and disappeared. Both times it had been when a vote had come up to revoke the sanctions, which had commonly become known as the "Knowledge Law."

Before that memory returned in full, she heard her father clear his throat. Her eyes focused, and she found her parents staring at her. Without averting his eyes, her father picked up a meat tenderizer and pounded the table three times with it like a gavel. Loud cracks filled the kitchen. For a man nearly eighty years old, he was still strong in his arms. She'd thought he was simply being impudent, but shortly, a young man she scarcely recognized emerged through the kitchen's rear door.

"What's the matter, Da?" Then her brother Mendel looked up at her. Fifteen years her junior, he'd grown taller and thicker than their father.

Mendel's face rushed through an initial smile of pleasant surprise to a look of concern, and then—she thought—a hint of distaste.

"Helaina, dear, you're all crippled over with rheumatism," her mother observed. "Are you drinking green tea? Try turmeric powder, dear."

Helaina smiled. Her mother never stopped being a ma.

"Please show the regent her way out," her father said.

"Gemen," said her mother with mild reproof.

He cracked the meat tenderizer down once more for good measure. "Merta, don't cross me on this. Storalaith hangs by a thread because of that girl." He jabbed a finger at her. "We're just this side of crooks, as they see it. Law always sniffing around. Conducting audits of our inventory. Threats all the while." His own words seemed to drive his anger to new heights, and he slammed the tenderizer down again, this time on its flat side, producing more a crack than slam. "And that's on the commerce of *information,* dove. It's madness!"

She hadn't heard her father call her mother "dove" since she'd lived here.

Mendel put a hand on his father's shoulder to try and calm him. "Helaina, it's late. I assume you're here for personal reasons, and not as regent?" His tone turned up at the end, as in a question.

Helaina nodded. "A little of both, actually."

"Can it wait 'til tomorrow?" Mendel suggested, looking down at his father and back up.

Her brother meant that Gemen Storalaith would be engaged in trade tomorrow. She'd do better talking to them if he wasn't here.

Not seeing the exchange, her father closed his ledger, took a long draught of his cold milk, and leveled his appraising eyes on her. "Then let's have it. Start with the regent bit; I'd like to know why you grace our warehouses so late on an official errand. You can't hardly tax us anymore than you already have. Or maybe we should just get to it and sign over our stock to you now."

She waited while her father vented, giving her mother a patient look. "I need access to the family vault."

Her father brayed out a caustic laugh. It sounded wet in his chest, like he had the blood cough, but he didn't fall into any spasms. "Unbelievable. Access to our vault. That's what you want? Is that an official request? Or is it my daughter needs money? Maybe to bribe a few votes to pass another trade law."

"I could make it an official request," she said coolly. "But I don't want to do that."

"We might need you to, Helaina." It was her mother, trying in her own way to smooth the divide between daughter and father.

"Why do you need to get in?" Mendel asked. He showed no suspicion, and it was a fair question, besides.

She stepped forward and placed her hands on the edge of the table, mostly for support—she'd been walking and standing a long time. "The day I was named regent, I came here, do you remember?"

Her parents both nodded.

"I had something with me. Something I placed in the Storalaith vault, because to me there's not a safer place I could have kept it, not even in the deeps of Solath Mahnus."

"What was it?" Mendel's curiosity was piqued.

She gave them each a long look. "A letter," she said. "Now, will you let me in?"

Her answer seemed to surprise them. And none of them spoke while her father considered her request. *He* led the Storalaith Merchant House, after all was said and done. It was a vast operation, with gatherers in most cities and towns across the Eastlands. In fact, to hear the merchant houses tell it— trade legends being what they were—Gemen had sent gatherers over the seas in merchant ships and into the Bourne itself.

Her father waved the tenderizer dismissively. "Very well. Let's get you your letter and the hell out of my warehouse. Bad for business," he muttered.

As he started to stand, Mendel gently pushed his father back into his chair. "I'll see to it, Da. You finish the day's ledger, and your milk, too."

"No horsing around back there," her father admonished. "In and out." He jabbed the tenderizer forward and back in emphasis. "And be mindful you're escorting your *regent*."

Helaina tried not to let the snide way her father used her official title bother her. She had certainly had worse from others. And if she was honest, she'd expected it, even understood it. But that didn't lessen the sting of it one jot. Her father's skin bore the large dark spots of age. Though he still had a steady hand, he'd go to his earth soon. She might have just lost her last chance to reconcile with the da she still loved. The man who'd given her the keen wit and values that accounted—as far as she was concerned—for any of her success as regent.

Mendel motioned her to follow, and he disappeared through the rear kitchen door. She paused next to her father as she passed. She longed to bend and kiss him one last time, put her arms around him. Tell him she loved him. She sensed any of those things would be too much. The gulf between them had widened too far. Instead, she simply reached down and put a hand on his forearm, feeling the warmth of his aged skin. She didn't look at him as she did so. And he didn't look up. But neither did he pull his arm away.

The moment passed in a breath. And it broke her heart with the suggestion of closeness she had forfeited for thirty years. Her da.

She wondered. If she could go back, would she shun the call to be regent, and stay at her father's side?

Get moving, you old dotard. Looking back's a fool's game.

She stifled a grin as she left the kitchen for the Storalaith vault, since the pragmatism she scolded herself with belonged to her father—maybe the best thing she'd inherited from him.

Down a short hall Mendel waited at an iron door for her to catch up. This was the first, simplest barrier to the family depository. The thickly cast portal had a rather plain keyhole. By rote, Mendel inserted a key into the lock and turned.

But this was all show. As her brother performed the obvious task, he also subtly pressed a small section of the doorjamb a hand's length below the lock. This was the true key.

After they'd stepped through, Mendel closed the door promptly, and turned into a small antechamber. A few chairs were situated in the corners, where attendant tables laden with a few books and low-wick oil lamps stood. A decorative rug spun by a Reyal'Te weaver covered the floor from wall to wall. This room had been one of Helaina's favorites as a child—quiet, removed from the bustle of warehouse inventory and kitchen conversation. It was great for reading in peace any of the wonderful books they meant to sell—stock, her father called it.

Helaina smiled at the term—*stock*. Even as a child, she'd seen through her father's insistence that she view the books as collateral. The man had a passion for knowledge. He could have chosen a hundred other ways to earn coin. And many of his own family argued there were simpler needs to fill, merchandise they could move more quickly and at better margin.

Gemen Storalaith would have none of it. Much as it filled his coffers, too, he had it in his head that he was doing his clientele a service. *Trading in knowledge,* he'd say, *is ennobling.* He wasn't wrong, either.

Her smile soured. She'd inherited that same sense from the man. And it was that feeling that had led her to pass the Knowledge Law. She'd had her judicature counselors draft it, which meant it was filled with a bunch of six-plug words only an academy graduate would understand. But in essence: New information didn't *belong* to anyone; so it couldn't be sold. The profitability of her father's trade had taken a severe hit; the law required Storalaith to turn over any new *understanding* it sourced to the Library of Common Understanding. They'd been forced to do commerce in the grey area of scholarship that reevaluated existing knowledge. It was a specialized market. A good one. And her father was expert at it. But her law had crippled his growth and profit potential.

The Knowledge Law had been the right thing. It made Helaina extremely popular with the people. And she liked to believe that maybe somewhere in his heart, her father was proud that she'd tried to help make enlightenment more widely available. But she'd lost her family because of it, and hadn't sat at the kitchen table for chilled milk since.

Mendel approached a second door. This one had no lock at all, just a handle. And when he knocked, it sounded as thin and light as balsa wood. But she listened in sweet memory to the tap. *Tap. Tap tap. Tap tap tap. Tap tap. Tap.* The same chiastic rhythm repeated three times.

Nothing happened. After a few moments, Mendel looked back at her, smiling. "Do you remember?" he asked, his eyebrows arching.

After a half moment to remember, she returned a grin, then repeated the rhythmic knock. But this time in its proper pattern: Left. Left, right. Left, right, down. Down right. Right.

Beneath her knuckles, the door swung slowly open on hinges that used gravity to pull it back. She smiled, happy to have remembered on her own.

The short hallway beyond chilled her skin. Cold stone surrounded them on every side; another dim, low-wick oil lamp burned at the corridor's end. Here forward, all was thick granite. She and Mendel came to the last door. She marveled now at the piece of genius stonework—practically seamless, set on a near-soundless caster system, graven with a simple undecorative word: so.

So was a Dimnian word meaning "speech-song," and an archaic connotation at that. This last door could be unlocked only by the sound of the voice. But the ingenuity of the lock went beyond mere *so*. The door had been attuned to the voices of the Storalaith family. Speech, it turned out, had qualities that followed family lines. Like a tonal fingerprint. It was as distinctive and different as one cloud is from the next. And for the price of a very old Masson text, Gemen Storalaith had bought the service of a Dimnian who knew the art of fastening the door with a speech-lock only a Storalaith could open.

Mendel parted his lips to speak. Helaina put a hand on his shoulder to stop him. She wanted to do it. She felt like a child again, and that didn't seem so bad a thing. He smiled and gestured grandly for her to take over.

Helaina stepped closer to the door and said, as they always had, "Don't let me in."

The childish joke of it made them both laugh, since the door, of course, rolled back at the sound of her voice.

Once the half-stride-thick granite slab had opened fully, her brother picked up the oil lamp and they went in. "Don't let me out," Mendel said, and the portal rolled shut again—vault doors were never left open.

Mendel lit several oil lamps to brighten the vault, as Helaina noted the receiving desk set beside the door, where a handy copy of the ledger was kept. Her father was a stickler for such redundancies.

Then she looked up, and came to an abrupt stop. Her father's trade had expanded. Where he'd begun with texts, the vault now showed tidy sections of various information goods. In one corner a tall cherrywood rack—much like a wine rack, but deeper—held a vast assortment of maps.

Next to the map rack stood a table laid out with dozens of different kinds of ores and minerals. She hadn't mastered mineralogy, but she'd gotten streetwise in their value and uses. Her father had no interest in platinums and golds and qualens, it would seem. Useful as those metals were in commerce, it appeared they hadn't the *leading* qualities these ones did.

Helaina caught whiffs of aqua fortis, strong water, and vinegar—reactants that could be used to test mineral authenticity.

Beside the table stood a large cabinet with glass doors. Inside it, on tall shelves, were glass bottles with cork stoppers.

The bottles held powders and liquids in various quantities. She knew her father better than to think he'd peddle false nostrums to the ignorant, or even useful ones to the sick— nostrums weren't his trade. Mendel saw her quizzical stare and crossed to the cabinet, opened the left door, and drew down a bottle. He opened it and dabbed a finger in a pale magenta powder, then put his finger in his mouth.

"Rhubarb powder. Good drink flavoring." He grinned.

Helaina laughed softly. She knew the cabinet held more than culinary ingredients, but before she could ponder it further, her attention turned to the dead.

On the left wall hung several large anatomical sketches. Beside them, from a series of spikes driven into the stone, hung intact skeletons. The sizes and shapes varied; these were the bones of different races—human, Tilatian, Far, Mal, Dimnian, and others. She was no anatomist, but she'd swear on there being at least those races. What disturbed her most, though, were the sketches themselves. They'd been marked up in odd places. *Strategic places.* It looked to her like the biological frailties of each race had been meticulously noted—information that had a certain buyer.

Looking around, she had the sudden realization that Storalaith had moved beyond simply acquiring and reselling understanding. It had gone into the business of discovery. They were using what could be learned in the books, and advancing the knowledge themselves.

The wall opposite the door stretched from one corner to the other with bookshelves, save a bureau over to the right.

This had been the meat of her father's trade when she'd still been a part of it. She ambled close and began perusing titles. A forlorn smile rose on her lips as she saw volumes by Shenflear and Hargrove and Malekel and Ara and Deleni—books almost certainly a violation of the Knowledge Law.

She pulled herself away from the books. She needed to focus on her task.

Rather than wait for Roth to make a move, she'd decided to take an offensive posture. She would reassert the office of regent, and her own regency, and do so by publishing . . . the letter.

Helaina went to the bureau. She opened the third drawer and pressed a hidden panel, revealing a hollow in the drawer from which she pulled an envelope.

Mendel had replaced the glass bottle in the cabinet, and stood back while Helaina removed with gentle, trembling fingers a letter, and laid it on the bureau's marble top while she read:

On this, the fourth day of the fourth cycle of the year 899 in this Fifth Era, I, King Nevil Sadon, end the line of Kings in the kingdom of Vohnce. I do this not because I have no heir. Rather, I admit that too often in our great realm's history have my forebears taken too much liberty as Lords of these lands simply because they were born in the line of succession. And we can no longer afford the inconsistent rule that proceeds from the unpredictable disposition of a single man.

Neither, though, will I relegate ruling power to the farmer who knows nothing of war and politics. It is not fair to him, nor to the rest of the people he would need to lead.

So I frame a new government, where in place of a King, Recityv and Vohnce shall have a Regent, whose responsibilities shall be like unto a King's but moderated by a Council, and a system of Courts. All this I will set forth in detail with my advisors, so that we may avoid confusion as we embark upon a reform of how we build prosperity, protection from invaders, as well as an industrious people.

The Regent will be appointed by recommendation from a new High Council, comprised of representatives from all the orders of influence and industry. That same High Council will then serve for the balance of their lives, so that the winds of change in the economies and fraternal politics of our many important brotherhoods do not blow us hither and yon.

So begins our new future. Each of you now has a voice. And you may trust your Regent to hear them all with fairness and sympathy and grace.

May you know fair skies.
Your King and Brother,
Nevil Sadon

Then just below this copy of King Sadon's Epistle of
Change, the following had been scrawled:

We, the High Council, in the year 431 of the Seventh
Age, do appoint Helaina Storalaith as Regent of Recityv and Vohnce, with all the rights and powers of that
office. Under her leadership, we will dispense fairness
and mercy, and will stand as an example to all other
realms.

This we do in line with the Epistle of Change issued
by King Nevil Sadon.

Beneath it were the names of all the council members, save
a Child's Voice, which was a role that had, until recently,
fallen out of favor.

Helaina's letter of succession.

She'd been a very young woman when it had been signed.
She could still remember how ill-prepared and anxious she'd
been. Her predecessor had reassured her: *Ruling is having the
conviction that you are right.* And if she passed away before
she had the chance to impart that same wisdom to whomever
would eventually follow her, the Council would perform the
selection process just as it had done with her. It was more tidy
if she could hand over the keys, but not necessary. A majority vote would see a new regent installed. But only when she
was ready to step down.

Convocation was just days away. She'd place herself firmly
in the minds of the people, her councils, and the visiting kings
she summoned, by publishing this letter. . . .

Something struck her head hard, knocking her to the stone
floor of the vault.

CHAPTER TWENTY-SEVEN

The Write Words

What did authors do before quill and ink?

—Provocation meant to establish the hierarchy
of an author's five gifts

ROTH ARRIVED AT Author Garlen's door. The smell of burning lamp oil wafted through cracks around the window on the left. The man's modest home stood down a small cobblestone alley, and was Roth's second stop since Helaina had refused to step down from her regent's seat. He hadn't really expected that she would, but asking her first had been the right order of events. Politics was about saying and doing things that could be recorded, seen, and judged proper, while taking private initiative in the interest of the greater good. And so he'd begun to make his rounds, visiting members of the High Council.

He'd started with General Van Steward, a Helaina loyalist. And while it would have been good to have the man's support, the general hadn't been persuaded. No matter. The man would, by law, follow the orders of whoever held the regent seat.

He knocked at Garlen's sagging lintel, like so many others here at the south edge of the central district—not a slum, but only a few years from becoming one.

"Go away!" a crotchety voice yelled from behind the door.

The old author was known as a high-order crosspatch. This visit would be interesting.

"Author Garlen, it's Roth Staned from the League of Civility. It's important. Please, may I have a few minutes of your time?" Roth smiled. No one turned him down when he came in an official capacity.

"Didn't you hear me the first time?" The author's reply came more caustic still. "I've no time for politics."

Roth had to handle this delicately. He must insist on an audience, but mustn't alienate the man before the door was even opened. "Garlen"—he used just the man's name, more personal that way—"odd as it sounds, I'm not one for politics, myself. That's just where I've wound up. I promise to be brief, but of all the authors in Recityv, you're the only one I can talk to."

Some cursing ensued, followed by plodding feet toward Roth from within the small home. Then the door snapped open with judgmental haste. "It's not the politician's flattery that pulled me from my writing, leagueman. It's my eagerness to have you come in and prove yourself a liar."

Roth gave a smile, thinking of how to win the man's approval. "That's fair."

Garlen retreated inside his home, leaving the door ajar. Roth stepped in, shut the door, and surveyed an absolute disaster of paper, books, maps, art, shoes, dirty plates, pens, ink, magnifying glasses . . . utter chaos. A few lamps burned low on desks set against the walls. The brightest hung over a tall lectern that Garlen was now ascending with the difficulty of advanced age.

"Will my honesty offend you if I tell you that you keep a pigsty of a home?" Roth put on his charming smile.

"Honesty never offends me," Garlen said perfunctorily. "Now, get to it. What banal, nonpolitical, conversational topic brings you to my pigsty? Or have you cheapened yourself with a lie to buy a few minutes of my time? I really hope it's the latter." At that, Garlen offered his own smile, and picked up a quill as if he was only ever comfortable when holding one.

Roth walked a narrow pathway between the clutter, deciding how to begin. Then he found an approach. "What made you take up the author's pen, Garlen?"

"First, stop calling me Garlen. You and I aren't friends, and that's unlikely to change. Second, I didn't have a choice in the matter. No true author does. You do it because you must.

Because *not* doing it will drive you mad." Garlen leaned forward and stared down over the lip of his lectern, smiling. "Suppose that frustrates the angle you wanted to take, doesn't it. Get me all nostalgic and maudlin about my craft, about the idealism of my youth and how I thought I could change the world with my pen."

Roth put up his hands as one giving up. "All right, I confess, yes. I'd hoped to do precisely that." But Roth's intentions had a second, deeper layer. "Tell me about this 'not having a choice in the matter' business."

"This is what you came here to talk about?" Garlen leaned back, scratching something on the parchment in front of him.

"In a way, yes," Roth replied, and stopped to show his attentiveness.

Garlen hunched his shoulders. "All right. We'll see where this goes. But it's not a long conversation. Men and women who are given to creating story have two choices: contentment or unhappiness."

"But never *happiness,*" Roth interjected.

"Not if they're worth their salt, no." Garlen dipped his quill, beginning to write even as he explained. "If a person is really a writer, then the tales come to them, needing to be written. Those tales don't let you alone until you write them down. The author may do it badly, but that doesn't matter so much; just getting them out and committed to some parchment will give the author contentment. Then, with time and some work and a little luck, the stories will be good enough to share with other folk."

Roth nodded, dissecting the author's words for how he could relate this back to his purpose for coming.

"However," Garlen went on, "some who would be and should be authors don't ever put those stories down on paper. They get busy with washing floors or milking cows or running a kingdom, and the stories build up like poison inside them, making them bitter or angry, and often they don't even know why. At the end of it, they're just unhappy, miserable creatures to be around."

Garlen stopped, finished with his explanation. His quill continued to scratch out words in the silence.

"I see," Roth said, filling the quiet house with resolute tones. "Then here is my gambit, Author Garlen. You and I are not so different."

That got the author's eyes to lift from his parchment, and his quill to stop. "I won't be insulted in my own home, league-man."

Roth stared at the man for a moment, and then shared a part of his past. "My mother died giving me life. My father never said it that way. But I knew. He was a deckhand in a port city. Mopped boards, scraped fish guts. Needless to say, we didn't have two coins to rub together. When he lost even that job, he and I went into the bedroom, and he got out my mother's few 'nice things.' My father told me about them. A thin silver ring—her mother's betrothal ring, which she and my father also used. An ivory pinch comb that she wore to feel pretty. A rosewood flute, because she thought music helped brighten the evening. And a small pen set, because she liked to write poems—thought one day she'd put them together in a book."

"That last part true?" Garlen asked, skeptical.

"I don't lie about my mother," Roth replied. "My father told me that they were just things. That Ma lived inside us. And that with no money, he needed to take them to a skiller, get what coin he could for them."

Garlen eyed him. "There are lots of stories of poverty."

Roth ignored that. "But he didn't take Ma's nice things to a skiller. He took them to a gambling boat. He lost them all. He might have been swindled. Probably was. But he lost her nice things in a game of placards."

A taut silence stretched between them.

"I was the reason she died. And to feed me, my da gambled away his last tokens of who she was." He gave Garlen an honest look. "I don't tell you that for pity. I tell you that because most people who have it rough like I did don't get the chance that was given to me."

"With the League," Garlen surmised.

"With the League." Roth smiled, not wanting it to seem that he was trying to play on Garlen's sympathies. "I know the League isn't terribly popular. But to be fair, neither has any other government or society been popular that has tried to introduce change. Even when the end results prove the merits of their cause."

"Clever," Garlen said, shaking his head with wry amusement, and maybe a little to dust off the lingering feelings of Roth's story. "But other societies, not unlike the League, have thought themselves enlightened when they began, but proved rather more odious when it was all said and done."

"For instance?" Roth asked, inviting an example.

"Well, at the risk of being unoriginal, how about the Whited One?" Garlen barked a laugh.

Roth held back his irritation at being compared to the dissenting god. He maintained his smile through the slur. "I'm at a disadvantage trading insults with a crafter of words," Roth submitted, with as much self-effacement as he could muster.

"Oh, I think you do just fine, there, leagueman." Garlan jabbed his quill at Roth, then started again to write.

"My point is this." Roth began to pace, thinking more clearly as he moved. "In many important ways, what you do chose *you,* just as what I do chose *me.* And, whether you admit it or not, at least one aim of your work is the edification of your readers."

"I think 'edification' is a strong word for what I do," Garlen said.

"And I think that's false modesty on your part." Roth pivoted and retraced his steps, pacing now as he often did when he found his rhythm. "I won't argue with you about that, however, since I can't prove it. But I *will* say that I know many who own your books or retell your stories. And they do so with a clear belief that your stories *matter.* That they provide moral guidance, enlightenment, and a much-needed escape from the hardships of their own lives."

"A happy consequence," Garlen said, testily. "I write for myself."

"Maybe." Roth offered an incredulous smile. "But if you didn't want an audience for your writings, you'd become a diarist or historian, or hells, even a scrivener."

Garlen glared down on him, apparently too angry to speak.

Roth noted the author's wrathful expression and modified his approach. "Forgive me for presuming why it is you write."

The author's next words came out in a torrent. "You take me for a cheap entertainer who seeks the adulation of the crowds. Or worse still, a sycophant who craves the attention of those who trod our vaunted marble halls."

"Not exactly," Roth corrected. "I think you believe what you do can shape attitudes and opinions. That's why I think we have at least something in common. And, if I may be so bold, Author Garlen, that's not a bad thing."

The aged author put down his quill. "So you're here to form an alliance, is that it? You believe that what you attempt to do with the League is the same as what we authors attempt to do with our pens." He shook his finger at Roth. "And for that, we should find ourselves in cahoots. That about right?"

Roth dropped his arms to his sides and looked up as submissively as he could. "That's about right. I want you to understand, though, that this isn't about power or control. I've been thinking about this for a long time. You know our own order has a faction devoted to history; these men and women prize the authors' work, often finding more truth in it than they do in historical texts."

Garlen sneered with skepticism. Roth pivoted his argument. "The authors are a powerful lot. They enjoy the affection of the people. They represent knowledge, learning, intelligence, and wisdom. These values perfectly express what I wish the League to be known for. The alliance of the author's society and the League would be a powerful step forward. Together, the work we could do would provide great value and direction. It's an ambitious vision, but not an unattainable one. And it begins—perhaps ends, if I may wax poetic— with discussion, even disagreement in small rooms like this, between men like you and me who prize honesty and have passion for what we do."

Author Garlen slowly stood. Though not a tall man, standing atop his pedestal he loomed large in the room, his head casting a shadow over Roth. "Comparing what authors try to do, working through the small hours of night, hunched over parchment we can often ill afford to buy, dizzy with the smell of our own ink, scribbling out the musings of our hearts . . . with the political power-brokering of the League, that tramples those who oppose it, and puts men to death—even members of its own fraternity—to advance its own interests . . . is perhaps the greatest insult I've received in my long life."

The author did not rush or rant, but offered his comment evenly, his eyes leaden upon Roth. And when Garlen had finished, Roth knew his maneuvering had failed. He let his prevarication drop from him like a mask. But he was not done.

"Very well, Garlen, then let me make something plain, with the words of a mere politician who cannot dream up stories and metaphors to teach and enlighten. I *will* have your allegiance as we reconvene the Convocation of Seats, and as the High Council prepares to vote on some important topics. Or the society of authors may find itself in the same position the Sheason did some few short years ago."

The old author barked laughter. "Extermination? You think you can push through an order that would see storytellers burned or crucified for stringing together a bunch of words? You really are drunk on your own power, Roth." He laughed again.

The old man's cackle infuriated him. His composure dwindled further, and he thrust his fist into the author's stand, rattling the pens, sending papers fluttering, and spilling the ink down the side of the lectern. "I won't be laughed at, old man!" Then Roth calmed himself, adopting the same coolness the author had used in denying and berating him a moment ago. "You have the choice, here and now, to seal a kinship between our two societies that will build the right future . . . or you may choose to damn all those who find themselves . . . content."

The two men glared their threats at one another across the small space, until Author Garlen picked up his quill and raised his right hand. Without so much as a blink, he began to write upon the air, his hand moving swiftly, surely, as though he saw some parchment that Roth could not.

And while he stood watching, the words the author wrote became slowly visible in midair. A dim yellow at first, tinged at the edge with umber, the words gradually glowed a tad more radiant. They hung there between them, slowly undulating as though stirred by gentle, indoor winds. As Garlen continued to write, his face shone in the unearthly light of his words, which had not just height and width, but also depth. They floated in the air like insubstantial sculptures.

It's true. Written glyphs, on the very air we breathe.

The author's intensity as he wrote spoke of passion and deadly zeal. A moment later, he finished, breathing heavily while staring through the words that glowed faintly between them. Then, Garlen waved his quill and the glyphs ceased to shine, though he could see they were still there. He'd have missed them if he hadn't seen them written, since now they appeared as little more than the slight disturbance of heat rising from a candle.

"Strikes you hagborn, doesn't it?" Garlen grinned. "We don't share it. It's old. Be careful not to awaken it and turn it against you. You wouldn't like the words we'd find for you and your League."

Roth stood in awe. But quickly composed himself and strode to the author's door. He turned back and looked at the old man, who stood poised with his quill in his hand, ready to write something more that Roth both wanted and did *not* want to see. One thing he knew now for certain, however: Whether or not Garlen and his society joined him, they weren't through with each other.

He smiled at the thought. He now knew better what he was up against.

And what to do about it.

• CHAPTER TWENTY-EIGHT •

Secrets in a Vault

Who a woman sells to is more telling than what she sells.

—Old merchant proverb

HELAINA FELL HARD on the vault floor. Sharp pain shot through her head, and she could feel warm blood flowing over her scalp. She struggled with her arthritic joints as she turned over, sure another blow would be following the cowardly first attack from behind. She stared up in shock—Mendel stood with a short, heavy cudgel in his hand.

"Why?" She tried to shout it, thinking to bring help, but her voice sounded weak and thin even in her own ears. She knew it was hopeless anyway—the vault was solid granite, a full stride thick.

She tried to stand, a wave of dizziness tumbling her back to the ground. Mendel circled toward her. She scrambled away from him on her hands and knees, the stone floor hard on her bones. Behind her, she thought she heard Mendel mumble something. Then another blow landed on her upper back, dropping her again. Her chin smacked hard on the stone and she bit her lip. Blood filled her mouth with the taste of iron.

Mendel took hold of her garment and spun her over. Instinctively, she raised her hands to ward off another blow. She was lucky; her wrist took the force of a strike that would have landed in her face. She had the sudden sense that she would die here, now.

Not without a fight!

Before the cudgel fell again, she kicked up as hard as she could, aiming for Mendel's tender parts. One foot flailed wildly, hitting nothing. The other caught him in the thigh, and drove him back. It gave Helaina time to scramble a few strides and look for a weapon. But there was nothing at hand. She had only the long sturdy pin she used to hold up her hair. She pulled the pin out, dropping her white locks to her shoulders, and glared up at her attacker.

Seeing her feeble weapon, Mendel smiled, laughed. Shaking his head, he said simply, "I expected some resistance."

"You're a fool," she said.

He looked from her to the cudgel in his hand for a moment, then back. He tapped it against his cheek with enough vigor to redden the right side of his face. "I'll scramble out of the vault. I'll puff and tell Da we were attacked. I'll call in your Emerit dog who stands outside waiting. We'll rush back in to find you lying here. I'll carry you myself to the blackcoat and the Sheason, shouting for their urgency and attention. But it will all be too late."

Helaina stared bitterly at him. "They'll find you out. And you'll hang."

"Maybe," he replied, unconcerned. "But maybe not. If they do, they'll need to do so quickly, since I won't be in the city long." Then a dark look stole over his face. "And if they learn that it was me who sent you to your final earth and execute me at first sight, I will have died a good death to put your weak, superstitious rule to an end."

Superstitious rule. It sounded familiar.

He started forward. His look of concentration chilled her. She clenched the pin in her hand, ready to do as much damage as she could before the cudgel did its work.

As Mendel circled in, her mind raced. Had her father known? Was he part of a plot? What had turned her brother's heart against her? Certainly the Knowledge Law wasn't enough to cause *this.* If she died, what would happen with Convocation? Would anyone step in to lead it?

"My regent," Mendel said, and leapt.

She raised her pin, stabbing upward with all her strength. The pin bit his flesh. His eyes widened in a look of surprise and increased madness. A moment later his cudgel struck her shoulder. Sharp pain ran down her arm and up her neck. She tried to twist the pin sticking in his side, but her sweaty palm slipped around it.

Then her brother's left hand was on her throat, clenching painfully, cutting off her air. She beat at his wrist. Tried clawing at his eyes. His grip tightened. She tried bucking him off, but he was twice her weight and well muscled. He started to raise his cudgel, holding her in place now for a death blow.

Helaina tried to talk, hoping to appeal to their shared, kinder past. But her words were choked by his viselike hold on her throat. She thrashed, seeing the cudgel reach its pinnacle high above her.

"Good-bye," said Mendel.

She braced herself, hoping to weather one blow and strike out when it was done.

His eyes widened and his skin went bright red. It didn't look like madness or anger. It looked like the pain of fire.

As her brother fell dead on top of her, a gust of hot air passed across them both. The brief, scorching wind whipped her hair about her face and was gone. Then a scalding hot drop of blood fell from Mendel's mouth and landed on her neck. Her heart pounding, she shoved the lifeless body away and sat up. Standing on the other side of the vault was Artixan, one hand still raised toward her.

"How?" she managed to ask.

Artixan stared back, looking more gaunt than she remembered. "His blood was already hot, my lady. I simply brought it to a boil."

He crossed the room and knelt beside her, breathing hard and sweating. He was spent, his hands shaking. From his robes he produced a small bag and took out a bit of wet cloth that smelled like sage and balsam. He gently wiped her wounds with the herb rag.

Artixan was her closest friend and confidant. He never pushed her. His contradictions were never biting. He had the uncanny ability to be near when she needed to talk something through, and absent when she wanted privacy. And none of this, she knew, was because he stood in her court. Were she to step down and take up a trade role with House Storalaith—if they'd have her—he'd be the same friend he was today. The kind that when real arguments occurred between them—

and they did—they still walked to supper together and spoke of idle things. He was also the man responsible for reviving her child when it came still. Her debts to him were many.

"You know you could be hanged for rendering the Will," she said, trying to use some levity to quell the racing of her heart. She had come so close. . . .

"That I could," Artixan replied. He made a bad job of smiling. Then in an earnest tone he asked, "Are you okay?"

Helaina took several deep breaths. "A bit unsettled. But I'm fine." Actually, her body hurt like hell. Her joints were screaming. But she said none of that.

Artixan nodded his relief. "You're lying. Eat this." He handed her a small sprig.

She dutifully ate.

"Good," he said. "And I won't be healing these." He touched her lip and the back of her head. "They should remain for others to see. They'll help us implicate and charge those behind this plot."

She nodded in return, the movement intensifying the pain in her head. "How did you know I was here?"

He gave her an incredulous look.

She managed a weak smile. "Thank you."

Artixan stood and went around to the other side of her dead brother. He began to search his pockets, even pulling off Mendel's boots. After several moments, he'd produced nothing save a few coins.

"He was careful not to carry much." Artixan sat back, appearing to consider what next to do. "I should alert the Emerit. Perhaps his coconspirators are close by."

Helaina noted the closed vault door, and looked a question at her Sheason friend.

"Another rendering offense," he offered. "I was in a hurry. I couldn't be bothered with doors."

She turned to the lifeless body between her and Artixan. Anger and grief battled inside her. She hadn't seen her brother in years. They'd never been particularly close. But she loved him in the way you love someone who's part of your past. A good part.

Why?

She began to unlace Mendel's tunic. Even when it was fully undone, she didn't see what she thought she might.

"Your dagger," she said, holding out her hand without looking up at Artixan.

He handed her his weapon—only ceremonial anymore—and she cut the tunic from laces to hem. She ripped the flaps open, exposing Mendel's muscled chest and the tattoo his remark—*superstitious rule*—had brought to mind.

There, on the man's right side, between his armpit and waist, in black and red ink, stood the insignia of the League. Not all leaguemen had the tattoo, but the devout almost always did. And it would take extreme devotion to attempt what Mendel had risked today.

She looked up at Artixan, whose face shone with dark anger.

"Did you know?"

She shook her head.

"The League must have a standing kill order on you." Artixan gave his thin smile again. "This is political suicide for Roth."

Helaina thought, then shook her head again. "He'll create distance between my brother and the League. Documents will surface suggesting he was a fanatic or insane, or that it was a sibling hatred. Other leaguemen will be coached in testimony that Mendel was a loner." She laughed caustically, immediately sorry as pain shot through her head and lip. "I'll wager that if we investigate, we'll find all manner of letters, too. One will state that he was acting alone, for the good of the order, which Roth will condemn publicly. One will be an official document stating that my brother had been expulsed from the League."

Silence then stretched between them as they both returned their attention to the symbol on the dead man's body. Artixan interrupted the quiet with a dark thought. "We now know how far Roth will go . . . your brother won't be the only one looking for his chance at you. Solath Mahnus is rife with leaguemen keeping counsel."

Her stomach churned with worry. She'd have a hard

time being effective if she must always be watching over her shoulder.

After several moments, Artixan again interrupted the silence. "What do you want to do?"

Helaina forced herself to stand. Her head spun for a moment, and she used the bureau to steady herself.

"Take this." She handed her succession letter to Artixan. "Have a thousand copies made and posted throughout Recityv." She then pointed to the parchment she'd just handed him. "I want the original placed on display in the Recityv public hall. Encase it in glass and surround it with ten Emerit guards."

Artixan gave Helaina one last look. "And what of Ascendant Staned?" He sneered the appellation comically.

Feeling once more like the iron fist inside the velvet glove, she said, "I'll deal with him."

Catching sight again of her brother's League tattoo, a dark suspicion gripped her. She slumped to the receiving desk and leafed through the ledger set there. Page after page, the entries were dominated by the same sales recipient: the League of Civility. Varying names signed for goods sold; often her brother's tightly scrawled signature inked the page.

It left her with a sinking dread, considering the things behind her in the vault, as well as the countless items listed on the pages beneath her fingers.

She might have to ask her father about this. It wasn't a crime to do trade with the League, but selling *information* to them . . . She wondered if she should lie about her brother to her da. Maybe let him believe his son had died trying to protect her.

She cast a look at Artixan, letting him know he'd have to find a discreet exit. Then she hefted the ledger and said grimly, "Don't let me out." The door swung open and she went to face her father.

CHAPTER TWENTY-NINE

Memorial

When sung properly, a Leiholan song has implications for both the listener and the vocalist. So, exercise caution when singing of mortal matters.

— Lesson in "form and content," Leiholan studies, first year

WENDRA STEPPED LIGHTLY through the corridors of Descant Cathedral; she didn't want to muddle the distant hum of the Song of Suffering that emanated from the very stone of the place. Two young students conducted her solemnly through the half-lit halls. She actively kept herself from singing, she was so excited. She'd recovered from the sickness of the Telling more quickly than the others, and couldn't wait to see Belamae and learn more about Suffering.

After many turns, they passed through a set of doors and entered an immense, circular hall. Wendra looked up and her mouth fell open in sheer wonder. The wide chamber rose higher than she could guess, and was crowned by a great dome. All around the walls stood bronze statuary depicting vocalists in the act of singing—some on this level, and more on levels above, where walkways circled the chamber. Hallways radiated from each story of the room like spokes on a wheel.

At the center of the room stood a small raised platform, a circular dais three strides across. The dais was a stage, with a modest, walnut-brown lectern, atop which lay several sheets of music. This great round theater would be a wonderfully resonant place to sing.

The chamber appeared, today, to be set for a recital of some kind. Several dozen rows of chairs faced the podium. Only a few were currently occupied.

As she approached the room's center, a familiar white-bearded man entered from one of the anterior hallways. Belamae, head Maesteri here at Descant. He smiled and came forward with open arms.

He folded her into his embrace. The man warmed her, holding her tight for several moments. His robe carried the scent of sandalwood and sage leaf, a clean smell that reminded her of home. Then he put her at arm's length, still holding her hands, and looked her top to bottom.

"You look well. How do you feel?" he asked.

"Tired." She smiled weakly.

"Just so," Belamae replied, and gently shook her hands side to side, obviously very pleased that she had come. "We won't sing today. But let us talk."

She nodded, eager to talk with him, and noticed an insignia woven to his robe. It appeared as two shallowly formed S's written side by side—the first written backward—with their bottoms connected to form a letter V.

He patted the mark. "Descant's emblem. Denotes the song form: sotto voce. Sotto voce is soft singing, under the breath. Nearly whispered, to draw meaning."

"And this?" she asked, gently touching another insignia beside it.

"Emblem of the Leiholan," he replied.

This second insignia still looked like two written S's, but *both* formed backward and written on top of each other so that their intersection created a slightly twisted oval with a point on each end. The top and bottom tails of the insignia also flared in an extra swoop.

Belamae smiled. "You'll find we like our meanings. The Leiholan mark suggests that doubling one's musical expression creates something more than volume."

Wendra became suddenly apprehensive. *Anything I learn will make him expect more of me.*

Belamae turned and offered her his arm. Wendra hooked her hand around the old man's elbow and the two began to stroll the circumference of the domed chamber.

"This is a replica of the Chamber of Anthems." He spoke in hushed tones as he gestured to the hall and cupola above.

"On the other side of the cathedral is the true chamber, where we sing Suffering, which is drawn from the Tract of Desolation. It's a history of the dissenting god, Quietus, and the events that saw him and all he created sealed inside the Bourne."

"And singing Suffering keeps the Veil strong," Wendra added.

"Some say without Suffering, there is no Veil." He then gestured to the wide chamber again. "We use this replica to rehearse. It takes much training and preparation to sing Suffering. And even then, the toll on the singer is great." The old man looked over at the many chairs set before the lectern—a few more now had occupants. She sensed he was remembering someone specific. He fell silent for several moments as they continued to walk, then shook his head, as if clearing his mind. "The hall is acoustically perfect. And it offers some protection from badly rendered song, so that you may safely practice here."

"Do Leiholan in the actual Chamber of Anthems ever make mistakes?"

He gave her a thoughtful look. "They do. Not often, but it does happen. Usually, they're not mistakes of craft or memory, but of fatigue. The song requires seven hours to be fully sung. And there are only a few who have the knowledge and gift to render Suffering. Even then . . . some offerings of the song are simply not as vivid."

Wendra could see she had asked a troublesome question. But the man brightened some as he looked back at her.

"But then there is you, Wendra. Your gift of song is unique. It would not only provide more rest for the other Leiholan, but it would lend strength to the Veil. I'll be more insistent this time that you make Descant your home." He smiled paternally at her.

Rather than resistance to the old man's suggestion, she found herself warming to the thought. He clearly cared for her. And though he also had a practical need of her, his affection couldn't be misunderstood. It had been a long time since she'd felt that. Or maybe a long time since she'd *let* herself feel it—because of the Quiet, because they'd taken so much from her, from people all across the Eastlands. Her song stirred deep inside her.

Belamae must have sensed her resentment. "This isn't a place for harsh or angry thoughts, Wendra. Guard yourself against them here. This may only be a replica of the Chamber of Anthems, but part of your training is to do here what you'll do in the actual chamber. Start now." Mild reproof edged his tone.

"You're telling me that my songs are the wrong ones. That I'm reckless." She thought about Vendanj as she said it.

Belamae surprised her when he said, "Not entirely." He smiled again. "Oh, you're reckless. You know this well enough. But I believe you'd like to stop being reckless, even as I know you'd like to keep the dark songs that live inside you."

Wendra narrowed a puzzled look at the old man. "Then what do you mean, *not entirely*?"

He took a few moments to consider her question, his eyes lifting past her again to the rows of chairs set at the chamber's center. More Descant students had taken seats there. The low hum of conversation buzzed now in the hall.

"Songs of mourning and anger and dread and frustration aren't *wrong*, Wendra. These are powerful emotions, and they have a place in how we sing about life, in how we create melodies with the intent to answer some need."

She again had the distinct feeling Belamae was referencing something in particular, some event from his own recent past. He turned the focus on her.

"Your songs of destruction and malice, are they intended to harm those who threaten you or someone you love? Or . . . does your despair make you sing to gratify a need for retribution, to purge your heart of some regret?"

He went on, not seeming to expect an answer. "Wendra, there are subtleties to the power you've been given. Leiholan spend a lifetime examining the nuances of melodies and the relationship those melodies have to their own feelings." He laughed softly then. "It gets easier. But you're at an important crossroads. How you come to understand and use this gift will set a course."

"So you want me to stay. Study here," she said.

"You make it sound like a sentence." He smiled warmly. Then his face became more serious. "Deciding to stay and study and *understand* won't be easy. You'll have to leave behind the vengeance you harbor in here." He tapped his chest.

She shook her head. "You tell me my feelings aren't wrong, then you tell me to let them go. You're as hard to understand as the Sheason."

He showed her a patient look. "You need to listen closely, Wendra. I said to leave behind the vengeance, not the pain or memory that stirs that vengeance." Once again he glanced at the dais and lectern. The rows of chairs were now nearly full. "And I asked you to let go only *part* of the song that grows inside you. I can hear that part even now. It's a powerful song. But it's blind, Wendra. It makes *you* blind. It's born of fury, and will become harder to control each time you use it." He hunched forward and fixed her with a flinty stare. "If you ignore everything else I say, heed me on this one thing."

Chills ran down her arms. And she recalled what had happened in Naltus when she'd sung on the shale. She looked away from him, his scrutiny making her uncomfortable.

Then his demeanor softened. "Besides, haven't you ever paused and just . . . marveled that you can do things with song that others can't?"

She fell quiet for a long moment. Then nodded with a small but genuine smile. "Sometimes it doesn't seem real." She looked at him more seriously. "How long would it take me to be ready?"

The Maesteri raised his head, looking down as a man does who intends to make an appraisal. "Hard to know. Now, some of the training is learning to read the language of music; that's easy enough. Another part is understanding the elements of music: melody, rhythm, dynamics, meter, pitch . . . there's more to it than simply making sound. Then you must marry this knowledge to the gift you possess. That's when you will transform music into something that can change the nature of things. To do that," he said, pausing so that she would focus on his next words, "there are two essential parts. There is the power of it. Finding within yourself the source that gives your voice its Leiholan quality. On that score, I sense you're already rather adept." He raised a finger of warning between them. "However, its use, how you render that power . . . its *intention* . . . that, Wendra, is something over which you've not learned control. And if you don't, the untrained use of the first part of your Leiholan gift will consume you. It will lead you down paths. . . ."

Belamae's words trailed off between them. After a few moments, his gentle smile returned. "Don't dismay, though, my child. At the risk of some conceit, the one thing I'm rather good at is teaching Leiholan. And you have such great potential."

Just then, one of the Descant students came up to them. "Maesteri," the young man addressed Belamae in reverential tones, "we're almost ready. We're just waiting on Telaya, then we can begin."

Belamae nodded. "Thank you, Alder. I'll watch for her arrival."

The young man bowed slightly and returned to the crowd seated facing the lectern.

They began to stroll again. "What's happening here today? A recital?" she asked.

"A memorial." He left it at that for the moment. Then, with a topic-changing tone, he asked, "In your time with Vendanj and Grant, how much have you learned about your family?"

Unease filled her belly.

"My child, here." He motioned to a pair of chairs set against the chamber wall. They sat together, Belamae settling himself before turning to gather her attention again. "Wendra, your parents didn't always live in the Hollows. For most of your childhood, they lived here, in Recityv."

The revelation struck her deep inside, like the first time one truly acknowledges mortality. But she showed none of it to him. Later, she knew, she'd mourn in some way. For now, she wanted to hear it all.

The crowd waiting at the chamber's center grew expectantly louder. Their collective hum buzzing in the hall.

"I knew your parents when they lived here, your mother especially." He eyed her closely, as if waiting. . . .

The realization hit her. "My mother was Leiholan."

"Indeed she was," he confirmed. "One of the most gifted I ever taught. It was a tearful day when she told me she was leaving Descant for a life in the Hollows. I won't tell you I didn't try to convince her to stay. Part of that was selfish— she and I were good friends—but most of it was the Song of Suffering. Even then the number of Leiholan was not many. Her departure placed more burden on the rest of us."

"Then why did she go?"

"She and your father were asked by Denolan SeFeery to take his son, Tahn, to a safe place and raise him as their own." He paused, letting the revelation sink in.

A kind of relief that she had not expected filled her heart. "Tahn isn't my brother."

"Not by birth," he clarified. "But she agreed to help hide him. She wouldn't have let your father go alone, anyway, if only to keep your family together."

Wendra concentrated, trying to remember any part of what he was saying. She sensed it was true, but could recall none of it.

Again he must have divined something of her thoughts. "Don't fret your lack of memory. You were helped to forget, to make the transition to the Hollows easier for everyone. What's important is that you learn more about your mother. She was some woman."

Reluctantly, she let pass a stream of questions, and focused on his invitation. "Tell me."

He looked in the direction of the memorial. "Telaya hasn't come yet. She's usually quite punctual." Apparently deciding he had time to share, he turned back to Wendra, his best smile returning. "You look just like her," he began. "I guess you know that already, but for me it's like looking into the past. I walked this very chamber with her. She was willful, too." He gave a soft, warm laugh.

"Before you and I became acquainted, I'd never met anyone whose gift of song matched Vocencia's. Such beauty and power. I watched halls like this, overflowing with people, weep, then laugh, then fill with rapture while listening to her songs. Never a better student, either. To her natural ability she added expert understanding. It speaks deeply of her love for you that she left Descant behind."

She loved hearing him talk about her mother. The few things she could remember of Vocencia were Wendra's fondest memories.

Then something occurred to her. "You said there were only a few who could sing Suffering. So wasn't it irresponsible for her to leave?"

Belamae's expression was unreadable. "Perhaps," he said. "But she made the right choice. I wasn't supposed to know about Tahn. Your mother confided in me because it mattered to her that I understand the reason she chose to leave. I've not spoken of that conversation or her reason for leaving until just now. But I think the time is right to share it."

Wendra thought a moment. "And my song, did she know?"

He shook his head. "No, the Leiholan quality is not passed down from parent to child. Otherwise, we would surely have more singers here. You're either a miracle of improbability, or something about the magnitude of your mother's talent made your inheritance of her gift more likely. Either way, you are Leiholan *and* the daughter of one of my very best friends. Both good things. I look forward to getting to know you and helping you cultivate your song."

Wendra stared back, feeling tentative again. "What if I choose not to stay? Or to sing the Song of Suffering?"

A look of shock and worry rose on the old man's face. Belamae gathered himself and fixed her with a serious look. "Wendra, you need to understand a few things before you ask such selfish questions. First, the Veil weakens. There aren't enough of us to sing Suffering to maintain its strength as it should be maintained. The effort is taking its toll on those Leiholan who offer the Song."

The Maesteri gave a long look at those seated in the hall. "This memorial is for a young woman, Soluna . . . a Leiholan. She died singing the Song of Suffering."

Wendra stared back at him in shock. "Died *while* singing?"

"The song is exacting at the best of times," he explained. "But when the Bourne pushes at its chains, the Song requires more. Suffering is no tavern song. It's not even a well-intentioned history cycle. Your whole self is required each time you sing it. You need to understand this before we start teaching it to you."

Wendra looked over at the large crowd waiting to honor a Leiholan who'd died singing Suffering. The weight of future needs pressed down on her, narrowing her options, as if she must replace vacancies—the vacancy left by her mother, the vacancy left by this young woman who'd just died.

Belamae softly cleared his throat. When she turned back to him, he gently cupped her chin, the way a father does when he wishes to convey both affection and the need to be understood. "And my child, I am dying."

Her chest tightened. "Belamae?"

A regretful smile spread on his face. "Oh, not today, or tomorrow. But soon. I can feel it. My time to offer you what wisdom and training I can . . . well, it's not without its limits. And a good singer knows when to leave the stage."

Belamae's revelation hit her harder than she might have expected. He'd only ever treated her with kindness. He'd never given her bad guidance. And now he was dying.

And yet, beneath it all, Wendra remembered Penit, who Sutter believed was still alive. She also thought of the countless others who'd been herded and sold into the Bourne as slaves. Just as the highwayman Jastail had tried to do to her. How many others had been taken over the years? How many were there now? She wanted to stay and learn, cultivate her love of song. But she also wondered what became of someone traded into Quiet hands. Wondered if she could help them. Wondered if she could do so with Suffering.

A door opened, echoing through the chamber. Wendra followed Belamae's gaze to see a lean woman, with a beautiful intensity about her, stride to the front row of the assembly and take a seat.

"We can begin," Belamae said, and led Wendra to the middle of the rehearsal chamber. "Wendra, this is Telaya." He gestured back and forth between them. "She's one of our finest Lyren here at Descant, and in many regards my right hand." He guided Wendra to a seat beside the woman, who gave her a terse nod.

Seeing the puzzlement in Wendra's face, Telaya explained, "Lyren are music students who have no latent Leiholan ability."

Wendra heard a hint of resentment in her voice.

Belamae then ascended the dais and came to stand behind the lectern. He waited a long while. Not for voices to quiet— the chamber had fallen silent in expectation. He seemed to wait for inspiration. His eyes might have met those of every mourner who'd come to pay respects. But rather than words, when the Maesteri opened his mouth, he sang. And what he sang was a long, drawn-out, monotone rendering of the fallen Leiholan's name: Soluna.

Wendra's heart beat fast just hearing it. The slow, low sound rang tortured and reverent and powerful. It filled up the Chamber of Anthems like nothing she could have imagined. And when he was done intoning her name, he paused, allowing the resonances of the room to carry the name to silence. After many more moments, he started again to sing. His words weren't scripted—this was no rote burial dirge. And he made no effort at rhyme. But neither did he search or falter in finding words to sing. They flowed as easily as his notes did. Slow. Processional. Sometimes heartfelt and heavy. Sometimes light and mirthful. Remembrances.

"So, a new Leiholan." It was Telaya beside her, speaking just loud enough to be heard.

Wendra looked over. "I have no training."

The woman shared a dismissive expression, one that said Wendra's admission was false modesty. "You're Souden, then—one training her Leiholan tendency. Nice that Belamae has a quick replacement for Soluna."

"I'm not a replacement."

Telaya's brows went up in an appreciative look that fell just as fast—more dismissiveness. She clearly didn't believe Wendra. "Learn your Suffering well, or we'll be here memorializing you next."

Wendra began to get a clearer picture of the woman, and decided to set the right tone early. "And why were you late to this memorial? Is it all Leiholan you dislike? Or just Soluna?"

Rather than appearing affronted at the accusation, Telaya

smiled, but only enough that she didn't appear to breach any memorial decorum. "I was late because a Leiholan needed a music lesson—clarity on the Shehalis scale, just before she walked into the *real* Chamber of Anthems to sing Suffering. We can hope she gets it right, so we don't have a double funeral today."

"I see," Wendra said, giving back with equal iciness, "then it's just the fact that you, yourself, can't sing with any real power."

The woman's face returned a flat stare. "I don't dislike people. I dislike some of their ideas. Like the idea that being Leiholan is some kind of birthright." Telaya then turned her attention to the lament Belamae was now singing. Real loss and regret touched her features. "Or will you embrace this as your fate, too?"

Wendra sat listening for a moment to the Maesteri's song. As it filled the great chamber, a thought struck her almost painfully. This Leiholan had recently died singing Suffering, to fortify the Veil against the Quiet. And only a few days ago Wendra had stood against an army out of the Bourne, who'd come through that Veil. She'd later check the specific timing of both, but she knew they'd fall in line with each other. This Leiholan, Soluna, was a casualty of the same battle Wendra had just witnessed and fought on the Soliel plain.

Had the Quiet army passed through the Veil because there'd been a lapse in its protection when Soluna died? Or had that army pressed at the boundary, and the pressure of it taken a mortal toll on her? Or was it some other external factor that had contributed to the weakening of the Veil? Of Soluna?

Whatever the truth, the risks of Suffering became clearer in those moments. More reaching.

• CHAPTER THIRTY •

A Fifth Man

You never want to face a Mal. They live for pain.

—Colloquialism captured in *Cruciations, The Use of
Torture to Prepare for a Life of Service and War*

FOUR LEAGUES EAST of Recityv stood the ruins of
Calaphel. Hazy light fell in slanting patterns from a midmorning sun, warming crumbled stone and dusty surfaces.
Motes lazed in those shafts of light, kicked up by Roth's
thoughtful pacing. He made slow turns in a roofless room,
passing before large windows where he watched the horizon
for the others to arrive.

Generations ago, Calaphel had been a small but important
lookout post, guarding against invasion from the Wynstout
Dominion. "Invasion" was a generous term for it, though.
Those attacks had rarely been more than raids, organized to
strike hard and fast and seize things the Dominion believed
itself entitled to. Calaphel had fallen to disuse when Recityv
signed a trade agreement with the Dominion. Since then, the
handful of feldspar buildings had been toppled by vandals,
much of the stone harvested by range herders to build cattle
pens near the oak forests up northeast of here.

Roth stopped in front of a gaping hole in the northern wall
and stared out on the long, unobstructed view. *Industrious
folks, those herders,* he thought. They'd hauled the pilfered
stone another ten leagues before setting it down. He liked
that. Reminded him of his father—a man not afraid to push
a mop on a fish-stinking trawler deck to put mash on his family's supper table.

He nodded to the memory, and to the wisdom of choosing
this site as a lookout post. In the light of day, it would be impossible to approach over the long, flat plain without being

seen. It was a good place to meet in secret with his Jurshah leaders.

He looked up into the deep blue sky, and found himself grinning. This decrepit outpost. The trade agreement that put an end to its usefulness had come by recommendation of the commerce and finance wing of the League. *From war preparedness to cattle pens.* He liked that flow of events. It also made Calaphel the right place for today's discussion.

Within the hour, the leaders of each of the four Jurshah factions arrived, and each from a different direction.

From the east came Nama Septas, leader of the League's political agenda; from the south rode Wadov Pir, the League's finance and commerce secretary; from the north, leader of justice and defense, Bellial Sornahan; and out of the west rode Tuelin Cill, master of history.

Riding in from the four corners had always seemed prudent to Roth, giving their detractors less reason and ability to worry or follow; but Roth also liked its symbolism. It pleased him to imagine his men and women, adorned in clean, pressed, chestnut-colored cloaks, walking the streets in the four corners of the Eastlands, models of civility.

The League leaders tied up their horses and exchanged quiet greetings. Then they came inside, each nodding to Roth before sitting on one of several stones set in a broad circle at the center of the room.

Roth began to pace the outer circle, small plumes of stone dust rising around his boots and further hazing the light. He did a full circuit before beginning.

"I've given the order, and all the right leaguemen now watch for an opportunity . . . the regent will soon be dead." He paused, allowing the declaration its moment to breathe. Each of his leaders nodded, generally pleased. "There will be an outcry, a call to find the villain. They'll marshal Recityv resources to investigate. Helaina's friends will suspect us. We'll deny. All the while, they'll be forced to plan for her successor. Amidst this chaos, we will act."

Nama Septas spoke first. "The High Council will need to replace the regent quickly; the Convocation of Seats is set to begin." She then offered a thin, lawyerly smile. "The Council will call for immediate nominations to replace her." Looking at Roth, she finished, "How many of them do you have in your pocket?"

Roth thought a moment. "Securing the Regent's Seat may prove somewhat more challenging than I thought."

"Perhaps not," Wadov Pir chimed in. "I've just come from her treasury office. There were . . . discrepancies. I've agreed to a mutual silence with her treasurers, which should be worth their support."

Roth nodded his thanks to Pir, a master at introducing digit falsehoods to a tax ledger. The man's mousy accountant's smile hid deceptively sharp teeth where pecuniary matters were concerned.

"But what of the vacant Council seats?" Nama asked. "We were going to see them filled with the right kinds of people."

Roth continued to pace around the outer circle of his Jurshah leaders. "The authors won't be joining us," he announced, frowning. "They're loosely organized anyway. And their unofficial leader is a cantankerous old fool who won't be persuaded."

Roth stopped behind Tuelin Cill, and placed a hand on her shoulder. "But I learned something about this disorganized guild of scribblers." He bent forward and pretended to write, as if on a chalkboard. "They seem to have an alchemy that gives them the ability to write on the air. Cill, we need to know about this. What are they capable of? And if they turn that sorcery against us, how do we stop it? Go to your archives. Enlist your brightest historians. We need answers."

Cill nodded. "The moment I return."

"But not having Author Garlen's support may not harm us, since I doubt he'll cast his vote for *anyone,*" Roth concluded. "I'd say he's hidebound, but I think he mostly just wants to be left alone. We have more work to do where authors in general are concerned, but we'll make do without his vote."

"You won't have the vote of the Church, either," Nama added. "They may not be able to prove you burned Bastulan, but they believe it anyway." Nama's voice grew strained with impatience. "And why, may I ask, did you find it necessary to add arson to the list of allegations against the

League? Wouldn't it have been simpler to convert the Reconciliationists to some better purpose *after* we've assumed control?"

Roth stood straight, and began again to pace. "You know the myths about Bastulan, its hidden relics. Its destruction will help many look for different answers to their questions. Answers the League can provide."

"And if the relics are real?" Tuelin interjected. "The simplest rule any historian worth his binder's glue will follow is that anything recorded by more than three chroniclers has some basis in fact." She gave Roth a slightly judicial look. "The relics qualify."

He nodded patiently. "Of course. And Bastulan is half stone, isn't it? I imagine anything of great value is kept in—or was moved to—some safe place where fire's no threat. So, let us tally. Bastulan's pews are now ash. That's a meaningful start." Roth got Nama's attention. "And it has the wonderful result of helping us gain control, don't you think? Reconciliationists will need a new touchstone." He then narrowed his gaze. "If it makes you squeamish, perhaps you and I need to reconsider—"

Nama stood. "I'm not squeamish. But it would have been wiser, *politically,* to avoid raising the ire of Bastulan adherents until there was nothing they could do to affect our ruling position." She pointed in the direction of Recityv. "It could galvanize them. That's all I'm saying."

Roth smiled and nodded. "Noted."

"What of Van Steward?" Bellial Sornahan asked. "Have you spoken with him yet?"

At the mention of the general's name, Roth began to pace more quickly, his excitement mounting. This got to the heart of why they met today in Calaphel. "I did. Van Steward, as you might have guessed, is absurdly loyal to the regent. What is more, he's said that our own efforts at policing civil conduct in Recityv must cease."

"We can contest that," Nama offered quickly. "There are laws that we could cite—"

"Indeed," Roth said, "but it won't be necessary."

Bellial held up his finger, as he often did when making a

point. "Your Leadership, I beg to differ. They need to know we can enforce law and correct misconduct when we see it. If the people no longer fear—"

"Respect," Roth corrected.

Bellial made a sly grin. "The enforcement of civil standards relies on the people's *respect*. If Van Steward's men alone have the authority to keep the peace, I'm afraid civility is at risk."

Roth smiled, but said nothing, waiting. Soon, the sound of hooves rose from beyond the cracked and ruined walls of Calaphel. An unseen rider came to a stop, the horse chuffing beyond the doorway. And, momentarily, into the ruins strode a fifth man—Losol Moirai, Roth's surprise for his other Jurshah leaders. In tow, Losol brought another, who was bound and gagged and had obviously been beaten. He settled the captive on a vacant stone around the circle. Recognition lit in the faces of the Jurshah leaders. They knew the prisoner, but said nothing.

Then, Losol stepped forward, his tunic and trousers close-fitting and made of countless, tight braids of sylph thread—a rare fiber that grew stronger the more it stretched. It was a variant of banded mail, running in tiny vertical lines. His blackened boots and gloves covered his ankles and wrists as closely as the rest of his armor. And over his shoulders hung the chestnut-brown cloak of the League, though dyed a shade darker, to set him apart. Losol wore two weapons, on one hip a sword with a handle of black ivory, and a trishula on the other. His head and face were cleanly shaven. A line of neat scarification ran in a vertical column of symbols up his chest and neck and onto his cheek beneath his left eye.

In every respect, Losol was Mal, the pattern of his face marking him from Mal Reeve Lux, specifically. The scarification was part of a lifelong Mal tradition called Talenfoier, a ritual of pain and constant humility. And yet, because of it, and their devotion to the art of battle, the Mal were almost myth. Some even considered them Quiet, or at least sympathetic to those who lived inside the Bourne. A common children's rhyme stated, *Every Mal worth* masal *men. Masal* was the Ebon word for "five."

"Gentlemen," Roth announced, feeling rather pleased, "let me introduce you to Losol Moirai."

Losol received the appraising gaze of each faction leader. He returned the stares evenly, with just a hint of challenge. *Good,* Roth thought. But he would wait to explain the intrusion, letting the men also wonder at the prisoner seated among them.

"Once my letter of succession as regent is written and placed in the vaults of Solath Mahnus, I will call the Convocation of Seats to order. I will eulogize Helaina, and announce a great celebration of her life and contributions. I will thank kings and rulers for leaving their homelands and journeying to Recityv to answer a call that would bind us all in a common cause. But . . ." Roth paused, making sure each of his faction leaders attended his words closely, "that cause will have nothing to do with old gods and their dire creations. Not even as a child's rhyme to inspire the obedience of curfew. No, I will focus them on the important work of education in our slums, new kinds of trade to take whores off their backs and children out of workhouses. And a creed that ties together the knowledge we have with our pursuit of the knowledge we don't. Through inquiry, not entreaty." He looked up at the deep blue sky above, as his leaders applauded, the sound of it resounding in the ruins of Calaphel and ascending into the open air above.

"I will begin to unify the nations," Roth continued, his voice growing strident, his pace quickening. "The Convocation of Seats will not be an event only once every several ages. It will be a perpetual ruling body, and I will lead it in the formation of a confederacy, founded upon our own creed, and maintained by our own diligent stewards." He looked down at his faction leaders. "We will walk the streets in League brown and answer the call to assist and chasten."

Roth didn't bother to tell his Jurshah leaders that some of his vision he'd stolen from Helaina.

His practiced words echoed about them until silence came again to the abandoned remains of the outpost. He liked the way the resulting quiet lent his speech a touch of the historic.

There was some bombast in his delivery. There were appropriate moments for bombast.

It was Nama who broke the silence, doing so with a question, no less. But Roth was grateful for the woman's endless, critical probing; it kept him sharp. "Kings are not often inclined to relinquish authority to a ruling body. How will you compel those that would sooner return to their homeland and reject your vision as political opportunism?"

Roth pointed at Losol Moirai. "There is your answer, Nama." Roth strode now into the center of their ring and motioned Losol to join him there. He then walked a tighter circle around the Mal, capturing the gaze of each of his old friends as he went, drawing the attention of a few away from the captive.

"The instrument of change, my friends, is war. Some nations will join us immediately. Those who need our help and protection, I suspect. And there are a few where we already exercise influence." He softened his voice, filling it with inference. "Others will need help seeing what we have to offer them."

Tuelin Cill, master of history, spoke with the reluctant tone of one who hated to be a reminder. "Your Leadership, superstition or not, the annals and archives mostly support the rumors of what lies beyond the Pall and in the far west past the Rim." She swallowed, looking around at her colleagues.

"Speak up, Cill. Let's hear your concern," Roth said, reversing direction as he paced back toward her.

Cill blew a long breath out through her nose, buying herself a moment. "We've called for an end to the Song of Suffering as a backward practice. I only want to raise the question: If the histories are true, and there are races and legions long spurned in the unmapped lands . . . and if this Veil that is spoken of ceases with the end of Suffering . . ."

Roth stopped in front of Cill, unsmiling now. He hated the lack of vision, but maybe he could forgive it in one who looked only into the past. No matter. Roth had considered the options.

"My friends," he began, focusing on Cill, "let us first

remember who we are and what we stand for. It isn't the reality of races beyond the Pall that we object to. Why would we think there *aren't* people there? I'd actually be surprised if there weren't. No, it's the myth and fable that has grown up around these distant places that we challenge. It's this business of dark gods—any gods—of reliance on others for things you and I aren't blessed with." Roth waved his hand back and forth between himself and Cill. "Singers and Sheason and Veils. They're allegories, morality plays, child-book rhymes."

Bellial cut in, his voice deep and rough from endless pipe smoke. "I don't know about singers and veils. But I can vouch for Sheason conjury. Seen it myself. Mostly helping folks. I don't like to think of it turned against us."

Roth forced himself to wait before replying. It tired him to remind his faction leaders of League cornerstones. "Again, my friends, it's not the existence of things. It's people feeling dependent and incapable because of them. It's the fear they inspire. It's the idea that anything is a foregone conclusion. It's irrational." He paused, looking around at each of them. "It cheapens us. We deserve better. We *are* better."

The prisoner shifted on his stone, his eyes more alert now, wider, as if from hearing Roth's words.

Roth turned back to Cill, fixing her with an iron glare. "I don't need any special sorcery before I lend a hand to one who needs it. I don't need a fairy tale to force me to behave. If in the reaches beyond our maps there are hordes whose sole aim is to do us harm . . . then let them come. I'll wager their motives are more selfishness than anything else. And that's not so strange a thing."

He stopped and took a long breath, looking around at the crumbling walls of Calaphel. "A war like that would hasten our plans, actually. And so much the better, my friends, that the League of Civility be the force that puts a literal end to the origin of such foolish worries."

He nodded at his own logic. "Regardless; as I said, the instrument of change is war. I would rather change come through discussion and treaty. But I'm not naïve. And we've been patient long enough. And so, just as the League will lead

Convocation once the regent is dead and we've assumed her seat, we will also be its shield and sword."

Those seated around him all looked at Losol. Roth nodded and thought again, *Good.*

"Today I announce the formation of a fifth faction of the League, an equal part in the formation of any Jurshah. Today, my friends, the League begins a new era . . . with a leader of war."

And perhaps a Mal alliance at some point. But one thing at a time.

Roth put his hand on Losol's shoulder in a gesture of endorsement. One by one, the others stood and crossed the circle to the new man, taking him in the League handshake. No words were exchanged, and Losol's eyes remained hawkish as he appraised each of his new colleagues. This, too, was good. The League's instrument of war would keep them all honest.

Each of them eyed the captive nervously as they retook their seats.

Roth directed Losol to join the circle, and once all were seated and attentive, he began. "Cill, I'm actually glad to hear you have a solid working knowledge of the Bourne. We'll have need of that. You'll spend time with Losol on some very specific questions, where his unique history will play a helpful role." He looked at Bellial with a knowing grin. "The results of those inquiries, my friend, could put to rest your fear of fighting the Sheason."

His leader of justice and defense raised his brows with interest and nodded as he began preparing himself a pipe. "And what history is that?"

Roth didn't know it all himself. And what he did know, he held close. But he offered this much: "Losol has an understanding of how things are on the other side of the Rim."

That fetched several concerned looks, but no further questions.

The prisoner's feet shuffled, as though he were preparing to run.

"So now, Calaphel," Roth said with some satisfaction. "We will rebuild it. And a hundred more just like it, near and far.

To provide protection and warning." He smiled openly. "I hope you appreciate the symbolic progression: a Recityv military outpost. Brought to ruin when the League negotiated a trade treaty with the Dominion. And now, a *League* military outpost."

Of course it was Nama who was the one to ask, "What is the symbolism?"

Roth gave her a patient look. "What is old can be made new. What we tear down, we build back up." He became more serious, and finished, "That tolerance has a price, nor are we always tolerant. Especially when our own regent decides to try and spy on us." Roth nodded toward the captive.

Losol stood, walked around behind the captive, and casually inserted a knife up from the base of the man's neck into his brain. He rotated the weapon, then pulled it free. An incredibly efficient attack; there was remarkably little blood. The spy's eyes were closed before he hit the ground.

"But not just a spy," Roth added. "Look close."

His Jurshah leaders eyed the body, the same recognition in all their faces.

"He was one of us. A leagueman in good standing not long ago." *And now a good example.* "Be sure your people understand where their allegiance should remain. Share the fate of our guest here with them."

With his own house now in order, he could give his full attention to Convocation.

CHAPTER THIRTY-ONE

Parchment War

To win, you must be willing to do what your enemy will not.

—First Precept of Conflict, from Himshawl's *Art of War*

THAELON KNOCKED SOFTLY at his daughter's door. *Softly,* because such a knock could be ignored, since he'd come to her in the heart of after-dinner study hours. Ketrine was his only child, and well on her way to becoming Sheason. But she hadn't been given the gift of rendering yet. And for the Sulivon—those who studied but couldn't yet command the Will—the hours after dinner were spent reading, rehearsing, and taking private instruction from Sheason mentors.

"Come in." The voice was muted by the door, but seemed distracted even so.

He gently depressed the latch and eased into her room. Several lamps burned. His "little girl"—a term he didn't even bother to shake loose—liked it bright. She sat at a table against the far wall, setting up a test of some kind. Whenever possible, Ketrine created practical demonstrations of the things she needed to learn. Seeing the effects of what she studied was her way. And it put her ahead of most of her peers.

Beside her sat Sellena, her Sheason mentor, who was asked, more than a little, to do some rendering to bring to life concepts Ketrine found in her books.

Tonight, atop her table, there were a dozen small parchment golems. walking with an amusing *crickle-crinkle* into a standard battle formation.

She didn't look up at him, remaining focused on the placement of the paper warriors. She pointed, giving Sellena instruction on where to position the golems. Thaelon smiled. It was a game. One he and his little girl had been playing since she was five. "Parchment war," they called it. Originally, it had been a simple strategy game, paper soldiers with various movement constraints. And back then, it was played mostly with a whimsical sense. His wife, Haley, had provided Ketrine's rendering.

A stack of thin parchment was placed in front of each player, and with a modicum of Will, that parchment could be rendered to take the basic shape of a person, and given a simple purpose. Initially, that purpose would be to fight. With time, the game had changed, as Ketrine learned deeper strategy and collaborative attack techniques. The game board became open terrain and the golems became soldiers with distinct rank.

Tonight, he could see his little girl was combining the lessons of combat with those of imparting, specifically imbuing—rendering skills she'd have to understand to become Sheason.

"I need to speak with you," he said. "I have a favor to ask."

She nodded for him to continue, as she instructed Sellena to stand up a few more golems and position them opposite her staggered line. She reached out and shifted the placement of a few, somewhat impatient to have them precisely where she wanted them. After doing so, she referenced a handbook—a copy of Himshawl's *Art of War*.

"It's not something to be taken without real thought," Thaelon added, coming around to the other side of the table so he was directly in her line of sight. "But I wouldn't ask you if I didn't think you were the right one to ask."

Still she did not look at him, indicating to Sellena where she wanted a few of the golems to move relative to her first line's flank.

"I'm listening." She continued to study the layout of the broad table and the position of the two opposing paper forces.

Thaelon smiled with understanding. "You let me in to test yourself. To see if you could run your battle scenario without being distracted."

He saw a slight crimp at the corner of her mouth, a hint of smile, before her concentration took hold again.

"Very well, let's just have us a game, then." He sat with a

flourish opposite his daughter and began to fashion his own paper army from the stack of sheets before him.

The sound of parchment rustling, ripping, and bending had a kind of humor in it. Maybe because the little figures looked so harmless as they prepared to fight. The paper soldiers he brought to life had legs and arms, but no real head. Height and width became their rank designations. Ketrine's eyes gleamed with anticipation, and she had Sellena reposition all the golems from her stack into a unified force.

Thaelon looked over how she'd laid out her general and soldiers, and gave her a mischievous smile. He'd make this a greater test still—he animated every parchment in his stack to fight, save his own general. His paper force outnumbered hers three to one. In response, Sellena began to try and match his numbers, but Ketrine held up a hand, as he knew she would. His little girl would see if she could outthink him with fewer golems.

"If I win, you'll finally endow me? Make me Sheason?" She showed the smile of a challenger.

"If you win, I'll let you keep your paper scraps." He laughed. "And I'll stop trying to sing you lullabies."

"Don't make promises you don't intend to keep." She knocked the table's edge, indicating she was ready.

He nodded, and held a palm up for her to go first.

She went at it with energy. First, she drew her line back into a near circle, removing the possibility of being flanked. Smart maneuver, given the ratio of golems between them. She whispered to Sellena, and a handful of her figures refashioned into barricades that she placed strategically, to force Thaelon to attack in only two spots. Not bad. But Thaelon crumpled several sheets of parchment, and had pairs of his golems heave them over the barricades, where they landed and rolled and scattered her circle.

She gave a small laugh, while her expression remained focused. Her army re-formed its circle each time it was hit. But she didn't counterattack. Instead, a few of her golems rolled the paper balls to extend her barricade, further limiting access to her paper army. She'd taken a purely defensive posture.

Thaelon wanted to force her strategy—not to mention he did still need to talk to her—so he made a push with most of his golems. A sheer crush of paper bodies moved in a wave against her buttresses. The golems used one another to climb over barricades and paper boulders. He meant to simply wash her under, or force her offensive mind to take command.

As his stampede of golems reached her circle defense—the *crickle-crinkle* of paper arms and legs like the sound of a rain shower—they all suddenly stopped. It took Thaelon a moment to see. While he'd been pressing his advantage in numbers, his little girl had lulled him into believing that her strategy was defense, preservation, limiting damage. Really, she'd been buying time to execute a deeper, more effective strategy.

He looked down at his general. The golem had torn a bit of his body away and held it aloft like a surrender flag. While Thaelon had imagined Ketrine would be forced to consider one of very few counterstrategies, including surrender, instead she'd changed the game. She'd leveraged another of the disciplines of imparting: realignment. His general had been brought in line with her own interests. It was a classic "move the head and the body follows" approach. He'd focused so much on the point of attack, he'd left little energy to look after his commanding paper man.

She'd passed his test more impressively than he could have hoped. Albeit with a questionable strategy. He held up his hands. "You win."

In a great unfolding, all the golems fell, their paper bodies flattening.

"As though it could have happened any other way." Ketrine got up from her chair and came around to give him a hug. When she stood back, she added, "You'd have seen through it, though, if I hadn't made you believe I was just trying to outlast you."

"Maybe." He gave Sellena a nod, letting her know she could go.

Once Ketrine's mentor had drawn the door shut on her way out, he let out a long breath. "You *are* close, you know."

"I know. I'm in no hurry. I'll be Sheason when it's right."
She returned to her chair.

When he had her attention again, he gently admonished,
"Realignment works fine for items with no real will. With
people," he held up a finger, "it's almost impossible, carries
immense risk . . . and it's not permitted."

It made Thaelon think of Vendanj, a Sheason who would
see no ethical issue with using realignment if he thought the
need was just.

"I know," she said. "But we're talking about parchment
war. Now, what's so urgent that you came during study
hours?"

Thaelon gathered his thoughts. "Our tension with the
League must be addressed." He paused, regarding his little
girl before asking this. "I need you to go to Recityv. As my
envoy. To speak with Ascendant Staned."

"And what do you want me to say?" she asked, gentle sarcasm in her tone.

"Simple enough: We want the Civilization Order repealed.
We won't sit idle anymore as Sheason are killed. Don't
threaten him, mind you. But that's the crux of it."

"And why do you think he'll listen now? Many have been
asking the League this same thing for years." Ketrine began
to shuffle the parchment back into stacks.

"Because you're going to offer the resources of Estem
Salo to help the League establish its schools, train beggars
in trades, build physic shelters to care for the sick." He
handed her some parchment from his side of the table. "If
Roth is genuine about his creed, he'll listen."

She stopped her straightening of parchment, and eyed him
thoughtfully. "And if he doesn't?"

He sighed. "Then we'll know that their Civilization Order isn't about self-sufficiency for citizens, but aimed at
eliminating the Sheason. That's still good knowledge to
have."

"In which case, you'd like me to do to him what I did to
your general." She held up the sheet she'd realigned to win
their parchment war.

"No," he blurted, rather too forcefully. "No," he repeated, softer. "I think the partnership is something he'll be eager to have."

"I love you for your optimism," she said, giving him a genuine smile. "And maybe you're right." She tapped the parchment into a neat pile and set it aside.

"If you're unable to convince the Ascendant, don't push too hard. Just gracefully leave Recityv." He paused a moment, realizing she wouldn't be alone. "And by no means let those who go with you render while you're there. Or if they must, be sure they're not found doing so." Thaelon kept as much real concern out of his voice as he could.

"Others are going with me?" She spared a look in the direction Sellena had exited.

"Four. You may ask Sellena to be one of them. The others will be a few of Odea's best."

"Because we may have to fight. Defend ourselves," she observed.

"Just to be safe," he clarified. Then thought better of that answer. "Yes, in case you have to fight."

She fell silent for several moments, rubbing at the binding of her Himshawl handbook. "I should mention the Quiet to the Ascendant," she said, speaking firmly. "He should know that if they come, he'll need our help."

Thaelon stared back at his little girl, unsure how to respond to that. How to meet the Quiet had a lot to do with Vendanj. And he didn't want to talk about him just now. If not for Vendanj, there'd likely be no Trials of Intention. No need to send Ketrine to Recityv. Damn hells, half of the League's distaste for Sheason was Vendanj's fault!

"If the Quiet come . . . yes. But when and *how* to address that, we'll save for later. For now, just be sure the Ascendant knows that Vendanj doesn't speak for us. Focus on mutual goals. I wouldn't offer if we didn't believe in some of these things, too. In at least a few respects, we stand on common ground. We can build from there."

She looked up at him, a grateful smile on her face. A second time she got up and came around to hug him. "Thank you for trusting me with this. I won't let you down."

He hugged his little girl back. "I love you. You know that."

"I love you more," she said. "Now, let's find Ma. She needs to know you lost our parchment war tonight."

He laughed, and together they left her room in search of Haley.

• CHAPTER THIRTY-TWO •

The Bourne: Fugue

Men swear on their lives. The Quiet swear on their dam-nation.

> —Response of an Ir-Caul footman, in the days after
> the War of the First Promise, when asked,
> "Do you think the Quiet will return?"

KETT HAD NEVER been this far from home. He wound his way north and west on the old roads, walking for three days now without seeing anyone he recognized. There was a change in the air and sky and landscape around him. The air had a thick, still, close feeling. Heavy like a storm might soon break, but never did. The sky seemed farther away, the canopy of charcoal grey like one endless blanket—no white, no black, no wind. The landscape wasn't stark, though. All was not basalt and crags. Things grew. It just took a great deal of work to ply the fallow land, tame soils that preferred the wild grasses and brambles.

Peeling ailanthus trees occasionally shed a curl of bark. The soft, woody sound as it struck the roots below was loud and unsettling in the silence. Once in a while he saw the ailanthus silk moths fluttering in the tree's long, pointed leaf-lets. The moths made no sound, the beating of their wings as silent as everything else.

On the road itself, other than the encroachment of brambles,

Kett met only bones, which he thoughtfully stepped over or around. He could tell from their skulls that these were mostly Inveterae. The bones might have gleamed—so picked clean—if not for the absence of sun. It all gave Kett the feeling that he moved deeper into a land—the whole of it—that served as nothing so much as an ossuary.

It also made him think Lliothan was right. Inveterae living in the south of the Bourne—treacherous as it was—didn't understand as much as they thought about this side of the Veil. Walking toward his induction into the Quiet ranks, Kett glimpsed the fuller condemnation of the Bourne. But rather than weaken his resolve, it fortified him. The Inveterae didn't belong here. It was a mistake. He'd correct that error . . . or die trying.

The afternoon of the fourth day, he emerged from a canyon road, which snaked its way down into a broad valley. At the valley's center spread Kael Ronoch, a vast city. It simultaneously inspired his awe and fear. The sheer size and organization of the place was a wonder. From here he could see the clean lines of roads set at perfect right angles, and waterways carefully laid out as irrigation canals. But the city itself looked like the brambles he'd been treading past for three days. Spires rose in profusion from city walls and rooftops and obelisks and immense halls. From a distance, it all looked like a thicket of bulrushes growing from a lake of brackish water.

He started moving again, keeping his same unhurried pace. Other, larger roads began to intersect with the one he traveled. As he neared Kael Ronoch, he finally encountered a few travelers. None spoke to him, though a few did cast sidelong glances his way, measuring. Some of those he encountered were Quietgiven races he knew—Bar'dyn, Yarshoth, Wole—but others he didn't recognize. And at least once, he was sure he was seeing an *Inveterae* race he'd never seen before—something in its eyes. The thought that there might be other Inveterae not known to him left Kett with the same mixed feelings as he'd had about the city itself: awe . . . and fear.

He arrived at the gate, where six heavily armed Bar'dyn stood perfectly still, moving only their eyes. One finally stepped out to block his passage.

"What's your business here, Inveterae?" the Bar'dyn asked, a deep and lilting derision in its voice.

He considered several replies before saying simply, "I am Kett Valan."

A look of recognition, if not approval, lit the sentry's face. "Basilica's fingers reach the highest." The Bar'dyn pointed up at the spires that topped every building, and then away into the city. "Keep moving."

Kett nodded and took maybe three steps past them before the Bar'dyn whipped a heavy pike across the back of his head. He stumbled forward and nearly fell. No laughter came, no further challenge. Kett didn't look back or curse. And he didn't check to see if the blow had drawn blood. He simply walked on.

As with the old roads he'd traveled to get here, Kael Ronoch lay steeped in silence. Quietgiven walked the streets, but rarely spoke. They moved with a sense of dark purpose, but it wasn't exactly malice in their eyes. More that they seemed humorless. The feel of the place hung in the air like a suffocating smoke.

Kett saw many more Bar'dyn as he trod the stony road, which had been laid out not in cobblestone, but great slabs of rock seamlessly fitted together. And just as often he saw Quiet races he knew only from the spoken stories. Laedan moved along, sometimes strolling on four feet, sometimes on two; their brushed shorthair twitched the way an animal's does when bitten by blackflies. Always near the Laedan were Rimaan Brode. Their long necks turned fast at the clop of every heel; skittish things with a long gait that made them appear always to skulk. Kett spied a pair of Kausellots, seams of bone protruding from their skin like stitching. The bone ran up their necks and over their cheeks and around their eyes. It looked extremely uncomfortable.

And more Quiet races yet, a dozen more, maybe two dozen. Some with wings folded against their backs. Others with reticulated tails that seemed more like long additional arms.

But the look and variety of species wasn't what bothered him. Not by half. What left him unsettled was the dark shine, one to the next, of the same burning intensity—intelligence, focus. It reminded him of the way anger settles into calculation for those who won't forgive a wrong.

And even that wasn't all of it. Not until he saw another Gotun Inveterae like himself did the realization come to him. *We look the same. Inveterae and Quiet.*

What he felt here—different from Inveterae lands—might be nothing more than another half turn of a stick-and-wetcloth tourniquet. It was the deeper sense of ruin, and demand for vengence. He understood the bitterness of those feelings. It lived inside him, as well. But somewhat paler. Still, he wasn't afraid here, as he'd thought he would be. And that proved to be the most unsettling thing of all.

The buildings had been raised of roughly hewn stone. Great care had been taken to create symmetry. Mortar cemented together dark basalt rock chiseled into precise rectangular shapes. But surfaces remained jagged. Doorways were no less than four strides high, and equally wide. Some led into structures large enough to accommodate Quietgiven much bigger than Bar'dyn. The doorways had no actual doors, giving the street and main level of the city an interconnected feeling.

Up the street, a forge emanated heat into the chill air, lending it an acrid smell that soured in his nose. Inside the forge, several fires burned—eight in all—as muscled Bar'dyn wielded huge hammers and beat rhythmically at orange steel. The shop reminded Kett that Inveterae weren't allowed to carry weapons.

It wasn't until after passing countless barracks that he realized Kael Ronoch was little more than a garrison. It made sense to him now that they'd summon him *here* to be installed among their ranks. But he had to believe the city served other purposes. Though if it did, those purposes escaped him.

What didn't escape him were the random spills of blood on the street. Most had been tracked through by the passage of feet and hooves, and were now dry. A few were more vibrant red—more recent, more wet. One remained in a pool, as though spilled that very hour. It left him with the impression that disputes and punishment were dealt with instantly, severely. He might have expected as much. What he hadn't thought he'd see was a detail of human men dressed in gunny cloth with blood-pink rags strapped to their knees. These men hunched and knelt near buckets of water, scraping up the blood with flat knives. Behind them came a few more men with mops and fresh water buckets. The stone shone and smelled again of wet basalt before they were through.

Then, as soon as they'd sponged away one mess, they went searching for the next spill.

He moved through the city for another hour, cataloging as much as he thought he could remember. Without trying, he found himself at the basilica. As massive as the other buildings were, this structure loomed above the others as though it had sired them all. The dark grandeur of the place came in not just one towering hall, but a collection of six. Kett approached the nearest gate, staring up.

Against a slate-grey sky, the basalt stone rose, ascending as if it might touch the clouds. From the street, several floors rose, more than Kett cared to count, and each larger than the last. Each successive rooftop bore sharp spires that stabbed heavenward like accusing fingers.

He was just noticing the many large glassless windows of the basilica, when a Bar'dyn approached.

"You're Kett Valan?" he asked, hints of both satisfaction and disgust in his voice.

"I am."

"The assembly waits on you." The Bar'dyn turned and started to disappear back the way he came.

Kett spared a thought for Saleema—to quicken his own resolve—and followed close behind.

Just inside the main gate, they strode down a wide outer corridor, dimly lit by windows on the outer wall. The carvings in the black stone on each side of the passageway were difficult to make out. And he had little time to discern such things, as the Bar'dyn came soon to an inner door and abruptly turned.

"Down this corridor. You will enter the Assembly Hall. Step onto the stand at the center." The Bar'dyn promptly turned and left.

Kett had questions, but sensed he shouldn't ask. As he

began walking toward a rectangle of light at the hall's end, his gut tightened and his legs grew weak. He knew broadly what he'd come here to do, but an expectant silence spread with every step he took. He had to think now of his children to steel himself against whatever awaited him at the corridor's end.

Without pause, he strode slowly but confidently into a great round arena. From the main floor where he stood, tier after tier rose, each wider than the last, like a great indoor theater. At even intervals around the circumference of the main floor, eight stairways ascended to the very top, some fifty tiers high. And every tier was completely filled with seated Quietgiven, silently staring at him. The aggregate feeling of ill will was crushing. Kett had the sudden impression of a great many deaths witnessed in this place.

Pushed back against the wall of the main floor stood several types of apparatus: basic stocks, a gallows, a pile of chains, racks, tables of edged instruments and pliers for gripping things that wouldn't stay still. None of these things were new, but they were all clean.

He began to feel the flutter of panic, wondering if Balroath had meant all along to lure him here. Here, where he could be dealt a meticulous death in this theater of pain.

He remembered Taolen, slowly crucified to provide a warm, salty drink for Praefect Lliothan. With the memory still fresh, he went directly to the center of the round. He stood, waiting, trying not to look defiant—a hard thing when one's thoughts linger on the crucifixion of a friend. He noticed that the basalt floor around the front of the stand was wet, newly scrubbed. The smell of wet stone and washed blood began playing at his nerves. That and the unnatural hush. If a single Quietgiven shifted in his seat or shuffled a foot, he didn't hear it. The silence was deafening.

Then, like a clarion call, a deep voice shattered the stillness. "Kett Valan, you are here today of your own choice, a member of the Inveterae, to give yourself to Quietus. Is that correct?"

The words struck Kett like a spike maul. The powerfully

low pitch. He knew the owner of that voice. Kett turned to see Balroath.

Looking at the Jinaal officer, the reality of what he was about to do descended on him like a rockslide. *Give myself . . .*

But he managed to nod to Balroath, who stood in the first row of the first ring.

"Very well," Balroath said. "Let us make clear your intentions, and then we'll make clear what it means to be given to Quietus."

Again, Kett nodded.

Balroath addressed the assembly more than he did Kett. The Jinaal looked over the hundreds of gathered Quietgiven, representing races Kett knew and more that he did not. And again, to his surprise and dismay, he saw some he recognized instinctively as Inveterae but could not name.

"You were tried for your part in a movement to lead Inveterae out of the Bourne. In exchange for your life, and the lives of your children, you agreed to use your knowledge and influence with these separatists to convince them to abandon their plans. Is this your understanding?" Balroath pointed at Kett.

"I will convince them that we all seek the same thing, to live beside those beyond the Pall." Kett watched to note the Quietgiven response to what he said.

Most of them remained expressionless, but a few turned to look at Balroath with slightly more interest.

Balroath dropped his chin. "There are consequences should you fail or try to deceive us."

"I understand." He could feel the assembly's scrutiny, as they sought to discover any falseness in him.

"No, I don't think you do, Kett Valan." Balroath stood beside one of the stairways, and now stepped down onto the main floor. He raised an arm to point at him. "Which is why you will give yourself to us." Balroath's deep voice resonated in his chest. It carried an intonation of harm.

So when Kett spoke, he didn't equivocate. They had to believe he wouldn't betray their confidence. He would need that for his ruse to work. "I have given you my word on my family's lives. I have pledged to help put an end to the hope my people have of escaping a captivity unjustly thrust upon them. Have I not already given myself—"

"No, Kett Valan, you have not." Balroath came halfway between Kett and where he'd been standing, his footfalls loud in the Assembly Hall. "Your oath to join us will mean more than betraying your friends or losing your family. All of us here, including you," he pointed at Kett, "have been abandoned. But we," he gestured to the assembly, "are born to this work, given life by Quiet hands. To be given means something more." Balroath smiled. It was an awful thing to see, as though the Jinaal's face didn't know how to form it.

Kett said nothing, waiting.

The Jinaal squared his shoulders to Kett. "It means consecration. Do you understand? Of your every thought. Of your every action. You have nothing else we can't take from you, or from your Inveterae coconspirators."

Kett nodded gravely.

Balroath went on. "It is a binding of your soul, Kett Valan. It is a surrender . . . of Forda."

He tried to maintain a stoic expression, but *a surrender of Forda . . .* dread bloomed afresh in his chest. "How will I do what you ask if I'm dead?"

Balroath smiled his awful smile again. "It is not a separation of body and spirit, Kett Valan. We will bind your heart to ours. If asked, you will gladly allow the Velle to render your spirit. More importantly, when you act contrary to your new heart, we will know, and we will come to redeem our right to the spirit within you. You can now always be found."

Kett's heart sank. How would he finish what he'd begun if he gave himself to the Quiet this way?

"No barrier or distance nullifies this vow, Kett Valan. So, if you have been playing us false thus far, I will generously grant you death even now."

Kett held in his mind the image of his children, and did the only thing he could. "I believe in the common bond Inveterae share with you." He looked up and around at the assembly, then down at Balroath. "I will take this oath." He hoped it sounded convincing.

He also hoped that once sworn there'd be a way to undo it.

"Very well," Balroath said, seeming neither pleased nor disappointed.

The Jinaal came forward and put a hand on Kett's chest. In a resonant voice, and in a tongue Kett didn't recognize, Balroath began a low chant. His chest warmed under the other's touch, and he could feel that warmth spread through his entire body. A searing pain grew inside him. He believed a portion of his soul was being rendered, that he was being bonded to the Quiet somehow. To Quietus. Then, something happened inside him. The closest way to describe it was that the feelings he'd had for Saleema . . . faded some. But that wasn't right, either. In his mind he saw bark peeling from ailanthus trees and falling slowly to the ground. He saw the tough silk of ailanthus moths woven into braided bonds.

He couldn't name it. But in himself he did feel a kind of indifference that he'd not known before. He didn't even care about the pain in his body.

Balroath removed his hand. The warm feeling faded. And Kett was *given*.

Silent stares of approval came from many of those seated in the hall. A few, Kett saw, still wore the intense disdain of Quiet who had only one idea about how to handle Inveterae.

A few of the Inveterae who sat in the assembly . . . their expressions were unreadable. He suspected they'd stood where he did now, and had felt the warm touch of the Jinaal.

The gallery then began to stand and exit, climbing the stairs to archways at the very top of the great theater. None came onto the floor to either exit or talk to him. As if by tradition, Balroath stood beside him until the theater was empty. It was hardly more silent now than it had been when the many Quiet had sat in their seats.

• CHAPTER THIRTY-THREE •

Handsong

There are other proofs of erymol that we could bring to Succession, but the College of Mathematics would laugh us from the discourse theater.

—Nanjesho Alanes, on the mathematics of movement, during the most recent Succession on Continuity

TWELVE DAYS AFTER departing Naltus, Mira led Sutter out of the shale stretches of the Soliel and into the rolling hills of Elyk Divad. The kingdom had once been a proud nation, united under a blue banner bearing the white sigil of a lance.

They skirted just south of the Sotol Wastes for another three days, enjoying a warm spell of sun, and avoiding small towns, riding wide of them and staying off roads for leagues afterward.

Mira found new admiration for Sutter; he hadn't complained once. Most of the time, when they weren't on the move, Sutter practiced with his sword. Mira taught him the Far Latae dances—a fluid anticipation of movement and striking only known to the Far. He took to it well. Surprisingly well. Sword mastery had become an obsession with him.

Each passing day more of her Far nature escaped like steam from a cooling boilpot. She'd begun to believe that she would no longer die when she came to the end of her eighteenth year. Instead, she'd live a human's lifetime and go to her earth with a human's blemish, never to inherit the promise given the Far of a life beyond Aeshau Vaal. If true, perhaps it freed her in ways she hadn't anticipated. Like knowing Tahn better, longer. Perhaps she'd even have the chance to be a mother to a child for *all* its life.

But only if I cannot find an answer. . . .

On the morning of the fourth day since entering Elyk Divad, Mira caught sight of a forest of aspen on a low mountain to the north. Several wide fissures could be seen at a distance, as though the mount had been cloven repeatedly by a wood-splitter's wedge. It looked just as it did on the map Elan had given her.

Leagues from any road, any town, she turned north and led Sutter to the last range of mountains north of the Sotol Wastes.

THE FRESH SCENT of aspen bark and the sound of rustling leaves soothed her as they climbed the moderate slopes. With the dapple of sun and shadow over the ground, the world about them became gentle, calm. The hint of danger that resided in the Soliel and even across Divad vanished as they entered the boreal forest.

At midmorning, the slope flattened, the trees ended, and she found herself looking out over a city nestled into a low summit. Smoke lazed from chimneys, and absent was the hum of merchant voices barking or wagon wheels creaking.

"Laeodalin?" Sutter asked. "I thought you said they guard their privacy."

"They do. We wouldn't have been allowed this far if they didn't trust that we would behave." She gave him a scolding eye. "Don't make a nuisance of yourself."

She got moving again, catching Sutter's exaggerated shrug as they rode toward town. Looking ahead, she noticed that no one rode on horseback. At the last stand of aspen, she steered them to the side of the road and they tethered their mounts back in the trees. They then entered the quiet community on foot.

There was no bustle to the place. The residents moved here and there, most of them wearing pleasant expressions. Some looked at Mira and Sutter with easy smiles, some simply walked by, unrushed and unworried.

They passed many simple structures, most fashioned by the hands of expert carpenters—wood seams were hardly visible, and engravings were simple and smooth. A

few limestone buildings likewise showed care in every chiseled detail, and in the formation of corners and steps—nothing
appeared too small to have deserved attention. Even the road
they walked had been cobbled expertly, the fitting of stone to
stone immaculate.

And yet there was no pretense in any of it. Just care in
craftsmanship, in the good use of hands.

After walking through several streets, they turned into a
plaza where a crowd had gathered around an amphitheater
recessed in a broad circle at the plaza's center. As they approached, a soft, indefinable music rose in Mira's ears. Perhaps it wasn't music at all, except that it carried the same
legato feeling, and seemed to rise and fall in pitch and rhythm.

Walking as quietly as she could, and shushing Sutter with
a silent gesture, she crept to the lip of the amphitheater and
looked down. At the center of the theater where a young
woman wearing no clothes stood gracefully moving her
hands and arms in patterns and gestures. The girl never
spoke. Her wrists and elbows seemed to intertwine, but never
touch, as they wove elegant shapes in and around each other.
Her fingers, too, danced in slow, lissome ripples. The entire
spectacle was almost hypnotic, as the woman bent at the hips,
forward, to the side, weaving her beautiful dance.

The Soriah song, Mira thought. *And a handsinger. Deafened gods, it's true.*

She looked at the gathered crowd, and could see the rapt
attention and pleasant smiles on their faces at the sounds the
young woman was producing with her song. But when she
looked at Sutter, she saw a different kind of delight. Not un-
seemly, but rather as though he watched a marvelous dance,
but did not *hear* the performance.

She looked back at the handsinger, drawn into the sound,
grateful her Far ears still possessed the ability to hear this
song. It came like the subtle stirring of the air, where the
girl's hands and arms moved through space, creating harmonics few would ever perceive.

In some moments, the handsinger's fingers were spread far
apart, sometimes cupped together, and still other times held
close to one another, producing higher, tighter intonations.

Then her forearms would roll past one another and sweep outward from her body, carrying deeper tones. The girl would slow, her limbs barely moving, making a song like unto silence, the beauty of which Mira would find difficult to describe. And then the movements would begin again—faster, though never frenetic—her arms passing near one another, stirring and playing off the ethereal notes they created as she pulled them in flowing rhythms.

Though the music was sublime to watch, Mira pitied Sutter that he couldn't hear it: melodies created by a stirring of the air, notes sounded in an acoustical realm that his human ears simply couldn't reach.

The handsinger gradually slowed, her arms and hands coming to rest at her sides. When her movement had completely ceased, each member of the crowd raised a hand toward her—applause, Mira realized. Then they began to disperse, and the young woman at the center of the amphitheater pulled on a modest white chemise, and began to climb the stairs from her cobblestone stage.

Mira motioned Sutter to follow, and moved to intercept the handsinger where she would reach the theater rim. They arrived at the top of the stair just as the young woman did.

"Excuse me," Mira began, speaking softly.

The girl started at her speech, a look of concern rising to her face.

"Please," Mira said, "I don't wish to alarm you. I heard your song. It was beautiful. Is there somewhere we can speak more privately?"

The handsinger still looked uneasy. Then it came to Mira—not uneasy, confused.

"Do you understand what I am saying?" she asked.

The handsinger said nothing, staring back.

She stood there awkwardly for a few moments, trying to think of how she could communicate with the young woman. Then she lit on something. She motioned gently for the handsinger to follow, and led her and Sutter to a strip of trees and flowers growing to the side of one building. She knelt near the flower bed, and with her finger wrote in the loam the word "friend." She looked up, hoping to see understanding in the girl's face.

The girl watched, but her puzzled expression remained.

Spoken words broke the silence. "I think I can help."

Mira turned to see a middle-aged man with an easy manner. He wore a light brown tunic, and had thinning black hair over a tanned scalp. He smiled kindly at them, one hand out and palm up in greeting.

She stood and took the man's hand in a clasp of friendship. "I'm Mira Far, this is Sutter Te Polis. We're not wanderers, or merchants. We come with a request."

"Visitors always do," the man said, and smiled. "We're too far south across the wastes for the Pall folk or, gods forbid, the Quiet; and too far north for Divad-kind to stumble upon us. No," he said, smiling a bit wider, "those who find their way here know about the Soriah. Intentions vary, but that's why they come. I'll say, though, it's rare to see a Far."

Sutter came forward and put out his hand to shake. Mira liked this Hollows boy better every day—for simple things like extending a hand in greeting. "I'm Leelin," the man said, and shook both their hands. "Eledri isn't impolite; she just doesn't know the languages of man."

Sutter looked at the girl. "Is she mute?"

"Hardly," Leelin said. "Most of us simply have no use for speaking anything other than our own languages."

Sutter's brow furrowed, but he prudently held his tongue this time.

"You can interpret," Mira assessed. "Are you also able to make the Soriah song?"

The man nodded. "Yes, but not as beautifully as Eledri. What you call the Soriah is something most Laeodalin can do. How expertly is another matter." His smile became charmingly modest. "And I suspect it's the latter that brings you to us?"

It was Mira's turn to nod.

"And if there's something we can do to help the Far," Leelin said more solemnly, "we will. Come, we should have this conversation in the shade of blooming trees. I only hope whatever old story brings you to us hasn't been embellished to silliness."

Mira heard a note of warning in the man's words. But returning her gaze to Eledri and recalling the young woman's song, Mira still hoped the girl could make her whole again.

• CHAPTER THIRTY-FOUR •

Those Left Behind

We should acknowledge that the pain resulting from a loved one's death is quite possibly more than internal anguish. Mechanical systems may well be affected.

—From *The Science of Absences, a Physicist's Model for the Pain of Loss*, found in the annals of the College of Physics, Aubade Grove

THE SECOND DAY after falling through Wendra's Telling, Tahn could sit up without much pain. And he didn't tire from conversation. Rithy had kept a kettle of willow tea hot. Tahn had had little else to eat or drink. And she seemed to know when he was finally strong enough to talk about what had happened before he'd left the Grove eight years ago.

He'd just handed back his cup, which Rithy placed on the bed table before turning her attention back to him. "My other friends didn't know how to act, either."

Tahn didn't need any context. He knew what she meant. Nanjesho, her mother.

"Rithy, it wasn't me. My father thought I should leave the Grove." How could he explain this? "They worried that the rest of you might be in danger if I stayed."

She was silent a long time, looking at him. "I found her at the end of a rope. It was made of hemp. Looked like one she'd braided herself—an eight knots, she liked the number eight.

She did it in her closet where no one would see." Rithy's voice trembled, just barely. "But I found her."

"There wasn't anything you could have done," he said. "And it's not your fault."

"I know." She looked away from him. Got better control of her voice. "But I could have used a friend for a while. The ones I had here, they stayed away. Didn't know what to say, I guess. Or maybe they were afraid or ashamed. A few teased, when they could get away with it."

Tahn listened, and after a few quiet moments took her hand. "I didn't want to go. And I'm sorry for not being here."

Tahn then realized that Alemdra might have felt the same way. Vendanj and his father had sent him out of the Scar to protect him from many things, among them the despair that follows the suicide of a friend. They'd even removed his memory. He'd left Alemdra behind to suffer Devin's loss without his friendship.

He'd failed Devin. He'd failed Alemdra. And he'd failed Rithy.

That's when it hit him. Really hit him. The suicide of Rithy's ma. He'd loved her, too. She and Polaema had filled a void for him. One where his own mother should have been, whoever she was. Nanjesho had shown him care that went beyond being the mother of a friend. She'd listened to his no doubt naïve astronomy advice and input. She'd welcomed him at their supper table, laughed at his jokes.

She let me talk to her about the "third purpose."

Tahn suddenly missed Nanjesho. A powerful missing. The kind one feels in his chest and throat and eyes.

Rithy squeezed his hand hard, a griever's grip. "After she failed her Continuity argument in the College of Astronomy, she never left the house." Rithy's stare became glassy, as though she were seeing it all again. "She worked day and night at her table. Countless sheaves of paper. Writing and rewriting proofs and equations. She wouldn't let any of her Succession team in the house. I think because she was ashamed. But she was so sure she was right."

Rithy looked up at Tahn again. "It was like watching math poisoning, Gnomon, when an unsolvable problem grips the mind and forces it into a loop of proofs that can never be solved. She wouldn't eat. She wouldn't talk. Those last days she wasn't even aware when I was in the room. She rarely answered when I spoke to her."

"Rithy . . ."

She shook her head. "It was frightening. It was like living with a ghost. I could see her, hear her. . . . She produced brilliant math in those days before she braided her rope. But even when I would try to take her hand, it was like she couldn't feel my touch." Rithy spoke through her tears as they began to come. "I watched her die, Tahn. Hour by hour for days before she gave up."

Tahn wasn't sure what could be said. He settled on, "She was a brilliant woman, Rithy. Succession can be hard. . . ." It sounded dumb, and he wished he'd kept quiet.

"I know," she agreed. "Succession *can* be hard. Hard on the one arguing. And hard on those who are forced to watch." She stopped, considering. "And when you fail . . ."

Tahn gave her a strong look. "I won't fail. I can't."

"*Can't* because you have ironclad proof? Or *can't* because you have a just cause?" She gave a small, bitter laugh. "Because all sucessionists have the second of these."

"You'll help me get the first," he answered, and tried a smile.

Rithy ignored his attempt to lighten the mood. "The argument that killed her was Continuity, Gnomon. She tried to show the existence of an ever-present element that connected all things. Erymol. Do you remember?"

"Yes. You and I sat up nights. Late. Helping her with bits of math and astronomy."

"I'm sure we were more of a nuisance to her than anything." She paused, swallowed. "But I think she liked having us around."

"I'm sure she did," he agreed. "And I liked *being* around. She had a sense of humor. Something I think she'd want you to use more."

Rithy had become silent again, staring away. "She left a note," she finally said. "I've never been able to read it."

It was the mention of the note that brought Tahn's two

worlds into sudden, painful resonance. Wards of the Scar who walked into the barrens with their knife or to Gutter Ridge always had a note in their pocket when their bodies were found. The notes usually said much the same thing: *I'm sorry. I love you all. But I couldn't take another day in the Scar. I pray you have better luck finding your true home. I'll hope there's a next life, as the dead gods promised. If so, I'll see you there. Love . . .*

So, the Scar had followed him to Aubade Grove. Rithy's mother's despair may have come from a different place. But it was her own Scar that had led her to surrender to the emptiness.

And like a ward of the Scar abandoning a friend—one they'd huddled with in a dry, wide place—Rithy's mom had abandoned her little girl. She'd done so even before she pulled the noose tight and let her body hang down.

Tahn leaned over and drew Rithy into an embrace. "I don't think they realize the pain they leave behind." He shook his head. *Thirty-seven.* "I think they're too in the middle of their *own* pain to see anything else." He drew back to make sure she saw him. "She loved you. I saw it from the outside. That's an objective observer's data, so you can trust it." He gave her a better smile this time.

Rithy blew a weak gust of air from her nose in a mild laugh. "I know. And most of her life she was the best mother I could have wanted. But . . . Tahn?"

He raised his brows, waiting for her question.

"What makes you think it won't happen to you? You knew my mother. You know how strong she was." She looked away toward where the Grove towers stood. "Even members of her college said, 'Nanjesho is as solid as her math.'"

Tahn understood better now. Some of this was fear for him. That he might fall into the Succession sickness, as Rithy's mother had.

He gave her shoulder a squeeze and sat back, feeling a bit queasy from sitting up so long. "I don't. But I have to try. Not because I want to make a name for myself in the Grove. I don't care about that. It's what I told you before. War is coming. War on a scale I don't believe we've ever seen. The nations will try to meet it. But Rithy . . . I don't think we can win. And if we don't, what will be left won't be a place. . . ."

It'll be a great wide Scar.

She stared at him, her brow pinched in concentration and concern.

"In a numbers game," he tapped his chest, "my life doesn't mean a damn compared to the thousands who'll die if the Veil falls."

"You might do well with that argument in the College of Philosophy." She smiled weakly.

Tahn didn't know what else to say, or how to say it. Mostly, he was eager to get out of this bed and get on with declaring his intentions. Start Succession. But godsdamn, just sitting up was proving to be too much for him. He lay flat again.

The room settled into a long silence. Sun fell across the bedcovers. Motes lazed in its rays.

This time Rithy took his hand. Her tears were bright in the sunlight. Like the motes. "Have you ever found a loved one who'd done such a thing? Who took her love away? Who robbed you of any more days to love her back?"

Yes. Many times.

The sunlight suddenly seemed heavy. The bedsheets seemed heavy. His chest tightened with the sob he held back. He'd left her alone to face it. It hadn't been his choosing, but he'd left a friend behind to the empty house and memories of a mother who hadn't cared enough to live for her. Succession had meant more to Nanjesho. The math had meant more.

He could have told Rithy that those were false things. That an illness had gotten into Nanjesho. That was true. And Rithy, grown now and filled with better logic, knew that for herself. But the little girl he'd left behind hadn't known those things. And Tahn ached inside to think of how she'd suffered alone when he'd left her. Yes, she would have had adults showing her their concern. But everyone knows that when the heart fails, what's needed is a friend who doesn't falsely reassure, and can walk a road with you just because. Doing things because. That's what friends do when the heart fails.

Tahn knew the truth of it. He'd found his share of friends lying dead in the Scar.

He sat with this friend now. A lot of years later. And he mourned with her a mother who'd made her own death's rope.

And when Rithy, having let out something she'd held a long time, fell asleep lying against his bed, Tahn's heart continued to pound.

By every dead god, he would go hard at this Succession!

No more quiet endings to personal suffering.

No widening of the Scar.

He started to push through his sickness, needing to get to his purpose for coming here—Succession. He was eager for the argument—and perhaps discovery—he was about to make. He would prepare. The colleges of Aubade Grove and its savants would listen. He would argue until they did. He would prove a unifying principle that could strengthen the Veil. *Resonance.* Which would mean tens of thousands would never be asked to stand up and fight the Quiet.

And he would pray to those absent gods that this time Succession went differently than it had the last time he'd been in Aubade Grove. He'd pray that Rithy would stand with him, when she had every right to tell him to burn.

He understood the raw feeling of losing someone who made the choice to die. Calling for Succession on the topic of Continuity would tear that wound open again, for all of them, but especially for Rithy and Polaema.

But Tahn held on to the idea that if he succeeded, there would be fewer who died fighting the Quiet. And fewer loved ones who walked into their own personal Scar to do death to themselves.

CHAPTER THIRTY-FIVE

The Child's Voice

We need a child to help us see past our own glaring self-interest.

—King Nevil Sadon, of Vohnce,
on the establishment of representatives to
his new government, ending the line of kings

From his window in Solath Mahnus, Roth Staned surveyed the northwest quarter of Recityv. His office didn't sit as high as the regent's, and its windows faced but one direction—things he meant to change—but for now, in the twilight of day, high above the city streets, he breathed fresh air as he waited and considered.

"It's hardly the squalor of a slum, is it?" Roth asked, his tone rhetorical.

Nama Septas, his political advisor, shook her head, confused.

Roth leaned on the window ledge and drew another deep breath, smiling to himself. "I grew up in the port city of Wanship. Along the docks. Mornings were filled with the stink of the catch. Lazy fishermen gutted their take and tossed the guts into the harbor waters."

Nama shriveled her nose.

"You always knew when the catch came in," Roth added. "The shrill cry of gulls could be heard all across the wharf. Damn things grew bold enough to peck at the fish as men prepared the catch for market."

Roth's lips twisted with disgust. And remembrance. "Even the fish blood was dull under Wanship's cloudy skies. All I wanted as a boy was to escape the wharf. Figured I'd wind up a shipwright, maybe work inland on timber or tar. Start off in the ship trade."

His political advisor prepared her pipe. Cherry sage leaf. "How'd you manage to escape that career?" Nama paused. "There are days I could do with a tar career."

Roth smiled. "The simple wit of fishermen and ever-grey of Wanship made me hungry to get the hells out of the company of dullards." He held up a finger. "That's not fair. My father was no dullard. Just unlucky. Seaside slums are unlucky."

Nama stopped puffing on her pipe, and turned to him. "Your father wasn't a leagueman, then? You're a family first."

"Da was a deck-slopper, poor gambler, and young widower," Roth said without any shame. "Knelt in front of me and told me we could survive. Told me he'd find his way back to me after exchanging me with a leagueman for a quick and dirty pardon."

"You were a marker?" Nama's jaw fell. "Silent hells, I had no idea."

Roth nodded with some satisfaction. "They didn't give Da a choice. In fact, it was my father's quick thinking to propose the swap."

But it had taken a long time to get over his separation from his father. Roth missed him still. He'd loved his da the way a boy does. Or should. Leaving Wanship and his father behind hadn't been easy. But he'd believed the man would have approved.

"He knew," Roth went on, "that the League would give me a better life." He laughed out loud. "And by the time I was old enough to take the oath, I knew more about the politics of the League than most leaguemen ever will."

Looking back at those days, he really only ever thought now about his father. And Leona.

He smiled again, the feel of it wistful on his face. The slums had taught him lessons worth remembering—about men, what they'd trade for. And Roth could yet recall the feelings of the boy he'd been, pinching purses in the street when he could, and lifting day-old haddock for meals his father wouldn't have mop-coins to buy. But the slums hadn't taught him a thing about a woman's heart, apparently.

"I don't eat fish anymore, though," Roth said. He and Nama laughed together over that.

Then they fell into a quiet moment. Waiting. He'd summoned the winner of the Lesher Roon—a race run by Recityv youth to qualify one child to sit on the High Council and represent the interests of the young. It was an outdated practice. And one the regent had recently reinstituted, he guessed, to outbalance him in council votes. *Smart,* he thought. But he'd anticipated her and set plans in motion. He would see to the work of steering the Council, just as he was seeing to the steering of Convocation.

Nama spoke up through a haze of her smoke. "Securing Council votes is important. But remember Convocation. The regent will have supporters who won't be turned."

Roth nodded. "We have the names of those invited—"

"I'm not talking about seat holders," Nama said, squinting at him. "I'll remind you of our last Dissent in Judicature. Her old friend from the Scar showed up to make an argument. I'll lay odds he'll be there. He's an artful speechmaker. Scary as a church bell, too."

"I have an idea for him," Roth said, nodding.

A moment later the patter and stride of younger feet echoed lightly down the hall beyond his door. Roth turned when the knock came.

"Come in," he said.

Two leaguemen escorted a boy of maybe ten years of age into his office. They looked for further orders, to which Roth waved a dismissive hand. The two retired immediately, and Nama joined them, shutting the door behind her.

"Our Child's Voice," Roth said, looking down. "Come, lad, announce yourself."

"I'm Dwayne," the boy replied. "Dwayne Alusel."

"Welcome, Dwayne. Would you like something to drink?" Roth crossed to his desk, where there sweated a cold pitcher of water, flavored with fresh lime.

"Yes, please." The boy came forward tentatively.

Roth noted the boy's hesitation. "You've no need to be nervous here, Dwayne. I'm your friend. You have a new responsibility as the Child's Voice, and I imagine it's all rather sudden for you. But that's precisely why I've asked you here for a visit. I'll help you navigate the problems and discussions that you'll soon be asked to have an opinion about."

The boy nodded and took the glass of lime water Roth extended to him. He sipped and looked around the Ascendant's office. "Why me?" he asked.

Roth smiled patiently. "Why not you? You won the race. And yes, I know there was some contention over who the true winner should be. But that's behind us."

Dwayne shook his head. "No, I mean why was I spared the trader blocks in Galadell. Was it because I run fast? Were you drilling a winner for the Roon?"

Roth raised an eyebrow. "What are you talking about?"

"All the children were made to run. We raced constantly," the boy said. "And then others were brought to race at Galadell. It's a trader's camp, you know. The new ones were brought from other camps. And when I won them all, they brought me here to run in the Lesher Roon."

Then Roth understood. Someone had conspired to cull a fast runner and place him in the race with the idea of being able to control one of the council votes. That didn't sound like Helaina. It might be one of the less scrupulous merchant houses. But what troubled Roth more was the boy's story of trader camps.

Suddenly, in front of him wasn't the Child's Voice. In front of him . . . was a boy. Roth was no longer thinking of the politics or what he wanted to accomplish.

His political maneuverings gone, he asked, "You lived in one of these camps?"

The boy nodded. "Longer than most kids. They sell us fast. But the ones who won the races, they weren't sold. They were kept so they could keep racing."

"What about your family?" he asked. "Your parents?" He thought again of his father, who'd given Roth up so that he might have better things, real food. A chance for more than dishonest wharf games to fleece unwary marks.

The boy stared a long moment. "I haven't seen them in . . . I don't know how long. A long time."

"You were taken?" Roth gently pressed.

Dwayne nodded. "I'm lucky, though. I got out. Got out because I run fast, I guess. That's why I was thinking . . ." The boy went quiet, his face pinched in thought. "I don't feel right about being the Child's Voice. I'm not even from Recityv. And I think putting me in the race was dishonest."

"But you could have said this before," Roth observed with mild challenge.

"I was afraid," the boy said meekly. "Afraid the man who brought me to the Roon would do something to me. Or my family."

Roth nodded at the logic. "And you're not afraid anymore?"

Dwayne gave him a long, thoughtful stare. "I was hoping you'd help me with that. People say that's your whole plan. To help folks who need help." He paused. "I need help."

The boy had real courage. And Roth no longer simply wanted the boy's vote. This had become more than politics. It wasn't so long ago that he'd been this kid. He wanted to give him the same help the League had given Roth when he'd been young. "Come to the window here, let me show you something."

At the window, they looked out together on the vast northwest quarter of Recityv. Even from this height, it wasn't possible to see the city's end. Rooftops stretched away out of sight, towers and spires jutting up here and there. The sprawl of Recityv seemed to end at the horizon.

"There are countless families out there, my young man. And they depend on the wisdom of those who sit in council in the Halls of Solath Mahnus."

The boy continued to look out over Recityv. "The Lesher Roon is meant to select a boy or girl that comes from the people, isn't it?"

"Well, yes," Roth admitted. "But we are *all* people, are we not? Any child may run. Any child may win. It isn't required that the winner have any kind of schooling or trade skills." Roth laughed easily, trying to put the boy at ease. "I'll grant you, though, most would prefer a child from the working districts, rather than the merchant or military houses."

"You want me to stay as the Child's Voice on the Council," Dwayne said, not exactly asking a question.

Roth settled a thoughtful look on the lad. "I was born with a window not so far from the stench of the street. And I'd prefer that anyone who sits on an important council and votes . . . know what it's like to live like I did."

Dwayne watched Roth closely, waiting.

"You've been through your share of hells recently," Roth said, shaking his head. "Slaver cities, traders . . ." He knew of the camps. It was something he'd told himself he'd deal with, when time allowed.

"And you think that means I'd make a good Child's Voice," the boy said, finishing Roth's thought.

"I do. Wait, no, I don't *think* it," he amended, "I *know* it."

Dwayne drank more liberally of his refreshment. He wiped his lips and looked out the window again, questions seeming to return to his eyes. Roth studied the boy's face. There was indeed a great deal of discernment in the lad. Perhaps he shouldn't have been surprised, as spending time in a place like Galadell would teach any child to detect guile. This boy had that ability, and added the calm courage to simply say what he thought.

"You didn't know I came from the camps, so you weren't the one paying the man to pretend to be my dad." The boy licked his lips, perhaps nervous. "But you still invited me here for something. Probably to ask me to vote the way you want me to." He turned to Roth, rushing his words a bit. "That's why I don't want to be on the Council. Everyone has been to see me. Telling me their story. Asking me to vote with them." He paused, composing himself. "You can find someone better than me. And if you're the man they say, you'll help me get out of it. You'll help me get back to my family. Isn't that what the League is for?"

The dread in the boy's eyes struck Roth with a pang of remembrance. It was the fearful lesson a child sometimes learns: that he's dependent on his elders . . . elders who abuse his fragile need and trust.

Roth knelt on one knee in front of the boy. "I make you a promise, young master Dwayne," he said in a low, confident tone. "I will find your family. I will bring them here, and make them safe."

The boy's brow furrowed in question. Doubt, maybe.

Roth looked up at the door. "Dimond."

His attendant entered the room. "When Master Dwayne and I are finished here, you will gather every detail he can give you about his family. You will then commission ten of our best men to find them and bring them safely to Recityv. They'll be given quarters in the League strong house until further notice."

Leagueman Dimond nodded and closed the door on his way out.

His meeting with the boy had taken a completely different path. He'd prepared for Dwayne as he did for every other politician. And in the course of a few minutes, he'd been reminded of the reason he'd wanted to be Ascendant in the first place. Reminded of the reason he wanted to steer the Council and Convocation.

He patted the boy's shoulders. "I have a lot of confidence in the votes you would cast. Stay. I'll take care of the rest. And in no time you'll be sharing evening dinner with your father." A smile crept over his face, sincere and full of remembrance of his own da.

Dwayne smiled with relief and gratitude. He lunged forward and hugged Roth. It wasn't something Roth was used to, but he put his arms around the boy and shared the embrace.

"Glad to have you back," Roth said.

The boy let go, offered a nod, and took another long drink of his lime water. He looked out the window to his left, and asked, "What's the first thing for us to vote about?"

Roth smiled, and turned to share the view with his new comrade. "Well, Dwayne, we need to talk about the regent. . . ."

CHAPTER THIRTY-SIX

Call Your Vote

*One can make private hatred acceptable, if it can be pub-
licly fashioned in the interest of others.*

> —*Axioms of Inveiglement,* a rhetoric reader
> authored by Dimnian separatists

FROM THE STREET to the heights of Helaina's High Office, Solath Mahnus boasted twenty-seven floors, most of
which required three hundred strides to cross from one side
to the other. The Court of Judicature and its attendant offices
resided in the southeast corner, occupying many Solath
Mahnus levels. And elsewhere, her other council constituents
held their own meetings in their own halls and offices. But
at the center of the fifth floor, a modestly sized room, surrounded by thick granite walls, hosted Recityv's most important discussions—the High Council Chamber. Today, she
prepared for a war of words.

She arrived early to ease herself into the room and to limber her body a little before the Council session began. In the
stillness of the chamber, she strolled slowly over the carpeted
floor, circling the table at its center. To her left, the chamber
walls had likewise been draped with heavy rugs, each depicting moments of Recityv history.

Fresh pitchers of water and goblets had been set before
each seat at the table, fourteen in all—one for each member
of the Council. She hoped those she'd lobbied to retake their
place at her table would come. She guessed Roth had also
been having private meetings with Council members, seeking a majority to forward his agenda.

But it might take more than votes today. She would see.

A moment later, Roth entered smartly through the door.

She straightened, making sure he didn't see her in any pain. One blessing she enjoyed was that politics gave her vigor.

The two shared a look, like combatants preparing for battle, and Helaina gently touched the bruise on the back of her head in a suggestive manner.

Before either of them could speak, the others began to stream into the council chamber, their footsteps hushed upon the carpeted floor.

One by one, they found their seats.

Artixan, her loyal friend, and the ranking Sheason in Recityv, took his chair next to Helaina's. First Sodalist Rochard E'Sau followed Artixan close and sat beside the Sheason. General Van Steward strode past her and touched her elbow gently before taking his seat on the other side of her chair from Artixan. These men were her staunchest supporters.

Soon after came the People's Advocate, Hemwell Or'slaed, voted into his position here by general election; he plodded in and sat heavily—the man ate free at every mealhouse in the city. Jermond Pleades, First Counselor of the Court of Judicature, came in escorting the new Child's Voice, Dwayne Alusel; the sight of them together tightened her stomach for reasons she couldn't explain. Behind them came the Commerce Chair—as they'd deemed it—Krystana Surent, who waddled in, a ponderously large and formidable woman with short hair and a forward-leaning gait. Krystana represented all the merchant houses, but she descended from Helaina's own family's most bitter commerce rival. The woman had been her fiercest enemy on the Knowledge Law.

In quick succession came the rest: Belamae of Descant Cathedral, with whom Helaina shared a warm smile; Lead Scrivener and scola Cheyin Grase—quite simply the smartest woman Helaina knew; Ambassador of Vohnce, Patrelia Calon, whose beauty belied her shrewdness—the latter serving Helaina well in matters of state; and lastly Prelate Noleris of Bastulan, who was assisted to her seat by two of her clergy, her hands and most of her face wrapped in fresh bandages that showed only a hint of stain.

Author Garlen hadn't come. Helaina could have guessed

he'd be the one to deny her appeal. He simply cared for nothing but his words.

Thirteen of the fourteen seats would be occupied. Despite A'Garlen's absence, it was still better than Helaina had hoped.

She looked back at Roth, assumed a stately air, and moved to her own seat. The rustling of Council members settling into their places ceased as all eyes turned toward her.

"Let us begin," she said, and sat ceremonially, completing the circle. "Not all of you have supported my recalling of the Convocation. But the law grants me the authority. And we're nearly ready to commence."

Roth muttered something. Helaina ignored him.

"I've asked you here to put our own affairs in order, so that our example might set the proper tone for Convocation. I believe solidarity here," she tapped the table, "is needed for Convocation to succeed. And to arrive at solidarity, there are some things we must discuss. I'll have candor. Put grievances behind you or set them in their rightful place, the courts."

"Yes, let us have candor," Roth interjected. "The laws are old and no longer safe that give the regent the authority to act alone in any matter of civil responsibility." Roth looked around the table. "I fully admit my quarrels with our regent, and I respect the office she occupies. This isn't about Helaina, personally. But it's irresponsible for us to have allowed the known world to send its kings and queens to our door for reasons we can't validate, for myths we are better to dispel than encourage with our politics."

Helaina turned and nodded at Cheyin Grase, who pulled several parchments from a leather bag at her side. She handed them to Ambassador Calon on her left and indicated that she should review them and pass them on.

"What trick is this?" Roth asked, light skepticism in his voice.

The scrivener leveled an academic eye on him—neither critique nor appeal—and spoke with quiet confidence, and perhaps sadness. "Almost a month ago, you'll remember we had a report of an attack on the library at Qum'rahm'se. We dispatched twenty scriveners to accompany several dozen of

General Van Steward's men to investigate the testimony contained in the letters now being passed between you.

"It's all true. The library has been burned to cinders; the mountain that encased it is now little more than a flow of melted stone."

"What's your point?" Roth asked, his polite impatience a common form of his condescension.

Scrivener Grase's head tilted to one side, as though she meant to talk to a child or dullard. "We didn't build the library on a volcano, Ascendant Staned. Besides which, a volcano would have burned away a mountainside, or more. What we found was a burn focused on Qum'rahm'se. And nothing occurs naturally in our world that could seek and destroy a labyrinth of stone with such incendiary heat." She paused, as if to allow Roth the chance to answer the question himself.

Roth would obviously not be baited.

Cheyin looked at him with contempt. "The only plausible answer is that the rendering of the Will brought destruction to Qum'rahm'se. That would indicate that the Quiet have come deep into the south. And they clearly desire to put an end to our search for understanding of formative languages."

Roth cast his eye at Artixan. "And how do you know it wasn't the Sheason? Internal strife has them competing with one another for position and dominance. Their credo is vexed by the schism in their own order."

Helaina watched as Artixan turned toward Roth. The Sheason's kind brow remained unfurrowed. Artixan would know, as she did, that Roth didn't really expect the Council to associate the attack on the library with his order. But it gave Roth the opportunity to remind those seated here that the Sheason Order was in disarray. He'd tipped his hand on at least part of his own agenda for today's Council meeting.

Artixan smiled. "I'll no more be goaded into argument than you will, Roth. Let's not descend into groundless accusation. No one here is going to believe it."

Cheyin continued. "With the help of General Van Steward, we've spent several weeks searching the mountains of the Lesule Valley. We've found no survivors and no evidence of any remaining books or journals. We did find, however, tracks we couldn't identify. A great many of them, actually. If they don't belong to creatures from the Bourne, then I don't know what they are."

"There, now that's a sensible conclusion," Roth said, with a patronizing lilt.

"But there's no question in my mind that Quietgiven are close and moving in secretive paths," Cheyin finished.

Roth cleared his throat. "The loss of Qum'rahm'se is tragic. Even if I didn't share the purpose of piecing together a dead language, I supported the effort. And there were many scholastic pursuits at the library that the League even financed." He looked around the table. "But we have, what? Some melted rock, some obscure tracks, and the written accounts of two criminals as evidence of the Quiet? Is this proof sufficient for us to stand before the leaders of nations and call for war? War against what?"

Roth paused, theatrically, and gathered himself. "Even if there are races in the north beyond the Pall, and even if they have passed the borders of a dozen kingdoms, we don't know that their intentions are malicious. And we certainly don't know that they bow to the will of a storied god sealed deep inside the Bourne.

"Don't you see? We're about to take actions that will impact the lives of a generation, maybe several, on the strength of little more than a tale told to corral the impetuous actions of youth. Let's not be impetuous ourselves. Our appointments to this council require that we have more wisdom than this."

He'll formally call for my resignation, citing my age. Not today, Roth.

Helaina produced a copy of her succession letter and placed it on the table in front of her. "For once, I agree with our Council leagueman. Impetuous men plot in the shadows to advance their own political power. Some would even kill for it." She fixed her gaze on Roth. "You will have seen that I've broadly published my regent succession letter. Many of you, I'm sure, find it odd that I should do so, particularly at this late stage in my appointment. I did it for two reasons. First, to assert my place in the governance of Vohnce, and to remind our people of that fact as we enter this age of rumor. But more importantly, it's meant as a reminder that the office of regent itself is not to be seized or assumed. It's filled by a majority vote of this very Council."

Roth smiled. "Correct, a *majority* vote. And a vote we shouldn't call a moment before it's needed." He nodded his head deferentially.

He needs a good horsewhipping. Helaina put a hand on Van Steward's arm, indicating that it was time.

The general rose and rounded the Council table. He knocked at the chamber door, and presently two men-at-arms pushed through, carrying the body of Mendel, stripped to the waist.

Mutters were heard around the table. Helaina watched Roth's face closely. Would he betray anything with a look? The Ascendant showed shock. *A nice affectation, Your Leadership.*

"Yesterday," Helaina began, "I went to retrieve this letter." She thumbed it forward on the table. "In my family's vault, my own brother tried to kill me."

Several soft gasps were heard.

The general had his men shift the body, and pointed beneath Mendel's right arm. "This traitor," Van Steward said, "bears the mark of the League. Can you explain this, Ascendant Staned?"

Roth stood up and went to the body, bending to inspect the tattoo, then the man. "I don't know him. Since I assume you mean to accuse me of conspiracy, General, I'll also assume you've found that this man was, in fact, a member of the League, and not just a pretender with a tattoo."

The general nodded.

"Then I can tell you that he was quite mad. The tattoo itself is a sign of extremism, since it isn't required and is a practice of those leaguemen who are prone to . . . zealousness." Roth turned to address the Council. "We're not a perfect order. Within our ranks, there are those who misinterpret our objectives. They're usually men who perceive some imagined wrong, and exploit League resources to try and correct it." He looked over at Van Steward. "Did you find anything in his quarters? Men who plot often record their plans and ravings."

Helaina waited intently. Indeed, as Artixan had predicted, they'd found just such a journal. A perfect ploy to show that her brother had acted alone and was stark mad besides. But Van Steward had lit upon a brilliant idea: suppress the journal and see how the Ascendant responded.

"No," the general replied. "We found nothing."

Roth didn't hesitate a moment, his composure never faltered, but his reply revealed as much as she'd hoped his reaction might. "A very clever individual to leave nothing behind," Roth said, and locked gazes with Helaina.

Helaina kept the smile off her face. "We'll need to be convinced that he wasn't acting at the direction of someone inside the League. You have three days to do this. If you cannot, your seat on this Council will be revoked."

Roth stared back with smoldering defiance. But even that passed quickly. "As it should be," he said. "Our disagreements, Regent, are political. Your personal safety is as much my concern as General Van Steward's. Please trust that it is so."

Roth then returned to his seat, as Van Steward directed his men to remove the body.

Helaina looked down at her succession letter. The gambit had been elaborate, but it had produced the desired effect: Roth was on the defensive. Or so she thought, until he spoke again.

"I would like to come to my purpose today," Roth said, his formal tone now more strident. "I've had this conversation with our regent in the privacy of her High Office. And I've called on her most trusted advisors, who, as you would suspect, have shown complete loyalty to her. But the time has come for new leadership. Regent Helaina Storalaith," he said, addressing her directly, "in the company of this Council, I formally request that you step down as regent."

Several of those seated around the table began simultaneously to speak. Roth raised his hands to quiet them. "Please, hear me out. I know it's not how things have been done in the past. The regent's office is a lifetime call. But do we believe it's in the interest of the people that the regent occupy her seat until her dying breath?" He looked around the room. "I want you all to understand, this isn't a bid to replace Helaina. It's a trying thing to be regent, something I don't think any man or woman would knowingly seek if they knew the demands of the office.

"But I look ahead at the challenges we face. And I worry that we don't have the right vigor in the regent's seat to meet them. Quiet or not, there is unrest. Our slums are growing. And there are obviously dangers in our countryside that we don't understand." Roth brought his gaze back around to Helaina. "One might argue that the regent is at fault for the state of things. But we must share the blame, since we govern with her. We've allowed the slothful and lawless to go unchecked. It's time to put right the omission of our duty, even if it means rewriting the laws that have guided us for so long. It's a new time, and we need a new way of doing things."

To Helaina's surprise, Ambassador Calon spoke next, turning to face Helaina. She addressed her more personally. "Helaina, I've served you for many years. I spend most of my time in the halls of leaders far from our own borders. You know how much I respect you. But maybe it's time for you to rest." She glanced at Roth. "There's real tumult and question in the hearts of those you've called here. They wrestle with their own court intrigues, and conflict on their own borders. They hear reports of violence and the taking of women and children from their homes. There's discord in many of the nations you expect to uphold the First and Second Promise." She paused a moment. "They may say no."

Helaina held back her surprise at the ambassador's words. Not that she distrusted what Patrelia said. They'd been friends a long time.

Her ambassador wasn't finished. "Your example has set the tone for whomever replaces you, Helaina. You needn't feel you must see this through. It won't be done in days or weeks or months. These problems are deeply rooted. To cut them out will require more than you should be expected to give at this time in your life."

Patrelia spoke with a warmth of affection, where she

usually spoke with a diplomat's tone. Helaina believed the ambassador to be genuine. She didn't feel as if Patrelia was one of Roth's pawns.

But it didn't change her response. "Thank you, Patrelia. But I'm many years from being a feeble woman who can no longer direct these affairs." She smiled graciously. "I'll be fine." She turned to the rest. "In fact, I've never felt more invigorated by the work set before us. And I'll challenge any vote that tries to rewrite law pertaining to the office of regent."

It was Roth's turn to nod to an associate. He turned to Jermond Pleades, First Counselor to the Court of Judicature. The severe-looking Jermond simply sat forward and began to speak.

"Regent, Council, at the Ascendant's request I have reviewed the laws that govern the office of the regent. Indeed, Helaina, the succession letter is a critical document that seals the vote of the High Council and gives testimony to a process that departs from the way of kings that preceded it. However," he cleared his throat, "in my research of the details around tenure, I've found no evidence that the calling has a duration, either short or long."

"What are you saying?" she asked, beginning to feel a tightening in the pit of her stomach.

Jermond stared back, unblinking. "It's my opinion, based on the procedurals I've read, that the office of regent can be voted upon at any time."

"That's outrageous!" Van Steward said, his voice booming in the chamber.

"In fact," Jermond continued, "it makes sense to me, since it would ensure that the regent, whose discretionary power exceeds that of the other Council members, would feel compelled to remain collaborative and benevolent, so as to retain the office."

Cheyin spoke next. "Lack of lifelong tenure for the regent would create a frenzied political environment. Council members with aspirations would be constantly vying for position and leverage." She then gave Helaina a remorseful look. "But it *is* reasonable that those who departed from the line of kings would have wanted to avoid the entitlement that lifelong tenure might create."

"The point is moot." The words rang with inarguable intonation—Belamae. "Who here would vote to unseat the regent, besides the Ascendant? Some of us have only returned to this table because she still occupies her chair. And I can tell you that we don't have seated among us any that can take her place. I can hear the songs created by each of you as you move and talk and think. I respect these stirrings. But they're not the songs of one who can unify us in the way we must be unified."

Roth chimed in. "It's no surprise that you cling to these myths. The only reason for your group of singers is to preserve the memory of our shared history. But look at the very house of those songs, Maesteri. Dilapidated and pissed on. It's a forgotten shrine at the heart of our slums. The poor cower in its windbreak, recalling fanciful stories of no use to them in finding another meal or warm bed. It's a beacon that leads them in the wrong direction."

Belamae listened patiently, his gentle old features unflappable. He even offered a smile. "I might suggest, young man, that the light of your youth is the beacon that misleads." The Maesteri stood and with a soft, deep voice sang his next words.

The sound of his voice and the lyrics he chose were a music made uniquely for this moment, for each of them. In a strangely right way, it was *their* song. The Maesteri gave it life, gave it resonance. It seemed he was singing a part of them, making them feel a value they might have left behind when their own youthful lips ceased to sing.

When Belamae finished, the room fell to utter silence. The power of song had conveyed more than all their debates ever might. But Belamae didn't leave it there. Into the silence he said just above a whisper:

"The Veil weakens because the Leiholan are too few to sing constantly with the strength that is needed to maintain it. While you talk of convocations and squabble over where to sit at a table, while some prepare to commit countless lives to war, we cling tenuously to the only thing that separates us from the Bourne itself. We're balanced on the tip of a knife, and something must be done. Who here has the experience and wisdom to stand in this breach?"

Helaina watched Roth allow Belamae's words to dissipate before he, too, rose.

"Maesteri, your song is rousing. I believe in its message to remind us of where we've been. We should remember the past as we illuminate a better path forward." Roth let out a mild sigh, perfectly offered. "I mean no disrespect. There'll always be value and a place for the exceeding talents you possess. But you must know that more than once I've called for an end to the Song of Suffering."

The prelate gasped.

"Too many of our people listen for the song like a miracle that will redeem their ruined lives. Rather than deal with their own fears and admit their poor treatment of others, they blame the threat you sing about. The Tract of Desolation that you use to create the Song of Suffering is itself a document that gives our criminals an excuse not to reform, and our slothful an excuse not to aspire."

Roth purposefully looked around the table at each member of the High Council. "Just as I've called for Helaina to step down, I likewise call again for a vote to end Suffering. Bringing an end to this song will signal a bright moment in our people's acceptance of their own responsibility. It will breed enlightenment and enthusiasm. A new era of scholarship and hope will replace the rumors spoken of—"

"And if there are Quiet beyond the Pall, beyond the Rim, and they flood into our world like a black tide, then what?" the question came from the First Sodalist, E'Sau, who had yet to speak.

"Then we'll meet them together, unified with a brighter purpose than living in the shadow of these gods you speak of, and their abandonment of this world so long ago." Roth's words came more genuinely than Helaina ever remembered.

E'Sau wasn't done. "And in meeting this threat, what help would you have of the Sheason?"

The air in the council chamber seemed suddenly very heavy. Helaina put a hand under the table on Artixan's leg. The Civilization Order had already seen more Sheason killed than she dared count. She'd fought the law, but Roth had conjured a magic of his own, formed of threats, to secure the votes he needed to enact the Civilization Order.

Before he spoke, she knew this would be his third request of the day.

"Artixan," the Ascendant said, turning to face the Sheason squarely. "I respect the creed of service you've sworn. You and I differ only on *how* to serve. But the time for conjuring is through. It makes men lazy, reliant. It breeds false security. And the ability to do it cannot be granted to all, and so is necessarily elitist. Anything that places one man above another is something we must eliminate from our society."

Artixan asked simply, "And would you accept *anyone* into your League of Civility?"

Roth looked back at Artixan, unspeaking.

Helaina had had enough. "Take your seats," she said, with a tone that would brook no quarrel. She then stood herself and narrowed a sharp gaze on Roth, feeling the rage of a woman half her age. "I find your requests contemptible.

"Let me tell you what is going to happen." She pointed at Roth. "A formal inquest will begin to discover how much the League knew about my brother."

"I've already said—"

"And a separate inquest, with all the same zeal, will investigate how it is the League went about poisoning the child of one of its members. You remember that, don't you, Ascendant Staned?"

"That is not at all what—"

"Silence!" she commanded. "Do *not* interrupt me."

Roth's face relaxed, as he sat back, biding his time.

"And last," she continued, "a third inquest will look into the burning of Bastulan Cathedral. The same fire that left Prelate Noleris with burns over most of her body, and killed dozens of others."

"Are you suggesting the League is filled with arsonists?" Roth asked with icy calm.

"I'm suggesting that you should hope the League is innocent of these crimes. I will exercise the full power of my office against the perpetrators we find." Helaina sat again.

272 · PETER ORULLIAN

After several moments, Roth said, "Are you finished?"
Helaina nodded.

"Very well. Then I now make the formal request for a vote on the office of regent. I think First Counselor Jermond will confirm that, by law, the request of a single member of the Council is enough to force a vote."

Helaina looked not at Jermond, but at Scrivener Cheyin, who reluctantly nodded that she believed it to be so.

"My lady," Jermond said, drawing her gaze toward him, "it's not personal. It's simply what the laws allow."

Helaina took a hard look around the table, trying to gauge the heart of all those seated here. Men and women with whom she'd served for some time. All save the Child's Voice, and she trusted the boy's wisdom. When she came around to Artixan, she said, "Very well, call your vote."

Ascendant Staned put his hands on the table and knitted his fingers. "With the state of affairs as they are, and given all we've discussed here today, I propose that Regent Helaina Storalaith be removed from the office of regent. I further propose that I, Ascendant Roth Staned of the League of Civility, take her place to lead the free city of Recityv, the nation of Vohnce, and the immanent proceedings at the Convocation of Seats." He paused, then sat back into his chair. "I would remind you that only a majority vote on either question is needed to succeed.

"On the question of Helaina's removal from the regent's office." He raised his hand, the indication of his vote.

Helaina watched as the People's Advocate, Hemwell Or'slaed; First Counselor Jermond Pleades; Ambassador Patrelia Calon; and Commerce Chair Krystana Surent, all raised their hands, as well.

It appeared the vote would fail, when reluctantly, Prelate Noleris raised her bandaged hand. The look in her eye as she stared back at Helaina told the regent much about who had burned her cathedral and the fear in her heart.

But even with just thirteen of the fourteen members present, Roth had lost . . . until the Child's Voice likewise raised a reticent hand.

CHAPTER THIRTY-SEVEN

More than Scales

*It's said he found the resonant note of a whole people, and
singing it, destroyed them all.*

—A recent song myth believed to originate
from current Maesteri

WENDRA AWOKE TO the sound of someone humming.
It drew her from sleep just moments before the knock
came at her door. She lit her lamp and went to answer it. She
found Belamae there, humming a lightsome tune through his
smile.

"Come, my child, let us begin your training." He didn't
wait for a response, and turned away, strolling up the corridor as if he hadn't a care in the world . . . as if he weren't
dying.

Wendra hastily pulled on a bedcoat left on a hook beside
the door, and hurried after him, smoothing down her hair
as she went. The old man continued to hum as he led her
through the cathedral in these wee hours of morning. He
paused at the bottom of a set of stairs, before going up. It
was a long climb, and at the top he paused again, coughing
and looking a bit pale. When it had passed, he smiled and
led her to a room with a grand view over Recityv.

"For inspiration," he said, pointing out the window to a
vista of the eastern part of the city and the reaches beyond.

Wendra briefly noted the view before her attention turned
to the room itself. Instruments of all kinds rested on stands
or hung on the wall: lutes, lyres, flutes, violins, a harpsichord,
trumpets, horns with circular tubes, drums of all sizes, a
piano, and other instruments she hadn't names for. Most of
them she'd never seen. She was drawn to them all, to the different possibilities of sound, music.

Around the room, set on small shelves, were reams of musical scores, some labeled in languages or musical notation she couldn't read. To one side, a slate stood with various scribblings rendered in chalks of different colors.

Belamae took a seat at the harpsichord, and directed Wendra to stand at the center of the room behind a wooden stand that held several sheets of music.

"Can you read any of that?" he asked.

Wendra glanced at it. "Yes, most of it. A few are in systems I haven't seen."

"Good. That's the easy part. Now then," he said, shifting himself on his small bench, "you are Leiholan, my girl, which means 'wrought by song.' And the techniques I share will prepare you to sing Suffering. I mentioned the Song takes a good seven hours to be sung. Those seven hours come roughly in nine movements. Their names are like so:

Quietus
The Bourne
The Placing
Inveterae
War
Self-slaughter
Vengeance
Quiet Song
Reclamation

"Sometimes 'Self-slaughter' is called 'Self-destruction,' but no matter. Each has its own feel, and its own portion of the story taken from the Tract of Desolation." Belamae eyed her, seeming to check if he was moving too fast.

Wendra smiled. "So one of the things I'll be learning is stamina."

"Just so," he said, and gave a pleased laugh. "Stamina with purpose. Direction . . . *intention*. And some internal fortitude on your part. The movements of Suffering are not just athletic to sing, they're an emotional journey. A hard one. Stamina of the spirit is maybe the better part of it."

She heard some caution in his words.

"But understand, my girl," Belamae held up a finger, "singing sadness and pain has its place. It can heal as well as harm. We'll teach you the difference."

He then played an ascending scale on the harpsichord, its plucky strings resounding pleasantly around the room. "Now then, music is the *quickening art*. It can stir the soul to peace or anger, even when rendered without Leiholan influence. It goes inside." He tapped his chest. "And it does this better than . . . well, anything. Music speaks to the heart as nothing else does, is it not so?"

He spoke with such gentle but sure passion. She began to lose herself to the instruction. For the next few hours Belamae taught her several music techniques: the turn, portamento, crescendo, pianissimo, and a handful of others. Wendra was soon combining these techniques in snatches of song.

Near midday, he invited her to sit and rest. "All these things, and so much more, are a part of the Song of Suffering. Every known musical, vocal skill is needed to sing it. You must have mastery of them all."

She frowned. As thrilled as she was to be learning so much, she hadn't decided to stay. In fact, she'd already begun to consider how these new vocal techniques might help her achieve a very different goal.

The man's keen insight was sharp as ever. "You haven't decided to stay, have you?" The old man looked on from his player's bench.

Wendra wouldn't lie to him. Not simply because it would do no good—the man would see through it instantly—but because she didn't want to. He was as near a father as she had now.

"No," she said. "I know you said my mother was Leiholan, and sang here. And I know you believe in my voice. But I'm not sure it's the right thing for me."

"Are you afraid because Soluna died while singing Suffering?" he asked.

She thought a moment. "It's not that." Belamae was watching her intently. "It's . . . sometimes I think my voice was meant for something else."

A look of disappointment rose in the man's face. "You are,

of course, free to choose. And I should say that if this is your feeling, you may not be the voice I'm looking for."

The words stung, though Belamae hadn't spoken with any real malice.

"At the heart of it all, a Leiholan tries to be selfless." His tone darkened, the delight of their musical exchange gone. "I learned that a very hard way. Your own wounds and losses must be put aside for Suffering." He swiveled in his seat to look at her directly, a firmness entering his face now. "You think about this, Wendra. We've spoken of it before, but only briefly, and since then things have gotten worse."

She stared back at him, feeling uncertain. "What if I can't control my song? Would you still want me to stay?"

He gave her an appraising look. "Tell me about your song."

Wendra shared with him the battle on the Soliel. She told of Quietgiven losing form in the sound of her dark song, which was little more than a series of screams drawn together with just a bit of melody. And all of it wrought with a coarseness in her throat that gave rise to a powerful shriek.

"Things, even people, become bright and dark and little more. Until I sing them down . . ." she finished.

The old man surprised her with a smile, and raised a finger. "The rough sound of abrasion in a singing voice has power. We call it a dysphonic technique. It's most often used in war, and well suited to songs of anger and violence and vengeance."

She nodded, understanding better than he knew.

"I don't want you to lose or forget this ability, Wendra. It's a part of your art and should remain a tool to you. You'll have need of it. The danger, however, is that it has a way of consuming the other parts of song, the other ways of singing. It tends to lead the vocalist onto a path where they find little need of other sounds. The song takes over. You've felt this."

She *had* felt it. Nearly every time she sang with Leiholan influence. "Can I control it?"

Belamae's smile changed, became more serious. "Yes, of course. It's not easy, though. And it brings us to the larger part of the Leiholan gift: attunement."

She stepped closer, eager to understand this new idea, especially if it could help her control her song.

"Now, attunement," he explained, his eyes locked on hers, "is a state in which you recognize the sound in all things. The *vibrations* of life that exist even in a rock or mountain, in the waves of sound that emanate from trees or rivers . . . or people. Being attuned is hearing song in *everything*. And once you do, then you can learn to direct your song, and resonate with other songs you hear. When you can control your song, Wendra, so that its vibration matches that of the thing you sing to or about, you will have become truly Leiholan."

I can learn to control it. Relief flooded her. "How do I become attuned?" she asked, trying not to sound too eager.

Belamae gave her a long look. "*Resonate* with me."

She began shaking her head, more from confusion than from fear or defiance.

"I can keep myself safe, and guide you besides. So, what shall it be?" He thought a moment. "Your mother. You and I both have a fondness for her, do we not? Sing to me about Vocencia. Find that song in you that best captures how she makes you feel. And then share it with me. Use it to seek that place in *me* that feels the same. Do you understand?"

Her hands felt suddenly cold. She was nervous and excited to try. "I think so."

"Much of this is intuitive," Belamae said. "In the beginning, anyway. As you find the song and focus on me, you'll begin to hear how to modify the sound to bring these parts of each of us into resonance. I'll help you. Now, let's begin."

He sat back and showed her an encouraging smile. Wendra took a deep breath and began softly to sing. The melody that came first was from her song box—a tune she'd sung with her mother often. But it didn't take much for the memories of Vocencia to shape the song. Wendra saw images in her mind of the woman working despite her tiredness, placing a cool wet rag on Wendra's forehead when she was ill with fever, laughing as their family took turns dancing the three-foot jig while her father clapped his hands to keep time.

The song she sang wasn't mournful. It became lively and

quick, and sung with open vowels that let her scoop up and down easily to the memories that cascaded in her head.

And when she had the song, she added the thought of Belamae, and the many warmths he had shown Wendra. She imagined he'd done the same for her mother. She let her song flow over him. Into him. And sooner than she might have imagined, she could feel a part of the Maesteri amplifying her song.

Perhaps it had happened so fast because their mutual love for Vocencia was so strong. But whatever the reason, the song grew. Not in volume. Though there was some of that. But in strength. In weight. Like a physical thing that could be used as a shield.

And when she saw Belamae's wet eyes, she knew he was seeing and feeling every good part of that song with her.

Then an image flashed, bright and hot like a stroke of lightning. It came again, longer the second time. It left an afterimage, too, just as lightning does: Wendra, as a child, angry and crying for having to leave Recityv.

She stared at Belamae, confused, her song drifting into a new melodic signature, more halftones, darker—the sound of threat and confusion. Belamae stared back at her as she sang. She sensed he could stop her at any moment. He did not.

And as her music unfolded, she saw Belamae sitting knee to knee with her mother, teaching her a song technique—something outside the regular lessons. Something he'd learned, used, in open battle. It was a dysphonic song. Rough and abrasive sounding. He'd sung it in war, and with it . . . killed indiscriminately. Like Wendra had on the Soliel plains.

Only his song . . . *Oh my deafened gods . . . he refashioned Suffering . . . for war.*

Her song coaxed the music into this shared moment and memory. She *heard* Belamae teaching her mother this weapon-song before she went away to the Hollows. He thought she might one day need it to protect her little family. Protect Wendra, and Tahn.

She felt it in him now, like an impossibly deep-toned string plucked and resonating. He understood her dark song beyond the power of it. He had a song of his own. One he was ashamed of. One that had changed him.

Without realizing it, Wendra pushed her song toward Belamae's private shame and sound. She sought to resonate with it, caught in a reverie of shared pain. It was the pain of accidentally slaughtering innocents when the intention of one's song was actually to satisfy the grief of losing a loved one.

She and Belamae sat together in their grief—hers new, his quite old. But it was a common chord to them both. And Wendra sang the sweet, awful sound until he finally nodded that it was enough. His eyes told her that this lesson had taken a turn he hadn't expected. But one he'd allowed.

She didn't want to stop, though. The song was teaching her. Teaching her Resonance. Teaching her Suffering. Teaching her something about her own song. She'd found a new voice. The very sound of grief. Its purest tones. So, she didn't stop, but sank deeper into the vibratory notes she and Belamae shared.

As though far away, she saw him shaking his head. A moment later he was singing. And his own song found hers— in tempo and rhythm and melody—and began to guide it, shape it.

But she wasn't ready to let go. She shook her head and sang more forcefully, invoking the strongest song she knew to keep hold of this resonation—her own rough, dark song. She lost herself in its sound. Lost control. As she always did. And did not care.

Dark and bright filled her eyes.

The joys of new sounds and new ways to craft her song were displaced by the song she'd learned naturally. It shot forth from her mouth in shrieking waves. Only this time, she sang with new understanding, giving her song life with crushed notes offered in violent staccato.

The force of it should have killed Belamae. But the sound of his own music must have blunted the attack, so that her dark song only pushed him brutally back against the far wall. His old body crumpled to the floor, blood running from his mouth. He looked up at her in shock and disappointment.

A moment later his expression turned to fury unlike any Wendra had ever seen, except maybe in the eyes of Vendanj.

Holding her in a firm stare, the Maesteri began to sing a deep bass note. The unwavering sound was so resonant that the air itself shimmered with it. It touched Wendra's skin, pressing in on her, forcing the air from her lungs, robbing her of the ability to produce song. It then lifted her from the floor along with sheets of music and began to spin her like a wind-up doll. Parchment fluttered around her, revealing a vortex with her at its center.

The world swam in her vision. Images of grief and destruction and murder filled her mind as the physical world whipped by—Belamae, instruments, the harpsichord, the window and a sky brightened now with sunrise.

Like a pirouetting toy, she spun faster and faster. Then the deep-pitched song ended, and she fell to the floor amidst the music notations, which fluttered down around her. Her head was spinning, her gorge rising. When her equilibrium returned, she looked up at Belamae, whose bloody mouth began to move again, his words coming in a singsong cadence.

Belamae smiled sadly. "Even when we look for a smile, your song finds the darkness, doesn't it, my girl." He must have seen the worry she was feeling, because he bent and put a hand on her shoulder. "Don't fret, Wendra. We've only just begun. And this," he motioned toward her chest, then his own, indicating the Resonance they'd shared, ". . . a strong first step to Suffering."

She stared back at him, unsure how to take what had happened, or what he'd said.

"It's always dangerous to train Leiholan," he added, seeming to talk mostly to himself. Then his eyes focused. "You're gifted, my girl, and have such great potential. But it's not going to be easy, is it?"

She pushed herself onto her knees, nearly afraid to ask. "Belamae," she said softly, "can one be attuned whose songs . . . whose intentions . . . are like mine?"

His smile returned. "Come Quiet or chorus, we'll keep at it."

CHAPTER THIRTY-EIGHT

It's Not What You Hear

"And when the creature unfurled its every limb, and began to move in its strange rhythms . . . the echoes. There were silent echoes, if you can believe it. And living things died."

—Historical account of the Sotol Ravages, a largely forgotten series of Quiet battles, written by Robart Mcamin, and largely discounted due to his narrative flourishes

MIRA FOLLOWED LEELIN and Eledri a short distance through the streets. The sun tracked high overhead, warming the mild air. Sutter kept pace just behind her, commenting to himself about everything he saw. He sounded like a child at a midsummer festival. Another time, she might have joined him. But not today.

They came to an area where the cobblestone ended, replaced by trimmed grass. Around the green, low buildings hemmed the area in. Several old broadleaf trees grew in the enclosed park, casting dappled shadows on the lawn. From the limbs fell the occasional late bloom; these trees would bear winter-fruit.

A pleasant look rose on Leelin's face as he led them onto the grass and beneath one of the large flowering trees. Mira noted the sweet scent of the blossoms as both Eledri and Leelin sat near the trunk of the tree. Leelin gestured for them to do likewise.

When they were all seated on the ground, Mira regarded Sutter a moment. What she meant to ask the Laeodalin would raise doubt in his mind—he didn't know she was losing her Far gifts. But he had a right to know what was happening to her, in any case.

She spent a moment regarding Eledri, who sat with almost musical poise. The young woman's body was her instrument, and had been carefully tuned. When a subtle wind pulled gently at the chiffon shawl loosely draped around her shoulders, she swayed with it, as though similarly stirred. The simple movement reminded Mira that Far training figures were patterned after Soriah dance.

With old stories about the power of the handsongs in her mind, she turned to Leelin. "Have you heard rumors of Bourne races crossing the Pall?"

Leelin's easy manner faltered briefly. "Is this why you've come? We did receive word of the Convocation. But we live outside your governments. Even Elyk Divad doesn't require tribute of us." The man's smile returned. "Happily, the Laeodalin are only stories to most. And those who know us aren't sure how to think about the Soriah. We very much want to keep it this way. The Laeodalin don't go to war anymore."

He related Mira's words to Eledri, speaking in a tongue Mira had never heard before. Eledri's expression shifted to concern, and she glanced at Mira.

"We're not here to ask you to attend Convocation." She shook her head to try and put Eledri at ease. "Our stop here is personal."

Leelin quickly gave Sutter and Mira an assessing look, as one might who expects to find injury or madness—something that needed the handsong to mend.

Mira spared a last thought of concern before revealing her condition. "My natural Far ability . . . is fading."

She watched as understanding bloomed in Leelin's face. But she needed what she wanted to be perfectly clear. "For many reasons, I need to stop this. Reverse it." She gave Sutter an apologetic look. "I should have told you sooner. I'm sorry."

Sutter's mouth had fallen comically agape, though his eyes showed real concern.

"More than once I've been late to a fight. And my blade is slower when I get there. So it's a good thing you're practicing so much." She gave Sutter a weak smile and turned back to Leelin.

"How did you lose your Far gift?" the man asked.

She stared, unspeaking for a long moment. "I broke my oath for a friend." She tried to keep her stare from hardening. "I don't regret it. What I did was necessary." She stopped, sighed. "But now there's an imbalance inside me I cannot mend."

Leelin was nodding as she spoke. "And you've heard fireside tales of Soriah handsong used to restore balance. You believe we can cleanse you."

"That's my hope," she admitted.

"So that you can claim your inheritance when you go to your earth," Leelin surmised. His face showed a father's tenderness.

"And give my king an heir," she added.

Sutter showed her another look of surprise.

Leelin quietly relayed it all to Eledri. The girl's pleasant expression slackened, and she turned to look at Mira. Gently, she raised her hands and began to sing with them a lament so piteous that Mira, who hadn't cried since the truth about Far motherhood had struck her, wept silently. The subtle intonations of air, moved delicately by the turn of a hand and curl of a finger, came to her like so many sighs. It was the sound of disappointment. And the sound of seedling hope. Not of reclaiming the swiftness of her step, but the willingness to bear a child she wouldn't live to know.

The song wove on. She lost track of time listening to the bittersweet music. Sometime later it ended, and the young woman's hands grew still. Mira was left looking into the faces of Eledri and Leelin, sad and thankful. Some few blossoms fell around them, plucked free by gentle winds. She didn't dry her eyes or cheeks. She wasn't ashamed of the tears wrought by the things that burdened her heart. She would simply have to turn them into new determination.

"What did she say?" Sutter asked.

"She said she cannot heal me," Mira answered softly.

It wasn't until that moment that the full weight of her loss came to her—the inability to produce a Far heir, perhaps restore the Covenant Tongue . . . see her family again when she passed this life. Her flesh weighed heavy on her bones, and she sank down, shutting her eyes. She should be grieving more for her people, more for the danger of war the Far no longer had an answer for. But more than these things, she grieved at the loss of her inheritance, of meeting those who'd given her life and loved her first and best.

A small smile touched her face at an ironic thought: Were her priorities all wrong because she was more human now than Far?

She sat in the self-imposed isolation behind her eyes for a moment more. Then, she opened them again. "We'll leave as soon as we fill our waterskins and find some flatbread." Mira extended a hand to Leelin. "Thank you. You were kind to interpret for us."

He reached out a hand, and when Mira took it, he covered their clasped hands with his other palm, and gave her a searching look. "For what it's worth, Mira Far, I don't believe in any oath that robs you of its promise when the offending sin is sacrifice. The First Fathers may have left us to ourselves, but I'm not convinced they're bastards besides."

She started to thank the man, when he spoke again.

"I'll ask you to remember that Eledri's song wasn't all sorrow and regret. Her hands also sang of the hope you brought with you to Laeodalin. I'm no great songmaster. In fact, it's your good fortune not to have heard the songs of my rough, clumsy hands." He gave an easy laugh. "But I'm wise enough not to ignore the notes of a song. On the roads away from here, I trust you'll recall them properly. Will this be good enough?"

Mira placed her other palm over her and Leelin's intertwined hands, a particularly warm gesture, given the company.

"I think you're plenty wise," she said.

They all stood, and just before leaving, a question rose in Mira's mind. "When we began, you said that the Laeodalin don't go to war anymore."

"That's right. And I'm grateful that's not why you came. Might've had to get ugly with you." He showed her a wry grin.

"Was there a time when you did go to war?" she asked. "I've never read or heard of it."

Leelin took a deep breath, and the music in it occurred to

Mira like a song of weary disappointment. "Yes, but the scola and biographers haven't the ears for our contributions. So they aren't captured in annals or authors' tales." He raised a hand and scratched his chin thoughtfully. "But we're grateful for their deafness. Otherwise many would be tramping through our aspen groves looking to take something they can't understand. You, at least, came with respectable intentions. I like that we met this way."

She smiled weakly. "Thank you. But it would be wrong of me not to say that we could use your help."

She took time to tell them more about Convocation, more about how she'd come to break her oath—going to Tillinghast. This last part brought worry to Leelin's face. She decided not to relate the losses in the Naltus library. And stopped short of explaining where Tahn had gone.

She looked Leelin in the eye. "If the Laeodalin can fight, you need to think about what you'll do if the Bourne breaks free."

The man seemed to look through her, his gaze troubled and distant. "I never want to hear Laeodalin hands move that way again." Then he focused on her, his eyes like those of a man arguing with himself. "Come with me," he finally said.

Mira and Sutter followed Leelin and Eledri through streets dappled by leaf-shadow. For the first time she noticed that a few of the residents had no hands; at the ends of their arms most of these had strapped likenesses of hands fashioned of wood. A few had attached simple, blunt implements—hooks, two- and three-tined prods, and the like. She guessed that even the mild Laeodalin had severe punishments for the abuse of their gifts.

Eventually they came to the foot of the mountain, which rose abruptly at the city's northern edge. Directly in front of them a corridor had likewise been chiseled into the rock. Looking up the cliff, she saw that several dozen square caves had been cut into the rock face. Leelin led them into the dimness, taking a lit handlamp from the wall as he went.

Twenty strides in they veered left and began to climb a set of stone stairs. Every fifteen steps let out on a lamplit hallway running parallel to the cliff face. Several flights up, Leelin moved down one of these corridors, where stone doors remained closed every twenty strides. At one of these, their host stopped and grasped its iron handle. He motioned them forward, so both she and Sutter could look in. Then he slowly pushed the door open, whispering as he did, "Soriah Maal."

The heavy iron hinges groaned, and bright light flooded toward them from the open mouth of the square cave. At the center of it all sat a dark-silhouetted figure, statue-still. After a moment, it stood, seeming to unfold itself against the light as a flower unfurls in the warmth of the morning sun.

And when it stood fully up—the smooth lines of its body showing no clothes—it raised its arms out from its sides. Against the brightness of the day beyond the cave, small appendages rose on its arms like long, elegant fingers. It gave Mira the vague impression of a bird stretching its wings and feathers. A moment later, more of the thin, smooth extensions rose from the Laeodalin's shoulders. The unfolding struck her as beautiful. And terrifying.

Leelin didn't have to explain. The handsong this creature could create, stirring the air in so many combinations, would be stunning, powerful. It left her with a feeling of beautiful menace. These were the handsingers that would go to war if it came to that. Mira imagined the dark dance and movement of these Soriah Maal as they wove silent strains against their enemies like a rush of cacophonous wind.

Then the short appendages relaxed, giving the figure a more human form again. She never saw its face or eyes, as it remained in silhouette until Leelin pulled shut the door. He then led them from the mountain, through the town, and near to where they'd tied their horses—all without a word. There he and Eledri turned.

"Thank you for the warning," Leelin said, offering his warm smile. "We will talk about this. If the Quiet do come, I'm sure you won't find us idle." He shook his head and added, "And we're sorry we couldn't do more to help *you*."

He made a half bow. But Eledri stepped close and took Mira's hand in an embrace that she would never forget. The touch of the handsinger's fingers felt like . . . *touching music.*

The two shared a long moment, searching each other's eyes. Then the young woman gave Mira the barest smile, a peaceful thing she'd not soon forget. Shortly after, she let go and stepped back. The disconnection was almost painful.

Leelin directed them to a spring and storehouse where they provisioned themselves before returning to the trees, gathering their horses, and descending out of the riven mountains through a forest of aspen.

As they rode out, she took time to tell Sutter more about the Draethmorte sigil-glyph he carried. She cautioned him to find an opportune time to show it to the smith king. She explained it as thoroughly as she could, though her mind was elsewhere.

She hadn't found the answer to make herself whole again. She wondered if there was another way. But they needed to get to Ir-Caul and convince the smith king to join Convocation, and then on to Estem Salo. There was no time to even consider alternatives to mending her condition.

She felt strangely mortal. As a Far, she would have been dead in less than two years. No longer truly Far, she might live to old age. And the thought terrified her. But nothing hurt as bad as the loss of that moment of reunion she'd looked forward to all her life—reunion, after death, with her mother. Her true mother. That blessing was gone. The bone-deep grief was new to her. She now understood the crippling nature of it. The Far lived their lives immune to such feelings. Mira now thought she understood what drove men like Vendanj.

She took away from the Laeodalin only the memory of a music rendered by beautiful hands, and the touch of a living instrument whose song, she now believed, played like her own personal accompaniment. She also took with her the memory of a silhouette—*Soriah Maal*—unlike anything she'd ever seen.

She was still thinking about the handsinger's song as they came to the base of the hills. Sutter pulled on his reins and dismounted—resting his horse and his aching back. He waited for Mira to find a place to settle herself before he came to her.

"Why didn't you tell me?"

Mira removed her oilcloth and began to work at her blades. "I'd hoped to find a remedy here. Then it wouldn't have mattered."

"You should have trusted me," he said, mildly reproving. "I would have kept your confidence."

Neither angry or smiling, Mira nodded. "You're right."

"It's more than that," Sutter went on. "If you'd told me, maybe I could've helped."

"I'm sorry," Mira offered. "I'm not quite myself." She gave a slight smile at her own joke. "What's your advice?"

Sutter laughed, being caught without an answer. "Fair enough. Let's get to Ir-Caul. Maybe there's wisdom there to help you. Hells, I was starting to think all that back there was a just a big dumb show. Seen too many of those stupid things on the pageant wagons. Usually performed by the trouper who can't memorize worth a tinker's damn."

"The rootdigger speaks." And she laughed with him.

"Damn right."

Through the smiles, she guessed this was how men and women got through their grief—they laughed.

• CHAPTER THIRTY-NINE •

Divestiture

If man is like a violin, then let us mute a string or two.

—Epigram inscribed into the cover of *The Vibratory Nature of Life*, an exploration of imparting silences as opposed to execution

THAELON SAT AT a table in the far corner room of the art gallery. Several books surrounded the chalk rubbings he'd made of glyphs carved into the granite stone deep inside the Tabernacle of the Sky. Glyphs that explained how a Sheason could be divested of the authority to render the Will.

A few lamps burned, lending a yellow cast to everything he'd been reading—all his efforts to understand how this thing was done. Around him, on the walls of this gallery room, hung depictions of the first Trial of Intentions. A chaotic time not long after the Framers had left the world behind. A difficult period in which the Sheason had effectively split: some following Maldea into the Bourne; the rest remaining here, in Estem Salo. He hoped these depictions would lend clarity to his preparations. Or at least focus.

He stood, stretched, and began to pace, taking a closer look at the paintings—maybe the first to do so in years. This room didn't receive many visitors. The gallery had several floors, and this area was tucked away on its highest level, in its farthest corner, behind doors that remained closed, though not locked.

Tonight, this room was Thaelon's study as he tried to recover a lost practice. And maybe, in part, convince himself that the course he'd set was the right one. Surrounding himself with books and art often helped him do just that.

A few moments after he'd started moving, Raalena entered quietly. "Pacing again?"

"How long have you been outside the door?" he asked without looking at her.

"How long have you been here?" she answered.

He smiled over this rote exchange. He then stopped, pointing to the painting before him. "They didn't use divestiture at the first trials."

She came up beside him and regarded the painting. It showed a woman being held on each side by a Sheason, as a third figure raised a rendering hand. There was alarm in her face. There were bodies behind her. Sheason bodies.

"Bad intentions met a final judgment back then, didn't they?" Raalena observed.

He looked around the entire canvas, which measured three strides on each side. "It was a different time. These dissenters had sympathy for Maldea. Their intentions were to follow him. Not much else to do but destroy them."

"A rather black view." She gestured to the left, where it appeared the children of dead Sheason wept. "I think you've been at this too long. You should step away for a while. Get some food."

He shook his head. "The first trial is soon. I need to understand how this is done."

Raalena took gentle hold of his arm and turned him to face her. "I don't think you're struggling with *how* to do it, just *why*."

He smiled without any real amusement. "Let me first tell you how—as much as I understand, anyway—and then I'll explain why."

She let go his arm, and he continued to walk, regarding the gallery paintings. Each told a Trial of Intention story. Lives lost. And other lives forever changed. After he'd viewed another handful of the paintings, he crossed back to his makeshift desk. As he stared down for several long moments at his rubbings, the glyphs began to take on clearer meaning.

"One of our oldest names, what is it?" he asked, still staring down at his papers.

"The Sheason?" Raalena asked. "Helpmate? Palamon's own? Inner Resonance?"

He looked up and wagged an encouraging finger at her. "Yes. Inner Resonance. Why do they call us that?"

"Because you render the Will," she said, squinting as though trying to see ahead to where their conversation was going. "Because you move things by drawing on your life's energy."

Thaelon let his own thoughts settle. He wanted to state it as something irreducibly true. "It's the vibratory nature of life. That's why."

"Vibratory?"

"Think of it as that which stirs us. As our capacity to *be* stirred." He tapped the rubbings for emphasis. "A Sheason's authority to render the Will grants him the power to cause the resonance between two things. He begins by causing the vibration of his own life's Forda and then touches something outside himself with it."

Raalena came to stand opposite him at his table-desk. "It

wouldn't be only life, then, that has a vibratory signature, would it?"

"No, it's everything. And it wouldn't necessarily be seen as a vibration. But it helps explain the possible connection between any two things." He traced a few of the glyphs with his fingertips. "A Sheason's control over his own Forda is unique. It's something that must be studied and understood before it's awarded. It gives him the power to manipulate his own inner resonance so that he can affect almost anything."

She looked around at the paintings surrounding them. "And kill, when necessary."

"But that's not our course." He turned the rubbings so that she could see them in their right order. "Divestiture is nothing more than returning a Sheason to the possibility of only one vibration, one resonance. The one he knew at birth."

Her eyebrows rose. "Giving you another reason to hate Vendanj: He's taken a young man to Tillinghast. A young man who was born dead. But revived, given the resonance of a Sheason in order to live."

Thaelon stared at her. Not with anger, but candor. "Tahn should never have been."

A long silence followed. A silence in which the paintings on the walls seemed perfect company. He didn't need to explain further that the boy represented a violation of the Sheason way. Or that his life resulted from a misuse and misplacement of inner resonance. Or that Vendanj, and those like him, were dangerous because their moral compasses didn't always point in the same direction, but changed as their needs changed.

She finally nodded. "It's the difference between you and Vendanj. And why you're going to strip the authority to render from those whose intentions are like his."

"It will go harder for them than that," he said, his voice thick with regret. "Once a Sheason has rendered the Will, his own life's resonance changes." He thought a moment. "A violin doesn't sound the same fifty years after it's made, any more than the musician plays it the same way. Each is different after so much time and use. And they can't be again what they were in the beginning."

She glanced at the rubbings, searching as if she might understand their meaning.

Again he offered his weary smile. "When they lose this part of themselves, they won't simply go back to the way they were before. In a real way, they'll stop being who they are."

She nodded understanding. "They deserve to know the consequences before they stand trial."

"Ironic, I think." He sat back down to finish his preparations. "The quality that brings them to trial will likely be the one that prevents them from being dissuaded by consequences."

"And what's that?" she asked.

"Pride in their belief that they're right," he answered, and hunched again over his rubbings.

He heard her say as she started away, "Doesn't make them too different from us, does it?"

• CHAPTER FORTY •

Convocation

We forget that Convocation failed the second time, until Sheason went into realm courts with grim threats and reminders.

—From *The Failure of Perception*, a study of
the divide between aspiration and reality,
a book banned by the League of Civility

HELAINA TRIED TO catch Dwayne's eye, but the Child's Voice wouldn't look at her. He held his hand aloft, staring at the table in front of him. The boy's vote had cost her the regent seat. Roth had succeeded with his political grab. She now understood the uneasy feeling she'd had at the sight of the boy with First Counselor Jermond. Dwayne had been coached, threatened probably. She wished she'd spent more time with the lad.

Her hands began to tremble. She'd gathered her High Council to prepare for Convocation and now she faced expulsion from the office that could make it a success. *All hells, I'm tired. Too damn old for this.* Artixan grasped her hand to help calm her. Van Steward did likewise on her left side. Her general gripped hard, as if he readied to do something rash. Before anyone could speak, the outer door to the council chamber slammed open. A few slapping steps sounded in the short hall between the two doors. Then the inner door was unceremoniously pushed, knocking back into the carpeted wall.

In the doorway stood A'Garlen, an annoyed expression on his face. "Your stewards are absolutely useless. I had to ferret this place out on my own."

The author surveyed the room, and seemed to divine what was happening, as he then visibly counted the hands in the air with little nods of his head.

"I suppose," said Garlen, "since I'll be voting with the lady, that your proposal is dead, Exigent."

"We are no longer called the Exigency," Roth said calmly, but with obvious displeasure, "and haven't been for a very long time."

"Oh, well. I'm too old to change such habits. I'll beg your forbearance." The author smiled over his use of the old name, then padded along to his seat. "Will there be food?" he asked, and winked at Helaina.

He'd shown. Relief washed through her like a floodwater.

Artixan laughed out loud. Van Steward beat an open palm on the table three times in approval. Scrivener Cheyin, E'Sau, Krystana, and the others on her side of things all smiled openly.

Roth's face only dipped a moment into anger. Something one might not have seen if they weren't watching closely. "You and I disagree," he said, his voice conciliatory, "but if this Council believes in you, then the full allegiance of the League is yours. My lady." And he made a show of an elaborate nod.

Helaina wanted to slap the man into honesty, but graciously received his pledge.

Meanwhile, A'Garlen had taken his seat and begun complaining about the lack of food. The old storyteller had a bit of theater in him. He'd made his appearance at precisely the right moment. She was sure that hadn't been an accident.

She'd gotten word from her Emerit that Roth had begun paying visits to Council members, applying pressure . . . securing support. Roth wasn't one to leave a vote to chance. She'd determined to do her own rounds. A few of her supporters would never turn. A few had soft places that could be pressed for effect. Roth would know the same pressure points. But the real game would be for those who no longer attended Council, those who had effectively relinquished their seats.

The Maesteri was one of these. Her good fortune was that her friend Belamae led the Maesteri at Descant Cathedral. That left the author's seat. And in the fraternity of authors, the unquestioned voice belonged to Garlen. Mostly because no one dared cross him.

She'd paid Garlen a visit, laying out her plan, convincing the codger to place his pen on her side of things just minutes before Roth had arrived at Garlen's home. She'd stood in a rear closet, listening to the two men bandy words. She'd seen the faint glow under the bottom of the door when the author had written his glyph on the air.

Maybe Roth couldn't have earned Garlen's support. But then again, maybe he could have. Short of that, the author might have decided to leave the whole affair alone. Leave his seat unclaimed. But she'd outmaneuvered Roth. Gotten there first. Made a convincing case to a hard man to convince. But until Garlen had walked through that door, she hadn't been sure.

I've still got some political salt.

Now, there was the Convocation of Seats. It had been ages since the Second Convocation. As difficult as it had been to try to put her own Council in order, it was a trifle next to what lay ahead. To succeed, she would need every whit of shrewdness and determination she'd ever possessed. She'd need more than political salt. She'd have to be every bit the iron hand she'd once been known as.

And Roth was surely not done with his plots.

VENDANJ LED BRAETHEN and Grant through the crowds. Streets were clogged with Recityv citizens, pilgrims, and banner-holders for major and minor houses from nearly every realm and country across the Eastlands. There was excited talk and anthem singing and roadside carts with spiced meats and roasted nuts. Men dispensed sharp ales from barrels by way of liberal spigots. If one didn't know Convocation was taking place, one might think Recityv was holding an enormous festival.

And more than a few men had cobbled together armor from disparate suits and woven a homespun banner to pretend at valiance, likely seeking a squireship. These worried Vendanj the most. Clearly there was a rising class that anticipated—even looked forward to—war. Because war gave men an opportunity to rise in social station. And there were many who needed an opportunity.

It was unlike anything he'd ever seen—an effervescent atmosphere sitting atop a grim purpose. And its celebrants had widely different ideas on the value and meaning of the gathering. He was thankful for their general ignorance. Masses turned to mobs with very little suggestion.

Vendanj wove through the crowds, and got to the Wall of Remembrance. He had to raise his voice to be heard by the Solath Mahnus guard, but he and his friends were quickly let through. A courtyard, staircase, and inner vestibule later, and they entered the long corridor that connected Solath Mahnus with the Hall of Convocation.

The passage rose ten strides high and as many wide; a column of soldiers could march it without having to jostle elbows. They moved briskly, boot heels clapping the white marble floor of the wide concourse.

Statues of kings and queens and regents lined the corridor, rulers who'd shown courage during the First and Second Promise.

Seats had been taken at sunrise, just minutes ago. Vendanj

had deliberately arrived late, and without announcement. He wanted those who would oppose him to have no time to prepare counterarguments. The Convocation would likely last several days, but Vendanj needed to frame the discussion from the beginning.

At the end of the corridor, great oaken doors rose five strides high. Emerit guards took note of the three-ring emblem around Vendanj's neck, and pulled the right door open enough for him and his companions to slip through.

The feeling of the place was like that of a great altar. Immense windows set high against the walls admitted wide shafts of morning sun. And at the hall's center stood a large circular table, set with high-back chairs. The scent of dusty stone and dry wood and newly dyed wools filled the air. Voices came in whispers.

He'd been in the chamber once. Alone and at night. Just to think. Seeing it here, now, filled with kings and queens called to answer the room's purpose, chilled him. The number of lives represented here . . . He remembered Illenia, and went in.

They made their way around the outer part of the room, as those seated at the central table were announcing themselves after a call for names and office. He knew many by sight. Some only by reputation. And most of the governmental seats were occupied. As were those for significant fraternities who also had a place at Convocation: Sheason Artixan, who stood in for Randeur Thaelon; First Sodalist Rochard E'Sau, here on behalf of sodalist leader Raalena Solem; and Ascendant Roth Staned.

But some seats were vacant. Absent was the smith king, Jaales Relothian of Alon'Itol; Elan of the Far; the Mor nations—they wouldn't have been expected—and the Sedagin, the Right Arm of the Promise. The Sedagin would never answer the regent's call; not after the betrayal they'd suffered during the War of the Second Promise.

The war kings of the Mal nations were also absent. Their seats were token, anyway. The Mal didn't consider themselves part of the Eastlands. Old rumors suggested that Quiet and Inveterae alike had slipped through the Veil west of the Mal lands, and coupled with mankind, siring new breeds. To some, the Mal were the same as Quietgiven. Their wars were too many to name. But Vendanj had spent time there, and found many of the rumors to be so much bad poetry.

Three strides behind each seat at the table were a few short rows of chairs where vassals and attendants sat. Many lords and ladies also had a scrivener who took notes, documenting their part in the proceedings.

And several strides behind these attendant rows were tiered galleries where lesser lords sat showing fealty to one crown or another. These peers and nobles held a great deal of power—more than their kings and queens at the center table gave them credit for. These *lesser* aristocrats supervised holdings, managed banks, reviewed accounting ledgers for merchant trade, and conscripted men for military service. Most of these gallery seats were occupied by men and women with "dirty hands," as the saying went. They did the *business* of government. And there were more than four hundred of them in all.

Vendanj and his companions came around to the chairs set back behind Helaina. She acknowledged him with a quick nod, before she glanced toward Grant. He saw the two share a look. Grant nodded. A brief touch of relief crossed her features. *Tahn's alive,* it said. And more than that. Something more tender.

Then Helaina adopted a regal air, raising her chin to speak. "First, thank you to those who have answered my request to reconvene the Convocation of Seats. It is neither trivial for you to come so far, nor for me to request that you do so. We're honored that you are here." She raised her gaze to the gallery. "All of you."

Then she leaned forward, placing her hands on the table, seeming to take the Convocation participants into her confidence. "I won't delay or dissemble. Our purpose here is as it has been before. And while I don't know how dire the threat seemed to your predecessors who sat where you do today, I believe if we can't again find unity, we will suffer. Suffer from this new and perhaps last threat from the Bourne."

Mutterings rose at her use of the word: *Bourne*.

She put an end to it by resuming with a vigorous tone. "There have always been Quiet who've crossed the Pall. But these have been small and isolated occurrences. We've suffered them as readily as the border disputes that rise among ourselves. Only twice has the threat been large enough to call this Convocation."

The regent looked around the table, her face intent, serious. "It is so again." She then stood straight and motioned Belamae forward. The Maesteri got up from his chair and came to stand beside her.

In a deep, resonant voice, Belamae addressed the Convocation. "For ages the Tract of Desolation has been rendered in song. That rendering is known as the Song of Suffering. Since the Placing, when all those created by Quietus were sealed inside the Bourne, the music has been made. Day and night it's sung." The old Maesteri looked up into the great vaults of the Hall of Convocation, as though supplicating gods long since gone.

Looking down again, he drew a long breath through his nose, and resumed. "But the gift to render that song is no longer abundantly found in men. And the Leiholan tire. I'm here to tell you . . . the Veil weakens."

More muttering. It came loudest from Maester Westen Alkai. Westen loosely ruled in Elyk Divad. His formal robe bore the subtle stitching of a musical score. Divad had a rich musical tradition kept alive in a handful of conservatories, which sent the occasional student to Descant. Westen's eyes were cloudy with cataracts, but he seemed to see Belamae well enough to share a look of concern.

The murmurs abruptly stopped with the scrape of chair legs across the stone floor—Roth rising out of his seat. "Gentle kings and queens and rulers of nations, I cannot sit by another moment without speaking. I live and serve here in Recityv alongside our regent and the skilled Maesteri. I have great respect for their contributions to the people of this city and the nation of Vohnce, whether it's done by clever governance or the art of song that ennobles us all. And I agree there is good cause for us to convene and discuss a new kind of unity or alliance to make our borders more friendly, safer. But in the spirit of openness and debate this Convocation must represent, I tell you that the original motivation for this Convocation of Seats is baseless."

Roth began to stroll behind the seats of the attendees. "I don't deny reports of violence. But have we not progressed beyond the tales of caution captured in stories of myth and legend? And if there are great hordes living beyond the Pall, beyond the Rim, then they are great hordes; lawless kingdoms bent on domination that we may unify against if it's necessary. But we inspire nothing but fear and regressive ideologies if we maintain this belief in unseen veils, dark gods, and evil creations, whose sole desire is our annihilation."

In his slow stroll, Roth passed behind the regent and Maesteri. "There is power in song, to be sure. But not of the sort being described here today. If there is indeed a concerted threat to the wide Eastland nations, then we can discuss a response, even war. But the time has come for us to root our decisions in what is real and practical. And I would suggest that any action anointed from our Convocation here must let go these superstitions, which I warn will only lead to unsound choices."

Vendanj surveyed the faces of those seated at the convocation table. Many remained impassive. But just as many appeared to find reason in the Ascendant's words. Roth's eloquence and logic had set a new tone for the Convocation. And he couldn't let it pass unchallenged.

"It's not simply a few reports of violence," Vendanj said, turning a hard eye on Roth. "I've just come from Naltus Far, where more than ten thousand Quiet came to destroy it. Thousands of Far died to turn that army back."

The table erupted in conversation. Some protesting that Vendanj had spoken at all, since he wasn't a seat holder.

Helaina touched Belamae's arm, and the Maesteri returned to his seat.

She then held up a hand to quiet them. "Civility, Ascendant Staned, does not mean abandoning traditions that have kept us safe." She looked around the table before continuing. "You should all consider that we sit here in safety, able to have this conversation, because of nations like the Far, and because of the very things the Ascendant would put to an end. We have hard-earned wisdom, passed down to us, that has helped preserve the way of life we know. That wisdom includes the songs and stories that remind us of delicate balances.

"We're on a precipice, my friends. Our next step is precarious and crucially important. I ask you to hearken to the histories which tell of your nations' part in the struggles of the First and Second Promise. Let that guide you as we consider a promise of our own."

Discussion then began. Leaders speaking, sometimes shouting, either in defense of Helaina's proposition or taking up Roth's practical stance. It became clear to Vendanj who Roth had spoken with beforehand—phrases and logic were repeated with too much familiarity. And in the space of minutes, the divide between two camps became clear and wide. That fast, the historic third call of the Convocation of Seats appeared on the brink of collapse.

Vendanj shook his head and strode to the table, deliberately standing directly behind Roth.

"I must speak," he called loudly, over several ardent debates currently taking place. As voices quieted, he added, "And you must hear me."

Roth leaned to one side and turned to look up. Vendanj caught a glimpse of disgust, before the man turned faceforward again. "Only those given leave by a seat holder may address—"

Helaina motioned for Vendanj to continue.

"Besides the Quiet army that has destroyed the Language of the Covenant," he paused, letting that revelation sink in, "there are three things you each must know and consider. What the regent has spoken here is not myth or mystery. I've spent the last several years of my life on the roads, traveling to cities far from here. I've been in all your own lands and capitals. With few exceptions, I've found the Quiet among you."

"It's no surprise that a Sheason—" Roth began.

Vendanj put a heavy hand on the man's shoulder. "You've

had your turn." He went on. "More than once I've fought those given to the Whited One. Usually, I've been able to turn them back. But I've seen their strength and resolve. And each year they come in greater numbers. They are a mortal threat. Make no mistake."

He then began to pace, as Roth had, meaning to draw near each Convocation member as he spoke. "Second, you need to understand that this isn't merely another race or discontented people. It is *many* races. And it is more than discontent. They believe they belong here, in the east, with us. They believe they are our kin, and that they're meant to test us. Even by war."

Roth again tried to speak, but Helaina pointed at him to be silent.

"But in one important way, they are *not* like us," Vendanj went on. "The oldest stories are true. They were not created as our equals," he paused again, looking around the table, "but as our betters: in strength and speed . . . and resolve. Given to many of them are qualities the League would find uncivil. Gifts of Will. And about their intentions, there should be no question. They will come to destroy."

Vendanj stopped behind the empty seat of the Sedagin and gripped the heavy posts of the chair back. "The Bourne is vast, and the Quiet that have come so far, even this ten thousand, are but a trifling of what will come if the Veil falls."

Calene Pammel, queen of Kuren, then spoke with a patronizing lilt one didn't possess without a great deal of practice. "You'll forgive us, Sheason, but yours is just another claim. And even if this army marched on Naltus, as you say, what evidence is there that it's anything more than a conflict between those two nations, or that *we* should get involved?"

Elerion Saradolay, queen of Balens, a woman so obese her jowls shook when she spoke, joined Queen Calene. "Much as we may dislike it, kingdoms go to war. But we don't need to be a party to every battle."

Elerion's army was token. Her allegiance hardly mattered.

Vendanj returned Calene's condescending gaze. "Your Highnesses, consider what you're saying. Your own histories tell of the great alliances forged by Convocations past, to meet massive threat from beyond the Pall. Would you prefer to have war upon you, before you *commit* your armies? If so, you'll be too late. In the past, we've prevailed because the Right Arm of the Promise went into the breach early, and for us all. But we betrayed their trust the last time, and they'll no longer take their seat among us." He lifted the chair up and slammed it down. "We may fail precisely because we did not *commit* the last time this table of rulers sat in this hall!"

The queen seemed unmoved, but said nothing more.

General Kaleth Weren chimed in, a man with more beard than face. "I agree we should always be prepared, Sheason. But you'll understand if I'm skeptical of *your* testimony."

Vendanj gave the general a thoughtful look. "You've heard of the rift that threatens to tear my order apart. I'm largely to blame for that. I don't care to curry the Randeur's favor, or the regent's, or yours." He looked around the room. "Any more than I care for reputation or my own *ascendance*. I pursue one thing, at any cost: the preservation of our way of life against real threats. And I won't be moved from that course, regardless of what you decide here."

He began to walk again, gathering his thoughts. "The third thing I ask of you: Choose here, now, to stand together against whatever threatens us. You still possess the freedom to meet and debate and disagree. You should unite if for no other reason than to protect that freedom."

His words resounded in the great hall. When they'd echoed their last, he paused, then spoke again, with a hint of finality. "If you don't, the Quiet will come. They will bring down the Veil, and the Bourne will stretch itself to every land and people."

Some moments later, into the stillness, Baroness Asari Redall of Ebon said softly, "I believe you."

The woman bore a haunted expression. Her cheeks were hollow, her eyes rimmed with dark circles. She ruled a kingdom that bordered Destick'Mal, and so she knew more intimately the ravages that affected those near the Veil. Her realm's history was a series of wars with the Mal. Ebon was a nation of halves, bright and shining near the coast of the

Soren Seas, but thorny and blasted by scouring winds in its northern regions.

Roth drummed his fingers twice on the table. "We're at an impasse. So for the moment, let's put aside the question of the Quiet and our response to it, and focus instead on *any* threat from *any* quarter of the world. Since if we believe the old myths, then across the Soren Seas there are other dangers, the Rim hides secrets of its own, and far over the ocean beyond the Mor nations there are things about which there aren't even stories to tell."

Roth sipped from his goblet, pausing dramatically. "But I don't believe in myths. I see enough evil in the actions of men, even if that evil is nothing more than negligence and selfishness. Our own *known* world, the many nations on this side of what you call the Veil, is varied and wide. Our nations are disparate kingdoms with no concern for each other. Openly hostile, in fact. We raise armies to defend ourselves or war with each other. Our greatest—or at least our first—fear should be of ourselves."

Fists pounding the table interrupted Roth. It was Jeshel Solomy, king of Nallan, whose ears looked like cauliflower from a lifetime of helmets and beating. "May the deaf gods hear you," he shouted. "I do nothing but defend my people against your beloved smith king of Alon'Itol."

Jeshel was a warmonger. The smith king was likely not here because he was busy even now fighting back Nallan advances.

Roth nodded thanks to Jeshel for the endorsement. "I have long sought peace and camaraderie across borders through a common set of manners and principles. And I will remain tireless in their defense and evangelism." Roth paused again, raising a contrary finger as if he might argue with himself. "But I have likewise seen that manners and principles by themselves won't be enough to forge the peace we all deserve and expect."

He drank again from his goblet, setting it down empty this time. "Today, there are but a few of your kingdoms where the League of Civility isn't welcome, where it doesn't already have men and women educating people on courtesy and lawfulness. In most places we're part of your ruling councils, and help create and enforce your laws because we prize nothing higher than civility."

Roth stood again, his posture as one prepared to make a historic announcement. "So today, after all that we've been told, and all that I have myself heard and seen, I announce the formation of a fifth contingent of the League's Jurshah. Alongside politics, justice and defense, history, and finance and commerce, I have established . . . a faction of war. This division will be separate from those who police laws and ensure justice. They will be trained in warfare. Their ranks will grow from within the League, and from recruits who will take up the cause. They'll stand with your own militaries if there is need, or they'll be the first footmen to meet an aggressor that comes to your border."

The Ascendant looked thoughtfully around the table. "No matter what threat arises, whether political enemies, strange encroaching hordes, or heaven and hell themselves, the League will stand on your soil and defend your people and their way of life."

A tall man clad in black armor entered through the hall doors. His confident gait spoke of battle and ability. The man came to stand directly behind the Ascendant. Vendanj caught a worried look on Van Steward's face. He studied the newcomer—clearly Mal—and had the feeling he knew or had seen him before.

"You're creating your own army." Vendanj didn't hide his contempt.

"I think of it as an army of the people. Yours, mine, everyone's here. They may report to me, but," he added, "I've made my goals and philosophies clear. And these do not, will not, run counter to the will of rulers whose borders we serve. Lawfulness, mutual respect, safety, these are the things we care about. If anyone disagrees with these, there are larger issues to discuss."

Vendanj restrained the desire to denounce the Ascendant. At least for now. He still hoped to convince the Convocation to ratify the regent's strategy. But before he could speak again, Roth continued his politics.

"If any of you wish to combine your own military with the League's force in your home nation, we welcome it gladly. The united power will make our mutual cause stronger." Roth then offered an easy smile, relieving the tension of weighty matters. "My friends, I believe this is all precautionary. I would have us prepared for the worst. But in my heart, and from the reports I receive from my men who live and work beside your own people, I believe our only danger is from lending fanciful stories more meaning than is their due. So, yes, let us prepare. The League of Civility will create this martial force as a safeguard against any that might march against us. But its presence will more practically put an end to border disputes. It will end civil unrest, and draw us all together in our mutual desire for peace and progress."

Vendanj shared a look with the regent; they both knew Roth's unspoken intention. He meant to create a hegemony under his own rule. Not today, perhaps not even this year. But the monstrous ambition of it was clear. Had those seated at the table likewise recognized it? He feared that many would allow Roth's army a garrison in their lands, believing they could control it and still benefit from its presence.

"Ascendant Staned." Volen Chraestus, king of Kamas, stood and faced Roth. He leaned forward, his hands spread on the table. "The Kamas Throne has no need or desire for League presence. I want you to acknowledge that you understand me."

The Kamas Throne defended the Divide mountains, Estem Salo. Its army was the reason the Mal had never succeeded in expanding farther east. Holding back the Mal . . . that was deadly work.

Roth remained poised. "We should discuss—"

"Acknowledge that you understand me." Volen's eyes burned under a heavy brow. But he never raised his voice.

"I understand."

Roth was as rattled as Vendanj had ever seen him.

Volen sat down, and Helaina rose to stand beside Vendanj. She wore an expression as stern as the Kamas king's, and likewise focused it on Roth.

"This Convocation will not become the pulpit for your

expansionism, Ascendant. I won't allow you to use our pressing need to further the League's agenda. Take care. The
recalling of the Convocation is *my* duty. Those seated among
us will hear from *me* the advisability of what you propose.
But not at this table. Not in this hall. And your war faction,
we will discuss whether this is permitted under Vohnce
law. Others here may wish to do the same."

She looked around the room then, calling each king and
queen and ruler by name, until she had spoken them all. "The
corridor you walked to enter this place is lined with the me-
morials of men and women who, like you, came to this place
for one reason. I ask you to honor their memory, and commit
yourselves and your defenses to the threat that has reawak-
ened.

"*This* is why we are here. It is *your* sovereignty"—she shot
Roth a glare—"that is at risk, and your sovereignty that I
would enlist in a common cause. Let our banners fly together,
stronger collectively than any one or few flown separately;
and stronger, too, than a single banner flown by one who
holds no throne." She finished, still holding her glare on the
Ascendant.

Roth only smiled and nodded. "Nevertheless, a fifth faction has been created. Five arms now, instead of four. For
peacekeeping. Not war with a myth."

Vendanj's anger boiled over. "You ask for proof of the
Quiet." He thrust his hands forward, and concentrated on the
space above the great round table. In the air materialized an
image of Zephora coming upon him and his companions in
the Saeculorum. He caused the memory to unfold in such viv-
idness that one might have imagined he could reach out and
touch the things he saw.

The sights, smells, voices, and sounds—everything was recounted for the Convocation. The dreadful feelings of hopelessness and hatred filled the room as though the Draethmorte
had appeared before them. Vendanj expended great energy
to relate every detail of their fight. The air itself stirred, as if
the winds of the mountains were blowing here, now.

Like a tempest it raged before them, blocking out mutters
and gasps. Vendanj deepened his call of the Will, creating a

full vision that engulfed every man and woman seated here today. The hall seemed to disappear. It was as though they sat in the heights of the Saeculorum, personal witnesses to the battle.

His companions were thrown and beaten. Zephora shot great bursts of darkness from his hands, blackening stone and air and minds. Vendanj shared the filth that Zephora's touch of darkness had left on them.

The storm and battle raged as real as he could command it, until he was spent, and he let the vision recede. The room around them came into focus again, the images dissipating.

Profound silence settled around them all as Vendanj collapsed over the front of the Sedagin's empty chair. Braethen rushed forward and eased him to the floor, where he lay on the stone in the quiet. Vendanj hoped the nightmarish sight had moved proud and cynical hearts.

At the sound of the first words to break the silence, he shut his eyes.

"A parlor trick that insults our intelligence. And having rendered the Will, the Sheason has broken the law." It was Roth, speaking coolly. "Helaina, will you call the guard, or shall I?"

Vendanj then heard steps, and a sword being drawn. He didn't need to see it to feel the power of the Blade of Seasons raised in Braethen's hand.

"Leave him alone." There was real warning in Braethen's voice. Vendanj knew the others could hear it, too. The sodalist was not just a man with a sword. The blade had infused him with a sense of authority that went beyond steel alone.

"Obstructing the rule of law, my young sodalist friend, will only earn you your own prison cell. And raising your sword here is not only caddish, but unwise." The Ascendant sounded as though he spoke while smiling, though his voice remained solemn.

Braethen replied with measured calm. "Test me."

Then another stepped forward and spoke to Braethen in a soft voice. Vendanj opened his eyes to see Grant standing next to the sodalist. "Now is not the time," Grant said, and put his hand on Braethen's sword-bearing arm. "You're of no use to the Sheason, or anyone, locked away in the pits of So-lath Mahnus."

The sodalist sheathed his sword, then knelt beside Vendanj. He reached into the folds of Vendanj's cloak, found the small wooden case, and produced one of his sprigs. After placing it in Vendanj's hand, he asked, "What should I do?"

"Grant is right. Now is not the time." He quickly ate the sprig, and had Braethen help him to a sitting position. He then turned to the regent. "We won't be a distraction."

Helaina nodded appreciatively. Shortly, three more guards came to escort him from the hall. With Braethen's help, Vendanj got to his feet. Before leaving, he spoke to Grant. "When the time is right, say what must be said."

A look of eagerness rose on Grant's face. Except for his deeply weathered skin, Grant looked very much like Denolan SeFeery again, the man who twenty years ago had defied everyone, even his own wife.

Vendanj went with the guards, Braethen accompanying him to the door. They passed those seated at the table, including Roth, who eyed them with indifference.

"Go see E'Sau when you have time," he said softly to Braethen. "You'll appreciate his perspective."

Then he left Convocation for the darkness and stench of the dungeons below. He went with some anticipation, though. There was a man in the depths of the Recityv prison that he wanted to see. A man who stood on the other side of the rift in the Sheason Order. He wondered if seeing him again would help Vendanj see a way to bridge the schism that divided their order. Or make it clear that such could never be done.

CHAPTER FORTY-ONE

The Bourne: Canon

*When the Mor houses escaped the Bourne with the Refrains,
they managed to sweep the very memory of song from the
minds of those they left behind.*

> —*Studies in Exodus*, a Quiet chronicle of Veil crossings,
> and resulting suppositions

BALROATH SAID SIMPLY, "Follow me," and led Kett
from the Assembly Hall down a different passage than
he'd entered by. They traversed dimly lit corridors, Kett in a
bit of a haze. He was trying to reconcile what he'd just done—
giving himself to Quietus—with the larger plan he still held
in his heart of liberating the Inveterae from the Bourne. He
focused. He needed to find out what he could about these
rumors—that the Quiet had discovered a way to pass over
the Pall into the south.

Soon enough, Balroath halted at another door, which stood
in deep shadow somewhere in the depths of the Assembly
Hall. He knocked once and entered. Inside, a small office was
lit by two double-wick candles set on either side of a bur-
nished ilexwood desk. The walls were entirely covered with
bookshelves, deadening their footfalls.

The room had a quiet, studious feel. Behind the desk sat
another of the Jinaal—smaller, with rounded shoulders as if
slumped from long hours hunched over his desk. Only when
Balroath and Kett had come to a stop in front of him did this
new Jinaal finally look up.

"Is he given?" he asked, his voice also deep like Balroath's,
but more coarse.

"Yes," Balroath replied.

The other nodded. "Kett Valan, you are a more important
Inveterae than you know. I am Stulten, and I've some things

to tell you." The Jinaal tapped the parchments on the desk in front of him and sat back into his chair, which groaned beneath him. "But let me start by asking you a question: What do you feel now, having given yourself today?"

He had the feeling Stulten knew his answer already. "I didn't understand what it was until Balroath put his hand on me. I feel some grief over the vow."

Stulten laughed. The sound became a hoarse cough. When he'd gotten control of his voice again, he looked up at Kett. "I think you are well sworn, Kett Valan. Now, I will reveal to you your true purpose. We know who your friends are. We know the extent of your plots and plans. If it had seemed prudent to us, we would simply have brought them all here and put them on the Assembly Hall floor for slow execution. We would have received their confessions and any additional names they might cry out to end their own prolonged suffering. Or, if we hadn't the time, we would simply have sent tribunals to their various homes, as we did yours, to try, convict, and execute them as quickly as possible. Can you guess why we did not?"

He stared hot grief across the desk at the old Jinaal. "Because you want me to do it for you."

Stulten looked pleased. "You were the right one to enlist," he said. "Of course, you're right. Your responsibility will not be to convince these Inveterae separatists—indeed all Inveterae—that we seek the same thing. Most would laugh at you, and certainly distrust you."

Kett meant to argue with him. But before he could speak, the Jinaal lifted a hand to stay his tongue. "Oh, I know your kind has great respect for you. But few would believe your words, and most would come to doubt you. Soon enough, your access to those who interest us would be compromised."

Stulten then picked up a piece of parchment and handed it to Kett. In the weak light, he could see it was a long list of names—friends, and those who'd worked beside him pursuing escape from the Bourne. When Kett looked up, a gratified smile rested on Stulten's lips. "A bit shocking to you, isn't it?" he said.

"These are my friends," Kett answered. "There's no need to kill them. They'll listen to me. Let me convince them.

They're worth more to you as allies than as dead martyrs to other Inveterae."

Stulten laughed again. More coughing ensued. "A true leader you are, Kett Valan. But I think you overestimate your coconspirators' influence—they are not martyr-worthy. And we don't believe ages of distrust and hatred can be changed, even by you. No, the example of their execution is far more valuable to us." The elder Jinaal leaned forward, a few bones in his neck cracking the way knuckles do. "More than that, Kett Valan, the example *you* will make of them is what will matter. One of their own, one who has led their hopes of separation, one who knows them, is now with us. It will demoralize them to learn that you have sworn to us your allegiance. And when you have scratched out the last name on that list, not only will you have rid us of the separatist threat, you·will have sent a message to the rest that we are watching, that we cannot be deceived."

Kett looked over the list names of again. Without looking up, he asked quietly, "What if I can't do this?"

No laugh came this time, only a silence into which candles burned. When Kett looked up, Stulten stared without emotion. "You already know the answer to this, Kett Valan. But I *will* tell you that the rendering of your spirit is a pain you cannot imagine. And beyond that—" He paused dramatically. "—it unmakes you. Whatever hopes or beliefs you have of a life after this life . . . forget them. The essence of what you are is stripped away, and you are returned to the void shapeless, nameless. You cease, Kett Valan, to be."

Stulten let his words hang in the air before adding, "And if you think you can suffer this, then consider your children."

Kett stared, disbelieving, and shook his head.

"Quite so," Stulten affirmed. "But there's another path for you. And as unsettling as it may be, if you succeed, you'll find prominence here. Trust me when I tell you, things are going to change." The old Jinaal tapped something on his desk that looked like a star chart.

"Think about where you want to be standing when it comes," Stulten said. "Think about where you want your children to be standing. You, Kett Valan, have the chance not only to be on the right side of this old quarrel, but to stand with distinction. Because the truth of it is this: We really do want the same thing. We want to live where we decide. We want to undo the unfairness that sent us here so long ago. These are things everyone inside the Bourne should agree on, should work together to change. The difference between us is only that we are no longer patient or gentle in how we do that work. This is what you will learn; it is what you will help us do."

"Then the rumors are true," Kett said, getting to his true purpose in giving himself to the Quiet. "You've found a way out of the Bourne."

Stulten eyed him closely. "We believe so."

"A way to bring down the barrier." Kett's voice sounded very nearly reverential, despite his effort to show no interest.

"Or open a way through, anyway." Stulten smiled with some satisfaction. "Now that you're given, there's no harm in sharing some of our plans. After all, you're part of that now." He took a deep breath, his eyes becoming distant. "For ages we've discounted the stories of the labraetates, the song-makers said to keep the barrier strong from somewhere deep in the Eastlands. I'm proud to say I've helped amend that notion. More evidence that we're not what we were."

Understanding bloomed in Kett's mind as he thought of all the humans brought into the Bourne. "You're trying to breed one."

The Jinaal laughed without any hint of mockery. "Well of course. But that's not even the better part of our efforts with the humans. We'll talk of that some other time. But our plans," he said with gentle correction, "don't hinge on successfully breeding a labraetates. I'm not sure we could train one if we did. The Mors took that knowledge with them when they fled the Bourne, the selfish bastards."

The final piece of it locked in place. "You're bringing one here. From the south."

"And that plan is under way. But before you're a part of it, we have this work for you to do." He indicated the parchment in Kett's hands. "It will prove you to us, while it also brings the Inveterae firmly in line."

Stulten then reached into a drawer in his desk, and pulled

out a dark chain necklace bearing the signet of the Sedgel, the Quiet leadership ranks. He handed it across to Kett, then nodded and waved a dismissive hand.

Kett looked down at the small medallion: an inverted letter *V*—a fulcrum—and atop it a line. He knew the symbol, an archaic emblem for a balance scale. The line in it did not tilt or lean. It meant equanimity, fairness. He might debate that. He might argue the Sedgel weren't fair or balanced at all. In fact, the symbol was better described as indifference. But whatever he or they *thought* it meant, it marked him as given until they either branded or scarred the same signet into his skin.

Balroath took Kett by the arm and led him out of the small office. He'd thought his heart a stony place, hardened by a life inside the Bourne, subjected to countless indignities. But this . . .

He followed Balroath blindly, as his mind and heart raced. He hoped there was yet stonier ground in his soul, as he stared down at the list of names.

• CHAPTER FORTY-TWO •

The Smith King

No mystery there. Jaales Relothian was a smith before he was a king. Good one, too. Brought every smith and tinker worth a damn to Ir-Caul and started his gearworks. Real war.

—Excised from an interview with an Ir-Caul gearsmith for the *Biography of Kings,* intended as a work of slander by pacificists

SUTTER AND MIRA rode another seven days. Every moment he wasn't on his horse, he practiced with his Sedagin blade. It had become an obsession. He rested only when they rode or slept. The overland stretches held some respite for him. More than friends around a table, more even than a long road traveled in silent company, an open endless field could rest a man.

Near meridian of the seventh day, they passed from a leafless wood, and far ahead saw Ir-Caul rise on the plains like great bones jutting up from the land. White spires and immense towers stabbed at the sky. Even at a distance they seemed old, their whiteness perhaps wrought by the bleach of sun and time. Sutter imagined the city having lain dormant in the earth, and being slowly excavated, over the ages, by the sweeping winds that scoured the long plain.

As they approached, they encountered no market or tents outside the city walls. The perimeter lay deserted. There weren't even travelers to be seen coming in or out.

What he did see were countless plumes of black smoke rising up into the sky all across the city top. These weren't from cook fires, or hearths lit for warmth. This was coal smoke. Had to be. He'd never seen so many burning at once. *Smith king.* Could this city really have so many active smithies?

They came to a stop at the gate, a sudden silence forming with the ceasing of hooves on the road. Mira made no attempt to knock or hail someone. The silence got to Sutter.

"Hello!" he called. "Anyone home?" His words echoed across the face of the outer wall, which rose twenty strides and stretched far in both directions.

Mira shot him a disapproving look. Sutter shrugged. "I don't get all this ceremony and mystery. We want to go in. We're no threat to them."

Mira shook her head. When she'd returned her attention to the gate, Sutter shook his own head in amused mimicry.

The groaning sound of massive hinges interrupted him, and he turned to see the gate pushed open wide enough that three men could slip through. They came adorned in badly stained armor—breastplates over shirts of chain. The symbol of a gauntlet balled into a fist on a field of white could be seen on the shields they carried. The lead man held a sword and had suspicion in his eyes.

They formed a rough line in front of Mira and Sutter. "Why do you make noise at our gate? Are you dullards?"

Sutter stifled another smile. But the humor faded fast in looking at the lead man and his sword. He knew instinctively that the other wasn't posturing, nor even threatening. Wrong answers would mean conflict, simple as that.

"The Sheason Vendanj sent us," Mira said. "My friend here is from the south. Forgive his ignorance."

The sword-bearer looked past them down the road, then both left and right out along the wall. Satisfied that they were alone, the man lowered his blade. "We've not heard that name in many years. What does the Sheason want?"

"He asks that we speak with King Relothian," Sutter said carefully, having seen some slight distaste in the man's face when Vendanj's name was spoken.

The lead guard cocked an eyebrow. "Is that right? And what business would you have with the king?"

Sutter dismounted and walked close to the man. They were roughly the same height, but he had no intention of starting a fight. He just wanted to see the man's eyes when he spoke, gauge his reactions. "That would be our business."

The man stared back flatly. "That so. And mine is to keep the riffraff out of Ir-Caul. Everyone wants to see the king: make complaints, seek mercy, claim privilege. He's not a counselor for the masses. He's the king."

Sutter saw earnestness in the man's eyes, no bluff, no bluster. "I don't mean to be a pain in the ass. But we've ridden from Naltus Far, and the ass pains are ours. I'd prefer to be back home, not serving as errand boy for the Sheason. No insult to your king. But Vendanj . . . he has a way of *requesting*. Anyway, what we have to say is important enough that King Relothian will want to see us. If I'm wrong, I'll buy you eight drinks and walk you home."

The man looked up at Mira, seeming to gather for the first time that she was Far. Then he looked back at Sutter, and his face softened just noticeably. "I met your Sheason once. He does have a way about him. Very well. Keep yourselves mannered." He and his men then stepped aside, and the massive left gate swept open. Mira led Sutter inside.

At the edge of the city, just inside the fortification, a second wall rose. Sutter hadn't noticed it from beyond the gate.

This wall stood a few strides taller, and thicker. From this rampart, countless ballistas appeared ready for use. Men could be seen watching the horizon every ten strides. It all gave Sutter a feeling of dreaded anticipation, though the soldiers didn't appear uneasy, which only heightened his anxiety—it appeared this city's routine was war.

Not much farther inside Ir-Caul, building stone showed pockmarks from siege-assault. Towers and spires stood truncated, as if severed or destroyed by assailing rock.

As they moved farther into the city, what struck Sutter more than anything he'd already seen were the caskets.

On every corner a stone casket stood on end, the likeness of a man carved in relief on its face. Torches burned on either side, sending shadows dancing across the road. The more of these they passed, the more Sutter believed these weren't permanent caskets, but new ones, new deaths. Which led him to conclude that the custom here in Ir-Caul was to put their dead on display. Perhaps to honor them. Perhaps as a reminder.

And the men were all clad in various accoutrements of war. The only exceptions were the merchants. Not a single beggar or urchin crawled in the streets or alleys. Sutter didn't get the feeling this was due to charity, as much as the fact that people here had a purpose or they moved on.

And perhaps because the entire city seemed to revolve around its military, they'd yet to see an inn. Sutter hoped to find a room, and get some decent sleep before calling on the king. But sleep would have to wait. It didn't seem Ir-Caul often had visitors.

They wound through the streets until they came to a magnificent building Sutter guessed must be the palace. Another thick wall protected the structure, this one the height of just two men. Along its circumference, men-at-arms stood watch, some talking to each other as their eyes scrutinized passersby.

Before Sutter could ask, one of the soldiers came forward from the inner gate and took his horse by the reins. "I'll lead you in."

Sutter didn't protest, and the man stepped lively, conducting them to a stable yard and directing them to dismount.

"Your horses will be cleaned and fed," the man said, then motioned for them to follow, as he got moving again.

Past an unremarkable door at the base of the palace he guided them, then through half-lit stairwells and halls, where in the stillness their boots sounded loud on the stone. The decorations on the walls were all of a sort: weapons, armor, paintings depicting battle or men in full war dress. None of these things appeared ceremonial or celebratory. The implements of war were all nicked and stained; the images brutal and specific as if historical and not imaginative; and the portraits of men weren't solemn or glorious, they showed gaunt faces, haunted eyes, and ugly scars. These were the commemorations of real lives, placed in plain sight as real reminders.

Feels like a damn crypt.

Farther on, they began to encounter other soldiers, whose hard gazes followed them.

Sutter muttered, "Happy bunch."

Mira seemed unaffected by the scrutiny or morbid décor. Sutter reflexively gripped his Sedagin blade more tightly.

When she saw him do this, she put a hand on his sword arm and leaned close to whisper, "You've improved. In fact, I'm impressed with your blade work. I've never seen anyone take to the Latae fight dances as you have. But don't be rash. Not here."

Their guide then stepped in front of a door and turned to them. "You'll hope you haven't misused the Sheason's name. And don't assume it makes you well received."

Sutter stared with frustration at the man who then pulled the door open, admitting them to an inner chamber. *Don't assume it makes you well received?*

Sutter's question slipped away as he looked into Ir-Caul's throne room. All the relics and ossuaries they'd seen thus far seemed like intimations of what stood at the far end of this hall.

He steeled himself and went in, Mira at his side.

The room was empty of people, leaving him with the impression that the king wanted to talk to them alone. Rectangular stone caskets, like those on the street, lay near the walls, a single bowl of oil feeding a lit wick atop each. On the wall above these tombs, weapons had been mounted. The variety suggested that each entombed man had a penchant for a different instrument of war. And far above, in the heights of the chamber, windows allowed the late hues of sunset to illuminate the eastern wall in patterns of russet light.

The caskets, the weapons, all of it focused toward the room's far end, where three stone steps rose to a platform on which sat a great throne composed entirely of bones.

Sutter couldn't remember ever seeing the bones of a dead man. But to his untrained eye, they were the bones of men.

The great chair had been erected with care, the curve and shape of its hundreds of parts fitted together like a puzzle. It gleamed dully in the light of braziers that burned on either side. It horrified him, and at the same time taught him something about this warrior nation—they revered their dead. At least that was the impression it left on him.

Yet, it chilled him to look at the throne. And it took him a moment to understand why: it was the casual acquaintance with death. He thought he now understood why Vendanj would want Alon'Itol's support at Convocation. But it also felt like there was more to their coming here than requesting an alliance.

They've forgotten who they are.

From behind the Throne of Bones, a giant of a man stepped out and gazed down at them. "Only a fool uses the name Vendanj to call on this throne."

Over his long, oiled hair, the barrel-chested man wore a thick crown of tarnished steel. Its prongs were fashioned in the same gauntlet emblem they'd seen throughout the city. And names had been engraved upon it. While not an ornamental piece of jewelry, it nevertheless answered the question: This was King Jaales Relothian. The smith king.

Mira prepared to speak, but Sutter placed a hand on her shoulder and stepped forward. "The Sheason is your enemy, then?" he asked.

From the depths of his great chest the king bellowed laughter. "Gods, no. There's real salt in Vendanj. But I wouldn't call him a friend, either. Does he even have friends?" The king laughed again.

"He knows Vendanj, all right," Sutter said quietly to Mira. Then he spoke once more to the king. "He was called south by the regent of Vohnce to a Convocation of Seats."

The king came around the Throne of Bones and descended one step of the throne platform. He appraised each of them. "One boy, scarcely old enough to cut his beard, and a Far, come out of the east, arrive at Ir-Caul with the name of Sheason Vendanj on their lips, and talking of Convocation." He pointed at them. Laughed loudly from his chest. "You, my friends, are on a fool's errand."

"You know why we're here, then," Sutter said, his voice strident in the hall.

King Relothian looked down at them. "My young friend. I know why *you* think the Sheason sent you here: to petition that I take my seat in the Hall of Convocation. I received my shrike from the regent, as did all those like me who sit in dry rooms and make *talk* their only weapon. The bird was tasty."

More laughter escaped the king's heavily bearded face.

Perhaps because he was tired, or mocked, or both, Sutter strode forward, placing one foot defiantly on the bottom stair of the throne platform.

"It's not actually taking your seat that brings us here. We know you'd never arrive in time. Convocation may already be done." Sutter made sure the smith king was looking at him when he clarified, "It's pledging *support* to Convocation. Being a part of it."

"I know what it means," Relothian replied in a low, cautioning tone, though still wearing a faint smile.

"I don't think you understand what's at stake." Sutter pulled his other foot up, standing fully now on the lowest step. "Or the sacrifices made just so that we could come here to be laughed at. It's vulgar of you to mock us. What king does that?"

The man's smile faltered, replaced by a heavy glare that showed scars across his brow that Sutter hadn't noticed before. He studied Sutter for several moments.

"For a Sedagin, you're young to be so far from home." He pointed at Sutter's blade. "Let me see it."

Panic ripped through him, but Sutter kept his composure and drew the blade. He'd barely gotten it out of the sheath, when the king spoke.

"You weren't born Sedagin, were you?" Relothian's gaze was locked on Sutter's sword hand.

Sutter couldn't find anything to say, so he just stared and waited.

The king gave a soft laugh. "Your grip is wrong for a Sedagin who grew up learning the longblade technique."

"It doesn't matter who we are," Mira cut in, her voice as calm as it always was. "Your help is needed. We've been sent to ask for it."

Relothian hadn't ceased to look at Sutter's sword hand. "And yet, you have their blade and glove. So either you're one hell of a fighter, who bested a Sedagin and took his things—which would be noteworthy. Or these were given to you, which is *more* noteworthy. What I have little patience for is that Vendanj used these to get to me. Bastard."

The king paused, looking at Sutter as though remembering something. "Don't profane this place with talk of sacrifice, or think whatever you've lost gives you a right to speak here. You don't know sacrifice. You don't even know Vendanj well enough to understand his true intentions in sending you into Alon'Itol." The king looked at Mira, then back at Sutter. "Irreverent boy. Vendanj knew I wouldn't take my seat at Convocation. That's not why he sent you to me." He looked at each of them. "But I think I'd like to find out."

• CHAPTER FORTY-THREE •

Sky Proofs

*Rumor had it that Lour was working a proof . . . of the gods.
Brilliant, crazy bastard. You don't see him around though,
do you? Have to say, zealots got nothing on scientists where
ostracism is concerned. I think he raises corn now.*

—"The Myth of Objectivity," a survey focusing
on self-critique in the science community
following the death of Nanjesho Alanes

TAHN'S THIRD DAY after falling through the Telling
hurt a little less than the day before. A little. He was now
convinced a good part of the pain was simply from the fall,
rather than the Telling itself. He'd enjoyed his cocoon for a
few days. He and Rithy and Polaema talked, ate, talked, and
talked some more. It felt to Tahn like standing beneath a great
falls, knowledge and memory like water crashing down. Connections came at lightning speed, and constantly: astronomical concepts, computation, debates over physical law.

They laughed happily when one of them made a simple
error in logic, then pounced on the problem together to find
new, *unassailable* logic. And through it all, he made liberal
use of the Dimnian study techniques Grant had taught him.

And he moved beyond what he'd known before, practically
swallowing new books whole: Savant Lumen's volume on
the varying qualities of light; a few philosophical tracts on the
Mal people; a theoretical math text by Herbel, a Wynstout
calculist; and another ten or twelve books—he lost count—on
new geomechanical models, entire volumes on skyward observations and phenomena Tahn could never have seen on his
own.

But he grew a bit cabin mad, and needed to get outside.
Needed to get Succession under way. Each day he imagined

the Quiet crossing the Pall. Imagined more wards walking into the Scar with their knives. Desperation stirred him. *Stop the Quiet before everything is Scar.*

Rithy helped him out of bed and led him on a slow, ambling tour to reacquaint him with Aubade Grove. Before leaving her home, he'd instinctively looked for his bow, finding it propped in the corner. He wound up leaving the weapon where it stood, and followed Rithy out.

He estimated the small city to be roughly half a league from one end to the other. Around it, in a great circle, a solid stone wall rose maybe seven strides—enough to form a defense, but not enough to weather a siege. The Grove wasn't likely in any jeopardy of assault, though, since it held neither political significance nor ambition.

The five towers, set in a broad pentagon, rose at the center of the Grove. In fact, the towers were largely the reason for the name, forming an imposing kind of copse on the long plain. Three hundred strides up they went, bearing at their tops not banners or pennants, but great glass domes. For observation. Of the stars. Each tower had a particular focus, too: astronomy, physics, mathematics, philosophy, and cosmology. And each of the five colleges was led by a savant of unparalleled understanding in their area of research and study.

Between each of the towers, lecture halls and libraries had been erected, forming a pentacle at the center of the city. If one wanted to peruse a volume or hear a discourse on a certain subject, they had only to find the halls closest to that tower.

But the Grove wasn't an academy in the way others were. There were students, to be sure. But only a few. And pedagogy wasn't its purpose. *Working* physicists and mathematicians and astronomers lived here. And they placed the highest importance on research and discovery. What few students there were had to contribute to the advancement of their college's body of knowledge, or they were asked to make room for those who could.

Those who were cut loose usually wound up buying drinks for *real* researchers, to try to curry some favor. That, or selling Grove supplies. Things like Ebon-shore lenscrafter sand, shaped loden stones, brass-tooth gearwheels, and sheaves of weathercut—a good paper for recording calculations when the air turns damp. And they often took up trades that served the Grove's purpose. Hard to shake a stick and not hit a bookbinder or ironmonger or glassmaster—the last being former glassblowers turned to lens and mirror work.

And these same merchants often brokered the knowledge produced in the Grove for a healthy sum, shaving a small percentage off before returning the rest to administrators to keep the Grove in lenses and ink.

Beyond the merchant ring were the houses where Grove residents lived. Interspersed throughout were small handcart markets selling fresh beets, potatoes, carrots, butchered hog, wheat, rice, and sometimes wool cloth and ankle-high tanners' footwear. As far as Tahn could tell, the only shops with stone walls in the residential areas were those that traded in the instruments of science.

Despite having to climb a short set of stairs, which proved a bit painful, he insisted on entering Perades, an astronomy mercantile, so named for a meteor shower that came yearly in early autumn. With Rithy supporting one arm, Tahn made his way into the shop.

He paused a few steps past the door, surveying the many tables and shelves around the store. The closest table on the right lay stacked with quadrant maps, lined parchment for making one's own charts, and journals for recording findings. On the same table stood a box filled with graphite sticks, styluses, and vials of ink—black, crimson, cobalt, and green.

Against the wall to the right a series of bookshelves stood, heavily laden with thick volumes whose spines were well creased from many reads. These weren't for sale; it was a lending library of books that hadn't yet been accepted as scientific fact. "Scientific apocrypha" they called it, just to give it a sense of danger. You'd not find these in the larger libraries near the towers. Tahn itched to peruse them.

But his attention quickly passed to the next table, across which astronomical sextants, dioptras, equitoria, and torquetum—all things to measure the position of the stars and moons and sun—had been neatly organized. Tahn shuffled to the table's edge to take a closer look. He could remember Mother Polaema teaching him how to sight in a star and convert the angles to distance and measure its closeness. Countless nights he'd stood out in the chill darkness, a hooded lantern set on the ground to dimly light his charts and personal journal. The memories were strong and comforting.

Then he saw the third table, and fell immediately reverent. Set there in neat rows were astrolabes, astronomical clocks—astraria, Tahn recalled—and at the back side, farthest from the door, a short line of armillary spheres.

My skies . . .

He stood staring at the devices, admiring the spherical framework of metal rings, centered on their world. The rings represented lines of celestial latitude and longitude—the ecliptic, meridians, parallels—circles linking the poles and representing the equator. All to demonstrate and map the motion of the stars as they moved about Aeshau Vaal.

Of course, the Aeshau sphere had been largely replaced with a similar armillary that took the sun as its center. Better science. But he had a fondness for the older instrument that was hard to explain. Perhaps it was little more than him not wanting to see the past made irrelevant.

As he slowly came around the last table, gently fingering these astronomer tools, he took in the scents of polished brass, leather bindings, sanded oak, and the mild aroma of ink.

At the back wall, on a series of hooks, rested at least a dozen skyglasses of varying length and lens and mirror size; in the corner a lone skyglass stood on a tripod, this one twice the length of the others, its glass spanning two hands at the end. Lenscrafting had taken a major leap in the last few decades. The use of Hidan sand off Ebon shores had been found to have an effective scouring quotient for good polish.

Tahn stopped again, overwhelmed with a feeling of being someplace . . . *right*. He'd been young when he'd stood here before, but the years of separation faded more each passing moment.

He smiled at his own nostalgia, and looked up to find *the*

chalkboard on the right-side wall, where it had always been. On it the most recent deep sky findings were noted. Like a running list of winners, numbers and hashmarks beside names told of who had found what and where they'd found it.

And finally, opposite the board, near the left wall, sat a squat desk, where a man nigh onto fifty years old sat waiting patiently for their inquiries.

Tahn tugged Rithy toward the proprietor, feeling the kind of glee a child might when given a surprise gift. As he neared the merchant, the other's brow progressively tightened in the lines of scrutiny. When Tahn came to stand in front of him, the man's knitted brow unfurled, and he stood up with a big, sloppy grin.

"Gnomon, my stars, you're back!" Martin Tye quickly rounded his desk, and had nearly taken Tahn in a mighty embrace before Rithy held up a hand.

"He's hurt," she said. "Best not squeeze him."

Martin's enthusiasm welled up inside him until he finally threw his arms up and hollered, "Welcome, my boy! Welcome!"

His old friend's booming voice brought Shaylas, his wife, from the back room. Dark wavy hair fell past her shoulders. She stood as tall as Tahn, and used a grin to say hello. Seeing her again reminded him of his childhood infatuation with her. He could feel heat rising in his cheeks.

Shaylas was as lean as she'd ever been, and held in her arms a child. It made him think of Sutter to see her with the babe. Martin and Shaylas had traveled and performed with the pageant wagons in their young lives. They'd come to Aubade Grove to play the old stories, and never left. Now they'd begun a family. It was the life Sutter might have written for himself.

"Welcome back, Tahn." Shaylas came close and kissed his cheek.

The whole thing left him a little shaky.

"Oh my skies," Rithy mumbled under her breath.

"A son," Tahn said, looking first at Shaylas, then Martin, who gave an exaggerated smile of pride.

"And why not. We're able-bodied," Martin offered with mock defensiveness.

Shaylas laughed. "I know what's coming next, so I'm going to excuse myself. A pleasure to see you again, Tahn." And she sauntered into the back room, speaking softly to the child as she went.

Tahn smiled, and turned to face his old friend. "It's good to be back, Martin. How are you?"

"That's all you've got to say? You disappear for eight years, then stroll into my shop and ask me, easy as you please, how I've been? I've a mind to smack you with my newest reflecting skyglass."

Tahn remembered that Martin had nearly made a religion of using reflectors, eschewing refracting telescopes as an unnecessary hindrance in observational astronomy.

Martin dashed away and returned with a skyglass that could have been no less in length than hip to toe. Its mirror spanned a full two hands across. "Feast your eyes on that, my boy." He handed the skyglass to Tahn, who took it gently in his fingers. It fit his hand as naturally as his bow did. He desperately wanted to try it, but he hadn't the coin for something this grand, and he couldn't let himself be distracted. What he really needed was to find Polaema. Now that he'd left his cocoon, he had to get started on Succession. Mother Polaema would be the one to help him get it under way.

But the draw proved too strong. He raised the glass and aimed it out the front door, across the street. The mirror pulled in the image of a man standing just inside the shadow of the horology shop across the way. The figure had its unwavering attention trained on Martin's place. Whoever it was couldn't know from this distance—and from outside Perades, no less—that Tahn saw him.

No one knows I'm here, though.

Perhaps he'd left his cocoon too soon.

"Not bad, right?" Martin asked rhetorically.

"Not bad," Tahn agreed, handing back the glass.

"Well, don't get *too* excited," Martin said with heavy sarcasm. "I was planning to make a present of it to you for your return. But—"

Tahn reached out and gently gripped the man by the elbow. "I'm still recovering, Martin. Don't be offended. And there's no need to give away merchandise, even to your best deep sky observer." He smiled.

Martin returned the smile. "Why *are* you back, Gnomon?"

Tahn hesitated a moment, but in the warmth of Martin's smile remembered the man had been as good a friend to him as Rithy. "I'm going to call for a Succession of Arguments."

Martin's smile erupted into agreeable laughter. "Of course you are! And by my best glass, you'll win this time." He started to give Tahn a slap on the back, but remembered Rithy's warning and turned it into a gentle tap. "Let me know if you need some help. I could stand a bit of fun in the theaters."

"I'll do that," Tahn said, imagining that he might, in fact, need Martin at some point—the man considered the discourse theaters where arguments were made as just another stage to play. He then caught a look of Rithy's face. Mention of Succession had stolen the smile she'd been wearing.

A new voice startled them all. "I could use a bit of fun in the theaters, myself."

Tahn turned to see a stranger standing less than two strides away, a pleasant smile on his face. He gave them all a look like he belonged to their conversation.

"Darius Franck," Rithy said, announcing the man. "Philosopher. Leagueman. Jackass."

Tahn kept himself from laughing.

"Ah, Gwen Alanes." Darius stepped forward, pulling gloves from his hands one finger at a time. "It's very interesting to hear you're going to be party to a Succession. Given your unfortunate history with the process."

Martin raised one of his beefy limbs. "You can close your gob, if you're going to use it that way. These here are friends of mine, and I don't give a piss for anyone in my place who won't respect that."

Darius held up his arms as one being robbed. "Peace. Peace. I was entitled to one barb for the jackass comment, wouldn't you say?"

Martin held his tongue on that, but had a cudgel-like hold on his skyglass.

Darius looked Tahn up and down once. "So this is Tahn SeFerry? Refiner of skyglass parabolas. Finder of planets who lose their way. Kissing boy for savants in their glass towers. Skittish mule who runs when things get tragic."

Martin lifted the skyglass threateningly.

Tahn put a hand on the glass, gently pushing it down. "You have me at a disadvantage. All I know about you is you're a jackass."

"I believe Gwen said philosopher and leagueman," Darius corrected.

"That's what I said." Tahn smiled and drew the moment out for effect. ". . . jackass."

"I see." Darius cleared his throat and set his feet like an orator—probably the only offensive stance he knew. "Then, you'd know nothing about another young man by the name of Tahn Junell who goes about shooting children and dismissing it as an unfortunate circumstance of battle."

The Quiet don't always fight in open battle, Vendanj had said. *They will use our own kind against us, spread rumors.*

Tahn marveled that the rumors had spread this far in just a few handfuls of days. But he didn't marvel long. The effect of the verbal barb was like a coward's punch—made while one's opponent isn't looking—and left Tahn a bit dumbstruck.

"What do you want, Darius?" Rithy made his name sound like a blight on all of philosophy.

"Answers," he said glibly. "There are stories on the road. And then our long-lost astronomer shows up seeking a Succession of Arguments. I'm just trying to reconcile these rather disparate happenings."

Tahn finally found his voice. "Makes sense to me."

"Ah, a reasonable fellow," Darius said, his tone thick with condescension.

"Of course, that's the work of philosophy." Tahn gestured comically. "Since you don't actually do any real science, you feel it's your place to reconcile the work of those who do. Perfectly understandable."

Darius's smile never faltered. "And yet we occupy and manage twenty percent of Grove assets—"

"Sounds like you ought to be a moneylender," Tahn said, smiling back.

Darius was nodding the way a man does when he's enjoying a good debate. "What will be your topic for Succession, then, if I may ask?"

"Well, see, I'd explain it to you, but it involves theoretical math. And it sounds to me like you're best with share numbers and profit margins. How's the Grove export business these days on philosophy tracts. Brisk? Or does the Grove make her money on actual scientific knowledge . . . as. It always. Has."

Martin spewed laughter, sending a sizeable bit of spittle onto Darius's forehead. The philosopher removed a kerchief as decorously as possible and wiped the spit away, making a gift of the kerchief to Martin.

Amazingly, he'd never lost his smile. It grew more tense, appearing harder to keep on—Tahn figured it was because of the spittle—but if he were any judge, the prospect of a worthy rival actually thrilled Darius.

"I love a good mystery to solve as much as anyone," said Darius, "even a murdering astronomer. I'll wait for the formal announcement, then. And I have to tell you"—he leaned in toward Tahn—"I hope you get past the Colleges of Physics and Mathematics."

"Because you think I'll lose to the College of Philosophy in turn?" Tahn surmised, shaking his head at the obviousness.

"No," Darius said, clapping him on the back. "Because you'll lose to *me*. I'm the lead panelist for Succession in our college."

"Is that all, then?" Tahn asked, clapping Darius on the back in return.

Darius trimmed his smile to something more officious. "Well, not really; you see, I'm here in a somewhat formal capacity."

"Oh?" Rithy rounded on Darius.

"Yes, and not as a philosopher, which should please you, but as a member of the League." Darius stepped closer to

Tahn, his expression becoming serious. He looked at Rithy and Martin. "Did you know Tahn here is a friend to known outlaws and exiles? He, himself, has recently been held in the pits of Solath Mahnus. I'm the ranking leagueman in the Grove, and my charge is to help keep her safe, administer her laws." He gave a thin smile. "And I will do just that . . . with every means at my disposal."

"Threats? In an astronomy shop?" Tahn laughed. "How long have you been waiting to catch me out in public?"

Darius's face brightened to its former jovial look. "Just so we're clear, my friend. The politics of the Grove are unique. A complex mix of science and law. Let's keep you on the right side of things, shall we? You wouldn't want to jeopardize whatever Succession you plan to bring."

The threat in Darius's last words hit Tahn hard.

Darius then bowed to Rithy, saluted Martin, and tapped his temple in farewell to Tahn. *Keep your wits,* he seemed to be saying.

Darius positively strolled from Perades, whistling as he went. When he was gone, the astronomy shop seemed rather too quiet.

"Well, you *were* the best, my young friend," Martin observed, jokingly.

"He's that good?" Tahn asked.

Rithy answered for them both, "I hate to say it, but yes." She then turned to him. "When were you planning to tell us about these fascinating friends of yours—outlaws, exiles?"

Tahn pointed after Darius. "He makes it sound quite different from the reality."

"As he will to Grove savants, if we give him an excuse," Rithy countered.

"Okay, peace. I'll give you the lowdown on all my friends, since it's of such great interest." He smiled. "But I wouldn't worry about it."

Martin put a hand on Tahn's shoulder. "Just mind that bit about jeopardizing Succession. Darius might be able to do it. Walk on your toes."

"Well, let's not get ahead of ourselves. We haven't even

asked for Succession yet." Tahn was feeling rather in good spirits.

"Right. And we need to catch you up if you're going to get back in the game." Martin showed a competitive grin and ushered Tahn to the chalkboard behind him. "Let's get right to it, shall we?"

Martin stroked his thin grey beard, a glint of glee and caution in his eyes as he looked around his shop, making sure they were alone. Afterward, he raised a hand and fingered a simple hook latch on one side of the chalkboard. With a slight push, the chalkboard rolled up, revealing a second slate behind it. Another wave of remembrance hit Tahn, who'd seen this hidden board before, long ago.

Martin said nothing, allowing Tahn to read what had been written there in yellow chalk. The observations were coupled with several mathematical equations. Beside him, Tahn heard Rithy make a sound in her throat. Surprise? Concern?

They were computations that might explain the stray course of Pliny Soray—the cause of her departure from her orbit.

He turned to Martin. "Are you the only one who knows this? Why do you keep it hidden?"

His old friend laid a finger aside his nose. "That, my young friend, is a very good question. And one I'll happily answer. But not here. Not now. You go about your way, and keep remembering what is left unremembered, and if you still want to know, find me after any sundown in any of the usual places."

Tahn studied the numbers a while more. His math wasn't as strong as Martin's, and certainly not as strong as Rithy's, but what he thought he saw there might tie to the reason the Quiet were able to cross the Pall and attack Naltus. Might tie to Pliny Soray's stray course.

Martin then held out a small ring dial—a kind of portable version of an armillary sundial. "You'll let me give you this much, eh?"

Tahn smiled and took the dial, a simple tool to mark the time. The rings folded flat so that it could be carried in the pocket, but that was not why Martin had given it to him.

He could see it in the man's eyes as Tahn stowed the ring inside his shirt. This dial had a movable gnomon to cast its shadow. The advantage of such a tool is that the gnomon didn't have to be aligned with the celestial poles. The meaning of the gift was clear, and a bit like Martin himself—since he hated to be forced to align with anything.

Tahn's smile widened. "Itinerant gnomon for an itinerant Gnomon. Clever."

Rather unceremoniously, Martin pulled down the outer chalkboard, latched it, and returned to his desk, where he placed spectacles on this nose and bent forward to stare into a quadrant map.

Tahn smiled at this, too. Rithy, though . . . she still had a look of concern, staring at the chalkboard as if she still saw the math on the hidden slate.

Looking with her, Tahn suddenly noticed the scrawl on the top piece of slate. "Martin, is this right?"

His old friend looked up from his map as Tahn pointed. "Ayeah. Somewhat rare, but not nearly as interesting as what I showed you on the inner slate." His nose returned to his map.

"What?" Rithy said, obviously hearing the concern in his voice. "It shows the date and time of the lunar eclipse."

"But of the second moon," Tahn said. "I saw the eclipse of the first moon not long ago. They don't usually follow one another like this."

"No," she agreed. "But like Martin said, it's not *unheard of,* either."

Tahn stared at the slate, probing for connections. The first lunar eclipse had occurred when the Quiet came to Naltus. If these two things were related, then that eclipse had brought thousands of Quiet through the Veil. And the second moon, Ardua, while smaller in the night sky, was denser. Tides flowed farther in and out at her phases. If his budding supposition held any merit, they needed to get to work. And fast. In part because of Ardua, but more so because of the observations scrawled on the secret slate. And they were on a fixed clock until the next eclipse. Until another Quiet army . . .

"Let's go," he said, and got moving. His muscles protested his vigor, but he struggled through the pain. There were inquiries to make, and it felt damn good to be about it.

He'd forgotten the man standing across the street before they'd even left Perades.

• CHAPTER FORTY-FOUR •

Everything's a Fight

The dysphonic vocal approach is often considered only a battle technique. Not so. Think of it more as "unyielding." In that light, it has every use you can imagine.

—Advanced Vocal Theory, Descant Cathedral, a rare course of instruction, premised off of Mor stylings

WENDRA ENTERED THE music room to find Belamae sitting in a lone chair amidst the clutter and wreckage of yesterday's vocal lesson. Most regrettably, the beautiful old instruments had been destroyed. He waited with a sullen look as though he'd been there a long time, thinking. To one side, Telaya knelt, gathering pieces of a shattered lute—something she did with care.

"That will do, Telaya." Belamae was nodding. "Leave it be."

"But Maesteri, the instruments need to be gathered—"

"I'll see to it," he told her. "But thank you."

Telaya nodded deferentially, stood, and started across the room. When she came abreast of Belamae she stopped. "Will you be coming?"

"Soon," he said. "Have Luela look after Dalyn and make him comfortable until we arrive." He then wiped his forehead with a kerchief.

Telaya leaned in. "Maesteri, are you all right?"

After a moment he smiled and put a reassuring hand on her arm. "I'll be fine."

Telaya nodded, and before leaving the music room, shot Wendra a look of contempt.

Once the door shut behind her, Wendra sighed with relief. "I'm not making a lot of friends."

Belamae smiled as he said, "Telaya's been assigned as your personal music mentor."

"Oh, wonderful."

His smile widened some. "Telaya's only real affection is music. And she works harder than most—maybe harder than anyone—at perfecting the techniques we teach her." He cocked his head a moment. "Hard to fault her for that, I guess. But she's Lyren—doesn't have the Leiholan gift—which is something she simmers about."

"Seemed more than that," Wendra observed.

"It's been a rough morning already." Belamae shuffled into a new position behind a harpsichord. "One of the Leiholan, Dalyn, fell during Suffering. The Song got the better of him. He had to be replaced."

Belamae seemed done with the topic, as he poised to run a scale on the harpsichord. She interrupted before he could begin.

"Maesteri, I'm sorry about yesterday. I didn't—"

"Never mind about it," Belamae returned dismissively. "I told you, training Leiholan has its risks."

She wasn't quite sure how to ask, but she needed to know. "I saw your song. I saw—I heard—how you reshaped Suffering . . . for war."

Belamae lowered his hands to his lap, his eyes becoming distant and apologetic.

"We started our resonance with your mother, didn't we?" He paused, staring at her now with some sympathy. "I will restore your memory, so that you might have more of the parents you've lost. But later, after our day's lesson. Right now, we have music to make."

She quickly sat beside him, resting a hand over his fingers before he could start to play. "You showed my mother how to use Suffering as a weapon. In case she needed to protect us."

He reversed their hands, firmly clasping hers between his own. "I loved your mother. As much as her father did, I loved her. I couldn't bear the thought of what might happen. . . ." He cleared his throat. "It was a mistake, though. My own mistake. When I was your age, I took Suffering and went back to my own country to answer war's call. I misused the Song. And when I'd returned and started to train Leiholan . . . I had a moment of weakness. I shared what I'd learned with Vocencia." He gave her a steady, unquestioning look. "I won't make that mistake again." And that was the end of it.

And yet, she could still hear part of his Suffering song. It wasn't a sound she could forget. Nor would she want to.

He visibly shook off the heavy effects of their conversation. "You and I, though, we still need to get to attunement. To resonance. Here, let me show you."

Belamae pointed toward a fiddle a few strides away whose neck and body lay shattered after yesterday's lesson. He began to sing, and the broken instrument rattled and rose into the air. It held there a few moments. Then he ended his song, and the fiddle fell back to the floor with a soft crunch and atonal bark.

"All I did there was sing the resonance of this room, the air, the wood and gut and bone of the instrument. I influenced what I needed to, to move it, raise it. The material the fiddle was made of responded to these vibrations. Now, observe."

He began to sing again. This time, the fiddle shuddered, rose, and slowly the fragments of wood began to draw themselves together again. Over the course of a few moments, the fiddle re-formed itself, appearing just as it had been. The strings pulled taut and began to hum. Belamae then softly ended his song, and the instrument fell again into its shattered pieces on the floor.

"Can you tell me the difference?" he asked.

Wendra couldn't take her eyes off the fiddle, but she knew. "You sang the fiddle's song," she said. "You found resonance with more than the fiddle's materials. You found resonance with the *idea* of the fiddle. Its own vibrations."

When she finally returned her gaze to the old man, he was smiling. "Precisely so. The oldest laws, Wendra, are that matter can be neither created nor destroyed, only changed or made new. By finding the vibrations that exist in the combination of wood and strings, all the things that give it"— he smiled—"its fiddle-ness, I restored it to itself, if only briefly."

Wendra nodded, excited. "But why didn't you leave it whole?"

"Oh, that's just me. I enjoy instrument repair the old way. I'll show you my lutherie sometime." He waved a hand for them to move on. "Now I want you to remember our goal is Suffering. That song has its name because the Leiholan who sings it must give voice to an awful series of historical events—the entire story of those who were placed inside the Bourne. There's languor and war in parts. And plenty of real suffering. You'll need to sing that. Resonate with it. Like I did with that fiddle there."

It awed her, thrilled her, and gave her a sense of dread she couldn't explain, just like the first hunting knife given her by her da. She'd been happy and proud and excited, and then realized what that knife was for.

"But here's what you must know, Wendra." Belamae held up a finger of warning, his countenance darkening. "Every time you sing in resonance with something, or someone, your own vibration changes, ever so slightly."

This time, she understood perfectly the lesson, even before he said it.

"It is the nature of song. The nature of Suffering. It's always changing—"

"Is that why Soluna died?" The words were out before she could think better of them.

He regarded her a long moment. "I don't think so," he finally said. "And before you ask, I don't *know* why she died. Except that Suffering's demands grow. They always have."

"I meant no disrespect."

He smiled the smile of a patient teacher. "I know. The point is that song is never stagnant. And so the effects of attunement, of resonating with a fiddle or me . . . or anything, will not only cause the change in what you sing to, but will shape your own life's song. By degrees, of course. But that's why I worry for you. Because just as you can do this to restore, you can do it to destroy."

Wendra thought about the battle on the Soliel. "I've already done that."

"No. You haven't." He shook his head once. "Oh, you're filled with dark vibrations, sure enough. And we'll work on that. But what you've done is more like raising the broken parts of a fiddle. You've yet to find the resonance of a thing and truly sing it."

With some reticence, she asked, "If I sing the resonance of another person, what will happen?"

"That will depend on your intent. We'll have a whole lesson on intent soon enough." Then he nodded the way her da used to when he needed to explain something undesirable. "For now, understand this: Once you're attuned, and can identify the resonant vibration of a thing, it's possible to sing in tune or *out of tune* with that vibration. We call the former harmony. We call the latter dissonance. The effect can alter the very nature of the thing you're singing to or about . . . can end it entirely."

The way Belamae used the word "entirely" left a feeling of cold dread in the pit of her stomach. Then his eyebrows went up again as he emphasized his next words.

"And every time you tear down or destroy, *your* life's vibrations are altered in a way that make *you* more dissonant; while each time your song lifts or inspires, the vibration of the song that is you becomes a more powerful melody."

She nodded understanding, thinking about all the times she'd wrought song to tear down.

Belamae offered her a reassuring smile. "I tell you this so that you see the responsibility you bear with this Leiholan gift."

"Is it too late to give it back?" She raised her brows with the questioning jest.

Belamae laughed hard from his belly. His laugh was cut short by a pained expression and a series of hard coughs. He took a moment to compose himself. "Just so," he finally said. "Now, becoming attuned is the great first step. It will make your song stronger. Give you more control." He paused a long moment. "Even if you decide not to stay with us at Descant. Which is something, my girl, I hope you are no longer considering. We very much need you here."

She looked back at him. And said nothing. She did want to learn all there was to know about being Leiholan. And she wanted to learn and sing Suffering. But few hours passed when she didn't think about the people captured and sold into the Bourne. Like she and Penit had nearly been. She couldn't stop feeling as though she should do something about that. That she *could*. And maybe more so after some time spent here with Belamae. Perhaps learn more about *his* song, the one she'd found in him during their moments of resonation.

Belamae then nudged her to stand up. "It's time for another practical lesson."

Wendra stood, feeling unsure. "You think I'm ready for this."

Without another word, he led her from the room and on a long, silent walk through Descant. They passed countless doors behind which music instruction and performance of such vigor and variety was taking place that she wanted to stop, ask a hundred questions. Down stairs, across atriums, through tunnel-like corridors they went. She'd be lost on her own. Eventually, they came to a door, one in a private-quarters area she hadn't visited before, though she knew this to be where Leiholan lived.

He gave her a single, searching look before ducking into this private chamber and motioning her inside. A man roughly the age of thirty lay in his bed, sleeping fitfully. At his side sat an older woman, cooling his skin with a rag dipped in a water basin on the bed table. On the far side of the room Telaya sat writing in a ledger; she looked up at Belamae and Wendra, open disapproval on her face.

Belamae drew near the bed. "How is he, Luela?"

The older woman kept at her task of cooling his forehead and cheeks with her rag. "He's in no mortal danger. But I haven't been able to use the sickness to ferret a cause for what happened in Suffering. He's got a fever I can't break with willow or balsa root. He sleeps, and can't be roused."

Belamae nodded, then motioned Wendra to his side. "This is Dalyn. One of our newest Leiholan. Though don't mistake new for weak." He paused, putting a hand on the man's chest. "Still, he fell sick while singing Suffering this morning."

Her stomach dropped. "You want me to try and take away the sickness, don't you?"

"That's the wrong way to think about it." He showed her his patient smile. "I want you to resonate with him and the idea of health. Draw on your own sense of well-being."

"What if it . . . goes *wrong*?"

"I'll be here." He placed his free hand on her shoulder. "But if you're to sing Suffering, I need you attuned. And not just for dissonant effect. Do you understand?"

"The practical lesson is to restore rather than tear down," she said. "Something besides *my* song."

He shook his head. "It's *all* your song, Wendra. You've just chosen a particular refrain most of the time. Sing something new today. Something Dalyn." His smile brightened, and he moved aside, gently nudging her closer.

Wendra sat at the man's bedside. *I can't do this.* She cleared her mind. If she was going to fail, it wasn't going to be because of doubt. For several moments she studied his face, searching for an entry melody. Finding nothing, she started as she often did when singing something new—she sang her song box melody.

The box had been a gift from her mother. Its melody had been how she healed herself that first time in the caves beneath the Sedagin plain. And several phrases into the song, she found a new course. She imagined the pressure of Suffering. She imagined Soluna, the Leiholan who'd died under that pressure. And note by note, her melody grew. It started to come in bold phrases, the way fight songs do. She lent strength and volume to it, not caring that it sounded too loud for the little room. What she sang wasn't the simple restoration of health. It was a challenge to sickness, a declaration of wholeness inviolate.

She inclined, singing loud into Dalyn's face. She thought for a moment she could feel the sickness pushing back, wrestling with her for purchase over Dalyn. She sang louder. She invoked the roughness of her song. Dysphonia, Belamae called it. She got up onto the bed, nearer this sick Leiholan, and shouted down her song not a finger's breadth from his nose and mouth. She was challenging this godsdamned sickness. This sickness in Suffering that put him down! She called with her shout-song for Dalyn's strength to return.

And a moment later his eyes fluttered open, a broad smile lighting his eyes and mouth. It was as though he'd heard every screamed note and was thankful as all hell. He reached up and took her in a bearish embrace. There was certainly no lingering weakness in his arms.

When he let her go, he turned to Belamae, his wry grin a mark of approval. "Leiholan?"

Belamae didn't seem to hear him. "Fight song. I'll be damned. You made even health a battle."

She shrugged. "Seems to have worked."

He laughed hard at that. "Used your mother's song as a start, too." His eyes lit when he mentioned Vocencia. "Come. One last thing for you and me."

They said good-byes. Telaya gave an appropriate level of thanks, a cool reserve still in her voice and expression. Then, in the hall, Belamae took Wendra by the arm.

"Now it's time for you to remember your mother . . . entirely. Vocencia, more than any Leiholan I ever taught, understood what I'm trying to teach you."

Wendra had forgotten about having her memory restored. Hearing her mother's name again brought another rush of sadness for stolen memories. The Maesteri didn't wait for a better time or place. He guided her to a seat in the hallway, and promptly began to sing. It was a soft, slow air, sung with tenderness and a pang of loss, but also of glad remembrance.

She found herself swept away, the present moment lost, and a kind of emptiness filling her mind. Then, slowly, like a flower blooming in the rays of daybreak, images drew into focus, and bittersweet feelings consumed her.

• CHAPTER FORTY-FIVE •

The Uses of Youth

*There's more to be learned from what an adversary won't
do, than what he will.*

—Maxim from *Exposing Indicative Behavior,* a recovered
text from the east of Mal'Tara, now in the possession of
League leadership

THE MEALHOUSE HAD been cleared for Roth's meeting
with the envoy from Estem Salo. He wanted privacy
for the discussion that would follow. Helaina was having
him watched by her Emerit guard, so meeting in a public
place where his own men could secure the doors and windows was the safest course. When he finally entered the hall
and saw the very young woman, he did something he rarely
did. In taking her hand, he placed his left palm over their
clasped fingers. It was a rare sign of warmth and familiarity that would put the young politician at ease.

"Let's sit," he said graciously, extending an arm.

A long table had already been set with plates. Warm wheat
bread generously spread with butter steamed beside pitchers
of cool water flavored with slices of cucumber. The young
woman smiled and took a seat at the head of the table.
Assuming a dominant leadership position.

But it was an amateur tactic. She'd been sent, no doubt,
because she was bright. But he guessed she wasn't seasoned
at politics.

As he sat along one side, in the middle, where he could turn
to face each of them as the need dictated, other Sheason sat
next to and across from him. His own Jurshah leaders filled
out the rest of the seats.

"Now then," he began, tearing a piece of bread and passing
it along, "I'm Roth Staned." He deliberately left his title out.

A half grin tugged at the young woman's face. He wondered if she smiled so he could see that she was keen to his desire to keep things informal. At first, anyway.

"I'm Ketrine. My friends and I are here at the request of Thaelon Solas." The woman took the bread handed to her and tore a piece.

"Your Randeur," Roth clarified. "I don't wish to sound ungrateful or overstep myself, but did he not come himself due to the troubles Sheason are having . . . internally?"

Ketrine laughed so delicately that it almost disarmed him. Almost. "Skies, no. Not any more than the difficulties the League is having with the many inquests it's facing."

Roth kept his composure, but was ready to accuse her of rendering to divine this information, when Nama, his political advisor, cleared her throat. "The regent published the inquests earlier today. The entire city knows we're under scrutiny."

In response, he turned to Ketrine. "I'm somewhat embarrassed. But this will pass. Our fraternity is swelling, and our influence attracts suspicion." He shifted his focus, scanning the other Sheason. "I assume this is why you've come to see us. To seek our help with something?" His tone sounded of invitation and readiness to help.

It was Ketrine who spoke—the youngest of the Sheason envoy at the table, and clearly the one the others deferred to. "In some ways, *we* have come to help *you*. But that's not the whole of it. And I don't expect full bellies to make our request any more palatable to you, so I'll simply share Thaelon's proposal."

Roth took a bite of his bread and chewed through his smile, putting on his best ordinary look. "I like your honesty. How can we help?"

She leveled her eyes with serious intent, but spoke in an unhurried and unsettling calm. "We can no longer suffer Sheason deaths. They have to stop. This means the Civilization Order must be repealed."

He gave her a look of surprise, but not at the request, exactly. "You realize that the League didn't pass this law alone. We certainly raised our hand to it. But it was ratified by the High Council. I can't speak for—"

"The League proposed the law. And you lead the League." Ketrine took a sip of water. "You can call for a retraction. And in exchange, Thaelon will commit the resources of Estem Salo to help build the schools and physic shelters and trade academies the League is working to establish across the East-lands."

The offer stunned him. He sat staring at the young woman, remembering suddenly the reason he'd begun his deliberate ascent through League ranks in the first place. How much faster, and better, could he see his desires fulfilled if this of-fer was true.

Ketrine pressed on. "For our part, we'll continue to exer-cise discretion in our use of the Will, since this is the center of our quarrel. But we won't *stop* rendering when it is in the in-terest of those who need our help. That *will* continue as a companion to the work we do with the League in these other ways."

This last bit snapped Roth out of his momentary reverie. *Rendering. Dependence.* He took a moment to drink from his own cup, preparing his thoughts.

"You're rather direct, my young lady. May I ask," he said, swallowing, and giving each Sheason a quick look, "what if we say no? What if we believe we don't need your help? Or that the Sheason should fade in the same way the First Fathers have faded—into the pews of the mausoleums we call churches."

Ketrine raised her cup as though he'd issued a toast. "Then we remain at odds. Which, I imagine, means that eventually we'll fight openly. If the Quiet haven't come and put an end to *all* our quarrels."

Roth put his cup down, nodding as though he'd fully ex-pected this. "Is that your true intention? An alliance to stand against these people from beyond the Pall?"

The woman took a long moment to study him. He could see that she didn't believe he was ignorant about the reality of the Quiet. Humanizing them, though. Calling them *people.* He looked forward to her reaction to that.

She leaned forward, continuing to chew casually. "My father is Thaelon," she began.

He hoped she didn't see the delight it gave him to hear it.

"I don't share that as a threat. I share it in the spirit of earnestness. We need to find compromise between the League and Sheason. My father wants that." She stopped, seeming to consider her next move. "And you should want it, too. Whether or not the Quiet come, you should want it. But let me tell you," she leveled a grave look on him, "whatever you choose to believe lives beyond the Pall, they don't have kind feelings for you. Or for me. Or any of us. You should trust me on this."

Roth did a fair job of maintaining his nonchalance. But if anything anyone had ever said to him about the nature of the Quiet struck him, it was this. He couldn't say why. Maybe it was because the young woman didn't behave like a politician. She didn't seem to care about repercussions. She seemed only to care about getting to the heart of matters. Which he applauded. But which he could also manipulate.

With a nod, Losol stepped from a rear shadow and put a knife in the back of one of the Sheason. It wasn't a mortal insertion, but a painful one. The man cried out, his back arching. Losol slid back with two graceful steps, sheathed his knife, and drew his sword.

The table around Roth erupted as Sheason sprang to their feet, chairs clattering back. His Jurshah leaders did the same, falling into a vague line behind Losol as the air thickened and took on a faint hum.

A focused push of force swept past him, riffling his collar, as it struck at Losol. Roth saw one of the Sheason's hands draw in and thrust forward again. But these bursts of Will broke and faltered against Losol's sword. There were no bright lights or shouts of pain. Just a warm wind that dissipated to nothing.

The wounded Sheason slipped to the ground. Seeing him fall, two of the other Sheason, both seated nearest their fallen fellow, raised upturned palms toward Losol. A moment later, the others joined them. All but Ketrine. She'd gotten to her feet, a look of concern and frustration on her face.

She can't render, Roth concluded. *Oh, this is lovely.*

The young diplomat hunkered low and rushed to her

friend's aid. She examined the wound, pressing a cloth against it, and nodding in reassurance. She'd recognized that it wasn't fatal. Would she think Losol a bad assassin, or recognize it for the ploy it was? Didn't matter. Roth sat in that suspended moment, as one might at a mummers' play, waiting for the rest to unfold.

All the Sheason, save the one who'd fallen, were now showing the same stance. They were combining their efforts. The floor began to rattle. Dust streamed from the rafters above. Lamp flames inside their glass guttered, a few extinguishing. Windows cracked, glass tinkling to the floor. Bottles fell, smashing into liquid pools filled with shards. And the wood of the mealhouse groaned. Roth fought to take a breath. They were like bugs in amber. A few of his Jurshah leaders looked about them, real concern in their faces. Only Losol kept a steady, unwavering focus. And a thin smile. His sword still held forward like a shield.

"Enough." Ketrine stood, and said again with equal calm, "Enough."

Neither side heeded her, but the fight did not escalate, either.

She turned to Roth. "An overzealous leagueman, no doubt. Not a sanctioned action."

She was giving him an excuse. This young woman was exceptional at diplomacy. Roth made his best apologetic smile. "That's right. My deepest regret for his rashness."

He held up a hand for Losol and the others to lower their weapons, which they did, slowly. "Losol?" he said, with a clear question in his voice.

"I thought I saw the man rendering where you couldn't see. A hand gesture like they do when they command a heart to go still." Losol wasn't good at faking sincerity, and fortunately he wasn't trying. "I took him for an assassin, Your Leadership. There was no other choice."

Ketrine didn't address Losol; she spoke directly to Roth. "This man is either a dullard, or a liar. The only real question is whether he acted on his own authority," she paused, fixing him with an iron stare, "or someone else's. You're telling me it's his own zeal, and I will take you at your word."

Roth didn't let the smile touch his face. She knew. And she was looking past the incident in hopes of fulfilling her father's desire to have the Civilization Order repealed.

He nodded as she spoke. And when she'd finished, he showed her a different kind of regret. "There's a law against rendering in this city." He sighed as though it pained him to say it. "A law that comes with a heavy penalty."

Ketrine took slow steps toward him, drawing near. She was two hands shorter than he was, but it didn't feel that way. He doubted she could be intimidated at all.

"I've looked past a murder attempt. Also something that comes with a heavy penalty. What we saw," she said in a voice loud enough that all could hear, "was the League Ascendant trying to kill a Sheason who came with an offer of peace. Reconciliation. Five witnesses to this." She turned her cool stare on Losol. "You have interesting weapons, Roth. They turn aside the effects of the Will. At least until we adapt to them." She looked back at him with cold assurance. "And we *will* adapt. So, now, what shall it be?"

Roth let none of his thoughts give him away. His showed her a patient expression as he began, "I can't, of course, make promises on my own. I'll need time to talk with others who will need to vote on this. But here's how you can help." He put a hand out and gently squeezed her elbow—another sign of warmth and familiarity. "Write me a letter of endorsement. Set down what you told me: the Sheason commitment to the League ideals of training and schools and physic shelters. I can share these with those I'll need to convince—"

"I'll go with you," she said. "It'll carry more weight if they hear it from me."

Roth was shaking his head. "No, in fact some of the Council members are fearful of your order. They wouldn't receive you." Her offer dismissed, he continued. "Maybe a hundred copies of the letter I mention. Something we can carry into all the places that need our help."

Ketrine fell silent for a moment, appraising him. "You'll have these letters once the Civilization Order is repealed. Until then, one copy. To use with your Council."

"Fair enough," he said. "And it's a good bargain for

Thaelon. Not simply because of a change in the law. Your fellowship is distrusted and feared in most places. You know this, don't you?"

"That, my new friend Roth, is the propaganda of the League." She smiled so imperceptibly that it nearly aroused him. "And part of what you will set down in a letter that expresses League commitment to repairing the damage done to our reputation. In fact," she added with satisfaction, "you'll want to write about how you'll stand in defense of Sheason if and when it's necessary."

Roth returned her thin smile. "It'll be hard for us. You have the better of the compromise." He patted her arm. "But I'd have it no other way."

The letters from the Sheason would help Roth open territories that had resisted League presence. And he'd get them, despite having no intention of repealing Civilization.

The Sheason lowered their hands. The hum and rattle stopped. One of the women turned and put her hands on her wounded companion's back, healing it.

"All's right again," he said, clapping his hands together. "Now, it's late. I have things to attend to, and you'll want to rest. Losol," he said, calling his war leader forward, "as a sign of good faith, you'll escort our new friends to a safe place to wash and rest."

"We don't need a guard." Ketrine looked up into Losol's Mal features, scrutinizing him closely but with dispassion.

"Of course not. I'm simply playing a good host," Roth said. "You'll allow me, won't you?"

She extended a hand, waiting for him to take it in token of an agreement. Roth did so, offering a small, deferential bow. "Rest up," he said. "We'll talk soon."

The Sheason and the daughter of the Randeur followed Losol out of the mealhouse, as Roth smiled wide at his good fortune.

CHAPTER FORTY-SIX

First Sodalist

Some say darkness breathes.

—Unattributed folk saying

NIGHT HAD FALLEN. The streets of Recityv resembled a festival now more than they had during the day. Opportunists had flooded the city with the start of Convocation. Braethen took to alleys to avoid the crowds. Vendanj had suggested he visit the First Sodalist of Recityv, Rochard E'Sau. But he'd have been headed there anyway. *Ask the person who knows,* his father used to say. And with what Braethen had learned about his sword and the origins of the Sodality, he had questions.

He took only a few wrong turns before finding the narrow alley that led to the rear entrance of the Sodality manor. The frenetic hum of the city faded behind him as he found the locked gate. He climbed the fence and crossed a small inner court, set around with chairs, to the door.

He knocked softly and waited. Nothing. The windows were dark, but they'd been dark the last time he'd visited here. Since the Civilization Order, the Sodality had been forced to maintain a low profile, assuming their every move was watched, scrutinized.

After several moments, Braethen simply tried the latch. The door opened. He found it slightly odd, believing they'd observe simple precautions like a locked door. But he slipped inside and quietly closed the door before turning to view the kitchen.

No lingering smells of supper hung on the air. All was still and quiet. Everything appeared in order, properly placed. And yet Braethen had the feeling something was wrong. Tonight, there should have been lighted lamps, evening talk, sodalists reading and studying, especially with Convocation under way. But as Braethen moved through the first story of the large house, he found the sitting room and small library as dark and empty as the kitchen.

He quietly walked the entire ground floor, and came to the base of a stairway. Looking up into shadows, he hesitated. As a boy, he'd been afraid of the dark. Bad afraid. Maybe because he'd read so many of his father's books about evil lurking unseen. He smiled, defying the old fear, and began to climb the steps. Though he did place his feet at the far side of each step, near the wall, to try to avoid creaking stairs.

Slowly he climbed into deeper darkness. He reached the second story, where heavy drapes hung over windows, blocking ambient light from the street and sky beyond. Panic grew inside his mind. He tried to reason through it; he wasn't a child anymore, afraid of the dark. There were *real* fears in his life now.

Logic didn't help.

As quietly as he could, he drew his sword. Then he began to creep down the hall, peering into rooms whose doors all stood open. As his eyes fully adjusted to the gloom, he recognized these rooms as personal quarters for sodalists: beds and drawers and writing desks. Braethen passed another small reading area, two large bookshelves standing like silent sentinels, forgotten in the shadows.

Relief filled him when he'd fully searched the second floor. And found nothing. He then came to another set of stairs rising to the third and last story. Smiling didn't work this time. He stood there, paralyzed.

What little light shone around window drapes only seemed to make the darkness more complete. His tried to rationalize his feelings, convince himself of his foolishness. But he'd seen too many living nightmares since leaving the Hollows not to be apprehensive. His heart drummed—a warning, urging him to flee. The heavy silence seemed unnatural. Perhaps the manor was empty precisely because of this heavy silence. Wise sodalists had run from what he could only describe as a density of dread. It compacted the very air he breathed.

Sweat beaded and ran down his cheeks; perspiration slickened his grip on his sword. He panted, finding it hard to fill his lungs.

And still . . . he began to climb.

The stairs beneath him groaned twice as he ascended into another layer of darkness. The sound of it seemed loud in the silence. If someone or something lay in wait, they'd know now that he was coming. He paused at the last step and looked down a long hall identical to the one he'd just searched. Doors stood open, like black gaping maws on either side of the corridor.

Looking the other way, Braethen saw more doors and rooms, equally still and abandoned.

Could they all be at some event together? I'm jumping at shadows. Calm yourself!

Chastizing himself didn't help. His heart raced faster, and he switched his blade to his other hand long enough to wipe dry his palm and the weapon's handle. On a table close by rested another lamp. He thought to light it, wondering if light could dispel the dread that gripped him. But that would truly alert whatever was here, and he'd need both his hands if he encountered an intruder. He hoped the darkness concealed him as much as it did anything else.

He smiled nervously, thinking how like so many author's tales this was: foolhardy adventurers going into the lair of a beast, testing themselves against unseen adversaries, reluctantly challenging the darkness. But he wondered then if maybe authors told such tales because there was a truth about the dark and men's fear of it—about the kinds of things that preferred not to be seen.

Sword in hand, he crept door to door, peering in, expecting some sudden, violent encounter. His arms and legs ached from the constant tension of preparing to fight.

At the end of one hall, he looked into a room and caught the movement of a shape just a few feet away. His legs weakened, but he reacted swiftly, swinging his sword. The shadowy figure did likewise. Braethen put all his strength into his stroke, hoping to beat the other back with the first blow.

A half second later his blade struck something and the

sound of shattering glass exploded in the silence. Shards fell over his hands and clattered to the floor. He realized he'd caught sight of his own reflection in a darkened mirror. He might have laughed but for the pounding in his chest.

He whirled around. If something lay in wait, there could be no disguising his presence now. *But by hells, I won't be scared off.* He started down the hall to examine the other side of the third floor.

The far end of the corridor ended at yet another open door. This last room was larger than all the rest; it had to be the quarters of the First Sodalist. In one corner, high-back chairs hunkered around a hearth, in another corner stood a large chest of drawers, and in yet another a private set of book-shelves.

In the last quadrant of the great room a four-post bed stood in the shadows. Of all the cots and mattresses he'd seen thus far, only this one seemed disturbed. The shadows made it difficult to see clearly, and Braethen ventured in, his sword held out in front of him.

As he approached the bed, he thought he saw a shape lying there, motionless. Sleeping? He crept closer, straining to see through the darkness. When he'd come within a stride, he lowered his sword. The bed was empty. The coverlet had been rolled back and the pillows displaced, appearing from a distance like a sleeping man.

Braethen turned and surveyed the room. The entire manor appeared empty. The tightness in his chest eased, and he took a deep breath. But he didn't sheathe his sword. Not yet. He began walking the rest of the room, to be thorough. As he went, his mind finally relaxed enough to frame the question he'd come here to ask: Was he on the right side of the schism that had torn the Sheason Order in two?

As he came around the nearest chair, he saw him. Slumped into its high-back embrace, E'Sau sat dead, a knife protruding from his neck. In the shadows, dark blood stained the man's shirt a deep shade of black.

Braethen fought the urge to cry for help. The First Sodalist was beyond the assistance of a physic blackcoat. And in these times of rumor, Braethen knew that being found alone here, a virtual stranger, would make him a prime suspect in the man's murder.

Why would someone kill the First Sodalist? Staring at the lifeless shape, he struggled with the senselessness of E'Sau's death, the injustice. Then he noticed something lying in the dead man's lap, his lifeless fingers curled around the object. He knelt and leaned close. A book. With care, Braethen gently pulled the tome from the man's hands. He turned back the cover, but darkness made it impossible to read the book's title. Braethen backed away to the nearest window and drew aside the curtains.

Despite the light of the stars and a bright moon, true dread crept inside him for the first time that night. His heart began again to pound in his chest. It was his father's book: *The Seamster's Needle.*

Is this just awful coincidence? Braethen wondered. Or had E'Sau expected Braethen to come? Maybe someone or something had placed the book in the man's hands. A sign or message to him. This last thought resonated with the most truth.

When the shock of it abated, Braethen returned his eyes to the page, and noted blemishes there—it was the same book Vendanj had given him.

After wandering the raucous streets of Recityv, and ascending through the dreadful shadows of the sodalist manor, and finding E'Sau dead with Braethen's father's stories in his hand . . . after it all, the most frightful moment came in a scrawled bit of verse below his father's name:

A bloody treasure you now hold,
Earned rightfully and willfully,
By following, with actions bold,
A man who will not see.
But patient are the rest who wait
To know if you will learn,
And find the courage that will turn
To peace what now is hate.
For boys will come to manhood
And wonder if they could

Follow paths that they might change
If they but understood
That death is just a consequence,
An easy thing, a recompense,
Of parents who may learn death's sense,
Which comes they know not whence.

Braethen looked up and, staring at the night skies through the dead sodalist's window, began to understand the poem's message. A threat. On his father's life.

· CHAPTER FORTY-SEVEN ·

An Illicit Diarist

The Dimnians are a thinking people, but still knew civil war once. Over a book. The ideas in it were said to be contagion. Well beyond thought riddles. No extant copies are known. The book was also, apparently, unattributed.

—Drawn from *The Conspiracy of Words*, anonymous

WHENEVER HELAINA WAS awakened after dark hour, she knew the news was bad. This summons came on the first night of Convocation, making her dread that the two things were related. And if that wasn't bad enough, the message came on the lips of her once-husband—the man had a way of being at the center of dire events.

She hastened to get dressed, her arthritic fingers fighting with the buttons of her gown. The task was none the easier with Grant waiting just outside the door for her to finish. She could feel the man's impatience. Finally, exasperated, he came in, as though he knew what was causing the delay. He gently pushed her hands away and began to fasten the buttons up the side of the garment.

"This isn't proper," she said. Even to herself, her voice wasn't convincing.

"It's nothing I haven't seen before." And though he didn't dawdle in the effort, he added, "And I don't believe there was ever an official annulment of the wedding. So, according to the law, I'm committing no crime."

"Precisely the kind of bedchamber talk a lady likes to hear," Helaina replied.

As though he hadn't heard, Grant commented, "You're well preserved."

She looked at him, shaking her head. "Your charm is boundless. Why have you wakened me?"

"We shouldn't discuss it here." Grant fastened the last button.

"Tell me where we're going?" she insisted.

Grant leaned in. His warm breath caressed her ear when he whispered, "To see your First Sodalist."

She drew back, looking a question at him: *Why a late night visit to see E'Sau?* But the man offered no answer. Helaina leaned back toward him, putting her own lips near to her estranged husband's ear this time.

"Summon Artixan and Van Steward to join us." She lingered a moment, enjoying being so near the man again. After all these years, the scent of him still aroused her.

From a sense of propriety, she pulled herself away. He looked at her and said softly, "I already have. I'm afraid, my lady, you are as predictable today as you were twenty years ago."

He smiled then, the lines of weather and sun around his eyes and mouth making him, to her mind, the handsomer. It was infuriating that he possessed such raw magnetism, while simultaneously proving to be so objectionable. She remembered that his passion and obstinacy had been no small part of his appeal when she'd first met him.

They made their way out of Solath Mahnus without drawing any attention to themselves. Much of that had to do with her Emerit guards making the way clear. And by the time they'd walked the streets of her city and arrived at the residence of the First Sodalist, both Artixan and her general were there, standing with Vendanj's young sodalist. None of them spoke as they followed Braethen inside.

Helaina prepared herself for a meeting with E'Sau. There'd likely been some development in the rift that divided the Sheason. The First Sodalist had been good about keeping her apprised of the rising tension, since it could potentially affect Convocation.

When she entered E'Sau's room, and rounded the chairs set before the hearth, her heart sank. Her trusted friend had been murdered, the weapon still protruding from his neck. A lamp set on a table between the hearthside chairs lit the awful sight, showing pallor in E'Sau's skin and coagulated blood across his neck and chest.

They held a collective silence as they viewed the grisly scene, internalizing what they were seeing, honoring the loss. And for her part—though she hated that her mind went so fast to it—she considered the implications for her Council and Convocation.

Helaina spoke first. "Who did this?"

Braethen answered, speaking in the reverential tones one uses at a barrow yard. "I didn't see who did it. After Convocation, I came here to talk with E'Sau. The manor was empty, no lamps were lit, and all the inner doors had been opened. This is where I found him. I went back to Solath Mahnus and waited for Grant. I didn't trust the news to anyone else."

Helaina nodded. "In the future, you may trust any of us here."

Braethen nodded in return.

Artixan stepped forward and knelt before the dead sodalist. "You were a good friend. Rest now. Others will carry the mantle you bore so well." The Sheason then put his hand over E'Sau's, as though bidding the sodalist farewell. Still kneeling there, Artixan's voice changed, an edge replacing the thoughtful remorse. "This isn't random. No house thief came here sniffing for coin. And it doesn't feel like revenge. E'Sau had enemies—my enemies—but the object of their scorn was me, not him."

Van Steward offered an angry sigh. "It's not really a

mystery, is it? Who profits most from E'Sau's death?" Her
general proceeded to answer his own question. "E'Sau's
vote always aligned with Artixan's—not from compulsion,
but from oneness of mind. And Artixan's vote typically sup-
ports the regent for much the same reason. There are important matters to be decided soon, and some recent decisions
that Roth may call to be voted on again. It will take time for
the Sodality to name E'Sau's successor. Meanwhile, the balance of votes shifts in Roth's favor."

"The Sodality will move fast to replace E'Sau," Artixan
assured them.

"It's more than the High Council," Grant reminded them.
"It's also Convocation. Losing E'Sau, we lose a vote on both."

Grant looked directly at Helaina. "You've lost a strong
voice for bringing rulers together a third time. Whoever replaces E'Sau won't have the same credibility, simply because
he'll be new and untested."

Anger blossomed in the pit of her stomach. "If Roth is responsible for this, I'll have him executed this very day. Justice won't be cheated. E'Sau's death will not be made a matter
of politics."

A shocked and horrified whisper from Braethen interrupted them, "Dead gods."

The sodalist crept to one side of the chair and bent down,
inspecting the dagger sticking out of E'Sau's neck. He then
turned to Artixan, who still knelt on the floor.

"You should look at this," Braethen said to the Sheason.

Artixan stood and shuffled to one side, inclining toward
the weapon. Helaina watched as some revelation stole into her
friend's face. Without waiting to hear what they saw there,
she stepped forward to look for herself. On the flat, round end
of the dagger handle, graven on the steel, was the three-ring
emblem of the Sheason Order. The implication was obvious.
Apparently, removing E'Sau from the balance of power
wasn't enough for her enemies.

Grant seemed to have no need to inspect it for himself.
"The three-ring knife is mostly ceremonial, but it's manufactured individually for each man or woman taken into the
order. There'll be a hunt for the renderer who has lost his

knife, but the real hunt isn't about one man. That's plain enough."

Van Steward spoke, his voice loud and resonant. "We'll find the one responsible. This very hour I will mobilize—"

"We've already started that process," came a voice from the hallway. Roth entered the room, followed by Jermond Pleades, First Counselor at the Court of Judicature. "Your men are welcome to join the League in pursuit of justice on this matter, General."

Helaina adopted a more formal posture and stepped between the Ascendant and Artixan, knowing emotions would be running high. "And how did you know to start such a search so fast, Roth?"

A smile so faint that Helaina wasn't sure she'd seen it at all crossed Roth's lips. "Rather simply. E'Sau and his second-in-command, Sodalist Urieh Palon, were scheduled to meet with Counsel Pleades and myself directly following Convocation today. Palon arrived as scheduled, and we spoke idly, waiting on E'Sau. Eventually, the three of us came here, thinking the First Sodalist had perhaps forgotten our appointment. To our dismay, we found this brutal scene. We went directly to inform his family, and bring them here to verify—"

A small woman pushed past Roth. Her honey-gold hair was coiled in a bun, her expression a griever's frown. She drew after her two children.

Shameless bastard even brought the children. This wasn't verification of the dead. This was waging the war of public opinion.

"Artixan?" E'Sau's widow spoke his name with a pleading voice. *Tell me it's not so. Make it not so,* that tone said. They knew each other, of course. Artixan and E'Sau were as close as she and Artixan were.

"Deliah, I'm so sorry." He stepped past the body, putting himself between her and E'Sau. "There's no need for you to see this. Don't remember him this way."

"Artixan," Roth interjected with a reverence Helaina knew to her bones was an affectation, "this is a serious matter. She needs to verify—"

The look Artixan gave Roth was heavy and hateful. "Ascendant, I knew and loved this man like a brother. It is E'Sau. And this woman," his throat thickened with emotion, "is my friend. I would spare her. . . ."

Deliah rushed forward into Artixan's arms, and buried her face in his chest. She sobbed, as behind her the two children stood near Roth's legs with wet cheeks. Seeing them, Artixan motioned for Roth to step back, and gently drew Deliah to her children. There, he slowly knelt, taking them all into his embrace. After a long while, he pulled back enough to speak to them.

"Let me tell you what I believe." He gave them a reassuring smile through eyes glassy with his own tears. "I believe there's a good place reserved for good people. A place they go to after this world, where they wait with great anticipation for the day their loved ones join them." He placed a hand alongside the older child's face. "That's where your father is, Alon. And until your time comes to see him again, you have me to help you."

Their mother reached out and wiped her children's eyes, a brave smile on her face.

"That's the promise he and I made to one another," said Artixan. "And I keep my promises."

They fell silent again for a while, sharing a series of hugs.

"Now," Artixan finally said. "There's some work for me to do. We have some justice to see to. And when I'm through here, I'll come and look in on you."

Van Steward gave a hand signal, and two men came into view. Escorts.

"He loved you," Deliah said to Artixan. "We all do."

He seemed momentarily incapable of words. "And I you. Anything you need."

She gave him a parting embrace, and gathered her small ones on her way down the hall, past Roth and the first counselor.

When the door below was heard to shut, Artixan's face changed visibly. Helaina could feel the man's anger. "How dare you use Deliah and her family as an opinion ploy."

"It was poor judgment on my part," Roth conceded with a politician's regret. "I'm sorry. I seem to compulsorily return to procedure in times like this."

"That's a load of horseshit," Grant said. "You apologize after the fact, but still hope the news of it spreads. Builds public sentiment."

"I assure you nothing could be further from the truth," said Roth.

"And careful of you, Ascendant, to take the company of one sodalist while you have another killed." Artixan had squared his shoulders to the man.

Roth showed Artixan a sympathetic expression. "My friend, you and I have had our differences, but I would never endeavor to do what you imply. I understand your need to assign blame, and, knowing your grief, don't hold it against you. But please refrain from pursuing this line of thinking. I'm your greatest ally in this, and we should get started, since it would seem someone in your order is the culprit. And I would assume you'd want to know who this person is and expulse him from your ranks."

Van Steward stepped near to Helaina's side, seeming to likewise want to create a barrier between the men. "One day, Staned, I will cut out your crafty tongue."

The Ascendant didn't even bother to acknowledge the general's comment. "My lady," he began, addressing Helaina, "I think I can add some light of understanding to what has happened here." He beckoned the first counselor forward, who she noticed now carried a book in his hands. "The topic of the meeting E'Sau set with us, but to which he never, unfortunately, arrived, was the schism in the Sheason Order. While we hadn't yet spoken of it in depth, he suggested to me that he feared the rift had grown so bitter as to be a threat to the safety of the people and his own order."

"Take care, Ascendant, not to defame this man," Artixan said, his voice strained.

"I would do no such thing," Roth replied, his voice a model of sincerity. "But, apparently, the infighting has become so severe that E'Sau's own sodality was at a loss as to how to continue to serve."

"What do you mean?" Artixan asked, the threat clear in his voice.

"I mean that he realized he had to decide which side of this Sheason schism his people would support." Roth showed them all a sympathetic expression, as one who might appreciate the difficulties of leadership. "But as an advocate of civility and a keeper of the law, the First Sodalist had intended to unify his followers behind those Sheason who had renounced their arcane practices."

"How do you know this?" Helaina asked. "You said yourself that he hadn't spoken deeply about it."

Counsel Pleades stepped closer. "When we came here earlier this evening with Sodalist Palon, and found E'Sau dead, we conducted an initial search for evidence. We, of course, found the three-ring emblem of the Sheason on the murder weapon, but we also found this." He raised the book in his hands. "It is the First Sodalist's personal journal. In it, he goes into some depth about his fears for the Sheason Order, for his own followers, and for the people both orders are meant to serve."

Helaina looked at the diary, then to Roth's face, scrutinizing the man for any momentary hint of duplicity or falsehood. The Ascendant maintained an immaculate façade of regret and officiousness.

Roth wasn't finished. "And I'm afraid he even provides a list of names of those Sheason whose radical behavior he fears most. It would seem, my lady, that the schism is deeper than we thought, and that most Sheason have chosen a path contrary to the law." Roth paused dramatically before saying, "They are now not only a threat to civil peace, but to your work at Convocation."

Helaina leveled a wrathful stare on the man. "And how is that, Ascendant Staned?"

"My dear lady," the man replied, "it's simple. The Sheason defy the Civilization Order, and in doing so, mock your own decree. They undermine the authority and respect you need to possess if other nations are to commit themselves to your cause."

"A cause, I might remind you, Ascendant, that you don't believe in," Helaina said.

"I don't deny it, my lady. But I, for one, respect our differences. And more importantly, I respect your office. I would be remiss as a member of your Council if I didn't advise you as I do now."

"Where is Sodalist Palon?" Artixan inquired.

"We took Palon back to the League house; the man is distraught," the first counselor answered. "We've made him as comfortable as possible, while we set in motion an investigation of this matter. Artixan"—Counsel Pleades looked at Helaina's closest friend—"this is a serious indictment. And . . . your name is written on these pages."

Bastard! She wanted nothing more than to exercise the power of her office to excise—with prejudice!—the poisonous element of her ruling council. *Iron fist in a velvet glove.* She prepared to loose a savage tirade on Roth when the young sodalist, Braethen, cut in. "May I see the diary?"

The first counselor looked momentarily hesitant before handing the book over. For several moments the room was quiet while Braethen looked through the last pages of the journal. An expression of focused concentration impressed her with some new hope. The young man then handed the volume back to the first counselor.

"I assume," Braethen said rather indifferently, "that as part of your investigation, First Counsel"—Helaina smiled inside that the young sodalist addressed Pleades and not Roth—"you will verify the authenticity of those entries in the diary that make these claims about the Sheason."

Counsel Pleades showed a look of momentary confusion, as though such had not occurred to him. Helaina noted, too, that when the young sodalist asked his question, he was not looking at Pleades, but Roth. At this, a thin smile did cross her face.

Then the counselor gathered himself. "We will be thorough," he replied.

"Are you suggesting that these entries were not made by E'Sau?" Roth asked, glaring at Braethen with incredulity.

"I am suggesting you be . . . thorough," Braethen returned.

Grant laughed openly, drawing a sharp look from Roth.

Braethen continued. "These pages aren't consistent with what I know about the man, and I'm guessing those who knew him better would say the same."

"I think, my young man, that this is precisely the point. E'Sau's secret conflict was what to do about his concerns. They were worries he kept private, until reaching out to me. A meeting that it would appear someone had great motivation he never attend."

Van Steward had grown impatient with the discussion. "My men will be paired with every leagueman and counselor assigned to investigate this matter. Nothing happens unless we're present. Is that understood?"

"I would have it no other way," Roth agreed. "Thank you, General."

Then Roth and Pleades exited the room, leaving them again in the company of her murdered friend. Grant put a reassuring hand on Helaina's arm, and spoke over her shoulder.

"What have you waited for the Ascendant to leave to tell us, Sodalist?" her husband asked.

Braethen looked over at them, drawn, it seemed, from his own inner reasonings. "If Counsel Pleades does as we've asked, and checks the authenticity of those diary entries, he won't find any inconsistencies of penmanship or ink or paper or style. They'll seem in every regard the writing of E'Sau."

"Grand news," Grant said.

"But I didn't ask the question because I believed he'd find anything." Braethen shifted his eyes to look at Artixan. "I asked to gauge the Ascendant's reaction to the request. I could be wrong, but I thought I saw an instant of doubt in his eyes."

Helaina turned to her old friend. "Did you see this, too?" she asked Artixan.

The old man's composure had returned, the hint of a smile beneath his beard. "I did. Go on, Braethen. I like your wit."

"My father taught me that among those who follow the Author's Way, there are some whose gift is counterfeiting. It's a skill that comes not only in the stroke of a pen to imitate another author, but in his expressions and choice of words. It's as though this forger *is* the author."

"Then we'll find this imposter," Van Steward said with quiet anger. "And we'll have his confession to conspiring with the Ascendant. To murder. And treason."

Braethen hadn't looked away from Artixan. "It's worse than that. Or it would be to my father," Braethen clarified. "It might suggest something he talked to me about once or twice. Sometimes, his work . . . sometimes it became a burden. Not like field harrowing or well digging. But still a burden. And there were a few times, when he'd been through a full carafe of sour mash, that he talked about a sect of authors who'd given themselves to confabulation—"

"Isn't that what all authors do—"

"Stories meant only to disrupt and darken," Braethen hurried on. "Words that would give life to chaos and mistrust and fear. He called it propaganda. He called it the indictment of the innocent."

"Like providing evidence that the Sheason would have a motive for killing E'Sau before he could turn the Sodality against them." Helaina sickened at the sound of her own words.

Braethen turned his eyes back to her. "And they're happy to intimidate us, too." He showed them the poem in his father's book.

Helaina promised to dispatch a band of men to watchsafe over Braethen's father. A look of genuine gratitude filled the young man's face, but dropped away quickly, as something seemed to occur to him.

"I think this proves that this sect of authors is real. And that the League has recruited them. Dead gods," Braethen muttered, "the sect *is* real. The power of an artful lie. It's probably been happening for a while now, and we just haven't seen it."

Helaina chilled at his words. But her anger fast burned away that chill. She might be in her twilight years, but she was thinking clearly. And standing in the presence of a close, dead friend, she knew what Roth would do next. *He'll seek control of Convocation.* And the thought made her fear for more than her own life's end.

My move, then.

She turned to Grant. "I suspect tomorrow holds more League surprises for us at Convocation. We may need your unusual brand of diplomacy."

Grant's face slowly spread into a lopsided grin.

• CHAPTER FORTY-EIGHT •

A Private Audience

There's credible evidence that warring cultures also excel at carnal pleasures. What is less certain is which precedes the other.

—A Study of Cultural Appetites, Volume 2,
the Northern Kingdoms—Practical Research

IN THE RUSSET hues of dusk, Sutter stood on a large balcony outside his room, practicing with his Sedagin blade. An easy stillness lay over Ir-Caul, the streets empty, leaving a calm upon the city. In the cool evening air, looking out at fiery western skies, Sutter made slow, deliberate motions with his weapon, the exercise more meditation than combat training.

They'd retired without even taking supper. The rather Spartan quarters—no decoration save a broken pole-arm hung upon the wall—suited him fine. He was exhausted physically from so many long days and short nights, but his mind raced with questions after their introduction to King Relothian. The king had seen that he wasn't a true Sedagin, which had darkened Sutter's mood, reminding him of the many Far who'd died because of his inexperienced sword-work. He'd hoped running his sword drills would relax him. . . .

On his quiet balcony, he methodically rehearsed the maneuvers Mira had taught him. In the midst of his drills he considered a kind of strength in his father—the man who'd raised him, not the one who'd sired him—in working a plot of land day after day to yield up a crop to feed a few mouths. And the man did it without complaint, without ever expressing the need to do or be more than what he was.

Sutter gave a sad smile, recognizing that he hadn't that same strength of character. Mostly, it made him grateful. Despite the bad joke of it, his years there had grounded him in what he thought of as the *right* things—loyalty, honesty, the ethic of work, suffering well.

He lowered his sword and stared into the past. He saw a bitter winter. The kind where the smallest pebble or dirt clod had frozen to the ground. He saw his father's skin steaming in the deep cold, as he tore at the rock-hard soil beneath the pear tree behind their home. He saw himself pick up a shovel to try to help with his own weaker arms. He saw the form of his little sister lying beneath their best blanket, dead from winter fever. She was four. He saw redness in his father's eyes, and maybe gratitude for the chance to swing a pick to release his anger and sorrow. He saw Renae laid in the cold, hard ground, and his da linger to say a prayer, unwilling yet to throw back the dirt.

The grief swelled inside him again, and Sutter raised his sword with renewed determination. As he completed a quick stroke with his longblade, a shoe scuffed the floor behind him. He froze. Looking out toward the horizon, he tightened his grip on his sword, his heart drumming. He imagined Quiet-given behind him, some beast, perhaps a tracker, having stolen its way into his room.

He whirled, bringing his blade around in a deadly arc. As he swung, he caught the image of a blue chiffon chemise, and pulled back his blade. He narrowly avoided cutting a woman, who stood looking at him with wide eyes.

Sutter growled, mostly from his fear that he'd almost attacked a woman of Relothian's court.

"What do you want?" he blurted, realizing as he spoke that he could see through the sheer fabric of her garment. She wore nothing beneath. Her hair—a deep auburn color—hung in slow waves to the tops of her breasts. And her fair skin made green eyes and brown freckles brighter.

"I am Yenola, King Relothian's sister. I've come to be sure you're comfortable." She bowed in a stately way, but the look in her eyes seemed less formal, more . . . *suggestive.* "You are Sedagin," she said, her voice carrying the hint of a question.

Sutter looked down at his blade and the unique glove on his right hand. He raised both, smiling, his heart returning to a normal rhythm after the brief scare. "Sure looks like it, doesn't it. But no, these were gifts."

The woman's eyebrows rose. "The Sedagin made a gift to you of their blade and glove? How did you earn these honors?"

Sutter thought, then smiled again. "I surrendered a dance with a beautiful woman."

Yenola returned his smile, a bemused confusion lightly knitting her brow. "Of course a woman would be at the heart of it. Are you bound to this woman?"

"Not to hear her tell it," Sutter replied, finally sheathing his blade.

The woman exuded the kind of serenity Sutter associated with royalty. She'd likely never had to dig a root. And she showed neither offense nor seductiveness when Sutter's eyes stole glances at her supple form. He gathered the impression that her being seen this way wasn't indecent for either of them. Still, from a sense of propriety, he turned to look back toward the distant line of mountains to avoid embarrassing himself.

She stepped close, her arm brushing his own, as she joined him in looking out from his balcony. "Keep your secret," she said.

"It isn't a secret," Sutter replied. "She and I simply haven't made any commitment to one another."

"Not the woman, your relationship to the Sedagin. It's assumed that you were born to the Right Arm of the Promise."

Sutter turned to her, questions rising in his mind. Relothian hadn't revealed why he thought Vendanj had sent them. And if Sutter's experience proved anything, it was that when someone delayed the sharing of information, it usually wasn't good news. Or they didn't know.

"Is that why you came? You thought I was Sedagin?" Looking at her gown, Sutter guessed at the purpose of her visit, but didn't say as much.

"Of course that's why I came. Does that offend you?" Her voice never became agitated or incredulous.

More importantly, Sutter could see that she didn't condescend to him.

"I guess not," he said. "It's more of a compliment, really, isn't it?"

The king didn't tell her.

"I would think so," Yenola replied. "It's the only reason you were admitted through the gate. Not even the Far woman would have moved the tower to allow you to pass." Unexpectedly, she took his hand, running her own over his fingers and palm. "So, your secret . . . You're not a born fighter, but you've the good use of your hands. How is that?"

Sutter didn't feel any shame to say, "I've spent a lot of years playing in the dirt."

The woman offered him a gracious smile that warmed him. Without her actually saying so, he knew that it pleased her to learn this about him.

"How did a farmer find himself on the Teheale dancing and earning esteem enough to be taken into the Sedagin family?" Yenola didn't let go of his hand, her touch soft and inviting. So much so that it took Sutter a few moments to register the implications of her question.

"Taken into the Sedagin family? What does that mean?" He momentarily forgot that this beautiful woman was nearly naked.

"I will tell you, and then you will owe me a favor. Bargain?" Her smile became uneven, one side of her mouth crooking up mischievously.

"Fair enough."

"It's really quite simple. This blade," she grabbed the handle of his sword with her free hand and gently shook it, "is considered by the Sedagin an extension of their body. They're never separated from it once they begin to learn its use. They take extreme care in the crafting of each one. And no low-lander is ever to bear their blade, unless he's made a part of their family."

"And the glove?" Sutter asked, holding up his right hand.

"Much the same," Yenola replied. "And it marks you as one of theirs. In some places, like Ir-Caul, it's a sign that earns you consideration you wouldn't otherwise enjoy. In other places, you'd do well to remove it; it would provoke an-ger or draw those who wish to test themselves against you."

Sutter looked at the strange glove on his hand with new appreciation and concern. "All I did was remind a man that who a woman dances with is her decision."

"If you think about it, you made him remember more than proper manners." She gave him a thoughtful look, still smil-ing. "You may not have been born on the High Plains, but they consider you one of them. Which means *we* consider you one of them. That's the only reason the king agreed to speak with you."

The woman must have seen the question still in Sutter's eyes. She laughed as she asked, "Do you know where you are?"

"What do you mean? I'm in Ir-Caul." Sutter looked up and around at the city.

"Alon'Itol's northern border is the Pall. Beyond it lies the Bourne itself. And to the west is Nallan. . . ." She trailed off, seeming to weigh whether she needed to say more about that place.

Sutter had heard of the Nallan Kingdom, but remembered little about it, except that its own western border ran onto the Darkling Plains. But something in the way she'd used the name—*Nallan*—led Sutter to believe she didn't speak of mere facts.

Again, Yenola showed an astute read of Sutter's under-standing. "I'll leave the king to speak more of our western neighbor. For now, and for you, the thing to understand—and use to your advantage—is that our gates are closed except to known friends."

"We used Vendanj's name," he said, hoping to understand more about the Sheason's relationship with Relothian.

Her beautiful mischievous smile came again. "Anyone could have used the Sheason's name to call on us. And I don't know that Vendanj truly *has* friends. As for the city of Ir-Caul, and for my brother and his generals, we may owe the Sheason a debt of gratitude. But how he earned it has made his name a curse here. I wouldn't use it again."

"That's just lovely," Sutter said. "The leper of Ir-Caul sends us here to do his bidding." He looked back at Yenola. "Why are your gates closed?"

A look of genuine surprise rose on her face. "Sutter"—it was the first time she'd spoken his name—"we're at war." She then led him by the hand back inside his room and to his bed.

Sutter awoke early. He hadn't slept much; he had Yenola to thank for that. But the night of lovemaking had refreshed him in a way a night of sleep never had. He'd never lain with a woman. He spared a long look at her lying beside him, wrapped in the sheets of his bed. She stirred, and opened her eyes, kissing him as naturally as if they'd known each other for years.

"Can't sleep?" she asked.

"I guess I'm used to an early start."

She sighed deeply, contentedly. "What you told me about your words with the king. I've not heard anyone speak to him like that. Not a stranger, anyway. I wish I'd been there."

"I'm told I'm too brash," Sutter said, smiling through the dark of morning.

Yenola kissed him again, and this time there was some meaning to it. Sutter admitted to himself that his own inexperience with women left him completely unable to decipher the kiss.

"You should talk to the king again," she said, her words sounding like thoughts spoken aloud so that she might hear them and weigh their practicality. She seemed to arrive at a decision, her gaze focusing. "Most nights, the king sleeps on the roof. He listens better there."

"The roof?"

Yenola nodded. "Get dressed."

He slipped out of bed and dressed in the dark. From habit,

he pulled on his sword belt and Sedagin glove. Then he looked back at the woman, suddenly more than a little curious. "Why are you telling me this?"

"A single staircase lies at the end of the corridor." She sat up, the bedsheets slipping from her shoulders to reveal her breasts. In the dimness, her beauty still pulled at him. "Don't tell him I told you how to find him. And come back when you're done." A thin smile rose on her lips, less carnal and more glad, he thought.

He nodded and got moving. He passed down the silent corridor of the keep, and found the narrow set of stairs. He climbed upward in the tight spiral through several floors of the castle, dragging his hand along the wall to guide him in the darkness. The steps didn't let out on intervening stories, but rather continued upward. Sutter followed them quietly, setting his feet lightly on the stone, until he reached a heavy door that brought an end to the narrow stairs. Sutter pulled the latch and pushed open the door.

He stepped out onto the fortress's smallest, highest rooftop. There resided a still, cool air at this castle peak, and a grand view of Ir-Caul. Sutter could see from this vantage that he'd underestimated the size of the city, and hadn't had a true sense of its garrison-like function.

Streets radiated in all directions and were dominated by large barracks and drill yards. It was a city built for war, peopled by warriors. At the far edge of his sight, he thought he saw several tracts of land where war machines he couldn't name sat in wait of use. It left him with a feeling like he'd had in Naltus Far, but here the underlying sense of hope was absent. Not that it was hopeless; only that the residents of Ir-Caul seemed to live for today's moment, with no expectation of another.

Sutter turned a slow circle, surveying the city's every quarter in the dark of predawn. His heart started to pound when he saw a figure lying huddled on a bedroll against the wall to his left.

He drew his sword as a precaution, and approached warily. He hadn't seen a single beggar or vagrant on the streets of

Ir-Caul. But that was what the heap reminded him of, tucked into the nook of the wall and rooftop the way it was.

When he'd come within a few strides, the figure spoke. "Put away your weapon."

He relaxed and sheathed his blade. It was, indeed, the king, sleeping on hard stone in the cold atop his own keep. Shortly, Relothian sat up, resting his back against the wall.

Sutter stared at the man a moment, then peered into the darkness at the stretch of plains beyond the city walls, expecting he might see a reason for the king being here. Seeing nothing but the occasional light of some window in the city below, he turned back to the man. "What you are you doing here?"

"I might ask you the same. You've no reason to be wandering my castle alone. A proper king would be insulted." The man didn't seem insulted.

"I couldn't sleep," Sutter lied.

"Nor can I. Not on feathered mattresses beneath heavy linens, anyway." The man pushed away the thin bedroll that lay across his lap. "And not by the warmth of a hearth." He patted the stone beneath him. "I must have firmness beneath me, and cold air to chill my cheeks. When the comforts of my throne start to please me, I will hand them back and step down."

Sutter thought he understood, but said nothing.

The king got up and walked to the edge of the rooftop. "A fighting man learns to sleep lightly, and appreciates a rough bed that keeps him from his dreams. I'll be ready when my enemy comes. So tell me what wakes *you* so early."

Sutter didn't join the king at the rooftop's edge, but stood where he was, trying to decide how much he should share. "My dreams are bad. Maybe I should try a harder bed."

The king laughed softly. "What dreams could a *Sedagin* have that frighten him?"

He didn't bother to explain his Sedagin gifts. Later, maybe. Instead, being in no mood to lie, and knowing how it would sound, he said, "Lately? Faces of soldiers who will soon die."

Relothian turned toward him, wearing a scrutinizing look.

Sutter strode forward then, to see the king more clearly in the gloom. "What do you think the call to Convocation is for? What has it always been for? I'm no great warrior, and I don't know the problems of a king, but I won't leave Ir-Caul until you stop being a jack—"

"Take care," the king said softly.

Sutter stared back, his impatience growing. "If a boy will cross kingdoms and borders to share a message in the name of a Sheason you hate, maybe you could spare a few days to hear what the regent has to say."

"You have no idea what you're asking," the king replied, a restrained anger in his voice. "Look there." The king pointed west.

Sutter looked into the distance, seeing nothing but a dark line of mountains beneath a starry sky.

"I'm at war with Nallan. A realm that takes what it wants. Kills without remorse or honor." The king looked south, and continued. "For years we have entreated nations to join us. I've sent countless letters, emissaries. And still we fight alone." He grew quiet for a time, his gaze turning east then again to the west.

"The forges will be lit soon." He gestured out over the city. "Smoke will fill the sky with hope. We were losing this war when I took the throne. Our men carried badly crafted blades. Their armor and shields were laughable. And the gears for war, siege weapons"—he shook his head—"we had few. That's why I am called the smith king. My first order was to bring several hundred blacksmiths to Ir-Caul to build forges and start smelting proper steel. That was twenty years ago."

Sutter remembered the countless rising plumes of smoke he'd seen the day before.

"But these last few seasons, my men are falling in greater numbers. Nallan pushes closer. Something is wrong. I can feel it in my bones. None of my entreaties to seat-holders have been answered. I may have to finally allow the League a garrison here." He turned back to Sutter. "So don't speak to me of Convocation. Your own people don't support it. It's a mockery of allegiance, just as it was in the past. Kings and nobles vying for power and influence, toying at politics. You know the Sedagin don't support it, either." He laughed.

Sutter impulsively reached inside his cloak. The king quickly grasped his arm in an ironlike grip. "I won't play games with you, boy. What do you hide?"

He ripped his hand free and dug into an inner pocket. He pulled forth the Draethmorte's sigil and held it up in front of the king's face. "You must listen to me."

Sutter's voice rang out in the stillness, echoing down from the top of Relothian's castle. A few moments later, the silence returned, heavier than before.

The king cupped the pendant with one hand, staring at it with disbelief. "I've never seen this, except in the paintings that hang from my walls. It's profane. How did you come by it?"

Carefully, he shared the story of Tahn's fight at Tillinghast. He added as much detail as he could remember from Tahn's account. Then he told about the battle at Naltus, and the loss of the Covenant Tongue. But he didn't repeat what Vendanj had said about the pendant: *The people there have forgotten who they are. Make them remember. The glyph will help.*

When he'd finished speaking, the king gave Sutter an unreadable look, leaving Sutter to wonder if he'd made a mistake in confiding so much.

The king never moved, never spoke.

"There are more sacrifices than I care to think about behind this piece of metal," Sutter said. "I've seen Velle, fought Bar'dyn, and looked over a field of dead so wide I couldn't see its end. The Quiet are coming." He stopped, unsure if he should say what he really thought about Relothian's army. In the end, Sutter decided to just say what he felt. "And to tell you the truth, I'm not sure even if you join Convocation . . . it will be enough."

Sutter put the pendant back inside his inner pocket, the king's eyes fixed on him as he did so.

"We'll talk more." The king left Sutter standing on the keep's uppermost rooftop in the light of daybreak as smithy fires began to lift their smoke into the morning sky.

CHAPTER FORTY-NINE

Gearsmithing

*Build your gears first as toys for children. You capture the
inventiveness of play without the encumbrance of adult consequences.*

—Gearsmith instruction received by all Alon'Itol smiths

T HE DOOR TO the gear house opened, and Mira stared
into the face of a short man with an almost entirely bald
pate. Beyond him, she could see the broad workshop had no
windows—this was not a place King Relothian or his generals wanted casual gawkers to see. But lamps kept it brightly
lit, and the sweet smells of freshly cut wood and wet hemp
drifted on the air.

"Oh my gears," the little man said. "You're the Far girl everyone's talking about. Superb. Superb. Come in."

The man stepped back, let Mira pass, then shut the door
and dropped a cross brace that fell into a kind of locking
mechanism she hadn't seen before. The brace was thick, solid
iron, and no clever thief was going to raise it from outside.

"I'm Gear Master Mick. You're Mira," the man announced
with bright enthusiasm. "You're a Far. And I design gear.
You've come to see my work, no doubt. Superb. Superb."

It was, in fact, why she'd come. In part, anyway. She had
other questions, but she imagined she might find answers to
some of those in the gearsmith's work.

"If it's not an inconvenience." Mira was already examining a table laid out with models of siege engines unknown to
her.

He shook his head, rather more violently than was necessary, and limped to the table she'd been surveying. On one
end lay heaps of freshly cut wood in a variety of lengths and
thicknesses. At a glance, it could have been mistaken for a

stack of child's blocks. Near it, spools of hemp twine stood on vertical rods poking up from the table. Carving knives and chisels and hammers and nails and iron couplings and other tools lay near the raw materials. But most of the table showcased scale models of things that looked like trebuchets, ballistas, mangonels, battering rams, assault ladders. *Like* them, but not quite the same. Without spending more time examining them, she couldn't say what was different. But she could see that they'd all been *modified*.

"Oh, lots of ideas," he began. "Maybe one in a hundred I can make work."

Closer to Mira, countless designs for swords, daggers, axes, hammers, flails, spears, shields, helmets, armor, and more had all been rendered in miniature. She noticed that the man wore a leather belt with pouches all across the front, filled with various wood-carving knives.

"You're a busy man," she observed.

"And why not," he replied. "Wars don't fight themselves."

He fingered a counterweight on an elaborate trebuchet and launched a small stone at her. Mira caught it, fingering the ore. "Your forges. They're casting iron to build all this." She slipped the rock into her pocket, and pointed to the table.

"Oh my gears, no. They're building *proven* engines. This is all . . . guesswork." His smile suggested playful deceit.

Some of this had been battle-tested, no doubt. But she didn't get the feeling the gearsmith took delight in war, so much as invention. He exuded a kind of energy that made her sure he never sat idle.

"You're at war, then," she said, fixing on a strange model that appeared as though it might shoot multiple arrows at once.

His silence seemed an answer. He moved around to the other side of the table and turned a wooden crank on the model she'd been eyeing. On one side, the device had a few wooden wheels with interlocking teeth that began turning when he started to rotate the crank. A clever mechanism drew back a string across two pulleys. The string itself had been threaded through two further endpoints. It created a straight line of the string where it would fit the nooks of six arrows resting in shallow grooves. When the tension on the string reached a certain point, the mechanism let go, and the six arrows sailed simultaneously across the table of models.

The gearsmith kept cranking, and she watched as another set of arrows was fed up in a rotation of six trays. Over the space of seconds thirty-six toothpick-sized arrows sailed over the table and onto the floor.

"That one works?" she asked.

"Superbly," the gearsmith admitted, beaming. "The battle version flings twelve arrow sets, and has ten trays. One man to feed the arrows. The other to crank."

"Who are you fighting?" Mira picked up one of the model-sized arrows, inspecting its nock. The design was ingenious; rather than containing a single groove, it appeared more like a crown, so that a string could easily catch it no matter how it was laid in the machine.

"Nallan, of course. Who else?" The gearsmith bustled over to the raw materials. He picked up a length of wood, and began carving as if he'd just that moment had a new idea.

Mira put down the small arrow and looked out over the rest of the gear house. "How long have you been at war?"

"Goes back longer than *my* life," the gearsmith said. "Generations, to be sure. Nallan . . . not nice people. Not nice ideas." He nodded at his own statement.

"Then I'd say you don't appear to be having a lot of success," Mira observed. "Being at war for so long, I mean."

The man looked up, momentarily ceasing to carve. Seeing the slightly more sober look in his eyes, an odd question occurred to her. "Are you trying to win?"

He stared back at her, his thumb running crosswise over the edge of his sharp whittling knife in a bit of a nervous tick. "I think what I wonder more is who's running the damned thing." A sheepish look rose instantly in his face. "Oh, there I've gone a'cursin' in front of company, and a lady Far, no less. Sorry for that."

Mira shook her head at the apology. Then said simply, "The *king* commands the army."

Even the gearsmith's fidgeting thumb stopped. He stared

at her for a long time. "You didn't really come to see my work, did you?"

"You're the king's head gearsmith," Mira replied. "I want to understand what moves when he asks it. The state of his warcraft." She paused, looking around again.

"And he knows you're here asking?" Gear Master Mick's playful smile slowly returned.

Mira let herself respond with a grin. "He knows that the regent of Recityv has called a Convocation of Seats. He knows he's been asked to attend. And he knows that it means these toys of yours could be built at scale and pushed by a column from Recityv, or Pater Ful, or Kali-Firth, or Masson Dimn . . . or Naltus Far."

The gearsmith's eyes beamed again. "That would be superb. Superb!"

With his knife hand, he waved her to follow, and he led her through his gear house, toward the far wall. They passed great racks, where the models became progressively larger, as though the applicable physics were being tested at incremental size increases. Going along, more metal was used in the larger iterations, and fewer designs appeared to have passed muster. Bins of broken gears stood beside each table.

They shuffled through sawdust and cast-off tools and stray wooden rods and bits of steel. The rafters seemed to heighten as the models became nearly the size one might take to battle. And at the far end of the wide gear house, racks of weapons and armor and a few smaller, strange-looking siege machines sat silent, ready for use.

Mira had seen her share of war weaponry. But this was new country. Master Mick must have seen something of that in her face, as he visibly held back a snigger, and led her toward the far wall.

They walked on for ten strides before he stopped and turned to her, a new look on his face—concern, maybe. "I'm no warmonger. I want you to understand that. But my gears . . ." His face took on the bright, gleeful quality she'd remember it for. "Isn't it grand to think of a thing, and figure out how to make it work." He shrugged his shoulder once, as though to say he was helpless to do anything but obsess about his gear work.

He then pulled a lever that released a locking hook, and slid back a great section of the wall. It rolled at the bottom, and glided at the top on an iron track. And beyond it lay a deep and wide courtyard, walled in by long-cut timber. Sitting here and there were the full realizations of the whittled models back inside his gear house. A few of them, anyway. Some stood the height of a man. Most were ten times that size, great, hulking, but elegant things, crafted of lumber and iron and rope. All were set on sturdy wheels for travel. And all, even in the bright sun of morning, hinted of menace.

Mira stepped into the immense courtyard, unable to name most of the war machines, though several appeared to have functions similar to others she had seen—casting boulders, iron balls, heavy spears. Others, though, she couldn't see how they worked. Some appeared to twirl large spiked balls. A few smaller contraptions were tethered to what looked like thin-canvased hot-air balloons.

And she realized there were yards like this all across the expansive city of Ir-Caul.

"Who takes care of these during battle?" she asked. "Do you go out with them?"

"Oh my gears, no. I'm a bit too gimpy for war business anymore. We have gearsmiths assigned to each machine. Usually come up through the smithy ranks. Fine crop of young men, I must say, to tend a fine crop of gears." He beamed with pride.

But the collection of siege weapons . . . they stole her breath. They spoke of devastation, and left the sunny courtyard feeling like a field of graves. As hand models hewn in the sweet smell of pine they were more a toy than a gearsmith's engine for war. But standing tall and throwing shadows the way a full-grown elm would . . . they had a silent roar of their own.

The gearsmith startled her when he came to stand beside her and spoke. "These were commissioned by House Relothian."

Something in that sounded off. "The king is Relothian."

"Yes," said the gearsmith. "And so are all the members of his family."

She turned to look at him. The playful grin seemed more knowing this time, and Mira knew where to call next.

▲

• CHAPTER FIFTY •

Thank You

We are the choices we make. So choose well.

—Sheason teaching most often attributed to Palamon

VENDANJ?" THE VOICE sounded very far away. "Vendanj?"

Slowly, he opened his eyes in the dimness. His circumstances rushed in—Recityv, Convocation, imprisoned in the pits deep beneath Solath Mahnus for rendering—and he looked back into the eyes of Artixan, the finest mentor he'd had in his early Sheason years.

"How long have I been asleep?" He looked around, finding himself the lone prisoner in the dark cell. "And where's Rolen?"

"Roughly eighteen hours," his old friend answered, "and I daresay your hope of being shackled in the same place with another Sheason was a bit fanciful."

He rubbed the back of his head, which had apparently taken several swift licks with a cudgel. "I figured I could find him if they didn't put us together."

"Mmmm, yes, that would have gone over well, too." Artixan shifted where he sat—on the bottom stone step that led up to the cell door. "Your politics haven't improved much."

Vendanj made a weak laugh, and instantly regretted it, pain spinning through his head as he did so. "I like to think they have. Everyone at Convocation is still breathing, aren't they?" He thought a moment. "So, it's what, third hour?"

"Round about. Safe time for an old man like me to shuffle down to see an old student. Give him another lesson or two, perhaps." Artixan's smile was playful, but still sad.

"Good trick if you can do it," he said, and tried to sit up. New waves of pain rippled through him.

"Stay still," Artixan ordered with a bit of vim. "Let me share the news that needs sharing, while you rest."

Vendanj nodded, and settled back.

"Convocation didn't get far after you were carted out. Lots of squabbling to establish a pecking order, if you ask me." Artixan shook his head. "Beyond that, there's some good and bad you should know about."

Vendanj braced himself.

"Randeur Thaelon has sent an envoy to broker peace with the League." Hope rang in Artixan's voice. "Sent his own daughter to do the negotiating. You know her?"

"Ketrine," Vendanj said, gladdening to hear this news. "Smarter than you and I together. But I didn't think she'd been given the authority to render yet."

"She hasn't. But she's not alone. I have to think Roth will take it seriously that Thaelon sent her on this errand." Artixan fell silent for several long moments.

"Out with it," Vendanj coaxed. "Whatever it is can't be worse than I've seen recently."

Artixan hesitated a moment more. "First Sodalist E'Sau was murdered tonight. The assassin has implicated the Sheason Order—left one of our knives in the poor man."

"Dead gods!" Vendanj seethed through gritted teeth. He welcomed the pain in his head that came with it. "Roth."

"Bastard dragged E'Sau's new widow and children to the scene." Artixan sounded both weary and angry. "Word of it will spread without the League itself as gossipmonger. That will all happen, I'm sure, before we can prove it was Roth behind it all."

Vendanj calmed himself in order to think past the act and toward intentions. "Who will replace E'Sau?"

"The Sodality will vote, of course," Artixan began. "But a young man by the name of Palon is the likely successor."

"I've met him. Urge the Sodality to replace E'Sau quickly. We'll need their support."

Artixan nodded as though such was already under way.

After several long breaths, Vendanj turned to his old friend and mentor. "And you're here on Helaina's behalf, too."

Artixan smiled. "She shouldn't be seen in the pits. Especially not with you. And especially not during Convocation."

Feeling a bit stronger, Vendanj propped himself up on his elbows. "Tell her Tahn is fine. He survived Tillinghast. And his memory has been restored."

"Where is he now?"

"Aubade Grove." Vendanj shared with Artixan that Tahn had stopped using the guiding words he'd been taught by his father. He also shared with him Tahn's enthusiasm to get back to the Grove and try to find a way to strengthen the Veil. "It's odd the path life takes, isn't it?"

"What about you?" Artixan asked, probing as he'd done when Vendanj had studied *knowledge* and *influence* with the man.

"Older. More bitter. Less trusting." The small smile that had spread on his face quickly faded. "Disappointed and angry that the Sheason are divided."

Artixan's brows rose, questioning. "Is that disappointment in yourself, then?"

The smile returned by half. It was good to have his mentor goading him again. He'd spent eight years under the man's tutelage. The first four as a Sulivon—mastering the requisite knowledge to command the Will—and the latter four learning the art of influence—the actual use of the Will. He remembered fondly that much of that time had been spent answering questions about his own motivations and feelings. When it came to Vendanj's decisions and actions, Artixan was a man who cared more about *why* than *how*. What had mattered to Vendanj was that Artixan cared at all. That concern was something even Vendanj's father had never bothered to show.

Vendanj left that part of his past alone. He had no time for it right now.

"Yes," he said. "Disappointment in myself. Not just me. But yes."

"Good," Artixan said, looking pleased. "Then I can trust that you plan to repair it."

He nodded, feeling new aches in his neck. "I do. Once we're through with Convocation, we're heading to Estem Salo. I believe, with Tahn and the others, we'll right this ship."

Artixan studied him for a moment, running his knuckles down his bearded jaw. "Don't bully Thaelon. I've a lot of respect for the man. He's reasonable, and unusually creative in his solutions."

"No bullying," Vendanj agreed. "I just need him to see things for what they are. Same as Convocation."

"And be careful as you do it." The admonition had the feel of a parent's caution. His mentor hadn't had children of his own, and Vendanj had been glad to fill that role as an unspoken surrogate. "But don't go in all milksop, either."

"No milksop. Understood."

After it all, this was how he'd originally bonded with the man. Artixan had a benevolent demeanor, and could be trusted to be fair. But he followed his conscience without fail, regardless of anything else. Even his Sheason oath. Just as he'd done when he'd revived Helaina's stillborn child, Tahn.

Vendanj shared a long look with the man he'd come to think of as his father in many important ways. "Do you ever regret it?"

"It" was another thing that needed no context between them. They'd spoken of it many times.

"No," he said firmly but without sharpness. He leaned forward, resting his elbows on his knees, his face softening a bit in the shadows. "Helaina was suffering. Just as one with leprosy or cowardice. Just as one who others won't allow to outlive a reputation earned by poor choices. And by some small miracle, she got pregnant, which was the answer for her suffering. So"—he hunched his shoulders—"when her child came still, and she asked me to help, I helped. I don't regret it any more than I would regret counseling a coward, curing an illness, or helping someone who needs to start over."

"Except that helping her was an illicit use of Will." Vendanj was more calling to question the Sheason oath than Artixan's choice.

His old friend sat considering a long while. "I suppose it makes you and I more alike than either of us might care to admit." Then he laughed, full and loud, the sound of it echoing in the pit cell.

Despite the pain it caused him, Vendanj joined in.

After their laughter subsided, he looked his old friend in the eye. "Did I ever thank you for sitting with me in those days after Illenia died?"

Artixan's smile turned sad. "Every time we meet. And you're welcome, my boy. You're welcome."

• CHAPTER FIFTY-ONE •

Pendulums

One must admit the possibility that the Veil and the Quiet weren't an unforeseen aberration, but part of the Framers' plans from the beginning.

—*A New Take on Reconciliation, an Argument for Design,*
from the office of the Third Prelacy of Recityv

IT HAD BEEN a long time. *Too long,* Tahn thought, as he stepped into the wide observation dome atop the tower of astronomy. He'd made the long ascent up the tower stairs in anticipation of this moment. Nowhere had he seen a view of the night sky like the one he had now. The view was, quite simply, magnificent.

In the shadows stood sky tools. The great skyglass dominated the center of the dome. But here, too, were armillary spheres, orreries, astraria, astrolabes, quadrant maps, and more. They sat silently waiting for an astronomer to make use of them to measure the sky above.

Polaema had ensured Tahn had access to college resources as he began piecing together his Succession argument. But that wasn't why he was here tonight. Before he formally declared Succession tomorrow, and got to the heart of his reason for returning here, he had one thing he wanted to pursue with his access to Grove annals and archives.

Quillescent.

Even that, though, faded momentarily from his thoughts. The vault of heaven opened above him as though near enough that he could reach out and touch it. He'd always loved the feeling here. A calm lay over everything. The patience of the stars. Thoughtful study and observation high above the rest of the Grove gave the domes a reverence all their own. They called it "walking with the stars" up here. Tahn smiled, relaxing more than he could remember since leaving the Hollows.

Slowly, he strolled the circumference of the room, looking out through the dome glass. He'd come at dark hour to be sure the sky was at its blackest, and because both moons were currently deep below the horizon. The long plain around Aubade Grove was uninterrupted by hills or forests, giving the widest possible view of the sky. Only the other college towers blemished a completely unobstructed field of view.

Tahn noted stars and constellations as he went, speaking them softly. And only when he'd walked a full circle, and drunk in the settled, patient feeling of the dome, did he turn inward to his task.

Quillescent.

The Quiet had used the word to describe him more than once. Vendanj didn't know what it meant. Tahn hoped he might find some reference to it here, in the Grove. He'd already visited the college annals, searching in the ways he knew how to find the word. Unsuccessful, he'd come here.

In addition to the great skyglass and other instruments used to map the sky, the domes were used to store a select number of volumes. They were both safer here and easier to access when inevitable sky questions arose that required reference to prior studies.

He found a hooded lamp, lit it, and began to peruse the rare books. By the time he got to the table used for star charting, he had four volumes: Jalen's *Reference to Celestial Movement;* a very old compendium of star charts; *The Language of Heaven,* author unknown; and the diary of Pealy Omendal. Omendal was considered by many the father of astronomy, being one of those to break off from the Sheason to establish the Grove.

Tahn sat and began to leaf through his selections. Jalen's reference book didn't appear to hold any clues. He moved on to the compendium, a book he'd retrieved more from curiosity than any sense that it could help him answer his question. But a third of the way in, he stopped, staring down at the name written under the pole-star: Quilesem.

He quickly checked the legend on the map, looking for any clarifications. The map was old. So old that it predated the tradition of noting the year of its authorship. Leaving the compendium open, he slid it to the side and opened *The Language of Heaven.* Surely he'd find a language reference here. This volume was like the astronomer's dictionary, but of a complete nature, before reductionists began to consolidate terminologies for consistency.

Tahn found nothing, and eagerly moved on to Omendal's diary. There was no internal reference guide to this book. Just daily entries. Tahn began to scan, but he didn't have to do so for long before finding an entry that felt close. His heart began to beat hard as he started over, reading slowly, carefully.

The diarist spoke of navigation by star alignments. He described the fashioning of a new instrument to assist the "men at sea." And then he spoke of the great pole-star, which never moved from its place in heaven. A star he called Quilesem.

The great star is the perfect guide, the perfect reference point. It is a gentle reminder and instructor in its motionless state. So, we call it Quilesem because it is at rest. It is quiet. It is still. From its unwavering point, we can measure so much of the sky, which may lead to the truest meaning for this name: Something from nothing.

Tahn looked up from the books to the pole-star, which to his recollection had never carried the name Quilesem. *I'm close.* He'd just turned his attention back to the diary, when a voice sounded from the other side of the dome. It came deep and clear as a bell heard tolling on a winter morning. But it came softly, as though its owner kept the same reverence for this place. The stars.

"Find what you're looking for?"

As the words touched the air, the air changed. Quickened. In the tower dome a feeling of danger spread. It felt to Tahn like malice born of disregard. Reflexively he reached for his bow, but he hadn't brought it with him.

From around the great skyglass a man emerged. Ordinary enough. His clothes showed no college emblem. He might be unaffiliated, but then how did he gain access to the tower? The man was Tahn's height, more slight of build, older by twenty years or more. He walked with casual certainty, his eyes never leaving Tahn. And his face . . . his face remained expressionless. Very much like the Bar'dyn.

That was the feeling. The Quiet. But this man looked like someone's father. Not a farmer like Sutter's da. More the way a struggling inn owner might. With a worn, weary face, but a focused, watchful stare.

It's the man I saw across the street from Perades.

"Who are you?" Tahn asked, closing his books.

"You want a name?"

"You're not with the college. Or you forced your way past the dome guards." Tahn slowly stood.

"No, I'm not with the college" was all the man said, coming to a stop a few strides from him.

"What do you want? Who are you?"

The stranger stared, made a slow blink. "I'm here to learn, just as you are."

Tahn shook his head. "I doubt it."

The man's head tilted subtly to one side, and Tahn's throat began to burn the way it did from a deep winter cough, when it had grown raw and every swallow seared as it went down. The man simply watched as Tahn's face pinched with the pain. Tahn struggled not to swallow, trying to avoid the sensation of a thousand stabbing splinters.

"Let's not speak any more about doubts," the man said.

Almost immediately the pain in Tahn's throat subsided.

"You're here to argue for Continuity." The stranger spoke with certainty. "It can be the only reason you'd come here, now."

Tahn stared back, his fear mounting, but with a grain of anger. This man had to be Velle.

"Leave Aubade Grove," Tahn said, keeping as much command over his voice as he could. "There's nothing for you here."

The man looked up at the dome above. Tahn felt a stirring, not of air, but something more subtle. A half moment later a pane of glass shattered and rained down around him. The sound of glass splintering as it hit the floor was loud in the quiet dome. Then, in rapid succession, several other windows burst, here and there. But it didn't seem random. And when Tahn looked at them, he saw it. The man had broken open views where several of the wandering stars could be found at this hour in the sky. *He knows the placement of the planets.*

But that realization faded fast beneath the simpler truth Tahn had just witnessed.

Resonance. The stranger was making a simple display of it. Just as he'd done with Tahn's throat.

"What shall we break next?" The man's voice held no humor. "So that we learn together."

Tahn's anger and fear swelled. He imagined drawing his bow, as he had done before, with no arrow. Just the idea of firing something of himself. From habit he made the motion as if raising his weapon, and let go a string that wasn't there. A rushing swept through him, a warm wave that exited his outstretched arm and struck at the man with unseen force.

But the energy of it broke around the stranger as a wave does on a breakwater. A disturbance in the air made the other appear watery for a moment, as though floating beneath the surface of a clear lake. Then the rushing was gone. Stillness returned in an instant.

The man's eyes narrowed ever so slightly. And this time the Resonance Tahn felt was not a burn in his throat, but an opening in his mind, his memory. He saw for the briefest moment a day at the edge of the Scar he'd spent with Grant, his father. He saw them laughing together, and sharing a pair of molasses sticks at the side of a river where they sat fishing. He saw his father listening to his questions and answering them and sounding hopeful. He talked about a day when they would leave the Scar. And in the dusk when light-flies lit the water's surface, he heard Grant tell him he loved him. And that he would never stop trying to undo the Scar—what it meant, what it was, what it had done to them.

Tahn's heart ached at the memory, one so deeply buried that it hadn't surfaced yet. Maybe never would have.

And then, after lingering a few sweet moments, it began to burn away. The stranger shifted his resonant render inside Tahn to erase the memory.

"No!" Tahn raised his arms as one might to ward off a blow, and pushed his own life's energy to resist. He felt the rushing again, but this time handled it better, focusing it on the attack.

Bits of the memory continued to go, like a paper puzzle left on a park table that finds itself caught in a light breeze. He'd loved his father. Through all the painful lessons, when it seemed the man had not loved him back, Tahn had kept loving him. And here, now, he could see a memory of a time that helped him know his father had loved him back. A simple memory. But one with clear feeling. He couldn't let it go!

Tahn pushed harder, feeling like he was wading upstream against winter runoff. But the stranger simply showed him another blank look, nodded, and the memory was gone. Tahn cried out again in anger and loss. He didn't know what it was anymore that had been taken from him, but the hole it left felt like love gone away. It hurt deep down where feelings start.

And it made him furious.

In a breath's time he summoned his memory of those six

small ones on the Soliel, of friends taking their own lives in the Scar—a place created by creatures like the one standing in front of him now—and he focused it all into a blind rush that he thrust at the man.

This time, Tahn's attack drove the man back hard against the skyglass. The loud thump resounded in the instrument's hollow body, and the man slumped to his knees. Tahn didn't let up. He brought to mind Wendra and Mira, their losses, his own failures, and shot another brutal wave of energy at the man.

The Quiet man raised a hand, deflecting the attack. He then lifted his head to stare at Tahn. The awfulness Tahn saw in the other's eyes was not malevolence, but ambivalence. The stranger simply didn't care about Tahn, his life, or death. The stare caused Tahn to falter and step back.

The next moment the man was searching Tahn's mind. Tahn tried to deflect it, but he was tired and cold. As the other stood, his face came the closest Tahn would see it to smiling.

"Resonance," the other intoned, the sound unmusical. "Of course. Like what you are about to feel."

The man raised a hand, fingers apart, and dropped his chin. Inside himself, Tahn felt as though his heart and lungs and belly had been pressed in a vise. The muscles in his neck stiffened. His jaw locked. And as his body clenched, memories began to draw together. Just a few at first. Then more. It reminded him of standing at Tillinghast, except now the associated images in his mind were . . . selective. Some came to him from the Scar. Some from here in the Grove as a young boy. Some from the Hollows. More than a few returned to him from his time since meeting Vendanj: his flight to Tillinghast, and his actions on the Soliel plain. Seen together, they told a different story about Tahn. And when he focused through the pain in his body and looked at the ordinary man standing across from him, resonating with Tahn along particular strings in his life, he began to understand. He and this man . . . were not so different.

But then why follow me here? What does it want from me? It could have killed me already.

He struggled, trying to muster enough strength to break

free. The other was too strong for Tahn to fight with brute force. It held him in this viselike grip, and wove a picture of who Tahn was that scared him to the bone.

Is this what Quillescent means? Feels like?

Then a sweet epiphany distilled in Tahn's mind. If the stranger was using Resonance to do this to him, then Tahn could likewise stir something inside the other. The moment he had this thought, his body jerked painfully back, rushing toward the edge of the dome. He slammed against the glass, breaking two broad panes. The bright, splintering sound of glass surrounded him again. A light wind swept through the opening here at the height of the tower. He lay crumpled on the floor, feeling a moment's relief from the pressing in his body and the story of himself he'd witnessed. He gasped, trying to breathe, as he heard footsteps approaching.

With no prior thought to give him away, Tahn imagined and brought forward simple images and feelings. Uncomplicated things. A green shoot risen near a trickling stream. The moment when light first brightens the east. Laughter with Sutter. Not knowing quite how to do it, Tahn probed the stranger, seeking to find in him a chord he could strike with these things. Something to resonate with. He thought he could cripple the man by making him see the better side of his life.

But either Tahn was completely incapable of this, or there was no such feeling or idea in the man with which to resonate. Tahn saw him slowly shake his head as he came.

A moment later, his body began to seize again. He stiffened, and looked up into the stars, trying to think of how to escape. The stranger dragged him through the glass a short way with an act of rendering. An act of Resonance. He was sure the man meant to cast him from the tower. He'd tumble hundreds of strides to his death.

"If you could kill me," the man asked, "would you? And how would you know if that was right?"

Tahn shot the man an angry stare. The stranger somehow knew that Tahn, for most of his life, had sought such confirmations.

"You should die!" Tahn spoke through clenched teeth, scared and angry. "There's no mystery in that!"

He had to do something. Trying to find something gentle inside the man with which to resonate hadn't worked. Brute force hadn't worked. Tahn was now weak and empty.

"You might be right," the other said, "but I'd like you to be certain."

Tahn began to feel something new, something blindingly painful. He felt as though parts of who he was were being stolen, remade. Just enough that he understood his life was being rendered. *As the children on the Soliel would have been!*

That's when he realized he'd fought this wrong.

He looked into the stranger's face, and began with the idea that this Quiet man was muscle and bone. Just like Tahn. He didn't try to shove the stranger back. Instead he sought to be one with the idea of the man's flesh. And he took hold of that idea . . . with animosity.

The other flinched, losing his grip on him. Tahn took a staggering breath, but kept at his own sense of Resonance. He slowly eased himself back from the edge of the dome and stood. For the moment, he had control, and he pressed his advantage, clenching the man with the notion of shattering his bones from inside his body.

The man began to fight through Tahn's grip. Tahn had anticipated it, and shifted his attack to the obvious Resonance he'd missed.

He reached out with the loss and loathing he'd known in his own life and sought it in the life of the stranger. He followed those strings to the bottom, their lowest note, found a chord in the man. And struck it.

In his mind came a new rushing. Images from the stranger's life, emotional resonance at a pitch Tahn couldn't explain. There was a level on which they *were* the same. It was a disquieting thought, but Tahn exploited it, pushed it, believing he could break the other's will.

Resonance thrummed inside him. The feel of it was like the vibration of a chilling melody felt more in the wood of the instrument that plays it than in its sound.

It's changing me.

But for the moment, Tahn had control, and he could tell

that finding something to resonate with inside this man was also changing the part of him that *could* resonate with the Quiet.

He deepened the feeling, seeking to crush the stranger. And as he did, he sensed that the energy he expended was greater than his own. But no glass shattered. No orrery metal bent or sagged. No wood seared and smoked. No strange winds engulfed them. No paper fluttered in warm funnels and whipped through broken windows.

The fight would have been a quiet one to witness. Just Tahn and this stranger, staring at each other, focused in a way no observer would understand. Yet a great, invisible storm was taking place. A flurry that tore at them. It filled his mind with noise and dread, like a tempest, images raining down hard as hail. But it was all a storm inside him. And inside the other.

The man gave Tahn a searching look, shook his head once, slowly, and the storm abruptly ceased.

Tahn was as still and calm inside as the dome around them. The man had simply canceled Tahn's effort at Resonance.

Had the man been playing a game? Testing him? Helping him?

The idea of Resonance had been made more real. More practical. More dangerous. And Tahn had learned that two very different people could be brought into resonance with one another.

If it had all been a lesson to Tahn, why?

With terrible suddenness, the man seized Tahn again, and began throwing him about violently. He hit his worktable, scattering his books. His body whirled left into the dome again, shattering more glass. Then forward, like a hurled doll, he slammed into the skyglass, ringing it like a deep bell. Tahn fell hard to the floor, gasping.

But through the attack, the man hadn't wounded Tahn's memory or touched his life's energy. Tahn had been rattled like a toy, as if to remind him where he stood.

The man casually walked to where Tahn lay on the floor, and looked down. He spoke softly, showing no signs of exertion for what had just happened. "Most have lost faith in you. But not me." The stranger looked Tahn over. "Not yet.

I'm interested in what path you're on now. What you'll learn about Resonance. What you'll do with that knowledge."

Silence fell across the tower dome, until the man simply walked away. Tahn could hear his footsteps receding down the stairs, as he lay bruised and beaten.

Dear silent gods . . .

Tahn's mind reeled at what had just happened, at how he'd reshaped the act of firing a bow, firing a part of himself. Resonance. He'd looked inside to find moments of ache and pain and used them to find the same in the Quiet man. And even now, he could feel the residue of the other's deep agony inside himself.

He shivered, realizing that his attempt at this new Resonance had been nothing. The other had handled him like a doll. What did it say about the resonances inside the Quiet?

Succession now meant more to him. He still intended to try to strengthen the Veil. More than ever, in fact. Especially if there were others like this man waiting inside the Bourne to descend into the Eastlands. But he now wanted to learn more about Resonance for himself. Just as he had during this fight. Because he had a feeling that sooner or later this Quiet man would no longer find him interesting. And it was clear he could end Tahn with little more than a thought.

He also wanted to understand what the Quiet man meant when he said, *Most have lost faith in you. But not me.* And something told him he'd only understand that by truly understanding his own Succession argument. He needed to *win* Succession, keep the Grove focused on the question until they found an answer. Until they could prove Resonance with every science. Use it.

But weary and hurting, he couldn't focus for long on the questions. He lay down flat, stared up through the dome at the stars, and slowly caught his breath.

CHAPTER FIFTY-TWO

A Touch of Resonance

A person's signature, to a Leiholan, isn't their name. Not some thing they write or say. Rather, it's the set of notes that defines who and what they are. It's their resonant harmonics at a fundamental level. Know these, and you have the all of them.

—Framing statement in the study of harmonics and personal signatures, Descant Cathedral

WENDRA STEPPED INTO an open atrium hidden somewhere deep inside the sprawl of Descant Cathedral halls and buildings. The young music student who had guided her here retreated without a word. Across the square, Belamae stood waiting. He'd not called for Wendra until after meridian, leaving her the morning to reflect on the memories of her mother that had flooded her mind.

Almost immediately, those memories had become like an old, familiar afghan that she might draw around her shoulders when the evening turned chill. The last half of the prior night, she hadn't slept. She'd sat at her bedside, mourning as though she'd lost her mother again. She was grateful to have memories of the woman returned to her, but it made her mother's absence a sharper thing to bear.

Belamae beckoned her to him. She crossed the atrium to a high table set with several tuning forks. He stood on the other side of the table like a barkeep ready to offer her a drink. He picked up one of the forks and struck it soundly against the tabletop. The fork began to hum.

"Vibration," the Maesteri said, and placed the fork in a hole drilled into a small box set on the table. While the fork continued to hum, Belamae picked up another tuning fork and set it in the hole of an adjacent box. He then put a hand on the first fork to still it. To Wendra's surprise, the second fork was humming at the same pitch as the first had been.

She glanced up at Belamae to find a satisfied-looking smile on his face. "The two forks are calibrated to the same pitch. The second one is humming what we call a *response note*. What you're hearing is the transfer of vibration, Wendra. We call this—"

"Resonance," she supplied.

"Just so," he said, grinning. "Incidentally, did you know that Sheason were once called Inner Resonance? Sheason exercise a power of Will that uses and affects this vibratory part of all things. Now, watch."

The Maesteri then repeated the demonstration, but used three similarly tuned forks to show further resonance from one to the next to the next. Wendra's mind began to race with applications for this new understanding. Though, before she'd gotten far, Belamae picked up one of the tuning forks and waved her over to a pianoforte whose cover had been removed.

It was a short walk, but when they got to the instrument, Belamae's breathing had a slight wheeze about it. He steadied himself, holding the side of the pianoforte, his features pinched.

"Belamae?"

"I'm all right, my girl. Sometimes my air and blood don't keep up with me."

He rubbed at his chest a bit. Wendra noted the pallor in his skin, and the hollows in his cheeks. He looked ill. But he saw her concern and smiled brightly.

"Now," he continued, "you might assume from our first experiment that resonance occurs only at the exact same pitch. Observe." He struck the fork against the side of the instrument, and passed it a hand's width above the strings in a slow, graceful motion. When he'd finished, he stilled the tuning fork and asked, "What do you hear?"

Wendra inclined toward the pianoforte. What she heard surprised her. Not only did she hear the exact pitch, she heard several of its octaves also resonating in the strings drawn over the soundboard.

"You're hearing octaves, my girl. Strings attuned to not just the same note, but to a numerically related vibration. See here." He pointed out several strings. "The lengths of these are all proportional, doubling in length for each lower octave."

She took the tuning fork from Belamae, struck it, and passed it over the strings again. After silencing the fork, she leaned in, listening close. "I hear thirds and fifths, too. But fainter."

"Just so!" Belamae exclaimed. "There are secondary and tertiary harmonics, and more still than that. Together, these do not always seem or sound harmonious, and yet they are related to the signature of a thing. Really, any two notes have a relationship; it's about a consistent structure. Has much to do with math."

They held a companionable silence until Wendra's mind turned to another question. "If any two notes have a relationship, this helps explain how a Leiholan is shaped by any resonance she sings."

He nodded. "In a real sense, you become what you sing."

"Then what of Suffering?" she asked, also thinking of Belamae's refashioned version of that song—for war.

Belamae's smile fell.

Wendra clarified her question. "You said Suffering is always changing." She followed the logic. "So if Suffering is changing, and a Leiholan—on some level—becomes what she sings, then Soluna . . ."

He held up his hands. "We've been singing Suffering for ages, Wendra. We understand how to adapt to its subtle shifts. But . . . it's different in these last few years. I'm convinced there's something more at work than the normal evolution of the Song."

"Any more of an idea what it is?"

He shook his head, his face drawn tight in genuine concern. "I don't know. But another Leiholan struggled last night. Worse than before. Suffering battered her something awful. I worry she might not . . ."

He looked up at her then, and took her hands in his. "But please don't fret. We've music to make. And today we'll focus on what I've just shown you: Everything has a resonant structure composed of many harmonic signatures. And it's possible to find common resonances along these signatures *in many things at once.*"

WENDRA WALKED THE streets of the Cathedral Quarter, alone. She hadn't left Descant since beginning her training, and was surprised all over again that the cathedral sat in the middle of a slum.

For the most part, the people were warm with their greetings. The pitiable shared the bond of struggling against life's bad odds. Half of those she passed followed their hellos with a petition for food or coin. And when Wendra shook her head, she typically got a "dead gods save you" before she passed on. The other half were equally warm in their greetings, but with a hint of larceny or madness beneath it all.

There was always music, too. Almost every mealhouse and tavern had some kind of performance taking place. Between the various strains of song and the meaty smells and the redolent stench of those who couldn't afford a bath, she nearly forgot that she was on her way to find human traders, like Jastail—who'd nearly sold Wendra and Penit. In fact, it was the highwayman she was specifically trying to find.

She had no real information about where she might locate him, but when he'd taken her before, he'd moved her a long way on the river. The same river that ran through Recityv. Her best guess was that if she could find a quiet dock, there'd be boats used for illicit trade—the kind that could push out into the current and be downriver with pickings before a general search was made.

So, she didn't bother poking her head into drinking holes down narrow alleys, or visiting brothels or gambling pits or auction houses. And she didn't alert anyone to where she was going, least of all Belamae. He'd see this excursion for what it was: a step toward knowing if and when she meant to leave her training. But she needed to at least start to inquire. She'd be happy if she found the Recityv river docks were little more than a travel port and fish market. Either way, she cut her path through the quarter, intent to find out.

The air grew colder as she neared the riverside district. The music here was slower, more often rendered in minor keys. And the voices less practiced, more broken, as from constant tobacco use or short sleep. In a way, this music was resonating with the feeling of the area. And its people.

She passed several inns and taverns before coming to an intricate dock system, like a series of streets and avenues on the water. Countless boats and barges sat moored in the night. The smell of old, wet wood hung thick over everything. Few people strolled the wharf-front. And those that did spoke in hushed tones, if they spoke at all. A fine mist hung in the air, enough to be a nuisance but not entirely hamper her ability to see.

Looking out over the scores of boats, she noted several with lighted windows. The kind of people she was looking for would be keeping their privacy, not standing around in taverns or mealhouses. Spending undue time in a place would be reckless. It's not what Jastail would do. With that thought, she started out onto the docks.

Reckless to go out there alone, she thought. But she had her song.

The pilings and dock edges were covered with a brown moss. In the faint glow of storm lamps hanging from iron spikes driven through the pilings, it looked abrasive, like coral. A few of the boats she passed appeared empty, despite the lamps burning inside them. The farther out into the dock system she went, the more frequently she heard voices gathered in what amounted to small floating taverns. Little groups huddled around flickering oil lamps doing the serious business of drinking.

The sound of rippling water. The smell of moldy wood and the vague odor of fish. The dim pool of light in a boat that could cast off to the river in a moment's time. Something told her she was getting close. At the farthest edges of the docks, a few of the boats had dockside strongmen standing like mute sentries. *One of these,* she guessed.

She approached two of the strongmen, but was shooed away before she'd even opened her mouth to lie. She finally turned left and wandered the far edge of the docks where she could scarcely see the lights of the wharf-front. The few tavern songs that carried this far sounded like an out-of-tune song box, warped and lethargic. Near the very end of the dock, she spied another strongman, this one sitting on a crate, staring ahead, motionless.

She took a long breath and approached him. Not fast. Not tentatively. She came to stand over him where he guarded the dock end of a short plank. "I have business."

The man looked her up and down, the way a farmer does a mule at auction. "I don't think so."

"I have business," she repeated, pushing her tone down her throat to give it a husky edge. "If I say it again, I'll be sure your employer takes the lost sale out of your ass."

Her threat seemed to do nothing to the man's willingness to move. "What business do you think you have here?"

"I have stock to sell," she replied, working to sound matter-of-fact. "I can do it here. Or I can go somewhere else. If you turn me away, I'll be sure to spread word that you did. And I'll make sure your competitors know you underpay. I suspect your employer will take that out of your ass, too."

His eyes narrowed on her. "I don't believe you."

"Or how about this." Wendra bent forward to look him levelly in the eyes. "How about rather than dim your employer's business, I just end it? How about I share the details of this boat with the Recityv guard, one of which had a daughter taken recently. His justice will be different than your employer's, I think."

The man laughed. "Go on in." He caught her arm. "And if you get lonely, later, I have help here for you." He clutched his groin.

"I don't think you have the stamina," she said. "But I'll remember the offer."

He let her go, and Wendra crossed the plank and descended two steps onto the deck. She moved to a large cabin forward on the barge. She took a deep breath and went in, not eagerly, not tentatively, just like one who had something to pawn.

Oh my, was she out of place. Her clothes weren't drabcloth, but were still several cuts beneath the garments these people wore. Brush cloth in rich drake and cobalt and crimson hues. Wide cuffs and collars. Belts encrusted with glass gems. Rose-oiled beards kept trim. The ladies with pearl necklaces in a multitude of lengths. It was no secret where some of their trade funds were spent. But the finery looked almost comic, out of place for sure, given the multitude of stains in each garment. And if the clothes didn't look odd by themselves, they were a sharp contrast to their owners' faces. The skin of these five had the weathered look of riverfolk who got the glare of the sun coming down and back up again as it's reflected off the water.

There were five of them, three men and two women. They didn't appear mean-spirited, or jovial in the way Jastail had. They struck her like a group of traders. The one difference was the bottle on the table. This wasn't mash, or kettle wine. This bottle had a gilded label. It was an aged whisky. The sharp tang of it hung in the air.

They waited on her, not as an intruder, but as if she were like any of a hundred others. Wendra could see knives and swords at their hips. Two daggers lay atop the table near the bottle.

"I'll have a drink of that," Wendra began, trying to play her part.

Without speaking, one man poured a mouthful into his own glass and held it out to her. Wendra took it and gulped it down, fighting the sting that rose in her nose and behind her eyes, then handed back the glass.

Still none of them spoke, waiting.

Wendra swallowed twice. "I have stock to sell. You buying?"

"We have no idea what you're talking about," the man who'd poured her drink said. He had a great belly. The kind that looked like hardened muscle.

"Three children," she followed, unflapped.

The man showed no curiosity. Wendra thought back to her own abduction, and an idea struck her. "And a pregnant woman."

The stoic faces showed a moment's eager interest. The drink-pourer motioned one of his fellows to move around behind Wendra to block the door.

"Selling people is reprehensible," the man said. "What makes you think we trade in such goods?"

Wendra fought her panic to run, and instead stepped farther into the room. She fingered the bottle, inspecting the label as one who knew the difference in label whiskys. "I can take my business elsewhere, if you haven't the stomach for it."

The man finally smiled, showing teeth gone brown as the moss on the pilings. "Have a seat," he invited.

"I don't intend to be here long enough to get comfortable," she answered. "No offense. The whisky is your company."

The man laughed at the insult. "You're brave for a pretty girl alone at the far end of the docks."

"What makes you think I'm here alone?" Wendra showed them each a challenging eye.

"Oh, I don't know." The man's chair creaked under his considerable weight as he reclined. "The docks don't hide much. And any help you have would arrive too late, I imagine. Don't you?"

Wendra decided to play a card here. One that would, she hoped, get a reaction she could use. "Does the name Jastail mean anything to you?"

The man's smile faded immediately. Wendra saw anger in a few faces.

"You're twice dumb to come out here *and* use that bastard's name." He sat forward, staring at her. "You're no trader. You'd know better than to threaten with Jastail's friendship. His closest friends wouldn't do it. So you're no friend of his." The man's smile returned. He poured himself another drink and licked the rim in a suggestion of tasting Wendra's lips, before downing the whisky.

"The real question," the man went on, "is why you're looking for him. Pretty thing like you."

From below the floor, Wendra heard a muffled cry. "Run! Get out!"

The big man shot a look to one of his men, who ducked out the rear cabin door. He then returned his attention to Wendra.

She didn't try to maintain her ruse. "Fair enough. The son

of a whore owes me. I will make him pay, you may trust that. But I need to know where to find him. I need to know where he trades." Wendra thought, and quickly added, "I have no quarrel with your trade in stock. And it's true that I aim to become a trader myself." Even saying the words sickened her some. "But for now, I'll settle for a list of places where the 'dust goes up.'"

Wendra had remembered the phrase for the auction blocks where captured stock crossed a makeshift stage with chalked feet that plumed as they stepped across. Shoes were taken to prevent flight. Their feet were chalked to keep them from cracking and thus limiting their owner's value.

The man nodded, appreciating both her intent to exact a price on Jastail and her knowledge of the trade.

"So, the three children? And the pregnant woman?" he asked, hopefully.

"A lie," she admitted.

A muffled slap came, followed by a cry of pain—again below the floorboards.

The man made a show of being crestfallen. "Pity about the pregnant woman. Wombs are our specialty." He smiled, and leaned close enough that Wendra could smell the drink on his breath. "But where the dead gods take with one hand, they give with another." He looked over her shoulder at one of his companions, who swept forward and grabbed Wendra's arms, pinning them behind her.

The man sat back, poured another drink, and sipped this time, while staring at her thoughtfully. "You're childbearing age. You'll make a nice price. And if Jastail has some squabble with you, he might pay half again as much for the chance to be the one to sell you in."

"In?" she asked.

The man waved away her question. "Put her with the others," he said, and returned his attention to his drink.

"Wait!" she shouted. Something in the sound of her voice caught their attention, and stopped the man holding her. "Just tell me where to find him, in the event that I escape. I'll make sure to kill him."

The man looked back at her and shook his head in further

appreciation. "The bastard really worked on you, didn't he? What did he do, force you to spread your legs? Our buyers don't care for that." The man sat forward, and ripped down her pants far enough to see her waist. Something dawned in his eyes as he saw the stretch marks in her skin from her recent pregnancy. "You bore a child, I see. Jastail took you for the child. That jackass has grit, I'll say that."

"Just tell me," Wendra pressed.

As she said it, the man who'd gone out returned, shutting the rear cabin door behind him.

"For all the good it will do you, my girl, Jastail is a man of habit. If you were in his company before, you already know where to find him."

Of course.

The man hadn't let go of her pants. And now eyed her skin, his gaze moving over her belly and up to her breasts. "Maybe you'll give us some fun, too. What a buyer doesn't know . . ."

Both women in the small deck cabin gave Wendra lustful looks. The one other man she could still see made no effort to hide the craving in his eyes. "Maybe she starts with the ladies," he offered. "We join in after."

Their trade in flesh. Their use of good whisky. The obvious carnalities these men and women shared. This crew had a deep, maddened sense of pleasure. Not unlike Jastail, who could only gamble anymore if the stakes were of the highest sort.

Wendra couldn't break the grip of the man holding her. And even if she could, running was useless. She'd never get through the door without them laying hold of her again, let alone past the dock man. *Sing them down.* But she didn't want to sing her shout-song. It would attract a lot of attention—loud and likely to shatter the deck cabin besides.

Resonance. In many things at once.

Without thinking further, she started to hum. It must have struck them odd, as they all froze where they were, staring at her.

She opened it up to song and reached out with it, caressing them, imagining the dark pleasures inside them—flesh on flesh, breath musty with bottles of fine rye, watching people lose their last hope as they were sold for coin to be dropped in a pocket.

Wendra worked to keep a quiet tone. A languid, seductive melody. She improvised lyrics that suggested unspoken sexual desires, winters of drinking from old bourbon reserves in front of fires with body after body in carnal combinations . . . and the lamentations of stock they sold to pay for it all. Control. It was an aphrodisiac at the heart of every trader. And Wendra sang the song of it. She found the resonant place in each of them that harbored those notes.

Like one tuning fork causing another to hum, then another, then another . . . Wendra's song caught them all in the embrace of what they wanted . . . what they felt most deeply. Most resonantly.

And she stroked that desire with her song.

She saw their eyes glaze as they became rapt in the visions she evoked in them. The man holding her let go. The glass in their leader's hand slipped and shattered on the floor—no one jumped. The women's brows pinched in the expression of pleasure felt in moments of great climax.

Wendra sang on, finding a further center to the song. A deeper resonance. She didn't rush, or sing louder. She sang *deeper*. She reached inside her own feelings for the pits of dark pleasure she enjoyed when she imagined rending the Quiet, who'd caused this trade. She found again the resonance of her own heart when her vision turned stark and her song ripped flesh from the bones of those who bought stock.

And she imagined it doing the same to the traders surrounding her in this dockside barge.

But this time, her song was not a series of rough shouts. This time, it was a slow, private melody. A strain that struck the chords of dark desire so forcefully that these traders began to slump where they sat or stood.

Wendra sang on. She reached deeper still, finding a depth of resonance she hadn't thought she could reach. It suggested dark desires to her own mind. Enticing things that wanted to be tried, experienced. She turned them on the traders, and found in them abominations of intent that even she couldn't imagine. But she didn't shy away. She embraced them. Sang them. Gave them life for these five. For herself. Making of them such an exultant, unbearable rush of fulfillment that she was only vaguely aware when they had all drawn their last breath with the intensity of their pleasure.

She'd killed them. She'd wrought a quiet rapture of body and spirit with her song. One that traded on the thrill of control and domination. On the thrill of pleasure.

She stopped singing as she smelled the unmistakable odor of a man's sex. And a woman's, too.

Then she sank to her hands and knees, shivering. Her face and body were coated with sweat. She panted from exertion, and the sensations still rippling inside her.

She had an afterthought that one of the women, in her final moments, had been glad to be relieved of the compulsions that bound her to the trade.

It might have been a full half hour before she could see clearly again. When she raised her head, she saw a small tube inside the dead leader's boot. She pulled it free, opened it, and found a map of stock trading posts.

As she knelt in the midst of these slavers, she shuddered with the truth of Belamae's caution.

Anytime you sing the resonance of a thing . . . you both are changed.

She could feel a dangerous, sensuous sound laughing around inside her. An irrational thought floated through her mind: *Go sex the strongman.*

You both are changed.

It made her wonder about singing Suffering. Had what she'd just sang been a kind of suffering, too? She didn't know. What had happened here seemed strangely unreal. And intoxicating. *What else can I sing . . . and who might it hurt?* But she wasn't sorry for killing the traders. There was none of that.

It was a long while more before she stood. Quietly, she searched the dead and found a set of keys on the man who'd briefly left their company. She slipped through the rear door and found a deck hatch. She keyed open the lock that fastened it shut, and pulled back the portal to find a stair that descended into a dark hold.

She climbed slowly down into the pitch black. She had the impression that she was being watched, evaluated. A moment later a small oil lamp was lit deeper in the hold. What she saw made her heart pulse hard with sympathy and anger. Seven women chained to wooden cots. Three of them were with child. These babies would come in a matter of a cycle or two, if she had any guess.

Without a word, she found the key to unlock their chains. They watched her with reticence. What surprised her most was that none of them rushed from their cots, from this hold, from this boat.

The youngest among them must have seen the question in Wendra's eyes. She shivered in the chill, her belly showing a child nearly ready to come. "They'll find us again." It was the fear that kept them bound. Probably a threat they'd heard repeatedly since being captured.

"No," Wendra said. "They're done taking women."

She wanted to sing something for them. Something soft and reassuring. But all hells, was she tired, and still cold inside. So instead she lay down by the young girl, hoping she had enough body warmth to calm the girl's shivers. She smiled a small smile in the dim light, thinking that *she* might need more warmth than the girl.

"What do we do?" another of the women asked.

"Let me rest a little while. Then, we'll leave the docks, and you'll go home."

Two of the women shared a skeptical look. "What about the dock hound?"

Wendra gave one more small smile. "I have a song for him."

• CHAPTER FIFTY-THREE •

Trial of Intention

*Intention may be man's most defining quality. It gives him
the forethought to ignore his animal instinct for survival,
and thus the resolve to strive for an ideal.*

—Excerpt from the defense made of the first Trial of
Intentions, archived in the Vaults of Estem Salo

THAELON ENTERED THE trial theater to find every seat
filled and a buzz of quiet conversation. The broad hall
had several hundred seats in rows ascending a gentle slope,
and two balconies with hundreds more. Its ornate ceiling was
brightly lit thirty strides above. And beyond the stage where
debate would take place, an open vista of Estem Salo. The
theater had been constructed without that wall to give a poi-
gnant backdrop to the discussions this hall was meant to
serve.

Whispers fell quiet as he passed, some sounding deferential, some accusational. The rift in his fraternity was never
more clear.

He took note of the grand murals painted on the immense
walls on each side of the theater. Unlike in the gallery where
he'd prepared for this moment, these depictions were of civil
disagreement, animated at times, but not resulting in death.
The idea of this hall was dispute and deliberation.

On the raised stage at the front of the theater, and to the
right, sat four Sheason exemplars—those who oversaw argument, effability, discernment, and rhetoric—his panel of
judges. To the left, standing at a lectern facing the judges, was
the first Sheason who would be tried. A man of middle age,
himself a teacher of ethics. Toyl Delane was his name. A
father, and a man whose hair always looked windblown.

Thaelon mounted the stage and came to stand in front of his judges. "Are we ready to begin?"

He hadn't seen her all morning, but suddenly Raalena was at his side. She said nothing, but put him a tad more at ease for her presence.

"Toyl." Warrin, his exemplar best trained in history and belief, spoke the name softly. "He volunteered to be first. I think he intends to make a speech."

Thaelon gave Warrin a smile meant mostly to reassure himself, and strode to the center of the stage. He looked first out the rear of the hall at the wide vista of his city. A magnificent view. A thousand rooftops. More. And beyond them the great mountains and forested hills of the Divide. It settled him to his task.

He turned and faced the theater. Voices hushed. He waited several long moments, then spoke as a man does to a friend.

"I don't call for Trials of Intention frivolously. We're here because there's real danger." Thaelon remained standing where he was. He would not pace. He would add no theater to his words. "I've spent many long days preparing. While I've not doubted that this was necessary, I've wished it was not. And I take no pride in what's about to take place."

A few mutters could be heard from the second balcony. Thaelon ignored them.

"Trials of Intention are rare," he admitted. "In fact, only twice, to my knowledge, have there been formal proceedings among us. Once, when the Second Promise nearly failed. And before that, in the time after the Whiting of Quietus, when what we're about to do had no name."

He stopped, remembering from the gallery wall images of Sheason lying dead after makeshift trials of intent.

"There are consequences for the wrong intent," he said, scanning the assembly. "Consequences that in previous seasons meant death. But that won't be the way this time."

"Then what?" Toyl asked from his lectern to Thaelon's right. "Banishment? Ostracism?"

Thaelon didn't look at the man. He remained fixed on those before him. "Divestiture," he answered.

The crowd erupted in murmurs. A few loud cries pierced

the humlike din. Among them he heard: "It's a tactic meant to frighten us."

He raised a hand for silence. "Divestiture has long been a myth. One we happily had no need to try and prove." He paused. "Until now. I've been to the depths of the Tabernacle. I found the old glyphs. And I've discovered the way to remove a Sheason's authority to render the Will."

The outbreak was louder this time, with a few calling for death as preferable to divestiture.

Thaelon simply waited until they could see he wouldn't continue before it was quiet again. Eventually the hall settled down.

"It's the right consequence," he stated firmly. "The purpose of the trials is to determine if a Sheason's use of the Will is in harmony with our first Charter. Because if it is not, then he is not Sheason. And if he is not Sheason, then he has no claim to a Sheason's authority."

Again Toyl interrupted. "And you'll school us on this Charter, will you, Thaelon? Because as far as I know, there's no document to which we may refer to know what it says."

Thaelon said simply, still addressing the theater, "I will."

"That'll be a good trick," Toyl quipped, drawing a few soft laughs from the hall.

Thaelon finally turned to face the man. "You will remember I am your Randeur. Or is disrespect also a quality of those who follow Vendanj?" Staring coldly at Toyl, he announced in a loud voice, "Every Sheason will have a Trial of Intention, to declare themselves. And I'm glad our first trial has a sharp wit to defend the dissent against us."

"I'm not sure who you mean when you say 'us,' my Randeur," Toyl said with heavy sarcasm. "But I'll be glad to help you examine the ethics of this entire proceeding."

A long hush fell over the hall, broken only by a stirring of wind beyond the rear of the stage, where aspen leaves rustled against one another.

Thaelon decided to use a simple question to demonstrate the crux of these proceedings. "Toyl, is there nothing that guides a Sheason's use of the Will?"

"Don't you mean to ask whether or not I agree with or

follow Vendanj?" Toyl shifted his weight behind his defense lectern.

Slowly, Thaelon approached him, leaned in, and said, "I thought that's what I asked."

There came many muffled laughs to that.

Toyl smiled and nodded. "Clever, yes. The thing that guides—or should guide—the use of the Will is a renderer's own ethical center."

"I see." Thaelon turned to watch the assembly's reaction to his next question. "And the Velle—who also render—their use of the Will is right, then, since they follow their own ethical center?"

Toyl frowned, then raised a finger as one does to challenge or clarify. "They are not Sheason."

"You realize," Thaelon pressed, "that they began as Sheason. We were all once one order. In fact, the first Trials of Intention are what removed them from our company."

Perhaps we could be one again.

"These are an arguer's tricks," Toyl said, visibly relaxing. "The Velle are fundamentally different because they adhere to no ethic. You know this."

Thaelon turned and pointed at the man. "And how do you know?"

Toyl opened his mouth to answer, but found no words. A few moments later, he seemed to latch on to some prepared remarks. "Let's talk about some references we can all agree on, shall we? For instance, the aftermath of the Second Promise."

Thaelon saw where Toyl would take this, and knew it would be hard to defend.

"Sheason, angered when the Second Convocation of Seats betrayed the Sedagin and let them die fighting alone, went into the courts of men and killed. Murder, Thaelon. To coerce action." Toyl pointed back dramatically. "Was this in line with the Charter you claim as guide?"

Thaelon's mind raced, seeking a rebuttal.

Toyl gave him no time. "And what of our own season? What of the Civilization Order? How are you dealing with that? To my knowledge, you're letting our own die. So, if you're asking me if I follow Vendanj, who stands against the Quiet, against the League, and doesn't worry if he can reconcile defending people with some vague notion of a Charter . . . then yes, I follow him."

Thaelon found his voice. "An envoy, led by my own daughter, has gone to Recityv to negotiate an end to the Civilization Order. And the murder you speak of—at the end of the Second Promise—did result in a Trial of Intentions."

Toyl showed a look of satisfaction. "Which resulted in almost no Sheason being found to have violated the Charter. Is my history accurate?"

From behind his judge's table, Warrin nodded.

It was a smart argument, Thaelon had to admit. He walked to the edge of the stage and stared long into the faces of many. He held up a finger, leaving it there for several moments before beginning in a clear, soft tone. He needed them all to hear him. Really hear him.

"The Charter is felt, as much as it is understood. Any one of you would rush to protect a child in danger. You don't need a document to tell you what to do. And you know your actions are right, even if they cause you harm." He stopped and looked into the brightly lit ceiling high above. More murals there: stars and cloudy bands that crossed the firmament. He took some strength from them.

He looked back at his fellows. "We've been given a gift in the authority to render. It's a shade of the authority the First Ones used to frame this world. But we are *not* gods. And when we use this authority in a manner that suits our whim, or without regard to who it may hurt, it smacks of our own arrogance. As though we *are* gods among men. Giving and taking life simply by right of our power to do so . . . it forfeits our right to hold that authority. Or should."

He turned on Toyl. "That is what the Trial of Intentions is meant to determine. We will always stand against invasion or expansionists. But in the right way."

Toyl, teacher of ethics, shook his head slowly. Like Thaelon, he used an effectively soft voice when he said, "The thing that matters is preserving our lands, our people. It doesn't matter how principled we are if we lose these. War is not a social experiment, Thaelon. It is not everyday life. It's everything, anything, you can do to keep the life you have." He looked out at the assembly. "I'm with Vendanj."

Your ethics sound situational, my ethics friend.

There were cheers from the crowd for Toyl's words. Not unanimous. But many. It saddened Thaelon to hear them. As the theater quieted again, he recalled his parchment war with Ketrine. It helped him focus on what he should say.

"We teach *realignment* here. But we teach it mostly to instruct you in what you should *not* do. It's a rendering technique aimed at getting what you want by manipulating the choice of another." Thaelon's passion on this point bubbled up hot. His voice rose. "It is not for us to create or control life to fight for us. If there's a war worth fighting, then we should bear the cost of it ourselves." He thought of the boy Tahn that Vendanj was using. He thought of the very existence of that boy, a revived stillborn child. "To do anything else is the Quiet way. You don't need me to tell you this for you to know its truth."

Heads were nodding.

He stepped forward, declaring in a loud, firm voice, "We are not gods, but we can be god*like*. And to do it we must ask ourselves: To what lengths will we go and at what cost do we render before we are no different than the Quiet we fight against? We are better than that! We must *be* better than that!"

What followed was not the roar of crowds. It was a booming silence in which Sheason remembered their oath. Thaelon could feel their hearts. Most of them, anyway. And from those hearts, good intentions. Or so he believed.

It stirred him. Made him proud. It would be a difficult path, these trials. But all understood now why they would travel it.

Slowly, he returned to Toyl. He looked the man in the eye for several moments. "There's just one question," Thaelon said, his tone inviting Toyl to closely consider his reply. "Don't answer for those seated before you. Not for those you counseled with before taking this stage." He paused, took a deep breath. "Toyl Delane, would you render at any cost, do anything, to make good on your intent . . . would you follow Vendanj, were he to ask it?"

With no defiance, Toyl said simply, "I would."

These two words broke Thaelon's heart. For all Toyl's fine rhetoric, his dissent was genuine. He believed in a different way. A way that ran counter to the Sheason oath he'd taken. Close as he was now, Thaelon could see in Toyl's eyes how it all weighed on him. *A good man; even when he's convinced he's right, hates to disappoint a friend.*

Toyl leaned forward, and repeated with a whisper, "I would . . . and, my Randeur, so should you." The sound of it was like a plea.

Thaelon stood staring at him, his gut in a knot. How many? Half? Would he divest half of his people before these trials were through? Good people. All of them. But with an intent that went a shade too far. A dangerous shade. His order might not survive this. But what else could he do?

Thaelon stepped close, so that he might ask a question only Toyl could hear. He studied the man's eyes, his *own* words now a plea. "Toyl . . . what about your oath?"

They shared a long look before Toyl softly said, "Perhaps, my Randeur, it's time for the oath to change." The words were genuine, even hopeful.

The words chilled Thaelon. In his studies he'd found that these very words had been spoken by those Sheason who'd gone into the Bourne . . . and become Velle.

Thaelon showed Toyl kind eyes, and nodded. A signal. The man was ushered around to the center of the stage. And there Thaelon brought to life something that had only existed as glyphs carved on the sides of deep, dusty stone.

There was no great tumult or rending. Just Thaelon and a few of the judges, who put their hands on Toyl's body. The man shuddered as Thaelon removed the resonance that gave his life's song more than a single note and vibration.

When it was done, Toyl shuffled back toward a woman and child who waited for him near a door.

• CHAPTER FIFTY-FOUR •

A Civil Argument

Civility? Means smiling and nodding politely to a bastard you hate.

—Response to a League survey on the meaning of "Civility"

CHATTER FILLED THE hall as Roth entered for the second day of Convocation. If all went well, there would be no third day. All the kings and queens and other leaders had already taken their seats at the main table and in the gallery. Roth had come deliberately late in order to avoid any conversation prior to the official talks, but also to capture some attention from several of the attendees.

No less than six of the critical voters had received a folded and sealed sheet of plain white parchment. Each one had a secret or two explicitly described in their note. At the bottom of the private missive, a promise to publish these indiscretions came followed by an invitation to oppose the regent.

Some of those who'd received the notes weren't huge opposition risks to Roth's plans. But making sure of their vote made good sense. A few of the others receiving notes this morning were unsympathetic to the League; the ink had flowed more liberally when crafting the messages to these fellows and one queen.

He took his seat, and cast his gaze around the table at each man and woman, lingering a scant second longer on the faces of those whose eyes had reviewed his messages this last half hour. It would be a fine day.

Helaina stood. "I thank you all again for being here at this critical time. Already what we've seen and heard has been historic. I would now hasten our deliberations. And urge solidarity among us. We cannot afford to make the mistake that Regent Corihehn made so many ages ago, when he sent Holivagh I'Malichael and the Right Arm of the Promise into the breach of war with no intention of sending reinforcements." She pointed at the empty seat beside her. "The Sedagin do not join us. Our betrayal has cost us their kinship. We can't afford to dissemble here. Let's begin. I'm eager to hear your thoughts."

An uncustomary silence held for several moments. Roth understood the reluctance—one he'd caused—of many to speak. He took it as a sign that he needn't wait. This was his time. So he stood, and began to pace the outer edge of the table.

"My lady, perhaps it does fall to me to begin." He looked at those seated around the table, then cast his gaze out to the wider encircling gallery. He thought briefly of his time in Wanship on the wharf, and the injustices heaped on those who had no voice in a place like this, with its vaulted ceilings.

Raising his voice in strident tones, he said, "I make no pretense of our open disagreements, Regent Storalaith. Nor do you. I will confess here, openly, that I've sought these last few days to remove you from your office. Not, I hasten to add, because of any dislike for you personally, or even as regent. I simply believe that your time has passed. The brand of leadership you offer has ceased to be relevant. We need to move beyond tradition, and it will take new thinking and the vigor of a younger mind and body to see these things done. We should venerate you for your service." Roth stopped just strides from Helaina, modulating his tone to one of earnestness and near-compassion. "But I must challenge your stewardship over this Convocation."

Helaina let a measured silence stretch before saying, "You have no authority here. Take your seat, Ascendant."

"My lady," Roth continued, with the same appealing tone, "there are no laws that govern this collective body. Nor are there rules for how we should guide our discussions. We're all here of our own will. And I would ask if any of us is confident that you are stable enough to direct these talks, let alone capable of waging the war you would enjoin us to." His voice became patronizing. "Come to that, do any of us really even believe in your purpose for assembling us here?"

A wild murmuring shot through the hall—some members appalled, some nodding as if they'd been thinking the same thing. Still others sat staring, waiting for Helaina's response.

She stood, and slowly walked to face him. Tall as she was, she looked him eye to eye, and spoke in a clear, strong voice for all to hear.

"You distract us from important matters," she said, "and what's worse, you do it with your own political agenda in mind. Very well, let us put to bed the political maneuvering. This man," she said, her words bitter as she glared at Roth, "this Ascendant of the League of Civility, is an ambitious man. I've no doubt he's convinced of the creed he follows, a creed he would have us all adopt. But his ambition blinds him. Makes him dangerous."

Still she didn't look away, unflinching as she cast her aspersions on him. Roth admired her iron will. And he patiently gave her time to speak, before he would make his radical suggestion.

"Ascendant Staned and his League are under inquiry for poisoning a child in order to advance the constraints of their Civilization Order. Ascendant Staned and his League are under inquiry for the burning of the Bastulan Cathedral, a refuge and symbol not just to Recityv but to pilgrims from many of your own nations. Ascendant Staned and his League are under inquiry for attempting to assassinate me just days before he called a vote of the Recityv High Council in which he announced himself as my possible successor."

The regent paused, and Roth nearly spoke before she resumed. "And last night, after our first day of deliberations, First Sodalist E'Sau was murdered in his own bedchamber."

Another round of wild murmuring rose throughout the Hall of Convocation. Roth realized what the regent would say next a moment too late to stave it off.

"Ascendant Staned," she announced with a clarion voice that rang out over the whispers and gossip, "and his League are under inquiry for the First Sodalist's death, as well. Individually," she said, "any one of these things could be named a tragedy or crime or unfortunate accident. But taken together, with evidence in each case of the League's hand, they declare the maneuverings of a man bent on assuming a position of authority."

Roth fought to control his mounting wrath. He hadn't thought Helaina would soil the more stately proceedings of the Convocation with Recityv events or her own private battles. Always before, she'd shown a special decorum when leading large assemblies. Even as his anger swelled, he conceded more respect for the old bird. She'd adapted to his game. But her words were now threatening to swing opinions back in her favor. Whatever the congregants here thought of the old stories, they wouldn't find much sympathy for Roth's position if they thought him a political threat.

Before she could say more, he broke in on her litany of accusations. "Of course I'm under inquiry," he shouted. "I represent the change that would unseat the regent." He turned, starting again to pace, and to make his appeal directly to kings and queens and generals. "It's a difficult thing to embrace change. It means giving up comfortable routines. It means finding new ways of answering the needs of those for whom you bear a solemn responsibility. In the past, we did this by arming men and sending them to war, instead of arming men to enforce our own civil peace. The war, ladies and gentlemen, isn't out there somewhere beyond the mystical Veil." He swept an arm out grandly. "The war is in your own streets, with hunger and poverty and the mistreatment of one man to the other. Yes, if an actual threat comes from a nation, we can address that, ride to meet it. But suppose the source of even that conflict is misunderstanding, *assumed* wrongs rather than actual hate or bloodlust."

Roth stopped, turning a complete revolution before saying, "Wouldn't any of you trade your seat at this Convocation for real peace? Wouldn't the success of a gathering like this be to forge a collective might that is never needed or used, except to police just laws? Wouldn't that," Roth concluded, softly, "be the mark of true leadership . . ."

The silence in the hall was deafening. The murmuring that

had come before seemed to have turned inward. Roth kept his self-satisfied smile off his lips.

Only the regent would have the gall to break the profoundness of the silence his words had inspired. And she did.

"Roth," she said quietly, using his name, her words carrying in the stillness, "your words are hollow, spoken to convince rather than instruct or inspire. The ring of truth is different from the truth itself. And I can no longer sit by while your words confuse and frustrate the hard realities that force us to meet here. I hereby revoke your seat at this Convocation. You are dismissed."

Roth smiled. "My lady, of course you know you have no authority to do this. And even if you did, such a move would only validate our suspicion that you are unfit to lead these discourses. Since it would then be clear that you accept no opinion save those that align with your own."

Helaina didn't reply, but simply motioned. A contingent of spear-bearing guards filed in around Roth. It infuriated him, but only for a moment—this was something he *had* anticipated. With a raise of his hand, the doors opened, and Losol—leader of his newest faction—entered with a contingent of leaguemen, who encircled Helaina's guards with steel of their own.

"You see," Roth said, "it can only escalate. This is the way of the past, Helaina. Let us find a new road, together."

He, of course, knew she would accept no such collaboration. But suggesting it was all that was needed. Around the room, attentive eyes awaited her response to his thoughtful, heartfelt-sounding proposal. While he, too, waited, memories of his boyhood stirred, days casting about the docks, looking for an easy mark to run a flimflam, or a loosely watched catch that could be pilfered for a meal. Perhaps there *was* some dissembling in his arguments. But he'd bring about the right kinds of change either way. He meant for there to be less need of hope, and in its place more bread and training.

But before Helaina could deny his offer, which would bring him to his ultimate motion for this assembly of kings, the sound of bootheels on the table drew his—and all the Convocation's—attention. Looking to his right, Roth saw that a man, in supreme disrespect, had climbed up on the table itself, and was strolling its glistening surface. The fellow alternately glared down at those seated at the table, and then up into the ringed rows of second lords and princesses of lesser lands.

He looked familiar, this man with deeply sunned skin. But Roth could not place him, until he began to speak. Then he knew. This one had been expected.

• CHAPTER FIFTY-FIVE •

Grant's Defense

There is a time for social reform. But it is not when dealing with fathers who beat their children, or rapists, or in times of war.

—Language from the first League of Civility credo,
redacted by Ascendant Roth Staned

GRANT TOOK SLOW steps, walking the surface of the venerated convocation table. His hard-soled boots clacked a measured beat as he stared down into faces aghast at his insolence or fretting some action he might take against them. But he only walked, capturing the attention of the hall as he strode the entire circle without a word. When he'd come around near to where Helaina and the Ascendant stood in the midst of their armed guards, he offered a bitter smile and continued to stroll.

"You are a circus of fools," he began. "Answer the question of why you came here to begin with. If you no longer believed in the dangers that brought your forebears to this hall to discuss matters of war against the Bourne, you wouldn't have come. And yet you sit here and let a politician mock that purpose."

Grant shook his head in disgust. "Many of you may lack the grit your ancestors possessed, which would explain why this exigent hasn't yet been thrown out on his ass. Or, maybe some of you are *just like* your forebears, and would let others go to fight a war on your behalf. Whichever is true, wake up! You stand at a crossroads and you can't afford to waver. There's too much at stake."

"Another friend of the regent's," Roth exclaimed. "Is it any wonder that civility is lacking under her rule?"

There were a few low chuckles.

Grant whirled and strode back toward the Ascendant, causing the leagueman's band of armsmen to raise their weapons toward him. He lifted his gaze and looked at the wide round gallery of secondary seats. "Did you know that this leagueman has called for an end to the Song of Suffering?"

The muttering of voices now came louder than any that had come before.

"Yesterday, when Maesteri Belamae addressed this Convocation so eloquently, the Ascendant decried his testimony but carefully omitted this detail. Why? Because even if everything else Roth says is true, he would find it hard to convince you that we should let go the singing of the Song."

He looked at Roth, expecting rebuttal. None came. Grant showed the Ascendant a crooked smile.

"Why should we listen to you?" said Queen Ela Valstone of Reyal'Te. "You occupy no seat among us. Who are you?"

"I am Grant," he announced in a deep rough voice. "Known before as Denolan SeFeery, Emerit guard . . . and husband to Regent Helaina Storalaith."

Rather than a rise of gossiping voices, Grant received several narrowed, critical stares. He'd expected as much. His irreverence was part of the reason others wanted him here. But some couldn't accept what they were seeing when they looked at him.

Grant laughed bitterly. "Those of you who knew me before don't recognize me, because your own eyes have grown old . . . while mine have not. Friends," he said, softening his voice in appeal, "change is coming. The march of time in the Scar . . . has slowed. It's an effect that follows from when the

Quiet stripped those lands of life. The natural order of things is changing."

"This is foolishness!" Roth cried.

Grant turned on the man. "And it grows!" he declared. "The borders of the Scarred Lands are expanding. The silence of the heavens takes root in the earth beneath our feet. Soon—not today, or tomorrow, but soon—even the possibility of war as an answer to these changes"—he looked around at those seated at the convocation table—"will be lost to you. To your people."

"Fear," the Ascendant said, coolly. "Fear is the last refuge and manipulation of those who have no other argument left to convince you. It's the tool of dictators and religionists, and has no place in the halls of civilized men. You, yourself, Grant," the Ascendant said, pointing an accusing finger at him, "take your name from the defiance and denial of arcane practices. You are a hypocrite to stand before us and argue that we should bow to the same myths you rejected."

Grant leapt from the table. Roth's guards gave ground as he strode by them. In a quiet voice, he said, "Don't ever again twist my past to help your own argument." He then strode by the leaguemen to the open floor nearer the gallery. "You here in these outer rings, you're a step closer to the men and women and children who will die first when this tide of Quiet comes. What do you say? Will you condemn them to the life I have led, walking in dry places, waiting for death?" He looked back at the convocation table. "Or will you have greater wisdom than those whose chairs are larger and softer and further removed from the hard realities that common men must face?

"Because, make no mistake," he said, coming around again to the cluster of armed men surrounding Helaina and Roth, "a sea of trouble is coming. You have only to decide how you'll defend against it. Will it be as it has been in times gone by? Will you make a promise to each other? Or will you ignore the past, silence the Song and Sheason, and hope that this arrogant leagueman and his untrained, dispersed army can answer the threat when it steals into your homelands?"

As Grant glared at Roth, the other's face grew suddenly

relaxed. He turned, and in mockery of Grant's dramatic walk around the outer ring of the hall—appealing to the gallery of second seats—he began the same walk, retracing Grant's path, and offering his own argument.

"The exile is a powerful speaker," Roth complimented. "If I were sitting where you are, I'd be moved to consider his words. Certainly, you are nearer the families whose protection we are *all* entrusted to provide. But let me tell you something about this man who would ask your allegiance to unsubstantiated myths and rumors of war."

Roth looked down at his feet for a moment as he paced, holding his chin thoughtfully, as though considering just how to say what he needed to say. Then, raising his gaze again, he began in a solemn, almost regretful tone. "I think you mean well," he said to Grant. "Yours is a bitterness I understand. There is nobleness in how you care for children whose own parents cannot or will not. But your methods of guardianship make me wonder."

He raised a hand, whereupon the doors to the Convocation Hall opened, and a man entered. The stranger slowly came into focus, and Grant realized it was the adoptive father of one of his wards, whom he had visited not long ago. An abusive man. Roth pointed at the one-armed adopter now standing beside him.

"This gentleman took in one of Grant's foundlings, brought the child into his home and cared for him. Without provocation or explanation, Grant returned to this man's home and cut off his arm, because he believed him an abuser. He never sought to understand the circumstances in the home. He simply came and dealt his own brand of uninformed justice. And this is the gentleman whose persuasive tongue we have just heard call for your sons to ride into war without a hint of our foreign neighbor's intention. Never mind the question of whether there's an enemy at all."

Roth strode back to his seat at the great table and pounded his fists on the lacquered surface. "No! The regent and exile may mean well, but their sordid past has compromised their wisdom. And now they would compel us to wrong actions, *uncivil* actions."

The Ascendant took a long, steadying breath. When he spoke again, he filled his voice with reminiscence. "I've known the taste of bone broth as my only meal, listened to a moneylender offer a mere plug for my mother's good things when we had nothing left to pawn. . . . But it makes me want to be sure our own children never know such things. And so," he said, sitting with dignity and resolve, "not only do I question the intentions of this Convocation . . . I propose that we disband it entirely. Its purpose belongs to the past. We'll find new solutions to new problems, and we'll be better for it."

Grant laughed. It carried into the vaults of the Convocation Hall. It had nearly echoed its last when Roth simply said, "I call for a vote of dissolution."

Almost immediately, hands began to rise. Many around the great table, and one by one hands in the outer gallery were likewise going up. Voices began to mutter. The Convocation was going to fail to answer any promise at all.

Roth slowly raised an arm, and pointed at the man whose arm Grant had removed. The gesture brought silence again to the hall. In a low voice, Grant made one last argument. "This is your evidence. This *man* beat his wife. Beat the child I trusted to his care. Again and again he beat them. He's lucky I didn't take both his arms."

He then took a long, measured look at those seated around the convocation table. "Tell me that if you found someone abusing your child you wouldn't do the same. Tell me that your heart doesn't whisper that I was right to do it." Grant looked up at Roth. "You may once have known the ache of an empty belly and the hardships of poverty. But don't sit there and pretend you understand them now. Your empathy is a mockery, since you use it for political gain."

Grant looked around again at these kings and leaders. "A man can only truly know the state of another's heart if he bears the same condition at the same time. The rest is sophistry. Maneuvering. This *man* with all his tenderness," he pointed now at Roth, "claims the interests of the people, but would let a child die rather than allow a healer whose art he doesn't understand to restore that child's health. This *man* decries others as dictators and religionists, and yet has published his own creed and tried to have the regent assassinated. This *man,*" Roth sneered the word, "would let this Convocation fail and your people consequently die, to advance his own ideas of reform."

Grant's voice softened. "Think, my friends. Your ancestors came to this same place for this same purpose. They weren't deceived. They didn't always make right decisions. But they came here with an understanding that some threats are real, and need to be met. We don't wish it so. But we have strength enough to meet these threats. . . . If we do it together." He paused, coming to the simplest truth he knew. "You wouldn't be here at all, if part of you didn't believe that was true."

When he'd finished, there was a deep silence. The kind in which you can hear true things.

Roth must have heard it, too. He'd just begun to interrupt that silence, when beyond the doors and windows, the distant sound of trumpets filled the air, hailing some arrival. They continued their call for several moments, until the doors opened once again, and for the first time in the history of Recityv, a Far king strode the halls of Convocation.

Behind Elan came ten of his closest guard. They peeled off several strides back, leaving their king to approach Helaina alone. Roth and Grant stood back as the Far came on and extended a hand to the regent. Helaina received his hand and bowed her head. Then Elan, as if accustomed to the place, moved in beside the empty seat next to Helaina's and leaned forward over the convocation table, placing his hands on its surface and staring around at the leaders of nations.

Helaina retook her seat just as Elan began to speak.

"I am not a myth." He gave Roth a dark look. "Nor is the commission my people have borne for ages. We were entrusted with keeping the Language of the Covenant safe until the time came, if ever, that it should be needed. . . . That time has come."

Roth waved a hand. "Surely, you don't—"

"You will let me speak, Ascendant Staned; the blood of countless Far gives me the right." Elan's eyes invited Roth to challenge him. Roth waved his hand again for the Far king to continue.

"If it is not yet known to you, the library at Qum'rahm'se has been destroyed. Your attempts to reconstruct the Covenant Tongue have been burned to ash. This comes at the hands of Velle, dark renderers of the Will who believe that your only hope against them is the use of this forgotten speech."

"More magic and mysteries," Roth interjected. "When will this end?"

It was Elan's turn to hold up a hand, signaling his men to drag forward something Grant hadn't noticed. Before anyone knew what was happening, several Far heaved a great form and cast it on the table, ripping free the dark shroud that had concealed it.

Men and women around the table and in the gallery shot to their feet at the sight of the slain body of a Bar'dyn.

Elan waited for the muttering voices to calm, for most to reclaim their seats, before resuming. "The Quiet have crossed the Veil. Some of them, anyway." Elan shared a look with Grant, then stared back at Roth. "This very turn of the moon a host of them descended out of the Saeculorum, crossed the shale plains, infiltrated the heart of our city, and destroyed the Covenant Tongue.

"My friends," Elan said, casting his gaze around the table, "you see the proof of the enemy before you. These events are not random. The Quiet have destroyed the greatest weapon we possessed to fight them. The time for deliberation is past. War is coming, whether you choose to answer its call . . . or not."

In the silence that followed came the slow clap of a single pair of hands. Roth's. "Fine theater, gentlemen. Oh, I have great respect for the Far." He looked at Elan. "For your steadfastness, if not the reality of some lost language. But this"— Roth stood and looked over the body of the Bar'dyn—"proves nothing."

"Certainly looks like something to me," Grant said.

Mild laughter filled the table.

"A foreigner," Roth said, hunching his shoulders. "He looks different. Smells different."

More laughter.

"But," Roth said, raising a finger, "is he an enemy? That's the question, isn't it. He needs to be an enemy for Helaina's Convocation to succeed. But what if he's just . . . a foreigner?"

Elan stood tall. "Thousands of my people died at the hands of these *foreigners*."

"And what if that could have been avoided," Roth said, and started to pace again around the backs of those seated at the convocation table. "What if through negotiation no battle need have been fought? Or be fought again? This is what we have to decide. Do we arm ourselves again for some great war? Do you put your children in armor and stick a sword in their hands and pray to dead gods that they return?" He paced faster. "And when was the last time a dead god answered one of your prayers?"

"Roth—" Helaina began.

"No, think on it. I've never doubted there were nations beyond the Pall. I simply don't believe they mean us harm. Or there's some old misunderstanding. A misunderstanding I'd rather us fight with diplomacy and leave our swords home."

"Is this why you've armed a fifth branch of your Jurshah?" Grant asked.

Eyebrows rose at that bit of logic.

"Now that's a sound argument," Roth said, seeming genuinely pleased. "The League is arming to keep the peace. And as I've said, if hostility comes, we'll then be ready. But as a last need. Not our first response."

He stopped pacing finally, took his seat again, and spoke with the humblest voice Grant had heard him use. "What have we seen to convince us of this Convocation's purpose: parlor tricks, a dead foreigner, false accusations about me and the League, an appeal to us to do things today the way they were done ages ago." He gave a tired sigh.

"There may have been a time when Convocation for the purpose of war was right. In fact, I'm sure that's true. But now is not the time for it. We are better than this. We need to be. Let us dissolve this Convocation, and re-form it with a new purpose. I will personally ride to these people"—he nodded toward the dead Bar'dyn—"and broker peace. But please, let's not send our men and women to war again. It's a waste. And it is not the way to resolve differences. Not anymore. What say you?"

An overwhelming number of hands began to rise to the vote of dissolution. Grant shook his head, and came around to place a thankful hand on Elan's shoulder. While arms hung aloft, he spoke quietly, his voice carrying in the great hall.

"Days ago, when Elan's First Legion met the Quiet out on the shale, they found these *foreigners* had come with more than swords." Grant paused, staring across at Roth in the silence. "Like the Battle of the Round, which created the Scar I now call home, they came with renderers of the Will. Velle. Quietgiven with skills like the Sheason that Roth and his League are trying to abolish."

Upraised hands were returned to laps. Seat holders shifted uncomfortably in their chairs, waiting on Grant's next words.

"Do you know the difference between a Sheason and a Velle?" He didn't expect an answer, and he got none. But he let the moment draw out a good long time before going on. "A Sheason draws on his own life to do the things he does. Velle do not. They pluck the life from anything at hand to fuel their craft."

"Are you going to tell us more stories?" Roth said. This time, no one laughed.

He can't see beyond his own view of civility. Grant almost pitied the man. Almost.

"The Velle who came to Naltus knew the shale there holds little energy for rendering. So, they brought vessels."

Queen Ela Valstone of Reyal'Te asked, "What do you mean, 'vessels'?"

Grant turned saddened, weary eyes on her. "People. Children."

There was a new silence. A heavy kind. In it, Grant thought he heard some culpability.

"Every one of you seated here knows that highwaymen walk your roads. There's a human trade being done in the remote places of your realms. For some buyers," he said, "it's a slave to drive a plow or mop a floor or row a trawler when the wind flags. But the best coin is paid by *foreigners* who seek strong, mobile vessels that can be used to give their renderings life wherever they go."

Grant walked around near the dead Bar'dyn and looked down at the decaying body. "I would be moved by the Ascendant's words myself, if in my life I hadn't seen what they do to a captive when they use his spirit to render the Will. I've watched it happen to young men and women in my care. No one should ever know that pain. Or have to witness it."

He turned a slow circle, speaking mostly to the outer gallery. "They're not simply preparing for war. They're preparing for annihilation. They don't want to rule us. They want us dead. They're carefully trying to remove every defense or weapon we could use against them. And the strongest weapons on their side of it . . . are fueled by the lives of people they've bought or taken from among us. Thousands. More." He shook his head again, in rejection of Roth's diplomatic charade. "No, there's no peace to be had with them. I would rather not go to war. But the Quiet are coming. And they come with intractable intentions. If you let this Convocation fail, trust me, it will be the last thing you think about when the Quiet sweep through your homelands and thresh them like spoiled wheat."

Helaina let Grant's words linger a moment, then spoke quietly but firmly. "Who will answer this Convocation's call?"

Hands began to go up. And the clear indication was that there'd be no further need to deliberate. But before a count could be taken, Roth spoke again.

"My regent, I have one last argument to make. And then, I give my word, I'll be led by the crowd."

Helaina looked warily at him. "And what is that, Ascendant?"

"I can't present it today, I'm afraid." He smiled apologetically. "May I beg a day's indulgence? I'll be ready for tomorrow's session."

"She doesn't have to wait," Grant reminded them all.

"No, she doesn't," Roth agreed, and turned his appeal to the many leaders around the inner table. "But if I can show you that this isn't necessary, wouldn't you at least want to hear me out?"

Several turned to Helaina, nodding approval for a day's delay.

"It's a trick," Grant whispered to Helaina.

But Helaina was bound to honor the Convocation's general wish, and they adjourned.

As the hall cleared, Helaina stood and took Grant's hand warmly. "We can make it through one night. We have the votes. It would have appeared uncompromising to deny him. And I've a feeling a few of these seats are being pinched." She smiled at that. "My indulgence of Roth on this point will help us eventually."

Grant had a restless, uneasy feeling about it, but let it go for now, escorting Helaina from the Convocation hall, where it appeared his own brand of convincing might have helped them earn the day. Helaina's tight lock on his arm seemed to say as much, and proved a welcome reward for the effort.

• CHAPTER FIFTY-SIX •

The Bourne: Elegy

The problem of most messiahs is that the very compassion which stirs them to save a people also makes them faint of heart when there's killing to be done.

—From Sedgel writings, *In Search of Shelah*

THEY MARCHED INTO the town of Jopal in the broad light of day. Kett Valan's shoulders and chest still burned with the ritual branding he'd received after giving himself to Quietus. His skin now bore the same marks as worn by the six Bar'dyn he led, as well as the Sedgel leadership emblem. The painful scars raised by the meticulous application of hot irons wove in alternating swoops and jags across his skin. He chewed root after root of balsa plant to dull the pain.

His old friend Lliothan was with them. He commanded the squad, and took orders from Kett. But there wasn't much to say. Their assignment was simple. Kett suspected Lliothan had been assigned to him more to keep his eye on Kett than help him.

It was midday, a time when field workers were home to take meals before returning to dredge the rows of brickle grass after the morning's irrigation. There needed to be a lot of witnesses.

He didn't rush. News of their entrance to the Inveterae town needed to spread. And he was still trying to think of a way out of this. Before long, crowds did begin to gather along the dirt roads. Hundreds of Gotun, his own kind, looked on. He could see expressions of surprise, disgust, and worry at the sight of the branding that marred his skin. The size of the crowd made him grateful that Inveterae weren't allowed to have weapons. An armed mob of this size would slaughter him and his small Bar'dyn detachment in moments. But untrained, and against the vicious steel of the Quietgiven, they would not attack. Or so he hoped.

He stopped in the middle of the street and halted his new companions. He turned a slow circle, surveying the mix of buildings, some raised of ailantus and cercis wood bleached by rain and wind, others built of dark grey stone mortared with black clay. Everything appeared somewhat muted through watery light under a ceiling of low clouds. The air hung damp today, promising rain later. The same rains that gave rise to the grasses and ironwood trees and dark green brambles that suggested edible crops might be easier to raise here.

Around him, all had stopped to watch what he and his Bar'dyn contingent would do. The shuffle of heavy feet and the taking of midday meals had ceased. It placed him on an eerie stage, and yet this was precisely what the Jinaal sought—his own people's complete attention to Kett's commission.

A mild wind swept up the street, cooling his seared skin.

He nodded, mostly to himself, and turned to the building on his right, the home of Reelan Sotal . . . a friend.

Reelan had been Kett's first confidant. They had met as guards, both having been placed on assignment over one of the human birthing camps. Light duty—when men and women from south of the Pall came into the Bourne, they quickly lost their sense of hope. Inveterae had to do little more than be sure they were fed and that they worked at whatever menial task the camps had for them—cultivation of crops, quarry shifts, some iron work. That, and the captives needed to remain healthy enough to have babies.

It had been his time at that post with Reelan when he'd first realized he had to do something about his ideas of escaping the Bourne. It had taken seeing a certain light go out of human eyes—as their expressions came to resemble those of Inveterae—to realize what his own kind had lost. Human women and children held on to some hope of escape for a few days, maybe weeks, before it slipped away. Usually it occurred naturally, without any assistance or punishment by the camp guards; the Bourne had a way about it.

He'd seen that *human* look before, though. Saw it in Inveterae children, who knew no other way, no other place. They lost it too, in their late childhood, when they became aware of their world. Inveterae called that look, that feeling, *the music*.

He and Reelan had begun to talk about when they'd stopped hearing the music. And when they were far enough from others not to be heard, they had whispered heretical things: revolt . . . escape.

Looking now at the door of his oldest friend's house, he hesitated. But only for a moment; any more and his Bar'dyn detachment would question. Or worse, go to it themselves. He crossed to Reelan's door and knocked. He could feel the collective weight of stares at his back. That's what the Jinaal wanted: witnesses, to quell the thoughts of separation, and to destroy any loyalty the Inveterae might show Kett.

The door opened, and Kett looked down at Salah, a young Gotun girl maybe four years old. She still held in her youthful eyes the light of one who had not yet fully realized who or where she was. *The music.* Reelan's daughter immediately recognized him and hugged his legs.

"Salah," Kett said evenly, "please go get your father."

"Don't you want to come in?" she asked. "We have fresh roots. There's stew."

The meaty smell of their midday meal met his nose, and Kett fought back the memory of many such meals taken in this very home.

Kett edged his tone. "Not today, Salah. Go get your father."

Salah looked up into his eyes, confused and a little hurt. But she went, leaving the door ajar. He listened in the stillness. All movement of the crowd on the road behind him had stopped. The scurry of feet inside his friend's home receded. Then heavier steps approached, and Reelan pulled the door open wide.

His friend's face showed a pleased look at the sight of Kett, and quickly fell when his eyes moved past him to the Bar'dyn and the waiting crowd of onlookers.

Then, Reelan's eyes found the branding across Kett's shoulders and chest. In a soft voice, he said, "You're given. It's as you planned."

He shook his head almost imperceptibly. Reelan knew of Kett's tribunal, of his ploy to get close to the Quiet as a means to gain their confidence and the information that might help them escape the Bourne. But his friend didn't know why he came to his home this day.

"Close the door," he said. "Leave your family inside."

Reelan gave him a puzzled look, but did as he was asked. "Why have you brought Bar'dyn here?"

Kett wished he had time to explain it all. Together they might even have thought of a way out of this. But it had all happened so fast, and he hadn't had time or opportunity to communicate with any of his fellows.

He looked back at his friend, trying to convey as much with his expression as he could, but found his face incapable of saying so much. And further hesitation in administering his newfound duty would be reported back to the Jinaal. He must do this now, or not at all.

May the Fathers forgive me.

He spoke loudly, so all could hear. "Reelan Sotal, you are a known separatist and are charged with sedition against the Quietgiven who protect and sustain you."

Another confused look touched Reelan's face. "What are you doing?"

"There will be no tribunal, Reelan Sotal," he continued. "I know about your conspiracy, because I was part of it. But that was before I found a better way. The right way."

Reelan shook his head, and spoke low, so only Kett could hear him. "Is there no other way?"

Kett nearly faltered. He nearly gave up his ruse. His friend had a family. Just as Kett did. It was the reason he was trying to get them out of the Bourne to begin with. He had to hold to that. And he was closer now. He knew the Jinaal were seeking a labraetates, a singer with the same power of song the Mors had before they'd used that song to escape the Bourne. But he needed more information, and in the meantime he'd been given this task. To kill his colleagues with whom he'd plotted separation. To kill his friends.

But he could give them hope for their families before he did so. He would take that much of a chance for them.

As briefly and quietly as he could, Kett said, "Don't react to what I say . . . I know how to get us out. A labraetates. I'm getting close." When he spoke it, there was dim heat in his chest. He quickly let go his feelings of separation, thinking that somehow Stulten would know. *I'm given.*

Reelan stared at him a long moment. He could see gratitude there, though it scarcely touched his friend's face.

Then he continued with his task. "Step into the street."

The sound of a door hinge came loud into the silence that followed. Behind Reelan, Kett watched as Salah poked her head out from the opened door. A moment later, Reelan's mate, Cenell, pulled the door wide again and stepped out in front of her daughter.

"Kett, what are you doing here? Come in," Cenell said.

In the next moment, her eyes caught sight of the Bar'dyn and of Kett's branded chest. Her face hardened.

Reelan spoke without looking away from Kett. "Take Salah

inside, Cenell. Go to the back of the house, where you cannot see or hear."

Kett allowed a moment for this, risking uncertainty in the minds of his band of Bar'dyn. To his surprise, Cenell didn't retreat inside their home. Instead, she picked up Salah and came to stand beside Reelan.

"Kett Valan," she said, coldness in her tone, "if you come to take the life of one, you will either take the life of all, or you will kill a father in front of his child and her mother, and invite the scorn of the widowed and fatherless."

He kept a stony countenance. Cenell didn't know of this last deception in their plans for escape from the Bourne.

He shared another look with Reelan. He couldn't give his old friend leave to try to change her mind, since witnessing this execution was precisely what the Jinaal wanted. And he couldn't procrastinate any longer.

He strode back to the center of the street. There he turned and beckoned his friend. "Come forward, Reelan Sotal."

As he spoke the words, Kett silently began to offer old prayers to the gods. Prayers he'd submitted so often that he scarcely had to think to recite them. He ignored that not once had those supplications been answered. What faith could there be if every request were granted?

Reelan turned and gently touched Cenell's face, doing the same to Salah, before walking to the street's center.

Kett smelled a coming rainstorm on the air as he drew his blade. Behind Reelan, Salah began to cry out for her father, her young mind beginning to grasp the danger. He stared into his friend's face, blocking the sound from his mind.

Hardened though they all were by life inside the Bourne—beatings, executions, the use of humans, fear of what lay hidden deeper to the north—and hardened though he was by his new oath, Kett knew what he was about to do would haunt him.

Reelan looked back, sharing the tortured look in Kett's eyes. In that brief moment, Kett could see understanding in his friend's expression. Reelan would gladly die if it meant his family and all Gotun drew one step closer to life beyond the Bourne.

Salah's cries now pierced Kett's consciousness, sounding hollow as they fell on the hard ground and echoed up and down the street. Cenell held her fast, watching stoically.

"Do it," Lliothan said, his voice low like shifting earth.

Kett nodded. As a mild wind soothed his burnt flesh, he then hardened his heart and drew his sword.

Unarmed and silent, his friend waited. The best Kett could do for him was make it quick and sure. He took hold of his blade with his other hand. With all his strength, he thrust the heavy steel into Reelan's chest. His friend slumped forward into him. He buried his head in Reelan's neck, and whispered, "I'm sorry."

"Kett . . ." Then his friend was dead, and slipped to the hard ground.

"Da!" Salah cried. "Da! No, Da!"

It happened so fast, and yet the moments seemed to stretch like a nightmare. There was no fanfare or chorus of outrage or dismay. This town of Gotun had seen such before. Only the wail of a child made it different. And despite a distance that had entered him since being given, it broke Kett's heart.

None of the onlookers moved in retaliation or turned away from the awful scene. The silence remained on the street as it had been before.

Reelan had known he must die. And while Kett had more names on his list—people he knew and had been commanded to execute—none were friends like Reelan. This oldest of fellows.

He stared down at the body, his heart hammering with grief. This would drive him mad. Part of him wanted to turn on the Bar'dyn, tear them apart, invite the town to help him. But another part of him knew the only way to honor Reelan's sacrifice was to carry on. He swallowed hard, putting his emotions away.

All that was left was to put a capstone on it. "Spread the word," he called into the quiet street. "Separatists will not be tolerated. It's time that Inveterae accept their place alongside those who are given. We are equally captive inside this Bourne. And liberation is something we can only achieve together."

When his words had dissipated on the wind along the street of Jopal, he sheathed his sword. He avoided looking at his friend's family; not to escape scorn or shame, but because he couldn't bear the haunted eyes of a child who had learned fatherlessness so early. He had to remind himself that his skin burned from branding precisely because he meant to rescue others from the same.

But *he* was not the same. Even if he was right about it all. He was not the same.

He led Lliothan and the other Bar'dyn out of Jopal, up the road toward another of his fellows.

· CHAPTER FIFTY-SEVEN ·

Soil

There's not enough regard for dirt.

—*Carrots and Barrows,* a humorist's almanac on the changing state of agriculture in the Eastlands, commissioned by the society of Scriveners

SUTTER MADE A show of walking the streets of Ir-Caul with Yenola on his arm. He'd waited a lifetime to lie with a woman, and it had been everything he'd ever dreamed of. Strolling with her now in the broad light of day, he couldn't help feeling a bit more manly. He even found a bit of a strut.

They'd spent the better part of the day in his chambers, where he'd become convinced that Yenola had more than simply been with a man before; for her it seemed a practiced art. But he held no petty jealousies of her former lovers, taking it as a point of pride that she'd chosen to bed him. She was inquisitive, too. He was new to the art of love, but her questions were badly timed. They'd dampened his . . . mood.

But, pleasantly tired, they ambled the many roads of the great garrison city. In the streets, the questions mostly belonged to Sutter, and Yenola happily supplied answers. Most of her replies were superficial, until they happened on a home for orphans. There, Sutter stopped.

He'd known what it was before Yenola had named it. A few children sat against the front wall, playing in the dirt. A woman in a nearby rocking chair knitted slowly, working knots into a drab shawl. The woman was too old to have birthed these small ones, and there were too many of them, besides.

"What is this place?" he asked anyway.

For the first time, his companion's voice didn't brim with pride or enthusiasm when she replied. "There are fathers and mothers among the ranks. When they fall in battle, children are left behind. We care for them as best we can." Yenola looked across the faded wood face of the orphanage. "It's not our city's finest quality."

"How many?" he found himself asking.

Yenola gave Sutter an odd look. "The number is not great," she said, seeming reticent. "Homes with cousins or other family are found when possible. And a few are claimed by the close comrades of their lost parents."

Sutter approached the woman with the knitting needles. He didn't know why, but he wanted to know how many children lived fatherless here. "My lady, are you the nursemaid?"

The old woman looked up with milky blue eyes and smiled a toothless smile. She nodded vaguely and moaned out something unintelligible. She then promptly returned her attention to her knots.

Watching her knobby fingers work the yarn, Sutter said, "Is this the care these children receive?"

His lover came forward and grabbed his hand. "It's an unhappy place on a day meant for idle pleasures. Come, let us go."

Sutter would not be moved. He looked down at three small ones whose bare feet and shabby clothes spoke of neglect and, if he guessed right, cold nights.

That could have been me. . . .

Without invitation he strode past the old woman and

through the open door of the orphanage. The interior some-how appeared as washed and faded as the sun-facing outer walls of the place. A threadbare rug sat before a hearth that clearly hadn't known fire for a very long time. A few wooden toys lay in corners. A couple of small chairs sat here and there, two of them occupied by very young girls, five or six years old, maybe. They looked up at him briefly, before returning to their play.

Behind him, Sutter heard Yenola enter the room. To her credit, she didn't again entreat him to leave. Room by room he went, surveying the abject conditions. There were no books and scarcely a toy per child; most of these makeshift things he guessed the children cobbled together from garbage they scavenged from the streets. On more than one wall, graphite or limestone rocks had been used to draw directly on the wood. Most of the depictions were crude renderings of tall and short figures standing together. The young artists, he guessed, had sought to fix images of the families they'd once known, or hoped to know in the future.

He climbed the stair to the upper story, finding more children playing quietly, glumly. From one of these rooms, he looked through a window down at the rear yard, where more parentless waifs sat or stood, a few talking, many staring distractedly at nothing in particular.

As Yenola came to stand beside him at the window, keeping him silent company, Sutter couldn't help but recall his own earliest beginnings. He had no precise memory of it, but he'd imagined the story his father had shared of Sutter's birth parents. He'd imagined the bucket of water his birth father had very nearly dunked him in just after Sutter had drawn his first shuddering breath of life.

Pageant wagon folk. Slaves to their conceits and the roads and their humble audiences in town after town . . . and little time to raise a child, to raise Sutter.

He'd never have known a place like this. He would have died then, in that bucket, not even knowing what life was; Sutter was spared both the bucket and living a life in a place like this.

Still, these children were his kin in a way he couldn't ignore. And there was nothing he could do to relieve the bleakness that clung here thick as horseshit.

Then his eyes lit on a plot of ground in the far corner of the rear yard: a garden. Sutter's spirits rose, and he spun around, heading for the stair. Perhaps there was *one* thing he could do.

Out in the yard, he crossed hard-packed earth, well trodden by the feet of the orphans. His haste drew a few stares from the children. And their eyes brightened at the sight of Yenola until they could see she paid them little mind, as she simply tried to keep up with Sutter. He stopped at the edge of a large square of ground that had been formed into rough rows. There should have been green shoots pushing up through the soil by now—a fall planting. Instead, the earth was crusted, as though well watered long ago and then left untouched for weeks. He wondered if the garden was fallow, and hunkered down close to the hard soil.

He rooted around in one of the rows of earth, searching for seeds or shoots that might be growing up to the surface. Nothing. He tried again with a second row of dirt, finding only some rocks, and dead roots from vegetation long since removed. Sutter stubbornly tried a third row, aimless anger rising inside him. Still no sign of growth, but at least he found a seed.

Quickly, he pulled his hand back and brushed the dirt away, inspecting his find. It appeared to be a squash of some sort. But the shell of the seed had never opened; instead it appeared desiccated, the ground having sucked from it whatever nutrients it once held.

He looked up and surveyed again the barren little garden. He hated the mockery it must be to the children—the promise of food to fill bodies that clearly needed the nourishment, and yet no crop rose from the soil.

A garden wasn't an easy thing to manage. And if the crone with the knitting needles was these children's only caregiver, then he understood the failure to grow anything here. But that didn't feel right. The soil and the seed, on their own, could push a sprout to the light of day. A farmer's hand did most of its service or damage after that.

Sutter raised his fingers and licked at the dirt covering them. The soil held a bitter, acidic taste, slightly metallic, almost the way a field would taste if left unfertilized for several seasons. He wondered if the planter had known the state of the soil when he tilled the plot and seeded the rows. Likely not. And yet, Sutter found it hard to believe that this square of land was the only useless garden in the city. Others would likely be sharing the challenge of raising a crop.

He wouldn't be able to help. Not even to plant a damn carrot. Nothing would grow here. Robbed of doing even that much to assist a bunch of orphans, he felt miserable.

"Are you taking us on the walk?"

The voice startled both Sutter and Yenola. He turned to see a young boy—maybe seven years old—with a face pocked by scars. The lad wore a severe frown—the most emotion Sutter had seen from any of the children.

"*The* walk? What do you mean?" Sutter asked.

"We should leave," Yenola said. "We've disturbed these children enough. We shouldn't give them false hope."

"The walk," the boy repeated, with an incredulous, challenging tone, as though repeating the words would make it clear.

"I'm not from Ir-Caul," Sutter explained.

The lad eyed Yenola suspiciously. "Is this your lady?"

With a small bit of pride, Sutter said, "Today, yes. Why?"

"Do you know about the walks?" the boy asked Yenola directly.

She stared back, saying nothing for several moments. She looked ready to reply, when the boy spoke again. "Send her into the house."

Sutter shrugged at Yenola. "What can it hurt? I'll talk to the boy."

She stood for several seconds, obviously hesitant to leave them alone, then finally returned to the house, looking back once over her shoulder at Sutter and the lad. He sensed he'd made a mistake with her by indulging the boy's desire to share something in confidence, but it was done. And in any case, what harm would a child's secret do?

"Your woman is from the court," the lad said. "She knows

about the walks. And now she will know you know, and you're a stranger. Be careful."

Sutter shook his head. "What are these walks?"

The lad became quiet, looking around at the other orphans with whom he shared this place. Sutter got the sense that the boy was something of a parent to them. Probably the one who consoled them when sadness made them weep, and spoke for the group when it was necessary. Like now.

"Every few weeks," he began, his voice growing soft and distant, almost like he needed to separate himself from the things he said, "at night, men come and wake some of us. They take two each time, give them shoes so that they can walk."

"Where do they take them?" Sutter asked. "Have they found you homes?"

"They came again six days ago. I woke up and hid in the closet. I think they would have taken me if I'd been on my blanket. But instead they took my friend, Salman." A silent tear streaked the dirty face of the lad. "And while he dressed and put on the shoes they brought, I heard their whispers."

Sutter braced himself. Even before hearing it all, he began to understand.

"They're losing the war," the boy said. "They need better swords and faster bows. More of those big rock throwers they roll on wheels. The stuff to make all that . . . they trade us for it. None of my friends have ever come back from the walk."

"The walk," Sutter repeated, lost in his own dark musings.

"That's what they call it when they get us up. A walk to wear-in our new shoes. But we all know now what it means. Why would the king let them take us?" the boy asked. "He's supposed to protect us, isn't he? Him and all the great ones in the castle. My dad fought because of that idea. What changed?"

Under a hot sun, Sutter looked at the boy and had no answer. *But by every absent god, I will find one.*

• CHAPTER FIFTY-EIGHT •

The First One

When someone we know takes their own life, our natural response is, "What could I have done to prevent it?" Consider: While well-intended, this reaction does not sufficiently acknowledge the magnitude of the sufferer's pain. In short, it's beyond you.

—From *The Fallacy of Understanding,* an examination of self-slaughter, penned by Shurts Nephets, who failed at self-immolation

THEY WOVE THROUGH streets more crowded with merchants than Tahn remembered. But the walk grew pleasant despite the pain and torturously slow pace he was forced to keep. On top of his aches and pains from passing through the Telling, he'd had his ass whupped by a Quiet man in the astronomy tower. Not an easy thing to explain away. Fortunately, there were plenty willing to believe he'd been rather clumsy this soon after returning to the Grove. And his pains were mostly bruises that lay beneath his clothes.

But he limbered up the more he walked, and began to enjoy even the unique merchant district of the Grove. It had the agreeable feeling of people too consumed with intellectual puzzles to haggle over the price of beans or quality of workmanship.

He more often heard traders and customers asking each other questions about where they'd spied a certain star than he heard them making change on a silver coin.

He smiled to see pairs of researchers walking shoulder to shoulder so they could stare down at the same book and read as they made their way along.

And through the cobblestone roads swept the gentle scents

of juniper and cherrywood blossoms, and stone wet from recent scrubbing.

There was a hum of activity that could scarcely be heard, because it happened mostly in the heads of Grove residents. Which wasn't to say there wasn't also amusement. Tahn caught snippets of laughter, but usually after some misstep of logic.

As he passed, one man was laughing at another, younger man. "Next you're going to tell us it's true because no one has proven it false. Such an appeal to ignorance." To which the younger man aptly replied, "And next you're going to tell me it's false, because the college savants have always held that belief. Such an appeal to authority."

The two men shook hands over their logical fallacies.

Tahn breathed deeply as they passed, feeling more comfortable every moment.

Eventually, he and Rithy reached the main halls of study and observation. Old stone, blackened by age, crept up four stories. The doors, similarly darkened by time and fortified by heavy iron, seemed imposing to try to pass. But Rithy simply opened the door, which creaked some, and led him inside the cool and dampened air of the astronomy college, where long ago he'd walked and studied.

It was strange to be back. On one level it seemed as though he'd never left. On another level, it was like having a third life—a life different from both the Scar and the Hollows. In some ways, though, this place struck him as the most . . . real.

Rithy ushered him inside a discussion hall where Polaema spoke, her head cocked back as she paced and gave a discourse on solar and lunar conjunction. She only stopped when the attendees, on seeing Tahn shuffle in, one by one slowly rose to their feet.

When she finally took notice, she lowered her head and turned toward the door. "Your reputation precedes you, Gnomon."

He knew a few of those now standing and staring. Names returned: Goffry, Mikal, Saranda, Cholas . . .

But the number of those he didn't know was even greater.

And he became self-conscious as they stood to honor him. Though a few did hold guarded, rivalrous expressions.

He'd loved the work and study of the firmament here, had flourished at it. By the age of nine, he'd earned enough of Polaema's trust that he was allowed to ascend the astronomy dome at will. But that had been a long time ago. Why were they standing now? And why, all these years later, were they discussing conjunctive phases? It left him a bit stumped. Perhaps there were new understandings of sun and moon movements that required further investigation.

"Come in, you two." Polaema motioned them deeper into the hall. "I was just talking through the somewhat rare lunar eclipse of the second moon."

"We should talk more about Ardua soon. I think there's something to this dual eclipse." Tahn made a mental note of it. "But for now, perhaps we should find someplace more private," he suggested. "I'm ready to explain my . . . request."

"No secrets here, Tahn." Without looking at them, she pointed at those standing behind her. "And I think you'll find some help here, besides." She looked over at Rithy and winked.

Tahn followed Mother Polaema's gaze to his friend. "Had this planned, did you?" Tahn started to laugh, before wincing with pain and shutting it off.

"Tell them," Rithy urged gently.

Tahn gave her a thoughtful look, then without holding back, addressed Polaema and the other astronomers. "I'm going to call for a Succession of Arguments, and I ask for your help."

A chorus of murmurs followed his announcement. Tahn gladdened to hear in it a tone more of excitement than concern. It lent him a shade of confidence. Successions didn't usually originate out of the College of Astronomy. Willing supporters meant a lot.

But in truth, Successions weren't common from *any* of the five colleges at Aubade Grove. They happened infrequently. They had a specific purpose, and proved grueling for everyone involved. They even followed the Grove's architectural logic. This city of science had been thoughtfully and deliberately laid out. Five towers, five disciplines. Each tower was the point on a broad star or pentagon. And the relationship of each tower to its two nearest towers held a logic of its own.

At the northern tip, Cosmology—the study of the structure and origin of the universe. Then, moving counterclockwise, came the College of Philosophy, which more than the other disciplines sought to find meaning in the sky—akin to cosmology. At the southeastern point, Mathematics. All students at the Grove were required to achieve a base level of proficiency in math, as they were in all disciplines. Those that kept on at math, however, wound up using it to theorize at a level that made it a near cousin to philosophy. East cf that rose the tower of Physics, where researchers pursued enlightenment around the physical properties of celestial bodies and their interactions with one another. "Grand mechanics," Tahn liked to call them. Lots of math and astronomy in their work, thus why they were positioned between those two colleges. Finally, at the northeastern point, Astronomy—Tahn's own specialty. The College of Astronomy was one part physics and one part cosmology, making its position between those two disciplines sensible.

In his years here, he'd actually excelled at each discipline. But he had the heart of an astronomer: studying and describing the nature and position of celestial bodies, their motion—stars, planets, and other night sky objects—that was his best thing.

The Succession of Arguments was a rigorous process of discussion and debate among these colleges. Its intention was to find the heart and answer to a specific question or supposition. In an open and formal dialogue, Tahn would make his argument, appealing to each college in succession. He'd have to prove his supposition on the basis of each college discipline.

Since Tahn belonged to the College of Astronomy, Succession would begin with the College of Physics—the closest discipline in a clockwise rotation. The men and women of Physics would offer input, speculate and ultimately challenge Tahn's question with their science. Their intent was to find its flaw and thus end Succession, or help prove it should continue on to a debate with the next college in turn. As long as the argument prevailed, it continued to move around the five points of the Grove, finding more strenuous challenge in each debate.

These contests of scientific prowess and inquiry were draining and often combative. Fights had been known to break out on the theater floors. Ultimately, the answer to a particular question or position—its "proof," as was said— either found its way into the volumes of their libraries as fact, or died in the Succession of Arguments, exposed for its rational flaws.

It was their way to test hypotheses and assumptions and agree on first principles and common understanding.

Staring into the inquisitive eyes of these twenty astronomers, Tahn answered their unspoken question. He hadn't time or inclination to be coy with information. He needed their help, and quickly. So Tahn told them about the Quiet coming into the Hollows. He explained that the ground there had been hallowed—which meant that Quietgiven coming into the Hollows now suggested at least two things: their world was changing; and the Veil had weakened. Tahn believed the two were related.

He turned to face Rithy and Polaema, who now stood near each other. "We have to determine how the Veil works. So we can strengthen it."

"Strengthen it?" one of the young astronomers asked.

Tahn nodded and paced a bit, rather professorially. "The Veil is failing. I've seen an army of Quiet that obviously pushed its way through. Time's running out. . . . If we can strengthen it, we can stop a war before it begins."

Polaema sighed audibly. "I've been thinking, Tahn. We will likely fail when we come to the College of Philosophy. And that's if we can get past Physics and Mathematics. Humorless bunch—" The master astronomer cut her comment short, and nodded in silent apology to Rithy.

"Why?" Tahn asked, feeling a small flutter of panic.

Polaema offered a sad smile. "Opinions about old stories like that of the Veil have begun to change."

"But if we succeed in our debate with the Colleges of

Physics and Mathematics," he argued, "we'll have the support and evidence of the core sciences when we debate the philosophers—"

"Who will turn it against you that such a Veil should even exist," Polaema interrupted. "Yours is a difficult supposition, Gnomon. Even before the philosophical arguments, you must first prove the existence of a boundary that I'm quite certain no one in the Grove has ever seen or felt. Then you must suggest that this boundary is weakening. I assume this is because there is trouble in Descant."

Tahn shook his head. "No. At least, not entirely. I think what's happening goes beyond the Song of Suffering."

"That, at least, is good news. There are critical views of Suffering, as well," Rithy added.

Tahn didn't bother to respond to that. Skepticism over tales of the Quiet and the practices of the Leiholan, not to mention the Sheason, weren't new to him.

So, he finally, fully embraced the argument that he was about to resurrect from the long-cold ashes of a failed Succession. *The last time I was here.*

Still holding Polaema's gaze, he said, "We will argue the Continuity of All Things. But this time, it will be about Resonance."

The mutterings that followed sounded of curiosity and excitement. *Good!* He couldn't wait to get started.

But Rithy and Mother Polaema didn't seem to share the excitement. Their faces showed the shock and worry he'd expected. It was why he'd waited until now to even utter the word "Continuity." He was sure they'd suspected. His talk of Succession to find a unifying principle . . . they must have known. Hearing it out loud, though. Tahn declaring the argument. It seemed to bring the past whirling back, causing their worried faraway stares.

He had his own approach to Continuity, though: Resonance. He hoped it would be different enough from before that they would still support him. The outcome of the last Succession on Continuity, in which they all three had shared a part, had gone badly. It had to be different this time. And Tahn had to tell them why. He needed to make them understand his reason for coming here. If he was going to ask them to help with a Continuity argument, he owed them that. Because it would open that wound again: Nanjesho. Absent gods, he missed her, too.

He gave them each a sympathetic, reassuring look, and started to explain. Not by talking about armies of thousands who would be called to war. Or Wendra. Or Mira. Or his own choices about when he fired his bow. Not even by sharing the story of Devin or Alemdra, both of whom had died in a Scar created by the Quiet's stripping of the land ages ago.

"Before I came to the Grove, I lived in a place called the Scar." Tahn gave a weak smile of remembrance. "It's a dry place. Broad and lifeless. Except for a house where a man watches over children who are left in his care when their parents can't be found. He teaches them to fight, because the world is cruel. He teaches them not to trust adults, because adults lie. He teaches them that the Quiet will return, because the Quiet want what we have. And when the Quiet come, he says, the Scar will grow. Maybe everything will become Scar."

A few of the astronomers nodded, as though they'd heard of the place.

"I had friends there," Tahn said, his smile this time more of fondness. "It was the only way to make it through the training and heat and bad food. We became a family. A strong family, I think, because of what we endured together." Tahn paused a long moment, looking over these Succession helpmates. "So it was especially hard when one of us chose to leave."

Rithy and Mother Polaema stood listening. Their expressions of apprehension had softened a little.

He swallowed hard, not really wanting to say this. But they needed to understand this was about more than the interests of kings and Sheason and big armies far away.

"No one ever left the Scar to find a new place to live," Tahn added. "No one I knew, anyway."

There were puzzled looks, a few of his listeners framing questions. Tahn held up his hand, begging their patience.

"The first time I found one who chose to leave, I was four."

He nodded, remembering more clearly now. "My job was to see if any sprouts had sprung up near a small stream that flowed whenever rain fell. It wasn't far. And everyone who can walk has jobs to do in the Scar. So that evening I walked out to the streambed, maybe three hundred strides east of the house."

"Tahn," Mother Polaema said softly. "You don't have to . . ."

"I'm all right," he replied. "There were lots of brown shadows that night. Baked stone at dusk makes everything look brown. And most everything was stone or caked soil. Except the stream. It was trickling along from a storm that had passed through the day before. I remember liking that sound a lot. A trickling stream.

"In the dusk, I could see sprouts in the shallow water, which meant fresh greens that night for supper." Tahn could taste them even now, pan fried and salted. "So I hurried down into the gulley and began to gather them in. I had a burlap bag to carry as much as I could pick.

"I worked downstream until there was almost no sunlight left in the sky. The stars, I remember, looked watery and washed—not yet bright as they do when the sun is fully gone. That's why I didn't see her at first. Another dark shape on one side of the gully, like any mound of rocks. But I kept gathering, drawing closer. And eventually I saw the shape for what it was: my friend Tamara."

Tahn could see realization blossoming in his listeners' faces. The end of the story wasn't hard to know.

Tahn stopped. The feeling in the discussion hall was tight, full. His own emotion had risen high in his throat, the old ache made new and now touching his voice. He swallowed again and pushed on.

"She was twelve. She told funny stories. She said her mom and dad weren't dead, but that they thought she'd be better off in another home. And so she wound up in the Scar." Tahn shook his head, anger now accompanying his grief. "She did it with her work knife. She cut her veins lengthwise to make it fast. Her short note said that she didn't think her parents were alive after all, because if they were, they'd have come for her by now. She said that she couldn't take another day in the Scar. That she couldn't bear the thought of living with people again. And that she didn't want to be around when the Quiet came. And she said she was sorry."

A few of the astronomers sniffed. Mother Polaema had tears in her eyes. Rithy's head hung down.

"I found her there, because she liked to go to the stream when it was running, to see the sprouts. She loved the color green." Tahn nodded to himself, just able to hold back his own tears. "She liked the smell of them, too. And that they had the bravery to come up, ignoring what would happen when the stream soon stopped flowing. That's where she wanted to be when she left the Scar."

In a soft whisper, Rithy asked, "Why tell us this, Tahn?"

He didn't immediately answer, thinking about Tamara. She'd been the first ward Tahn had found dead. "Don't cry for Tamara," he said. "She's no longer in any kind of pain. But that's why I'm here. Not Tamara, in particular. But because if we don't find a way to make the Veil strong, the Quiet will come . . . and there'll be many left alone like Tamara. And the only home for them will be an even wider, broader Scar."

One of the astronomers spoke reverentially. "She shouldn't have done it."

Tahn looked in the direction of the man. "I wish she hadn't," he said. "But that's selfish of me. She escaped the Scar. In some ways, even then, I was a little jealous."

He turned again to Rithy and Polaema. This topic of self-slaughter held an awful poignancy for them. For Tahn.

Nanjesho had had a unique warmth about her. She'd never divided her attention. If she was taking to Tahn, the world could do what it liked; she remained focused on what she and Tahn were talking about. He'd seen the kind of mother she'd been to Rithy—patient, encouraging. And he'd seen the unique love she and Polaema had shared. Since he'd never known his own mother, it was the first loving relationship he'd ever witnessed.

But Succession had taken its toll. And she'd walked into her own Scar.

Believing that his old friends now understood, Tahn meant to get started. "I understand the mercy of death. But wouldn't it be better if it was the last option?" With a firm voice, he began to declare what he wanted to do. "I want to prove Resonance is the unifying principle of Continuity. I want to use Succession to prove that principle is true. And once we've done that, I want to use it to strengthen the Veil. Keep the Quiet at bay." He paused, softening his tone. "I want to help those like Tamara," *and Nanjesho, and Devin . . . and Alemdra,* "believe there's a good reason to be here for tomorrow."

The astronomy discourse theater came alive with a vibrant resolve Tahn could feel. They kept a silent respect for what he'd shared. But it was clear they wanted to help for new reasons. It was everything he'd hoped for. Gratitude filled him until he thought tears might come. These new friends would begin preparing for the astronomy argument—which would come last—as he went through the other colleges in succession.

When he looked over at Rithy and Mother Polaema, he could still see a hint of reservation. But it was different this time, from what he'd seen and sensed before. It wasn't about the past. Or, at least, about the past alone. The pressures of Succession were many. It wasn't only Nanjesho who'd felt its sting. The process had been known to cripple many of those who'd failed. Cripple them mentally. Emotionally. One tended to succeed at Succession only if he gave his whole self to it. Which came with a very real risk if the argument was lost. That was the concern he saw in his friends' eyes. It wasn't about Rithy's mother. It was about what it could do to Tahn.

But as the moment stretched on, their faces showed tentative smiles. They would support him. Despite the past. It was maybe the greatest act of faith he'd ever seen.

• CHAPTER FIFTY-NINE •

A Dangerous Endeavor

> *Unschooled Leiholan takes the stage, you see. Sings some-*
> *thing in a tongue none of us has ever heard before. We under-*
> *stand the song, though. In our guts, we understand. And*
> *some hearts couldn't suffer it. Eighteen people drop dead*
> *in their pork stew. Don't tell me music isn't dangerous.*

—Witness account suppressed by the League of Civility
in its investigation of several simultaneous deaths
reported by Rafters tavern patrons

EVENING IN THE Cathedral Quarter came on with raucous laughter, the shouts of men and women ready to
gamble coin, and music wafting on the air like strains of a
great, nightly symphony. Musicians of every stripe were either on their way to a venue, warming up, or currently performing. And tonight, in the company of Belamae, Wendra
was in the Quarter to hear music.

After the events on the docks the previous night, she'd gotten the women to safety and quietly slipped back into Descant. Those things played in her mind as they set out *this*
night. But not for long. Belamae's excitement for their out-
ing in the Quarter was infectious, and they were soon talking
and walking as two friends with someplace to be.

"There are the main roads of the Quarter," Belamae explained. " 'First stops,' the music jokesters like to say. Usually larger performance taverns. Lots of seats. Liquor bought
in casks. Not bad for that, but it leaves less space for curated
selections: what we call 'music drinks.' Libations found only
deep inside the Quarter."

They moved at a leisurely pace through the crowds.

Belamae gestured here and there. "Recityv has thirteen
other music 'quarters.' And for the most part, you'll only find

pay-to-play establishments in them. Musicians generally put up three plugs for fifteen minutes of stage time. The bigger places, where the crowds are larger, get four. Even field hands and butchers and farriers, who work ten days to earn three plugs to rub together, will buy time if they think they have the musical finesse to mount a stage." He nodded in appreciation. "It's true, though, that a fine performance can earn back double what is paid to play. Performance tavern folk can be generous when they think the coin is earned."

Then he paused a moment in the midst of the bustle, making sure she was listening to his next words. "Here in the Cathedral Quarter, musicians don't pay for stage time. And patrons come for more than entertainment and distraction. Folk here, they come to *hear* musicians play. Not just watch, or, by silent gods, ignore the music while they eat and look for bed company."

Wendra suppressed a smile, and they started to stroll again.

Belamae continued as before, giving her this private tour. "And folk who come to *hear* musicians play, they understand false notes and poor rhyme. If your need is a tune to dance to, go somewhere else. Maylains perhaps. Or Scrodulan Street." He raised a finger, as one clarifying a point. "But even the music in these districts is generally better than you'll find in other cities, save those with conservatories of their own."

She wanted to ask about other conservatories, but didn't interrupt Belamae, who was lively tonight like she hadn't seen in a good long while.

"But, music in the other quarters of Recityv happens in formal establishments, where concerts are announced days or weeks in advance." He shriveled his nose comically. "These concerts became *affairs,* events where people who can afford Hidan silk and the satins of Masson Gulf like to be seen. Vapid things," Belamae said with a bit of distaste.

"The best thing the other quarters produce musicwise is musicians with enough salt to play here." He raised a hand to indicate the Cathedral Quarter. "And that happens with enough frequency to make them tolerable." He laughed.

Wendra looked around at the slum.

454 • PETER ORULLIAN

Belamae put an arm around her shoulder. "I see the way
you look at it. Yes, it's the laborers' district. But it's the harbor for those who take care in the craft and consumption of
music. And that's what counts."

"No argument from me," she said. "But, if I *were* to argue, what would I say?" she asked, and smiled.

"You'd say that in Recityv's musical heartbeat, musicians
have largely one aim: to be asked, or have their petition accepted . . ." he paused, drawing it out, "to train at Descant. It
isn't about coin. And it isn't about patrons, either. Those are
worthy enough outcomes of solid musicianship. But those
are to be had in other places. Not *the Quarter*. Here it's about
the music. Here, about Descant."

They strolled a few minutes more, walking unhurried
through street after street, hearing instruments and voices
carry through doors and windows. Wendra began to feel a
sense of place, and folded her arm around the Maesteri's as
they ambled along.

Belamae hadn't summoned her for another lesson during
the day. Instead he'd waited until dusk, and then led her
on this tour of the slum and music enclave to a place known
as Rafters—another performance tavern. It sat back off the
main streets. She began to look forward to quite an evening
of music, and enjoyed the anticipation.

Out front sat two heavyset men on bar stools eyeing
down those who wished to enter. They collected a copper
plug from those who sought the opportunity.

Belamae paid the admission, and led Wendra through the
crowd toward the stage. The Maesteri received several deferential nods, which he graciously returned. And more than
a few eyed Wendra, wondering openly about her. There was
a little jealousy in many of those who stared after her, several of whom held instruments. Though just as many showed
a different spark of interest, like hope that she might be performing, given her companion.

From more than one table she heard whispers, all generally saying the same thing: *The Maesteri's here. It's gonna
heat up tonight.*

He stopped three times to exchange pleasantries and clasp

hands with men and women. These folk struck her as being rather like Belamae, probably music instructors. Or perhaps they were simply fixtures here at Rafters—like the Maesteri himself, it seemed. Soon they reached the stage, and moved to the right, where they passed a large slate, written on in cream-colored chalk. The night's playbill. It looked like nine different performances were scheduled. Belamae read down the list with excitement. Behind them, the room buzzed with anticipation from patrons a drink or two into their evening. She couldn't help but smile, and began tapping her own foot.

Then he led her up a short set of stairs and around to the side stage. Tucked just out of view from the crowd sat a table adorned with a small wicker basket filled with baguettes of pumpernickel, rye, and dark-grain breads. A generous bowl of whipped butter rested beside the basket. And behind it all, two empty chairs.

Belamae motioned in a gentlemanly manner for her to choose a seat. After she'd done so, he sat beside her and exhaled with delighted expectation. "Here we are."

"Wouldn't it be better out front?" she asked, more than a little confused.

"Oh, no, no. Out there we'd get caught up in the enthusiasm of the crowd. We'd hear the resonances of the room. We'd be more inclined to share a word with the next table. We'd miss the musicians' faces when they fret before taking the stage." He pointed across from them, stage right, where several musicians were tuning and running scales.

A dozen questions jumped to mind. But before she could ask, the Maesteri smiled and explained. "Back here, we get the unencumbered view and sound of the performance. No enhancements. Just whatever music they're making. We hear it *flat*." He ran a straightened palm through the air in a slow horizontal motion. "This way, we pick up intonation. We catch the places where the musician struggles. And when it's good from backstage"—he tapped the table, indicating the little nook they now occupied—"it's superb." He showed her a beaming smile.

Wendra nodded, as a mandolist began taking the stage.

A moment later, two glasses of a velvety, sharp-smelling

brandy were brought without the need of an order. Hardly looking away from the onstage musician tuning his mandola, Belamae said, "Board says Goffry's back in the city."

Their server leaned down, putting his head squarely in Belamae's line of sight. "So he is, you strummer."

"You know I only pick my strings," Belamae replied.

It sounded like a rote greeting, as the two men settled into shared chuckles. Wendra assumed some metaphor at work in the exchange, but whatever it was escaped her. It gladdened her, though, to see Belamae in such fine spirits. He had color in his skin and the glimmer back in his eyes. He seemed truly at home here.

"Wendra, this is Ollie, Rafters proprietor, rag-handler, insatiable gossip, and music . . . er, tone-deaf aficionado."

The man made a shallow bow. "A right fine pleasure. Though, you could find better company in a barn. You see where we sit him."

Wendra smiled.

Then Ollie turned back to his old friend. "Goffry spent some time down in Dalle, I hear. Comes back to us with some tricks, he thinks. All he gave me for his set selection was notation keys. A bit o' pomp in 'im now. All Dimn-like."

Belamae nodded. "He'll draw a crowd, though. You're not hating that. Man's got a talent for loud." He patted Ollie's elbow. "The slate also says there's a pair of pageant wagon players taking the boards. What's the story there? One of them offer you a kiss?"

Ollie's smile brightened briefly then fell down quite a lot. "Said they wanted to sing something from the Slaternly Cycle. I haven't heard that since I was a kid. League won't allow it anymore, neither. I wrote 'em up on balls alone." He mimed putting their names on the slateboard.

"Good news is the Reconciliationists have stopped recruiting sopranos out of the Quarter. Bad news is it seems their own music conservatory is doing right well. Can't say how many good voices are now singing to dead gods, but it makes one want to weep."

"Or convert," Belamae quipped.

Ollie laughed hard twice. "Well, hold your praise. I've had

more than my share of Rykian Church fellows in here scouting for canters. The whole world's turning their music skyward. Whatever happened to a good ole dirty-time jam-all?"

The Maesteri sat back for a moment, looking into his friend's face, as though the question had been a serious one. "Most musicians are too *rehearsed* these days. They play a thing to death before they stand up to play it for someone else. They know all the songs, and so haven't anything of their own."

A strange silence settled over them in their little backstage nook. Then Ollie's brows rose, his lips pursed, and he nodded as if it was the truest damned thing he'd ever heard.

"Harnell's closing it out tonight, I saw." Belamae nodded, approving of each selection as another man might test and approve of his glass of wine. "And Cris is first, I see," he said, motioning toward the mandolist.

"He's gonna make another run. You sittin' here's not gonna do much for his stage hands." Ollie held out his hand, splay-fingered, and made it all trembly.

The Maesteri shook his head. "I think that part's behind him." He then handed Ollie a coin. "Don't argue on the change. You're a damn sight better to these kids than they get on the main roads. That matters. Now get off the stage, I can't see."

Ollie stared at the full handcoin in his palm, looked like he meant to argue, then smiled and did as he was asked, nodding to Cris that he could begin whenever he liked. The lad thanked Ollie, and continued to tune.

"Tonight's lesson, my dear: sound versus meaning. Lend an ear." Belamae leaned forward in his chair, ignoring his glass, awaiting the song.

The mandola player finished tuning his instrument, then looked up tentatively at the large crowd. In a broken voice he announced, "'Green Fields,'" before quickly returning his eyes to his fretboard. He fingered his first chord and took a visible breath as the tavern quieted.

He strummed once. Let it ring out to silence. Then began a fingerpicking pattern across the twelve coursed gut strings. Wendra could hear the pairs of gut had been tuned mostly in octaves. Though she thought she heard a few tuned to harmonic fifths. The young man began to move through a progression of chords, his right hand continuing to pick a rhythmic pattern with each new combination of notes.

But as focused as he seemed to be, the player made a bad job of his song. Wendra could see his heel bouncing, not in time to his music, but with a nervous twitch. And he missed more than a few notes, unintentionally playing muted strings and striking some that sounded sour against the rest.

Perhaps worst of all, he seemed unable to find a tempo. And quickly the crowd began to call for him to get off the stage.

Wendra stole a glance at Belamae, and saw an intensity in him she couldn't name. Perhaps it was the Maesteri's patience for bad musicianship from earnest musicians. But she couldn't quite read him.

A wet rag flew out from somewhere on the floor, hitting the boy in the face. A patron wouldn't likely be carrying a rag; this would have come from a tavern worker.

"Why doesn't he stop?" Wendra asked. "Before they get more hostile?"

Belamae didn't answer.

A few of the patrons had walked near the stage and begun to heckle the lad. "Go home to your mother's teat and your 'green fields.' The city's no place for such poor fingers."

Then a glass hit the young man in the side of the head, breaking apart and splattering him with liquor. A deafening roar of laughter followed.

Wendra shot to her feet. "It's a damned song. What right have you—"

Belamae pulled her gently but firmly back to her seat. Her anger continued to mount, even as the Maesteri said, "It's a performance tavern. The crowd is what the crowd is. The boy knew what he was up against. Now, patience yet." And he returned his attention to the mandolist.

The player had stopped plucking his strings. Liquor soaked his shirt and instrument. A small runnel of blood ran from his ear into his collar. The mandolist's dejection seemed only to cause greater ridicule and mocking laughter.

She wanted the young man to slip away and save himself the embarrassment. It was then that she noticed the hems on his clothes. While she couldn't be sure, she'd have wagered that the wide gathering stitch and rough weave belonged to a field hand. Not someone who'd grown up on Recityv streets. She'd have bet her last coin he was here trying to improve his lot. Get into Descant and out of the muck fields.

Another thought then struck her. Maybe he wasn't doing any of this for himself. Maybe he was doing it for his family. Wendra's coarse music began to rush in her blood.

Then the boy's heel stopped shaking. And in the midst of the shouts and laughs, he started once more to play.

His first notes couldn't be heard above the noise. It took several moments for the crowd to realize they hadn't shunned him from the stage. The silence that followed had the feeling of a serpent ready to strike a hapless animal.

But this time, and with liquor dripping from sodden hair across the strings he played, the young man did not falter. She knew "Green Fields." It was a common tune, an old one, meant to strike a contemplative tone. She'd always taken it as a song men and women of the field sang to convince themselves that their lives weren't dire. A kind of self-deception, perhaps.

However, the young man ran at the tune with abandon. The fingers of each of his hands worked in a complicated dance that hastened, exposing the lie of the song's composition. It might take a simple theme, but the song itself was anything but.

After several refrains, the feeling in the crowd's silence changed. No longer did they wait for the lad to falter, but now sat in growing wonder at how the plain song had been given fresh life, the frantic pace of it seeming to express a common angst.

Belamae began to tap the table in front of him in half notes, striking a rhythm to the lad's song. The crowd began to do likewise, softly knocking on tables or clapping their hands—one beat for every eight notes the boy played.

Wendra joined them, feeling as though she were helping the young man create, while showing support and approval.

The lad looked up with surprise in his eyes, drawn momentarily from the world that had become him and his mandola. When he settled his focus back to his instrument, he widened his feet beneath him, as though he'd need the added balance, and hunkered more deeply over his fretboard.

And he played like Wendra had never seen a man play.

She heard frustration and loss and anger and disappointment in his notes. She also heard hope just beneath the music itself. His hands flashed over his strings, and when she heard the occasional erring note, it sounded appropriate, as if to say a field hand makes bad choices in a hard life.

But those were few. The song became a blur, and the pounding and clapping became a clamor. It all spiraled together, feeling like a song offered by them all, rising, quickening.

Until the young man began to falter. Not a lot. Just missing a note here and there. Dragging the rhythm, but not in a purposefully musical way.

Wendra spared a quick glance at Belamae, whose eyes showed a resigned concern. She looked back at the mandolist, listening closely through the din. The pace he'd played up to was remarkable. And slightly beyond his ability to control. The rhythmic dance of his two hands fell out of time. The boy pushed on, fighting through his performance, making his efforts all appear purposeful. There was a strong measure of raw emotion in what he did, how he played. And most of the tavern was alive with the energy of it. Only a few seemed unmoved, watching the way Belamae watched.

Finally, the young man stopped, panting, and clasped his hands together as if he might squeeze rhythm back into them. It left him looking like one in prayer, or perhaps begging alms. His face, though, held a hint of confusion, as if he asked himself how he'd lost control. But only a hint, as the crowd erupted in praising shouts and applause.

Under his breath, Belamae whispered, "Oh, my boy."

"What?" she asked. "They were all clapping. All he did was falter a bit at the end."

Belamae's reply surprised her. "He'll have no offer to study at Descant. Not yet. Not from this performance."

"But he moved this crowd. You saw it. He's got talent. Why no invitation?"

He turned to her, a thoughtful expression on his face. Then he showed her a patient smile. "Of course moving an audience is a fine aim. A very good thing in and of itself. But don't confuse that with being a musician. Some pluckers do well in front of a crowd. They seem to shine a titch brighter when folks are watching. Nothing wrong with that. But I care more about the music you make when no one is watching. Is it honest then? Is it right?" He paused a moment, as if clarifying his thoughts. "A musician, some would argue, can sell a song with more than notes. But you can't fool yourself. When you make song in your private chambers, there's no thrum and rattle of the tavern, no flowing liquor, no ready mind for escape. In your own rooms, there's just you and the song."

"Meaning what?" Wendra argued. "That you must be perfect in private?"

"Of course not." He patted her hand warmly. "Some call it the difference between musician and musicianship. I think it's closer to say the difference between musician and performer. Both are a treat. But they're not always the same. Mind you, I'm not saying one is best."

"Then what *are* you saying?" Wendra was now watching the young man under the scrutinizing eyes of the tavern crowd.

Belamae gave her hand a light squeeze, drawing her attention back. "I'm saying that a performer can get a crowd tapping their feet. But played or sung in private, that same song may not hold up. Only *you* know—when no one is there to shout your praises—if the song is worth a tinker's damn."

The young man cradled his mandola close and stepped slowly from the stage. Without a word to anyone, he made his way through the patrons and vanished from the tavern. A kind of stunned silence held for a while. Slowly, conversation returned, but more subdued than before.

Speaking as one to himself, Belamae said, "Stretch your limits, yes. But don't go beyond them. Don't compromise the song. Especially not to please a crowd."

The Maesteri sat back when the tavern returned to its usual

hum of activity. As he stared at the place where the lad had stood, he said, "But don't worry for the boy. The song broke down. But he had such marvelous intention, didn't he? I think he'll get to Descant soon enough."

They each took a drink of their brandy, Wendra more deeply than Belamae. A bitter-smooth plum flavor lit fire in her throat and belly. And Belamae began to explain.

"We've spoken about sound. It has natural behavior, and we do well to understand it before applying our *intentions*." He waved a finger at the stage. "Intentions are what we *mean* when we make music. This is where the gift of Leiholan takes root. For meaning to occur, there's conceptualization by the musician, the performance itself . . . and comprehension by the interpreter."

"What if there's no one to hear the song? Does it still have power?" Wendra asked.

Belamae gave her a puzzled look. "Everything, my dear, *everything* is an interpreter. You, me, this table"—he knocked it with his knuckles—"the glasses we hold, the liquor inside them."

Wendra spared a look at her brandy glass. *Because everything has a resonant signature.*

He smiled, and returned his attention to the stage. "Let's focus on vocal music. Meaning bursts forth when language is uttered. But true meaning has less to do with the words themselves, and everything to do with *intention*. We call this 'shotal.' You see, *powerful* meaning occurs when shotal is communicated regardless of the lyrics or story a musician is trying to tell."

Belamae began singing a sharp, angry note on an open "ahh" sound. He then stopped and sang a lullaby that sounded like a cooing baby. "Do you see? You understand my meaning with no words. My intent is clear."

Wendra nodded, excited to understand explicitly what she'd only ever intuited before.

"Shotal strikes the vibration in all creation." Belamae smiled with his own enthusiasm.

"Did the mandolist's song have meaning?" Wendra said, unable to shake the feeling of his failure.

Before the Maesteri could respond, a song rose up from the stage several strides away. By silent consent they turned and watched a flutist play a fine tune, by turns fast then slow. She added a percussive quality to the performance by blowing into her instrument in bursts. Wendra quite liked it. And so did the crowd, which broke into applause before she was even through playing. When the woman finished, she looked over at Belamae, who smiled warmly and shook his head.

This happened twice more: once with an older man who sang in a powerful baritone that resonated throughout Rafters like a sounding horn, and again with a woman who played a rather mean fiddle. Each received gracious applause, and then looked over at the Maesteri, whose smile showed genuine appreciation, approval even, as he shook his head.

"Are these auditions?" Wendra asked.

Before Belamae could speak, another voice lifted from the stage: a Descant student standing in front of the tavern, easing into a gentle air. It was Telaya. Her name hadn't been on the slate. She might not be Leiholan—a fact that Wendra knew rankled her—but Telaya's musicianship was impeccable. With perfect clarity and pitch, she caught the attention of Rafters' patrons as she sang the first notes of "Fit Men Do Not Wait." This song might have been as old as "Green Fields." But it had an entirely different lyrical message.

With strong alto notes she sang a chanting staccato, emulating a march with her music. The familiar fight song quickened the blood of even the elderly, who rose to their feet with the others as if hearing their realm's ballad of fealty.

Song selection, Wendra guessed, had much to do with a musician's success in a performance tavern. Telaya had chosen an anthem of the people, one that caused them to feel a common bond. But partway into her rendition of "Fit Men," she began to improvise the lyrics. Her words brought an unpleasant frown to Belamae's usually kind face.

> *The time of meek and patient hands*
> *Has passed and you will rue this day,*
> *If ever on your blitheful way*
> *You dare not taint your regent's lands.*

In marble halls like kings of old
They feast on firstlings and grow quite fat,
While you dine near where you have shat
And take your drippings cold.

Telaya's song fanned the flames of civil unrest that were spreading through the city. A Recityv guard slipped backward through the Rafters crowd and out the door, wisely excusing himself before he became the object of mob rancor.

A few leaguemen in their dark russet cloaks were among the many tavern patrons. They stood with the people, gratified but with watchful looks in their eyes, as Telaya's song turned again—her voice louder, her words more accusing.

Monarchs alone are not your foe;
You now neglect some in your midst.
Right here in slums where you resist
Lives music that might bring kings low.
But it is held above your heads,
As if like children you don't deserve
The blessing that it might preserve,
If it were shared with those who've pled
To have the song to share with you—

Belamae grabbed Wendra's arm, an iron grip belying the man's age. "Listen close. Telaya is a gifted musician, but she is not Leiholan—something she wants more than anything. She believes we keep it from her. She's grown bitter, and would use the tide of dissent in the city to try and seize Suffering."

Softer, and seemingly to himself, he said, "I didn't think she would go this far."

He squeezed Wendra's arm again, as if focusing them both. "We're moments from a mob forming and storming Descant. It wouldn't take much to incite the League to join them; they're openly critical of our purpose already. Fighting could spread across Recityv; we'd have little support from the city watch. Our only option would be—"

Telaya's words rose to them:

And whether Suffering could heal your wounds
Its melody belongs to you—

"What do you want me to do?" Wendra asked.

He gave her a hard look. "Sing," he answered.

Wendra stared back, fear rippling through her.

"Shotal," Belamae added. "Make them understand you; make them understand *us*."

"What song?" The only Leiholan songs she knew how to use wouldn't serve her here.

"Shotal," he repeated, then pushed her out of her chair.

She stood and moved quickly, trying to make sense of all this. She rushed up beside Telaya, who gave her a surprised, angry look, but kept at her song:

No, don't be fooled by tired men,
Who hold tradition like cambric dress.
It is a selfish foolishness
We must uproot if e'en we rend.

Wendra mentally sorted through all the songs she knew, briefly thinking that the tune from her song box might serve her here. But that didn't feel right. She glanced back at Belamae, whose face peered through the gloom with a desperate severity. Her brief training jumbled in her head— onomatopoeia, vowel clusters, phenomimes, psychomimes, velarized vowels, unvoiced stops, frictives. But finally, she pushed it all aside, and simply began to sing a solitary note.

Initially, it came like accompaniment to Telaya's song. Then it sounded like a duet, and she could see excitement rise on the faces of the hundreds gathered here at Rafters. Slowly, she began to find a melody line, standing there beside the woman who would tear down Descant to have its prize for her own.

Shotal.

Wendra didn't bother to find words. She sang whatever series of nonsensical vowels came into her head.

Beside her, Telaya began to sing more loudly, perfectly executing every note. The woman's strong song resounded throughout the tavern, resonating in its own way with every standing patron who felt run-down or cheated or hopeful of a better lot.

How do I combat this?

The crowd began to chant something. She couldn't quite make it out.

Telaya sang on, guiding them: "After we have found its song—"

Intention. They need to understand Suffering.

Then she heard it clearly: "Burn Descant. Burn Descant."

Wendra gave Belamae a last look, then turned to the crowd and let her note ascend in pitch and volume. It grew coarse in her natural dysphonic technique. Her one note heightened to a scream that drowned Telaya's perfect pitch. But she didn't leave it there. In the heights of her song, she began to shout in melodic rhythms, the strain still nothing but unintelligible syllables.

Except that she *meant* them. Every note she sang came with intention. And the crowd ceased its chant. Telaya tried to reassert her song, drawing on her considerable talent. Wendra turned to face her, crying out in the heartache of Suffering. The emotional force of it dropped the woman to her knees. Wendra swung back to the crowd, now making eye contact with everyone she could, singing to them individually.

She thought of Penit crying as he was carried away by Bar'dyn. She thought of other children dropped by Tahn's arrows. She thought of a stillborn babe that would never hear the lullaby she'd written especially for it. They were the cries of lost motherhood. Those thoughts formed the notes, and came out in a kind of improvisation she could never have imagined. She sang not a single known word, but she knew that, like tuning forks resonating with each other, these people understood her.

Then she changed her song, and made them understand that Suffering was their defender. That it did an awful work they should be glad they didn't have to do themselves. She gave implicit meaning to her sounds that they should appreciate those who performed this labor, and leave them to it.

There is some business you leave others to do, because it's heartbreaking, and because we're not all able or willing to sacrifice ourselves to it.

Her rough screams rang throughout the tavern, ascending into its tall rafters. Her song came in dense waves, speaking of war and lament and scorn, and the thin preservation they all shared from the same.

Wendra could feel the resonant power of what she sang. A new texture to her ability, where she chastised without tearing apart.

At last she gave all her energy to a long, powerful note that came out sounding something like, "SHYYYYYY YYYYYYYY!"

The sound of it lingered over them long after she had ended her song. The silence that followed was equally deafening. They understood. She could see it in their faces.

Then, slowly, they began to applaud. First one. Then another. Soon all of them, in a thunderous rush like she'd never heard.

When she'd made her way back to Belamae, he gave her an uncertain look. "Thank you," he finally said. A crooked grin followed. "That's what we call putting the fist in the glove. It won't be the last time it's needed, either. Telaya isn't alone among Descant Lyren. It's simply worse than I feared."

He looked over Wendra's shoulder. She turned to see Ollie. The fellow's eyebrows went up in a silent question.

Belamae nodded. And Wendra had an instant suspicion.

"You knew," she said, both angry and confused. "You knew the mandolist. And you knew that Telaya would bully her way onto the stage. Was it all a performance?" She jabbed a finger toward the footboards.

Belamae showed her a fatherly smile, replying carefully. "I only made sure they didn't keep you from standing beside her to offer your song. But yes, I knew who would play . . . and why."

She glared back at him. "You could send Telaya away from Descant. Why do you tolerate her?"

"She's an excellent musician. Marvelous desire for intention, if a bit misguided." He gave a patient smile. "I don't give up on good musicians. And now I have a new training approach for her. Besides, she has some interesting ideas. Particularly, she's trying to help us understand why Leiholan singers are failing at Suffering." His smile faded, and real concern rose in his face. "You might have heard: Another Leiholan fell ill today in the Chamber of Anthems."

Wendra hadn't heard, having slept most of the day after her evening on the docks. The news unsettled her, even as she still shook from her performance . . . and from what *could* have happened if she hadn't been able to control it.

"I'm sorry to hear it." She pointed toward the stage. "But you play a dangerous game, Belamae. They might have gotten hurt. I might not have kept control. . . ."

He returned a grave look. "Training Leiholan is a dangerous endeavor." It was all he said the rest of the evening.

· CHAPTER SIXTY ·

A Hard Choice

I'm not one who's ever believed in the Charter. Still, it's curious that in its disregard we've come to a point where a single choice can be regarded both noble and immoral.

—From *Governing Dynamics,* an open dialogue had each Endnigh in the College of Philosophy, Aubade Grove

A LIGHT MIST HUNG in the air, touching Roth's skin with a chill as he waited outside the Sodality meeting hall. Losol was nearby, as were a few other leaguemen, all discreetly out of sight. Distantly, he heard the voices of sodalists talking, arguing, deciding. They'd been at it three hours. Roth was patient. Important conversations took time.

A loud crack sounded half an hour later—a gavel perhaps. And shortly, sodalists began streaming from the doors. Roth kept a close distance, watching for Urieh Palon. It wasn't hard to see that the Sodality had moved fast to name him First Sodalist for Vohnce—the mantle of leadership hung on the man like a diver's weight.

"Sodalist Palon," Roth called, getting the young man's attention, "may I walk with you?"

Relief touched the young man's eyes at seeing Roth. The Ascendant had made every effort to comfort and advise Palon, E'Sau's obvious successor.

"I'm on my way home," Palon said, "if you'd care to go that way."

"Would be my privilege to accompany the new First Sodalist." He showed the man a smile of knowing regret, as only the leaders of men can.

"You heard?"

"You were the clear choice. I applaud the Sodality for naming you so quickly. No doubt," he said, looking away in the direction of Solath Mahnus, "other venues have helped their haste."

Palon followed Roth's gaze. "They want me sitting at both High Council and Convocation tomorrow."

Roth turned and gave the young man a steady look. "As do I. Come, let's get you home."

The two walked in companionable silence through mists that swirled around them as they went. The flat sound of their boots came muffled, absorbed by the thick Recityv night. Sensing Palon's insecurities, Roth began laying the foundation for his evening's goals.

"They elected you because of who you are," he began, using the voice of a father. "Don't fall into the trap of thinking you need to be someone else now. The quality that earned you their trust is the quality you need to go right on showing."

"Leading the Sodality isn't my worry," he said. "I would just have liked to lay E'Sau to rest first. Then serve for a while before going into something like Convocation."

Roth chuckled softly. "Oh, that. Never mind about it. Think

of it like a schoolroom filled with rowdy children, except their toys are armies instead of dolls and blocks."

"Not sure that helps," said Palon, and managed a smile.

Roth nodded to that. "About E'Sau, I know it's hard. So let me shoulder some of that burden, if you will. I'll take care of all the burial arrangements, and make sure you see and approve them. We'll also get to the bottom of the affair. Find the murderer. Bring him before Judicature."

Palon nodded to most of it. "I'll want a few of my people to participate in the search for E'Sau's killer. The Sheason are implicated. But I don't believe they're to blame."

"I can understand that," Roth conceded with an appreciative nod. "But I'll ask you to put aside your preconceptions in this matter. Leaders must, you know. Your best friend is objectivity."

They rounded a corner, and shortly came to a modest home. Roth walked Palon to the door, where the two men turned to face each other.

"There's something more?" Palon asked.

"I'm afraid so." Roth made an audible sigh, so that Palon might sense that Roth had no other course. "May I come in for a moment?"

"Certainly." Palon unlocked the door and led them out of the chill night mists.

The house was warm and homey. A mild cinnamon scent rose all around, and shortly a lovely young woman came in, carrying a child on her hip.

"Faster than you thought," she said, eyeing Roth.

"I think they'd decided before the assembly was called," he said to her. "This is Ascendant Roth—"

"Staned," she finished. "Yes, I know who he is."

Her tone was hard to decipher—contempt or appreciation. Either way, Roth was glad she was here. He smiled warmly. "My apologies for the intrusion. I'll make it brief. But I suppose my purpose will be your husband's first bit of business as First Sodalist."

She gave Palon a sideways embrace. "There's supper when you're ready," she said, and left them alone.

"Lovely woman," Roth observed.

Palon sat heavily in a chair beside a hearth crackling with a modest fire. "Thank you."

"Not at all, she seems—"

"No, for your help after E'Sau . . ."

Roth shook his head. "Leave that alone. It's only right that I lend whatever help I can. But I'm afraid I come to you with some hard business, my young sodalist friend."

Palon looked up, his face lined with concern. "What is it?"

Roth reached inside his oilcloak and drew out leathers wrapped around a document of several sheets. He handed them to the new First Sodalist. "You need to read that."

Palon took the parcel and placed it in his lap. "I'll read it later. Please just tell me what it says."

Again Roth sighed, as if reluctant to speak. Then he cleared his throat, making a show of bracing himself, and drew a chair over to sit across from Palon.

"It's no secret that I've had my contentions with the Sheason." He held up his palms as though there was nothing to be done about it. "And to some degree, I imagine, that means the Sodality, too. Though, from what I'm able to discern, your people don't make any attempt at these old ways of mysterium. You're protectors, helpmates. Am I right?"

Palon sat back. "Mostly, that's true, yes."

"You study rigorously. And then marry that knowledge with some weapons mastery. That about the size of it?" Roth asked, nodding while he said it.

"We do believe in the Sheason right to render the Will," Palon replied. "I can't lie about that."

Roth raised his palms again. "Fair enough. But there's a gulf between defending those who do so, and doing it yourselves. Let's not argue about that."

Palon put his hands on the document in his lap. "What is this, Roth?"

"The Civilization Order," he said.

"I already know it word for word." Palon picked it up and tried to hand it back to him.

Roth made no effort to take it. "It's been revised," he said softly, just above the crackle of the fire. He was keeping everything gentle, for a man newly and heavily burdened.

"Tell me," Palon said, his voice sharp now—there was obviously good reason for giving him the First Sodalist mantle.

Roth wouldn't be pulled into debate or sharpness, himself. Gentleness would be best here. Gentleness and suggestion. He leaned forward, placing his elbows on his knees and knitting his fingers together—the picture of a man about to reluctantly share something hard.

"The High Council—the one on which you now sit—will be voting to extend the Civilization Order." He paused, looking Palon dead in the eye. "It will no longer be required that a Sheason render the Will to be executed. . . ."

Palon sat forward, the papers falling to the floor. "What? You can't be serious!"

Roth nodded. "Once this is ratified, any Sheason living in the nation of Vohnce will be put to death. I don't doubt that this makes us enemies. But for my part, I've lost patience with men like Vendanj. His thinking sets us back a thousand years—"

Palon jumped right to the heart of the matter. "Do you have enough votes to pass this?"

Roth sat back. "Not yet. That's why I wanted to talk with you."

The sodalist stared intently. And by slow degrees, his anger turned to horrified understanding. "My deafened gods, you want me to sign it."

"I do," Roth admitted. "But not for my sake. And not even to pass the law—"

"Who all have signed it? How many signatures do you need?"

As if on cue, a knock came at the door.

"May I?" Roth said, and got up before Palon could answer.

He went to the door, and pulled it open, admitting a runner. The young messenger wore a Recityv court uniform. Specifically *not* League garb.

"Yes," Roth said, once the runner was in. "What news?"

The fellow handed Roth an oiled leather, which he opened, reading from a single sheet of parchment that had been folded within. Roth looked up at Palon. "The authors will sign," he lied. "I have the votes I need." He crossed to Palon and handed him the paper to read himself.

The young man took the message with trembling fingers and read the expert forgery that bore Author Garlen's mark. Roth could only hope that in his fragile state, the new First Sodalist didn't decide to corroborate the news. To keep him off balance, he pressed on.

"I suspected as much," Roth said. "The authors and scriveners and poets and the rest have no real love for the Sheason. Not that I've seen, anyway. So you see, I didn't come seeking your signature to pass this expansion of the Civilization Order."

Palon had a bit of terror in his eyes. "Then why?"

Roth bent and gathered the fallen Civilization documents. He ordered them neatly, and placed them back in the man's lap. "My young friend, I want to give you the opportunity to strike the Sodality's name from this revised law."

The blood drained from Palon's face. His jaw visibly slackened. "What are you saying?"

Roth sat back down, leaning forward again, as a man advising a friend in a dire hour. "The expansion here names the Sodality alongside the Sheason. Once it's passed, the executions will include the men and women who now follow you."

Palon's mouth worked wordlessly for several moments. Finally, he found his voice. "You can't do that. We could fight you on this."

"Legally?" Roth said. "You're outnumbered. Physically? Well, yes, you could. But the Recityv army is bound to uphold High Council law. So, you'll be outnumbered there, too."

The man sat still a moment, thinking. A measure of calm entered his face. "Do you really want to declare war on the Sheason? You may hate their old abilities, but I don't think you can stand against them."

For what he believed would be the last time, he sat back in a self-assured motion. "We've found ways to compete with what I'll call your Sheason's *thrall*. You don't have to believe me, if you choose not to. But I want you to understand what is going to happen."

Palon seemed to steel himself.

Good.

"Once the order is signed," Roth said, taking care not to sound as delighted as he felt, "it's unlikely that your people will always stand in the protective company of the Sheason." He waved a dismissive hand. "Oh, you're plenty capable with a blade yourself. All sodalists are. But you'll be outmatched. And as days roll by, Sodality numbers will dwindle. In Vohnce, anyway. That's where it will start."

Roth stopped. He could see Palon reasoning ahead, and decided to let the man think it through. Moments on, Palon opened up the expanded Civilization Order. To the crackle of the fire, he read a long time.

When he looked up again, his eyes were haunted and distant. "And in exchange for my signature, you'll strike the Sodality from the law."

Slowly, Roth looked past Palon toward the kitchen, where they could now hear the man's wife humming a tune as she worked at something there. "You need to think beyond the lives of your own order," Roth invited. "Yes, of course they're your concern. But they're not your *only* concern. Or maybe even your *chief* concern."

"We're meant to serve the Sheason," Palon said, his voice flat.

Roth now shook his head, adopting his best fatherly warmth. "That's how you began. It isn't how you need always be."

"What choice is this?" Palon said, running his fingers over his own emblem—the dancing quill atop the horizontal length of a sword.

"It's an awful choice," Roth admitted. "And I'm a bastard for putting it to you. But that's a name I'll gladly accept to push us all forward. Past the henpecking of these Sheason. Past their theatrics that frighten us into believing falsehoods. Past . . . the past." He steepled his fingers beneath his lower lip, narrowing his eyes judiciously. "I will understand, and even admire, your choice to stand your vow. Die with the Sheason. But"—he pointed at Palon—"I'm offering you a chance to lead. A chance to choose that your followers *not* die. Right here, you can sign this document, strike the Sodality from the order, and chart a new way to serve."

Palon stared dumbly, caught in his own inner loops of logic and worry.

Roth watched him a moment. "You may be thinking that if you stand with the Sheason, you can defeat this expansion of the Civilization Order. If nothing else," Roth said with resounding confidence, "you need to reject that possibility. Trust me on this."

The man's attention was drawn toward the kitchen when his child babbled something. It was as though he suddenly realized how close his family might be to a predator.

Roth smiled graciously. "The order doesn't extend to families," he said. "But that will hardly comfort the fatherless, will it."

Palon's face was now coated in a sheen of sweat. His lips and fingers trembled. "And the High Council all support this?"

"Of course not," Roth said. "Helaina has her cronies. But if you look, you'll see the signatures I've already secured." He let sharpness enter his voice for the first time. "And I'm losing my patience."

Palon stared back at the document for a moment. "Isn't it really the regent's seat you want? So you can direct Convocation? Why not gather signatures to replace Helaina? Leave the Civilization Order as it is now?"

Roth tapped the parchment in the sodalist's hands. "Some who are willing to sign this are yet unwilling to side against Helaina. Most of her friendships go back a lot of years. And I've a feeling that the expanded order will be disruptive enough to Convocation to help them see my point. At the very least, I'll have two more votes for dissolution: yours and the absence of Artixan's. I'll deal with the rest during the adjournment of Convocation that will surely come once this is signed into law . . . which happens tonight."

Palon looked pleadingly at Roth. "If I do this, Estem Salo will forsake us. The Randeur. The Sodality leadership—"

"Then you become your own Sodality," said Roth, pointing

at Palon's chest. "Better to decide your own damn fate, any-way, isn't it!"

Palon's eyes were distant. "I can't decide this alone. It takes the support of the Second and Third Sodalists—"

"Who I've already met with," Roth interjected, "and secured their support."

Then all fell quiet. Palon, who'd been the First Sodalist of Recityv and Vohnce for all of a few minutes, stewed in the cauldron Roth had placed him in.

"How would you do it?" Palon asked sometime later.

Roth had considered it carefully. He couldn't announce the change broadly and proceed with incarcerations and sched-uled executions in due course. It would have to be a hammer stroke. Quick and sudden. The whole thing might fail if he left time for due process, debate, or for the Sheason to mobi-lize and fight back. He'd long ago conceived a cleansing sweep of Recityv. The methodical plans for that were laid out and waiting. He'd even selected the time and place to alert Helaina. There might be complications with so many visiting dignitaries in the city, but success was just a matter of timing.

"Leave that to me."

Many, many long moments later, the man's head bent for-ward. There was the barest of nods. Roth coaxed a pen into Palon's hand. The word "Sodality" was stricken from the doc-ument, and a loose scrawl added to the last page.

It had gone as he'd hoped. But he didn't rush to leave. He stayed sitting by Palon after he'd won the signature. It was the strangest thing; the home seemed smaller. Tighter. It re-minded him of his own boyhood home that morning when he'd been dragged away from his father in exchange for a debt. It was a wounded feeling. A defeated one. That deep, deep ache. He hated the feel of it. But didn't abandon Palon to it. The young man had made a very hard decision. A right one. But it had cost him much. And would cost him more, when others learned of it. But for the time being, Roth spoke in hushed tones, sharing examples of how the young man's choice was a good one.

• CHAPTER SIXTY-ONE •

A Widening Schism

The question I ask myself is whether this is yet another branch in the Sheason Order, or whether it's the same division as occurred with the first Trial of Intentions.

—From the journal of Randeur Thaelon Solas

VENDANJ WOKE TO the feel of a cool wet cloth dabbing his forehead. Through the gloom, he looked up into a gaunt face he thought he knew, but didn't immediately recognize. After a few moments, he realized he'd been moved during one of his deep sleeps—which often came after prolonged use of the Will—and placed in a cell with Rolen after all.

"Artixan had me moved here?" It wasn't really a question.

"Came with the turnkey himself," Rolen said, wiping his brow again with the wet cloth.

"How long have I been asleep?"

"Several hours," Rolen answered. "I'm guessing the cumulative effects of rendering and endless parading around the countryside have gotten you into this condition. You should rest."

Vendanj made no effort to sit up. Instead, he lay still, allowing Rolen to dab more water over his skin. "You don't look well, yourself. You'll die of disease if they don't execute you first."

"I always could count on you for a cheery thought," Rolen said, his hollow cheeks pulling into a grim semblance of a smile.

Vendanj offered a weak but genuine smile in return. They might have fundamental differences—Rolen was of Thaelon's mind—but they were also good friends.

"Why *haven't* they executed you yet?" Vendanj asked. But

before Rolen could speak, he added his own answer: "They use your ability for their own needs."

Rolen nodded, his head a bobbing silhouette. "An execution day has been delayed several times. Leaguemen find their way into my cell late at night with injuries and ailments. A few come raving, as though fractured in the mind. I mend them all. It seems I've become a pet."

Vendanj frowned. "We'll share this with Helaina. She'll use it to strike the Civilization Order from the Library of Common Understanding." He finally sat up.

Another faint smile shone from his old friend's face. "They'll deny it, and I have no proof. Besides, I'd offer the help even if I were sitting in my own home."

"That's not the point, and you know it," Vendanj argued. "If it suits their needs, the League is glad to exploit even those things it condemns. We need to expose their hypocrisy. Otherwise," he sighed, "otherwise the Civilization Order will destroy the fraternity we both swore to preserve."

Rolen fixed him with a grave expression. "The Sheason Order is already dead, my friend. At least as it existed when you and I took our oaths. What it becomes . . . we'll have to wait and see."

"You won't live to *see* any of it," Vendanj observed, without malice. "You deplete your own Forda to heal these dogs. Without sleep and food, you can't properly replenish what you expend. They're killing you, sure enough. They're just doing it slowly."

"If I'm going to die," Rolen offered another of his smiles, "I'd rather do so returning health and peace of mind—"

"To your accusers and jailors?"

"Yes."

"Even though you know their intention is the end of *all* Sheason?" Vendanj stared through the dimness, feeling his anger turning toward his friend.

"If I follow the dictates of my conscience only when it's convenient, then my oath means nothing." Rolen shook his head. "I think we've said all this before."

"I'd hoped mealy bread and daily beatings might make you sensible." Vendanj smiled through the darkness.

"Is that a joke?" Rolen said back, delighted surprise and humor in his voice. "Maybe there's hope for you, after all. What have those Hollows boys taught you that I couldn't?"

Vendanj struggled to his feet. "You know I won't stay here. You'll be left to your slow death unless you come with me."

"Again, I think this is ground we've covered before," Rolen said, smiling weakly. "What of the Randeur? I've not heard where his heart lies on the matter."

Vendanj rubbed the back of his head, feeling the bruises there. "I don't know if he'd join you in this prison cell, but I'm not sure he'll see my logic, either."

Rolen nodded, seeming neither pleased nor grieved. "You know what that means."

He did. If the Randeur decided he and Vendanj weren't aligned on the Sheason path, it would leave Vendanj at the head of a Sheason faction that must part ways with the order.

"I'm not alone," Vendanj replied. "There are many who believe we should give men what they need, not what they *think* they need."

Without condescension, Rolen replied, "The danger, my friend, is you thinking you know what they need most."

Vendanj held his silence for a long time. It was too late for rethinking any of this. He wasn't wrong. He lived in a confusing time, in an age of rumor. Even good men, guided by conscience, had fallen into a way of thinking that threatened them all. Like Rolen. How could he make his friend see?

Ultimately, he left it alone. Rolen was as stubborn as Vendanj himself, if in a quieter way. He only hoped that before it was all done, Rolen hadn't gone too soon to his earth.

He smiled as he considered that his friend would be thinking the same of him.

"Perhaps you're right," he said. "But think of the Castigation during the Second Promise. Think of Siwel Trebor, when he defied the Randeur, and nearly brought destruction on the Tabernacle of the Sky. Think of the Commiseration of Soljan, when he took a dangerous view of the Whited One. Think of Jo'ha'nel himself. Be careful of complacency in your service. It's worse than daring to challenge, even if you're wrong."

Rolen seemed hesitant to ask some question. Finally, with a cautious tone, he said, "You say there are many, but are you organized?"

"I've no Sheason army." He gave a low laugh that sounded darker than he'd intended. "But that's not what you want to ask."

"No, it's not." There was a moment when it seemed Rolen wouldn't ask after all. He heard his friend swallow hard. "Do you, or any of those who follow you . . . seek Solemnity?" Rolen kept a hard, fixed gaze on Vendanj.

Vendanj had considered it. A practice whispered about long after fires died to ash and the whisperers could be sure no one overheard. It was one of few Sheason abilities that could *not* be taught, and among a handful that were considered profane. The power itself was an acknowledgment that in the heart of every servant lived something coarse and bitter. Some said it was one side of a balance scale, a necessary side.

It was a secret within a secret. Its pursuit was tantamount to heresy, to being Quiet oneself. Just the thought of it chilled him.

He stared back through the gloom. "I hope none of us ever goes so far. . . . But don't mistake me. There's only one response to the Quiet. And I'll use any means. . . ."

It was his friend's turn to draw out the silence between them. "That's where you and I differ, I suppose."

Unreconciled, they began to laugh.

Vendanj would soon leave his friend to his suffering. But he wasn't ready to go yet, fearing that he might never see him again.

They spoke of simple things for a while, old memories, the missteps of their youth, time spent together in Estem Salo. Sometime later, Rolen asked, "So what precisely did you do to get thrown in the pit?"

Vendanj explained. Rolen nodded, and shared that he'd been Tahn's First Steward at his Standing, which had taken place in this very cell.

"Glad it was you to guide him into his years of accountability," Vendanj said.

A long stretch of silence fell between them again. They each seemed to be deep in their own thoughts. Vendanj spoke first.

"The schism may be too wide to bridge." His own voice hinted that he hoped Rolen would argue with him.

Instead, Rolen nodded and smiled sadly. "The divide is our intentions. I'm sure you know that."

"You don't think I can convince Thaelon to help me."

Rolen sighed, and shook his head as a parent does when talking to a defiant child. "I've touched the boy's soul. I know about his birth. I know it flies against the principles of the Charter Thaelon holds in his heart." Subtle judgment came with his friend's next words. "And I know how you would use Tahn. The difference between you and Thaelon is your regard for the boy."

"Then the gap is too wide." He clenched a fist. "But I will still try to bridge it. Someone must speak sense to Sheason who wallow in thought and won't choose the right fight."

"You realize," Rolen said, tapping his temple to emphasize that he was going to share a *thought*, "you've offered Roth the best possible argument for broadly fulfilling the legal allowances of the Civilization Order. Maybe you're overdue for a good wallow."

Just then, the door at the top of the cell steps opened. Passing into the harsh glare came three silhouetted forms, quickly descending the stairs. When Vendanj's eyes had adjusted to the intrusion of light, he saw that one of the men carried a heavy black bag—the type placed over the head of one being executed.

"It would seem you're right," he said to Rolen, "about the Civilization Order. Not the wallow." He smiled, keeping his eyes trained on the leaguemen who circled around him. "Good-bye, my friend."

The men rushed in, seizing him. He concentrated, calling a minimal amount of Will to swell each of the men's throats, closing off their air. They all stumbled back, clutching at their necks, struggling to breathe. Gasping sounds resounded against the high ceiling of the cell as Vendanj unfettered himself from his chains and hastened from the pits of Solath Mahnus.

CHAPTER SIXTY-TWO

Bargains

To succeed with a buyer, establish if he's caught in a condition of fear, whether personal or societal. The fearful man is a practical buyer. Men with no fear are impractical.

—*Merchant Fundamentals,* a guide for stock and trade,
published by House Callister of Ebon South

B EYOND THE WALLS of Recityv, Helaina wandered slowly from cart to cart along the market road. The bright of day had yet to fill the sky, leaving the world in a palette of chill blues. The barkers and beggars hadn't awoken or arrived yet. Only the industrious small-shop owners moved through the early morning, silently preparing their wares and foods for sale.

Wearing her hood up, she liked to come before the crowds arrived. She'd casually shop for small items that most would find unbefitting her office. It was a good way to limber herself for the day ahead, too. Always, Artixan walked at her side, more friend than protection. And he kept the silence, seeming to take pleasure in the speechless industry of early-morning preparations.

Many here knew her. A few for her true self. But mostly as a customer who came often and paid generously. They were vagrant merchants who capitalized on the traffic of the road. And lately, traffic had been brisk.

These morning strolls, handling vegetables and fruits, looking over kitchen tools and fabrics both coarse and fine, had become her best way to stay connected to the people. Prices inside Recityv walls had driven the poor to this market road beyond the walls to buy their salt and shoes. The state of her politics and the health of her economy could be understood most clearly in the exchanges heard here. What's more, she could deduce the needs of her people by the items available for purchase and their prices. It was a simple practice her father had taught her, and one that somehow escaped the understanding of so many merchants.

Today, she was disturbed to find an inordinate number of weapons dealers. Carts of handknives, small swords, armbows, axes, and short spears abounded up and down the market road. For the most part, the workmanship was poor, but it probably matched the skill of their buyers. And while the threat from the Quiet was real enough, she didn't think the demand for weapons came from those rumors alone. Regardless, citizens who were scared and armed would prove a dangerous mixture.

But more alarming than the weapons was the small number of carts displaying food—it had dwindled significantly. Seasonal fruits were either coming late this year, or not at all. In either case, a simple apricot bushel was priced at three thin silver, nearly eight times its usual rate.

The man at the fruit cart smiled vaguely at her, and she gave him a single thin realm mark, taking two apricots from his display. She handed one to Artixan, and rubbed the other against her overcloak. Then she bit through its rather crisp skin, her mouth filling with a tangier-than-usual nectar. The fruit had been harvested too soon, rushed to market. She didn't mind the taste, though, and took another bite, savoring the freshness and wiping some juice from her chin.

It was a delightful moment, and her favorite reason for coming here. "The people might blame us for these prices," she said to Artixan.

"You don't give them enough credit," he countered. "They know it's you who makes commerce on the roads safe and keeps taxes low."

"And what of this weapons trade?" She motioned toward a cart loaded with knives.

"Troubling," Artixan said. "But the people will also remember that it was you who changed the laws about private knowledge and made it accessible to everyone, not just those who could sell and profit by it. My guess is there are more new tradesmen than citizens carrying knives."

"I think you're pandering to me," she said, and grinned.

"And I think you should hear the excitement I do when I speak to the merchant houses who no longer talk to you." Artixan took a bite of his apricot.

Her brows went up. "Oh?"

"Your Convocation has them excited at the prospect of trade across many nations and king roads." He wiped his chin. "Your vision is winning you new respect."

She hoped it was true. "Speaking of trade across nations, I haven't heard from the Mors yet. I'm going to send an envoy. I've spoken with Belamae at Descant, and he says he has a young student who should go with us. Apparently her song is something like the Refrains. He believes it will help."

Artixan nodded. "Sounds promising."

"Now, if I could just get *Roth* to see that we share some common ground." She took another bite of her fruit.

At the next merchant stand up the road, Artixan showed more than casual interest in a variety of personal items set out on a broad swath of black felt. Helaina continued to enjoy her apricot as she watched him thoughtfully pick up several items and examine them at arm's length with his aging eyes—a pen set, complete with sander; a better-than-average hand mirror; a walnut-wood snuffbox; a silver locket large enough to hold a small item or two.

He kept at it, shopping with a will now . . . until he picked up a pinch comb with a pearlescent finish. He turned it over in his fingers twenty times before a satisfied smile touched his face. He raised a hand to the merchant, inquired on the price, and paid the man without a single word of dickering.

"It's not even my name day," Helaina said, joking over the intention of the purchase.

He turned with a bit of apology on his face, then saw her smile, and laughed. "It's for Yolen. We've been together . . . my skies, must be fifty years. Just a small token to celebrate."

She looked at the fine pinch comb in his hand. "You're a dear man not to have resorted to buying an older woman practical things."

"My Yolen ought to have a chest of these for tolerating me," he said, holding up the comb.

"I won't argue with you on that."

His easy laugh came again. "Our friends will bring practical things. They think she needs household items. We have enough stoneware for one of your midwinter receptions." He shook his head with good nature. "But they mean well."

"I have a gift for you both. Delightfully *im*practical."

He half-bowed. "Thank you, my friend. And though you'll think me ripe with sentimentality, waking up to Yolen each day is gift enough."

"You're a rare one. But for all the right reasons." She hooked her arm in his and they continued on.

And despite their small diversions this morning, her interests were more than casual. A few carts down she found one of the usual traders. A good man. Nonperishable items. And one of the rare merchants who worked the realms east of Vohnce.

"Timothy," she said warmly.

The man stood up, bracing his back a bit and uttering a small groan.

"You," he said, keeping her identity secret, as was their standing agreement. "What'll it be this morning? I have a few hand vases, turned in Kuren." He uttered a rough squeal. "Oh, and a poem book out of Naltus Rey. *Pain poets,* wouldn't you know." He finally turned and winked. "That one would set you back several full real marks."

"I'll take the poem book," she said, and stepped close enough that she could whisper without being overheard. She handed him ten thick silver marks. "And your understanding of the best trade route into Y'Tilat Mor." She quickly added, "Keep your voice low, and just look bored."

The old merchant didn't miss a stitch. As he plopped the coins into a purse at his waist, he fumbled for the book and spoke softly. "One day, you'll tell me why, since only fool traders go that way. But the best road starts at the south of Falett Range. Cardal Point. Hard to miss. But also hard to follow once it hits the forests of the Mors."

He then proffered the book. She took it and turned away casually, raising a hand of thanks. She wasn't sure she'd need

Timothy's information, but she knew enough to be ready if she did.

She'd returned to her routine and gotten past another handful of carts, when in the distance, the sound of urgent hooves broke the morning's peaceful spell. When she turned, she saw three riders moving fast in her direction. In the predawn light, she couldn't make out their garb, though it appeared uniform.

Helaina turned into the road and waited, Artixan beside her. A few moments later, out of the dark of early morning, Roth and two of his ranking lieutenants appeared, coming to an abrupt stop before her. Their horses chuffed in the chill, their nostrils flaring. Roth didn't step down, but rather bent forward, extending a hand filled with papers.

"You'll want to read these," he said.

Even before she received the parchments, she noted that the leagueman had known where to find her. He'd likely been tracking her movements for months. She might have guessed it, but was disappointed her Emerit guard—hiding somewhere out of sight—hadn't discovered that she was being trailed.

Roth gently shook the parchments once. "Please, my lady."

Helaina stepped forward and took hold of them. "Do you intend to make me read these, or will you simply tell me what they say?"

He sat tall again in his saddle, resting his hands on the horn. "The time has come for more decisive action, my regent." He looked at Artixan. "You have remained lax on issues that concern your people. I've taken their interests to heart, and secured the votes I need to act on that order." He pointed to the parchments in her hand.

"And what is it?" she asked.

"The Civilization Order," Roth replied.

"Which is already law." She glanced at the parchment, confused.

"An amendment has been added, witnessed and signed by over half of the High Council." Roth softened his voice, adopting a more personal tone. "Whatever you may think, Helaina, I didn't really wish to do this. But there have been rumblings since this Vendanj conjured his abomination in full view of your Convocation. Even I feared riot if we didn't take action."

"What action, Roth?" she demanded.

He stiffened. "No longer will abstention from rendering the Will be sufficient. Members of the Sheason Order will be killed on sight." Again he softened his voice, playing both sides of this game. It sickened her. "Their very presence unsettles the people, makes them distrustful, even violent. There have been fights these last two days between those who support the order and those who fear it. Fights, my lady, with steel." He pointed a finger toward a nearby cart, where Helaina had a moment before been browsing a selection of weapons.

Artixan's calm voice rose from beside her. "This isn't binding," he said. "Such an order must be discussed in chambers. How are we to have full faith in these documents and signatures? Any more than the diary of Sodalist E'Sau? No, Ascendant, this will not be considered law until it can be heard in Council."

Roth drew forth another parchment and threw it at Artixan's feet. "A transcription from the books of Judicature by First Counsel Jermond himself. I'll spare you having to hunker down to pick it up," he said mockingly. "It says that witnessed votes of the members of the Council can serve as proxy for a meeting had in chambers. And before you ask, Jermond himself validated the urgency of immediate action, and witnessed every signature. It is law. I do you the honor of letting you know before the order is executed."

"A coup," Helaina said, her voice distant. "Why haven't you used this maneuver before?" Her question was aimed at herself, as she began thinking of her next step.

Roth dismounted, and came to stand before her. "Let's you and I be honest. You hate me as much as I do you. But I don't tamper with the proper order of things. I will avail myself of every possible avenue to see the civil mind arise in Recityv, and elsewhere. But I won't do so by immoral means."

Artixan gave one of his mild, derisive laughs. "You have a double tongue, Roth. But worse than this, you—of all people—force civil unrest at a time when we should be forging common bonds. Your purpose is political gain. No one's deceived about that. But would you really risk civil war now? When the Quiet presses across the Pall? It's madness. Even if you still believe the Quiet are a child's rhyme, help us prove it. Help us prove it before you tear down the halls of servants that would stand with us to defend against the onslaught."

"Artixan," Roth said coolly, "the only *Quiet* I believe in are Sheason, who play at arcanum and keep men subservient and indolent."

Helaina rested a hand on Artixan's arm to calm her friend before he said or did something that might get him killed.

"Roth, I will return to the city, and I'll visit every witness to this decree." She leveled a look on him that bore all the weight of her office. "I want you to acknowledge that the execution of any Sheason before I can attend to this matter will be treated as murder, and you, as the Ascendant of the League of Civility, will be held fully accountable."

"I will not—"

"Moreover," Helaina pushed on, "I will expel the League from Recityv, from all of Vohnce. Even if it means that the fires that burn in our squares carry the smoking offal of their broken bodies."

Roth raised a defiant chin, but didn't speak. The time for further speeches or councils had passed. They had each stepped over a line, and would either keep their grim promises or recant.

After several moments, he gave a slight mocking bow of deference to her, and climbed back into his saddle. Before reining around and galloping back to the city, his face relaxed again, becoming frighteningly impassive.

"I do you the honor of giving you time to say good-bye to your friend, Helaina." Roth nodded toward Artixan. "Though you should know that many suggested he be the first taken. When we meet again," he warned, "my honor will be to the will of the people, as should yours."

Roth kicked his gelding into a full gallop, his men doing the same. Behind them, Helaina dropped the damned document and began to run as fast as her aching legs would carry her back toward the city gate, Artixan at her side.

CHAPTER SIXTY-THREE

Fields of Wheat

*An attack of Will, which is Resonance, can take many
forms. The least-consuming of your own energy is to drive
an attack through space at your target. Much more of you is
required to cause spontaneous and immediate Resonance
inside your enemy.*

—Allocating Forda, a senior course of study in Estem
Salo for Sheason studying Influence

THAELON ARRIVED UNANNOUNCED to Exemplar
Odea Ren's battle training sessions. Her preparations
were taking place in a meadow high above Estem Salo that
was flush with unharvested mountain wheat. Warm sun
touched everything with a golden hue and lit chaff raised
from the shuffle of feet through knee-high grasses. A group
of Sheason stood behind Odea, watching their fellows take
turns at the meadow's center. Thaelon stood a stride back, so
as not to interrupt or distract them.

A woman had just taken position out in the meadow, surveying several rough scarecrow figures fashioned of white
pine limbs and aspen branches. Near each scarecrow stood a
Sheason who would provide the actual attack on the woman
taking her turn.

"Defense first," Odea called, her voice carrying with a
single echo. "Simple barriers to deflect what's thrown at you.
And remember, it won't always be an attack on your body.
Smart opponents will try to cause change around you to
distract and disrupt what *you* are doing."

The woman nodded and turned back toward the five scarecrows, preparing herself.

Odea gave one last instruction. "Once you've withstood
their initial barrage, strike back. Keep it focused and specific.

Conservation of energy, remember. This is one fight. You could have several in a day."

The woman nodded, and slightly raised her hands.

A moment later, the tops of the wheat whipped, as though a gusting wind traveled along a narrow chute. With immense speed, a burst of energy cut toward her in a straight line. She got her left hand up, but not in time to begin a defense. The attack knocked her back hard on the ground. She stood fast and saw another racing line of disturbed wheat tops. This time she got both hands up and partially defended against it. Partially. A deep-toned boom sounded when the renders met, causing the wheat around her to whip outward. She was knocked back, but kept her feet.

Two of the Sheason standing near the scarecrows made small, coordinated gestures with their fingers. This time, no wheat stirred. Thaelon watched as the woman's breath began to plume on the air. Thin at first. Then thicker. And a few moments on, her coat began to whiten with thick frost.

She lifted a hand, rotated it—a rendering indication for warmth. The frost ebbed, then returned, thicker. The woman dropped to her knees, shivering.

Odea held up a hand. The attack stopped. Two Sheason rushed forward to help the woman back to the group. Odea didn't speak to her, and motioned for another Sheason to step into the meadow.

This man was well into middle age. He had a calmer face. *The confidence of years,* Thaelon thought, and was eager to see how this one would perform.

Odea didn't repeat her instructions with him. She said simply, "Begin."

The air shimmered, like the look of a long plain baking in the heat. The man's hands went up, but not to render a barrier. He grabbed his head as if feeling a sudden sharp pain behind his eyes. He gathered himself, and pushed his hands out as though meeting the resistance of thick cords trying to constrict him. Once his arms were fully extended, he focused on one of the scarecrows and clenched his fists. The figure shattered into splinters.

A few of the Sheason near Thaelon commented on the

strong counter. But the man wasn't through. He whirled to face another of the scarecrows and pointed. A crack sounded, but was cut off when the earth beneath the man's feet shifted violently, causing him to fall.

Rather than try to stand, he got to his knees, his shoulders and head visible above the wheat. He swept his arm out. *He's creating a rendering blockade.* Direct attacks wouldn't reach him. It was a simple defense, but effective. While the man concentrated on his next action, the earth beneath him softened to thin mud. He sank to his neck. Then the earth hardened again, fixing him there. To prove a point, the wheat around him lay down over his head, suggesting he could have been buried alive.

The attack stopped. Again a few Sheason went forward. They got the man free and helped him back to the group.

Odea held her comments. The Exemplar of Battle was letting these failures do the instructing. For now.

Sheason after Sheason went forward. All with little success in defending against the varied attacks. Finally, Odea seemed to have reached the limit of her patience.

"Tuomas." It was all she said.

A young man, perhaps near his thirtieth year, walked to the center of the meadow. His head slowly rotated as he noted the exact positions of the scarecrows. There was no call to begin or whipping of wheat or low boom of clashing Will. What came was silent. And something Thaelon only saw because Tuomas flashed in and out of view.

An immense rendering of force pressed down on him. Compaction. If he wasn't up to the task, his every pore would begin to leak blood. In response, Tuomas stood still, focused on the scarecrows. The young man was exerting great Will in a protective layer against a weight that could crush him. Clearly his attackers knew his level of skill.

When Tuomas no longer flickered—the first attack over—he widened his stance. He made no effort at counterattack. He waited. But not long. A funnel wind descended, ripping at his cloak, stirring leaves and wheat stalks and small stones in a painful spout that began to riddle his body and obscure his vision.

The young man extended a hand, creating a bubble inside the spout. He didn't try to end the wind, just survive at its center.

Moments later the funnel wind dissipated, rocks and torn wheat falling in a sheet around him.

The ground softened. Tuomas floated a hand's width above the ground.

The air grew chill. Tuomas sped his heart to pump blood faster, warming himself.

Arrows were fired. Tuomas brought them to a full stop in the air just an arm away.

Painful memories reared. Tuomas brought to mind simple images of kindness.

It was as impressive a demonstration as Thaelon had seen since . . . well, since Vendanj.

The attacks let up, for a moment. If the pattern held, things would escalate. Tuomas apparently had no intention of waiting on that. At a look from him, the scarecrow on the far right splintered and exploded. The next one had a sudden break where its neck would be, the head lolling back, held only by a bit of green bark. The next scarecrow blackened, seared with heat. Smoke rose on the air. The scarecrow to the far left began to spin. It gained speed until it hummed. Until it was torn apart by the force of its own spinning.

Then all fell to silence. Tuomas slumped. Spent. The Sheason who'd been attacking Tuomas all sat where they'd stood, then lay down, disappearing in the wheat.

Odea turned to the group of Sheason around her, finally seeing Thaelon. Her face told the story of her disappointment.

"Tuomas is ready." She pointed at a woman on her far left, who Thaelon hadn't seen tested. "Glenna is ready. The rest of you would die if you went to battle today. I know you understand strategy, tactical offensive and defensive measures. I know you study war. And you appreciate the ramifications." She looked them over, her stare hard and telling. "But understanding these things from books is different from understanding them in practice. We've been to the meadow a dozen times. From most of you, the progress is unacceptable. Pair off. Keep it simple. Keep testing each other relentlessly. The pressure of constant defense will create the right habits. Go until you've no more energy for the exercise."

The Sheason dispersed, finding areas of the meadow to begin their sparring. Odea gave Thaelon a sour grin. "How did you like that?"

"Tuomas was impressive," he said.

"And he has Leiholan talents, too. I use him to shame the others." She looked back at the many Sheason behind her. "Mostly it doesn't work. There's a sense in which this kind of rendering is something you're born to. Or not."

Thaelon came up beside her, surveying the crop of Sheason. "I don't believe that. Where survival is concerned, most will find the mettle they need. We just have to find a substitute for real threat to help them reach that deep inside themselves."

Odea gave a laugh. "You sound like the books I'm asking them to leave behind."

Thaelon smiled. "Maybe I do, at that. But have more faith in them. It's been a long time since Sheason were needed this way. They'll answer just fine."

She sighed with a bit of exasperation. "These are basic tactics. We mostly use attacks that travel. And we do it here where they can see it coming." She pointed at the wheat field that had been stirred by many of the renderings. "This is like learning to pluck a single string on your way to playing a symphony."

"We all start by plucking a string," he said, pretending to do just that. "And the only gift you possess that matches your rendering is hyperbole."

"That must be why you're Randeur," she said.

"What do you mean?"

She gave him a genuine smile this time. "Your optimism. What will it take to see your pessimistic side?"

He shook his head. "Oh, I've my share of that. Visit the intention trials with me if you don't believe it."

They stood in silence for a time, watching Sheason test their ability to defend against one attack or another. Many fell. Many stopped to rest. The sun made the training a hot affair. This, along with the trials, and the envoy to Recityv . . . they were doing the right things. And he relaxed long enough to take in the smells of wheat and pine and aspen. He enjoyed the sounds of rustling grasses and humorous falls as Sheason failed some defense. This high mountain meadow above Estem Salo had helped him focus. There was work to do, but he trusted Odea would get them there.

"I want to show you something," she said.

She led him back beneath a large quaking aspen and produced a ledger from a bag. She opened it as they stood together.

"What am I looking at?" he asked, scanning page after page of names.

"A list of Sheason," she answered, seeming to wait on his questions.

"And the circle beside some of these?" Thaelon turned several pages, noting that few bore the circle notation. Maybe one in twenty.

"The circle means they're ready to fight." She placed her finger beneath one circle, which had a line drawn horizontally through it.

"And the line?" he asked.

"Means they've had their Trial of Intention, and been found guilty of sympathizing with Vendanj." She looked up at him. "They've been divested."

Thaelon's stomach sank hard. "We're eliminating our own best defenders."

"Not just defenders," she clarified. "But those who can actually render the Will to fight. In a manner that would be helpful, anyway."

He looked up to where Tuomas still sat, resting. "Do you know the leanings of those who can fight but haven't yet been through trial?"

Odea hesitated. He could tell she wanted to say something larger than she finally did. "My sense is that seven of ten who have the ability to use the Will in combat . . . sympathize with Vendanj. I can't say whether they've had some kind of training I don't know about, or if there's just a fighting nature to those who believe as he does. But if we're preparing for the possibility of war with the Quiet, your Trials of Intention are drastically reducing our numbers."

"Do I hear dissent?" he said with a slight smile.

She gave him an incredulous look.

Thaelon took a deep breath. Shook his head. "We're not gods, Odea. We don't satisfy our whims. What we do can't start from selfishness. Or personal desire." He held up a hand before she replied. "But it can be done with power. And indignation, if need be."

"You want me to teach them to be indignant?" she said, jabbing a thumb at the practicing Sheason.

"With you as their instructor, I assumed indignation was a given."

They shared a quiet laugh over that. But when the laughter faded, Thaelon found himself staring at Tuomas, wondering what side of all this the young man would take. Wondering about sides. And hating that he had to question the intentions of his own people.

· CHAPTER SIXTY-FOUR ·

A Quiet House

Wherever you think the bottom is, it's usually deeper. And darker.

—Familiar commiseration used by coastal laborers, believed to have originated on the decks of Wanship trawlers

THE SUN HAD not yet set, the skies bright with streaks of red as sunset came. Soon the blue and grey of twilight would fall, and a chill would rise on the air. Sutter was spent. He'd visited other orphanages, hearing more stories about these "walks." And now he made his way back toward the king's keep. He had no appetite, and no desire for company. So he said goodnight to Yenola and returned to his room alone.

They'd moved his things. A house servant said something about the king wanting Sutter in a middle room—no windows. He guessed Relothian was simply being cautious, and followed the attendant to his new quarters.

By lamplight, he undressed, propping his Sedagin blade against the wall beside his bed, and stowing the Draethmorte's pendant beneath his pillow. After blowing out the flame, he stared up into the dark for only a moment before sleep took him. And for the first time in he couldn't remember how long, he dreamed. Nothing sobering or evocative of all the revelations he'd had today, or even of his pageant wagon parents.

Instead, he dreamed of twilight in the Hollows as seen from the porch of his boyhood home. He saw light-flies dancing near the trees, winking here and there. He smelled the sweet, tangy smoke of his father's pipe lazing around them. He heard his mother singing a soft tune, neither mournful nor merry, but simply lending a gentle accompaniment to the end of day.

He tried more than once to join her, but always made bad harmonies that got them laughing with each other. His father had prepared his special drink, water flavored with several sour fruits and a stem of spearmint.

And as light fled the sky, the crickets began to whir, laying in a soft chorus to his mother's song and their unhurried chatter about whatever crossed their minds. Vaguely, they remembered Renae, his sister who died in the winter of her fourth year. And without feeling somber about her absence, they mentioned how good it would have been to have her there. His father raised his cup to her memory and sipped at his drink.

The western rim slowly lit with an array of scarlet, auburn, and orange hues. Clouds came to look like puffed-up, colored lanterns near the horizon. And his father would begin to rock in his chair, which meant he was about to share a story.

And so, with the labors of the day fading from their muscles, Sutter listened, feeling contentment settle inside him—

—The sound of a boot on the floor near his bed ripped Sutter from the dream. He gasped from the sense of vertigo, his eyes darting around the pitch-black room, finding nothing. That same moment, the sound of stretching fabric left him with the impression of one raising up their arms.

To attack!

Sutter rolled to his right as something struck the bed where he'd lain a moment before. The sound and impact left him thinking not of a sword, but of a heavy mace that might have crushed his skull. His mind went to his blade, but he'd rolled in the opposite direction. And he still couldn't see.

He dropped to the floor on the other side of the bed.

Can it see me?

He assumed whatever or whomever had come into his room could navigate the dark better than he could. He needed help, but he'd have to pass whatever it was to get to the door.

As he reached the end of the bed, he heard something coiling again in the darkness. He crouched to avoid the blow. But the heavy, spiked weapon had been aimed at his legs, and took him hard in the right shoulder, knocking him to the floor. Warm blood flowed immediately from a gash in his flesh. Sutter rolled back, holding his wound, desperately trying to focus his eyes in the darkness.

"Mira!" he screamed.

A low chuckle rumbled from a human voice. Then more deliberate steps, coming for him.

Sutter leapt back toward the bed, thinking to bound across it and grab his sword. In mid-jump, he was struck by the other's weapon again, catching him in the hip. Shards of pain fired brightly through the bones around his waist. The blow knocked him into the heavy wooden side of the bed, his left shoulder jouncing off the bed frame.

Sutter tried to stand, but his hip wouldn't allow it, his right leg tingling with numbness.

Over his own labored breath, he thought he heard fabric stretching again. He dropped to his back just as a hard blow hit the bedside. He rolled on his injured shoulders to get under the bed, and forced himself to keep rolling until he'd reached the far side.

Hurried steps skirted the bed, rushing to meet him. Sutter raised his hands, feeling for the far edge of the frame, and pulled himself out and up, his shoulder burning with the strain. He then swept out blindly with his hands, grasping for his weapon. Behind him the attacker had given up all attempts at stealth.

But when the indistinct form drew close, it didn't pounce on him. Instead, it bounded onto the bed, riffling through the covers.

The Draethmorte's pendant!

Sutter's hand finally found his sword. He locked his left hand on the grip and tried to raise the heavy length of steel. Pain flared in his shoulder, and he nearly dropped the blade.

A moment later, he heard a guttural cry of glee, and knew the intruder had gotten hold of the sigil-glyph. Just as it did, the door slammed open.

· CHAPTER SIXTY-FIVE ·

Civilization

It's remarkable to consider that, by some accounts, the purpose of Mal aggression is reform. And remember, this is a people whose path to enlightenment is paved by ritualized torture of their own.

—*Reformist or Expansionist, a Correlation of Motives,*
a text broadly deemed apocryphal

THE FRONT DOOR of the Sheason house crashed in and heavy footsteps rushed down the hall. There were shouts and the clang of steel and cries of distress. Braethen shot up from the endfast table and drew his sword. He could see none of the fight from the kitchen at the back of the Sheason home, where several of the order lived. They'd met this morning to discuss what should be done about Vendanj's incarceration and about Convocation.

Several Sheason joined him, racing toward the hall that led to the front of the house. Almost immediately, they were pushed back into the large kitchen, where smells of fried pork and potatoes still lingered in the air.

A large man suited in League attire drove a dagger into the belly of the closest Sheason, a good man named Uuliah. The leagueman twisted the steel inside Uuliah's body, dropping him to the floor.

Shock paralyzed Braethen as another Sheason fell to a savage thrust from a long sword wielded by a second leagueman. In other rooms, and from the floor above, more cries and shouts erupted, filling the home with chaos and terror. Surprise seemed to have immobilized them all, before Sheason Marrot, standing beside Braethen, broke through the panic, and shouted, "Stop this! Or by every absent god, I will—"

The leaguemen didn't yield and came on fast, hewing down two more Sheason—Thera and Felinal, two women who had befriended Braethen over the morning's meal.

"Please, we can discuss—" The words ended when a sword pierced Dulan's throat. From the room above came the words "We've done nothing—" followed by a ghastly scream. The sounds of death and dying washed over him. And all of it come so fast that Sheason were lost before they could defend themselves.

He flung aside the table between himself and a murderous leagueman. "I am I!" he cried, invoking the darkness of the blade.

But no darkness came. No doubt. No fear. No memory of loss. Only indignation. He trembled with it. He launched himself at the closest attacker, who was pulling his sword back from the chest of a woman. In a vicious, elegant stroke, he opened the man's belly and left him to bleed out.

Another browncloak turned on him, but Braethen continued his momentum, carrying the blade around and tearing open the throat of this second murderer. The man fell to his knees, surprise in his face, blood filling his mouth and pouring out over his chin.

Braethen kicked the man in the side of the head and moved

quickly to the third leagueman. This man had had time to set his feet, and brought a heavy mace around into Braethen's side. Though a weak strike, pain shot through his torso. But it only made him angrier, and he focused all his strength into another sweeping blow. The other raised a shield in defense, but too late. Braethen's attack hit home across the crown of the man's head, burying deep and dropping him instantly to the floor.

"Get to the others!" he cried, and dashed toward the front of the house, where moans and the shuffling of feet could still be heard.

He and the others from the kitchen arrived too late to save any of the Sheason who'd been on the first floor of the house. Bodies lay ravaged and bloody. Hovering over each of them were leaguemen, confirming their kill and just starting to come in search of more.

Braethen met them head on, anger flowing through him. His side burned each time he used his arm, but in the midst of the fray, it seemed a distant thing. He took a cut to the shoulder, but hewed down another browncloak. Behind him one of the Sheason drew the Will and hit two leaguemen with a pulse of energy. The men struck the far wall and slumped to the floor, their necks at impossible angles.

Braethen paused, listening. The only movement they heard was on the upper level. He sprinted for the stairs, leaping three at a time, his sword seesawing the air with the pumping of his arms. At the second story, he shot left, the Sheason behind him moving to the right. He jumped over the bodies of two more Sheason lying dead in pools of their own blood. Only one leagueman lay on the floor.

Ahead, in the library at the end of the hall, he heard commotion. He ran harder, taking hold of his sword with both hands. He burst into the room to find four more dead members of the order. Only one intruder had gone down, though he still breathed where he lay. Three leaguemen turned, startled at his entrance.

Braethen realized he'd be overwhelmed. And he had too many steps to close on the first man.

In that instant, without thinking, he raised his sword—

impossibly early to hit anyone—and felt a strange, almost imperceptible shiver. In the blink of an eye, and with the sound of rushing wind in his ears, he was five strides closer. Right in their midst!

He'd not run or jumped, and had no idea how he'd traveled the distance in an instant. *The Blade of Seasons*. He stumbled, out of balance from the strange leap, and nearly fell. But he managed to keep his feet, and swung his sword at the first leagueman, catching the man in the belly.

Then as Mira had taught him, he spun, keeping his momentum, and pulled the sword through the man's flesh, out again, and around into a second enemy.

The man's eyes showed surprise and fear, as though he were seeing a ghost, or maybe Quietgiven, his own action stalled as Braethen drove his sword into the man's chest.

A third leagueman raised his own blade, a similar shock in his face. Braethen didn't hesitate, taking advantage of whatever had just happened, and kicked the man hard in the groin. The other doubled over, and Braethen brought his knee up into the man's chin.

Blood and teeth exploded from the leagueman's mouth, and he went down, unconscious. Braethen quickly finished him.

As the last of the leaguemen fell, a Sheason ran into the room. Braethen quickly surveyed the carnage. All were dead—Sheason and leaguemen alike—save one. The chestnut-hued cloak lay spread out beneath one exigent who had fallen back; his lips quavered as he lay too hurt to assist himself. Braethen lowered his sword, its quiet authority ebbing. He stepped close to the downed leagueman.

His anger nearly got the better of him. "What madness is this?" he asked through gritted teeth.

The man looked up, fear for his life plain on his face. "The Civilization Order—"

"The Civilization Order is enforceable against Sheason who *render*. You came here unprovoked. Why?" Braethen asked with forced calm.

"A v-vote," the man stuttered. "The High Council voted to amend and expand Civilization. All Sheason are now criminals, they don't have to render. . . ."

Braethen dropped to one knee, took hold of the man's collar, and shook him. "Without a right to dissent, or even imprisonment first? This law grants the right to immediate execution?"

The leagueman nodded, blood issuing from his mouth and nose as he did so. "The Ascendant commanded us to go into the city and purge it of all Sheason. Locations were given. Orders say not to return until all are dead."

Two more surviving Sheason came into the room and limped to the other side of the leagueman. Looking down in disgust, one asked, "How many have you killed this morning. . . ."

"Our dispatch was to this house first. Others were sent elsewhere," the leagueman said.

Braethen dropped the man's head back to the floor, where it struck hard, causing more blood to gush up and out of his mouth. "And what of your own conscience? Did you think to ask why peaceful men were being sentenced to execution? You're nothing but a murderer."

A look of defiance settled into the man's face. "Not all Sheason use the Will to serve others—"

Before the leagueman could finish, one of the Sheason pointed a hand at the man's throat. A moment later bones snapped, and the leagueman's head lolled to the side.

Braethen hadn't time to wonder what the man's words might mean. His mind raced, considering the implications of the expanded Civilization Order, what it meant for the Sheason, for the Sodality. Citywide, perhaps nations-wide, death for all Sheason. War between the League and the order. How many would die before ever getting to defend themselves? Even now, all across Recityv, Braethen imagined rooms like this one: unprovoked, secretive attacks at dawn that would leave most dead before the sun was up.

They mean to annihilate them.

The Sodality would stand against it, but they were hopelessly outnumbered by the League, and the attacks were happening *now*.

Then Braethen remembered Vendanj, locked beneath Solath Mahnus. He got moving that instant, flying down the stairs and out into the street. The few others who'd survived fell in behind him. As he rushed toward Solath Mahnus, only one other thought plagued him: How had he crossed the distance to the leaguemen so quickly? One moment he'd been in one place, in the next . . . another.

HELAINA AND ARTIXAN reached the Recityv gate. Her joints were on fire. Several leaguemen had been left to watch for them.

"Seize them!" she yelled to the gate captain—one of Van Steward's men. The man returned a puzzled look, but immediately called to several footmen to arrest the Ascendant's men.

Before the city guard could move, the leaguemen were ripped from their feet and sent crashing into the stone wall. They crumpled to the ground in a series of painful, crunching sounds. None stood back up as Helaina and Artixan ran through the gate and into the city.

Without needing to confer, they angled left to a small horse stable where the gate guard kept their mounts. The guard captain shouted no protest as they scrambled atop two of the horses.

"No leagueman leaves this city!" Helaina shouted. "And seize any that you come across."

She and Artixan kicked their mounts into a full gallop and made for Van Steward. The ride jounced her hard, but she held on tightly, watching for signs that the bloodbath had begun. She saw nothing, and could hear nothing save the pounding of hooves and wind in her ears. Twice she looked over at Artixan, whose face had drawn itself into hard lines of worry and anger.

Faster than she might have imagined, they arrived at the center house of Recityv's main garrison. They hadn't yet dismounted when Van Steward shot out onto the steps. "The attacks started ten minutes ago. My men are moving into the city now. Come."

Her general jumped onto his own horse, and together they raced back into the main streets, followed by several of Van Steward's men. Artixan took the lead, directing

504 • PETER ORULLIAN

them to the home of the closest Sheason—he knew them all personally.

Helaina struggled off her horse, her old body not accustomed to the exertion. Artixan seemed buoyed by his anger, moving like a man half his age—*perhaps an infusion of Will?* Van Steward drew his weapon and they went quickly into the first house.

They were greeted by the soft mourning cry of a new widow, who held her husband in her lap. Helaina thought her heart would break when she saw a young girl peeking out from behind a doorway at the far end of the room. Tears wet the girl's face. The child had learned too young—and without reason—the loss of her father. Artixan knelt, offering some words over the broken body of one from his own fraternity, and then shared a look of regret and resolve with the dead man's wife. He put a hand over hers and spoke something low Helaina couldn't quite make out. Instead, she heard the mumbling curse of her general, who moved back into the street and began shouting new commands to his lieutenants.

A few moments later, Artixan was up, and together they went out, climbed into their saddles, and went hard to the next house several streets deeper into Recityv. They arrived just as two leaguemen emerged, their weapons bloody, their brows wet with sweat. They looked up as Helaina and the other riders bore down on them. This time, Artixan was robbed of the chance to take his revenge, as Van Steward and one of his men pushed their mounts faster and rode the two leaguemen under. Two others from Van Steward's contingent leapt off their horses and finished the job.

Inside the house the leaguemen had just exited, there were hysterical cries that echoed out onto the street and brought neighbors from their doorsteps. Or was it the commotion and death of the leaguemen? Or both? Helaina looked around as chaos broke out in her city—distant cries, the panic of rushing feet, angry shouts.

Artixan went quickly into this second house. The cries stopped. When he emerged, there was a gravity in his face that Helaina had never seen. It was the quiet countenance of vengeance. A terrible face to see on her friend.

Riding from house to house was pointless. She was of no use in that effort anyway. She had to think past the slaughter of innocent Sheason. She had to imagine Roth's next move—the man would have anticipated her reactions, he would have planned and prepared each detail carefully. But so had she. He'd surprised her with the sudden escalation of the Civilization Order. It seemed a bit reckless to her. But every good politician was a bit reckless.

And while thinking past the deaths of friends and servants struck her as irreverent, she had to move quickly. But not haphazardly. She slowed her mind, absently rubbing her rheumatic hands, which had begun to cramp painfully from managing the reins.

She could get to her councilors, reason with those who had voted and witnessed to an enlargement of the Civilization Order. She knew she could turn back the law. But by the time she did it would be too late. This had been a coordinated massacre, everything happening nearly at once.

She began to feel the awful weight of the events surrounding her. Perhaps Roth had been right. Perhaps she was too old and should have stepped down—yielded the regent's seat not to him, but to a younger leader who might have prevented this slaughter. She would accept responsibility for allowing it to occur. But not today.

As she rubbed her crippled fingers, she began to see a way through. She needed to exercise some control amidst this mindlessness. *Balance.* She needed to restore balance. It was the root of her strength, just as it had been in her youth when she'd been the pride of her father's merchant house.

She still had Van Steward and his army as her right arm. But the Sheason had provided the unspoken power and threat that had kept Roth in check. With the order's power so totally impoverished, Roth might ignore formalities like Councils and Convocations and votes. Besides, she couldn't establish civility between factions who would now be sworn, open enemies. Peace would have to come another way. Before all those she loved were dead. Before her city burned to ash.

She looked down at Van Steward, who had just started to

speak, when a distant roar went up. A crowd or mob. They all turned to look in the direction of the great plaza several streets over. Voices echoed along storefronts and cobbled roads around them.

Van Steward turned questioning eyes on her.

She gave a private signal to one of her Emerit guards, who nodded and raced ahead. As soon as her friends had mounted again, she took hold of her reins and kicked her mount, racing toward the tumult.

ROTH SAT ATOP his gelding, carefully selected for its color—the chestnut brown of the League. On his right, likewise sitting on his own mount, was Losol, his new leader of war. They had taken position at the east entrance of Solath Mahnus. On each side, the Wall of Remembrance stretched out. And before them, the great plaza had begun to fill with herded Sheason.

It had all gone as planned. The moment he'd handed Helaina the change to the Civilization Order, Losol had raised his left arm—a signal that had set off a coordinated effort to rid Recityv of the arcane arts of the Sheason. Striking fast and all at once, they would allow no time for Van Steward or the Sodality or the Sheason themselves to respond. Roth did regret that there would be innocent children left heartsick at the loss of loved ones—he knew that pain—but you must sometimes cut to heal, he reminded himself. And as Ascendant, he couldn't afford a weak resolve.

There was a better day ahead for men once they found their way beyond the superstitions of the past, and tackled their problems carefully, logically. The enemy was not truly the ghouls and gods that lived in story; the enemy was empty coffers when food was needed and the idea that one's ills could be remedied with a simple touch. Education and discussion had failed to achieve the necessary change. History would record that Ascendant Roth Staned showed unnatural courage to lift men to a new consciousness, even if it came by the loss of life.

And the last act of today's historic effort would come here. While some of the cleansing had taken place in the bedchambers and homes of the Sheason, the important part would happen on the great central plaza of Recityv. He'd directed his men to usher the rest to this place. Along the way, citizens' and onlookers' curiosity would rise. And they'd follow.

As Roth looked around now, he nodded to himself. Indeed they had. As dozens of Sheason were herded into the center of the plaza, the periphery filled with hundreds of Recityv men and women and children. Soon it would be thousands. A low babble rose, words shared behind the backs of hands or close to the ear of a neighbor. His men, some with blood on their hands and arms, firmly held a perimeter, allowing through only other leaguemen who escorted more Sheason to the center of the square—Sheason, accompanied by sodalists.

This was regrettable. He hadn't given Palon time to share with his order what he'd done. Men and women of the Sodality were still protecting Sheason. Many of them would die doing so. But it was an acceptable loss.

There wasn't much time before Van Steward would arrive in force. But Roth breathed deep, savoring this moment. The air was crisp, the sun full now in the eastern sky ahead. The rays of light struck his face and warmed him, though most of the plaza lay yet in cool morning shadow.

The scrutiny of those gathered for Convocation would come. He'd been losing his argument there, and the seat holders would likely see the escalation of the Civilization Order as a political maneuver. They'd accuse him of trying to control not just the Recityv High Council, but Convocation, as well. That couldn't be helped. The time was now. He didn't look forward to what was about to happen. But he was eager for what lay on the other side of it all. This was the boldest move he'd made so far to give his vision life. He'd see it through.

When it seemed most had been gathered, he raised his hands to quiet the crowd. *Indeed thousands.* "There is doubt and fear in your hearts," he called, his voice echoing across the throng. "That is to be expected. Since what we do today is not trivial or easy. Today, the Civilization Order has new strength, and requires more from us. The Order of Sheason has been condemned, commanded to be executed. It is the vote of the High Council, made thoughtfully and in consideration of what is best for Recityv, for Vohnce."

Some murmuring arose. Roth waited until it died back down.

"I take no pleasure in enforcing this law," he continued, lending his voice a touch of regret. "Death is not the means by which I would seek civility. But we've wasted countless words trying to bring rational, needful things to you. We've tried to stop the foolish, uneducated rumors of this Quiet and their aim to enslave and destroy. If we ever find truth in this, then we'll approach the problem responsibly and with real force. But we will *not* call on myths and the dangerous practices of those who seek to deceive or control."

One of the Sheason cried out. "This is shameless! You know these people. They've only ever tried to *help* you." The appeal had been directed at the crowd, but Roth took it personally.

"You see," he said, looking around the great square, "even now they would rather lie than admit the truth."

He paused, knowing that eventually these remaining Sheason would strike back. They would seek first to persuade their captors to let them free. But then they would do as all animals do, and fight to survive. So, even here, his actions would need to be swift.

The Sheason who had called out came forward then—Ketrine Solas, the Randeur's daughter. It was poetic in a way he hadn't dared hope.

Drawing near Roth, she said, "You claim to want what is best for the people, and yet you condemn our efforts, even when we leave the Will out of it. This is madness. Where is the regent? Let us hear from her and her Council that what you do is lawful. Before another sword is raised!"

He stared down thoughtfully at her, knowing that in her case he needn't fear rendering. "My dear, appeals are done. We've been patient with your kind since the order was first passed, and men like Vendanj continue to demonstrate that it wasn't enough. Really, we have no choice."

She glared up at him. "If you do this, or even attempt it,

you'll wake my father's anger. Do you want to risk putting him on Vendanj's side?"

Roth laughed behind his gloved fist. "I have it on good authority that these two will never share a pie."

"Good authority?"

"Out of House Storalaith, Helaina's house, as it happens," Roth said, taking some satisfaction in sharing it with her. "Seems we common folk are rather resourceful, doesn't it? And the real value of a Storalaith is not in ruling but in information trading."

Ketrine's eyes turned plaintive. "Let me take them away from here. We'll leave this very moment. There's no need to kill them."

But there is.

"Oh," Roth said, pulling her letter of endorsement from his inner pocket. "And thank you for this. It should make rounding up Sheason in other cities a *cleaner* matter, before we execute the order."

Her face twisted in rage and horror. "You bastard!"

At a small hand signal from Roth, Losol moved his horse forward, circling Ketrine, who did not move or flinch, but stood steadfast as Losol circled her, twice around. Then, while at the young woman's back, he silently drew his sword and hewed her head clean off. It rolled backward toward her fellow Sheason, silencing the crowd.

As the headless body slumped to the ground, Losol lifted his chin and declared. "We *are* the law. We do the will of your ruling Council, and we will not suffer a single insurgent." He pointed his blade at the headless body. "The consequence of defiance."

A powerful sense of certainty and calm settled over Roth. So different from the tentativeness he'd known as a boy. He kept the satisfaction off his face as he focused his attention on the several dozen remaining Sheason. He could see horror and anger in their expressions. The time was now. A public display of the new Civilization Order—the entire reason for driving these Sheason to a public place—was necessary. It would make his resolve clear. And the tale of it would spread, grow. Some would hear of it on the road. Others would read it in the pages of authors. It began here in a morning of cleansing, but would move beyond Recityv. The days ahead filled him with deeper purpose and pride.

This time, he wouldn't raise an arm to cue his men—too much warning in it. Instead, by design, when he raised his eyes to the sky . . . it began. He liked the many ironies of this signal.

From vantage points atop buildings surrounding the plaza, expert archers began to rain down arrows. The penned Sheason dropped quickly to the cobbled stone. Sodalists, too. The air whistled with the flight of shafts and feathers. Shadows darted in the morning rays of light. Cries of pain and surprise rose up, as did sounds of horror and shock from thousands of onlookers.

The arrows continued to fly, shot with expertise, few missing their marks. Some of the Sheason raised their hands to some profane use, only to be struck by a deadly point before they could do anything more.

The sight of death didn't particularly please Roth; the face of it left him feeling empty, even when he knew it was justified. Bitter bile filled his throat, and the nature of his cause and war overcame him.

Well-intentioned men and women would die. Those few who knew him, and for whom he cared, would misunderstand him, label him a monster and traitor—no better, perhaps, than the illusions he fought to destroy. His effort to elevate men beyond the need to steal or beg or rely on anything but their *own* best effort would require more brutality. So be it.

As Sheason fell, a cry rose up behind Roth. He turned to see Vendanj rushing from the doors of Solath Mahnus.

EVEN AS VENDANJ raced toward the gate where Roth and his warmonger sat in their saddles . . . he knew he was too late. The air rang with the vibrations of bowstrings and the slip of arrows toward men and women sworn to the same oath he'd taken. They fell in waves as their bodies became little more than targets for archers firing from rooftops. They'd been caught unaware, probably in a mild state of shock and panic.

He raised a mighty cry, filling the sky with anger and threat, hoping to scare or startle the assailants. His alarm did little more than draw the attention of Roth himself and his new Mal general. Their pitiless faces settled his anger deeper inside him. He thrust an open palm at them and forced their mounts violently apart, throwing their riders to the stone yard just before he passed into the plaza proper.

He'd deal with them later; right now he must try to protect those Sheason and sodalists still alive.

He caught sight of Helaina and Artixan entering the square directly across from him, and at the same moment, to his right, Braethen shot into view. His sodalist carried a bloodied sword and led a Sheason man who came a few paces behind. Grant appeared beside Braethen, assessing the scene.

More arrows were released; Vendanj sensed they targeted Artixan. He quickly raised his hands, palms skyward. Wind swept up from the ground in a thunderous burst, and arrows sailed harmlessly away from their targets. The howl of wind brought sudden silence to the square.

Nearly every Sheason and sodalist had been killed. All but a few were dead. Those fallen, but not yet silenced, uttered mortal cries in whispers.

"Take him down." The words pierced the relative calm, and a new volley darkened the sky. Vendanj wheeled around to see Roth standing with an accusatory arm raised toward him. His war general stood at his side, a sword in hand. Losol's face shone with eagerness to take the fight to the ground, a thin smile playing on his lips.

Behind him, a forceful word was uttered in a deep, calm voice. In the air, arrows lost their form, disintegrating to sawdust, and fluttered down like a soft rain across the plaza. Artixan.

The spectacle of arrows brought to dust in the open sky caused a new silence, broken only by the rush of Vendanj's companions driving toward the center of the great square. He looked back down at the dozens of bodies, their forms pierced with so many arrows that it looked like a riverbank overgrown with reeds. Beneath it all, blood coated the plaza stones, spreading slowly in the morning light.

"Again," the command came, Roth's voice calm, assured.

"No!" Helaina cried out with the authority of her office. "Any leagueman who strikes will be tried as a traitor." Her words echoed up the building faces to their attackers.

She and Artixan came alongside Vendanj a moment before Braethen and the Sheason with him.

They all stood, chuffing hard from their run. In the crisp morning air, their breath steamed, very much like the warm blood that oozed from the dead around them. The slaughter brought quiet rage to his mind, an anger like he'd known only when his wife and child . . . His arms and hands trembled with the need for vengeance. He would save Roth for last, and watch the man's face as he crushed the life from his body.

"Don't listen to her." Roth began to walk the perimeter of leaguemen that held the crowd at bay. "We act in good conscience and in accordance with the law. More than this, we act on the moral authority of defending the civility of the people."

Artixan stepped past Vendanj, his elderly form quaking as he cried out. "This is murder! What law is civil that calls for the death of those who do no harm?"

"But that's where you're wrong," the Ascendant countered conversationally. His calm demeanor lent his words authority. "Grave as it seems, we know from sad experience that there are times when the very existence of a thing is harmful." He held up a finger as one preparing a metaphor. "When an arm or leg is filled with the poison of a serpent, do we not often remove the appendage to save the life? So it is now." Roth paced, looking past his army to the throngs of Recityv citizens that stood silent, watching, listening.

Vendanj could see standards far back in the crowd— members of the Convocation come to see what was happening. They'd come too late to stop this. And even if they'd arrived in time to help, he knew that governments were slow to intercede in the civil affairs of other realms.

"Listen to me." Vendanj lowered his voice, but gave it a sharpness that would carry. "Some things *are* harmful in and of themselves: prejudice, selfishness, pride. To say nothing of those who prey on our little ones for their own pleasures. We've always stood with the League to oppose these things."

He paused, turning a slow circle, the copper smell of blood in his nose. "But I ask you, when you're in your homes, and you're quiet, and you think about the old stories . . . when you think about the Sheason who've lived among you"—he raised his arms, palms up, gesturing to the countless dead around him—"does this *feel* like the truth? Never mind the logical arguments made by *anyone*!" Vendanj shot a withering look at Roth. "I ask each of you to hearken to your *own* wisdom. And then decide," he called out strongly, "do you know for *yourself* the legitimacy of these actions. Or will you be led by others who would silence the voice of opposition." He pointed simultaneously to the murdered Sheason at the center of the plaza and at Roth. "Will you be led by those who coerce others to pass immoral laws."

"Beware," Roth said with cool caution to both Vendanj and the crowd. "These are careful lies from one who would prefer you remain enslaved in ignorance. I'm no deathmonger. But neither will I stand idle any longer. There's a new promise now," Roth declared, "a final promise. The League and I will be its right arm. We'll establish a new standard of life and defend it against any who threaten to tear it down. And that begins today with the enforcement of a law that I take no pleasure in upholding. But I'm bound to it, just as I'm bound to each of you. Your children will grow up safe and have opportunities to learn. They'll no longer be dependent on anyone. They'll have no need to fear." Roth looked at Vendanj, the man's eyes smiling, even if his mouth did not.

When Roth finished speaking, men and women muttered. It sounded to Vendanj like assent. He could feel the tide of opinion turning. The people would sanction this slaughter because they wanted to believe in the immediate answers Roth offered them. Vendanj looked away to catch the eyes of a few Convocation seat holders who looked on. Helaina's efforts would, indeed, fail here today. He could think of no rendering that could stop that now.

His anger began to rise, replacing horror and loss and appeal. He meant to give every last measure of his energy to render an attack, tear apart the flesh of Roth and Losol and all the League.

Before he could begin, a low rumble, like thunder heard far away on a rolling plain, began in their midst. He looked around. It wasn't Artixan with some act of the Will. It was Braethen, who, rather than stepping toward Roth to speak, stepped carefully into the midst of the dead Sheason and raised the Blade of Seasons. The sword shone darkly in the morning light. Its unrefined length normally appeared merely tarnished. Today it held the crimson blood of leaguemen.

Braethen raised the tip of his blade to the heavens, and with his free hand pointed to the fallen Sheason at his feet. The crowd grew silent. The sword trembled in his unsteady hand. With a quiet voice that carried far in the stillness, he spoke just one word.

"Remember."

The air above the plaza swirled, weaving itself into a vision of the Placing—those events that followed the Whiting of Quietus. Creatures moved like waves over plains, pushing north and west into regions beyond nameless mountains.

The images were terrifying. Legions of unremembered races. They didn't howl or caper about madly in petulant protest. There was no gnashing of teeth or rending of clothes or apocalyptic battles. Most walked quietly, somberly, their eyes telling of acute minds and long memories, of malice tempered by patience.

Vendanj shivered. Those being herded were *aware*. Aware of their mistreatment. Aware of the injustice. And though the languages they spoke were foreign, the oaths on the lips of these forgotten races were clear: vows to come again into the Eastlands, and to come without mercy.

The images coalescing in the air above the plaza changed, and new scenes from the Placing drew into form. In these, Quietgiven fought their confinement. With powerful grace they stood against the hands of renderers, their faces calm with defiance. And while some raised makeshift weapons of stone and wood, most defied the Placing with nothing more than questions. Without ceremony, these defiant ones fell.

Renderers simply put them down with an act of Will and moved on.

The images shifted again and again, showing more scenes of numberless creatures being marched into new geographies. Into far places deep inside the Bourne.

Among those driven into the distant lands were some whose protests struck a sympathetic chord. Inveterae races, who had no ill-purpose concerning the people of the east. There was a pleading tone in the questions they asked that was heartbreaking to hear.

The many images of the Placing reminded them all of the precarious balance between the Eastlands and the world beyond the Pall. And if races herded there had hated man then, what must their bloodlust be like today?

Vendanj shivered again, knowing that behind that bloodlust lurked an equal measure of reason. They would be fierce, but also calculating.

The smell of soil after a rain shower rose on a wind that blew out of the vision above the plaza. *We smell the very winds that blew over the Placing.* It coursed over the throng that pressed in around Solath Mahnus. "Remember," Braethen called again, his voice clear above the sibilant rush.

It had carried them to the edge of this history, threatening to leave them stranded in that past when the promise of the world would soon be abandoned. The Blade of Seasons had bridged the ages, giving them all a firsthand account of those sealed behind the Veil.

A moment later, Braethen collapsed. His sword arm fell first, his body following as he tumbled amidst the dead Sheason. The images dissipated in an instant, leaving the air cut through with shafts of light out of an eastern sun. The throng now had clear doubt in their eyes—doubt about Roth's claims of safety. Braethen had given them the reason to doubt.

"Don't be deceived," Roth called out, dispelling what had happened. "These are more tricks. If I wanted to deceive you, I could create visions that refute these myths. But I won't. I will just tell you that it's time to look ahead. The realities of this day represent the change I offer you, that a new High Council offers you. It's the only right way forward."

The crowd became restless with its own struggle to make sense of it all. Vendanj could see citizens beginning to argue with each other. Some stared into the sky, confused. Others pointed at either Roth or Vendanj or Helaina.

Regardless of what came next, Sheason in Recityv had been hewn down, almost entirely destroyed. How soon before the Civilization Order, with its expanded power, reached other realms?

He forced the thought back as Losol started toward him. Other leaguemen followed. Still standing were Vendanj, Artixan, and the Sheason who had come with Braethen.

A dark smile spread on his lips. After all that had happened this terrible day, he would take pleasure in confrontation. The time for talking was over.

But before the first blow or act of Will could fall, Helaina cried out to her people. "Friends of Recityv! Decide for yourselves. If you honor what I have offered you all my life, if you believe that the murder you've seen today has no place in our city, then stand with me now and fight this menace!"

The drawing of steel from sheaths and hidden pockets surprised even Vendanj. More men and women than he could have imagined carried weapons. And when one of the leaguemen tried to seize a woman's handknife, the struggle broke out in earnest.

Van Steward's men rushed into the crowds, fighting alongside citizens who battled the League. An unbelievable number of leaguemen came, too, bolstering citizens who stood with them around the broad plaza.

"Civil war," Helaina whispered.

Vendanj barely heard, as he strode toward the Ascendant and his man of war.

• CHAPTER SIXTY-SIX •

Just an Evening Stroll

*So, Jon Petruc wrought two mandolas from one, giving the
second to his beloved Jaane when she was asked by the
Randeur to visit the Sellarians. Each night, he'd play his music. And Jaane, half a world away, would listen to her mandola ring with song.*

—Drawn from the Dimnian instructional text *On the Nature
of Instruments,* Chapter One, "The Mandola or the Man"

A WINDLESS EVENING settled in with the onset of dusk.
Tahn, Rithy, and Polaema strolled westward from Aubade Grove. In the sky ahead, the constellation Anolees, the
crippled king of Masson Dimn, slowly rose into view. Tahn
smiled. He could name them all. Every last glimmering light
in the night sky.

They enjoyed a companionable silence, taking in the stars
with the kind of awe once reserved only for childhood. The
fresh scent of sage lingered on the air, coupled with the pleasant smells of green grass and cooling stone.

"Why are we headed away from the Grove at suppertime?"
Tahn asked with playful challenge.

Polaema gave him a motherly look. "Because I've something I want to show you."

"All right, Gnomon," Rithy said, breaking in. "I've been
waiting to ask . . ."

Polaema gave a wry smile that held its own kind of glimmer in the gathering darkness.

Tahn likewise grinned. "Why Resonance?"

"That'll do for a start," she replied.

He focused a thoughtful look at Polaema. "You say the
College of Philosophy has a new view on the entire subject
of the Bourne. Easy for them to sit around and theorize. But

I've seen the Quiet. Seen what they can do. What they *are* doing."

"And what are they doing, Gnomon?" his astronomy mother asked matter-of-factly.

"Killing, mostly," Tahn answered without humor. "I think you know the regent at Recityv called a Convocation to try and stop it, raise an army . . ." He paused a long moment. "Prepare for war."

"How does proving Continuity with Resonance help us win a war?" Rithy asked with enough distraction that Tahn knew she was already theorizing about it at a math level he'd never understand.

"Not win a war," he reminded them, "prevent a war." He smiled, feeling excitement begin to prickle his skin. "How would our philosophers feel about that idea?"

"Don't lump all philosophers into the same ideological camp," Polaema suggested. "But go on."

"Fair enough," Tahn said, eager to share his idea. "If we can prove Continuity through Resonance, I believe we'll find a way to strengthen the Veil. Make it impenetrable by the Quiet. No Quiet. No war." He dusted his hands as if finished with a dirty chore.

"Elegant in its simplicity," Polaema admitted. "But the philosophers will argue about the very existence of a Veil."

Rithy laughed at the truth of it.

"Won't matter," Tahn said. "It's conceivable that if we prove Continuity, we could erect a barrier of our own, right? The Veil's a consequence of Resonance, not the other way around."

"Why Succession, though, Gnomon?" Polaema skirted a low, broad sage bush.

Tahn was nodding. "Succession will force rapid preparation and focus. All the resources of Aubade Grove will concentrate on one question. Otherwise, I could spend a year trying to do this with *willing* contributors, and still not get so far."

"Makes sense," Rithy agreed. "But the topic has been through Succession before and put down. And not just by my ma. . . ." Her words got lost on the soft evening air, her thoughts turned inward.

Tahn said nothing, and they walked a while in silence.

Rithy got them started again. "Just how do you plan to go about proving Continuity through Resonance?"

"We'll build on—"

"You don't have time to *build* an argument," Rithy argued. "And what we did before won't be much help. Plus, you've just dropped out of the air, returning to an area of research you suffered for maybe four years."

Polaema's eyebrows rose. "Suffered?"

"My apologies, Savant Polaema. I just mean that it's not easy here. It'll look to many like Tahn walked away rather selfishly. Now he's back, and asking for help. Many will resent him for it. They'll be less than accommodating."

Polaema gave Tahn a questioning look. "I hate to agree with a mathematician, but she's right."

Tahn shook his head absently. "They'll have to get over it. I'll appeal to them to focus on the science, not their own feelings."

"I'll sponsor the Succession," Polaema offered, "since it appears your diplomacy hasn't improved much. But I'll need you to answer Rithy's question about how you plan to prove Continuity through Resonance, since that's what we'll be taking to the discourse theaters."

As they continued to walk through the sage, he looked at them each in turn, and started talking it through. "Bear with me, it's been a while." He took a long breath to gather himself. "In the past, Continuity supposed the existence of an omnipresent element. This element was first called *omnilesch erymol*. Erymol is said to exist as much in you or me or this sage or the Grove towers, as it does in the air and deep sky. It's the most subtle, most attenuated, most . . . volatile substance. Continuity then assumes that even air is matter, that erymol binds all things, and that this connection is what ultimately gives gravity and magnetism their power."

They bolstered his confidence with silent nods.

Tahn went on. "Erymol's natural condition is restful, still.

520 · PETER ORULLIAN

But because it's everywhere, in everything, and so . . . fine, it's easily disturbed, easily . . . manipulated."

Tahn became flush with his own excitement. Not over erymol, but just rational thought on complex ideas.

"It would mean that the flying bird is connected with the earth below it, that we are connected with the stars above. If prior arguments on Continuity hold true, then light, heat, sound, color, magnetism, gravity, would all have a means of transference. And so it would suggest that there exists an understandable and demonstrable mechanism for this invisible barrier along the Pall that we call the Veil."

Neither Rithy or Polaema said a word, but he could see them reserving judgment.

"Any movement, any vibration would cause resonation along this erymol—"

"That's the essence of *prior* Successions on Continuity," Polaema affirmed. "The trick will be evidence to support and prove your new hypothesis on Resonance. You're a gifted astronomer, Gnomon, but the best minds failed to prove Continuity after long years of study. What's your fallback plan?"

Tahn remembered that the mother of astronomy had often preached such preparedness.

Rithy appeared to be doing calculations in her head, her lips moving as she silently mouthed numbers and signifiers to some equation. Her eyes wide with a thoughtful glaze, when she spoke as though to herself: "I think you might be on to something with Resonance. . . ."

"I don't have time for a fallback plan," Tahn said, answering his old mentor, but still watching Rithy.

Polaema made a soft, disapproving sound in her throat. "You'll first argue the physicists, Gnomon. In some ways, they're going to be the most difficult. If memory serves, that's where Continuity died in Succession last time."

Rithy rejoined the conversation. "The physicists would like to have a unifying principle to support the laws of force that keep them in chalk and slate." She frowned up at him. "Proving air is matter isn't the principle they're hoping for."

"Right," Tahn said. "We won't come at it from that angle. With Resonance, we'll show that the whole world is connected without the need of a medium. One leaven, not one loaf."

"And then," Polaema said, making them look ahead, "if you're successful in all this, you'll need to use this new understanding to determine how it can be manipulated. Don't forget your ultimate goal. To strengthen this Veil no one's seen or felt." She smiled.

Tahn allowed himself a small smile in return. "But that's the purpose of science, isn't it, Mother Polaema? First we seek to understand. Then we can *apply* that understanding."

She raised her eyebrows; part, he thought, in reproof of his slight conceit, and part, he decided, in esteem. "Are we really going to do this again?" she said softly into the twilight.

They fell silent once more, returning their attention to the sky briefly before Polaema held up a hand to halt them. Her mouth and brow were pinched, lines forming around each. He recognized the look: It spoke of inexplicable phenomena. Tonight, though, the look had a dark cast to it. When he followed her gaze—like an invitation, like the reason they'd come away from the Grove—he saw her expression's cause.

A field of dead birds . . .

• CHAPTER SIXTY-SEVEN •

The Bourne: Toccata

The problem for a messiah is that not everyone who suffers wants to be rescued. Nor can they be.

—The Second Inference reached by Sedgel leadership in
Dissent and the Introduction of Humans to the Bourne

THEIR FACES HAUNTED him.
Since the death of his friend Reelan, Kett had walked the empty roads of the Bourne with six Bar'dyn—Lliothan,

his old friend, among them. They'd ranged far and wide to the regions of the other Inveterae houses that had pledged themselves to him at the shores of their mourning lake. And one by one, he'd executed them in the company of their friends and families.

The irony, he thought, was that he couldn't have suffered the memory of the friends he'd killed if not for being *given*. It had gotten inside him. Made his heart stonier.

Or perhaps his resolve flowed from the look of understanding and acceptance each of his fellows had shown him. They'd realized why he'd come to them, realized what their sacrifice could mean to generations of Inveterae if Kett could lead them from the Bourne.

Even for his love of his children, he didn't think he could have continued his march across the endless, lonely sweeps of the Bourne to kill.

So, perhaps it was the misery of the Bourne itself that gave him strength—the strength of an unfriendly reach of land that knew no conscience or concern.

Just before dawn, he crested a low rise in the long road. All around, rocky terrain stretched, dotted here and there by ailanthus trees and sagebrush. A bitter wind blew at his back, as down the far side of the hill he saw the sprawl of another Inveterae town, Waeland. The last name on the list would be found here. Sool, who'd forged the union of the central houses at Saleema's burial. Like the others, she would see the wisdom in her death, and go to her earth gladly. She was the most important Inveterae on the list. Perhaps as important to their movement as Kett. Perhaps more so. Her influence came from unimpeachable wisdom. Killing her would be a crime on more levels than he could count.

With the wind goading him forward, he descended the hill with his Quietgiven in tow.

The clouds raced low and dark over nearby bluffs, but the wind broke in the little valley. He inquired of an elder Raolyn and her son for directions to Sool's house. They hesitated a moment before grudgingly pointing and muttering a few instructions. Without incident he came to a well-worn path that took him to her modest door.

He knocked. Waited. He'd ceased to pray to the gods at these moments. His prayers in these circumstances hadn't produced anything more than the prayers he'd offered in all the years prior.

It pained him when she pulled back the door of her small clay-brick home and smiled at his arrival. Her expression faltered as she caught sight of the Bar'dyn a few strides behind him.

He watched as she pieced it all together: the branding across his chest and shoulders, the fact that her home lay the farthest east—he'd killed many before arriving here.

"Is our hope dead?" she asked softly.

With this last of his fellows—and especially with Sool—he wanted to share what he'd learned. He needed word to spread. Those close to Sool would be best to do it.

As he stood, trying to figure out a plan, she asked, "May I say good-bye to my family?" Sool's words stung him—they were the plea an executioner hears.

He nodded, and found a believable enough excuse to go in with her. He turned to his Bar'dyn companions, addressing Lliothan. "I believe she hides other separatists. I'll go in and force them out. Be ready."

Before an objection could be raised, he turned and followed Sool inside. There he found her lighting lamps and candles and opening windows. Odd, as daybreak had just lit the sky. His attention shifted to the many paintings hanging on the walls—images rendered in browns and greys on thin, flat rocks or the inner side of tree bark stretched flat. Some were faces. Most were portraits of Inveterae races it was unlikely she'd ever seen. A few were of places she could never have visited, places south of the Pall.

"They're my reminders," she said. "All my life, I've dreamed of people with sun on their faces, of cities that fly colorful banners that rise high against a clear sky." She looked from one painting to another. "And I paint the Inveterae who might one day lead us there."

His eyes lit on one painting in particular. He picked up a lamp and approached the wall, where he held up the light. "Me," he said.

"I painted that the day before your tribunal. To remember you once you were gone." She crossed to stand beside him in front of the simple painting, which held a crimson-rust tint. He could think of only one source for the color.

"When I heard you'd survived, I decided my painting was more than a portrait of another Gotun. It's why I gathered the others and followed you to the Mourning Vale." She placed one hand on the painting, and the other on his shoulder.

The Bar'dyn would get restless soon. And Kett had to guard what he said and thought, still unsure what it might give away to the Quiet because of his oath. "There isn't much time, Sool. You must tell your family good-bye."

"My family's dead," she replied. "Killed by Quietgiven three moon cycles ago."

The sound of her voice was the sound of the Bourne. There was some sadness in it, but mostly resignation. Her heart, like his, had become stony.

She went on. "I just wanted a moment to show you these." She looked around at her modest portraits. "Most of them are dead. And the cities? I hope they're real places. I hope our people see them with their own eyes someday. And this one"—she tapped the image of Kett lightly—"you, Kett Valan, are the one to lead them there. Whatever happens, whatever your plan, promise me you'll take the Raolyn with you."

Kett had no firm plan yet. But he'd gotten closer. He still needed to gain the absolute confidence of the Jinaal. To do that, he'd had to hunt down the Inveterae leaders who had pledged to support and follow him. Like Sool. He hoped when he returned that he'd have earned enough trust to ask about the Quiet plan to bring a labraetates to the Bourne, sing their way across the Pall.

"Because," she said, interrupting his thoughts, "you realize you can't take them all. The Inveterae, I mean. It's a simple problem of logistics."

He hadn't considered it before. Not fully, anyway. Foolish of him not to. But he'd become slavish to only the next step in escaping the Bourne. The realization descended on him now, though. The Bourne stretched for leagues he couldn't count. There was no practical way to organize all Inveterae.

Whatever the final plan turned out to be, he'd have to be selective, realistic.

He might not have that plan yet, but he'd let Sool die believing he was more prepared than he was. "I won't leave the Raolyn behind," he assured her. Sool's smile would be something he'd remember a long time.

She then nodded and lowered her hands. "Let's get to it." She didn't linger for a farewell word, or a final look around her home, or any other last preparation. She'd only wanted to bind him to a promise. That done, she walked out, ready to face death.

He went out after her, finding the clouds had broken in the east, allowing daylight to stream down. The rays of sun seemed foreign, but shimmered on the cold, dew-covered ground. Steam rose in thin streams as the soil warmed.

He followed her to the street, the gravity of the moment filling him. She came to a stop in front of the six Bar'dyn, who stared at her with reasoned indifference. In the light of the sun, their muscled bodies hinted at menace.

He raised a hand to the branding on his own chest, so much like that of his band of Quiet.

She waited with her back to him. She might expect him to make a formal declaration of her crimes, perhaps call them out loudly to draw the town in to witness the execution, make her a public example. That had been the way of it for other names on the list.

He would do her a final favor. He'd kill her unexpectedly, so that the moment wouldn't linger, and her people wouldn't have to watch. He'd later explain that he'd feared she had some weapon or insurgency planned, and he'd had to kill her before things got out of control.

Kett drew his blade, catching a glint of sun off its flat edge.

Just as he began to imagine scratching the last name off his list, dozens of Raolyn stepped from behind houses and buildings and trees. They didn't rush. But they came on, holding implements used to turn the ground or cultivate what crops could be grown in the rocky soil.

Lliothan and the Bar'dyn unsheathed their blades.

Sool didn't start or turn at any of this. She stood still as her people walked toward them.

Then, without a shout or call, the Raolyn crowd rushed in, their large forks and picks and shovels raised. The Bar'dyn whirled to face them. Several of the Raolyn were cut down so effortlessly that Kett despaired of countless, senseless deaths. They would all die. Their inexperience at combat—with farming tools, no less—would fail against Bar'dyn training and steel.

In those moments, the sight of Inveterae fighting back stirred him in a way he couldn't explain. And he saw in his mind the painting of himself Sool had just showed him.

He charged past the Raolyn woman, his sword in hand, and plunged it into the neck of one of his Bar'dyn brothers. The Quietgiven slumped to the ground. And fire erupted in his chest. *Abandoning gods, is this because of my oath?* It left him weak and trembling.

To his right, Lliothan cursed. "Betrayer." His old friend turned and brought a great hammer stroke down on him. Kett managed to get his blade up in time to ward off the blow, but the power of it knocked him to the ground.

Lliothan raised his blade again, gripping it with both hands. Before he could strike a second time, two Raolyn farmers tackled him to the ground.

Kett stood, heaving breath into the cold morning air. Around him, dozens of Inveterae had swarmed the five remaining Bar'dyn. A few of the Quiet were on the ground, grappling for their lives. Grunts and the scrape of metal rose into the morning. Blood flowed onto the ground with the dew, taking a bright fiery hue in the sunlight.

Faster than he would have thought, four of the Bar'dyn lay motionless, their bodies still taking the sharp ends of tools, as if death wasn't enough justice for their former villainy.

The sound of pounding feet drew Kett's attention. He whirled again, preparing to take a charge. Instead, he watched as Lliothan disappeared over the hill at a dead run. Bar'dyn could run faster than a horse. Much faster than a Gotun.

A sickening dread filled his stomach as he thought about Marckol and Neliera. They were still being held by the Jinaal.

In that long moment, he felt something he hadn't before . . . godless. Because no father or mother should ever abandon their child, not even the First Ones.

What have I done? What do I do now?

After the Bar'dyn disappeared over the rise at the far end of the vale, he turned back toward Sool. "You signaled them with open windows and lamplight," he said.

She nodded. "We've been tracking your approach for days. News of the executions has spread over the roads of the Bourne faster than you were able to travel them. We decided the time for separation was now."

"But what if I'd . . ."

Sool smiled—a rare enough thing in the Bourne that it caught him off guard. "I had a feeling that once the attack began, you'd be on the right side of it. But," and she looked back up the road, "we hadn't expected one to escape. It changes our path."

"It changes *my* path," he corrected. "I have to go back. If I don't go, they may decide annihilation is the only way to deal with Inveterae. Maybe I can convince them that killing a few Bar'dyn was my way of earning your trust. To get more information about the exodus. Besides, I've only learned a little of the Jinaal plan for crossing the Pall."

"You'll fail. And you've already done most of what they asked. They won't have any use for you. And you'll arrive as a betrayer. We should begin now, spread the word, gather, move south." Sool gestured for the others to remove the Bar'dyn bodies from the road.

He sheathed his sword. "We'll meet more Quietgiven. What will we say to them? And if we *do* reach the Veil, how will we cross it?" He shook his head. "Our patience may have its price, but without it there's no hope of success."

Sool smiled with understanding. "Go get your little ones. But we can't go with you. Raolyn will be killed on sight after word of this spreads. We'll prepare to leave, and gather the other Inveterae houses." She put a hand on his shoulder. "Be careful. Remember your responsibility to *all* of us."

Without another word, he set out under the morning sun. He strode briskly westward, his shadow preceding him up the road.

• CHAPTER SIXTY-EIGHT •

A Clash of Wills

It stands to reason that any force which must traverse space may be met, counteracted even.

—Sheason battle corollary and preface to simultaneity,
also known as synchronous resonance

VENDANJ BROUGHT HIS hands together, clasping them before him as he strode toward Roth. He'd remove the League head first, then deal with the rest. Roth smiled as Losol stepped into Vendanj's path and held up his blade. Around them civilians fought leaguemen or Recityv footmen or even each other. Many had already fallen from their lack of skill or the inferiority of their weapons. The sounds of combat and struggle enveloped him, but seemed distant as he thrust his hands toward Losol. He sent a violent burst of resonance at the man. It shot fast, little more than a distortion in the air.

Losol held his sword out straight, and the force of Vendanj's attack traveled around him, like a river current flowing around the prow of a ship. He remained untouched. A half moment later, rocks exploded in the stone wall behind Losol, as the resonant push found a surface.

Vendanj stared in shock and concern. Losol's smile tightened.

Silent gods, he's found a Talendraal.

The leagueman moved swiftly toward him, his sword still held out like a shield. Vendanj knew of these weapons, forged with the power to deflect a rendering of Will, but he'd never encountered one. There existed only one place where such a weapon would be necessary or allowed—the Bourne.

He drew his long knife and set his feet. Losol came on, feinting a strike then kicking up with his left leg. Vendanj took a hard boot in the gut, and dropped to the ground. The whistle of a sword's edge sliced through the air, and he rolled. The ringing sound of steel hitting stone rose just behind him.

He kicked hard at the warlord's shins. The man fell to his knees with a painful groan. Then Vendanj was up and whirling, ready to end this. Impossibly, Losol had already gotten to his feet and swung his blade at Vendanj's chest.

The sword edge tore through his garment and skin. Blood flowed free and warm down his front. He stumbled back, checking the wound, and looked up in time to avoid a second strike that would have met his throat.

He then slammed his fists together, causing his own flesh to split and blood to spatter into the air. With a word, he fragmented the blood into a fine mist and whipped it toward the warlord like a stinging, abrasive funnel. The man flailed at the biting blood-wind, deflecting some, but not all, his skin peppered with deep pricks that began to bleed.

But Losol smiled through the red mask that became his face, and extended his sword again as a shield. The wind parted, and he came on hard.

Vendanj was weak and lost momentary focus. He backpedaled, seeking time to consider a countermove. Losol's face twisted with delight, and he surged forward. Vendanj lifted his knife again, and began to draw a greater rendering of Will than he'd used for some time. He was through with this! But before the other could reach him, a dark flash erupted in front of Vendanj as steel struck steel. Grant stood between him and Losol, a look of calculated violence on his face.

"Find Braethen," Grant shouted, "and get off the plaza."

Vendanj glared at Losol. He hated not finishing a fight, especially this one. But Braethen still lay unconscious and helpless in the midst of the fallen Sheason. And killing Losol wouldn't stop the fighting that had broken out all around them. The League itself needed to fall, and that meant dealing with Roth, who was now nowhere to be seen.

As Grant and Losol began to fight, Vendanj hurried to Braethen's side. The sodalist drew ragged breaths, but he *was* breathing.

"Braethen."

The sodalist opened his eyes, looking disoriented. Vendanj

showed him a satisfied smile, then sheathed for him the Blade of Seasons. He folded Braethen over his shoulder, and looked for a gap in the fighting. Only the entrance to Solath Mahnus through the Wall of Remembrance appeared open. He moved fast in its direction, trying not to think about how this civil war had just put everything so much further away.

HELAINA STOOD IN the middle of her city's grand plaza, surrounded by the dead, the dying, and the living who were trying to kill the rest. Civilians swung bad weapons badly. Shouts and clamor filled the air. Maybe she could still avert all-out civil war. But she'd need Grant's help.

She caught sight of him locked in battle with the League's new war leader. Her estranged husband held his own, but this warlord fought with a dangerous elegance, his movements almost hypnotic.

Losol brought his greatsword around in a vicious arc. Grant easily stepped out of the way, as though he anticipated the attack. It was the same with almost every attempt Losol made. Grant had spent twenty years studying the art of battle, learning more deeply the mechanics of the body with weapons and position and stance.

But each time Grant prepared to counterattack, another leagueman was there, hammering at him, too. Man after man went down as he stepped back far enough to keep the odds even. But it meant little progress against Losol himself. The Mal seemed pleased that his Jurshah was doing their part, and annoyed he didn't have the fight to himself.

At one point, Grant shuffled back and went at a whole group of leaguemen, wading through them. It appeared almost choreographed, as four men fell in mere moments. When he stood and looked back at Losol, the war leader nodded and finally held up a hand, signaling for his men to fight elsewhere. Grant advanced on Losol with a determined look on his face.

They locked in combat, trading blows without pause. Each went down more than once, but rolled to his feet like an acrobat. Before long, a few leaguemen, who hadn't seen Losol's command to leave them alone, waded in. Grant's face hardened, more focused. And he began a series of sweeping turns, swords flashing out, dropping the newcomers without giving ground to Losol.

His strikes were quick, efficient, pulling through a man's throat or manhood, whatever was easiest and most debilitating. A few of the attackers caught his flesh with their steel, but the cuts were small. It was the most amazing thing Helaina had ever seen, watching him fight. He crouched, lunged, all in a continuous series of turns. But the numbers against him were rising again, and this time Losol didn't call his men off.

"General," she called, "there!" She pointed toward Grant.

Van Steward rushed to double the attack on Losol. Together, her general and her husband pushed the man back. Van Steward fought the leaguemen. Grant, Losol. When Van Steward whistled in several more of his men, the warlord offered a conciliatory smile, one that spoke not of defeat but *postponement,* and quickly disappeared into the throng.

When she turned, she saw Artixan helping several women and their children to safety inside a building fronting the plaza. He moved people aside with a wave of his hand, showing little regard for League, solider, or civilian.

When Van Steward and Grant returned to her side, she raised a hand, pointing. "Get me up there."

Grant followed her outstretched arm to the top of the Wall of Remembrance. "They won't listen to you," he shouted. "They won't even hear you."

"I'll take care of that." It was Artixan, coming up behind her.

She got moving as fast as her old, tired legs would take her. Van Steward and Grant ran just ahead, brandishing their weapons. Artixan followed close at her heels. It sickened her that twice they jumped over the bodies of fallen citizens. But she remained focused.

They passed through the entrance into the inner courtyard, cut sharply left, and stopped at the base of the wall. Grant hunkered down, mumbling under his breath, and Helaina put her feet on his shoulders. With her hands against the wall for balance, she told Grant to stand. A moment later, she could see over the top of the wall into the plaza. Helaina then hauled herself up with great difficulty, and carefully stood, overlooking the violence and growing number of dead or wounded in and around the great square.

"Listen to me!" she yelled. "I command you to stop!"

Her words didn't rise above the tumult. "Artixan," she said. The Sheason extended a palm toward her, and she called out again. This time, her words echoed loud, like a deep brass horn. A few heads turned, but went back to the fray almost immediately.

"Will you die over nothing?" she asked angrily. "You fight because you're afraid, but you're afraid of the wrong thing! We must not be divided!"

Her words rang out again like a clarion trumpet, piercing the din. But still the fighting raged. Never had she lost control like this.

"Enough!" she cried out. "You kill neighbors and friends, when our cause is a common one!"

The sound of her voice fell across buildings facing the great plaza, across thousands locked in conflict, across the bodies of dozens of executed Sheason, across a growing number of dead. But ultimately it fell useless.

She'd stayed a step ahead of Roth. But this. She hadn't anticipated that he'd try this. He was inviting the wrath of the entire Sheason Order. But he wouldn't do that if he didn't feel prepared. *What defense does he possess?* The thought caused a cold shiver deep in her bones.

She'd believed her authority as regent could stem this tide before it washed her city under. Now, she believed all might be lost. But for one thought, she might have broken down and wept.

For what might be the last time, she raised her arm, the regent sign for silence.

Then, in a dreamlike moment, she heard the sound of a bowstring being released, a deep pluck followed by a low whistle. Her eye caught a sliver of movement, and then a sharp pain struck her body. She looked down and found an arrow buried in the center of her chest.

As she tumbled back, a series of images swept through her vision: her people at war with themselves; Sheason lying dead across the great square; women and children trying to escape the danger of the crowd, the grand architecture of granite-stone edifices facing the great plaza, and blue sky. . . .

A weightless moment followed in which she seemed to float, looking up now at tree limbs carving intricate patterns in the vault of heaven overhead. Vaguely, she knew she must soon strike the hard stone of the inner courtyard below, but didn't fear it. Perhaps her time was done, after all. If so, she might have liked to see Tahn before going to her earth. To hold him the way a mother would. She might have liked to tell Grant that even though she'd had to banish him, and couldn't understand his fanatic observance of old principles, she respected him more than any man she knew. That she might even still love him.

Darkness came to her eyes before she felt anything more. And even then, it seemed more like strong arms catching her than a hard impact on cobbled stone. But she was too far down a black funnel to be sure.

• CHAPTER SIXTY-NINE •

In the Company of Eggbirds

The pole-star glyph isn't inherently corrupt. Quite the opposite, in fact. And many believe it to be first among symbols. But to try and "possess" it is like trying to claim a part of the sky for your own. Madness.

—The Dimensionality and Consequent Relationship Between Glyphs and Matter, Primary Text in Semiotics and Symbols, by Examplar Susforth

TO AVOID DRAWING suspicion, Mira didn't ask anyone for directions to the residence of the Relothian House. Nor was it necessary. The manors in Ir-Caul flew their family colors the way a tanner displays a cleanly cured hide from the eaves of his cottage. Sitting in her bedchamber that morning, she'd noted the bold lion crest embroidered on a vibrant scarlet coverlet; the same escutcheon and heraldry as everywhere else in the king's palace—a lion on scarlet belonged to the Relothian family.

In less than an hour's time on the streets of Ir-Caul, she'd found an impressive smooth-stone manor with banners of the Relothian lion hanging from the eaves on either side of a great porch. The stately mansion sat amidst several of equal grandeur, each similarly displaying a coat of arms, but flying their colors beneath the Relothian crest. Only this great house bore the single shield.

Her plan was simple.

She'd always believed that secrets were the only real power men had. But men were bad with that power, because they were bad at keeping secrets. Divulging hidden knowledge, she thought, made men feel superior to those who hadn't secrets of their own. Relothian folk, she guessed, were no different. So, her plan was to steal her way into the company of the king's family. And listen.

Checking the streets, Mira found an opportunity to slip unseen over the wall to the south of the house and drop quietly into the large enclosed gardens. To her surprise, she found the outbuildings and grounds of the city estate rather rustic: a woodblock for chopping wood, a chicken coop, an overgrown hedgerow garden. Amidst the oddly farmlike yard, a fountain statue and basin stood dry, its stony flesh patched with dead, blackened lichen.

Mira crept along the base of the manor, looking and listening for signs of movement. She'd nearly reached the rear entrance when the sound of footsteps approached. She scrambled to the chicken coop and got inside just before the rear manor doors were pulled wide. A man led a woman by the hand down a few stone steps and across the uneven lawn, directly toward her.

She whirled, quickly surveying the coop. Chickens clucked and stirred at her haste, chaff rising thick into the air from the flutter of fowl wings and her own shuffling steps. There was little room to hide, but she opted to duck in behind a wall of wood boxes where the chickens laid their eggs. If anyone came far enough inside the shed, she'd be in plain view. She'd just drawn her swords when the door opened again and the man and woman stepped inside. Then the door closed, leaving them all in the musty dimness.

Over the sound of clucking hens, the strangers began quietly to speak. Mira caught herself smiling at the sound of conspiratorial whispers offered in the company of chickens.

"Who are these strangers? What do they want with the king?" the man asked.

"Don't panic. It's ugly and makes you foolish," the woman replied. She cleared her throat and sniffed. "They're little more than messengers. Someone thinks a personal plea will succeed, where the regent's request failed cycles ago. They'll be leaving soon. The king is sufficiently convinced that his only duty is to his war with Nallan."

"I think you're overconfident," the man said. "Why would they send a Far and a Sedagin? Her kind hasn't been seen outside the shale in ages. They may have suspicions. Perhaps they know we've been filling the traveling army with loyalists."

"Then they will test those suspicious and find them wanting. Or, these messengers will go *missing,* and the king's attention will be drawn back to important matters. Are you prepared to make that so?"

The man didn't reply, and began to pace the small coop. He cocked his head back slightly, and stared upward as he passed directly in front of Mira. She remained perfectly still in the shadows, ready. The man wore a tabard, richly embroidered with the Relothian lion, white on a red field. Chaff and a few feathers clung to his recently oiled boots. His wavy, golden hair touched his shoulders. He reached the wall, pivoted, and walked back, passing before Mira again.

"Already, the boy has spoken to the king a second time." The man paused. "Relothian may listen. The Sedagin doesn't have the practiced words of a politician. He's crossed borders without a military escort. The personal risk will impress the

536 • PETER ORULLIAN

king the more he thinks about it. But more than any of this, the lad bears an emblem no man should hold."

"What emblem?" the woman asked.

In the quiet of the coop, the man spoke as if sharing an omen. "Draethmorte."

Silence stretched for several moments. The feeling in the coop tightened. Even the birds seemed to quiet with the mention of the Quietgiven name.

"Are you sure?" the woman finally asked.

"The king has seen it. He confided this news to us at war council. He believes it speaks well of the regent's chances at Convocation. He may join her if these messengers aren't dealt with." The man's boot leather creaked as he shifted his stance. "Which is why I sent Delos to take care of the Sedagin, and bring the sigil to me."

The woman made a soft, feminine sound of approval. "I should have more confidence in you," she said. The sound of a kiss came and was lost in the noise of the clucking birds. "When you have this sigil, bring it to me. We may leverage it to hasten our trade."

Another kiss, this one longer, louder. "The crown will dress your head nicely, but it's your mind that I love."

"It's the seat beside the throne that you covet," the man answered, and Mira heard the sound of his hands rustling through the folds of her dress. "But," he added, "as long as your maiden box is mine . . ."

The woman made a seductive sound, in which Mira found more humor, mostly because of the place and company it kept—high romance had here in the stench and impertinence of eggbirds. Though some of her mirth grew from understanding that this was an affectation. The man's hands hadn't coaxed this sound from the woman, as he no doubt assumed. Any woman could hear the difference.

The man was a dolt. If these conspirators succeeded in displacing Relothian from the throne, this aspiring king would be dead as soon as his queen could devise the plot. She'd then ascend the throne herself.

But she left all that alone. It was the woman's words that bothered her: . . . *leverage it to hasten our trade.*

"We need to consider what comes next," the man said. "The lad *is* Sedagin. The Right Arm of the Promise won't like hearing of his death. They'll want answers."

The woman laughed. "While you were planning his death, I asked Yenola to become acquainted with this boy. I've learned he's not truly Sedagin. He bears their sword and glove, but they're little more than gifts. And he's taken more interest in my sister than in being a Recityv envoy to the king."

The man made an appreciative sound deep in his throat. "Still, his Sedagin emblems will mean something to the king. As for the Far, her presence gives their entreaties credibility. She won't be easy to kill."

"But you'll find a way, with both of them," the woman said. "I have faith in you."

Mira sat in the shadows of the coop and listened as the man and woman worked at each other like rutting pigs, until the sighs of climax faded beneath the sound of distressed chickens. Then, the coop door opened and shut, leaving her alone again with a choir of clucking eggbirds.

She sat a moment, reflecting on what she'd learned. This deception meant Ir-Caul, even all of Alon'Itol, had been compromised so deeply that it might be useless for Relothian to join a Convocation army.

When she thought it safe, she began to stand. Just then, the door opened again. Lighter, less confident steps shuffled slowly from one chicken box to the next. The delicate sound of eggshells clicking against one another rose as someone collected eggs into a basket.

Mira crouched, ready should this new stranger try to raise a call of alarm. When the old man shuffled around the wall of chicken boxes, he caught sight of her and stopped dead in his tracks. He didn't yell or try to run. He just stared, one hand holding a wicker basket, the other hand holding an egg. Mira thought for a moment that he might try to throw it at her. He didn't. He just remained there, frozen in place.

Eventually she stood, the floorboard beneath her groaning slightly. The birds had quieted some, the coop mostly still. Sunlight fell through a few windows and the cracks where planks had stretched or yawed with time and weather. In the shafts of light, the chaff lazed.

Mira didn't like the thought of needing to kill an old man. He would try to yell with his feeble voice, showing loyalty to his duplicitous masters, and she'd have to cut him down. Just an old man collecting eggs. Once more the feeling in the old chicken coop drew taut, but this time with nuances Mira hated to consider.

Then the man spoke, softly, meaningfully. "Don't let them get away with it," he said. He turned with his basket of eggs and left the coop with his shuffling steps. Sometime later, Mira followed, racing to find Sutter, taking with her the image and memory of the old man, whose entreaty had the sound of both hope and hopelessness.

BLINDING LIGHT FLOODED the room. Sutter could see only a silhouette rushing in, a blade in each hand.

The figure went past him, swords descending in vicious arcs toward his attacker.

The glee in his assailant's throat shifted to surprise, and one great arm brought around the heavy mace toward the sword-bearer that Sutter could now see was Mira.

She got her swords up in time to block the blow, but the force of it slammed her against the thick headboard. She quickly caught her balance, and thrust both her swords into the man's throat. A strangled, gurgling sound bubbled up from the other's gaping maw, as he sliced his own hand trying to remove Mira's blades from his neck.

A moment later, Sutter's attacker fell back onto the bed, his hands still clenched tightly: one around Mira's sword, the other around the Draethmorte's pendant.

Sutter and Mira stood, catching their breath, each massaging their own wounds.

When the large man on Sutter's bed had taken his last breath, they shared a worried look in the light from the door. Sutter had only told one man of the pendant—the king. What did this mean?

Mira went and shut the door. When she returned, she didn't light the bed table lamp, but sat on the edge of the bed. Sutter did the same, and took the sigil from the hand of the dead assassin. With his thumb and finger, he pinched the floating disk at the center of the charm, and spun the outer circle—it spun quickly, smoothly.

In the dark, they each whispered of the things they had discovered that day in the garrison city of Ir-Caul. Mira told him about Gear Master Mick. She also told him the things she'd heard in the king's sister's chicken coop. Sutter shared his conversation with Relothian on the rooftop of the castle, as well as everything about the orphanage and the children's "walks" in new shoes.

He began to think he understood the real reason Vendanj had sent them here. But had the Sheason really thought that a rootdigger and a Far who was losing her inheritance could do anything about it? He couldn't answer that. But he knew one thing: Tomorrow the king would answer the question of betraying Sutter's confidence about the sigil.

• CHAPTER SEVENTY •

Placing

In all of Suffering, the most difficult movement to sing may be the Placing. Being brought into a state of sympathy with the countless who were sent away into the Bourne, it's hard to remain on this side of it.

—A customary reminder offered in memorial of Leiholan who succumb to the third movement of Suffering

WHEN BRAETHEN HAD raised the Blade of Seasons and said *Remember*, the air above the plaza had woven into a vision of the Placing. It had been meant as a reminder of how precarious the balance was between the Eastlands and the world beyond the Pall. It had carried them to the edge of history and shown them real events, shown them races driven into the Bourne.

But for him, it had been more real even than the sounds and smells seen by the throng on the plaza. Braethen . . . had gone there.

THE DARKNESS SLOWLY receded, allowing light to bring the world into focus. Braethen squinted into the distance, the world a patchwork of grey and white under low, menacing clouds. Hilly tracts of land alternated between dimness and swathes of weak sun streaming from cloudbreaks. The smell of rain on dry ground rose, suggesting the dark clouds had stormed recently. And a gentle wind came in occasional fits, leaving stillness in their wake.

Dark shapes in the distance marched in lines or crowds over gently sloping hills, moving north. Braethen's boots ground the dirt as he pivoted and looked to the east, where in the distance other numberless lines of unknown races slogged northward, their heads hung down.

The Placing. Dead gods, I'm in the past. He was there. He was watching races formed by Maldea being sent away into the Bourne.

The air and land and sky held the feeling of betrayal and uncertainty. It pressed in on him as he breathed the warm air and watched from afar as life was sent to a vast prison. Some were sent because their maker had overreached his calling, others because their makers had no faith in their potential. Far from the lines of the migrants, Braethen unwittingly began to walk north, his own steps loud in his ears.

He needed to see these migrants. To know the faces of those condemned to the Bourne. Lost in thought, Braethen crested the top of a hillock and almost stepped on the body of a slender creature lying dead between two blooming sages. When he drew nearer, he saw that a child sat beside the fallen female. The child's tears were dry on its cheeks. It looked up at him, languid, sad, as though weakened by the unanswered cries that had caused its tears.

Both the mother and child had smooth, dark brown skin. The mother's form was tall and slender, and lean, her muscles giving her a comely appearance. Braethen saw no hair to speak of on the creature, and patterns of branding wove around her middle with lettering he couldn't read. Her breasts were exposed, lying full and firm on her narrow chest. Her long arms ended in fingers tipped with short, sharp talons. And he guessed by the shape of her mouth that he'd find large teeth should he peel back her lips.

But her face in death was peaceful, beautiful even.

The child at her side stared up at him with a quizzical look that wasn't hard to interpret: The girl child wanted him to help rouse her mother. The babe's large eyes pleaded, even as they showed some fear of Braethen.

There was no one to help the child. It would fall victim to predators who would come prowling. He couldn't help but imagine the frightened cries of the babe, who wouldn't understand what was happening, wouldn't understand anything save its fear, wouldn't know why its mother continued to sleep.

The mass exodus from the Eastlands had been only a reader's tale to him, a subject for authors, not historians. It meant something entirely different to see it in the face of a child, even if that child belonged to a race created for the sole purpose of fighting man.

Did it know such things? Was hate rooted inside it from its conception?

The girl child made a pleading noise.

There was a mercy he could extend her. But Braethen hadn't the steel inside him for that. And there was no rescue for the babe. He cursed himself for contriving such a dream, biting his tongue to try and wake himself—an old trick his father used to say helped him escape a nightmare.

Braethen's mouth filled with blood. A very complete nightmare, then, and one he wouldn't escape so easily.

He whisked up the babe and began to move as fast as he could over the long, rolling hills toward the moving masses. The babe emitted a weak mewling sound, raising its arms toward its fallen mother. But soon it stopped even that, unable to sustain the effort. The child laid its head against Braethen's chest.

He passed through patches of sun falling from the heavens in great murky slants over the wide expanses of the world below. Ahead, the distant roll of thunder echoed down from dark clouds.

On he went, alternately running, then slowing to a fast walk, catching his breath, then running again. It struck him that saving the child's life appeased only his conscience, leaving death—a slower, more spiritually rotting death—to the bitter world beyond the Veil. But at least he would have done something. Braethen slowly closed the gap between himself and the nearest emigrants trekking away from the Eastlands.

As he reached the line of creatures, the rain set in again. Mild, slow rain. It gave rise to a low hum, rather than the hiss of a downpour. The child in his arms wrapped its tiny fingers more deeply into Braethen's cloak.

He tried to capture the attention of any of the exiled beings, hoping to convince one of them to take the child from him.

"The child's lost its mother," he repeated to one after the other.

His words were of no use. Either they couldn't understand his language, or they were too focused on the struggle of their own departure, most carrying children or belongings of their own. Braethen couldn't even draw their attention. Perhaps this was part of the dream. Perhaps they couldn't see or hear him. He was just a silent observer in this vision.

But he kept trying, moving up the line, noting more races he'd never seen before. Some walked on two legs, some on four or eight. Some appeared to have no eyes. Some had coats of thick fur; others were hairless. Some seemed utterly like himself in appearance and potential. And all wore dour expressions, as though their minds were already caught in the Bourne.

He didn't know how far he'd gone or how long he'd been pleading with these banished creatures to take the child, when he came upon horrors of the Placing that had never appeared in any of the books he'd read.

Braethen stopped, exhausted and defeated. He chuffed into the slow fall of rain. He half-turned, looking up the winding column, and saw that many had broken ranks and stepped out of the line. Some lay on the ground already. As Braethen watched, two sat together, holding short, silent looks with each other, before one took a sharp knife and cut deep the throat of the other, who did nothing to stop it.

Mercy killings.

By the dozens, the hundreds . . . the thousands . . . hosts of these abandoned races had chosen not to go into the exile of the Bourne. As Braethen looked farther into the distance he saw masses lying dark and motionless beside the trail.

It took his mind some time to acknowledge the last horror that littered the plains and hills on either side of this column of slow-moving exiles. Little ones. Like the one in his arms.

Braethen shut his eyes against the images.

He wrapped his arms protectively around the Quiet child and grieved the failed efforts of the abandoning gods that had brought them to this. It left him feeling weak and powerless and wanting just to sit and let the dream run out, pass him by.

He turned to look away from the column of slow-walking creatures, and saw the same shafts of light slanting in long lines through the rain. Muted prisms over distant hills—bits of color in a world of heavy, dark greys. The scent of wet pine needles. An instant later he began running toward those who were killing one another. As he ran, a thought struck him: Do creatures without conscience fear anything enough to kill themselves? Could the Quiet actually dread the Bourne?

Perhaps they're not what we thought.

The child in his arms began to cry, its weak moan pathetic, just as he reached three creatures standing in quiet companionship, each with a knife in hand. Before they could raise their blades to undo one another, he called out.

"No!"

The forcefulness of his cry drew their attention, and the three creatures turned intelligent, somber eyes on him. Two were clearly female, one like the mother of the child he carried; the other thick in the waist, but just as lean, her breasts and loins cinched about with thick brown leather, long hair braided into a queue. The larger female also had horns curling back from just above her ears, and a heavy jaw. The male walked naked, his genitalia hanging down and beyond his concern. His entire body had been raised in brands of varying shapes and designs and writings. A shaven head, likewise, bore the painful art. And his eyes sat deep beneath a thick brow, so that Braethen could scarcely see them.

He came to a stop a few strides away, holding up one hand. "You don't need to do this."

"What do you know about it, grub? You have the fair skin of the makers. We should cut you first." The branded creature drew around to face Braethen squarely, its shoulders impossibly broad.

All he could do was shake his head. "Your own children . . ."

Whatever reason existed for their creation is lost.

Or was it?

A glimmer of logic rose up in the back of his mind. In the waking world, the Quiet had begun to slip their cage. Braethen found himself wondering: Why? Was it really retribution they sought?

Before he could ask anything in this dreadful dream, he sensed a new presence, and jumped when a soft, authoritative voice spoke. "You don't belong here."

Braethen turned, still holding the Quiet child, to see a robed figure standing behind him. The man's countenance showed him great scrutiny, and had a look of power unlike anything he'd ever seen, even in Vendanj.

My skies, this is one of the Framers!

Though in a dream from which he would soon wake, Braethen stood in awe of one who had strode the Tabernacle of the Sky, who had walked *innumerable* worlds.

A mere utterance from this founder could unmake him, and yet Braethen wasn't afraid.

"Couldn't you find another way?" Braethen motioned toward the masses moving in dejected unison into the northern and western quarters of the world.

The god didn't follow Braethen's arm or gaze. He simply continued to stare at him.

"Your sympathies are misspent, Sodalist," the god said. "You will become a danger to those you serve if you cannot discern which side of the line to defend. It might be wise to send you into the Bourne with the others if that's where your heart lies."

Braethen looked down at the baby he carried. When he looked back into the eyes of the god, he said simply, "I suppose my heart is with any who have no voice of their own."

The sound that followed felt like autumn's last gentle wind, as the god sighed. "Oh, my boy. That is a war that can never be won. The voiceless are too many. And their stories tend to break the hearts of brave men."

After careful regard, the god raised a hand toward him. Almost immediately, Braethen's neck began to burn, as though hot coals touched his skin. He could smell charring flesh and struggled to hold the child as the pain grew too intense to bear.

Then it stopped, and he raised his fingers to the spot. He gingerly felt what he recognized without seeing: an incomplete circle; a mark that started thick and strong, but faded as it neared closure at the bottom, never completing the loop. It was a brand like the one given all Quiet being driven into the Bourne.

"You may be their patron, and bear their mark," the god said, his voice soft and sympathetic, like a father finally apologizing after a bout of wrath. "But beware what mercies you show, and when." The other pointed to the Blade of Seasons Braethen still carried.

He looked down at the sword, and back up. "When?" A thought sparked far back in his mind, and a new dread filled his belly.

"You don't understand what you hold, do you, Braethen? You think this is a dream. Look around you. You're not simply seeing the Placing. You're *part* of it now. Don't toy with the power of that weapon. Go back to your time, and remember."

His vision began to rush with images. He dropped to his knees and set the child down. He clung to the Blade of Seasons as darkness wrapped him in its tight embrace and winds tore at his clothes and hair. Winds that carried voices that called after him, entreating him.

It all rose to a deafening scream, howling in his mind. Insecurities he'd once felt when taking hold of this blade were replaced by dreadful knowledge. He hadn't tried to do anything more than remind the people in Recityv of the reality of the Placing, and in a moment he'd traveled there . . . in time.

Then the screaming winds and voices ceased and darkness slowly receded, allowing light to bring the world into focus.

DARKNESS GAVE WAY to light, and Braethen returned from a time in history. In the space of a few short breaths, the world of the Placing became the plaza. But the Blade of Seasons had carried him into the past. It had been more than a vision. It had been *going there*. It left him unsettled, as the present moment crystallized into the satisfied expression of Vendanj, who had come to carry him from the fray that raged around him on the plaza.

The images of the Placing, though, weren't so easily left behind. And on his neck, he still felt the pain of a brand forming an incomplete circle.

· CHAPTER SEVENTY-ONE ·

New Alliances

Anything may be written upon. Anything.

—Statement made by an author witness
during his demonstration of Seriphic glyphs at the first
Succession on Continuity

GRANT CAUGHT HELAINA as she fell from the Wall of Remembrance, an arrow in her chest. Her eyes were closed, her body limp. He laid her gently on the ground as Artixan rushed to her other side, his wrinkled face taut with concern. Behind them, the sound of running footsteps could be heard, and Grant looked around to find a mob of Recityv guards and attendants hurrying toward them to assist the fallen regent.

Grant took hold of Helaina's left hand, and with his free hand, placed his fingers on her neck, feeling for a heartbeat. Nothing. He repositioned his fingers higher, and relaxed. His own heart raced with emotions he'd not felt in a long time. He'd always assumed that a reconciliation would come for them. That he or she would admit to being wrong where Tahn was concerned. That they'd recapture the feelings of the past. Now, he might not ever get to tell her. The swell of grief made it momentarily difficult to concentrate on his task.

Before he could regain his focus, the hand he'd placed inside his own gave a quick squeeze. Then again. *A ruse!* Somehow, she'd arranged this deception. It took a great deal of effort to keep the smile of relief and admiration off his face. *Crafty woman. No wonder I love her.*

Immediately, he could see the benefits of her gambit. They had to maintain the hoax. Grant gave Artixan a knowing look, and the man's brows went up in quick acknowledgment. The Sheason then made a show of putting his hands on her chest and speaking more loudly than he otherwise would have.

Grant leaned down close to her ear. "Lie still," he said. "Don't open your eyes. Keep your chest and belly as motionless as possible."

Then he stood and turned to the mob of attendants closing in. "The regent is dead," he announced. "The regent is dead!" he said again, yelling this time with mock grief and anger. When those racing toward them heard it, they slowed, dumbstruck. "The regent is dead!" Grant cried out a third time, making sure that at least some of those beyond the gate would hear him.

He strode toward the mob, not allowing them to get too close. "Go. Spread the news. I will see to the rest." After some initial hesitation, they went, exiting the courtyard in a loose pack. He wanted the city to know. And one citizen, in particular.

Grant turned and addressed Helaina's Emerit guards, who

still stood nearby. "Get word to every Convocation seat holder: The League has murdered Helaina. Tell them Roth will likely assume the regent's place, but that he will never speak for the Second Promise."

One of the Emerit moved to go around Grant, get to his regent. Grant stepped into his path. "You're the senior man."

The other nodded. "Crawford. And you're no longer Emerit," the man said, with no particular judgment in his voice.

Grant didn't bother establishing a pecking order. "Has Helaina kept an *accounting* of who at Convocation leans her way?" "Accounting" was the Emerit term for gathering information on someone, by any and all means.

"You know I can't answer that." Crawford shifted to look at Helaina, then back to Grant. "But to any Emerit, past or present, it's a silly question."

Grant kept from smiling for the second time in as many minutes. "Get to them. Every one. Don't be seen. Gather them in the Hall of Convocation at dark hour. No lamps. No candles. Escort them in at varying times, and by the rear entry hall. No discussion until I arrive."

The man seemed to weigh the set of instructions, holding an even gaze on Grant. "You will honor what she was trying to do?"

"That was my thought." Grant extended a hand, which Crawford received in the Emerit grip. "Now, how many men do you have in or near this courtyard right now?"

"The regent fell." It seemed at first to be all the answer the man thought necessary. When Grant didn't reply, he added, "Fourteen."

"Take your two closest men with you when you go. Signal the rest to come in close and be seen. I'll need their show of strength."

Crawford didn't hesitate before making a subtle hand signal that only an Emerit would catch. Within moments, several Emerit materialized in the courtyard as if from nowhere.

"They'll do as you ask," Crawford said.

Then he and two of his men left, blending into the world around them and disappearing fast. As Crawford himself passed through the gate at the Wall of Remembrance, Roth and Losol entered, striding directly for the regent.

Right on time. The one citizen Grant had wanted to see, and had known would come fast to verify Helaina's death.

"Here comes Roth," he said, loud enough only for Artixan to hear. The elder Sheason did something more in his ministrations over Helaina, then sat back, sighing with some exasperation and grief. *Good showmanship.*

Before the Ascendant got too close, Grant spoke softly to Vendanj, who had just sat Braethen down against a near wall. "Don't provoke him. I'll take care of this."

Roth and Losol slowed to a stop a few paces away.

"Come to pay your respects? You're a decent murderer to do it." Grant lent his words an edge of ready violence.

"It is a shame," Roth began. "Rest assured I will find the man responsible and hold him accountable."

"Even when you find him wearing League browns? I doubt it." Grant looked down at Helaina.

"You blacken this moment by politicking over the body of a woman so well regarded." Roth's smile was only in his eyes, but it was there.

"I blacken this moment, do I? Interesting. As I imagine your respects are really just to confirm her death. Am I right? Your tender farewell is to be sure you can safely take hold of the regent's seat."

"It's procedural," Roth replied. "Her death must be verified."

It was true, and precisely what Grant had counted on. Especially from Roth. "Maybe with two Sheason, a sodalist, twelve Emerit, and myself, we have enough *procedure* to put an end to you and your dog."

"That would be my preference," Vendanj said, his face grim with anger.

Behind Vendanj, Braethen got to his feet and came to stand beside him.

Roth waved a dismissive hand. "I would have thought you'd seen enough of my friend here to think twice about that. And an astute man would know that if I'd followed you here to do anything but verify the regent's death, I'd have come with more help." He made another dismissive gesture. "Besides, Helaina would want the city to move on with strong leadership. You know that's true."

"No arrogance on your part in that," Braethen mocked. "League politics seems to be: 'Give the people what they think they need, not what they truly need.'"

Roth turned toward Braethen. "You've recently lost your leader, as well, haven't you? Dangerous company you keep." Then he looked back at Grant. "Are we going to have sharp banter all morning? Or can I see to my duty as acting regent? I won't make any promises about what comes next." He eyed both Vendanj and Artixan. "But I'll promise to withdraw peacefully after saying my own good-byes to Helaina."

"The regent's seat is filled by votes, you'll remember. Helaina's death guarantees you nothing." Grant looked over his shoulder, not at Helaina but at Artixan, who nodded. "Have your graver's moment," he said, and stepped aside.

Roth settled to one knee beside her. He made a nice show of looking sad and thoughtful. He placed a hand on her wrist in a tender gesture, establishing a physical connection as he said his farewells. Grant knew the man was feeling for a pulse. Losol had positioned himself closer to the body, as well. But he seemed more intent on watching Grant and the others during Roth's inspection than in making an inspection of his own.

The moment became long. Grant could only hope that Artixan had managed some artful piece of rendering.

The Ascendant remained hunched over Helaina for an uncomfortable amount of time. At one point he drew out a knife and eased it under her nose, watching its polished flat side for the fogging of breath.

Finally, he stood back up. "I'll arrange for a ceremony befitting her life and station."

Grant shook his head. "That's *my* responsibility."

"You're not a citizen here," Roth reminded him. "And it's only right that the Council see to the disposition of her affairs."

"Check your records," Grant countered. "I'm her husband. If you want to take it to Judicature, fine with me. I'll wager the law still grants first rights to family, even over friends of state."

It was an unassailable legal position, and Roth's silence was the bristling kind—he knew he'd lost this niggling point. It would have been his chance to pretend great sorrow and leverage his false esteem in front of Recityv to raise his own image.

Grant sensed that Roth hated losing a battle of position as much as one of bone and steel—maybe more. So he softened it for him. "She wanted a small ceremony. Something modest. Nothing that would . . . excite people."

"Very well. I'll trust your decorum," Roth said, and bowed gracefully, insultingly.

Before taking his leave, he gave both Artixan and Vendanj long looks. "These two are criminals. The new law is clear on what to do about them."

Grant looked first at the two Sheason, then at Braethen, then at the twelve Emerit now standing in clear sight. Finally, he turned his gaze back to Roth and raised his eyebrows.

"I see. A numbers game." Roth smiled. "I could summon twice as many with a single call."

"And what of your promise to withdraw?" Grant laughed mockingly. "Forgive me, I forgot who I was talking to."

Surprisingly, Roth laughed with him. "As did I, a man who betrayed this fine dead woman, and—if my memory isn't failing—is also criminally back in Recityv. Wasn't the standing order death, if you ever returned here?"

Grant ignored that. "You'd need to triple us, don't you think? Or are the Emerit softer than I remember? And let's assume you do just that. You might kill us all." He paused for effect. "But not before you're dead, too." Grant then stepped close to the Ascendant, and spoke conspiratorially. "I'll tell you what. Why don't you trust these two criminals to me. I'll see they're rightly punished. And that way, you can maintain your dignity as you march the hell out of my sight."

Roth smiled. It looked genuine, too. He seemed to be enjoying their game. With a slight nod, he turned and left. His dog, Losol, gave them each a warning look before following.

Grant waited until the courtyard had cleared, then turned

to Vendanj and Braethen. "Get to A'Garlen. Bring him back
here as quickly as you can. Watch that you're not followed.
Artixan and I will see to Helaina. We'll be in the narrow
room."

Vendanj was nodding, but watching Artixan as the older
Sheason reversed some rendering action he'd performed just
before Roth arrived. Vendanj's face showed instant understanding, and he left immediately, the sodalist at his side.

Grant knelt again near Helaina. Word of her death would
spread. Many, too, had seen her fall after being shot with the
arrow. *Good,* he thought.

He slid his arms beneath her, whispering as he did so,
"Keep your body limp."

She was light to carry. And together, he and Artixan moved
quickly out of the courtyard and into the halls of Solath
Mahnus. Within the cool confines of Recityv's ruling courts,
the activity was frenetic. Many, moving past them, lifted their
hands to their mouths in shock and horror. Others looked
furtively at them. Still others grew solemn, bowing their
heads as they moved on to their own private tasks.

Tumult reigned, but Grant paid it no mind, leading Artixan
into hallways less traveled. In a quiet part of the palace,
tucked in amid the servants' quarters, he entered a dingy,
vacant room. He angled to the left wall and fingered a release
behind a decrepit closet. The closet swung out, and Grant led
Artixan into a long, narrow room with no other entrance and
no windows. After laying Helaina on the bed, he closed the
secret portal, lit a lamp, and returned to her side.

"Can you hear me?" he asked.

Helaina nodded almost imperceptibly.

"You can open your eyes," he said.

When Helaina did so, his emotions surged—admiration,
gladness, love. He regretted again his many years of exile.

Her face, on the other hand, twisted with pain. She clasped
her hands and began to rub them.

"Are you all right?"

"My bones hurt," she said, and shook her fingers.

"How long have you been planning this?" he asked, shaking his head and smiling.

"About twenty years," she said, and gave a small laugh. She pulled the arrow free from her chest. "Banded leather with an iron backplate, and sewn with fifty small pouches filled with sheep's blood."

"It was my design, remember?" Grant replied.

"I liked the idea of the irony, should you return from exile with revenge on your mind." She dropped the arrow on the floor. "And it only works if my archer doesn't miss. Which he never does." She smiled.

"You thought I'd come back to kill you? You know me better than that."

She shrugged. "A smart woman learns to ignore her instincts where men are concerned. Anyway, there's rarely harm in preparation."

"And you put this preparation into play when Roth went madhouse with the Civilization Order," Grant surmised. "What's next?" He honestly couldn't wait to hear it. He remembered again that more than her physical beauty—which was nothing to blink at, even now—he reveled in the beauty of her mind. She could outmaneuver a seer.

She looked at Artixan. "How did you convince Roth I was dead?"

The elder Sheason smiled with a gleam of mischievousness. "I dropped you into a kind of sleep. Let even your heart rest for a few moments. It's tricky work, but I'm no new pony."

Helaina chuckled warmly. "That was a gap in my plan. I should have considered that Roth would want to know for himself." She then spoke to both of them. "My 'death' gives us an opportunity." She shifted her position, sitting up. "Alive, I would have had to direct Van Steward to mount civil action against the League."

"You mean civil war," Grant clarified, not wanting anyone deceived about what was happening in the streets of Recityv.

"Which by itself would be challenging," she affirmed. "Van Steward is loyal to me, but by law he serves the High Council, which Roth now controls. Or will."

"Well, we'll see," Grant said. "But go on."

"Van Steward would fight the tide of civil unrest that the

554 • PETER ORULLIAN

League has fostered. And the High Council would be split, likely disbanded, and the rule of law in Recityv destroyed. All of which would lead to more death, and at a time when we have other concerns."

"But if you were thought to be dead," Grant offered, picking up the logic, "Recityv could remain whole, even if under the rule of the Ascendant and his League."

She nodded. "If I'm gone, the Council can continue. Van Steward will still have his army to protect the people. And more importantly, he'll remain close to Roth, which will be critical to us later on. We'll also have public sympathy on our side. My death and all." She smiled demurely at her own deception. "That sentiment will temper Recityv's optimism about the Ascendant's regency."

"Your martyrdom becomes our best ally. Clever." He showed a thin smile.

"'Martyrdom' is a bit strong, but yes, while we see to other things," she conceded.

"What other things?" he asked.

"The Mor Nation Refrains. I'll go and petition for their use." She paused, nodding as if to convince herself it was possible. "Now's the time. I sent a letter, but there's been no response. And we obviously can't wait here any longer. I believe I need to go there, personally. And if I'm successful, I'll renew a very old alliance." She nodded at her own plan. "One that should make reclaiming my regent seat rather academic."

"*If* the Council remains intact," Grant argued. "And you're right when you say that it must. Which is why I've invited A'Garlen here."

"Thinking ahead." She gave him one of her trusting looks. "We make a good team when we share the same goal."

Another surge of old emotion filled him. He remembered what it had been like—even before they'd shared the pleasure of each other's bodies—when they'd gotten into this kind of rhythm. Having her trust gave him courage. He guessed it was the same for most men with women they loved.

"Tell me," she asked, "why are we sharing my death with A'Garlen?"

Grant gave her a look as though it should be obvious. "The man's a walking disruption. If he attends the Council while you're gone—"

"Walking disruption," came a growly voice from behind them, "can I use that?"

They turned to see Vendanj and Braethen leading the old author into the secret bedchamber. A'Garlen puttered forward, looking generally put out to be asked to do anything.

Grant smiled. "The rest of the Council, in their ignorance, will continue doing what they've been doing. That'll suit Roth. A few members will vote against him, but they know he controls the majority, so no one's in any real danger. Roth will likely use the fact that there's disagreement as evidence of healthy governance."

Helaina jumped ahead of him. "But Author Garlen tips the scales in Council votes. And he'd vote against Roth just to cause the man distress." She shifted to watch the old author amble close. "Better he not occupy his Council seat. Otherwise, Roth might just dispense with the Council altogether. Or do something to Garlen. And we're going to need both the Council and Garlen after our visit to the Mor nations. That the size of it?"

"That's the size of it," Grant confirmed, giving Helaina a wide grin.

"Do I get one of those leathery smiles?" A'Garlen asked Grant, coming near Helaina on the other side of the bed.

"Not if I have to read one of your damned stories in exchange," Grant replied, keeping his smile on. It was good to see the old storyteller.

The author shot back a wicked grin. "You don't have to repeat your little speech," he said, waving dismissive fingers at Grant. "I'll avoid the High Council parties. But I'm afraid the Ascendant may not leave me be, even so."

Grant gave the author a close look. "Why is that?"

"Roth came to see me recently," said Garlen, making it sound storylike. "Looking for new friends, he was. Wanted my vote. But there's nothing to leverage against me, really, so I sent him away feeling sorry for himself."

"Sorry?" Grant asked.

"Well, that's the thing, see. When he came knocking, he made me mad, and I accidentally showed him a bit of why he'd better stop trying to coerce me." The old man's wiry eyebrows rose, lifting his forehead into a series of deep grooves. He seemed to be waiting for Grant to deduce . . .

"You wrote the glyphs," Grant said, knowing there could be no other answer.

"That I did, my boy. Just happened." He mimed doing so again here, weaving his hand through the air. "Then I warned him not to awaken that old power or this old codger against him. But, if I know the Ascendant, he'll be looking for a way to put it to his advantage." A'Garlen took Helaina's hand in his knobby fingers. "But don't you fear that, Anais. It can't be coerced, nor am I aware of any author who possesses the ability who would use it to help the League."

"That's a broad assumption, my friend." Grant looked over at Vendanj to get his sense of this news. The Sheason's brow was drawn tight, as though he was thinking through the consequences of this new revelation.

Braethen stepped closer, getting the author's attention. "I don't know if they're true or not, but I've read accounts of authors who practice the Seriphic craft, and who might actually be sympathetic to Roth. They're a loosely aligned set of authors, whose stories are grim tales with only one kind of audience. After starving for a reception of their words that never comes, these authors fall to other uses of their gifts." He paused, an almost comic expression of realization on his face. "It's the same sect of authors willing to do forgery . . . like E'Sau's diary."

A'Garlen studied the sodalist. "By the rotten gods, boy, do you have an answer for everything?" He glared a bit at Braethen, then turned back to Helaina. "Yes, there are rumors of these story hobbyists. But they are *not* authors. Their craft has taken them down another road. Don't lump me in with those bastards."

The old growler wasn't seeing Grant's point. "But you've shown Roth it's possible," Grant said, irritated. "Now he'll be searching for anyone willing to use it in his service. Old man, your anger makes you a damn fool."

"That's how anger works. Besides, didn't you hear our resident know-everything? Roth likely has them in his employ, and just doesn't know it yet." Garlen tapped his lip, nodding in concession. "But perhaps I was a bit rash at that. Still, what's done is done. About your strategy, though. I'll tell the Ascendant that the authors won't sit on his Council. That we object to his whole damn League. I don't have to affect *that* emotion. Our absence means he doesn't have to worry about my vote canceling out the vote of one of his cronies. That ought to suit him just fine. Then, you let me know when you're ready for me, and I'll drag myself back to Solath Mahnus again to see what I can do to help. Good enough?"

"No, Garlen, not good enough," Vendanj said. He went around the bed to stand near the old author, towering over him. "The Seriphic craft, dimensional inscriptions on the air. It's a rare use of glyphs, and one we may need before this is all over."

"Ah, damn," A'Garlen groaned. "Means you need some words for free, doesn't it?" This time, though, the old author grinned. "Vendanj, you, and maybe leathery over there, are probably the only two men I know who are as prickly as I am. That'll buy you a few."

Vendanj began to smile in return. "Not just yours," he added. "We'll need an army of scribblers with Seriphic talents."

"It'll be an army of a handful, my boy. It's about as rare as those who sing Suffering. But I'll go to work finding them. I suppose it'll get me down from my writing perch and out on the roads again. I don't think I'll mind that, actually."

Vendanj's smile sweetened into appreciation. "Thank you, Garlen."

"That leaves Convocation," Helaina said, sounding suddenly more magisterial. "I heard you give some direction on that." She looked at Grant, waiting.

"The Convocation is lost," Grant said bluntly. "In terms of what you'd hoped for, anyway. If it continues in full, Roth will use it to more deeply secure his hold on those nations who've come."

"But there were many who pledged support—"

"They're being contacted. I'll meet them tonight, and have their oaths to stand ready for when they're needed."

Helaina seemed satisfied. "Then we should begin preparations to leave."

Grant heard the "we" in her statement. "I'll need to stay with Vendanj. We leave soon for Estem Salo to meet Tahn and the others."

"You will take me to the Mors," Helaina stated matter-of-factly. "I'll need the strongest, most able guides. Plus, I'll want men I can trust. We don't know how the Mor nations will respond to my arrival. There may be old resentments."

"Helaina—" Grant started to say.

"It's decided," the regent snapped. "I see nothing in my request that violates your precious *Charter*. So unless you're also lawless, there's nothing more to discuss."

Vendanj was looking intently at Grant. "We must have the Refrains. And Helaina may be the only one who can convince the Mors that's true. It's critical she arrive there safely. We'll be fine getting to Estem Salo. And you know I'll watch after Tahn."

Grant saw the wisdom in it. "Fair enough. We should leave today."

"I have one other that I'll want to accompany us," Helaina said.

Before Grant could ask who it was she wished to take, Vendanj was dashing toward the door.

"What is it?" Grant asked, drawing his sword.

The Sheason reached the door, yanked it open, and turned back, impatient. "Your plan's a good one. But it also means Roth will continue to execute the expanded Civilization Order." Vendanj disappeared through the door, pulling it shut behind him more loudly than Grant would have liked.

But the Sheason hadn't needed to explain further. Like sheep awaiting slaughter, some Sheason were being held in the depths below Solath Mahnus. *Rolen.*

CHAPTER SEVENTY-TWO

Mending

Having the power to heal, or save, doesn't mean you should. That kind of singing has particular consequences. But so does keeping quiet.

—"The Sound of Silence," a discourse on Resonance
taught during the study of absolute sound

T HE QUIET LIGHT of morning bathed the luthier workshop. The lutherie occupied a place on the eastern side of Descant, high up on the cathedral's seventh story. Windows five times Wendra's height dominated the eastern wall. The slow drifting of motes in the slanted sunlight lent a kind of peaceful feeling to the quiet. The smell of milled wood and hand tools hung in the air.

She eased into the workshop, noting tables and racks laden with broken instruments. They appeared to be lined up awaiting the expert hand of a craftsman to repair them—violins with broken necks, lutes with cracked facings, drums with split heads, horns with crimped or missing valves.

As she moved deeper into the domain of Descant's master luthier, she heard the sound of something softly scraping. A moment later she came to find Belamae seated at a workbench, bathed in the warm light from the windows, and bent over a broken violin. She had rarely seen the Maesteri so relaxed. It puzzled her, given what she'd heard was happening not far away in the city.

"Come have a seat," he said, continuing to work at the instrument.

Wendra took a seat beside him, facing the great windows. Up close, and maybe because of the light, he looked weaker than she'd ever seen him. His kerchief was on the other side from her, sitting atop the workbench. She could see blood on it.

For now, though, he breathed easy. And she had questions. She started to inquire twice before realizing there was no delicate way to ask why he sat here while others might be dying. "Have you heard there's fighting on the plaza?"

He slid a handwritten note across the workbench and left it for her to read. It was a letter from the regent, asking Belamae not to be distracted by political upheavals or even open conflict. Helaina wrote of the importance of the Song of Suffering and Belamae's focus on training Leiholan and keeping them safe. She wrote that the Song was more important than politics. That it must endure. That he should stay put. Him and all those at Descant.

Wendra finished reading the letter and looked up at him. "But how can we sit here when there are people who could use our help? Some of them may be my friends."

She thought she understood enough about her song now that she could focus it, not harm anyone she didn't mean to harm.

"Helaina's my friend," he replied, still working at the broken violin. "I'll respect her wishes. In part because she's my regent. But mostly, because she's right. If we lost one Leiholan trying to defend Helaina's office, the Song would be harder to maintain. We can't have that. A great many more than those here in Recityv depend on us to sing Suffering."

In his own way, he was telling her she shouldn't go, that she wasn't ready. If she went, her song might harm those she meant to help, despite all she'd learned. For the moment, she let the idea go.

She took a long breath, taking in the calm of Belamae's warmly lit lutherie. She guessed he'd chosen to be in this place for that feeling of peace, given what was happening in the city.

"I remember you like to repair instruments," she asked, hoping for a bit of that peace herself.

"And I'm a fair hand at it," he replied. "But the real gift belonged to Divad, *my* Maesteri. He could coax an artistry from wood like no other."

She looked around, and couldn't see any instruments that appeared to be being built new. "Did he only do repair work?"

"No, of course not. But older instruments have known the touch of musicians, have played their share of music. The wood is tempered by practice and song. They've served us well. And so Divad took special pride in their restoration." Belamae smiled. "I'm glad he did. And I honor that a little by doing the same."

Wendra sensed a personal story in Belamae's words, but let it lie.

"I suppose I'm responsible for some of these here," she said, looking around.

Belamae continued to work at the violin. "No matter. You're not the first Souden to break an instrument." He stopped then, staring down into the maple shavings on the table before him. "I come here to remind myself that song can be restored. That few things are ever broken beyond repair. An encouraging thought, don't you think?"

She breathed deep, taking in the smell of the workshop. "It reminds me of my father. The man never gave up on a tool. He'd spend more time repairing a spade than it would take to make a new one."

"Just so," Belamae said with a pleased tone.

"Is that the lesson for today? Patience? Repairing what's broken?"

"*Impatient* to begin, are we?" He grinned at her.

She smiled wryly back at him.

"In part, yes," he finally admitted. "This Leiholan gift, Wendra, is often misconstrued as one that only *creates*. And please understand that it does. But a song is usually needed to amend something that has gone wrong. Or it bolsters something that needs bolstering."

"Like Suffering," she said.

"Just so. A musician might create for himself something from whole cloth, for the sake of the sound. It pleases him to do it. And that song may even serve a need." Belamae began to inspect the finished back piece of the violin. "But more often, a song is asked for because there's a loss or deficit that needs to be repaid. Or someone needs added strength or understanding. A song will fill the hole inside a man better than anything else ever will. Better than food. Better than prestige. And certainly better than coin. The thing that best stands him up when he'd rather remain down is a song."

"You sound a bit like Balatin about it." She put a hand on his shoulder.

"Oh, Anais. I'm old enough to understand how fanciful and sentimental all this sounds. But I'm also old enough to know it's true." He shrugged. "I've seen it too often to lie about. You know it, too. First time we met, you were in need of a song to make you well, remember?"

Wendra thought back, feeling like her fever in the cave beneath the High Plains was a lifetime ago. "I remember."

The smell of freshly shaved maple lingered around them as Belamae worked for a few more moments at the violin. Sitting there, watching him, easy contentment distilled inside her—something she hadn't known for a very long time. No thought intruded beyond the present—nothing of what she'd done, hadn't done, or should do. Nothing of the conflicts beyond Descant walls. Aware of this small, rare peace, she remained silent, simply observing, until Belamae spoke.

"But of course there's more to learn. Always more." He put the small wood chisel aside, and picked up a length of gut. As he began stringing the violin, he explained, "There are two types of song, Wendra. Or maybe it is more helpful to say there are two ways your song can have effect. Have you discovered these yet?"

She had a sense of them. Her own song had always been aimed at someone. But she'd thought often about the Song of Suffering, which was meant to influence something far away, on the other side of the Eastlands. The Veil.

He wound the gut string on its peg, and started to thread the second. "The first we call audala, audible song. It's a song that can persuade its listener, move him, even destroy him. But it must be heard."

"Song sung by Lacunae singers," Wendra said, matching the song type to the vocalist type.

"Just so," Belamae replied, smiling. "Leiholan can sing it, too, of course. Its resonance is the sound as it's interpreted by the one who hears it. That sound can touch deep inside.

And yet, this type of song is lost on inanimate things, or those who cannot hear it."

"Including one who is deaf," she guessed.

"That's right. And we'll talk about shoarden, who sacrifice their hearing to protect Lacunae. But for today, let's speak about a second type of song, one that doesn't need to be heard to have effect. We call it 'absolute sound,' or 'absolute song,' if you'd prefer. This song needs no listener, no interpreter. This is the music that can touch the sound or vibration that exists in all things, even at a great distance. It takes immense skill, but the resonance isn't bound by place."

"That's how Suffering strengthens the Veil, then."

He nodded and strung the third length of gut. "As a singer, you learn how to manipulate your voice and mouth and body to create harmonics and resonance. But knowing how the one who *hears* your song will receive it, how to produce resonance in *him*? This is the path to attunement, and becoming Leiholan."

"But we saw Telaya stir the crowd at Rafters. And she's not Leiholan." Wendra picked up the next length of gut string and handed it to Belamae.

He paused in his stringing of the violin to look at her. "Those weren't trivial feelings she caused in the tavern crowd, but they weren't brought about by true knowledge. A Leiholan possesses the capacity to *deliberately feel* and understand the resonant places inside another. And once she understands these, the song she offers is an *intentional* resonance. What you did last night, Wendra, was find such a place inside each of those who heard you. It was possible because some things resonate with us all."

"Like Suffering," she said again.

Belamae nodded, and went on stringing the violin for a moment. He then abruptly set the violin aside, and reached to his left, where a plate scattered with sand sat on the workbench. He placed it at the edge of the table between them, and promptly produced a violin bow. He began drawing the bow up and down on the side of the plate. It made no musical sound. But the sand atop it jounced and formed itself into distinct patterns.

"Sound vibration can rearrange physical things," the Maesteri explained. "Like this plate, which has signatures of its own. When touched by external resonances, it causes change. Here we see it in the patterns formed by the sand." He leveled a professorial gaze at her. "What else does this little demonstration teach us?"

Wendra leaned in conspiratorially. "The bow made no sound, but had effect anyway. So, I'm guessing you have a point about absolute sound."

Belamae grinned, and tapped her chin with the violin bow. "Just so. And it also suggests an entire course of study on inaudible sound. But that's another topic that will come much later in your training."

"I could be here a while," she said, smiling back.

"I hope so, my girl." He studied her, as one deciding if he should share something. "Late last night, Ian was silenced in the Chamber of Anthems."

She'd only met Ian once. He had a wry sense of humor for a Leiholan. "Silenced?"

"Not dead," Belamae added. "But Suffering echoed back at him in some way I can't explain. He still breathes, but he stares ahead vacantly as if he would like to *stop* breathing. He doesn't hear anyone or anything. His voice is gone. I don't know if I can restore it."

"But how?"

"Something is happening. Getting closer." He shook his head. "So *many* things are happening and getting closer."

He put the bow aside, and strung the last line of gut on the violin, tightening and tuning the full set. He hummed several notes, tuning to his own pitches until he had the instrument sounding the way he liked. Then he strummed it. Wendra watched a gratified expression touch his face.

Then, beyond him, lying on the workbench, she noticed another broken instrument. From the look of pieces and splinters, she guessed it had been a mandola. "Is it too broken to fix?"

Belamae didn't bother to follow her gaze. "With the right touch, anything—or very close to it—can be repaired, Wendra. It's just that . . . sometimes it's better that we choose not to."

She turned her stare on him. "Do you speak of the instrument or the musician?"

He took an audible breath in the silence of the lutherie. "Why do you think they're not the same?"

He handed her the violin. "What you did in the performance tavern. It was the sound of spirit striking the air and declaring a person's whole wish. And the wishes of all those present. A luthier's touch will mend a broken violin. A musician's hand will play it. Like both, a Leiholan will mend and play the souls of those she sings to . . . as you did in a drinking house in Recityv's slum last night. Never forget that. It's a finer resonance you sang there, Wendra, than I've ever heard you sing." He gave a slight grin before adding, "Dark as it was.

"And to bring our conversation full circle, this is the power of song I'm training in you. You're making fine progress, but you've still much to learn." He showed her a patient smile. "If you'd gone to the square today, joined the fight, I don't think you'd have been able to keep control of your song. Not yet. Not in open conflict. And you might well have harmed those you meant to defend. Your song is yet more Lacunae than Leiholan. Though you're on the path, my girl."

She wanted to argue with Belamae, but she knew he was right.

He looked almost frail in that moment. But he put his hand over hers with fatherly warmth. "And here's the last of today's lesson. I'm suffering. Oh yes, my body is failing. I'll go to my earth soon. But that's not what I mean." He tapped the regent's note, which still lay on the bench before them. "While I respect Helaina's wishes, I've had word . . . she has fallen . . ."

The news hit Wendra like a forge hammer in the chest. "What? When?"

Belamae shook his head in a slow, disbelieving motion, his face drawn in grief. "My girl, would you sing something to me? Something inside?"

His gaze was far away, as if he'd left her here, and could add nothing to explain his need. But she understood it well enough. And began to hum something in a sweet, low tone. *Something inside.*

She sought her own grief over things lost—that hollow

feeling left when someone you care for is taken away. She gave that feeling voice, not rushing, adding her every tenderness and empathy. She shared his suffering, gilding it with the assurance of better days that the grieving find hard to see.

She sang a full hour, filling the warm, sunlit lutherie with gentle sound. She stopped only when Belamae's hand tightened on her own.

"Thank you," he said, and smiled sadly. "It's not a lesson I'd planned, but it may be the most important one you'll learn . . . for that day when you sing the Song."

She narrowed her eyes in question.

"The Song of Suffering, my girl, is to a large extent about remembering the pain and injustice of those who were sent into the Bourne." He took a long breath. "The Song is sung every minute of every day, and those who sing it witness the very real suffering of those who went to that place. Don't misunderstand me," he said, raising a finger again. "It's a vital protection to maintain the Veil. But it doesn't make watching suffering any easier. The Leiholan draws on her own pains, and resonates with a thousand more. It's not easy. And it will change you." His smile brightened a shade. "For the better," he added.

She returned his smile, her thoughts beginning to pound an urgent rhythm.

My own pains? My lost child. Penit. And a thousand others lost to the godsdamned Bourne—taken there by traders.

And Suffering is changing.

Those who sing it are dying.

What Quiet pain is causing all this?

She could already feel a choice coming. Sometime soon. Belamae had said it would be selfish to consider leaving. He'd said she was needed here, to sing Suffering. She believed that was true. But if she stayed, and if she made the Veil stronger, wasn't she also making it harder to escape for those who'd been captured and taken into the Bourne? For anyone to try to rescue them? And on the other hand, wasn't it possible that if she went there, she might be able to use her song to help those same slaves? Get them out?

Maybe in some ways, the darkness in her song was better suited to that.

When she looked again into his eyes, he seemed to know her thoughts. "Wendra, I go to my earth soon. And I'm scared."

"Belamae—"

"I'm scared that when I leave this world, everything I've done here," he gestured high, to indicate Descant, "will fall apart. Fade. It's my life's work, you see. And I don't know who will replace me. I don't know who will hold it all together when I'm gone." He smiled with some regret. "I'd rather hoped it might be you."

Her heart slammed in her chest, as she realized his hope and her own desires might never meet. He must have seen that, too. His face slackened, and something bright disappeared from his eyes.

Disappointing him hurt. She didn't want to do that. And after a short moment, her mind latched onto a new idea. She gently took his hand in hers, gathered him in an intent gaze, and started again to sing. She found the wellness in her own heart and lungs and muscle and bone. She let her melody weave until she knew the resonance of her own health, and then she reached out to him. She let the perfect sound of well-being and vigor flow, until she'd identified the last vestiges of real health inside him, and then she let go.

With the love she felt for Belamae, she sang with all the strength she possessed. There was deep sickness in him. It had laid hold of his organs, not just his breathing. It was like a long-moored ship rife with barnacles. She felt its every surface and edge. But to the tissue and functions of his body she lent a song of restoration like nothing she'd ever sung or heard before. It wove gentle sweeps with the strongest dysphonic progressions she'd ever sung.

At times the song drew down to something low and slow. But more often it ascended and filled up all the space in the lutherie. She fought it. She fought his sickness with her song. She'd never resonated so intensely. There was a euphoric feeling in it. She embraced that feeling. That sound. And she sang the heart of him.

Then, sometime later . . . she simply stopped.

His eyes were wide and bright. In the warm sun of his lutherie, Belamae looked a different man.

"My dear girl . . . My. Dear. Girl!" He laughed deep in his chest and his belly, as if testing this thing she'd done. He was the same silver-haired elder Maesteri, but by gods, he had the heart and lungs of a man twenty years his junior. She could see it in him.

He took great deep breaths like a man suddenly freed from prison. And after the shock of it was gone, they laughed together. Loud and long they laughed, testing this new breath inside him. And when the laughter died to smiles, she could see in his eyes that he still hoped she'd stay. But there was relief, too, as if to say he could now manage if she did not.

There was still a decision to be made. And questions, besides. But she let those slip away. For now, she relaxed into the easy comfort of Belamae's company and the warmth of his lutherie, and tried to ignore a new feeling. The deep kind. The kind that whispered something had changed in her, as it always did when she resonated with someone.

· CHAPTER SEVENTY-THREE ·

A Succession Team

This inquiry is an embarassment to the Grove. If the argument for Continuity were defensible, then it wouldn't matter if a member of the Succession team was sharing her team's approach in advance of the discourse theaters.

—Statement taken during the probe that followed
the failure of Nanjesho Alanes's argument for
Continuity and her subsequent death

THOUSANDS OF DEAD speckle-backed sparrows, as well as several field hawks and starlings, littered the fields for as far as Tahn could see.

"What happened here?" he heard himself ask, surveying the strange sight in the failing light of day.

Polaema's brows went up. "We were hoping you might tell us." She paused. "It doesn't feel coincidental that it happens at the same time you return to the Grove."

"Hail? High winds?"

Rithy shook her head and squatted, taking a closer look at the nearest sparrow. "Hard to say how long they've been here," she said.

"We've had no storms for nearly the cycle of the first moon," Polaema added. "This is not the work of weather."

"Could it be the work of the Quiet?" Tahn asked, speaking softly and mostly to himself.

"To what end?" Polaema questioned. "The destruction of flocks of birds seems a poor use of their talents. Even as a warning. No, I don't think that's our answer."

Tahn hadn't meant to suggest the Quiet as a direct cause. But he couldn't help the feeling that what he saw here bore some relation to his larger worries.

"It's not a native bird to this region," he said, beginning to reason it out. "So, they were migrating."

"Exhaustion then," Rithy said.

"Except there are field hawks and starlings," Polaema pointed out.

Rithy stood up, her eyes seeming to calculate the sheer number of fallen birds. "Could they have been fighting? Or perhaps there was an eruption of dry lightning?"

Polaema's eyes narrowed in concentrated thought.

But Tahn dismissed these explanations quickly. He could see no blood. And the stretch of land covered with the fallen birds appeared too broad for a lightning strike to have brought down such a flock.

The shadows of dusk lengthened until darkness took all. And gradually, Tahn's attention turned east, then to the northern sky. Far against the horizon a faint luminous red glow could be seen. He studied it a moment, curious. Then a flash of anxiety and insight tore through him. *Lunar eclipse!* He sprinted away, heading back toward the Grove. He scarcely heard the voices calling after him.

BY THE TIME Tahn reached the College of Astronomy, Rithy had caught up to him. Shouts of protest followed them as they swept past sentries who sat at registry tables beside two sets of doors. Far behind they heard Savant Polaema silencing these evening clerks as she followed Tahn and Rithy into the annals halls. In the main room, they found a young physicist, a somewhat older philosophy student, and a cosmologist who looked young *and* old, depending on how the light caught her. They all seemed to have just arrived.

They were easily identified by the insignias embroidered on their overcloaks. Black thread on black cloth showed the symbol for the colleges, in the traditional subtlety. For physics, a gear wheel with eight outer teeth. Sometimes, Tahn knew, the emblem took on the vague form of the sun—a nod to celestial mechanics.

The philosophy sigil was a perfect circle with a single line vertically bisecting it and running a finger's width above and below the circumference. Some said it signified the intersection of the finite with the infinite, of recurrence with endless possibility. Some saw the rotating world and horizon, with night on one side and day on the other. And linguists were fond of a letter conflation: *I* for *istola* from the Divadian root tongue, meaning "simplicity" or "indivisible"; and *O* for *odanes* from the sister tongue, Itolous, a dead language, the word meaning "at last" or "found in the end."

Cosmology had, perhaps, the oldest insignia of them all—a swooping line that wove in and around itself to make what appeared vaguely like a three-petal flower. It was the cipher in it that made it uniquely cosmological. Most often, the symbol was rendered dimensionally, showing how the delicately curving line or tube wound itself into a loose knot. It could be hypnotizing to look at.

The three of them quickly jumped to their feet. Tahn didn't need to ask why they were here. Rithy had obviously been at work hand-selecting the members of each college who would help them. That was the way of Succession. He might have some core ideas, and even have a knack for finding the seams in arguments. But he'd been away a while. He would be glad of the critical thought from each college as they tried to prove Continuity this time. Prove Resonance. And this would be their core Succession team.

"You invite them?" he said, smiling.

"We were planning to come back here after showing you the birds and introducing you, yes." She shook her head, and returned his smile. "Figured you'd want to get started tonight. Just didn't figure on an evening sprint."

Tahn looked at each of these new additions and nodded greetings. Then he got moving again, his team falling in behind him as they leapt up the main stairway and onto the second floor: the almanac library. Its aisles and rows shaked like a warren fashioned of bookshelves.

They stood there, lightly panting. Soon they heard Polaema lumbering up the stairs behind them. She reached the second story, and swept out in front of them.

"What is it, Tahn?" she said, gasping.

"Commonalities," he said, his own breathing already settling into a natural rhythm.

Then he turned to his Succession team. "Remember one thing. Everything we do. Every hour of research. Every word you read. Every moment of debate in the Discourse Theaters. It's all about one thing: proving Resonance so we can strengthen the Veil. That's the lens to look through. At everything. We're going to prove that two things can resonate and be magnified by one another at a distance. The weeks ahead will be spent digging deep into the annals and our own understanding to find the mechanics and math and philosophy and ideas that can support this. We need to be thoughtful. And we need to be fast. Understood?"

Eager nods were had all around.

"Good. Now, do you all know the Karle Tonne categorization of astronomical phenomena?" he asked.

More nods.

"You, what's your name?" Tahn pointed at the physicist.

"Seelia," the young woman replied, giving Rithy a look that revealed some unspoken desire.

"Seelia, can you find the historicals that document significant conjunction in the deep sky, changes in the magnitude of the sun, recurrences of these kinds of phenomena?"

"How far back?" she asked, confident.

Tahn shook his head, impatient. "Everything we have. Go."

The girl disappeared at a fast clip into the almanac bookshelves.

"Myles," the philosophy student said before Tahn could ask his name too, and stepped forward, giving Rithy the same brief, wanton look.

Tahn began to explain. "Find a succinct and accurate timeline for any recorded social change or epidemic or upheaval—wars, riots, plagues—just anything unnatural enough that a historian would put it on a timeline."

"Historians generally don't agree—"

"Myles," Tahn cut in, "we're not yet looking for nuances. And you probably won't find this here. Search your own college's annals first. Go."

"And I'm Tetcha," the cosmology student said, introducing herself with a slight bow. "How about I gather everything we have from the last Succession run at Continuity?"

Tahn nodded agreement, glancing sideways at Rithy to see if the mention of the last Succession caused any change in her face. Not this time. Tetcha had gotten to the door when a thought laid hold of Tahn and he called after her, stopping her in her tracks. "And start thinking about whether Resonance is impersonal . . . or personal."

Tetcha's brows went up, surprised at the question. But eagerness lit in her eyes. "You're going to frame an argument that Resonance could be the personal touch of the abandoning gods, aren't you? Not just a principle of planetary mechanics. That we produce it ourselves—"

He smiled. "I don't know just what we'll do with the old dual argument. But I can tell you this much: We're not leaving it to philosophers to define for us."

She hurried away, nodding. Tahn wanted to start preparing now for the argument that Resonance was more than a vibration. That it was a principle meant for people, too, not just inanimate mechanical systems. It would have to be if he hoped to convince them not just of the Veil, but that they should strengthen it, keep races bound behind it.

Polaema gave Tahn a strange look. "It's bigger than just the Veil, isn't it?"

His mother of astronomy had seen to the heart of it. Something he'd begun to believe after his encounter in the astronomy tower. He gave both Rithy and Polaema an excited look. "I think Resonance might be the highest governing principle. Think about it. We're going to try and prove it's what makes the Veil possible. But if the Song of Suffering strengthens the Veil, then Suffering must work off the same principle." He began to talk faster. "Sheason, too. They're called Inner Resonance sometimes. They *move* things by the use of their own Will."

Polaema spoke, wonder in her voice. "Many different systems—"

"All accessing the same dynamic, vibratory power," Tahn finished. "It might be the unifying principle, the scientific basis for every form of magic."

"That which stirs," Polaema whispered.

"And *my* order," Rithy said, grinning, clearly feeling the excitement. Tahn turned back toward his friend, who seemed earnest enough. Maybe the scars from the last Succession were behind her.

"To tell me which one of these three has the sweetest lips." He pointed after his recently departed Succession team members. He held up his hands to stop her retort before she could speak it. "No, I don't want to know. And yes, I'm a bit jealous."

"You were the one who left—"

"The task at hand, please," Polaema chided them gently.

Rithy's face showed a moment of real regret and anger, but the look faded as quick as it came.

Tahn stood there, staring at his old friend, realizing that his observations about the physics and philosophy students weren't casual; he *was* jealous. Despite his love for Mira, he couldn't ignore the resurgence of the feelings he'd cultivated for Rithy in his years here. They'd been of a more innocent nature then. Time had given them the sweet, smooth bite of a good winter wine.

"There's a lot to do," Tahn said reluctantly.

Rithy nodded. "So, what about me?"

He quickly considered her strengths. Like him, she'd proven herself adept at much more than her college's central research. But above the rest, the clarity of mathematics had been her passion. He knew enough to play to that strength.

"The evening aurora, do you have solid math to explain it?" The rush of excitement immediately resumed.

Understanding lit in Rithy's face. She moved to a window and drew open the shutters. "That's what you saw that got you running from our field of dead birds." She pointed toward the horizon, where flows of red and green dimly lit the night sky.

"When I left the Grove, there was only a hypothesis as to its cause." Tahn came to stand beside her.

"Still just a hypothesis. Better accepted now, but I've no solid math for it yet." She turned to him. "What about it do you need to know? I could work up some statistical computations on frequency and relative strength—"

"Beneath you," Tahn cut in. "I can do that myself." He surprised himself to realize he could, in fact, do just that—base astronomy stuff. "I think I know how we're going to present to the physicists. What I worry about is the College of Mathematics. We need to start thinking about them now. I need to have you doing that."

"Oh, *now* you need me, huh?" She gave a playful grin.

"But work with us here. Some of what we learn may be helpful to you." Tahn reached out and put a hand over hers. He'd meant it as a gesture of thanks, but touching her soft skin made it something a whole lot more . . . intimate.

When he'd studied here as a boy, Rithy had been a very good friend—a girl who hadn't been put off by Tahn's obsession with the stars. Maybe because her own aptitude with numbers put her in a class of her own. And despite the lapse in years, and these new affections, he didn't feel the least bit awkward. Apparently, neither did she.

Rithy leaned in and kissed him. When she pulled away she remarked, "Five seconds of kiss, probably a half pound of lip pressure, and I'll get back to you on the relative friction of my tongue on your teeth."

"Math has come a long way in eight years." Tahn laughed.

"That's nothing, wait until you see my geometry—"

Polaema cleared her throat. "The task at hand," she repeated.

Tahn nodded and let go Rithy's hand. Then, the three of them cleared two long tables and pulled them together. Several lamps were brought and extra wick turned up to brighten the room. Polaema disappeared into the deep almanac shelves and returned with an armful of tomes that she set down in meticulous order and began opening to chapters about the aurora. Shortly after, Seelia wheeled in a book cart loaded down with more than twenty volumes. One by one they set them out, opening to chapter descriptions and finding passages that spoke of deep sky events and unexplained phenomena and recorded anomalies.

They had gotten all this organized to Tahn's liking when Myles came clambering up the stairs, huffing over an armload of books. He dropped them indelicately on the table and quickly took a seat to rest.

"Bottom one has the best timeline," he said, chuffing. "But the volume on anatomy is the most interesting." The philosopher then sat back to gather his breath.

Tahn looked a question at Rithy. "He can read a page at a glance," she explained.

Tahn looked back at the philosopher with admiration. His own Dimnian training—received from Grant in the Scar—made him an exceptionally fast reader, with great recall. But not like Myles. Tahn then put out the books, and went to the first one the philosopher had mentioned. Over the rough parchment, a line had been drawn across both pages of the opened book. Time-markers intersected this horizontal line, giving it the look of a quadrant map. And beside each marker, a tight-handed scrawl spoke of the event at that moment in the timeline. Prominent on the pages were the wars of the First and Second Promise. But similarly, other wars were noted, as were the famines of Thalese and Monalav. The historian had also captured important political changes like the establishment of the regency in Vohnce when King Nevil Sadon ended the line of kings for that nation.

The historian had made reading the chart easy, drawing the vertical lines that intersected the timeline at uniform lengths based on type. Wars were all noted at the top of the pages, at the end of the longest intersecting lines. Political change and unrest slightly below that. Notable religious movements and periods of pentacost occupied their own space beneath the row of political notations.

Surveying the time-map in this way showed that while there always seemed to be something significant happening at any point in time, there were clusters where this meticulous scrivener had been forced to catalog much information all in a crowded column on the page. These columns of ink always had at their top the name of one war or another.

Rithy ran her finger down one of these.

"The question you should be asking," Myles said from his chair, "is whether war induced all the other events, or if there are external factors responsible for these things independently."

"Thanks, Myles," Rithy said with mild sarcasm over the obvious observation.

"It appears the historian has classified the events in ascending risk or cost," Polaema observed, motioning from the horizontal line upward. "Perhaps another way to read this is that each occurrence contributed to the next, eventually leading to war."

"I think war breeds the rest," Rithy countered.

Tahn listened, but had ideas of his own. He glanced at Seelia, who stood at the end of the tables watching them, or mostly Rithy. "What do you think?" he asked.

"I think it's kind of obvious," the young physicist said. "You're looking for astronomical correlations, which is why you had me fetch these." She gestured at the line of books she'd retrieved from the almanac shelves. "But I doubt you're going to find any solutions in the deep sky, and," she paused, looking around at them all, "if this is the argument you're preparing for the physics theater, I don't hold out much hope for you."

Tahn laughed. "I see why you and Rithy are friends."

He then began to pore over the almanacs, lifting many and browsing to additional passages as he went.

Over the next few days, they worked tirelessly in the room, all but cordoning it off so that others couldn't enter. Polaema was the only one who left, and that was to put together grab bags of cheese and pumpernickel breads, along with apples and some dried thin-meats—pork mostly. She didn't allow wine in the almanac library, but a plum cider—only days from going hard—kept them loose, as they grew a bit cage-weary.

They began to smell one another, which Tahn might have imagined would become increasingly unpleasant. Strangely, with the women anyway, it became more of a *pleasant* musk. Could be that the continued excitement of their pursuit clouded his senses.

At first, before diving deeper into the annals they'd collected, they decided to see if they could put together some practical demonstrations. Physicists, after all, were more about the *see* than the *tell*. Book proofs, says a physicist, are for sophists and politicians. Building off what they found from the last Continuity Succession, they dialed in a few rather compelling physical models using lodestones and pendulum gears. But it didn't seem to cohere into a final argument. So, they made sure they could reproduce their material demonstrations with sufficient accuracy to be taken as proofs, then moved on to the books.

"When the Quiet came to Naltus," Tahn explained to them, as they started to peruse the many volumes they'd retrieved, "it was at the time of the lunar eclipse we just had of the first moon. It makes me think there are correlations worth exploring."

As they pored over the initial volumes, and several more besides, they slowly began to build something of a map. They copied out the original timeline on a half-dozen sheets of parchment laid end to end. And began to add more events to it: vague accounts, apocryphal bits, speculative information. Anything. Everything.

And then they lined up the almanacs around the time-map, laying them open to pages that cataloged various noteworthy astronomical events recorded over the last several centuries. Some, he noted, were inferred from astronomers who had determined the position of stars and planets and moons by calculating where they would have been, given their annual cycles and orbits. He appreciated the masterful work shown here. It reminded him how much he loved the study of the sky. The scratch of ink and graphite over the imperfections of old parchment . . . Memories filled him of perusing star maps all night here in the almanac library to prepare for discourse in the theaters. He missed this place.

Tahn forced himself to put the past away, and focus on their current preparation, this time for his own Succession. After staring at the opened pages for several minutes, Rithy spoke what Tahn had already seen.

"There's no real alignment. The significant events in the sky aren't occurring at the same time as notable historical moments. And frankly, tying them together would have been a neat trick, anyway."

Tahn looked askance at his old friend. "Whose side are you on, anyway?"

"Are there sides?" she retorted.

He shook his head, and laughed. "Thanks for your unrestrained honesty."

"And yet," Polaema said, still staring at the pages of the almanacs, "there do seem to be some patterns here."

Returning his attention to the books and timeline, Tahn refocused. And almost immediately, the patterns leapt out at him from the pages: There were heliacal rhythms. Sunspots had been recorded for millennia. These wouldn't have required a skyglass, and the astronomers of Aubade Grove had begun documenting any observable changes in the sun from the very beginning. Then, over the last few hundred years, after the Grove had invented the skyglass, constantly refining its design and reach, they'd made an interesting discovery. Sunspots produced simultaneous flares of light, as though by being cooler, the sunspots were causing more intense temperatures and activity at their edges.

Tahn looked up, making the simple deduction: These so-

lar flares had also been happening for millennia, and at predictable intervals of time.

But they didn't correspond to the columns of social activity seen in the timeline.

"Wait," he said, practically pouncing on the historical text
that contained the map of time. He riffled back through the
book to the front pages, where the legends and indices were
held. He read wildly, scanning, until he found what he'd been
searching for. "The timeline is demarcated using the Bael-
lorean Calendar." Tahn moved quickly to three of the almanacs, nodding as he went. "The College of Astronomy has
always used the Tonnian Calendar. They're offset by three
hundred and eleven years."

Rithy pushed in front of him, already finished with the
math, calling out conjunctions and dates. "The full alignment
of the eleven known wandering stars, TC 488."

He added the delta of time, his finger landing precisely on
the war of the First Promise. A shiver rippled over his skin.

"The passage of the Perades aéirein showers on the same
day as both Northsun and a full solar eclipse. TC 2043." Rithy
looked up as Tahn slid his finger horizontally across the timeline to the war of the Second Promise.

He paused there. The Scar had resulted from the last battle of this second war. It reminded him of his friends, those
living in that dry, wide place, and feeling hollowness. It reminded him of Tamara. And Alemdra. It reminded him why
he was here. The thirty-seven.

Stop this whole damned mess before it gets messier!

It reminded him there was another lunar eclipse in a few
short days.

"We're not letting this happen again!" He slammed a fist
down on the notation for the Battle of the Scar. "Not again."
He was overtired, but it wouldn't have changed his feelings
about it. Not one jot.

Seelia, Myles, and Tetcha gathered close, adjusting texts
from their respective colleges, where the annalists had used
chronological systems best suited to their lines of inquiry. A
master map began to take shape.

Tahn's heart pounded; his hands shook. He and Rithy did this awful dance back and forth across the history of Aeshau Vaal, until they'd reached the end of the time-map and almanacs.

"This is good," Seelia conceded, "but you're going to need to couple all this with the demonstrable models we built."

Tahn tapped his lip in a good-natured affectation of thoughtfulness. "You're right. Any ideas?"

Seelia stared at the maps for several long moments. Almost comically, her eyes widened and her mouth fell slightly open. "What if this Resonance you're proposing is more fundamental even than magnetism?"

He and the young physicist shared a long look, as though they could read each other's thoughts. "Let's pull it all together," he said eagerly. "I think we're going to be ready for the physicists."

· CHAPTER SEVENTY-FOUR ·

Contrarians

That for which you have no words is infinitely more powerful than that for which you do. This is as true of hate as it is of love.

—The first principle of ineffability, established as a model for irrational thought, Estem Salo

ONCE, THE VAULTS had been a much simpler structure, smaller. But that had been long ago. Today, they were a sprawl of buildings, many of them—though not all—interconnected. But each was devoted to the education and training of those who wished to become Sheason. In form and function, they resembled the colleges of the major cities, but were larger, and not as crowded. That, and the regimen of study went well beyond rigorous.

Thaelon strode through the Vault halls this morning, moving quickly on his way from the morning's first trials. He'd just left a young woman who he'd had to divest of her Sheason authority. A promising young woman. Gods, he was tired of this. And at her trial she'd explained how much of her opinion had been formed in the classes of . . . Exemplar Hanry.

So Thaelon had no time to enjoy the scents of ash and oak and old granite stone. Nor the great naves, or long history and purpose of the Vaults. He scarcely even noticed passing Sualen—students so far only allowed to pursue Knowledge, and not yet Influence—who offered him a nod of acknowledgment as he hurried past. Instead he rushed to a classroom where they would be exploring Influence in light of what was effable and what was ineffable—that which could be expressed in words, and that which could not.

He arrived, eager and angry. He pushed through a set of solid, well-worn oak doors into a small theater-style room. Here were twenty students listening to Sheason Hanry in a flourish of exposition on the topic of contrariness.

Thaelon managed a smile when the students rose to their feet in greeting.

Exemplar Hanry continued to ramble a moment, his eyes currently scanning talking points from the notes he kept atop the central lectern. The subtle change in silence—fewer bits of graphite furiously taking notes—brought his attention up to his standing students. He followed their gaze to Thaelon, and bowed slightly to his Randeur in acknowledgment and deference.

"My apologies for the intrusion," Thaelon offered cordially.

"No apology necessary," Hanry replied a bit tersely.

"I'd like to hear what's being taught here." Thaelon looked back at the students. "And I'd like to address the class."

Hanry paused a long moment. "I have a thought," he said. "Since this class is on the topic of contrariness, why don't you and I teach it together. Should lend itself to the topic."

Thaelon took a slow breath, and nodded.

Hanry gathered his notes, pivoted on the balls of his feet like a soldier walking a sentry line, and proceeded in a slumped shuffle to a lectern on the far side of the floor. Once situated, he raised a hand, inviting Thaelon to take his position at the rightmost lectern at the front of the class. They'd be on opposite sides of the room—very symmetrical.

The slightest of grins lit Hanry's face. Thaelon guessed it was because the exemplar couldn't wait for what would follow—Hanry was known for his antagonism. The man was the perfect teacher on the principle of contrariness.

Hanry cleared his throat to gather the collective attention of his students. "I will review, so that those of you awed by the presence of our Randeur might refocus yourselves and benefit from today's practical demonstration.

"Today we explore contrariness. For the dullards among you, it falls in the domain of Influence. And in our pedagogy, Influence comes after Knowledge. Since you're here with us today, you've all mastered basic logic and knowledge, which includes the study of *that which is arguable*."

Thaelon took his place behind the lectern on the far right of the room.

"It takes time, however, to become an effective rhetorician; language has nuances. Especially when it comes to . . . disagreement." Hanry grinned again, making a bad job of concealing his glee.

"Understand, mind you," Hanry was quick to add, "what we're talking about here is the coupling of the Will with your words in order to give them the power of their meaning and your intention—"

"That's right," Thaelon said, cutting in. "And what you *intend,* once you are Sheason, will be guided by your oath."

Hanry cleared his throat. "The crux of it, however, returns us to where we began before our Randeur interru—joined us. Anyone remember what that might be?" His voice lilted upward in a rising tone of mild condescension.

Thaelon took it upon himself to answer. "It was surely the difference between what is effable and what is ineffable."

Hanry's wicked grin faltered briefly. "Of course *you* know, my fellow, but I was hoping one of my students here could tell us."

Thaelon surveyed the group. "You all knew the answer, right?"

A spate of nervous laughter rose and quickly fell, silenced by a stern look from their instructor. Hanry then lowered his eyes to his lectern. The silence continued for quite some time while the man reviewed his notes. Finally, he cleared his throat; more, Thaelon believed, as the affectation of an orator than from any real need.

"The Principle of Influence—which is to say, our use of the Will—has many tracks of study. Among these is"— Hanry looked grumpily over at Thaelon—"*effability and ineffability.* This is nothing more or less than what can and cannot be expressed through written or spoken words."

A middle-aged woman in the front row hesitantly raised her hand. "Exemplar?"

Hanry waved for the woman to speak her question.

Tentatively, the woman asked, "So, ineffability means that even explicit language is sometimes insufficient to express what we mean?"

Thaelon raised a hand to stop Hanry from answering. He rounded his own lectern and surveyed the many students in the small theater. When he did, the importance of these classes struck him. Not contrariness, in particular, but all classes being taught by any who opposed the trials. The dissenters weren't standing idle. Particularly those who hadn't had their trial yet. These classrooms were being used to guide and shape intentions . . . intentions of people just like the young woman he'd just come from divesting. Thaelon didn't know for certain yet if Hanry was part of this, but he felt it as deeply as anything he ever had. In a way, trials were starting in classrooms like this one.

How many future Sheason might he lose to evangelists working their personal philosophies in these rooms? How many would he have to divest? A third? Half? Nine-tenths?

He had to fight for them. He had to teach them the true nature of being Sheason. They needed to know the right way of things. They mustn't follow a selfish path.

"This, my young friends, is *why* we study what is ineffable," Thaelon explained. "Some things are simply beyond our ability to adequately express. Like love, for instance. We will sometimes, however, need to give even these inexpressible things a voice. Do you understand?"

Most of the students nodded.

"You have no idea what you're nodding about," Hanry said, chiding his class. "But you will. One of the thought-forms in the track on effability and ineffability . . . is contrariness. My Randeur, shall we begin?"

"Contrariness?" Thaelon said. "I think you already have."

His colleague paid the commentary no mind and set forth the topic for their debate. It hit Thaelon like a smith's hammer in the chest. "How best does a Sheason serve? Is it by doing what he's asked by others to do? Or does he render the aid *he* believes others most need?"

What they were about to do was not simply debate. This was *contrariness*. This was the use of the Will to express a point of view in order to change the heart and mind of another. Of all the topics a Sulivon would study on the Principle of Influence, this came last. A Sheason must understand it. But like realignment, he should never use it on someone else, because it violated the most fundamental belief a Sheason tried to defend: every person's right to choose for themselves. Even now, Thaelon could feel doubt creeping into his mind, seeded there by the power of the Will. *Hanry's Will*. Subtle, gentle whisperings that pulled at him.

"Hanry," Thaelon said with warning.

Again the exemplar ignored him. "This is a relevant question, class, since we, as an order, face the question even now in the Trial of Intentions. And you've no doubt heard the rumors of the itinerant Vendanj, who cares little for the laws and institutions of the Eastland races, and chooses instead to follow the dictates of his own conscience when it comes to serving others."

"Service," Thaelon broke in, fighting back, "inherently means to voluntarily do the will of others. If we act contrary to that notion, we cease to serve." The gentle grip of Hanry's suggestion eased.

"Nonsense," Hanry blurted. "The person in need is often too steeped in their own misfortune to see clearly what is right or best for themselves."

Thaelon could feel the words begin again to take root in his mind, as soft as cottonwood seed falling to rest on a riverbank.

"That is arrogance," Thaelon argued. "It supposes we know better than those we serve. And it's a misuse of our abilities."

Hanry looked down, referring to his notes. When he raised his gaze again to Thaelon, his wry grin had returned. "What of the Civilization Order, my Randeur? How do you reconcile a government's decree that a Sheason not render the Will, with, say, the request from a parent to heal their sick child?"

These words gripped Thaelon's mind more tightly than any that had come before. He could feel himself losing the strength of his convictions. Hanry was a master contrarian. And looking into the man's eyes and slight, wicked grin, he realized this was more than a practical demonstration. His opponent here *believed* in Vendanj's approach to service. Thaelon had been deliberately drawn into this debate by a dissenter. Hanry abhorred the Trial of Intentions. Thaelon could now feel it as plainly as the shirt on his shoulders.

And his answer was . . . he had no good answer. Perhaps his anger clouded his reason. Or perhaps Hanry's gift for contrariness had stolen it from him.

Hanry took advantage of Thaelon's hesitation to offer his own opinion. "What you have here, my Randeur, is a conflict of interests. And, if I may be so bold, while you equivocate on the fundamental question of how best a Sheason should serve, many of the order perish. And I do not speak metaphorically. Men and women are dying. This is not good leadership."

Thaelon found himself nodding in agreement, and looked up into the small theater, noting the confused and expectant looks of the students. They waited on his reply. He was their Randeur. And he'd just been publicly criticized, humiliated. There might only be twenty young men and women in front of him, but what he said and did here, now, would surely reach the rest of Estem Salo. A second realization hit him: He was not the only one feeling the effects of Hanry's influence. The malleable minds of these young people were being shaped and directed just as his was. He had to fight for them.

That's all it took to break the suggestion that had begun to overwhelm him.

He didn't turn to address Hanry, but instead directed his response to the students. "It's not our role to coerce councils and kings, any more than I would coerce one of you to disregard the dictates of your own conscience—"

"More equivocation," Hanry chimed in from the other side of the room.

"What you decide to do when called on to render aid, only you can answer. It may have the consequence of law, as it has with Rolen, which is why you must feel certain of your choice. But always, it must be guided by your oath. You cannot be Sheason and wield your Influence at any cost. Some things simply go too far."

"These are platitudes," Hanry offered dismissively. "They're rote replies that ignore the realities of life for Sheason beyond the protection of Estem Salo. The world no longer holds any regard or respect for us. My Randeur, as you hide behind these antiquated proverbs, your order suffers. As a result, so do countless others. But . . ." Hanry's smile changed—less cynical, though still angry. "There are those of us who imagine a different way. Those of us who stand behind a Sheason bold enough to declare, 'Damn the costs!'" Hanry thrust a clenched fist into his lectern to emphasize his point.

In Thaelon's mind rushed a flood of Hanry's thought and Influence. Images of executed Sheason rose in his head. Images of Quiet, too. He could feel commitment to his own path waning. His legs weakened, and he saw Hanry's smile tug his mouth into a perceptibly wider grin. He was slowly accepting the master contrarian's logic. The rushing of Influence would soon erase his own objections entirely. And it would take place as nothing more than a practical demonstration for Sulivon students.

Sulivon students. The next generation of Sheason. Who were systematically being taught self-interest. By Hanry.

That realization stirred fresh anger. His own arguments formed and thrummed inside his head, but found no words. A mad, ironic thought occurred to him: *I've come upon the ineffable: hatred.*

He turned fully toward Hanry, silently judging him, letting his wrath for the man emanate outward. He thought about the many who had surely lost their way after listening to this exemplar's opinions concerning service. The many that would be divested. A broken order of Sheason. He thought about the long line of Randeurs who had never failed to keep the order aligned behind a common interest. He thought about his wife and daughter, and the world he would leave them if he couldn't unite the order entrusted to his care. He even thought of Rolen, and Vendanj, and the hardships that had befallen them.

He thought all these things, but had no words, only a feeling.

The bitter smile fell from Hanry's face. Doubt rose clearly in the man's eyes. It was different, Thaelon knew, from the self-doubt he himself had just felt. It was the difference between the effable and ineffable. Hanry had sought to change Thaelon's mind. The power of Thaelon's thoughts, on the other hand, drove a more fundamental contrariness: the question of Hanry's existence at all.

The exemplar's expression of doubt slipped to panic as he fell to his knees and raised to Thaelon a beseeching hand.

Thaelon's mind turned not to mercy but the many Sheason deaths already come. Preventable deaths. Sheason falling while Hanry stood here, lecturing, asking questions, preaching dissent. Thaelon's anger burned.

Only when it was too late, when Hanry managed a last, faltering, wry grin, did Thaelon understand. As the instructor of contrary Influence fell dead beside his lectern, a victim of his own contrariness, Thaelon realized that he'd been baited. Hanry had never intended to win a debate. The man's attempts at effability were strong, but not ultimately convincing—deliberately too weak. Hanry . . . had meant to die. Or more accurately, he'd meant for Thaelon to kill him and have that death witnessed by a classroom full of students.

The dark irony was that Thaelon had done as the dissenters would have done. Imposed his Will. With the deception of a practical demonstration, Hanry had shown him the heart of the itinerant Vendanj. He had also made Thaelon a hypocrite. And news of all this would now spread.

These thoughts spilled onto another more disturbing thought. *Perhaps I'm more like Vendanj than I realize. . . .*

When his hatred and anger had abated, the silence that consumed the small theater seemed deafening. He might have been grateful for any sound, except that when the door opened, and Raalena poked her head inside, he heard only this: "My Randeur, come, there's unsettling news."

• CHAPTER SEVENTY-FIVE •

Two Ways to Serve

Our failing, and why I frankly agree with the gods—real or otherwise—for abandoning us, is that we tend to care more about "how" than "what." In other words, "how" a man serves a fellow man unfortunately matters more to us than the fact that he tries at all.

—From a controversial tract entitled, "In Defence of Abandoment," published by the school of philosophy, Naltus Rey

ALL SOLDIERS, EVEN turnkeys, had been called into the civil conflict raging across Recityv. It left the dungeons and pits beneath Solath Mahnus unguarded. Vendanj raced down the halls, past doors that stood open. *Other Sheason holding pits.* Then, far up the long hall, he heard heavy thuds followed by weak groans. *Rolen!*

A few moments later he came to a stop at the open door to Rolen's cell. He stepped inside and looked down the stairs into the gloom. In the heavy shadows, he made out the rich hue of several brown League cloaks. Two men looked up at Vendanj; two others continued their work in the darkness where Rolen was chained. He could hear his old friend grunting as each blow struck him. Rolen could be glad these leaguemen had decided to beat him before killing him, else Vendanj would've had no chance to rescue him.

The click and hum of a crossbow struck the air. Vendanj raised a barrier around himself and a moment later saw the bolt career harmlessly off the unseen shield. Two of the leaguemen started up the stairs, swords held up defensively. Vendanj raised a hand toward them, then flipped it. The two swordsmen spun violently backward, their heads striking the stone staircase. They both fell immediately still.

He swept down the stairs. Another bolt whizzed past him, striking the stone wall with a metallic ting. When he reached the floor, he looked into the far corner, peering through the dark. There, at the back of the room, stood two more leaguemen, one with fearful curiosity in his eyes, the other loading another bolt. Vendanj concentrated on the high end of their spines. A moment later two muted pops could be heard from their corner, where the bones in their necks exploded from within. Their bodies slumped to the floor in a crunch of armor.

He then turned just in time to meet one of two leaguemen who'd been working at Rolen. The man swung a large warhammer at him. With no time to stop it, he braced for the blow, managing a thin protective cocoon around himself. The hammer struck the barrier, the force transferring across its surface and slamming Vendanj's entire body like a heavy fist. It knocked him to the ground.

As he tumbled, he caught a flash of light on an upraised blade. *The other is going to kill Rolen!* Vendanj pushed an angry fist at the leagueman's sword arm, and pulled the limb entirely free of the man's body. The leagueman screamed as his appendage dropped to the floor, the sword clattering away into the corner. The iron smell of blood filled the air, as the man tried to stanch the flow and raced up the stairs to save himself.

Vendanj had lost track of the last remaining leagueman, whose hammer fell on him again. The protective shield kept the blow from crushing his chest, but the energy traveled across it and pressed in on him again, bruising much of his body. He looked up into the angry eyes of his assailant and spoke a few words. The man's head snapped unnaturally to the side, and he fell motionless atop Vendanj—the barrier keeping the dead leagueman a finger's breadth away. Vendanj pushed him off before letting go of the protective shell. He rolled to his feet and cast his gaze into the darkened corner at the crook of the wall and stairs.

"Come," he said. "Let's get you free of this place."

A stirring in the corner brought the jingle of chains.

A weak, panting voice replied. "They wanted to know where to find you." A wet cough. "They wouldn't believe I didn't know."

Vendanj hated the thought that they'd worked at Rolen on his account. "Civil war is spreading in the city. The regent has been killed. And the League . . . slaughtered nearly every Sheason in Recityv."

Rolen's chains jangled as if agitated, and the emaciated, beaten renderer crawled into the light. "No."

"Many were killed in their homes," Vendanj said with more urgency. "Dozens more were herded onto the plaza and murdered in front of thousands."

"Why?" Rolen asked plaintively.

"The Civilization Order was amended. All Sheason are to be executed, whether they use the Will or not."

"The High Council wouldn't ratify such an amendment," Rolen argued, and began to cough again.

"The Council has changed," Vendanj said impatiently. "Roth has manipulated the votes. It's only a matter of time before Van Steward yields. He won't continue to fight . . . to kill civilians who just don't know any better. He'll hate it, but he'll yield. Then, any remaining Sheason will be sought out and put to death. Just as these men came here to kill you. If you don't let me take you away from here, more will come. You'll be the easiest to find."

The withered Sheason stared back, seeming to try to make sense of what he'd just heard.

"Do you understand?" Vendanj said more gently. "Simply belonging to the order is now cause for execution. The world is upside down."

Rolen got to his feet with great difficulty, and stood as though considering. But Vendanj didn't wait for the other to speak. With a concentrated look, he snapped the shackles binding his old friend.

"Since I doubt you'll join me to resist the League, you have very few choices. You can flee Recityv, and hope they don't catch you. You might also, I suppose, forsake the order. But I doubt that'll buy you clemency from the law. What will it be?"

His friend still didn't move. Perhaps he was too weak from starvation and beatings. Perhaps such awful news had stolen any meaningful words he might have. Vendanj hoped when his old friend finally did speak, he'd hear defiance and anger. Maybe this would give Rolen some clarity of thought. Maybe he'd understand what Vendanj had been telling him. Maybe this awful day would move his Randeur to stronger action.

"Perhaps," Rolen said, after several tense moments, "we must change, even as the times around us change."

Vendanj stepped close to his friend. He could smell cycles of sweat and human waste on him. And Rolen's unkempt beard had crawled over most of his face—he looked half mad. The Rolen he knew would never call the Will as Vendanj did. But to keep himself alive in this new world, his friend would have to embrace new ways. It was that simple. He could see his old friend struggling with the prospect of it.

Vendanj reached out and placed a hand on Rolen's shoulder, imparting a warm transfer of his life's Forda to heal what he could without overweakening himself.

Rolen stood a little taller, his eyes a little more focused. He raised a hand and weakly clutched Vendanj's outstretched arm. "You mean to convert me," he said, and smiled.

"Since when has that been a secret," Vendanj replied, feeling slightly diminished. "Can you walk?"

Rolen took a few tentative steps, looked up in surprise that his legs were useful, and together they mounted the stone stairs. As they went, Vendanj found himself wondering if he'd saved his friend from certain execution only to someday have to stand against him.

"Let's go," he whispered.

Vendanj got them to the stables, heaved Rolen onto a stout destrier, and took a golden bay for himself. He grabbed the destrier's reins, told Rolen to hold tight, and slipped through the large wooden gates of the stable yard into the city.

They passed several frays, but Vendanj kept them at a distance, turning down narrow alleys and only passing large streets when they needed to cross to some other smaller byway. They wove toward the seldom-used northwest gate.

"Raise the gate!" he yelled as they neared. "In the name of Van Steward!"

The surprised gate captain took a close look at Vendanj. Lines of allegiance had fast been drawn today, and the general's men were still loyal to the regent's friends. The gate began to rise.

Vendanj ducked through and led Rolen's mount a thousand strides onto the rolling plain before stopping. He wheeled around and came abreast of his old friend, facing the opposite direction. He handed Rolen the reins. The other took them with feeble fingers.

"Find what help you can," Vendanj said. "But be careful. Most larger towns have League garrisons, and they'll hear about the amendment to the Civilization Order."

Vendanj raised his own reins, readying to return to his companions. The danger was getting out of hand. There was yet another escape from the city to prepare.

"Wait," Rolen said, his voice husky. The tortured Sheason tried to clear his throat, but the effort only brought another wracking cough. Some blood oozed up onto his lips as he finally spoke. "The League . . ." He gasped for breath. "The League is seeking Talendraal."

Vendanj remembered Losol's sword. Dismay and terror

filled his chest. Talendraal were weapons that could turn aside a Sheason's rendering. Most renderings, anyway.

Rolen wheezed as he struggled for breath. "More than once, Roth's new Jurshah leader has come into my cell and commanded me to render against him." He swallowed hard. "I'll admit I didn't put much of myself into it. Down there, I hadn't much to spare. But what I did throw at him, his blade seemed to divert or dissipate as easy as sun off a mirror. I don't know any other way he could have done it, save Talendraal."

"How do you know they're seeking more?" Vendanj asked, anger replacing his initial dread of the League's interest in the old weapons.

"I overheard them talking once," Rolen answered. "The real question is whether or not the League has made an alliance with those beyond the Pall. Or do they simply seek the weapons forged there during the Craven Season."

Vendanj shook his head, thinking, disgusted . . . worried. "Between laws that make it a crime for us to render, and steel that can turn aside the effects when we do, the League will fear no resistance from us. Gods!" Vendanj cursed. "But Talendraal will not be easily had."

"No, they won't," Rolen agreed, "but a few may be all they need. They won't use them to lead armies. They'll put them in the hands of hunters. To track down Sheason. I wanted you to know. For Illenia's sake."

The use of her name left him without words. Vendanj didn't speak of his dead wife. Nor of the unborn child they'd lost when she went prematurely to her earth. Few knew this part of his past. Fewer still knew Illenia's name. But of course, her brother Rolen knew it, and had every right to use it.

Only now did Vendanj allow himself to fully acknowledge that this Sheason he'd rescued was family. It had been part of his need to save him. Illenia would have wanted it. But Vendanj had hid away connections to that part of his past, even from himself, and rarely gave them space in his own mind. They served no useful purpose. They were too painful.

But he understood Rolen's warning, and guessed that Talendraal were responsible for the rising number of residents at Widows' Village. That dreary place where the husbands and wives of fallen Sheason gathered together, lived, and remembered the ones they'd lost.

A bitter frown rose on his dry lips at the thought of Roth directing secret efforts to secure such weapons at the same time he was pushing for laws to execute Sheason. The Ascendant spoke of peace and civility, of putting away superstition, and simultaneously sought steel forged with superstitious intent.

He was a clever hypocrite. And dangerous.

After a long silence far from the city gate, his dead wife's brother spoke again with his bloodied lips. "Tahn surviving Tillinghast may not mean what you want it to mean, Vendanj." Rolen tried to straighten his back, but wound up more deeply hunched over his saddle horn—his wounds were having the better of him.

Vendanj didn't bother to ask what Rolen meant.

"Will you take him to Estem Salo?"

"He travels there now," Vendanj answered. "By way of Aubade Grove. With luck, the Randeur will be moved to support us."

Rolen exhaled, a hint of forbearance in his face. "Because you loved my sister, let me caution you. The Randeur is every bit as headstrong as you are." He offered a slight grin. A final joke between them.

Vendanj returned a thin smile of his own. But inside, a knot of dread tightened in his gut. The years. The leagues traveled. The lives lost. It all hung as though by a thread. He needed to unify the Sheason. The Randeur's help was crucial.

But as his dread rose, so did his anger. He'd vowed long ago, in a room not far from where Illenia died, that no cost would be spared to change the way of things. And no one, *no one,* would stand in the way of that vow. Not the Ascendant. Not the Randeur. Vendanj acknowledged a touch of madness in him when it came to seeing this done, but accepted—even believed—that madness might be the only thing that got him through.

To oppose the Randeur . . .

It *was* madness. But the right kind, if he could be any judge of it.

Vendanj nodded thanks to Rolen and spurred his mount, rushing back to Recityv.

• CHAPTER SEVENTY-SIX •

The Bourne: Vespers

If we believe the creation stories, then in the same way the benevolent gods failed when they created Inveterae, isn't it possible that Maldea likewise sometimes failed? And if so, what would those creations be like?

—Words spoken by a historian in the company of "low ones" at a Tenendra carnival

KETT FELL NAKED and trembling on neatly laid black terrace stones that ended overlooking a great chasm. Where his body didn't bleed openly, the blood welled beneath the skin from bruising that ached to the bone. He might have lost the use of one eye, and he could no longer feel the fingers of his left hand. Crashing down hard near the edge of the sheer drop, he thought the bones in his knees had cracked. He rolled onto his back and looked up into a cloud-darkened sky, and even then still hoped he would live to try to lead the Inveterae away from the Bourne. Save his little ones.

As if knowing his heart, the Jinaal Balroath made a sound of contempt and amusement deep in his throat. But Balroath said nothing. This wasn't his interrogation; this moment belonged to Stulten, who Kett could hear slowly approaching from the rear of the manor somewhere behind them.

He had run more days than he could remember, scarcely eating or sleeping, tracking Lliothan. But he'd never caught him. When he'd arrived back at Kael Ronoch, his children were not in the quarters provided for them. Several Bar'dyn had been waiting. They'd brought him here to the far side of Kael Ronoch, to the last residence before the land fell sharply away—no less than five hundred arm-lengths to a black river.

The wind came up the face of the cliff, carrying the scent of wet rock and dead roots. He could also smell the blood of others, which stained the terrace stone around him. But he'd seen no bodies. It wasn't hard to figure out the use the Jinaal had of the cliff so close behind him.

"You disappoint me," Stulten said, coming near and looking down at Kett. "I would not say I am surprised, but I *am* disappointed. Did you forget you were given? Did you forget we will always know when you betray our heart? Did you forget we will redeem our right to the spirit inside you?"

He *had* forgotten.

"Of course, this time, we didn't need to find you. We knew you would come."

Marckol and Neliera.

"For a visionary, Kett Valan, you failed to see the real opportunity for your kind." Stulten shook his head. "That homeland you desire? You'd find that sooner by following us than by separation. Do you see that now?"

"Killing my patrol was by design," Kett lied. "I was trying to earn the villagers' trust. Make them think I was still one of them, so I could learn their true plans."

Stulten made an indiscriminate sound deep in his throat and moved past Kett to the edge of the stone-cobbled yard, where he looked out at the great expanse. "The *truth* is, my Inveterae friend, we no longer need your kind. And as most shelah, you underestimate your own acclaim."

Kett sat partway up at the use of the old term: shelah, the old-tongue word . . . messiah. "You're mistaken. I'm not shelah. And my people don't see me as one."

"You are naïve," the Jinaal replied. "The murder of your friends was a test, Kett Valan. You knew this. We could certainly have killed these seditionists without your help." Stulten turned and came to stand over him again. "I had to know if you were truly shelah."

"I could have told you—"

"Yes, you could have. But it didn't take much to convince you to kill your friends. Don't you see, Kett Valan? As badly as I needed to know, you wanted to prove to *yourself* that you are shelah. Physical pain means nothing, proves nothing. Your willingness to claim the lives of friends . . . it's magnificent, Kett Valan. A great marvel."

Stulten looked away again into the wide open space beyond the cliff, lost in his own thoughts. Beneath him, Kett's pain deepened, crawling down into his soul where Stulten's words took hold, hinting at some truth.

He recalled countless stories offered by his own parents in the small hours before sleep, stories that as a child he'd hoped to see made real. They weren't tales of heroes or redeemers, or war or bravery. No, they were simple stories of a brighter shade of grass, ground-fruits that didn't taste of mineral and ash, and of walking free beyond the grey skies of the Bourne.

"I'm not shelah," he repeated.

Stulten ignored him. Then he squatted down, and spoke more softly. "After all our words and schemes, we want the same thing as Inveterae." Stulten smiled. An ugly thing to see.

Kett shook his head. "We don't want the same thing. We seek to live *beside* the races south of the Pall, not to dominate or destroy them."

Stulten's smile turned thin, angry. "You and your kind have cowered in the shadow of the Veil, feeling betrayed. The only difference between us . . . we don't cower."

Stulten grew quiet for a few moments, seeming to ponder. "Haven't you truly considered yet, Kett Valan, that we may want nothing more than a homeland that can yield a proper crop?"

He listened, finding it hard to tell whether the Jinaal's words were truth or lie. Perhaps the Quiet's final desire was, indeed, the same as the Inveterae's. Perhaps the way of things had been put out of balance precisely because of the Abandonment, and not because one zealous Maker had overreached himself.

"Do you see now?" Stulten asked. "I gave you a great

598 · PETER ORULLIAN

chance to see beyond the divisions forced on us during the Placing. Your redemption might have been more than the Inveterae houses escaping the Bourne; it might have been seeing done what the gods themselves had abandoned."

The thoughts swirled maddeningly. Had he been wrong from the very beginning? Had his instinct to be given to the Quiet really instead been a way to try to do what the Framers hadn't been able to do? Perhaps he *had* been too narrow in his hopes, thinking only of his Inveterae family.

He rolled onto his side, testing his strength and the wounds in his body. Excruciating pain shot through his loins and across his skin, but brought with it clarity of mind. Even if all Stulten said was true, a Quiet intrusion into the world of men would be an apocalypse from which it would never recover. Even if the Quiet's intention was to bring forward the finest virtues of the favored southern races, those imprisoned so long in the deeps of the Bourne would be unable to stem their bitterness. Countless men would die. He felt that truth as surely as he felt the fragments of bone shifting under his skin.

From the corner of his eye, Kett looked up at Stulten. "You're arrogant to think you know yourselves better than those who confined you here." He swallowed hard. "And as for my people, I suspect it isn't our exodus you want to avoid, but open rebellion."

Stulten laughed deep and long. "And why would you think that?"

Without hesitation, Kett answered. "Because many of us were created equal to Quiet races. We're not weak like those south of the Pall."

Stulten's face slackened, and he gestured back toward his manor. Promptly a familiar form came out, pulling tethers lashed to the small wrists of Marckol and Neliera, his children.

He wanted to scream, but he couldn't seem to breathe. And it would have frightened his little ones, anyway. But in his mind, he cried out, *No! No.* And suddenly he was reliving his tribunal—which now seemed so long ago—when Saleema had been struck down.

Grief and worry throbbed inside him at the sight of his

small ones, and what he imagined lay in store for them. Their pleading eyes fell on him as they approached. And he looked up at their captor, realizing suddenly who led his bound children . . . the Bar'dyn Praefect Lliothan.

• CHAPTER SEVENTY-SEVEN •

What Steel Can Do

Some believe Ir-Caul is where—after Palamon fought Jo'ha'nel—the last few men and women settled. They also believe it's why every child there learns the use of a blade, even still.

—Belonging to an apendix of uncataloged sword techniques and labled "unfriendly" or "unwilling" by the chronicler commissioned of the League to inventory known combat sytles

THE GRUNTS AND strains of a physical contest grew louder as Sutter emerged from a long tunnel onto the king's practice field. To the west of the castle, a broad stretch of land lay enclosed by a high fieldstone wall. Along the perimeter, various outbuildings stood: a forge, a stable, an armory, and what looked like quarters for trainers who lived to do nothing more than teach battle. In the strong afternoon sun, Sutter could see King Relothian refining his combat skills.

Three attackers worked at the king. It quickly became apparent that this was no idle exercise. A savage intensity lived in the faces of those trying to defeat him. More than this, the men—all of them—were bleeding from various cuts to face and hands and arms. It didn't surprise Sutter to see that in Ir-Caul, the training imitated real battle. It *did* surprise him to see the king wielding a sword . . . and a forge hammer.

Smith king.

The men were all sweating heavily from exertion. Even those watching were ripe at the armpits, as if they rested from a previous round of drills. They watched intently, seeming to silently root for one of their brothers to best Relothian.

The yard held spots of grass. But dirt dominated the area, kicked up into low clouds of dust that coated the men's faces with grit. Trails of sweat streaked down their cheeks, giving them the vague look of painted-face troupers from a pageant wagon doing the droll threshes—a comic set of plays that took whips and slapsticks as their main props.

Sutter came to the edge of the practice field and stopped. His presence drew a few questioning looks from the armored men seated and standing here and there around the current contest. He paid them no mind. He meant to know who'd tried to kill him.

The king caught sight of Sutter, and redoubled his efforts with the three men encircling him. In a matter of seconds he'd disarmed two of them, and put the third on the ground with a body-throw. He brought his sword up to the man's cheek and gave him a slight gouge that drew bright red blood in a small runnel.

The men at the edges of the field beat the blunt ends of spears on the ground or their sword handles against their shields in applause. The defeated trio stood together and bowed to the king, who did likewise, before they departed the field in different directions.

Breathing hard, Relothian made his way straight for Sutter. His gait suggested a purpose more than welcome, and he still held his hammer in one hand. Sutter held his ground.

"You don't belong here," Relothian said, drawing near. "You're a guest in my keep, but you're not a warrior in my army. Leave the way you came."

Sutter ignored the command, but kept his voice low enough—for now—that the king's men wouldn't hear him. "I'll go once you've told me why you betrayed my confidence."

The king's anger faltered, momentarily broken by Sutter's insolence. Then firmness returned to his face. "If you're making an accusation, then make it. But be careful, boy, this king doesn't betray a confidence." Relothian rotated the hammer in his hand.

"Then tell me how one of your men came into my room last night, trying to kill me and take the sigil I showed only you." Sutter stepped closer to the king, realizing how close he'd come to death in that attack. If not for Mira, he'd be dead.

Again the king's face showed a momentary hesitation, his gaze shifting from Sutter's eyes to his neck, which had purpled from the attack. Then the hardened resolve returned again—a leathery look that belonged to smiths who'd spent long hours near a forge. "You and I had no confidence or bargain for silence. The pendant you wear may bring danger to my people. I shared that information with my advisors. We had to decide what to do about your being here at all."

A grim smile grew on Sutter's lips—an expression that surprised him. "This is how a man becomes king, then, with careful words and betrayal?"

"Hold your tongue," Relothian said, his voice both soft and menacing, "or I will *show* you how I became king."

The man raised his hammer. Sutter didn't back down. "If you needed to share secrets you knew were meant for your ears alone, you should have told me. Your loose lips nearly got me killed."

Relothian's hard glare remained unchanged. "We live in perilous times. Now, is this why you interrupted my training, or is there something else?"

Sutter cast his gaze at the king's training companions, who eyed him expectantly. He knew what he must do, and doubt filled him. But then he remembered the dark plain of shale. He remembered thousands of dead Far, many of whom had died saving him. His inexpert use of his Sedagin blade had sent many to their final earth. He'd vowed not to let that happen again. Vowed to be worthy of the sword he carried.

He frowned back at the king. "There's rot in your city. And you're blind to it."

The king grabbed Sutter's tunic and threw him toward the center of the yard as easily as he might a doll. "You'll defend those words," Relothian said, stepping toward him.

Sutter pulled his blade from its sheath. This was mad. But *he* was mad. "Before we begin, I'll have your word that if I best you, you'll hear me out."

The king laughed.

Sutter shook his head. "It doesn't have to be this way. Let me take you and show you. There are things you need to understand."

"Your insult needs an answer." Relothian raised his sword and hammer, a kind of grimacing smile on his lips. Before Sutter could do more than raise his sword defensively, the king was on him, shoving him to the ground.

Relothian raised his blade. Sutter rolled, steel striking the dirt where his chest had been a mere second before. It rang out in the battle yard with a metallic ting. Unable to gain his feet, Sutter rolled again, sensing a second blow. And again the blade bit the ground where he'd just been.

He pushed himself up in time to ward off the third blow, blocking it with his own weapon. The ring of steel came brighter and sharper this time, his blade chipping where it was struck by the king's own.

Sutter reared to strike. Before he could, Relothian brought his hammer down in a brutal stroke at Sutter's left arm. He just had time to whip away, using an evasive Latae dance move. He backpedaled to gain control.

Relothian followed, and swung again. This time, Sutter parried the strike, and slipped his blade in under Relothian's outstretched arm, piercing his upper left thigh. Another Latae figure. The king made no sound, and came on undaunted as blood darkened his trousers. As Sutter pressed forward, the king whipped his hammer around, knocking Sutter's blade out of the way, and following with a powerful strike that cut deep into Sutter's left arm.

The slicing metal sent bright shocks of pain through his flesh. Warm blood began to flow down his sleeve. Every movement brought terrific burn, but he managed to raise his Sedagin blade to ward off another hammer attack.

The metal edge of his Sedagin blade chipped again, and the force of Relothian's blow sent him to the ground a second time. He blindly thrust his blade upward, just as another arcing attack came down at him. This time, the king's sword sundered the Sedagin blade in two.

Sutter stared at the cleanly severed steel, shocked and saddened over the ruined gift. The king likewise stared down at the stump of the Sedagin blade. The only sound in the training yard was their labored breathing. Sutter looked up at the sword in the other's hand.

What metal could cut straight through Sedagin steel?

Then Relothian's eyes focused again on Sutter, and the hard anger returned. Before the king could rear back to strike again, Sutter tossed the truncated sword aside and grabbed the king's sword arm. He pulled Relothian forward, lifting his feet into the man's gut and thrusting out hard with his legs—another Far Latae maneuver. Relothian went sailing, landing heavily in the dirt behind him.

Sutter grabbed his broken blade and rolled onto his knees just as Relothian gained his feet and took one charging step with his upraised hammer.

The king skidded to a stop, dirt and dust flying into the air. A look of confusion lit his face.

"You're mad!" Relothian shouted. "Would you die just to have me join a crowd of politicians in Recityv? Those farmers know nothing of war or the threat beyond the Pall. We're defending ourselves well enough without the help of gladhanders, boy! A *Sedagin* would appreciate this, and leave us in peace."

Sutter frowned in anger and frustration, and fought to catch his breath. "I'm not Sedagin!"

The king's brow wrinkled with impatience. "Yes, I know the sword wasn't originally—"

"I'm a rootdigger," Sutter shouted. In the long pause that followed, his frustration released him and he laughed at the look in the king's eyes.

The laughter disarmed Relothian, who looked confused and wary.

"And, my lord," Sutter said, nodding, "your court and army are not what you think. Take it from a working man."

Relothian's expression moved from confusion to wonder. Sutter guessed that a man who started life as a smith might appreciate one who started life digging roots. After several long moments, the king's own breathing returned to normal. He lowered his sword. "Show me."

• CHAPTER SEVENTY-EIGHT •

A Better Parabola

If we ever get the mirror shape just right, I'm convinced our skyglass will peer beyond space and give us a look into the past.

—Lore ascribed to Jahnes Plerek on the very same
night he invented the first reflecting skyglass;
though, regardless if it's true or not, it did give rise
to theoretical models on the nature of light

TAHN'S SUCCESSION TEAM had been preparing ceaselessly for their first argument—a tough one, with the College of Physics. He knew they all needed a night to relax and think about something besides Continuity and Resonance. And, maybe more than that, they needed, for an evening, to leave behind the things they'd been finding as proofs for their argument. They weren't easy things to learn. Or believe. After a warm meal of pheasant and roasted potatoes, Tahn led them to the place he remembered most for getting away from other cares: Snellens, a lens and mirror shop at the edge of the Grove.

He ducked through the door, and immediately heard the rhythmic sound of circular movement. It was like listening to a familiar tune. Shem, the shop owner, could polish a lens or mirror all day with minimal breaks. The man seemed never to tire. Tahn smiled. He loved this place. As much as he enjoyed the *higher*-minded problems of charting stars and making suppositions, he liked every bit as well the chance to sit with Shem and polish a mirror.

He made a small laugh in the dimly lit front of the shop, and led his Succession team through a second door. They emerged into a broad, well-lit workshop filled with all the instruments needed to make a lens or mirror. Neatly in their place were Shem's toolbench, buckets of grit, a box of Ebon white sand, cooling posts, pots of agent and coating metal. All of it had been situated relative to a small kiln in the corner, where Shem fired his own glass parabolas preparatory to them receiving their metal coat. The air hung with the scent of pine—pitch used for polishing. Tahn also smelled the speculum—a copper, tin, and arsenic mixture that comprised one type of metal layer used to make a mirror.

He took it all in at a glance as Shem looked up, his well-lined face smiling. The mirror-maker never stopped polishing the mirror in his lap.

"Gnomon!" He nodded with his head for Tahn to come closer. "You're a reflection of your younger you. Grab a pad."

Tahn sat opposite his old friend, took up a mirror pad, applied a dollop of pitch, and began polishing the opposite side of the mirror in Shem's lap.

"You're still using speculum?" Tahn asked, as though a day hadn't passed since his last visit to this place.

"Oh, I've got new alloys, and silver's popular. But some of the older star-fellows like the older reflections." His grin widened. "What's a mirror man to do? I just have to moderate the arsenic. It lends a shine, but not worth dying for."

"No, probably not," Tahn agreed with a grin.

Without any introduction, Shem spoke to Tahn's Succession team. "You may not know that Gnomon here is responsible for the single most important discovery in Grove history. In my time, anyway. And maybe in a handful of centuries." He smiled with the joke of it, and held his tongue to heighten their anticipation.

Tahn looked up at Rithy and his new friends, shaking his head in mock embarrassment.

"Pine tar," Shem finally said, sharing the mystery's answer.

He pointed at the bowl of pitch beside him. "Was a good admixture before. But Gnomon made it better. Poured oil and resin and what-all into a bowl, then went out and tapped a piñon pine for something to give it some viscosity and grit. Mirrors got twice as bright, by my eyes."

Tahn continued to polish, already losing himself in the steady rhythm of brightening the metal mirror. "I'll be famous for sap," he added.

To her credit, Rithy made none of the obvious jokes.

"Several mirrors need rubbing," Shem said, indicating benches around his shop. "You can see how it's done. Have a rub."

Tahn smiled in good humor. "Give it a try," he encouraged. "Work the metal in small circular motions. It's relaxing."

His friends all sat and began to polish various shapes of glass, each bearing a metal coating. With the proper amount of polishing, they'd become Snellens skyglass mirrors—best in the Grove. For several minutes, all that could be heard was the sound of pitch pads going around. Shem put an end to that.

"Now I won't diminish Gnomon's pine tar discovery. Truth be told, it's helped me fetch a fine return on my lenses." Shem often referred to all his skyglass work as "lens work." But he also sometimes called it "snellens," like the name of his shop, which was his own mirror joke—a palindrome with "lens" reflected backward at its beginning. "But did you know he's responsible for the new parabola?"

Rithy looked over at Tahn, who hunched his shoulders. He'd never bothered to share this, even when he'd lived here in the Grove.

"Ayuh," Shem went on, continuing to polish. "Got fussin' over the shape of it. Said his own skyglass had blurry spots. I let him have a mirror cast to play with. Next thing I know, he shapes it out a bit here and there, changing the curvature. Then he runs some hot glass into it, molds his parabolic mirror, coats it with silver, drops it into his skyglass frame, marches onto the east plain, and discovers the three-year comet. You named it Tamara, didn't you, Gnomon?"

Tahn nodded, memories of different kinds colliding in his

mind. But like an astronomer with a good parabola mirror, he was seeing clearly now. The deaths of friends were part of that. He relaxed even more into the fondness of being in Shem's shop, polishing. The smell of mirror metal, pitch, linseed oil, burning tallow . . . he'd missed this place a hell of a lot.

"I'd forgotten you found Tamara," Rithy said. Tahn heard admiration in her voice.

"A bit of luck," he said dismissively.

"No such thing," Shem countered.

They fell into a spate of quiet polishing. And from the looks on his Succession team's faces, he thought he'd picked just the right thing to help them clear their minds before the actual arguments began.

But the feeling soured when three young philosophers stepped into the room.

"We're closed," Shem said, hardly acknowledging the newcomers.

"I can see that," said the first philosopher, "by all the visitors you're entertaining." The sarcasm was subtle, but accusational.

Shem looked up. "I don't need to stand up, do I?" Shem's tone carried the right amount of threat. He was older, but his arms were like iron. Everyone knew it.

"No, no. Keep your seat." It was Darius, appearing from behind his two philosopher brethren. He stepped farther into the room, surveying the Succession team. "We just wanted to share a few words, then we'll be going." Darius smiled.

Tahn noted that beneath the philosophy college insignia, in the same subtle threading, the emblem of the League lay embroidered on his overcloak.

"I overheard a bit of your conversation," Darius finally said. "Pine tar, was it?"

Tahn nodded, not the least embarrassed. "Clever, don't you think?"

"Certainly. And also certainly the most important discovery you *will* ever make in Aubade Grove." He stepped forward, coming very near Tahn. "You see, Tahn, with the

College of Philosophy, it's not whether or not you can prove Continuity is a real thing." Darius paused, lending weight to what he meant to say. "It's whether or not your use of it is rational and justified. Like killing a child to save us from the monsters."

This time it was Darius's men who laughed. Tahn's anger flared—clearly Darius had spies. "Why don't we worry about the philosophy argument when the time comes. Here," he said, proffering his pitch pad, "would you like a rub?"

The loudest laugh came from Myles, Tahn's team philosopher. Darius silenced Myles with a withering stare. "It may be conventional for a member of our college to counsel the Succession arguer," Darius said with a biting tone, "but it earns you no credit with me." Myles dropped his eyes to his mirror.

"Still with the accounting language?" Tahn interjected. "Well then, can I get some credit with you? For my pine sap, maybe?" He was trying hard to diffuse the situation. He'd meant this to be a relaxing evening, and didn't want any trouble, particularly here in Shem's shop. The lenses all around were in a delicate state.

Darius leaned forward. "I don't think you understand the League's position on this."

Tahn looked down at the dual insignias on Darius's garment. "I watched leaguemen burn an innocent woman." He let that hang in the air a good long time. "I fought leaguemen for poisoning a child." He let that hang, too. "I don't give an absent gods damn what your position is." Then he smiled as dismissively as he was able. But even to him it seemed a grim smile.

Everyone had stopped polishing.

Shem stood. "I'm going to ask you to leave."

Darius seemed not to hear Shem's invitation. He smiled at Tahn. "As before, I'm here to see Tahn in a formal capacity. As Aubade Grove's ranking leagueman, I'm putting an end to your bid for Succession," he said, his voice gone cool. "There are many reasons to believe you're a fugitive. Among them, your unlawful escape from your prison cell in Recityv, where you were being held for interfering with the hanging of a leagueman. And the reports we have of you killing innocent children, while inconclusive, are ongoing. In the meantime, I'll have to restrict your access to college libraries and towers, and am considering assigning you a permanent guardian . . . for the safety of our community."

"You have your facts wrong," Tahn said, standing.

Darius waved away his objections. "Besides all this, and before we expend any further Grove resources on Succession, we'll want to feel confident that you aren't putting forward an argument . . . for the wrong reasons."

Tahn had lost the feeling he'd come to Snellens to find. And his hope of stopping a war was being torn away based on rumor and distortions of the truth. It was preposterous. And maddening. Perhaps Darius just needed to understand Tahn's purpose.

"Continuity and Resonance will help us understand the Veil. Which will help us figure out how to make it strong again. And stop whatever would cross that barrier to harm us." He offered it all as evenly as he could, his blood pumping.

Darius's brow went up in an expression of incredulity. But not surprise. He knew what Tahn's argument was going to be. "This is your Succession plan? This is what Aubade Grove is going to be asked to consider? Do you have any idea how antiquated you sound? How this demeans all of us here, who are trying to push thought forward? Real science?" The philosopher shook his head. "No, Tahn. Even if you weren't someone who'd escaped by dubious means from the pits of Solath Mahnus. Even if we couldn't hold you for killing children in the name of war. Even then, I wouldn't let this Succession proceed."

Tahn took a deep breath. "You don't have that power. I have a sponsor for Succession. The savants will hear it."

Darius's own smile at that was answer enough. Darius *did* have the power. Tahn's mood darkened. He saw in his mind the faces of friends, *thirty-seven*—what they felt, what they did—when the Quiet stripped them of hope. He saw Tamara lying by a stream.

And there stirred in him a bit of Resonance, not unlike

what he'd experienced days ago in the tower dome, fighting a Quiet man.

Tahn stepped forward, bringing his face close to Darius's. "You will wait for Succession," he said softly, slowly, moderating his own anger the best he could. "Because if you don't, I will show you, personally, what I intend to prove. And it will end your doubts about the Quiet."

He couldn't be sure, but Tahn thought the room fell into shadow then. Like something passed before the many lamps set around the workshop. Or perhaps it was a greying in his own eyes, as he focused on Darius to the exclusion of everything else . . . the way he did when he needed to find something with which . . . to resonate.

The League philosopher stared back a long moment, undaunted, and said, "Teach me."

Darius let that settle between them. A challenge. An invitation.

Tahn looked at this man who meant to block him, who might cause a great widening of the Scar and everything that followed from such a widening.

Then Darius added, "Because we all know what happened to the last Successionist to argue Continuity."

Tahn shot a look at Rithy, whose expression turned sour with remembrance. In that moment, his last bit of restraint melted away.

What came started like a cold ache down low in his gut. Then it filled him with a warm rush like blood returning to a numbed limb. Unlike when he drew an imagined arrow and let fly a part of himself, this time Tahn's Resonance was like the pluck of a tightly drawn string on a broken, unmusical instrument. He instinctively sought the crippling memory of Tamara in all its fullness. Funneled it into a pure feeling of helplessness and regret and reached out to something inside Darius that could know such a feeling.

Like a pot boiling over, the man before him drew a hundred instant connections to the Resonance Tahn was causing, and began to shudder. Tahn could see him hurting deep down. He could feel the ache that was spreading in him like a disease, quieting doubts, quieting resolve.

And Tahn kept on. Things he'd suffered. The ugliness he'd seen from the League. It was all swept into the Resonance he forced inside Darius. He followed it, let it grow inside himself, too.

Only vaguely was he aware of how cankered everything around him began to feel. As though the Resonance had grown beyond what he felt or caused Darius to feel. And only vaguely was he aware that he was being shaken, that the smell of pitch was strong in his nose. As though it was being used as a strong-smelling waking salt.

But he was far inside the feeling. Unsettling as it was, he didn't want to let it go. A morbid desire to see it through had seized him. Carefree delight tripped along with his blackest anger.

Tahn, can you hear me?

He would drop this man with the amplification of his own suffering.

Tahn?

Then he was seeing Shem before him, the man's hands on his shoulders—one holding a pine-tar pitch pad. Shem was speaking, asking Tahn if he could hear him.

Tahn shook his head, and pushed Shem gently aside. A few paces back stood Darius, staring, a guarded look in his eye. But not an acquiescent one. Not completely.

Tahn took a few steps toward him. "I will honor Succession, and make my argument the best I can. If I'm beaten in the discourse theaters, then I am beaten." He pointed a finger. "But it will not happen anywhere else. Not here. And not anywhere my Succession team will be. Until Succession ends, one way or the other."

Darius stared back at him, firm, but thinking—Tahn could see it in the philosopher's eyes. "Is this what you did to those kids near Naltus?"

Tahn didn't miss a beat. "No. Them I let die."

Darius looked around the room, then turned and left. As soon as the shop's front door closed, Tahn dropped to his knees. The shivering he'd barely kept under control now wracked his body.

"What in all my skies just happened?" Shem asked.

Rithy was there fast, wrapping her coat around his shoulders. "Tahn? What was that?"

He looked at her, having no way to explain that proving Resonance had begun to mean two things. At least two: strengthening the Veil, and understanding his own connection to Resonance itself.

When he thought he could move on his own, he got to his chair, took up his pitch pad, and continued polishing the mirror. "Please," he invited, "let's not let it ruin this night. We deserve some distraction."

"In the name of dead gods, you don't think *that* was a distraction?" Rithy exclaimed.

A few low chuckles followed.

He looked them each in the eye. They deserved to know. "A few nights ago, in the astronomy tower, I was attacked by a Velle."

There were gasps.

"I knew it was more than your clumsiness," Rithy remarked.

"At least I think it was a Velle," Tahn went on, shaking his head. "I'm not certain. But whatever it was, it could render like one. It could . . . control and direct Resonance. And so, it would seem . . . can I."

A heavy silence stretched in the little mirror shop. Incredulous looks.

Tahn nodded and managed a small laugh. "That's what I think, too. But, if nothing else, the stranger got me thinking about Resonance in new ways. I believe it's helping our Succession argument."

"How?" asked Myles, his team philosopher.

Tahn gave Myles a thoughtful look. "Made me think about the sound a person has. Made me think about ambivalence. Made me realize any two things can be brought into resonance." He looked over at Rithy. "Which will help us with our clock demonstration tomorrow in the discourse theater, won't it?"

"Is this thing still hanging around?" Rithy asked. *The visitor in the astronomy dome.*

Tahn took a deep breath. "Haven't seen him, but yeah, I

suspect he is. Leaving me alone for now, though. So, please, let's try to enjoy just polishing a damn mirror for a few hours."

Nervous laughter turned easy. And slowly, the others picked up their pitch pads. Soon enough, there was idle chat as they prepared mirrors and lenses for skyglasses big and small.

Tahn, though, battled back an unsettling thought. *I might have killed him.* And before he could try to fool himself that what had happened was Resonance *doing something to him,* maybe taking control of his senses, Tahn stopped himself. That would be a lie. He'd been aware the whole time. Deeply aware. And if Darius came again, and made the same threat, he might finish what he'd started.

So, aware? Yes. But not in control. He wondered if coming to understand Resonance would prove more dangerous to him. Since it seemed what he had inside to resonate with was little more than the Scar.

He took a long, stuttering breath, still feeling chilled. Looking down, he noticed his mirror had a crack in it. Several, in fact. He used it as an excuse to move near the kiln, its bed of coals a medley of bright red and orange, and good medicine for the cold inside him. There he set to work on a new mirror, one with a fresh coat of silver.

Eventually, the rhythms of polishing pushed troubling thoughts from his mind, leaving him and his Succession team a mild last evening before Succession truly began.

• CHAPTER SEVENTY-NINE •

Gathering Old Stories

There's a currency that all people share, that all people care about—stories. The ones they hold close and share only when nothing else matters. A smart merchant gathers these the way a fool gathers hats.

—The unwritten and unacknowledged commodity of the Storalaith House of merchants, a generational principle of their brokerage

THIN SHADOWS FELL across the room as Helaina slipped from her bed to the cold stone floor. The soft glow of a single lamp lit the chamber, where only Artixan remained. The others were gone, preparing for their departures from Recityv. Her old friend, sitting in the corner, looked very tired and very old as he sat vigil over her.

"You should get some sleep," she chastened mildly.

He gave her a weak smile, and nodded. "There'll be time to sleep when my body lies warmly in the earth."

"Nonsense. I'm doing fine. And you look like a bit of death." She limped over to where he sat in a deep high-back chair. "Besides, we shouldn't stay in this room long."

He nodded understanding. "The map of private chambers in Solath Mahnus is in the regent's High Office. Roth is likely to avail himself of its secrets, isn't he?" He looked up at her with anxious eyes. "When did I start being able to anticipate the actions of a murderer?"

She couldn't help but give a small laugh. "You've stood too long at this old lady's side not to. And thank you for that."

"What's your idea?" he asked with a heavy sigh.

"I have to go out briefly." She moved to a small table and drew out a short sheet of parchment and set to it with ink and pen. She rubbed her hands briskly before beginning to write.

"On my way, I'll slip an anonymous letter under the Sodality's rear door, knock, and leave before they answer."

"And your letter?"

"To First Sodalist Palon. Him alone. You need to be in their protective care while we're away."

He struggled to the edge of his chair. "I'm going with you to Y'Tilat Mor."

"No, my friend. I'm old, but you're ancient."

That fetched a genuine laugh. "I won't argue that. But do you think you should go without me? Just let me rest. I can make the trip."

She shook her head. "I'll have Grant at my side. He's a bit rough, but can you think of anyone better? Even you?"

Artixan conceded with a smile.

"Besides, if you're strong enough to travel, you should consider going with Vendanj to Estem Salo." She shot him a quick glance of emphasis.

"Because you worry even if his intentions are right, he'll offend the Randeur. Put our path sideways." Artixan nodded as he said it.

"I'm not sure why we verbalize anymore; we always seem to know one another's thoughts." She paused a moment, grinning. "Which should distress me more than it does."

He didn't share her smile this time. "If I don't see you again before you leave, remember that the Mors protect their privacy with vigor. And if they get news you're no longer the regent, you won't have the protection of authority. You'll just be a lone woman asking for their most cherished, most secret knowledge."

"That's a bit stark for a good-bye," she said, knowing she'd miss his pitch-perfect advice while she was gone. "But you're right. That's why I'm taking this nighttime stroll. There's something I'll need when I solicit the Mors. As for you, I suspect the Sodality will be here within the hour to move you to their daily strong room."

"I know the rotation," Artixan said. "It's close. I'll get there myself. And tell them to be discreet. A pile of sodalists will be a signal to the League."

She finished her note, folded it into an envelope, sealed it with a few drops of wax, and wrote Palon's name across the front. She then shrugged into a heavy cloak with a deep cowl, and turned to face him.

"Pull the cowl up farther," he advised. "No one needs to see that face of yours."

She smiled and crossed to where he sat, bending down to embrace him around the shoulders. "Take care for yourself. And if you really are able to travel, get out of this hell. Go with Vendanj."

His nod told her it wasn't likely. His family was here. He'd want to be close if they needed him. "You're as uncompromising as he is, you know."

She didn't have to ask to know he meant Grant. "There's a happy thought."

"Just something to think about." He sat back in his chair, clearly still exhausted. When he looked up at her again, his face showed a contented sort of thoughtfulness. "It's been an honor to serve you, Helaina. You're the finest person I know. A bit leathery at times. But more calfskin than sow's ear."

She had to work hard to keep herself from laughing too loudly. "And you, my friend, are nothing but dignity and self-lessness, miraculously evident in the body of a man."

"We're two doting old fools, is what we are." He waved a hand for her to be on her way. "Get going before we start competing over incontinence."

"Just one more thing," said Helaina, putting a hand aside his face. "Thank you. Thank you for restoring my son's life all those years ago when he came still."

He was shaking his head. "You've thanked me for this—"

"It was a breach of your Sheason oath," she went on. "A serious one, I've learned. I asked, and you said yes. You gave me my son back, knowing what it might mean for you. I don't know many . . . thank you."

He placed his own hand atop hers and gave her a warm smile. For a long moment their good-byes came in silence. She thought she could distantly hear the tumult of civil conflict in her city. But she'd have to navigate through it. There was one visit she needed to make, one thing she needed to retrieve.

She kissed Artixan's forehead, and moved to the rear of the room. She couldn't simply walk out the front gates of Solath Mahnus. She would need a less conspicuous exit. And as regent, she had some few secrets that she shared with no one. They weren't even listed on the documents in her office.

She moved to the far corner, where a high table stood with small statuary, some books, and an oil lamp. After quietly picking up the lamp, she crawled beneath the table and triggered a false panel in the wall. Beyond it lay a secret, narrow system of corridors connecting many of the chambers throughout Solath Mahnus. The air inside smelled of dry stone and rodent droppings. She lit the lamp and began to wind her way through the passageways.

In some places she had to duck low, even crawl, to pass. And more than once she slipped into a sideways shuffle to negotiate extremely tight sections of a corridor. Stairways between floors were rare; mostly she climbed very old ladders made from wood that creaked beneath her slight weight.

She pushed on through her weariness and pain, panting like a mongrel as she descended a last ladder that brought her to another false panel. On it, she traced a complicated set of numeric symbols in a pattern where each next symbol was separated by the sum of the previous two. The panel swung quietly open. As it did, she extinguished the lamp, and eased into deep shadows behind a great hedge of holly. She was outside. The cool, dry-earth smell, coupled with the sweet scent of holly berries, refreshed her. She put down the lamp, ducked low, and pushed her way through the hedge.

Distant shouts of anger made it clear the civil hostilities continued. She took them as a goad to hurry.

She made her way across a small garden to a narrow arch in the Wall of Remembrance. Even this would normally have been guarded. But tonight, all members of her guard were needed elsewhere. So she passed unnoticed into the broader streets of Recityv, just another older woman with her cowl up, trying to avoid trouble.

She slipped through the shadows of familiar buildings and

down narrow byways. These were avenues for deliveries to merchant shops. They were alleys for straw-drift folk, who piled cast-off refuse into makeshift huts.

Tonight, some of these back alleys were open graves where those first to fall in the civil conflict had been dragged to clear the thoroughfares. Helaina slunk past dead men and women and more than a few small ones who lay still in the shadows. She stopped more than once and forced back sobs at the sight of loved ones who'd obviously been alive to take each other in an embrace before dying. All of it galvanized her resolve. *Fist in the glove.*

She got quickly to the Sodality manor's rear entrance. The gate to the small courtyard was open. *Thank the deaf gods.* She slipped the letter beneath the door, then returned to the gate, where she selected a hand-sized rock and made a good throw at the door. It cracked loud, like a brash knock, and she scuttled up the alley. She was turning onto another small street when she heard the door fly open and the sound of voices.

With her chin tucked low, she hurried on, breathing through her mouth with the exertion. By alleyway, she came soon to the broad thoroughfare of Rel Mercantile, where all the merchant families kept residences and storehouses. The Merchant Quarter. Standing concealed just inside an alley, she spied men walking, hands on sword pommels, in regular shifts. They reminded her of trained guard dogs pacing back and forth. Only here, a handful of men—leaguemen, it appeared—walked long beats. Rel Mercantile stretched three hundred strides, at least.

After watching their patterns, Helaina timed her crossing to the Storalaith House, and got quickly to the delivery alley directly across from her. Tonight, she would be less formal. And she knew the trace lock to get her into her childhood home.

Inside, she drew back her hood and climbed a small set of stairs to the main floor. She headed directly for the kitchen. Unsurprisingly, two lanterns burned on the thick-block table, and seated between them was her father, reading over a set of ledgers.

When her da heard her footsteps, he looked up over the top of his spectacles. His face appeared more careworn than just a few days ago when she'd come to retrieve her letter. As she looked back at him, the parade of expressions was almost comical: initial indignation at being interrupted, distaste at seeing her—given their last meeting—and then grateful relief as the realization set in: His daughter was alive.

"I wanted you to know," she said. "I'm going away, leaving Recityv. But I wanted you to know I was alive."

Gemen Storalaith didn't move for a long moment, the light of the lamps reflected in the glasses far down on his nose. Finally, his face softened a tad more. "I'm glad, sweet one." He hadn't called her that in many, many years.

Then he added, "Where will you go?"

"I think it's safer for you if I don't say. I may have put you in some danger just coming here. That's enough."

He'd already been nodding, following her logic immediately. "Smart thinking," he said. She'd missed that, her father's turn of phrase whenever they got talking strategy over a thing, whether commerce or politics or rhetoric. *Smart thinking.*

"Da?" She hesitated. She should get what she came for before upsetting the man.

His eyebrows rose, awaiting her request.

"I need to go back into the vault. There's something I left there long before taking the regent seat. I imagine it will help me while I'm away." She then waited for an invitation, no longer feeling the right to simply enter. Though she would do so if it came to that. Ceremony had all but been abandoned in matters of state.

Again he nodded. "Need help getting in?" A grimace interrupted the man's softer look. *He's remembering Mendel.* She wondered if the pinch of it had to do with his son's death, or that Mendel had proved to be capable of murdering Gemen's only other child. Maybe both.

"I can manage," she said, and angled past him into the hallway off the rear of the kitchen.

She navigated the several doors and their clever locks again to get to the granite vault. After closing the great stone door, she turned up the wick on the low-burning lamp, and looked around.

Tonight, as before, she was seeking one thing in particular. She crossed to the bookshelves, and moved to the far left, where a crank was set into a series of steel flywheels. With a childlike anticipation she hadn't felt in decades, she began turning the crank. It didn't move at first, and she smiled.

"I'm cranky," she said, initiating the key to the voice lock. That pithy expression had been Mendel's idea, when their father had asked for a vocal phrase for the crank. Remembering it was bittersweet—she missed Mendel, the way he had been back then.

She tried again, pulling on the handle. The two leftmost bookshelves began to move. The one on the far left drew backward, and the shelf next to it began moving into its place. From behind the one on the right, another bookshelf started to move forward.

A very low, very quiet rumble sounded in the vault of goods. The shelf system moved on a special series of casters and tracks that were never allowed to fall into disrepair. Still, the low, toneless hum sounded like the voice of a lesser god announcing revelation. There were treasures secured in the shelves kept out of sight: valuable editions, Storalaith histories, ledgers of past transactions. There were too many to catalog or recall, spanning across no less than thirty shelves, which slowly came forward into the light of her lamp.

With a little tradesmanship, she'd long ago convinced her father to give her a shelf of her own. Books that she wanted kept safe, as much from the weathers of time as from malfeasant hands or just careless readers.

A few moments later, her own private collection cycled into view. She stopped cranking. The sudden silence seemed deafening, like the calm before important things take place.

Kneeling on the floor, fingering along the spines of the many tomes, she came to a very thin book with a cracked binding. She pulled it free and curled it into her lap. She knew its feel without having to strain in the weak light to read its cover. Just holding it gave her some small measure of hope for the trip they were about to make. And while feeling its aged leather beneath her aching, swollen fingers, she recalled how she'd come by these pages.

Helaina cherished scola—authors, readers, scriveners, even accountants—thoughtful entertainers and historians all. But to most merchants, books—much to the distaste of those who created and cared about them—had become a commodity.

The correlation between books and money adhered to the Merchant Rule of Reciprocity though—a rule most merchants failed to fully appreciate, which was why Helaina had fast surpassed her peers in financial acumen. The rule was simple: Buying was at least as important as selling. Helaina had devised a strategy of expending considerable amounts of Storalaith resources when the economy was at its worst.

In time, she'd become the wealthiest amongst them, because traders in goods and services wanted to deal only with Helaina.

With some of her wealth, Helaina had built a library, and followed soon with other libraries in other cities where her family did trade. She bought vacant storehouses in Vohnce and even in Balens and Kali-Firth. They were modest structures, housing at first just a few dozen books. But she hired troupers to give readings for children, and staffed these places with knowledgeable scriveners to aid those who still struggled to read. With time, the number of books in her libraries grew, as did those who came to read or listen.

She bought books by the lot, dealing with copyists, collectors, scrivener houses, authors themselves. And it all—well, most of it—went directly to her libraries. Rare items she often sold to show her father a profit. And occasionally, she held one back for herself. Like this book. She looked down through the dimness at the story she held in her lap. *The Pauper's Drum*.

She remembered hearing the story of the pauper's drum as a young girl. Not at bedtime from her parents or in play with her friends. She'd seen it acted out on a pageant wagon long before the League began to discourage the fancies of myth performed by the troupes.

This book, though, had been written in the Mor tongue. She'd spent the better part of three years in lessons from Maesteri Belamae—himself a Ta'Opin Mor—learning the nuances of the three-part speech. Doing so had taught her of the gulf between interpretation and the words of the actual story.

On the pageant wagon, a sweet tale of music and innocence had drawn tears from mothers, reverence from fathers, and fascination from kids like herself. In the book, the drum was terrifying.

If she didn't miss her guess, this very book had been stolen from a private collection belonging to someone of importance in one of the Mor nations. Though there were times over the years that she wondered if the book had been offered to her for some other reason. If, perhaps, it was an overture of some kind, or an invitation, or a reminder.

Regardless, Helaina believed this book might be necessary to their safe reception when they entered Y'Tilat Mor. Perhaps personally carrying it back to them would convey something about her reverence for the tale and help with her request for the Refrains. *The Pauper's Drum,* Belamae had taught her, was sacred to the Mors.

Her joints were aching, and got her moving again. She cranked the shelves back to where they'd stood when she'd first entered, and spared one last look around, feeling nostalgic for her merchant days. Then, she took herself through the several locked doors and back to her father's kitchen, where he still sat, poring over numbers.

"Find what you needed?" he said, not yet looking up. He marked the page with his graphite to hold his place, and finally sat back.

"I did, thanks." Helaina looked in the direction of the hall that led to the stairs and the upper living rooms. "Is Ma asleep?"

"I gave her a mild soporific to ease her nerves. She won't wake 'til morning." He smiled regretfully.

She nodded, though she would have liked to see her mother and let her know she was all right. She didn't know if she'd be coming back.

Everything else done, she finally came to it. "Da?"

Again, her father's brow wrinkled as his eyebrows raised, awaiting her question.

"First, I'm sorry about Mendel. I didn't really get a chance to say it when . . . It happened fast. And my Emerit wanted to get me someplace safe."

Gemen Storalaith swallowed audibly in the silence that stretched between them, and only shook his head. *A shame,* that gesture said. *A shame all around.*

She smiled weakly. "I also notice that it looks like your trade has . . . shifted. House Storalaith was a knowledge broker, mostly. At least it was when I was here."

Her da suddenly looked slightly less grief stricken, slightly more guarded.

"It's late, sweet one. Maybe we should leave the rest for another time." He tried to go back to his ledger.

His trembling hands took up his graphite and rule, and he began to etch another line of text and figures onto the page.

Helaina pressed on, but with a gentle tone. "I guess my own law forced you to evolve the business. From the looks of the vault, I'd say information discovery. That sound accurate?"

The man said nothing. The scratch of his graphite seemed loud in the quiet kitchen. He paused long enough to take a draught from a glass of chilled milk.

"I'm not angry. And I'm not the regent anymore, even if I wanted to take exception to anything I saw." She raised a conciliatory hand. "Please, I'm just asking."

Her father glanced up at her over the top of his spectacles and set to his ledger again. His jaw tensed. She could tell he wanted to keep the more familial exchange they'd had this night, and let that be their parting memory. He was struggling to keep his temper.

She hated that she couldn't let him have that much.

"Your transaction ledger shows the League as your main buyer." She stepped closer. "I'm sure Mendel's involvement with them is wound up in that somewhere." She wished she hadn't said it that way.

Her father stopped writing, but didn't yet look up.

"What I mean is, it would seem that Storalaith resources are gathering and producing information for the League. Current, available information here in Recityv, and from all the places where you have informants. But not just that, Da. By the look of it, you're testing, researching . . . uncovering new knowledge. And on the League's behalf, it seems."

Then it hit her, and a chill rushed over her skin. The League wasn't just buying information. They were looking for something. And her father was helping them.

Now she was making an accusation, not one with any legal bite, but one with ethical teeth that would tear at her father's sense of principle. "You realize it was the League that tried to kill me. The League that slaughtered hundreds of innocent people today."

With her father, she'd never been a good politician. She'd never learned to work hard at crafting the words just so. It was plainly spoken, and it was out there now. But it was also accurate.

Gemen Storalaith put down his graphite and rule and took off his spectacles. He worked his jaw back and forth a few times, as one might who needs to relieve some tension first. Then, he began, slowly. "I think what you mean to say is thank you. Thank you for providing sound information to a man who wants everyone to have the same access to information that my daughter once sought with her libraries."

"Roth—"

He held up a hand to silence her. "And thank yourself, while you're at it, for leaving me with nothing to do but re-scope my trade and find the only willing buyers available."

As he spoke, his voice began to quaver the way a griever's will when sobs threaten to steal his voice. Helaina watched with a grief of her own, realizing she was losing him again, seeing in his eyes that he knew he was losing her, as well. But neither of them seemed able to relent.

She wished they could just sit together and calculate numbers and talk trade strategy and drink cold milk. She wanted to be a daughter again.

"How can you do this?" she asked.

He smiled sadly. "I've often wanted to ask you the same question."

She guessed at his meaning: *The Knowledge Law*. Though something told her there were multiple meanings in his words. Finally, she had only one thing to say. "Will you please keep secret about me?"

Her da finally gave in to a deep sob, and nodded. They stood, a stride apart, appraising each other with thoughtful expressions, but never embracing.

In a hoarse whisper, she managed, "Thank you, Da."

Before she turned to leave, he held out a small envelope.

"What's this?" she asked.

"Mixture of tea and turmeric." He offered a weak smile. "Like your mother said, it'll help with those hands of yours."

She took the envelope, and stole a brief caress of her father's age-spotted hands. Then she turned and got herself out into the cool night air, which made the warm tears that followed all the warmer.

Be the fist in the glove.

With no small amount of determination, she turned her thoughts forward. She and her friends would all leave Recityv soon. But they had one stop to make on their departure from Recityv: Descant.

There was a young Leiholan woman there that Belamae had indicated might join them.

CHAPTER EIGHTY

Scores

All things have a resonant signature. And so all things have a song.

—Fundamental compositional canon, first articulated by Maesteri Elyk Divad

WENDRA STEPPED QUIETLY into the music archive. She'd found it, with some difficulty, near the southernmost portion of Descant's sprawling series of halls and vaulted cupolas. It occupied a smaller dome. But there seemed nothing small about it from where she stood.

High above her, starlight passed through a round of windows. The rectangles of night made the rest of the dome seem all the darker, except for the single lamp burning several floors above her.

As she watched, a figure stepped up to one of several podiums overlooking the open center of the domed chamber. The rustling of sheet music fell down from above. And then the figure started to sing. A sweet, foreign sound. Wendra listened, captivated by the music, and instantly knew the voice. She'd been directed correctly. It was Telaya.

Wendra didn't reveal herself right away, though. Instead, she remained quiet, listening, while the expert musician worked her way through several songs. Between each rendering, many of which came as snippets or phrases of much larger works, Telaya paused and scratched down some notes. The sound of the pen scribbling on rough paper reverberated as easily as did the songs.

It became clear there'd be no good way to interrupt the woman. So, after she'd finished one of her melodies, Wendra called upward toward the lamplight: "You're the finest singer I've ever heard."

In the silence that followed, Telaya spoke evenly. "So, my dissonant friend, you're both one of Belamae's puppets *and* an informer. Or are you simply guilty of the good manners of eavesdropping?"

The woman's words echoed out across the domed archive.

Wendra stood. "I only came to talk. I'm sorry if listening to your songs offended you." She paused, then added, "They really were quite beautiful."

Telaya did nothing for a long time. She simply stood there high in the archive at her podium. "Your music is strong," the woman finally said, the sound of it like a reluctant confession.

Wendra took it as an invitation, and made her way through the darkness to a long, winding ramp that spiraled up along the circular wall of the archive. She lit a lamp of her own, and started up.

"Why 'dissonant friend'?" she asked as she climbed.

"Your voice creates half-step overtones. Not always, but sometimes. I've never heard a singer do it before." Telaya spoke with certainty but caution, her voice still echoing out over the expansive dome. "Why are you here?"

Wendra reached the second level, continuing up. "Belamae said it was worse than he thought when he heard your song at Rafters. What does he mean?"

A caustic laugh reverberated suddenly around the dome. "So you *are* an informant. Or, have you come to join me in my sedition?"

"I haven't decided to join *anyone*," Wendra said, making her meaning clear.

More laughter. This time with genuine delight. "Wonderful. Does Belamae know this?"

"Why does his failure make you happy?" Wendra passed the third floor.

"This has little or nothing to do with Belamae. I'm sure he's convinced what he does is right." The mirth left Telaya's voice. "But he works from very old ideas. His concept of Leiholan is destroying Descant." A softness entered the woman's tone. "I can't let that happen."

"But you nearly incited a mob at the performance tavern.

They were chanting 'Burn Descant.' I think you're as much a danger to this place as you accuse him of being."

The bitterness returned to Telaya's words. "Don't fool yourself. And you didn't hear the end of my song. I would have steered them into a different course. I was . . . interrupted. My feelings about Belamae and Descant aren't a secret. But I would never let my dislike for one destroy my love for the other."

Wendra reached the fourth level, over halfway to where Telaya stood. Hearing the woman talk Wendra found her reason for coming here growing firmer in her mind. A decision lay ahead. She would have to either remain here, under Belamae's tutelage, or follow her heart. And despite her fondness for him, and the thrill of learning, and even the possibility of singing Suffering, her thoughts often returned to the blocks, those platforms where people were sold into Quiet hands.

"Tell me why you think Belamae's ideas of Leiholan are destroying Descant," Wendra said.

"Think of it this way," Telaya began with undisguised condescension. "If the gift of a Leiholan is a real thing, if she can render song to give Suffering a power that any silly tavern performer cannot, why aren't Leiholan also singing in orphanages and sick houses and the homes of widows? Or . . ." Telaya paused, as if for dramatic effect, "if the *gift* of Leiholan is no mythical or transcendent thing, but just expert musicianship, why would those who desire to sing Suffering be denied the opportunity?"

Wendra climbed through an entire floor in silence, considering the contradictions Telaya had shared. By the time she'd reached the level where the woman stood, she'd found an answer. She stepped toward Telaya, who turned from her podium to face Wendra.

"You know the gift is more than expert music craft. You knew it long before we stood together on that stage. But if you had any doubt, you surely knew it after I knocked you on your ass." Wendra smiled without any malice.

A grimace of distaste rose on the woman's lips. "I hear the dissonance in your voice again. Are you going to start shrieking at me?" Telaya stared at Wendra with chilly judgment.

It was Wendra's turn to give a laugh. "Careful. I don't have the same restraint toward you that others at Descant must have."

Telaya's face slackened with worry, but it passed quickly. "And still you come to me for answers. I find some poetry in that, don't you?"

Wendra disregarded the woman's posturing. "I can't tell you why Descant Leiholan don't go into the streets with their gifts. But I know there aren't many of us. And the Song takes a heavy toll. Even *training* to become Leiholan has its dangers. Perhaps the best help Leiholan can be to anyone is to remain healthy for Suffering."

Telaya was silent a long moment. "I would gladly take the risk of becoming Leiholan if it meant singing Suffering."

Wendra nodded, unable to deny how much she, herself, wanted to sing the Song.

"Looks like you're convincing yourself to stay," Telaya said, smiling. "How nice that Belamae will add a puppet to his play."

"I don't think you're here just for orphans and widows," Wendra said. "I hear a woman who is bitter because she isn't Leiholan herself. Is that why you come here late to study? Are you hoping to find something hidden in old sheets of music that will reveal the secret to you?"

Telaya stared back, anger in her eyes. "There, you're wrong. I come here to perfect my craft . . . because I care about the *music*. Yes, I hope to find some clue to what makes a Leiholan unique. But it's not the *reason*." She tapped the sheets of music atop the podium on her right. "I find a different kind of strength here, Wendra."

It was the first time Wendra could recall the woman using her name. It disarmed her a bit. Or perhaps it was the genuine tone of Telaya's voice.

"For instance," Telaya said, "I study the musical epochs catalogued on every floor of this archive." She looked around at the many floors obscured in shadow. "I learn about entirely different musical scales that have been used to compose music I've never heard. I find modes within those music systems unlike anything I've ever studied before. Hundreds of them. They're hard to decipher, but I can usually piece them together." Telaya's passion for music softened and brightened everything about her. "And when you hear the melodies and harmonies possible from these variants . . ."

Telaya seemed to drift into her mind, hearing some song Wendra couldn't share.

"And on these shelves," she gestured around her, "are the songs of things. The very music that describes and defines a tree, a cloud, the feeling of morning sun on cobblestone." Her voice grew softer. "More than this, if you look, you'll find the songs of people. The notes that make up their lives. Performing one of them is knowing who they were, and how they felt, and what they hoped for. The song of them. Some are songs of people you don't know. Others, you would. It's a resonant art to write the song of someone. Rare. And not often done anymore. But when you see it . . . when you sing it . . ."

Then the woman gave her an appreciative look. "Your song the other night at Rafters. Pure shotal. And offered in the Phrygian mode of the Elyk Divad system used thirteen generations ago. I don't suspect you knew that. But it was stunningly beautiful nonetheless."

"Thank you," Wendra said, feeling rather outclassed.

"It's also what makes me worry," Telaya added. "I have no idea what your real intention is. The shotal of *your* song. Its meaning." She gave Wendra a searching look. "You find resonant notes well enough. But I don't think you've decided why you do it. Or maybe it's that you haven't found *where* you should do it."

Wendra felt a mounting desire to understand these things the way Telaya did. She wanted to explore new scales, and the modes inside them that this singer seemed already to have mastered. But she caught herself, remembering that her reason for coming to this dissident Lyren was to try and find some clarity of purpose. She wanted to speak to someone who understood the cathedral's function, the role of Leiholan, but who saw it all with different eyes.

Then she stopped deceiving herself. What she actually

wanted was a way to justify leaving. She'd hoped Telaya could give her that.

The woman had been watching her closely. "You really *haven't* decided to stay, have you?"

Wendra looked back, but said nothing.

Telaya picked up a couple of the sheets of music and looked them over. "There was a time, Wendra, when thought and sound were taught as the same thing. Did you know that?"

Wendra shook her head.

"Not many people do. It's an old philosophy."

"Why are you telling me this?" she asked.

"Because we need to find new ways of doing old things. And maybe the answer is here somewhere." Telaya shook the sheet in her hand, then waved out at the great archival dome. "Particularly if those blessed with the gifts we need are uncertain of how best to use them."

Wendra caught sight of words carved into the shelving behind Telaya: *Descant,* then labels organized by epochal age. Telaya was studying the music of the cathedral itself. She had a sudden thought. "You're here because of Soluna. She died singing Suffering. And you're here looking for the reason. Or for a way to prevent it from happening again. Or both."

Telaya stared back at her, confirming nothing.

"Because the Song is changing," Wendra added. "Right?"

"All songs change over time," said Telaya.

She stared back at the expert musician, and had a new thought. "Maybe Suffering *needs* to change. And maybe we're just not evolving fast enough to compensate for whatever pressures are shaping the Veil." Something felt right about that. "So maybe," she finished, "that's what you're doing here so late."

Telaya didn't acknowledge this, seeming to stay focused on something she wanted to share. She held the transcribed music sheets out to her. Wendra gently took them.

"You may find these helpful," Telaya said.

"What are they?"

She humphed out a quiet laugh through her nose. "Two pieces. This one," she tapped the topmost sheet of music, "is a Telling for Descant. In case, should you leave, you need to return in a hurry. The other . . . is your mother's song."

Wendra pulled the second piece up close to look at it. "She wrote this?"

"No, it is the song *of* your mother." Telaya was smiling when Wendra lowered the music to be sure it wasn't a joke. "Belamae wrote this. It's the sound of who your mother was. Singing it . . . it's more than memory. I thought you should have it."

Stunned, Wendra looked at the music a moment, then up at Telaya.

"Vocencia left Descant. She left for the right reasons. It does happen." Telaya gave Wendra a thoughtful look. "When you hear that, you'll understand."

Wendra stared at Telaya a long moment. "Thank you."

The woman seemed uncomfortable receiving thanks, and quickly moved on. "And you're right. I'm here partly because of Soluna."

Wendra stared back, concerned.

Telaya pulled several music scores up from a satchel at her feet and laid them out across the lectern. She also went to the shelves behind her and pulled several more sheets of neatly notated music. She laid them all out together.

"Before Soluna died, we had Leiholan falling ill for days. Progressively so." She began organizing symphonies, choral arrangements, and other musical scores. "And you've seen what's happened over the last several days in the Chamber of Anthems."

Wendra nodded. "I assumed it was because the Song was changing."

"As we've said, all songs do. But after Soluna died, I started to research other times in Descant history when the Leiholan have struggled inordinately with Suffering." She tapped a symphony written in a Divadian mode. "I thought maybe I could identify some patterns."

"And have you?" Wendra felt her pulse quicken.

"What I've found is that at certain times, composers seem to write more nocturnes, more requiems, and more musical odes to the vault of heaven." Telaya began to talk faster, grouping the scores together. "It's as if there's something about celestial movement that has a direct bearing on the music that's written during specific periods in history. And these are the periods when Leiholan struggle, and even die. Sometimes it's a single day. Sometimes twenty or more days."

Wendra stared at the groupings of compositions on the lectern. "And Soluna died on the night of the last lunar eclipse," Wendra added.

Telaya looked at her, seeming impressed but also puzzled. "How did you know that?"

Wendra shook her head. "Doesn't matter."

"I think it does," Telaya said. She pointed up at the window high above them in the vaulted ceiling of the music archive. "We're about to have a somewhat rare second lunar eclipse. Of Ardua, tonight."

Wendra looked up and saw a wine-colored moon high in the night sky. Panic gripped her chest. *Like the moon on the Soliel when the Quiet came!*

Telaya put a hand on her shoulder. "I've asked for two Leiholan to be standing ready tonight should our singer go down. Particularly with everything that's been happening the last few days to those singing Suffering."

Wendra shook her head, wishing this weren't true. Believing that failure tonight might let another Quiet army slip into the Eastlands.

"I've got to go." She turned and raced down the long, sweeping ramp. Toward the Chamber of Anthems.

• CHAPTER EIGHTY-ONE •

Uncommon Understanding

Some say Mikal's brews were different on account of his apples. How a Wynstout man got hold of Su'Winde yellows, I'll never know. But I'll say this, he never turned a tasty yield until he started toting that spigot around on his belt. I half believe that spout gave Mikal's brew its edge.

—One of sixty-three accounts of unusually fast overland portage collected by House Storalaith for the League of Civility

BRAETHEN ENTERED RECITYV'S famed Library of Common Understanding. It was late, and the library was empty. Vendanj had suggested the basement for what Braethen sought—more information on the Blade of Seasons. Braethen had promised he'd be only an hour.

Crossing the atrium, he stopped and looked up. Eight stories above, through a glass pyramid that dominated the ceiling, he saw distant, distorted points of light—stars far away in the heavens. He would have liked to talk with his father just then. He longed for the simple, quiet evenings he'd spent with his da, doing nothing more than reading on their open rear porch.

He smiled at the thought, then moved to the outer perimeter of the main floor, and started around. There were many doors. But the rooms behind them held little more than water buckets, brooms, dirty rags, and once a selection of books awaiting repair.

Halfway around the main story a second time, he spied an inconspicuous doorway he hadn't noticed before. It lay tucked partway behind a tall standing bookshelf. Drawing it cautiously open, he found a set of stairs. He struck alight a handlamp set on a table just inside the stairwell. And with a single, clean whit of dread, he went into the bowels of the library.

Even the rough stone staircase was lined with books. Thin ledges had been carved directly into the stone walls, and dusty tomes sat patiently waiting for a reader. The selection seemed random, and made Braethen's descent slow, as he was forced to read every spine, looking for a title relevant to his search.

He judged he'd descended fifty strides of the slowly winding steps before the staircase opened into a subterranean level of more book stacks. Braethen had expected it to be cold and dank, but the walls had been paneled up with heavily oiled oak, sealing the cold of the earth out and the warmth of books in. The air hung still and silent. If there were secrets to be had, this certainly felt like the place to find them.

As he began to browse the first volumes, he came upon very old books by Shenflear with titles he'd never heard of, small handbooks by Celysias the poet, again with titles unknown to him. He realized he was browsing work and words carefully preserved in a place where they'd be protected from fire or other kinds of negligence.

Of the secrets and silences preserved in this vault of the earth, however, he couldn't see anything that might help him. It could be that the wisdom he sought *did* exist somewhere in one of the books. But he didn't have time to peruse every volume.

As he walked the perimeter of the deep floor, he let his eyes pass randomly across their spines, holding his small handlamp before him as he went. He had a sense that if he let himself relax, he'd notice the right detail. Something that *felt* right.

Just before turning at one corner, his eye caught something high up on a shelf. Graven into the wood at the top of one bookcase against the far wall were two words. It took Braethen a few moments to shift his thinking into the Falett tongue in which the words were written—a language he knew somewhat well from his studies with his father's favorite author, Macam.

They read: UNCOMMON UNDERSTANDING.

He paused, considering the preposition further. In Dimnian, *un* could mean "through" or "past." In Kuren dialects, it often meant "beyond."

It can't be that simple, can it?

Braethen crept close, reading the spine of every book in the stack beneath the foreign words. Though he knew few of the authors, the titles and subjects indicated nothing uncommon that Braethen could see. However, one book seemed rather out of place, a very thin volume set on the top shelf and almost unnoticeable for being pushed back between two thick tomes.

He reached up and retrieved the little book. Opening it, he found but a single page written on in what his father would call a "bad hand"—almost illegible—and with but a single phrase: *Put me back, down.*

A strange pamphlet. One page. One sentence. It wasn't even poetic. And the cover had a strange feel. Almost slick. He held it up in the lamplight, and decided it was a lightweight metal of some kind. Though it was so soiled it was hard to tell.

Did it mean anything? He read the line several more times before it struck him. The placement of the comma. The words already read like a command, but pausing where the author had placed that simple bit of punctuation . . . Braethen knelt and hunkered close to the bottommost shelf, running his hand along the volumes. And looking more carefully this time, found a very small slot where a thin book might fit. *Put me back.* And so he would. *Down,* on this bottom shelf.

As he slid the small volume onto the shelf, it began to feel as though it were being pulled. Just before coming flush with the rest of the spines, it snapped into place, like a link in a chain of lodestones. And as it settled, a sound like a tumbler rolling back grumbled behind the shelf.

A moment later, the bookcase before him swung open as though admitting a caller.

Braethen stepped through and raised his oil handlamp into a hidden room. The same oak paneling lined the walls, though the air here was slightly colder and carried the stale scent of upholstery. There was but one long bookcase in the room, covering the entire rear wall. And several tables sat around, so small that each would accommodate but a single reader, encouraging private study.

He moved deeper inside.

Leading with his lamp, he crossed to the solitary bookcase and read book spines as quickly as he could. Many were incomprehensible to him, written in languages he didn't know. But many others were written in languages that *were* known to him—Maerdian, Kamasal, Balensi. And halfway across he stopped, his heart pounding. His fingers traced the title of a book that he realized, without having to open it, was the object of his midnight search: *The Thousand-Fold Steel.*

With a trembling hand, he took down the volume. Then he turned and found the closest table. There he sat, placed the book before him, and slowly drew back the cover to the first page. The text had been written in an old tongue, but not one foreign to him—a Kamasal root. With some initial difficulty, Braethen managed to read a guide of topics: Origin, History, Purpose, Dangers, Uses . . .

There he stopped, his dread deepening. He read across to the page number corresponding to that topic: *Uses.* Part of him thought he already knew some of what he would find in these pages about the Blade of Seasons. This very day the sword had made certain impossible things . . . possible.

Before Braethen could turn another page, he heard something far behind and above him—like the door to the stairs that descended into these subterranean book stacks. *Did I leave the door open?*

He waited, listening, and heard nothing further. To be safe, he got up, checked to be sure the room's door could be opened from the inside, and quietly closed it. He then promptly returned to his book. This time, without delay, he turned the pages until he found the heading he desired, and began to read:

The Thousand-Fold Steel hath many names, and at least as many intentions. It is known by most as the Blade of Seasons. Though this name might be least instructive, as it is a weapon last of all. At least, as men define that word. It may be refolded and recast into whatever shape a tinker or smith sees fit to put it. This being true, it has held the forms of a rod, a rake, a hoe, a mace, a shovel, a spigot, a barrel band, and more. Regardless the form, the metal will yet possess its fundamental quality—to be a focus of thought, to give its bearer a window through which to view, even become acquainted with, those things he chooses to think upon.

In this way, it is the tool of a teacher, not unlike the book or rule. It is hoped that reminders of where men have been, and the things they should have done, can instruct their present actions. But for the bearer of the ThousandFold, the power of this steel brick is that its fundamental quality is not bounded. Linear qualities lay no claim to it. Think on time and place, how straight they seem. And yet "ThousandFold," as the Dimnis say, "pays not a jot for linearity."

In the simplest terms, looking back at the past from the present is a folding of time and place. However, it is said of ThousandFold that she can do more than take the mind a'gallivanting. But likewise send the body, too.

It is also said the steel can deliver what has been called a "consequence of time and place" on those it is used against. Such a consequence has never been documented, so most historians don't agree on the meaning of this.

What is known with more certainty is that calling the steel's influence has a consequence for the bearer. Time may yield her grip to he who invokes the steel's influence, but time requires payment. The cost, while not entirely known, is thought to be drawn from the days of the bearer. Though, it is also recorded that at one time, a member of the Inimicae carried the steel, and felt no such effects when, in the Craven Season, he raised the ThousandFold in the war against the Soundless.

Braethen looked up, his head swimming with information. In addition to what the text said about the steel itself, he shivered at the mention of the Inimicae. He'd never seen the name written down. Not even in Ogea's texts. He'd heard it spoken, once. Deep one evening when his father and Ogea had been hard at a bottle.

In some ways, it diminished the rest of the passage, giving it a fablelike quality. Back when he'd been a scrivener to his father, it wouldn't have been a source he'd quote when documenting primaries for a text going overland to a college's annals.

As he was thinking it through, a muted noise came from behind the hidden door. This time, Braethen was sure it was no trick in his ears. Someone had descended into the vault of books. He looked back at the entrance, thinking through his options. He considered tucking the book into his cloak and taking it with him—he needed to read and understand this volume. But it would be wrong to steal it. And really, it had answered his fundamental questions already. Though it likely explained other uses of the steel. Uses that would come in handy.

As Braethen struggled with the ethics of stealing something that seemed necessary, he heard several tiny pops, like glass shattering, beyond the door to the secret library chamber. He stood quietly, placed a hand on his sword, and crept toward the entrance. At the wall, he put an ear to the seam of the doorjamb and listened. Slowly, a quiet sound grew into a low roar. Moments later, he heard a crackling and noted the scent of smoke.

He threw open the door and saw the vault of books consumed in flames. He ached for the loss of wisdom burning in the lick and sputter of fire. The blaze climbed the stacks and blackened the walls and ceiling.

The heat became too intense for him to stand in the doorway, and he backed away. If he closed the door, he might wait out the fire and be fine, assuming the smoke didn't seep in and fill the room, suffocating him. His mind raced, trying to latch onto the best course, when he heard footsteps distantly beyond the roar of fire. That's when he put it together. *Pop. Pop.* Someone had tossed glass oil lamps into the bookshelves. The old parchment had been perfect tinder.

Maybe whoever did this isn't trying to kill me at all; maybe this is just vandalism on the past.

It made a disheartening kind of sense. The League wanted to put the past away. And in this vault of books resided legends and writings that represented the kind of folklore the League meant to quash.

This was a violation of everything he'd ever loved, a mistreatment of the values his father had taught him to observe and respect.

Without thinking, he raised the Blade of Seasons and started toward the fire. The heat became suffocating, but he was blind with anger and helplessness . . . until . . . he felt again that strange, nearly imperceptible shiver.

Suddenly he was standing at the foot of the stairs in the library vault. Disoriented and nauseous, he fell against the wall. It took him a moment to realize that the flames were gone, though he could still see them in his mind. Then he heard again the sound of the door opening on the library's main floor.

I've remembered this room as it was moments ago. He spared a quick glance at the Thousand-Fold Steel.

Then he whirled to look up the stairs. Realization bloomed in his mind. Though he didn't know how he'd done it, he'd stepped back in time. Just a few minutes. Just ahead of the vandal's cowardly act. Quietly he stole into the nook where the last turn of the stair came onto the basement floor. And waited.

He remained there, unmoving, until the intrusive sound of secretive footfalls came down the last few stone steps. A cloaked man stepped into the basement carrying four hand-lamps, each filled to the brim with oil. The intruder deliberately placed three on the last step, and prepared to throw the first into the shelves to his left.

Braethen stepped out and thrust the Blade of Seasons through the man's back, reaching for the lamp the man held, to keep it from crashing to the floor.

A look of awful surprise showed in the vandal's eyes as he crumpled, looking up into his killer's face.

"Courtesy of the Sodality," Braethen said, his anger still burning inside him.

With his boot, he pushed the man's cloak aside to reveal the emblem of the League. A caustic laugh burst from Braethen's throat. But then he was remembering the vague warning he'd just read about the consequences of using the Thousand-Fold Steel.

Time requires payment. . . .

• CHAPTER EIGHTY-TWO •

Pall Stones

The real gearworks of war are families. Not our siege engines. Not our steel. It's arms and legs traded for safety and honor.

—Spoken by Nojel Rroath, the second gearmaster of Ir-Caul, during the Age of Disdain—a court record held in the private library of Thalia Relothian

STREAMERS OF GREY smoke ascended into a clear sky above Ir-Caul. They rose from the forge chimneys of countless blacksmiths. Sutter turned in a full circle, trying to decide which plume to follow. Finding a smithy would be easy enough; finding someone who would talk to him would be trickier. Relothian had given Sutter leave to find proof of his accusations about his court and army.

Sutter got moving, and passed several shops prominently displaying the insignia of the Relothian lion hung from pennants or nailed to exteriors—king's men. He sought a man who shaped iron for the king, but took somewhat less pride in doing so.

A few hours after meridian, he came upon a small forge tucked into a deep alcove of a vacant alley. A crude piece of iron fashioned in the shape of a lion lay fallen in a spray of dirty straw. Sutter wandered in.

The smithy was dark, taking little light from the shadowy lane. A weak lantern, hanging from a rusted nail, burned dimly above a work area where an anvil and bed of coals and bucket of foul water stood like a trinity of low, earthy gods. The tools he saw looked as though they'd been mended many times. And to the side, three forges burned hot. Behind it all, back in deeper shadows, Sutter saw what looked like animal stalls. It made him think this had been a stable before the wiry smith had turned it into a place for iron. Several low carts loaded with ingots made it plain.

"You got coin? Or are you lost?" the smith said, glancing up once at Sutter as he shoveled some ore into a forge.

"I have a few questions—"

"You got coin? Or are you lost?" the thin blacksmith repeated, and grinned to himself.

Sutter put a hand in his pocket. "A little."

The smith made a noise in his throat as though his suspicions had been confirmed.

"You work for the king," Sutter commented, and moved just inside the forge work area. He spied a handcart where rods of metal and a stack of ingots had been piled. He also caught a hint of a familiar smell.

"We all work for the king. Are you looking for a piece of metal or not?" The smith turned toward Sutter and leaned over his shovel. "You're not another set of boots, are you?"

"Boots?"

"A soldier, I mean. Never mind, now. I can see you're not a lion." The man's smoke-dirty face creased with another smile, forming lines dark with soot.

Sutter ignored the observation. "You're not making weapons. And I don't see any farm tools—"

"Do you always say what's obvious?" the smith said, impatience edging his voice.

"How do you heat your forge?" Sutter asked, with some impatience of his own.

The man stood up straight, the way a man does when he's preparing for something.

"Who sent you here?"

Sutter pulled his severed blade from its sheath and held it up in the dimness. "I want to know what steel could do that."

The smith sauntered up, inspected the Sedagin weapon, and ran a finger down the smooth cut. "I don't sell swords. Just the raw stuff to make 'em."

It was a lie. Sutter could see it in the other's face. The man might mostly make ingots for other smiths, but he'd tried his hand at weapons. Sutter hadn't come for a new sword, though. He looked over the smith's shoulder into the shadowy depths of the forge. His eyes had adjusted enough now that he could see more clearly the repurposed animal stalls at the back. He looked at the blacksmith, whose large pores stood plugged with black dots. He then nudged past the man and stepped to the rear of the workshop.

The smith followed, coming to stand beside Sutter as he stared into two wide stalls heaping with piles of ore. "What's this?" he asked, pointing at each stall.

"You're a bit dense, aren't you? It's ore." The other chuckled low.

Sutter pulled a coin from his pocket and threw it on the ground in front of the left stall. "Not like anything I've seen. Where did you get it?"

The smith eyed Sutter closely, then looked down at the silver gleaming dimly near a large pile of black rock. "You could've had that information free. But I won't turn down a donation." The smith stepped forward, bent down, and picked up the coin. He wiped it and put it on his tongue, testing its authenticity. He then dropped it in a soiled pocket. "It comes down the Sotol River. It's hard ore. Harder than anything I've ever worked with. We calls this palontite. It's surely what cut your blade in two. You been fighting with lions?" He picked up a bit of palontite and tossed it to Sutter.

Sutter caught it. "Down the river from where?"

"The Pall," the smith said with matter-of-factness. "No place else I know to get rock like that. Hard as every hell to smelt down, too."

Looking around again, Sutter couldn't see or smell any charcoal or coke—things he'd learned about in Master Geddy's forge. "How do you do it?"

"Ah, that's the trick of it. Meet import number two." The smith picked up a large piece of rock from the second stall. He handed it to Sutter. "Call it chohalis. Burns hotter than coal," he explained. "Gets at the princely stuff inside that Pall rock."

Sutter turned the dark ore over in his hands. "Where's *this* come from?"

"Same place," the smith said. "Comes in loads on flat barges down the great river. One to burn the other. Works out fine. Takes several passes through the fires to burn it down to weapon steel. You'd think they'd pay me more for it, wouldn't you?" The man's ironic grin showed it wasn't a real question.

"You have miners in the Pall quarrying this for you?"

The smith became suspiciously dumb. A vacant expression told Sutter that he hadn't enough coin to buy this answer. He looked down at the rocks in his hands, turning them over several times. As he handled them close to one another, they drew more quickly together, almost like lodestones.

He looked up at the smith. "What just happened here?"

"Not to worry," the man said. "When we smelt down the palontite, we refine that magnetic nuisance right out."

On instinct Sutter asked, "When did your last load arrive?"

The seemingly harmless question took the smith by surprise, and he blurted, "Six days ago."

Several conversations began to connect in Sutter's mind. He rushed to the opening of the man's nearest forge. He leaned in, waving smoke from the burning Pall ore into his face, taking deep whiffs, and nodded—he knew this smell.

He shot an angry look back at the smith, whose eyes showed shame. Then Sutter raced out into the Ir-Caul streets, burdened with new secrets. He had much to tell the king.

• CHAPTER EIGHTY-THREE •

The College of Physics

Summary: A glass rod is formed, cut in two, and one half walked to the far side of the room. The first half is rubbed with silk. Near the second half a piece of parchment is scraped with a knife, raising paper chaff into the air which is immediately drawn to the second half of the glass rod.

—From Tahn Junell's notes—a possible demonstration in his argument with the College of Physics, should it be needed

FROM BEYOND ITS outer wall, the College of Physics discourse theater sounded like a beehive. Tahn might have guessed that everyone in Aubade Grove had packed into the hall to hear the first argument of Succession, except that was a physical impossibility. He stood with Rithy in the shadows of dusk, each of them holding a stack of books and carrying satchels with various items. They were waiting for Polaema to arrive so they could go in.

"You realize that this is the easy one," Rithy commented.

"I thought the first one was the hardest." He gave her a teasing grin.

"In some ways, yes." She poked his chest. "Getting over the hump of the first one is a chore. But statistically, the chances of passing each successive college will diminish by a factor of about six hundred."

"How do you figure that?"

"Algorithm. There's the simple percentage of the College of Astronomy versus whomever it's up against at the moment. Then, really, you have Astronomy versus the rest of the colleges, one in five. You'd be lucky if that were the end of it."

"But it's not." Tahn smiled, paradoxically comforted to have Rithy running down the numbers for him.

"There's the Werner principle, that compounds the simple percentage. It says that in a contest of multiple linear opponents, the victor has fifteen percent less vigor to meet her next adversary; while that next adversary has fifteen percent more incentive and determination to beat the advancing force. It's a predictive military computation. It's a great deal more involved than that, but I've shorthanded it for your benefit."

"Thanks."

"Then, there's the relative size of each college in the Grove. Enrollment size isn't uniform across them all. Philosophy and Cosmology are extremely large." She made a sound of disgust. "Everyone wants to play at high-mindedness instead of determination by fact."

"I see," Tahn said, grinning.

She wasn't looking at Tahn; her eyes were trained at his chest, while her sight had turned inward where she saw and worked the numbers.

"I know the relative college enrollment sizes, so I factored those in—the more minds working on a problem or argument . . ." She nodded to herself. "Then, there's the ambiguity of philosophical debate, and an estimation of your persuasiveness when it comes to the softer sciences." It was then her turn to grin. "Have you any idea what Succession is going to be like with the cosmologists, provided you get that far?" She blurted laughter.

"Factor of six hundred is all, then?" Tahn asked with his most cavalier voice.

Even in the dim light of twilight, Tahn saw Rithy's expression sober. "If you start this, you win this. Understand?"

"I don't fight to lose."

She looked away to the second moon, just rising on the eastern rim. "You realize tonight's the lunar eclipse of Ardua."

He sighed. "I know. It would be easier on my nerves to think my hypothesis was wrong."

"Because if you're right, the Quiet come through tonight? Is that it?" she asked, still serious.

"Something like that." He followed her gaze to the sliver of moon they could see over the top of the discourse theater rooftop. "Somewhere, someone might be doing battle tonight. I don't like their chances, if we're still doing odds."

Rithy looked back at him with an even stare. "If you succeed, what then?"

"Well, I guess we put our Theory of Resonance to work. Figure out how to strengthen the Veil before—"

"You'd be leaving again," she finished.

Polaema saved him from having to answer, bustling up in her most magisterial astronomy robes. "I'll make an introduction, as is custom," she said, brushing by them, and pulling them in tow down an exterior hallway. "You're lucky, Tahn. Up until even an hour ago, there was debate about allowing Succession to occur. You must have made an impression at one time on Savant Scalinou. A cosmologist vouched for you, hard to believe—"

Tahn smiled.

"—which necessarily means that if we make it that far, he may have to recuse himself from any judgment on the soundness of your arguments."

The humming sound grew suddenly loud, and became a wave of noise as Polaema opened the door to the Physics discourse theater and led them inside. The chatter seemed to both intensify and grow softer, but he soon wasn't hearing anyone. Instead, he stood on the floor of the theater just past the door, staring slack-jawed up at an immense gearworks model of the night sky.

The apparatus hung from the high ceiling. Fifteen strides up from the floor in the center of the hall, a replica of the sun hung at the epicenter of a great planetary system. At various orbits around it were the wandering stars of Solena, Contuum, Reliquas, Boul, Ansic, and more. Each of these had orbiting moons, too. At the outer edges of the hall, the Perades aéirein had also been manufactured into the model, along with several other deep-orbit bolides. All these were held in place by thin rods that emerged from the center of the apparatus like spokes. And at the end of each spoke, a short rod turned down and fastened to the top of the various orbs. It was a masterwork of manufacture.

He marveled at the engineering that had crafted this

articulated model of the heavens. Something he hadn't seen in years. As voices began to quiet, Tahn could hear the soft gurgle of water flowing down a chute up above. *It's like a water clock.* The water applied a slow amount of pressure to one of the gears, as it would a water wheel, and the whole system of stars would turn a click. Several wooden fly-wheels interlocked at various points to turn the wandering stars the correct amount for their orbital speeds. It was old, but it was genius! They probably kept it running for tradition's sake.

With his eyes, Tahn followed what he assumed was the water chute. One end disappeared out the side wall—water must pass that way once it had done its job—and one entered near the ceiling. It was there, high up above the gears, that Tahn saw a small box, where a young man sat reading a book next to several levers.

Nudging Rithy, he pointed up. She glanced toward the gearbox then back at him, understanding immediately. Depositing her books and satchel on the nearest table, she scratched out some numbers and disappeared back through the door, just as Polaema began to speak.

The crowd silenced.

"Succession will begin with the College of Physics, since the College of Astronomy is the one to pose the question. And the question: Is there now ample evidence to prove the Continuity of All Things?"

Whispers rose and fell.

"Each college savant has given assent to the inquiry. I am its sponsor. Our inquirer is Tahn SeFeery, assisted by Gwen Alanes and other members of the various colleges."

The murmuring that came again led Tahn to believe his return to Aubade Grove hadn't yet become common knowledge. But more than the speculation from the Grove scholars, Tahn was struck by hearing himself called by that name: *SeFeery.* It brought to mind memories of a hot and barren place . . . Grant. All his old friends. And the thirty-seven.

Polaema continued, and he forced himself to focus.

"We've not had Succession for several cycles. So let me

remind you. We reserve it for the most difficult and important questions. For the discovery of foundational principles that we believe will illuminate and enlarge our body of scientific knowledge. You will all treat these sessions with the proper reverence and attention. All are expected to participate. For the duration of Succession, each of you will put aside your studies to focus on this one investigation."

Polaema turned a slow circle, as though she would exchange stares with every student in the theater. "Lastly," she said, "after all that is shown and argued, we share a common interest here. Let us not forget in the heat of debate that we question one another to find answers, and not from animosity or the desire to see others fail. Succession is all of us. A failed argument well stated and defended is better than prevailing with arrogance and vindictiveness."

Polaema turned her eyes on Tahn. That last bit had been about him. The stories about Tahn had overgrown since he'd left. He could see it in their eyes: His opposing panelists would be studying extra hard to show any flaw in his argument. He thought of Aleck from the old story of Seletz Run— the last soldier left to defend the city gate at Mal point South against the press of the Mal nations.

Except Tahn wasn't alone.

Rithy returned, and Polaema took one of the somewhat larger seats, reserved for college savants in the first row of the theater. The mother of astronomy gave him a reassuring look and nodded.

It was time.

Tahn stepped forward. He caught sight of each savant; they were seated at even intervals around the theater, each in their finest robes, the emblems of their college in rich charcoal embroidery over their upper chests. Most of the college scholars likewise sat together in sections. It bothered him that they did so.

Then he focused again on his argument, and why he'd come to make it. He'd expected a rush of insecurity, doubt. Instead, exhilaration filled him. Damn, he'd missed making a formal argument.

"Continuity is simple," he began. "In the past, it's been the idea that there's a binding substance that runs through all things. Erymol. Some call it an element. I think that's a mistake, since if the hypothesis proves true, it's in and a part of all the rest. But whatever name we use, such a thing would provide a construct and medium for the passing of light through the air, as well as sound and heat and . . ." Tahn stopped, thought. "Vibration of any kind would have a conduit for movement. But in some ways," he said, "I wonder at the jumble of logic we use to account for such things. Because while erymol may help us establish some physical models, at the end, it's not necessary. What I hope to show is that Continuity is about Resonance, and isn't dependent on a medium. And that once we understand Resonance, we'll be able to strengthen the barrier commonly known as the Veil."

More whispering followed Tahn's use of the term. The Veil hadn't been accepted into the science canon as yet. But rather than upsetting him, it made him smile. He was just getting started.

And I haven't yet told them why the Veil needs to be strengthened. He was holding on to that for now. Sharing his intent too soon might cost him some credibility. He wanted his demonstrations fixed in their minds before he made the end goal explicit.

He gestured toward the door, and Seelia and Myles, physicist and philosopher, wheeled in two pendulum clocks on a flatbed cart. Per Tahn's prior direction, they circled the theater, clocks facing out, so that all could see. Then they came to the center of the hall, beneath the model sun, and faced both clocks toward the savant of physics. Tahn helped lower the two clocks to the floor.

One of the pendulum clocks stood seven feet tall and had a broad case. The other rose to Tahn's shoulder and had a much narrower width and depth. While his new friends withdrew the cart, Tahn wound both clocks, drawing up the weights. He set the pendulums in motion, and waited for them to settle into their own rhythms. He said only, "Please note the beat of each clock."

The discourse theater grew silent, all listening. After a moment, Tahn moved on.

"At this time, there are but a few known forces of nature in our shared lexicon, right? Among these is gravity, which is easy enough for us to all agree upon, since none of us floats away into the sky." He looked at Rithy, cueing her. "But what about magnetism?"

She pulled a couple of lodestones from a satchel, two lengths of wood from another, and brought them to him.

"We all see the effects of magnetism when we place a couple of lodestones near one another, right? They're drawn to each other. Or, we could roll such a stone through the dirt and it would attract bits of iron to itself." He allowed the two stones, which had been shaped into cylinders, to snap together. "But what about their effects through matter?"

He held up the two pieces of wood, each of which measured about a hand's width. "This is maple wood, crafted tongue and groove for the making of a simple frame you might use to wrap a piece of art." He inserted the tongue end of the first piece of wood into the groove of the other to demonstrate how they fitted together.

After pulling the lengths of wood apart again, Tahn placed one of the stones on top of the piece of wood carved with the groove. Next, he brought up the other stone until the magnetic force held it in place on the lower side of the same piece of wood, defying gravity.

"The power of the lodestones holds them in place on each side of this wood; their attraction spans the gap chiseled by our carpenter. But what happens if we now insert the other piece of maple, adding density between the two lodestones?"

Tahn fitted the two pieces of maple together, and raised the wood over his head to emphasize his point. "The attraction isn't changed by adding matter between the stones. But how can this be? If the separation by space or density of wood doesn't affect the magnetic pull, then what's facilitating these stones trying to draw together?"

Tahn slipped the pieces of maple into his pocket, and allowed the theater a few moments to anticipate the obvious solution. "Erymol might be *one* answer." He spoke with skepticism, to keep them attentive. "Consider that for a bird to fly, or a song to be heard, or for any of you to see me from

652 · PETER ORULLIAN

where you sit, there must be a vibration of wind or sound or color in one place that has an effect on another place. These all work through physical or known mediums. But magnetism maintains most of its effect regardless of what comes between the two endpoints.

"In the past, our best assertion was that there must be an unseen, subtle element—erymol—that conveys forces like magnetism. And why? Because we won't believe—or at least haven't been able to prove—that these forces have effect through a void. Or *without* a medium. And erymol was our attempt to explain what we've shown with these lodestones, that properties of forces like magnetism can pass through an obstruction." He paused again, feeling more confident.

"This isn't new territory." The lead physics speaker rose to her feet. She stood a hand taller than Tahn, her lapels showing several silver pins shaped in the form of gearwheels— decorations for new thought or discovery in the discipline of physics. "I hope you intend to do more than present again the arguments that failed in defense of Continuity the last time it was brought to Succession."

Now the fun starts. "Of course," he said. "And in the spirit of Succession, may I ask you to lend me a hand?"

• CHAPTER EIGHTY-FOUR •

The Patience of Friends

I'm a simple man. A wink'll do me in. But I deliver the kitchen goods to a place that fits your bill, all right. I'll swear it's the Academie of Persuasasion, so called. Overheard a lass talking about something named the "five circles of manipulation." Just her voice saying it made me feel slavish.

—Information gathered by a traveling merchant at a drinking house in the north of Kali-Firth

As dark hour came, Grant stepped into the Hall of Convocation. Utter silence. But he could see by the light of a high moon through the great windows that several figures occupied seats at the convocation table. *Moon's red tonight . . .*

Not all the seats were filled. Just those who'd supported Helaina from the beginning had come. Those who could be trusted. If Grant knew Roth at all, he'd move fast not just to secure the regent seat of Recityv, but to begin directing Convocation under new auspices. Before that happened, Grant meant to secure some support for what would come much later.

Moving quietly across the marble floor, he came to the table's edge, where he could make out faces in the dimness: the Far king, Elan; Danis Malethem, king of Masson Dimn; Maester Westen Alkai from Elyk Divad; Queen Ela Valstone of Reyal'Te; from Maerd, Governor Labrae; and from the Kamas Throne, King Volen Chraestus. There was also Vendanj, Braethen, and the new First Sodalist of Vohnce, Urieh Palon.

It was odd not to see Artixan or Belamae. But he imagined the elder Sheason was weary, and likely attending Helaina. And Belamae had worries of his own.

In the shadows, all were watching him. Waiting. The inclinations of their heads suggested that they wanted answers, and direction. He had half their need.

"A bloody day," he said. "Not one to forget. The Asçendant will try to seize control of the High Council. I suspect that'll be easy enough to do, given that he had votes enough to expand the Civilization Order."

Danis spoke up. "Has anyone seen the order? Did Roth publish it?"

"It'll have the required number of signatures," Vendanj said grimly. "Roth is manipulative, but he likes to stand on firm legal ground."

"We should visit the High Council members tonight," Danis suggested. "Perhaps we can turn enough votes to keep him from the regent seat."

Grant shook his head. "He'll have a grip on them that simple persuasion won't loose."

Even in the dimness, Sodalist Palon looked uncomfortable.

"What do you want from us?" Danis's question was forceful and genuine. The man had deeply respected Helaina. He also led a kingdom that rivaled Estem Salo for sheer knowledge, not to mention boasting the strongest fleet in the Eastlands. In war or peace, Masson Dimn was seen as a necessary ally.

"We'd ask patience," Grant said. "Helaina was preparing to visit Y'Tilat Mor. Solicit their help."

"The Mor Nation Refrains?" Maester Westen asked with obvious awe. "Dear deafened gods, even my own conservators would never ask their use."

Westen's homeland—Elyk Divad—hadn't the Descant Cathedral, but there were conservatories in Divad that taught music at a master level.

Governor Labrae spoke next. "They wouldn't have received her, anyway. We've tried to establish trade with the Mor nations. Even offered music relics out of our oldest archives and museums—items we believe belonged to the first Mors. Our ambassadors were killed."

A somber silence stretched in the darkened hall.

"Nevertheless, we're going," Grant told them. "We're not

asking your help with that. But it will take time. And while we're gone, if I know Roth, he'll also move fast with his expansion plans." He looked around the table, taking a mental inventory. "The League has garrisons in most of your major cities already. He'll press you for tighter integration with your standing militaries and law guards. Don't say no. We don't want conflict to escalate for any of you. But stall him. Hold open hearings and discussions. Delay. Make it all slow and procedural."

"Roth has no men in my lands," King Chraestus said evenly. "Nor will he."

Grant didn't debate it. The king of the Kamas throne was practically the military arm of Estem Salo. If Volen and the Sheason Randeur marched together, few armies would rise against them. Chraestus had won wars with both Nallan and the Mal. The latter was seen as an act of the dead gods. When the Mal went to war, there were usually two outcomes: destruction or surrender. Neighboring nations were happy that the Mal weren't expansionists.

"My point is, don't draw attention to yourselves by openly fighting with Roth. We don't want him to sense resistance." Grant made sure to look them each in the eye. "Because whether we succeed with the Mors or not, there'll come a day we will stand up in force to put down the League. We want that to come as a surprise to Roth."

Danis was nodding to the wisdom of it.

"I'll be leaving to enlist the support of the Sheason," Vendanj added. "It's no secret that there's some tension in my order. With some luck, I can resolve that." He paused a moment, his face filled with sad remembrance. "Today's events may actually make that easier."

Grant nodded with reverence, then moved on. What came next might be the delicate part of his request. "There are other nations who will look to you for direction, if only by example—So'dell, Ebon, Kuren. Their posture will likely mimic your own. We didn't invite them here, because we're less certain of them. But keep your spies active in their cities. Any information may help us when we return to take Recityv back and call another vote for alliance."

In the darkened hall, Grant half-smiled that none of them denied having spies deployed in neighboring nations.

"I'll be returning to Naltus," said Elan. "I have work to do at home. And I won't sit at Roth's Convocation."

Grant nodded. He didn't think even Roth would push the Far. Not at this time, anyway. Taking another inventory of support, he noted that all here tonight had spoken, save Queen Valstone. But though she'd been silent, her eyes were alive with thought.

"Ela?" Grant asked with a leading tone. He'd known her well in years gone by, when she'd come often to Helaina's court. "We've not heard from you. But there's always something on your mind."

She waved a hand. "I'm just thinking that one of us should go further with Roth. Get close. Embrace his ambition as their own."

"Are you volunteering?" he said, his smile full now.

"Reyal'Te is known as a champion of civility. Not the League's brand of it. But more genteel, shall we say. It wouldn't be suspicious for me to be the one to do it."

Grant liked the idea, but knew the risks. "Just be careful."

"Oh, please. I deal with confabulators better than Roth in my pastry kitchen." She laughed easily, and many around the table joined her.

As laughter was tapering off, Palon spoke, his face still screwed up tight. "I need to tell you something." His voice was small. "I need to tell you all something."

Grant leaned forward, bracing his arms on the table. "You have our attention."

In the dark and silence of the Convocation hall, he related the account of Roth's visit to his home the night before.

On his right, Grant heard Vendanj whisper, "My last god . . ."

"All I could think about," Palon explained, "was the lives of those I'd just sworn to serve. Their families. I'm so sorry. . . ."

"You must renounce it," Chraestus said, no judgment in his voice.

"No," Grant said immediately. "At least not formally. It

would put your people in danger. And the Sheason are already dead. Let's not ignore their sacrifice."

"What are you thinking?" Danis was nodding as though he already knew.

"Palon stands in a unique position. He's made a difficult choice as the new leader of the Sodality in Vohnce. Roth fancies himself a self-made man . . . *ascendant*. He admires the difficult choice." Grant pointed to the sodalist. "Palon can get close to Roth as a result. Earn his trust. We'll make use of that."

Palon was shaking his head absently. Grant understood the gesture—not a denial of the request, but self-condemnation.

"Listen to me, Palon." Grant gathered the man's attention. "I don't agree with what you did. I doubt anyone here does. But don't waste the opportunity we now have by wallowing in self-loathing. There's a good path from here. Take it."

The young man stared back at him. There was a moment of disbelief. But while they shared that moment, something hardened in Palon's eyes. It was a look Grant knew from so many wards in the Scar, from those who survived that place well. He nodded satisfaction back at the man.

But that hard look had another quality. Concern. Palon's jaw clenched.

"What is it?" Grant asked.

"Early this evening, I received a note telling me Artixan had survived the assassinations. That he'd be in today's safe chamber. I sent a few men. . . ."

The Sodality kept a strong room for consultation, which moved every day. Rarely the same place twice. It had become a method for securely sharing information since the Civilization Order had been instituted. The room was also where a Sheason was kept if there was any threat to his life.

"There's something more?" Grant pressed.

"Just before coming here, Roth came to me, wanted to know where today's safe chamber was." Palon stared at Grant with distress in his face. "He's been sweeping the city for any hidden Sheason."

Vendanj was already running for the door. "Where?!"

Braethen raced beside the Sheason.

Palon shouted to them the location of the day's strong room—right there in Solath Mahnus. Grant told Palon to stay put, and raced after Braethen and Vendanj through the darkened Convocation hall.

• CHAPTER EIGHTY-FIVE •

No Grey Country

The traditional belief of Alon'Itol kings is that they will one day meet every man, woman, and child that dies during their reign, and have to make an accounting to them.

—From the *Register of Devotions,* an index of avowals recently stolen from the Cathedral of Bastulen

STRONG WESTERLY SUN shone across the concourse in dusky gold and auburn hues as thousands of Ir-Caul men marched over the parade yard. Mira watched solemnly as rows of twenty moved in processional fashion, having left vacant spots where their dead comrades had walked. It looked like an endless, awful smile that had lost too many teeth.

They were returning from a broad sweep to the north and west. Rumor had arrived ahead of the army that they'd never reached the battlefront, and that many—too many—had fallen in the attempt.

The men needed no drum or caller to mark time for their measured steps. Nor did they stomp or make a show of their uniform lines and cadence. They simply moved past the mezzanine where the king and his generals looked on, unspeaking. It seemed a silent ceremony, one of mutual respect: soldiers for their monarch, and Relothian for his fighting men.

Just beyond the marching column, other men drove teams of muscled work-horses that pulled their war machines. The creak and roll of axles and wheels over the yard stone echoed flatly around them. Many of the gearworks rose high against westering sun, casting long shadows that slowly passed over the king and his coterie. Some of the great trebuchets and catapults had been ruined, making their shadows appear like strange, twisted creatures as they stretched toward them. Near these, men with tool belts walked like healers watching over ailing friends. Field gearsmiths, no doubt.

As the procession continued, Mira saw many men who had likewise been crippled. Some limped, and some were assisted by comrades or conveyed on stretchers—legs and arms lost or rendered useless. She grew angry, recalling the conversation she'd overheard in the king's sister's chicken coop: *Perhaps they know we've been filling the traveling army with loyalists.*

Mira had a suspicion that the corruption of Relothian's house was responsible for deliberate tactical failures in matters of war. Which would also mean that men were dying in battle because their generals were purposely making bad decisions. *Getting rid of loyalists.* Staring out over the returning army—so many lost, so many wounded—she thought about her own decimated people. She couldn't remain silent any longer.

Mira stood up from her seat far to the king's left. She swept past him, speaking loud enough for all to hear: "Come with me." She caught sight of Thalia, Relothian's sister, and her escort, General Marston. She'd recognized their voices—from the chicken coop—when they'd all gathered earlier this hour for the return of this Ir-Caul brigade. They rose at her invitation. *Good, let's make some accusations.*

She stepped fast down two sets of stone stairs and out onto the broad parade yard, where she waited for the king and the rest to catch up.

"Stop them," she said to Relothian when he came up beside her.

Relothian turned on her. "I don't suffer indignity on one of our oldest and proudest traditions. Tell me what this is about."

Mira stepped within arm's reach of the passing battalion. She reached out and grabbed one of the footmen, yanking him from the march and hauling him around to face the king.

The men broke ranks and began to draw their swords. The king held up his hand, and gestured for them to continue their ceremonial procession. "If you don't have good reason for this, Far, you'll never leave this yard."

She stared back at the king evenly, her own anger an easy match for his indignation. Still, she had taken a great gamble on her assumptions.

She eyed the man she'd pulled from the marching line. "You've lost many men from this brigade. Nearly one in three. Tell us how."

The man didn't look at her, instead staring directly at his king. "Sire, I'd rather not. I don't complain. I'm proud to serve. . . ." The footman trailed off, his voice thick with emotion.

"What's your name?" Relothian asked softly, showing a tenderness she'd not heard from him before.

"Lian, sire." The man never averted his gaze from the king's eyes.

"Lian, it's your duty to be honest. You have my pardon for anything you say." The king put a hand on the man's shoulder.

At Relothian's touch, the footman slumped a little, as if already bearing a great weight. But he then seemed to gird himself up, and stood straighter, always looking into the king's face.

"Sire, eight days ago at dawn we came to the Gallem Valley. Low clouds there. Silent as a grave." Lian stopped, appearing to consider what to say next. "We went in at the narrow end, sire, where the hills are steep on both sides.

"There was no sign of Nallan, but the men didn't want to travel by way of the narrow end of Gallem, sire. We'd be too spread out, too open if you take my meaning."

She guessed they all knew where this story led. But like nightmares in which you know you are dreaming and can only wait and watch as the horror finds you, the account of the attack began to unfold.

A voice interrupted the story. "My king, must we have recounted the losses of war when we should be celebrating the living who return to us in honor."

Mira shot a look to her right and found the king's sister, Thalia, stepping closer.

"I think we can forgive the Far. She doesn't understand our traditions. No doubt she's moved by the sight of such valor. We all are. But let us not make these men relive such atrocities."

Mira didn't wait for the king to reply. "My lady, you're right. I am moved at the sight of these men. But not for valor's sake. I will have Lian's story."

The king looked at his sister, whose brow knitted in disapproval—and concern, Mira thought. Then Relothian turned hard eyes on Mira again. "You've no more allowances from me, Far. We will have Lian's words here and now. You will hope what he says doesn't condemn you."

The man then looked at Mira for the first time, his eyes lit with a spark of hope. "You're a Far," he whispered.

Mira took the man's hand in the welcome grip of friendship. "Spare nothing," she said in a quiet voice.

Then Lian's head snapped back around to face the king. His jaw flexed as he prepared to speak. "Sire, the men didn't want to enter the narrow valley. Men loyal to the throne advised the captains, and were lashed for it. We went in. Marched quietly for several hours. Watched the steep hills on both sides. Soon, the low clouds made it impossible to see."

He paused, taking a long, slow breath. "Deep inside the pass, the hills came alive. Out of the fogs, every kind of weapon: arrows, spears, knives, rocks. The crash of drums filled the air. It was hard to think or hear. By the time we got ourselves to cover, Nallan men pounded out of the hills on every side. Up the trail behind us. Down the path ahead of us. It's a miracle we lost only one in three, sire. We owe that to the iron will of Ir-Caul men, and nothing else. But my king . . ."

"Don't hold back," Relothian urged.

"We should never've gone that way. 'Twas foolish. If I didn't know better, I would say—"

"You were led like lambs to slaughter," the king finished. "This is poor leadership. You have my apologies, Lian. I won't let this pass."

Mira gathered Relothian's attention. "It's not poor leadership. It's contagion in your court."

"Watch your tongue!" The king took a menacing step toward her.

Mira didn't yield, but instead met the king halfway, looking up into his glowering eyes. "More than this," she said. "It's contagion in your *house*."

Relothian seized Mira by the shirt, nearly lifting her from the ground. Weeks ago, she never would have allowed it. But she hadn't been able to react in time to stop him. She still managed to draw one sword as he pulled her face a finger's breadth from his own.

"Take back your words," he demanded icily. The king's closest guards drew their weapons and surrounded them.

Mira waited to retaliate. She didn't wish to harm the king. She also wasn't sure she could do much before his men cut her down.

"You must listen," she demanded, maintaining her composure. Softly, she added, "Please."

The simple plea changed the look on Relothian's face.

Far back against the mezzanine wall she saw the soldier she'd paid to keep an egg-gatherer company until she beckoned them. Those men were now being ushered away, and Mira knew Thalia had intercepted Mira's ploy to expose her plots.

"Stop them." She pointed at the soldiers and her informant.

"You there! Hold!" the king shouted. The soldiers abruptly stopped. Then he looked into Mira's face, and spoke just above a whisper. "Tell me what this is about."

Mira nodded toward the two men who'd almost been escorted from the parade yard. "Have them brought to you."

"Those men," he said to the nearest guard. "Bring them here. Now."

"This is outrageous, Jaales," Thalia protested. "They breed lies. I won't stand for it!"

A moment later, the soldiers returned, escorting a simple farmhand Mira had met lately in the company of chickens. She gave the old man a firm look and said, "Tell him."

As the man shared countless stories of secrets and private meetings held in his chicken coop, Mira realized the military parade had stopped. Men with blood-soaked bandages, a few with missing limbs, and others with grit on their faces so heavy that they looked like pageant wagon players, all had begun to gather around on the immense parade yard. No one spoke as the old man offered in his wizened voice the secrets of scandal.

The man finished by repeating what he'd said to Mira. "Don't let them get away with it."

Mira told what she had heard that day, as well.

Relothian's face fell slack and pale, even in the warm tones of sunset. She imagined him thinking of the countless men who had died, the many processions he'd watched here under westering suns that came with many gaps where men should have marched. When Mira finished recounting what she'd overheard in the chicken coop, a horrible silence fell across a place reserved for honor and pride.

Into the stillness, she heard a soft word of disbelief from the king. "No."

She turned her head and watched as Relothian went to his sister. General Marston came up beside them.

"Your Majesty, your wisdom is sharp to see through this plot." The general narrowed a hawkish look at Mira. "How else do you explain a Far arriving with these fantastic lies? Or a boy pretending to be Sedagin, come to curry favor on the strength of an old bond between us and the Right Arm? They're spies or inveiglers, sire. Let me execute them for suggesting such disgrace in your own house."

Relothian's expression slowly changed, as though he was becoming confident that he had escaped some coup. The touch of his sister's hand seemed to reaffirm his sense of purpose and direction. "Remove them," he said with an uncertain tone.

Two guards seized Mira. And a small squad began to take her and the chicken farmer from the parade yard, as the sun dipped fully beneath the western rim. A moment later, another voice pierced the twilight. "Let them go!"

Into their midst rushed Sutter, with a finely dressed woman and a boy in tow.

Seeing his other sister with Sutter, Relothian raised an arm and his men stopped. Sutter flashed Mira a look both reassuring and grievous. Then the rootdigger looked around him, assessing the situation.

After a moment, he took the young boy by the hand and approached Relothian. "I told you I'm not Sedagin," he began. "What I didn't tell you is my true bloodline." Sutter looked down at the boy with him. "I was born to parents who had no use of me. Pageant wagon folk. A farmer saved me from them and took me in. He gave me a bed and family, and taught me to appreciate soil—"

Relothian interrupted sharply, "The only thing I want to know about you is your relationship to my sister." The king pointed to Yenola. "If you've shamed her, your death will not be quick."

Sutter never looked away from the youth at his side, as if his courage and resolve rested in the child. "Your fields yield no crop," Sutter said. "The soil has a bitter taste. Roots won't take to it. You must have a healthy trade with distant farmlands to feed your men."

"Yenola," Relothian said, with rising anger, "tell me what this is about. Now. I won't suffer fools or liars a moment longer."

The lovely young girl returned the king's cross stare with a look of faint defiance and resignation. It made Mira think of the way a woman looks when she's reconsidering her loyalties. Instead of responding to Relothian, she came to stand at Sutter's side, opposite the child.

The smith king's jaw fell. Only a notch, but visibly for that.

Sutter hadn't looked away from the boy, a steadfast intensity in his face. Mira had never seen such determination in the young Hollows man. And yet, she noted some compassion there, too, like the look of a protective parent.

"King Relothian, do you know what robs your soil of the richness it needs to yield its fruits? No, you don't," Sutter said immediately, disallowing a reply and breaching every form of etiquette. "It's the very war you fight. It's the smelting ore you use to fire your steel, that fills the sky with smoke from a hundred forges."

It was then that Sutter looked up at the king, his countenance hard. The revelation brought surprised looks to the faces of many, including the king.

"But that's no crime. Soldiers and smiths wouldn't know the smoke from their forges might taint the air and soil." Sutter reached into his pocket, pulled free two dark rocks, and held them out toward Relothian. "The ores you trade for to get your steel, and melt it down."

The king took them from Sutter's hand and looked each over carefully, turning them with a smith's familiarity. Then he fixed his stern gaze on Sutter again. "What does this have to do with my sister?"

"Do you know where the ore comes from, sire, that makes your blade so superior to mine?" Sutter asked with some indignation, again ignoring the king's question about Yenola. "And do you know how you're paying for it?"

Mira noted worried looks on more than a few of those near the king. It was the look of men and women conceiving defensive lies to hide their guilt.

Relothian didn't answer, waiting.

Sutter nodded, not in satisfaction, but from a kind of sadness Mira hadn't seen in him before. He looked back at the boy, whose hand he still held tight. "Go ahead," he urged gently.

The king turned his attention to the child, and knelt, looking the boy eye to eye. "What's your name, lad?"

"Mikel, sire. I'm sorry to bother you."

A genuine smile touched the king's face.

"The child will have been instructed to tell you lies," Thalia said. "Please, Jaales, don't let this pageant go on a moment longer. It degrades you. It degrades us all."

"Shame," said the young woman on Sutter's right, her voice low and angry. "It's not the child that degrades us."

The king paid no mind to the exchange, focusing on the boy as Sutter did. "Tell me what your friend here means, Mikel."

The lad looked up at Sutter, who gave him a reassuring nod, after which the boy returned his attention to the king and started to speak. He talked about life in the orphanage, the way the garden didn't grow, how hungry the children were all the time. He talked about how afraid the boys and girls were to go to sleep, worried each night that they might be awakened and offered a pair of shoes and taken by soldiers for a walk. And he told of how he'd overheard the men who came to take the children away whispering secrets about where the children went, who they were turned over to, and what they were used for.

Relothian's face went first pale with shock and then red with anger, though he listened patiently and silently as the lad talked about his friends. Friends who ordinarily would have been happy to have a pair of shoes, but feared the gift, since they knew it meant they would be marched at dark hour beyond the gates of Ir-Caul and sent north on a barge into the Pall. Payment for ore to fight the war with Nallan.

Mira's heart ached hearing it, knowing what it was like to believe you would die young. But unlike Mira in her own childhood, this boy had no protector. The very men who were supposed to defend him had used him, betrayed him. A child. Mira seethed, placing her hands on her blades.

Sutter raised a hand toward her, wordlessly begging her patience.

When the child had finished speaking, the king's eyes remained on him for a very long time. A kind of serenity had seemed to get into him. The boy stared back, unspeaking. Finally, Relothian asked but one question. "I need your word that this is true, Mikel. Not a story you've been asked or threatened to tell. But the truth, you understand? I will protect you no matter what. You can trust me."

The boy's eyes became glassy with tears as he replied simply, "Help us."

The king stared back at the lad, his face like that of a father who has disappointed his child and knows the child won't ever forget. But Relothian's expression changed quickly, and he replied in a deep voice, with a king's command, "There will be no more walks, Mikel."

King Relothian stood, put a large roughened hand on the boy's head, and said to his nearest attendant, "A new pair of shoes for every orphan in Ir-Caul before you sleep." He then looked around, selectively calling forward a dozen of his private guard—men, Mira guessed, that had Relothian's highest trust. "A guard will be posted, day and night, on every orphanage. Every child will be counted, their names taken. I will visit these houses myself. A missing child will go badly for the man assigned to him. Go."

The king turned to the man holding Mira. "Release her."

As Relothian turned, Thalia spoke. "Surely you aren't going to believe these lies about your own house? It is preposterous, Jaales. The child is distressed, and we should help him. But it's a fancy born of deprivation. A way to make sense of abandonment and disease. Think hard, my king. It doesn't make sense. Who would do this?" She paused briefly, looked at Sutter and Mira, then added, "And remember who sent these two."

The king beckoned a general whose face had been ruined by more than one enemy blade. Mira sensed that this man would sooner put his knife through his own heart than betray his king.

"Send the men to their beds, Caldwell," Relothian said. "They've earned the rest. Then bring your most trusted and meet us in the throne hall."

The scar-faced general went immediately, and the sound of countless boots echoed across the parade yard, the men returning to their garrisons. With the setting of the sun, the world had turned a shade of blue. Through growing darkness, Relothian motioned for his coterie to follow.

"You will all join me," he said. "We'll talk in the company of the Throne of Bones, where our ancestors will witness what truth and lies there are."

The boy, Mikel, was escorted by another man Relothian clearly trusted. Yenola fell in beside Sutter. And Sutter shared a look with Mira that she couldn't quite put words to. But whatever it was, and whatever lay in store for them at the Throne of Bones, Mira guessed that the violence in Ir-Caul hadn't yet truly begun. Nor had they accomplished what they came here to do. Far from it. They'd learned the army of Alon'Itol had multiple masters, an ignorant king, and corruption in its ruling house. They were further than ever from the help they'd come to solicit. And Mira's time was running out.

▲

• CHAPTER EIGHTY-SIX •

Old and Young

There are limitations. First, each Sheason's measure of Will is different. Next, each Resonance you cause depletes it for a time. And some Resonances require much. But past all this, there is the Talendraal. It's not Will. It's a metal that seems to imbue its bearer with immunity.

—From a sequence of Sheason lectures that includes
conservation of energy and using the environment to
cripple the enemy, copies of which may have been
sold by disavowed Sheason

T HROUGH THE DARKENED passageways of Solath Mahnus they sped, their footfalls louder than Vendanj would have liked. It couldn't be helped. Twice they encountered Roth's men. Vendanj closed the leaguemen's throats with a minor act of Will, and dropped them unconscious as they hurried past. Down several sets of stairs and long corridors they ran, toward the Sodality's strong room.

When they turned right down the last hall, braziers burned, lighting the way past several doors to where two leagueman stood guarding another door. *He's alive,* Vendanj thought. Else, why would the League still be here?

He raised a hand to silence these two leaguemen. Before he could, at the far end of the hall, Braethen suddenly appeared between them. The sodalist stumbled, nearly falling, but righted himself quickly.

The first guard never saw the harsh blow coming, as Braethen slammed the blunt steel pommel of his blade against the back of the man's skull. The other had begun to turn at the crumpling sound of his comrade falling when Braethen performed the same move, this time landing it upside the leagueman's jaw, knocking him out cold.

As Vendanj closed the distance between him and Braethen, the sodalist himself crumpled to the floor, much the way his two victims just had. When Vendanj reached the three bodies, he nodded with satisfaction. But he didn't pause, instead stepping over the sodalist and pushing the door open in one fluid motion.

Inside, he stopped short, his hand still on the door latch.

There stood Roth, one hand gathering Artixan's robe in a fist to hold him, the other bearing a sword. *Losol's blade.*

"It was a matter of time, wasn't it?" Roth said. "Come in, shut the door, and put down the crossbar. We'll want some privacy as we come to an understanding."

Vendanj slowly closed the door and lowered the batten to secure the portal. When he turned back around he nearly stumbled over one of two fallen Sheason—men who'd obviously been here to try to protect Artixan. A charge still hung in the air from their efforts to render the Will, efforts which had obviously failed against the Talendraal Roth carried. Farther to the left lay two more bodies, a couple of Van Steward's men and sodalists—likewise dead from their attempt to defend Artixan.

Losol, the Ascendant's trained dog, stood on the other side of Artixan's chamber, holding a blade of his own, bloodlust in his eyes.

"We understand one another well enough, Roth." Vendanj caught the weary eyes of Artixan, who was still spent from drawing the Will to help Helaina. His friend would be no help in his own rescue.

"No, I don't think we do," Roth countered. "I'm the law now. Or I will be when the sun rises. But even now, both you and Artixan are condemned by virtue of the Civilization Order."

"It's an immoral law," Vendanj replied. "I don't recognize its authority."

The Ascendant laughed. "*You're* lecturing *me* on morality? From what I understand, your own order deems you an outlaw. It would seem you keep only your *own* council. I call such men criminals who recognize no authority but their own."

"As do I," Vendanj said with thick insinuation.

Roth grinned rather genuinely. "Clever. But under my rule, there's no tolerance for the lawless."

"What crime has Artixan committed? Belonging to an order? Drawing breath? There's madness in you, Roth, if this is how you intend to deal justice."

Roth smiled. "More cleverness. But to govern, to lead, a man must make unpleasant choices. You understand this. You're simply playing word games with me. Buying yourself a little time to conceive some plan."

Vendanj shifted his attention to Losol. "What's your part in this?" he asked. "Why do you stand behind a warmonger?"

From the half shadow where he stood, Losol smiled and said nothing.

"The world has changed, Vendanj," Roth said, drawing his attention again. "We're letting go of that part of our past which hinders us from reaching forward. Between you and me, there was a time—recently even—that your kind served an important purpose. Not you, in particular, since you observe no oath but your own. But the Sheason, certainly. It gives me no real pleasure to dispense with an entire order. It will make me unpopular with many of those I must lead and care for."

Roth's smooth tone sharpened. "But as a child must cease to suckle at its mother's teat, and find its own food, so must we stop relying on superstition that makes men indolent and dependent and silly. Wasn't this the design of your imaginary gods from the beginning?"

Vendanj glanced at Artixan, who looked ready to collapse. He needed to be quick when he wrought the Will here. He didn't know what unknown attributes Roth's weapon possessed. At a minimum, he'd seen it cancel his efforts to render. But perhaps the blade had a limit. He would need to be clever and precise.

He tried to catch Artixan's eye. Reassure him. But the elder Sheason was panic-blind. Vendanj also tried to calm *himself*. His dear friend was a quick moment from murder.

"Then you are now a god?" Vendanj asked. "Or how would you have me understand *your* designs, *Ascendant*?"

"Take care, Sheason," Roth warned. "I have a bargain for you to consider, but your tongue may ruin it for you yet."

Vendanj scarcely heard the leagueman now parading as a regent. "Your Leadership," he said, stepping nearer with implied threat, "I think you've only substituted your own creed for the beliefs you seek to kill. You're building an empire on the backs of men who fell bloodied and dead this very day in the streets you claim to protect." Vendanj pointed slowly at Roth. "You are worse than those you seek to replace. And I won't allow it."

An easy laugh rolled from Roth's lips. "You stew because your time has come to an end. And you resort to the logic of a hypocrite. How many have died to protect your way of life? How many of them do you mourn? Or do you see them as a necessary sacrifice to bring about the change *you* seek?" Roth paused, his eyes dancing but serious. "In this, Vendanj, we *are* the same. But we are stagnating. Why else do we dream of vast lands filled with dark enemies? It's because we only recognize brotherhood when we march against the Quiet." His serious eyes stopped dancing, and fixed on Vendanj. "Either these are the deepest and oldest truths, or they are ignorance and fear of something foreign."

Putting the blade closer to Artixan's throat, Roth spoke again, this time with a quiet, foreboding resolve. "Either way, I will be the one to put an end to them."

Vendanj remained quiet, thinking of the right instance of Will to use. As he was considering his move, the door behind him shattered inward and Grant leapt into the room.

Roth smiled. "Why, Denolan SeFeery, good of you to join us."

Grant took a step forward. Roth raised the sword high against Artixan's neck, and Grant stopped.

Vendanj clenched his teeth. He had to focus. *One render. Kill the bastard.* The thought itself caused lamps in the room to gutter. A glint of doubt passed over Roth's face. But it was brief, before his own countenance set like a mask of iron, and he spoke chilling words that Vendanj would never forget.

"For the crime of inhibiting the people's own self-reliance, and inviting belief in the irrational, in the . . . arcane, which does not promote civility, I claim your life." Roth held Vendanj's gaze as he set his blade against the wrinkled skin of Artixan's exposed neck and pulled.

Artixan's eyes widened at the intrusion of steel opening his flesh. Blood gushed immediately as the old man's hands went futilely to his neck to stanch the flow.

Vendanj tried to freeze every liquid in Roth's body, stop his movements. The rush of Will broke like a wave around the Ascendant and his Talendraal blade, allowing him to complete the slow, deathly pull of an edge across Artixan's throat. The elder Sheason dropped to the carpeted floor of this private chamber, clutching at his neck.

Grant started forward, sword in hand. But before he reached Roth, Losol took a position between him and the Ascendant. The war leader wore a look of satisfaction, as though anticipating a worthy opponent.

Behind Losol, Roth said, "We can have this contest now. Or, Vendanj, you could spend this time trying to save your old friend. Which will it be?"

"Grant," Vendanj called, "help me."

They circled left, allowing the murderous pair to move right, Roth holding his weapon out as a defense against another rendering. The war leader's eyes showed a hint of remorse—for the delayed battle. But they gave way, circling around to stand in front of the door, blocking it and having a ready escape of their own. Vendanj and Grant dropped to their knees beside Artixan.

Vendanj took a small wooden box from his inner pocket. "Put two sprigs from this on his tongue," he said to Grant, handing him the box. Then he put his own hands over the old man's bloodied fingers as they gripped his opened throat. Grant placed two sprigs from the wooden case in Artixan's mouth. Vendanj called the Will.

He focused all his energy into this rendering. He grew desperate, sensing life ebbing beneath his fingers. His body warmed, the transfer of his Forda rushing down his arms and through his hands into the dying man. His friend. *Dear dead gods, no!*

It might have been an hour or a few moments. He had no idea. Time lost all meaning. He only became aware of his surroundings again when a hand settled on his shoulder. "Vendanj." It was Grant, beside him. "He's gone."

Vendanj's eyes cleared, the intensity of his act of Will having blinded him in those moments. Beneath his hands, he saw the still form of a man and mentor he had loved and esteemed for most of his life. A man who'd been a father to him when no one else would.

His mind flew back to memories of his wife, who'd likewise died while he was near, unable to help her. With that thought in his mind, he rose. Grant came to his feet beside him.

"It gave me no pleasure," Roth said. "But to get where we must go, I won't flinch."

The Ascendant's words might have been mocking. Or earnest. Or both. Vendanj didn't care. He was done with words. Silently he stared, focusing his energy on a thought. A subtle suggestion.

The Sheason is beaten. Overwhelmed with grief. This he did to soften Roth's guard. And to it he added a simple *slowing. Of the man's heart. A beat less. Then two.* Fatigue would overcome him by degrees. He would sink to his knees, too weak to use his blade anymore. He would lie helpless before Vendanj, who would then decide the man's end.

He made no gesture. No utterance. He simply commanded Roth's heart to slow. He watched as the man slumped, ever so slightly. He watched the look of focus ebb from his face. He watched the man's grip on his strange sword relax.

Vendanj never moved. Never blinked. Never made a sound. And he did not rush. *A slowing.*

When Roth's chin dipped, as a man's does when he's fighting sleep, he jerked. The sudden movement brought fresh life to his eyes. For just a half moment. But it was enough. With what appeared a heavy arm, he raised his sword. His features pinched with new anger. Vendanj's rendering had been nullified by the Talendraal.

"You're clever," Roth said, taking a step forward.

Vendanj still said nothing, trying to prepare another act of Will, trying to resonate with Roth simultaneously this time, rather than across space. But he was so weary. Grant circled away from him, to give Roth a point of distraction. Losol stepped out, mirroring Grant.

Roth turned the sword back and forth between them. A taunt.

When his body bristled with the energy, Vendanj stepped into the attack and thrust his arms at Roth. A force of Will shot from his hands and arms and chest like an unstoppable tide. The attack again broke around the Ascendant's blade, but the impact knocked him on his ass.

Roth had the presence of mind to keep the sword held up, to ward off another strike. But Vendanj had a different idea. He focused on the stone beneath the man's feet, to change its form. But before he could do so, Losol leapt at him, disrupting his concentration.

Grant swept in, forcing Losol back. The clash of steel rang loud in the chamber.

Vendanj began drawing the Will again, when Roth rushed him, his blade held out like a shield. Instead of Roth, Vendanj focused on Braethen, who still lay unconscious in the hall beyond the door. He whispered a waking to Braethen's mind.

There wasn't time to see the results, as Roth's sword sliced down at Vendanj's chest. He was too taxed to do anything more than step back out of the way. His legs threatened to give out. He stumbled, nearly falling over Artixan. The reminder of his dead friend brought new anger and energy.

He drew what Will he had left and focused it on the ceiling above Roth. The stone shattered and began to rain down. Several large pieces struck the Ascendant, who scampered away. Vendanj glanced to his right, where Grant and Losol traded blows, neither dealing anything fatal.

He dropped to his knees, panting, bone-weary. The sound of boots over rubble brought his gaze up to see Roth's thin smile through the dust hanging on the air. He might have enough energy to do one last thing, but it wouldn't be forceful, and his mind couldn't lock on what might succeed against Roth's blade.

"How might it have been different," Roth asked, with an executioner's confidence, "if you hadn't wasted so much energy trying to save Artixan?"

Anger swept through him to think his friend's death had been little more than a strategy to weaken Vendanj for battle. But it was a dull anger, lacking his ability to act on it.

He'd begun to consider his last move, which he held little hope would save him, when a soft sound, like an eddy of wind that might stir a drape, shivered in the air. Braethen tumbled to the floor behind Roth, and looked up at them, disoriented.

Vendanj liked the look of confusion in Roth's face. The Ascendant had seen Braethen move instantly from one place to another. Vendanj would have laughed, if he'd had the strength.

"This isn't your fight, Sodalist," Roth said coolly.

"You made it my fight the night you killed E'Sau." Braethen got to his knees and pointed his sword at Losol. "Call him back. And get the hell out, before I do this again and put my sword in your back."

Vendanj could hear the strain in Braethen's voice, and could *feel* the strain in his spirit. Braethen didn't have the stamina to withstand the effects of what he was doing. Not again. But Roth didn't know that.

The Ascendant considered for a long moment. "Losol."

The Jurshah leader pulled back as effortlessly as he'd been fighting. He'd suffered a healthy cut on one forearm, and seemed pleased to have been wounded.

Roth looked past Braethen at Vendanj. "It's inevitable. But have your graver's moment." Then he and Losol backed halfway down the hall, before turning and striding swiftly away.

The silence of death took the room in its horrible embrace. Grief landed hard in Vendanj, sudden and gripping. The sense of irreplaceable loss struck him. *Artixan, no.* He looked up, wanting to plead, wanting to wail. He did neither. He only lowered his head again to his old friend and teacher, and found himself too weary even to weep. A long moment later he bent more deeply over his friend's body and kept a private silence.

In some ways, Roth's coup was now most complete.

He felt the hands of Braethen and Grant on his back in sympathetic comfort. *The losses are too many,* he thought. *And I am tired.*

• CHAPTER EIGHTY-SEVEN •

The Bourne: Requiem

But who then saves a savior?

> —Dimnian thought riddle; such conundrums are believed to be
> more than exercises of inductive reasoning, but actual questions
> with precise answers—this riddle being one the Sedgel had
> concerned itself with since the Placing

KETT VALAN CRANED his neck up to watch Praefect Lliothan leading his children, Marckol and Neliera, by black leathers lashed to their wrists. He saw them with just one eye, the other damaged beyond use by the beating he'd received. He tried to get up, but the shattered bones in his knees tore at his flesh and sent waves of pain up and down his legs. More than anything, his helplessness and the helplessness of his children tormented him. He should have been protecting his little ones. His notions of freedom from the Bourne seemed suddenly foolish and selfish, and he cursed himself to think of the consequences he might have wrought.

The praefect didn't rush, walking in the breeze carried up and over the edge of the chasm behind Kett. Lliothan's indifferent eyes remained trained on Jinaal Stulten as he came. Behind the praefect, the large manor rose up like a monolith against the slate sky. Kett was trapped. Not by the Bourne chasm behind him. Or Stulten. Or even the embittered city of Kael Ronoch. He was trapped by the threat being made to his small ones, and his own inability to stand and defend them.

"Is he shelah?" Praefect Lliothan asked as he came to stand a few strides from Stulten.

"Was there ever any question?" the Jinaal replied. "I think you mean to ask if his influence is finally given to Quietus."

Lliothan stared back, seeming to wait for Stulten to answer his own question.

"No, he is not shelah. Nor did I expect him to rise above his petty Inveterae dreams. But we were asked to try, weren't we?" Stulten then shifted his menacing glare past the praefect and toward Kett's little ones. "They are pathetic looking," he observed.

"They are Inveterae," Lliothan replied evenly.

Marckol and Neliera looked at Kett. His little girl's face was wet with tears of fear. His son's eyes . . . Kett had never seen Marckol so afraid; the boy silently pleaded with him to save them. Roughened skin, rubbed raw in places, around his children's wrists told of their struggles against their bands. The effort had seemed to teach them better of it.

Again, Kett tried to stand, if only to show some dignity in front of his children. But only his right hand was of any use to him now, and the moment he tried to put any weight on his legs, the splintered bones in his knees again tore at his flesh. He dropped back to the hard stone of the courtyard. His only hope of helping his children was to try to convince Balroath that he could still be of some use to him.

"There's no need to threaten the lives of my little ones," he began, trying to keep worry out his voice. "I was stubborn. I've been punished. I have no more will to oppose you. Instead, let me advise you. No more tests. No more visiting my friends with death squads. I'll live under arrest, and I can provide you information to help you with my people."

"No!"

Kett looked over and found his son staring at him in horror. Through his own fear, Marckol had spoken. "No, Father," Marckol repeated. "Don't help them kill the others."

Pride swelled in his breast at his son's act of bravery. But behind his pride came a wave of self-loathing—he'd just offered to betray innocent lives to save himself and his children. And his son knew it.

He averted his eyes from his son's gaze.

How far had he fallen from being the Inveterae who'd stood at his own tribunal and watched his beloved destroyed, and in those moments still plotted to use the trial as a way to further their plans of escape? Now, all he could think about was survival. Not for himself, but for Marckol and Neliera.

"It would seem your son has inherited the same courage that made you foolish enough to try and deceive us, Kett Valan. These are good things to know about the young, no?" Stulten's words carried an undertone of menace.

"He's a boy," Kett said. "He doesn't understand the way of things."

The Jinaal took a long look at Marckol. "He understands," he concluded.

"Stulten," Kett said, desperate to get the Jinaal's eyes off his son, "you could kill me now, and you could kill my children. But what purpose would that serve? Isn't your function to find ways to use us to achieve your ends? Of all Inveterae, there are none better than me that you might use. You know this is true."

"*Your* usefulness is done." Stulten raised a finger as one making a point. "But you make a keen observation: finding ways to use . . . a child. Yours, yes. We'll come to that. But you might like to know that we have another child, a human child, a trouper, being held in one of the colonies."

Kett looked back at Stulten, confused.

"This trouper boy means an awful lot to a particular labraetates, a singer. She is Leiholan, Kett Valan, and we believe she'll come for him." Balroath smiled. "Do you see how poor your timing may be? We could be walking south across the Pall this very cycle. We could be walking through a seam in the Veil rent by the power of this Leiholan's song. But you won't be walking with us, because you've clung to an old vision of who we are. A shame." He looked around at Kett, his face placid, considering. "Because the last question, Kett Valan, is this: Will the Inveterae ever join us to march against the Tabernacle's favored races? If, after it all, they will not . . . then death squads and any information you could give me are of no consequence. The only solution is annihilation of *all* Inveterae."

The words chilled him. He'd always believed that if nothing else, the Quiet would keep Inveterae around to run their camps and produce their crops to feed their armies. Though a bitter life, it was a life. And the Inveterae had learned to suffer it.

But perhaps annihilation is just as much a liberation from the Bourne as escape to the south.

An unexpected peace entered Kett's heart, and he stared up at Stulten until the Jinaal returned Kett's gaze.

"Then do it," he said, without fear or remorse or defiance. Just a simple reconciled reply.

A flicker of confusion passed over Stulten's eyes. Then a thin, awful smile twisted the other's lips. "You truly *are* shelah, Kett Valan. Tell me, are you bold with the lives of so many because you believe the gods have prepared a reception for you when you pass through the narrow way?"

The Jinaal didn't want a response. He wanted only to deride him, cast him further into despair. But Kett had never really considered his own relationship with the absent gods when it came to what followed death. His only business had been escaping the tyranny of the Bourne *alive*. But without the ability to stand, the smell of death rising on the air from corpses that lay far down the face of the cliff, and with his children looking on, Kett found an answer to Balroath's question that he hadn't expected.

He rose up on his elbows, and spoke more to his little ones than to the Jinaal. "I'm not the savior you think I am. I'm not one to give faith or hope." He nodded just slightly to his children. "But acknowledging the Framers at all reminds us that death is not the end of life. And if that's so, we have nothing to fear from you. Since the very worst you can do is to send us to our earth, where we will be free of your enslavement, and closer to those we care about."

His words seemed to comfort his children, if only a little. Just that much, coupled with the praefect's vow to kill them quickly—should it come to that—was good enough.

But his words hadn't the same effect on Stulten, who started to laugh. When he'd finished laughing, he squatted near Kett, looking over Marckol and Neliera as he spoke in a low, almost affectionate tone. "Ah, Kett Valan, don't you see? What I have in store for you is not so easy as that. Your punishment is not death, nor is it the annihilation of all Inveterae—though that is something we have already begun in the west. No, your punishment will be to live. To live with the images you will see here today. Images of your little ones, frightened. Images of them dying a very painful death while you watch, unable to help them."

The horror of it descended on Kett, suffocating him, seizing him with panic.

"That, Kett Valan, will be the suffering of the Inveterae shelah," Stulten continued. "I will keep you alive a very long time to wonder if the reunion you believe awaits you beyond death is real, or if you brought the premature end to the lives of an entire race . . . beginning with your own family."

Kett's mind raced as he struggled to find words that might change the Jinaal's course, some point of leverage or promise he might make. There was nothing. He'd already proposed everything there was to offer Stulten to stay his hand against his little ones. And he was of no use in his own defense or the defense of his children. He had to act while the Jinaal was close.

He buried his one good hand in Stulten's ceremonial robes and pulled him down to the ground, where he sank his teeth into his cheek. He ripped free a huge chunk of flesh. The Jinaal howled and kicked. One boot struck Kett's left knee, sending a new wave of pain through his body. But he fought through it, trying with his useless hand to knock free Stulten's knife. If he could just get it out and close enough to grab.

But before he could do much more, Stulten pulled away,

ripping his garments from Kett's fingers. The Jinaal's cheek bled freely, showing a glint of reddened bone where the flesh was gone. The wound oozed more when Stulten smiled.

"This is what I expected, Kett Valan. Not the supplicant you've shown yourself. You knew what would happen when you crawled back to Kael Ronoch. You knew we would bring your small ones. Would they not have been a better sacrifice with you still on the high roads trying to stir your kind into its separatist dream? You have cheapened their lives . . . and deaths. That, too, you will live with for a very long time."

Kett watched as Stulten nodded to Praefect Lliothan.

"Please," Kett pleaded. There was nothing else left for him to do but beg. And while he didn't expect any pity, he was helpless not to try.

But Stulten didn't even acknowledge him, stepping back to give Kett an unobstructed view and the praefect plenty of room.

"Father," each of his children whimpered, seeking help from the only source they could.

Their appeal brought new anguish and determination to Kett's heart. Against the excruciating pain, Kett forced himself to stand. He caught the praefect's uncaring gaze, and with all the conviction he could muster, spoke a request.

"Don't do this, Lliothan. There's another way." He had only the old desire left. It might sound weak to them, but it was all he could think to say. He softened his voice a shade. "What if there were no Veil? Could there not be just . . . life, day after day, in a place that knows death only after a lifetime of peaceful skies?"

The praefect didn't reply.

"Is there truly malice in you, Lliothan?" Kett continued. "Or could you have been told lies to stir your hatred against an enemy you've never even seen?"

The wind up from the chasm swirled around them with its awful smell and black dust. The praefect's countenance didn't change, and he regarded Kett with icy indifference.

"Kett Valan," Lliothan finally said, "you've been found guilty of betraying your covenant. The Jinaal have spoken your punishment."

As the praefect began pulling Kett's son in by his tether, the boy looked in pleading desperation at him. "Father," he cried.

Kett tried to get to his son, but after a single step his legs simply gave out, his knees unable to support the weight of his body. As Lliothan reeled Marckol closer, Kett pulled himself over the stony courtyard as fast as he could, trying to reach them. It took him only a few moments to realize he would never make it in time.

As he dragged himself forward, he looked into his son's eyes. "I love you, Marckol," he said. "Don't be afraid. We'll be together soon."

"Father!" his son screamed as the praefect put one mighty hand around the boy's chest.

Lliothan let go Neliera's tether, and brought his other hand up around Marckol's neck.

"He's a boy, Lliothan. Only eight seasons." Kett then saw an awful glint in the praefect's eyes. "Remember your oath to me, Lliothan." *Be swift!*

And in that moment, Kett knew the praefect's treachery knew no bounds. He began to squeeze his son's throat, cutting off his cries. Kett could only watch as his son struggled helplessly until a muted snap came from beneath the hand clenching his son's throat. Then Lliothan dropped Marckol, who fell to the hard stones like a doll, not yet dead, convulsing, his throat broken, useless. His boy fought to breathe, his eyes wide, looking plaintively at Kett.

And even as his son fought for his life's breath, Kett screamed, "Run, Neliera!" His daughter did not. She stood frozen in fear, crying. And where could she have run? But he yelled it again, bringing only louder sobs of helplessness from her.

Lliothan took two long steps, grabbed her up, and turned toward Kett again to be sure he witnessed this moment clearly. Neliera didn't struggle, her fear so complete that she could only hope for some rescue. Through her sobs she called to Kett meekly, as if a softer entreaty might earn her his aid. The sound of it seared Kett's soul.

"Lliothan, for the child's sake, swiftly, please," Kett pleaded.

While looking at him, the praefect performed the same horrific act, crushing his little one's throat just enough that she would gasp and bleed inside, her gullet swelling, her breath slowing. . . .

Lliothan dropped her beside her brother, where the two lay broken, drawing weak, strangled breaths, their faces pale and frightened. Kett pulled himself toward them, his ruined knees smacking stone edges that he no longer really felt. He reached his children in time to stroke their faces and see the questioning looks.

"Don't be afraid," he whispered. "You go soon to see your mother. Won't that be a fine thing?"

He no longer knew if he believed his own words, but he spoke them again and again until Marckol and Neliera ceased to breathe, their young, innocent faces motionless, their eyes glazed. He heard only the shrill whistle of the wind coming up over the lip of the chasm. "Receive them, Saleema," he whispered. "I'm sorry. I failed them."

He grieved, holding them tight in his arms, feeling an emptiness inside deeper than anything he'd ever known. Then he realized his punishment had just begun. Balroath meant for him to live a long life with the memory of what had just happened. A life that would likewise see the annihilation of his kind.

I won't suffer it, he decided.

Giving each of his children a last look, he quickly began to roll toward the edge of the courtyard that dropped away into the chasm. By the time either Stulten or Lliothan realized what he was doing, they were too late. Their commands to stop followed him as he tumbled into the open air and fell gratefully down. The black crags of the Bourne and its slate-grey sky turned in his vision as he dropped. He thought of the many losses and horrors that had brought him to this. He found himself impatient in his fall toward a death he deserved and welcomed. His last hope was that the fall would, in fact, kill him.

• CHAPTER EIGHTY-EIGHT •

Broken Will

*Aye, but there are many prisons. One of bars, sure. But
also of wit, or the lack thereof. Then expectations—yours
and others. And by every silent god, reputation. That one's
tight, she is.*

—From a written entreaty for relief sent to King Bomaan
of So'Dell by a dockworker in the years following the
War of the First Promise, when it was said, "all the city's
a slum"—required League reading

FROM HIS BALCONY high above the rooftops of Recityv,
Ascendant Roth Staned looked down with a heart
both heavy and full. Fires burned here and there across the
cityscape, where civil unrest and fighting had resulted in
arson and accidental infernos. While some of the rebels
still fought, others scrambled to control the blazes. Distant
shouts could be heard—cries of defiance, orders to com-
ply, and the agonized shriek of the wounded when steel
entered flesh.

Then came lulls in the faraway sounds, leaving the blanket of night to cloak the unrest that Roth had forced at the
break of day. Though some clashes rose up in pockets, and
the fires lifted their smoke in dark streams against the starry
night, the tumult that swept Recityv had fallen into relative
slumber. For a time, anyway.

It was a victory. One that left him with the sense of completing a path begun a lifetime ago on a wharf in Wanship.
He'd scraped by, earning plug-coin for gutting fish.

He'd trodden over estimable things, sanctified things, to
bring about a new understanding. He'd have to do so again.
He meant to give confidence to every street-laborer. He would
be sure every drudge could feel pride in his own contribu-

tion to his community, if that drudge just observed the proper civility. It was worth the breakage of estimable things. Sanctified things.

In real ways, conflict, war, would be his catalyst for change. He would continue to work his politics, but he knew sometimes diplomacy failed. The Civilization Order and other maneuvers were part of his social engineering; they'd likely eventuate in full, outright war. And he was preparing.

A door opened into the chamber behind him, and hard boots approached, stopping at the doorway to his balcony. "Your Leadership, I have the accounting."

"Please," Roth invited.

The captain strode forward to Roth's side and attempted to hand him a bit of parchment.

"Read it to me," Roth said.

The captain faltered a moment, then lifted the parchment into the light shining from the chamber behind them, and read.

"Initial and incomplete counts confirm two thousand eight hundred forty leaguemen dead or missing. Only eight of thirteen complements have reported in so far." The captain licked his lips.

"And how many of our opponents, Captain?" Roth asked, looking to the far, dark horizon where Recityv faded and the night sky began.

"Nearly sixteen hundred recorded deaths from Van Steward's ranks." The League captain joined Roth in looking out over the ravaged city.

"How many citizens?" Roth braced himself.

"It's hard to say with certainty, Your Leadership. We believe it's best to wait until dawn and then take a proper count—"

"How many?" Roth repeated. "Don't mince words with me."

The captain settled himself, swallowed. "We think the number is upward of four thousand."

Roth shut his eyes, a wave of grief sweeping over him. These were the people he had done all this for. The husbands and sons who barked in the streets to make a life for wives and children. Not that some civilian loss wasn't expected, but so many . . .

"There's more," the captain said softly, finding the need, it seemed, to be thorough.

Roth waited a moment before nodding for the man to continue.

"There's no easy way to say it, Your Leadership." He put the parchment away. "The fighting is chaotic, close quarters. Our leaguemen are defending themselves as much as they are rooting out insurgents." The captain paused, readying his next words. "The nonmilitary dead are not men alone."

Roth finally looked over at the young captain, anger beginning to simmer inside him.

"Explain," he said coolly.

Seeming to find some inner strength, the captain said quickly, "Women stand beside men, armed, fighting us. Boys, many years before their Change, likewise raise steel. . . . They are part of the accounting."

"You're telling me that we're killing wives and sons." Roth began to feel and see the blinding white that flashed in his mind when his wrath came upon him.

"I'm telling you that your League is defending itself against every insurgent," the captain said politically.

Roth looked away into the night again, high above the Recityv rooftops. He'd known death would accompany his plans. But it wasn't how he'd envisioned this change in Recityv rule. These losses could undermine what he sought to establish, tainting the new era he meant to usher in before he'd even begun. There would need to be accountability, but it couldn't belong to the League.

Without turning, Roth issued the orders. "Pull all leaguemen back. Disengage the fighting everywhere. Send word into the streets of a temporary truce. Every pair of hands we have will begin the immediate removal of the dead from the streets of Recityv. Contact their kin when you can. Involve them in where and how they'd like their dead buried. Any we cannot find kin for, take them just outside the city and give them a proper burial. Grave markers, too."

"Yes, Your Leadership," the captain replied, and turned to go.

"Captain," Roth called, stopping the young man in his haste to leave.

"Yes, Your Leadership."

"Start with the women and children," Roth added, hating the sound of the words from his own lips. "Take care with them. Be quick, though. By dawn, every fallen Recityv citizen must be buried. Is that understood?"

The captain nodded, his face ashen at the very prospect of the task.

"On your way, send in my Jurshah leaders. They're waiting beyond the door."

The captain nodded again, and hurried out. Roth composed himself, preparing now to strategize the second part of his plan with his closest fellows.

Presently, Nama Septas, leader of the League's political agenda; Wadov Pir, the League's finance and commerce secretary; leader of justice and defense, Bellial Sornahan; and Tuelin Cill, master of history, all entered Roth's chamber. Last came Losol Moirai, leader of the new war faction, a stern look on his face and blood on his clothes.

Roth took one last look out at the darkened panorama of Recityv, then joined his advisors.

"Nama, what's your assessment of the day's events?" Roth asked.

"I was surprised how easily the regent fell," Nama said first. "But it makes tomorrow's bid for the regent's seat a simple matter. Convocation, on the other hand, may not be so easy. There are letters of inquiry from several of the seat holders. They expect a reply."

"Get word to *all* those here for Convocation. Ask them to assemble in the hall at meridian hour." Roth nodded at his own plan. "By then, we should have the regent's seat secured, and I'll address them as Recityv's new leader."

Nama nodded with him. "But your challenge is with Van Steward and the Sheason. There'll be some rising sympathy for the Sheason after the public executions, particularly after a day where the dying had no recourse to Sheason arts to heal them."

Roth had considered all this.

"Van Steward has the right," Nama went on, "to declare military law when the regent is incapacitated. If he does so before you claim the office, we'll have to either stand down or declare war against him. I don't think the latter would be wise."

"Because we cannot win?" Bellial asked, a hint of challenge in his voice.

"No," Nama replied. "Because declaring war on a government will earn us enemies of every nation where we now have a garrison. Kings and councils won't like the suggestion that the League is willing to take control by force. They'll see it as a threat to their own thrones."

"We need to tread lightly here, gentlemen." Tuelin Cill, Roth's historian, spoke as he stared into the carpet. "The choices we make will brand us for generations. How the League is perceived here in Recityv, and throughout the known world, could well be decided in the next few hours." He looked up at Roth. "Your Leadership, I'm not simply talking about how these events will be recorded. I'm talking about whether or not these events will describe a League that exists only in written histories."

Roth looked back at Tuelin, the oldest of his advisors. "You're saying that our actions could bring an end to the League."

"Public outcry, the might of armies beyond Van Steward's, they could all force a conflict we can't sustain. Yes, Your Leadership, the League itself hangs in the balance." He repeated, "We must tread lightly."

No one spoke for some time. Then Losol strode to the center of the makeshift circle in which they sat. "Roth," he said, looking directly at him. Roth made a note of the familiarity his newest advisor assumed. He would later correct him. "I don't disagree that our next actions will have lasting consequences. But those actions should be decisive. We shouldn't have gathered Sheason to die this morning if we didn't intend to finish that work tonight."

Roth smiled. His leader of war might be rough—and need to better understand his place—but he shared much of Roth's spirit.

"Take a seat," Roth said, pointing for Losol to rejoin the others.

Losol's brows rose, but he complied. Then Roth stepped into the ring of his closest confidants, so he could pace. "I have ordered the bodies disposed of," he began.

"But we should leave them. They will discourage others—"

"Losol," Roth cut in. "It's decided. But I also agree that we mustn't lose our conviction. The right choice requires boldness once it is made. We have a few powerful detractors who may yet complicate things for us. We'll see to them."

Roth then strode to Losol and reached down, drawing the man's sword from its sheath. He watched a look of worry and resentment cross the war leader's face. *Good,* he thought, *we will strike the proper balance yet, Losol.* Once he had the sword fully in hand, Roth held the blade straight out from his body, twisting it in the lamplight.

"But we must do so carefully. These aren't ordinary men who oppose us." Roth smiled again, coming to the second part of his plan. "Tuelin, Losol, have you validated the existence of more of these Talendraal weapons?"

Roth listened as first Tuelin then Losol spoke of their unsuccessful efforts to locate any more of the apocryphal armaments known only to archivists and historians. He'd learned of the Talendraal from Tuelin when Roth had first conceived the Civilization Order. Opposing the Sheason would require more than a political document. And considerable League resources had been committed to determining if the Talendraal were anything more than an author's tale, and then following ciphers to try and recover the fabled weapons.

Over more than a decade, they'd succeeded only once. Roth stared at the culmination of that success as he turned it back and forth in his hand, catching light in the blade's edges. A weapon crafted deep inside the Bourne, as the histories told, to repel the effects of a Sheason's rendering of Will.

Their search would continue. Such weapons would suit Roth's more far-reaching plans. But for a few hours, he needed to get out of his offices. He needed to see the streets where the people were.

ROTH WALKED THE Recityv working quarter. Their worst slum. His lieutenants assumed it was a political maneuver, to put him close to the people he purported to serve. He didn't bother to correct them. He'd long since learned that changing someone's opinion was usually a waste of energy. The truth was, he liked coming here. He liked strolling through the bars and hostels and workhouses of the cathedral district. It lit new fire in his belly for the League and its creed. He could help these people. He knew he could.

The Cathedral Quarter apparently hadn't been a place of fighting that day. So there were no body removal operations taking place. Part of him was glad of that. But it was still rather desolate. The music and activity that usually thronged here was softer tonight by half.

Citizens nodded in his direction. He held no delusion that they did so from anything but a baseless fear. He knew the art of pandering, of quick glances to evaluate pecking order: threat, rube, or competition. He'd once strolled the wharf slums in the city of his birth. A place like the Cathedral Quarter. He was at home.

He ducked into the cool environs of a local tavern, the Hemlock. This liquor hole doubled as a gambling pit. A rare place in this district for its lack of music. The bar had been situated against the back wall, putting everything in line-of-sight for the drink tenders. Tables had been inscribed with various patterns denoting games of chance. Late as it was, the Hemlock was light with patrons. Stalwart gamblers were in their routine chairs. A few men with billowy shirts dealt placards or gathered dice or spun wheels. Gambling had been provisioned as a taxable entertainment. Roth knew men would gamble anyway, were he to strictly outlaw it. This way, those who ran a profitable parlor sent seventy percent to League coffers. The arrangement strengthened the League and kept seedy men from profiteering.

Roth sauntered to the bar at the rear of the Hemlock. "So'Dell wine in a tankard," he told the barkeep. He had no palate for ale or hard liquor, but wouldn't use a glass in a place like this.

With the mug in hand, he turned to survey the drinkers and chancers and the few women working the room for men with money.

Eventually, he would find a way to shut this down, too. But he reminded himself that things happen in due course. It was by degrees that a screw is turned and a knot tightened. His real hope was that the gradual strengthening of trade and commerce would naturally change the balance of activities in a place like the Hemlock.

Give men real work for real coin, and they lose the need to hope on a roll of dice. Let a woman decide for herself if her flower can be bought, and most will choose another way, many to be honest wives and raise honest sons.

As he relaxed into his drink, a man brushed his arm with a strange familiarity. "You're looking well, my boy."

Roth turned, not perturbed by the prospect of a little bar banter. He nearly dropped his tankard when he looked into the eyes of Malen Staned. His father.

"What in hells are you doing here?" he asked, losing his composure.

"Released from debtor's prison. You remember. Got rather deep into it trying to escape the wharf in Wanship." The old man winked.

"What I remember . . ." Roth motioned to his highest in command in this detachment. With the aid of his fellows, the leagueman cleared the Hemlock entirely, even the barkeep scampering out without a protest. "What I remember is you selling me to pay a gambling marker. I'm fortunate I wound up in the service of a leagueman."

"You're all upside down. No one sold you." His father showed him a patient smile.

Roth reached behind the bar and took the So'Dell wine bottle. He poured a glass and pushed it over to his father.

"No, son," his da said, and pushed it back. The man

proceeded to pour a cup of water from a decanter and take a long drink. "Love water that doesn't taste stale."

"You say I wasn't sold?" Roth pressed. "I remember you making a deal—"

"No one tried to sell you, Roth." His father shook his head, a hint of regret in his face. "I was going to prison, remember, after trying to turn your mother's nice things into some coin." Malen's gaze seemed far away. "I hated doing that. We just had no other way."

"But you lost them, didn't you?" In his mind's eye, Roth could see his mother's nice things even now.

"I was cheated, and nearly did a fool thing to get even. Nearly stole something that didn't belong to me." His father turned to face Roth straight. "But I staightened up before doing that crime. Turns out, though, the city guard was going to pin it on me anyway. They were in on the theft. All I did was a quick negotiation to get you placed with the League."

"In payment for being let off," Roth finished.

"Didn't turn out that way, did it?" the man said. "I wound up in prison anyway. But you . . ." He looked Roth up and down. "I was right about the chance the League would give you, wasn't I?"

Roth smiled at that. "Yes, Da. You were right." Then he looked at his father's shabby clothes and scraggly beard. "If you've come expecting money . . . I won't put coin in your pocket just to see it gambled away." He nodded toward the empty tables of chance.

"I see," the old man said, a disappointed look in his eyes. "Kind of forgotten how hard it was for me to take your mother's nice things to the river in the first place, haven't you? Or that you begged me to teach you the art of chance so you could put it to use on the wharf, running your rook and flimflam cheats."

"And you said no," Roth said, smiling at the memory.

His father smiled, too. Seeing the man again . . . it made Roth's heart thump in his chest. Much of the code he expected his men to live by had been born from the memory of this man.

His father took another drink from his cup. "The girl . . . she came back to Wanship."

Roth nearly dropped his tankard. There was no ambiguity in his mind who the old man meant. Leona. The dockside prostitute his father had given mash soup to. The first—the only—girl Roth had ever loved.

He didn't believe in fate. Those were outmoded ways of thinking. But he *had* always believed he and Leona would be married. Even now he could imagine the feel of her, the sweet lilac scent of her hair.

The former regent had obviously secreted Leona and her family away to start their lives afresh. Another beginning for her. Now here stood a man with several days of road stink on him, fresh from debtor's prison, telling him she'd returned to the city of her birth. Where her whoring had begun.

Perhaps I've been too hasty in my opinion of fate.

"Yes," his father continued. "She and I had a very nice chat not long ago over a half-bad lamb pie. Told me some of your mischief, she did." The man's smile fell off, then. He fixed Roth in the firm stare of the man he'd once been. A man Roth respected. A man who'd swabbed decks for honest pay, left the gambling tables alone, and honored the memory of Roth's mother. A man who'd fed broth to a door-to-door child-whore named Leona, rather than take her to bed.

"What did she say?" Roth asked, holding his father's hard stare.

"I hear about the poisoning of children. The murder of dissenters. The burning of churches. The execution of men and women who only want to serve. . . ." The old man's cheeks sunk with sorrow. "Tell me these are lies, Roth. Tell me she's a silly woman and not to be believed."

Roth's silence proved answer enough.

"You're a coward, boy. A shame. You stand with the ability to extend a hand, and you ball that hand up and knock the rest down. If I were a younger man . . ."

Roth endured the tongue-lashing. "I don't think it's fair for you to say these things without knowing the whole story." He gestured to a table for them to sit. A placard table. Like the one where his father had gambled away his mother's nice things.

"We used to play," his father said, shuffling the plaques.

"Let's have us a game," Roth invited. "Coin a hand."

Malen Staned gave him a long look, his mouth finally showing a tired smile. "How about we play for pride, son. For the skill of it. Like when you were a boy."

Before Roth could argue, the old man had dealt out three plaques to each of them. It was as he watched the man deal that the hard years of his father's life became most apparent—in his hands. Those hands hadn't begun to tremble yet, as happens to the aged. But they looked used, tired— knobby joints filled with the ache of latter years—moving more slowly, not bending quite so easily.

"Turn," his father said.

It was the first game his father had ever taught him. Simpleminded. High plaque wins. No strategy. Pure better's chance. Extremely hard to calculate odds on it, too. But the simplicity and luck carried a meaning he imagined his father meant to bludgeon him with. He'd go along. Because they both knew how the game would end. How it always ended. They each laid their first plaque face up. Malen's crow beat Roth's sparrow.

"Again," the old man said.

This time, Roth's hawk beat his father's arbor jay.

"Again," his father said, a strange light now in his eyes. "And this for all."

They turned their plaques, each showing a black mountain shrike. They began to laugh together. They'd both cheated, each turning the highest plaque in a deck. It was their way of getting comfortable again.

When the laughter subsided, they studied each other.

"I'm not going anywhere," his father said. "I promised I'd come back to you. And so I have."

"Tell me what else Leona said," Roth replied. "And I'll tell you of all the good that's come of your quick thinking to get me placed in a League home."

CHAPTER EIGHTY-NINE

Considerations

A good leader considers the most objectionable response when no one else will.

> —The second entry in the private journal of
> the Randeur office—a thin volume added
> to by every Randeur and handed down to each
> successor—this from Randeur Sorbena Gernelle

IN THE WESTERNMOST room of the ninth floor of the Vault of Story, Thaelon sat by a corner window in the failing light of day. Word had come from the Maesteri, who'd delivered a few letters by Telling. He stared into the wood grain of the table beneath his hands and mourned the loss of Sheason assassinated a world away in the streets of Recityv. He'd sent them there. Some to live among the people and help where they could. And recently, an envoy to Ascendant Staned. An attempt at diplomacy, to reverse the crippling Civilization Order.

Dear silent gods. Thaelon had killed them. Killed his little girl. Not by his own design, but the blood of their deaths was on his hands just the same. Hands he now turned over and over in the warm sunlight slanting through the window, as though he might discover a way to use them to change this black news.

That was how Haley found him. She took the seat across from where he sat, and reached out, grasping his fingers to try and quiet the inner storm he suffered. Of course she'd known where to find him. It was here that he'd spent years of his life studying and pondering exemplar teachings on his own path to joining the order. It was here they'd sat together countless times, sharing each other's company, keeping the counsel only a man and woman in love can keep.

"You're not to blame," she said, her voice on the edge of emotion.

"I was their Randeur. Of course I'm to blame."

"How many?" she asked, placing an emphasis on the many lives, as opposed to the one she would want most to know about.

"Does it matter?" His reply sounded harsher than he'd intended. He squeezed her fingers. "You want to know who they were." He nodded toward the window, where a list of names sat near the glass.

She took up the parchment with trembling fingers, and read it in silence. When she'd finished, her face showed a hint of relief. Their daughter's name had been left off the long list.

Haley looked up at him with deep sympathy, "Artixan, too."

He nodded. Every name written on the parchment was an indictment. Artixan's death . . . he'd been a dear friend, and maybe the best teacher Thaelon had ever had. It deepened his anger and grief to think of someone murdering him.

"We'll organize a celebration of their service," Haley said with solemn strength, honoring those who'd fallen before asking about the daughter she assumed had survived.

"Will you help share the news with these families?"

"I would have it no other way," she replied.

Thaelon shook his head, and spoke through clenched teeth. "Must our strength in this be to look past the slaughter of servants and sue for peace with the League?"

Haley turned the parchment around and set it before him so that the names were unavoidable. "No," she said simply. "Service does not mean servitude."

Thaelon looked up in surprise. His companion for twenty years now showed him calm, resolute eyes.

"What are you suggesting?" he asked.

"For now, only that we not trivialize their deaths by ignoring their sacrifice." Her eyes lowered to the names scrawled on the parchment. "Later, maybe more."

"Another envoy, then," he surmised. "We have discussed as much. The League is misguided in its understanding of who we are."

His helpmate showed him a sad smile. "You're a good man to expect understanding of those who ill-use you."

"You think it is a fool's errand." Thaelon looked through the window toward the western rim of Estem Salo. "That the League can't be made to think differently of us."

She reached up and drew his face gently back around toward her. "I think you need to consider the mind of a man who would herd men and women into a public square and slaughter them like animals. Let that guide your response."

It wasn't a good time to share the rest with her. But for such things, there never was. He took the second parchment resting in his lap and set it before her.

His beloved didn't look at it. She began silently to weep.

"I would give anything to undo this." He did his best to remain strong. Not as Randeur, but as Haley's husband, and the father of their only daughter.

But he wept. He wept with her. They held each other's hands and grieved for their lost daughter. A long time they sat like that, in silence, feeling the depth of that loss.

His wife didn't look away once, holding his gaze as firmly as she did his hands. "What will you do?" she finally asked.

Of all the moments in his time as Randeur, never had a decision weighed so heavily on him. If this mantle weren't his, he would already have set out for the capital of Vohnce, bloodlust in his heart. But his wasn't the only child lost, nor the only friend taken in this vile business. Families and friends would suffer the loss a hundred ways. Fear and doubt would grow. He had to consider the order. Its responsibility. How even this might bring about greater compassion and understanding between Sheason and men.

The warring needs and desires made him sick inside, especially as he stared into the grieving eyes of his beloved, who needed him—more than anything—to be her husband and Ketrine's father.

As he hesitated to answer her, she took both parchments and stood, the scuttle of her chair legs sounding like a gavel in the silence. "I love you, Thaelon. No matter what you decide, I love you." She opened her mouth to say more, but must have thought better of it. She turned and left him alone near their corner window in the upper level of the Story Vault.

Her departure felt like a judgment, and he looked back again at his hands, thinking now how useless they were against the volition of men. But he allowed that despair only a moment's purchase on his thoughts, before calling softly for Raalena, who was ever within earshot.

His most trusted advisor came into the room and sat where Haley had been just moments before. "She'll heal," Raalena offered in consolation.

"With time, and with the right resolution to all of this . . . perhaps." He folded his hands together on the table.

"You underestimate her. But that's not particular to you. It's a common failing of men where women are concerned." Raalena meant it as further consolation, he knew.

"No," he said. "I don't underestimate her. Any more than I underestimate you."

They fell into silence. After a time, Raalena asked in a somewhat softer voice, "How are you?"

The simple question nearly sent him into tears again. Gods, did he miss his little girl.

In the end, he wouldn't have the time he might want to truly grieve for Ketrine. That made him angry, too. And it was an anger he could use.

He steadied his gaze on Raalena, having found his certainty in a cauldron of grief and doubt and a day filled with contrariness.

"Issue a declaration that Hanry died from age and overexertion of his talents, even as he strove to train the next generation in the way of the Sheason."

"A lie. But a good lie. What else?"

"I want another envoy leaving tomorrow for Recityv to speak with Ascendant Staned and his Jurshah leaders. Let them know that I want diplomacy first. Their job is to begin the work of repealing the Civilization Order."

"What makes you think he won't cut down a second envoy as he did the first?"

He looked evenly at her. "The envoy has my permission and command to render the Will in any way it sees fit to broker this peace. Make it clear that they are not to seek retribution, but to quietly secure an audience with the Ascendant and begin negotiating that peace."

"And if they refuse the overture? Or manage to kill—"

"Then our response will be severe, but defensible." He gave her a steady look. "Diplomacy one more time. To repeal the Civilization Order. If that fails, our renderings are at least justified. Unlike Vendanj and those like him."

"I'll go with that envoy." Raalena began to stand.

"No, you won't. And we're not done," Thaelon said.

His friend sat back down, her brow drawn into a quizzical expression. "You've something special for me to do?"

He studied her for an uncomfortably long time, trying to decide how to explain his idea. It was the dangerous thought born when he'd called his friends together in the shadow of the Tabernacle of the Sky. It was the thought of trying to bridge a schism older even than the one that divided Sheason and League. It was a heresy of the first order. Truly unthinkable. And yet . . .

Something in him had changed. Through all this business with the League and Vendanj and the Quiet. Certainly it had all taken its toll. But his little girl . . .

In the place where he had first learned the difference between quiet contemplation and Quiet contemplation, where he'd studied argument and implementation, battle and the beautiful, discernment and the ineffable; where he'd fallen in love, and today mourned the loss of the only child to come of that union, Thaelon rendered a thin line of Will and turned the parchment notice of his little girl's death into a paper warrior, like in the games they used to play.

He made it walk a bit, swing its arms, raise its head in an attitude of prayer. It was a simple memorial to his child, but a fitting one, he thought. And as the paper man danced, Thaelon began to relate an idea so absurd that even Raalena looked at him as though he'd gone mad. It wasn't an immediate plan. They needed to conclude the Trials of Intention first. But the groundwork could be set. Groundwork for reconciliation . . . with the Quiet.

CHAPTER NINETY

A Case for Resonance

I woke up in the middle of the night and looked at my man-dola. I knew. I knew my beloved Jaane was dead. She was a thousand leagues away, but I needed no messenger or letter to tell me.

—Excerpt from the journal of Jon Petruc, captured in the Dimnian instructional text *On the Nature of Instruments,* Chapter Two, "The Vibration of Being"

THE PHYSICS SPEAKER showed Tahn a wary eye, but nodded and started toward him, ready to help with the demonstration.

Tahn held up his hand to stop her before she'd taken two steps. "I'm sorry, I don't know your name."

"Janel," she said.

"Janel," he smiled, "let's use your table." He joined her beside her colleagues at the physicists' bench. He wanted them all to see this up close. And doing it on their own table was bold. Almost bad form. Almost.

Rithy hadn't needed a cue this time. In a moment, she was there with all the materials they'd prepared, setting them out on the workbench now serving as the arguers' table: a lodestone ring, a smaller lodestone hemisphere, a small stick, a gob of pine tar, and a stiff piece of parchment.

One by one Tahn held them aloft for all to see. "Using these lodestones, this stick of wood, and this bit of paper, we'll show the unseen effects of Resonance."

He then handed the parchment to Janel, directing her to take firm grasp of it, and hold it just above and perpendicular to the bench top.

"Listen," he said, again gathering the attention of all in the discourse theater. "Listen to the rate at which the lodestone turns this bit of wood to strike the paper. Note how long it takes the stone to reach its maximum spin rate."

Tahn could see Janel trying to deduce where the demonstration would logically lead, trying to prepare her counterargument. He gave her a smile. "Ask your questions, but remain open to what we show you."

She frowned, but gave him a single nod.

He placed the lodestone hemisphere on its rounded side in the center of the workbench. It looked like half of an iron ball. He then pushed the wad of pine tar to the center of its flat top, and stuck the short stick lengthwise in the tar so that it extended a finger's length beyond the top of the hemisphere.

"Hold the parchment close enough that the tip of the wood hits its edge," he said to Janel.

Then he lowered the lodestone ring above the hemisphere until he'd positioned it just right. Slowly, the lodestone hemisphere started to spin. The stick began striking the parchment, producing an audible *tick* each time.

Tick. Tick. Tick tick. Tick tick tick. Tick tick tick tick.

Tahn counted to himself, just as he'd asked everyone else to do. Nine seconds. Nine seconds and the rate at which the wood struck paper had reached a steady rhythmic hum. He let it continue for a full minute.

Then he pulled the ring away, and the disk quickly ceased to spin.

Janel looked up at him, keeping the parchment in place. "It's a valid demonstration of the force of magnetism, one with applications we're investigating ourselves. But," she said, her own confident grin spreading subtly on her thin lips, "I'm afraid this does not show a causal medium. Let alone your notion of Resonance—"

"You're right," Tahn agreed, then turned to address the hall, "but someone tell me how long it took for the disk to reach its steady rate of rotation?"

"Nine seconds," an old physicist in the first row blurted. The elderly-looking researcher was leaning forward in his seat, eyes intent.

Tahn looked about the hall. "Anyone else get a different count?"

A few voices called ten seconds. A few eight.

"Close enough," he said. "These are just simple observations, of course, but they'll serve—"

"Are you now going to try to attach time theory to Continuity?" Janel called out. "This wasn't part of your erymol *or* Resonance statement, and frankly will require more than some tabletop lodestones."

Tahn held up the stone ring and playfully eyed her through its hollow center. He said nothing as he returned to the workbench, pointed for her to resume her pose with the parchment, and positioned his lodestone a second time. "Count again," he invited in a resolute voice.

Then he lowered the ring, and the disk began again to spin. *Tick. Tick tick. Tick tick tick.*

The stone disk reached its steady state at just over four seconds. He held the lodestone ring in place a while more, then stepped back, allowing the disk again to stop spinning. Puzzlement shone clearly on Janel's face. The entire panel of physicists seated at the workbench showed the same baffled expression. Tahn let the discourse theater hang in stunned silence, knowing that they were now trying to apply their understanding of physics to the variance in time.

He shared a satisfied grin with Rithy, who beamed over the simplicity of an integer divided in half: nine, four and a half.

A few moments more for good measure, then Tahn spoke softly, as if shouting out might be uncouth just now. He sensed that they felt a bit fragile—on the cusp of having foundational principles of physics challenged, rewritten.

"I'll leave you to replicate what we've shown you here today. A simple test. You'll want to ask questions about variables like the table surface, the air current. I invite you to do so. But as Janel will attest, there were no indoor winds buffeting her hand or the parchment she held. And the bench top is old, but well lacquered." He stopped for a moment, allowing it all to sink deeper into their minds.

"You're going to find that no variable will compensate for the lodestone coming to its top speed in half the time. And this, my friends, is the effect of Resonance."

Tahn stole a look at the savant of physics. The gentleman's

expression pleased him. He appeared delighted by the discovery, his eyes darting about as he seemed to be piecing other bits of information into this new story of physical law.

"I felt nothing," Janel said. "How . . ."

Tahn could see that she needed to believe that some medium had pushed the lodestone to accelerate faster the second time. "Wind isn't a true force of nature," Tahn began, ruling out the most obvious. "And would have done more to disrupt the spin of the stone than help it. But magnetism. Magnetism, like gravity, has its origins at a foundational level. It's part of celestial mechanics."

And he then drove the point home. "I'm arguing that magnetism is a function of Resonance."

She held up a hand as one does to slow an over-anxious child. "Let's not get ahead of ourselves with impractical hypotheses. What you've shown here might, *might,* help support an argument for erymol. But that's not your Succession premise." She strolled past him, brushing dismissively near. "You need to demonstrate induction of the lodestone's movement *without* a medium in order to prove your Resonance argument."

"But I have." Tahn walked in the other direction, closer to the other physicists, who stared up at him with looks of anticipation and resentment. He pulled the two pieces of maple from his pocket and held them up. "I showed you that magnetism works across distance regardless of what may lie between the two objects." He stuffed the maple back in his pocket. "Then I showed you—"

The physicist speaker held up her hand again. "Tahn, please. Everyone in this theater knows that if you place a good sheet of steel or iron between two lodestones, the effects of magnetism change."

He turned to face the speaker. "And a bird has wings."

"What?" Janel gave an incredulous laugh. "I think you've been away from the Grove too long."

Subdued laughter rumbled around the theater.

"A bird is subject to gravity, and yet it doesn't fall to the earth and die." He pointed skyward for effect. "Why? Because it has wings. Because the bird is using air resistance to affect its free fall and the acceleration of gravity. We'd see the same if we dropped an iron ball and a feather from a Grove tower; they won't land on the ground at the same time. My point is that every law has an impingement. A qualification or two. It doesn't negate the law. In fact, in some ways, it better defines the law."

Janel stared, at a momentary loss for words. He made use of her silence. "And as I was about to say, I also showed you Resonance causing a lodestone hemisphere to spin once. And then more quickly a second time. I—"

Janel had paced back to the table and found her voice. "Yes, and as *I* said, if anything, this argues for the existence of an element like erymol, which would then be spinning the stone. But erymol is *not* your premise."

Tahn was getting tired of the interruptions, but he forced himself to be patient. "You're not understanding the demonstration." He paused for dramatic effect. "Resonance is independently affecting both."

Her brow drew into lines. She opened her mouth to argue, but this time Tahn beat her to it. "While I'm not trying to prove the existence of erymol, what you're seeing is that Resonance is spinning both the lodestone and swirling some unseen element that continues to whirl after the stone stops."

Janel's brow unknitted itself, and her eyes widened with some internal understanding.

"What's happening," Tahn further explained, "is entrainment, or erymol drag, if you'd prefer. The vibratory motion of magnetism that spins the stone also spins some substance we've yet to prove. Like erymol. So, while Resonance may affect erymol, and thus have a secondary effect on the lodestone, Resonance is also having its effect on the stone itself. It spins more quickly the second time because of the *cumulative* effect. The ring simply doesn't have to work as hard the second time."

"Are the effects indefinite?" she asked with hesitation.

"No," Tahn confirmed. "If we'd waited more than a minute, we'd have counted to nine again. But as I said, I'm not trying to prove the existence of erymol. It may well exist. And

I find it a useful reference. But Resonance takes place in the stone, regardless; it's not dependent on a medium."

Janel shook her head—a motion that seemed to help her gain her composure. "Even if we accepted your logic, the force you're describing is magnetism. Not some new celestial mechanic we might call Resonance."

"Again," Tahn said with mocking slowness, "my argument is that magnetism is one facet of a higher law. What I'm showing you is that Continuity is based on Resonance. And Resonance is the higher, governing principle. It's the vibratory nature of all things."

He looked around the discourse theater. He had their attention, and took the opportunity to again connect Succession to his goal. "And if Resonance controls the vibratory nature of the Veil, whether by magnetism or some other force, we could devise a way to amplify it. Make it stronger."

Tahn saw understanding—if not full acceptance—begin to dawn in many of those who looked on. He smiled with satisfaction. Smiling might seem a bit smug. But he couldn't help it. As much as showing the inspiration and results of their research, he was simply enjoying the process of Succession.

From across the theater, Savant Jermane, head of the College of Physics, spoke up. "It would seem, though, Tahn, that with these demonstrations you are, in fact, trying to establish a basis for erymol." His eyebrows rose in a questioning expression.

Leaving the immediate company of his fellow Successionists, Tahn crossed to stand in front of Savant Jermane. He shared a long, thoughtful look with the older man, wondering if the correlations he was about to draw would weaken his argument on Resonance, but knowing he must do so regardless.

Tahn shook his head. "My point is that *if* erymol is an actual medium, it too needs to be stirred to movement. What stirs it? Magnetism. And what's the overarching principle of magnetism?"

"You believe it's Resonance." Jermane's wrinkled face was

a portrait of patience as he waited for Tahn to share more proof.

"We already have working models for the vibratory nature of things, and our ability to cause resonance through mechanical systems, like sound." He paused, lending just a little drama to what he was about to say. "I'm suggesting Resonance proves Continuity whether a medium exists to conduct a vibration from one thing to another . . . or not. I'm arguing that Resonance is the governing principle for *all* mechanical law."

Another wave of murmurs rose in the discourse theater. He'd just proposed a governing principle that sat above the laws of celestial mechanics. Above magnetism, gravity, and the rest. Some would embrace the intellectual challenge of his hypothesis. Some would reject it out of hand.

But he wasn't done. He'd debated with himself if it was appropriate or helpful in this Succession to tie Resonance to their other historical findings. But as he looked around now, he decided it was foolish *not* to.

Tahn pushed on. "Savant Jermane, if, after all our arguments, this Succession holds that Continuity is true because of Resonance, we will have to admit *other* truths. These truths will challenge our most basic understandings. But they may save us, too."

The gentleman sat forward. "What are you talking about, Gnomon?"

"A few days ago," Tahn explained, "I saw a field of birds that had fallen from the sky. Thousands of them. They were migrating in a time they shouldn't have been, and lay dead of no visible cause."

"How does this relate to Continuity?" Jermane glanced at the mother of astronomy.

Tahn smiled, enjoying this whole thing. "It's thought that migratory birds have a sense of where they fly because they're able to perceive the world's magnetic poles, similar to the way a compass does. I believe the birds I saw got . . . tangled up. That the magnetic signature of Aeshau Vaal is changing, shifting. Or at least being pounded by the sun. The birds' internal compasses failed because the force drawing them is in a state of chaos.

"It relates to Continuity because something connects these birds to the same magnetic reality of our world that we observe in a compass or lodestone. I'm saying Resonance is that connection."

"Birds die all the time," Savant Jermane said, more a statement than challenge.

"Not by the thousands," Tahn reminded him. Then Rithy was at his side, as if she could read his mind. She carried several books in her arms. Without being prompted, she laid open the book with the time-map, setting it on the banister before the savant. Beside it she set two almanacs showing the vault of heaven during the periods of both wars of Promise.

Jermane placed spectacles on his nose and inspected the pages.

Tahn gave him several minutes, while the discourse theater sat in expectant silence. He shared a look with Polaema, who nodded for him to continue.

"We know the sun has several predictable cycles. Among them sunspots. Sunspots and nearby solar flares, which exert an intensity of light and heat and magnetic influence. These cycles"—Tahn pointed to the time-map—"correlate with periods of human suffering and conflict. Is it coincidence that there are epidemics of supul disease when these times of magnetic change are most intense? The annals record masses of supul victims migrating to cities—even Aubade Grove—for care and relief during these sunspot cycles, as though their bodies are more sensitive to this change."

Savant Jermane nodded, his eyes far away as though remembering these migrations.

"And while I can't document it yet, what we could be seeing is an inversion of our magnetic poles." Tahn dropped that nugget just to stir the pot. "But what we *can* document is that during these cycles, the attacks from those who live beyond the Veil increase in frequency and strength."

Jermane sat back, a suspicious look in his eyes. "*The* Veil?"

Tahn ignored the question, driving his argument's momentum. "What we *can* document is that when these cycles of the sun correlate with conjunctions of our wandering stars"—he ran his finger along the lined-up planets in the almanac—"we move from illness and skirmishes . . . to war."

There were no mutterings around the discourse theater. In the silence, Savant Jermane's seat creaked as he sat forward again. "Are you saying war follows a weakening of the Veil, which is in turn caused by a planetary conjunction?"

Trepidation slipped inside him for the first time—like once he'd said this next part, it would be true in a way it hadn't yet been. He thought of Vendanj, the iron-visaged Sheason who did what he thought right without concern for who it hurt or upset.

Tahn drew a deep breath. *Here we go.* "These alignments"— Tahn again pointed to astronomical events where wandering stars aligned—"are thought to produce changes in gravitation, an amplification that is causing activity in the sun. Our own almanacs record that during these periods of activity, we see a dramatic increase in the phenomena of the aurora lights. Auroras, Savant Jermane, that have been recorded as great spectacles in the sky above the Pall Mountains . . . during periods of strife." This time Tahn tapped the time-map where war, disease, political upheaval, and social injustice all spiked at once.

"So let me understand." Jermane adjusted his spectacles. "You're suggesting that astronomical alignments affect gravitation, which causes rhythmic phenomena in the sun, which in turn affects the magnetic signatures of Aeshau Vaal. And that if such a thing as a Veil exists, it's weakened by these changes in magnetic signatures. . . ." Jermane's words slowed, as if he was beginning to believe the things Tahn had said and shown.

Tahn finished the logic for him. "And that magnetism and all other celestial mechanics are grounded in a higher principle we'll call Resonance. A principle that works across known mechanical laws, like acoustics, but is equally true in explaining the transfer of force we observe when there's no apparent medium." He'd been waiting a long time to say his next words. "Thus Continuity *is* Resonance. And it connects . . . everything."

The elder savant locked eyes with Tahn, a new line of reasoning seeming to dawn in his face. He sounded apologetic when he said, "It's an intriguing argument, Gnomon. But in the absence of the forces of nature, like gravity, like magnetism . . . how do we argue for Resonance?"

In answer, Tahn walked to the center of the discourse theater and the two pendulum clocks. He stood there, silent, simply holding an open palm toward them, inviting all to listen.

The clock pendulums did not swing left and right at the same time, but the clocks had begun to tick at the same rate.

Tahn watched as, one by one, those seated in the theater came to understand.

"My friends," he said, "the transfer of energy is known to happen in just a few ways. Matter striking matter is one. Through magnetic force is another, as we've shown. But here"—he gestured to the pendulums—"no gravity, no impact, no lodestones. Just two different oscillating systems in proximity to one another, which after a time come into a sympathetic phase. How else does this occur, if not through Resonance?"

Stunned silence continued for several moments. And in that silence he recalled that he'd arrived at this demonstration because of the resonance he'd felt—and caused—between him and the Quiet man in the astronomy dome—two apparently different things, brought into phase. *The Quiet.*

Tahn let the hush draw out a good long time before finishing in a soft, clear voice. "I didn't want to leave Aubade Grove. This is as close to a home as I've ever known. And I have friends here." He looked over at Rithy. "But others said I needed to leave. They said I was in danger. That the Grove might be in danger, too, if I stayed . . . so, I left."

Tahn focused on Savant Jermane, knowing that tonight this man's opinion mattered most.

"Since I've been gone, I've seen the Quiet. Not pageant wagon rhea-fols. Not authors or poets reciting their tales. I've seen living Quiet. Up close. Just as those before us saw them in the wars of the First and Second Promise." A chill ran up his arms, and he knew what he should say next. "They're not beasts, my friends. They're not mindless. There's reason in their eyes. Intelligence. But they come in strength now . . ."

He didn't finish that part. It wasn't his intention to use fear here. "They're starting to push through the Veil."

Tahn took a few long strides and pointed up at the gear-works orrery above them. "We're in the middle of a rare dual lunar eclipse. A syzygy of the sun, moon, and Aeshau Vaal. At the same time, another cycle of the sun is upon us. I believe this is why not long ago thousands of Quiet were able to march on the city of Naltus Far."

In his mind Tahn was seeing the Soliel plain. He was seeing small ones in the hands of Velle. He was seeing graves being dug by the thousands.

"As I stand here, nations meet at Recityv in Convocation to try and build an alliance to meet this new threat. Prepare for war." He began shaking his head. "But even if we could win such a war, how many would die? And if we lost . . ." Tahn left off again, thinking about the friends he had in the Scar. Thinking about the choices left to one who has run out of any real hope.

He turned a slow circle, looking at each savant. It wasn't good form in the discourse theaters to make nonscientific arguments—with the physicists anyway—but Tahn felt the need to do so. "There's a feeling about them sometimes . . . the Quiet," he began, softly. The theater held a thick silence, listening. "It's the feeling you have when you find someone you love . . . who's taken their own life."

Tahn turned and showed Rithy a look of apology. But he pushed on. "It's a heavy feeling. The helpless kind. You grieve for yourself, but you also grieve for the one who's gone, who couldn't find a reason to stay with us." He looked up into the theater seats, still believing he might have saved Devin if he'd been attentive. "Many of you have known someone who did this. And you've felt that ache inside. That deep ache. The Quiet bring that feeling with them. And what they're doing will cause that feeling to widen across our cities and fields."

Tahn nodded to himself, remembering Nanjesho. Remembering Alemdra and Devin. *My last god, thirty-seven wards of the Scar* . . . "The Quiet come with war in mind. And for those who don't fall in battle . . . the resonances of war that follow will often be quiet ones. But stronger than most of us have strength to suffer. It will be that deep ache. It will get inside people you know and love. It will get inside you. And you'll believe there's only one thing you can do."

When he stopped speaking, the theater was not simply void of mutters and mumbles, attendees were sitting perfectly still. He thought he might have succeeded in helping them feel a small measure of what was coming. Of the urgency to find a way to prevent it. He chanced a look at Rithy, worried he might see tears and lose some resolve. She did have moist eyes, but the smile she flashed him gave Tahn a charge of determination. Good gods, he admired her.

Then Tahn raised his hands in emphasis, and declared what he believed. What he hoped. What he wanted of all this. "But if we can prove Resonance, understand it—then we can find a way to strengthen the Veil, and keep the Quiet from pushing into the Eastlands. Keep *us* from having to fight another war like those recorded in our annals. Keep that ache from getting into the people we care about!" He pointed at the historicals that still lay open before Savant Jermane. "This is why I've come back. This is why I've asked for this Succession of Arguments. The time is now!"

Mutters flared. Some incredulous. Some with the sound of approval.

Then Jermane stood, bringing silence again to the discourse theater. He gave each of his fellow savants a long look before he spoke. "My friends, I don't believe we have definitive enough proof of Resonance that the College of Physics will adopt this new law of mechanics. Not yet. And on those grounds, I might end Succession here."

He gave Tahn an unreadable expression, then looked up at the model of their own sun and planets that hung above the theater. The orrery had been dialed back—at Rithy's request of the clock keeper up on his perch—to show a conjunction that everyone in the theater knew. It was a subtle thing. But those who looked saw the Valediction Conjunction, an alignment that corresponded with a time of scientific persecution out of the Mal.

"However," he said, still staring upward, "neither do I have good reason to do so. For while these evidences bear more scrutiny, they argue powerfully for Continuity. Or, as young Gnomon here calls it, Resonance." He lowered his eyes to Tahn again. "The larger context you share is compelling, Gnomon. But don't let it cloud your arguments. Your task is to prove this Resonance on the merits of its science. Not the pressures of a world that needs a scientific answer. We could all recite those times when our efforts were put to bad use . . . and mistreated. Let us have none of that."

Then he showed the barest of smiles. "Succession will continue in a few days' time with the College of Mathematics."

Whispers and muttering resumed in a frenzied wave. Except for among the College of Astronomy. His fellow astronomers erupted with cheers that filled the entire theater. Polaema would, no doubt, scold them later, but Tahn was glad to hear it. He wanted to shout and dance a little himself. Join them. But that would have been rightly seen as gloating. So, he kept his composure. For now.

Physics researchers descended to their fellows, and began immediately to replicate the lodestone tests. Men and women whose robes bore the insignia of philosophy hurried out together. A few—who, Tahn noted, bore the insignia of the League on their robes—showed him a wary look as they exited the theater. Among them was Darius, who locked eyes with Tahn. The philosopher subtly shook his head, then gave a glittering smile of anticipation and swept through the exit.

The rest of the assembly sat staring from their seats, lost in their own thoughts, or meandering out in huddled groups, chatting amongst themselves. Tahn could hear the postulates and debates and excitement as they went. The Grove was alive with Succession.

Relief and joy flooded him like nothing he could remember, save maybe waking from his moment at Tillinghast. *Feels damn good to make an argument!*

Rithy sauntered up beside him, watching those from her own college exit the discourse theater. "I told you this was the easy one."

"You did?" He smiled.

"College of Mathematics is going to come hard at you with numbers."

"I have you," Tahn replied, and elbowed her gently.

"My math is strong, but there are many minds over there. And now they have a framework to attack. What's the plan?"

Tahn had an idea, one he'd had since he'd arrived here. It seemed ludicrous. But filled with the excitement of Succession, of being back in argument here in the Grove, he couldn't help but grin. "Tell me, Rithy, can you sing?"

• CHAPTER NINETY-ONE •

Throne of Bones

Lore suggests that the first bone used to construct the Ir-Caul throne belonged to someone sent north during the Placing—Quiet or Inveterae isn't specified. Reports vary, though, as to why: some say so we remain watchful of our enemy; others suggest that at least some of those we fought were friends.

—Scrap from but a few surviving pages of
an uncopied Ir-Caul record

KING RELOTHIAN SHOVED open the throne room doors and strode inside. Members of the Relothian House followed, Thalia chief among them. Other courtiers and attendants filed in. Mira entered beside Sutter and Yenola.

The king ascended the three wide steps to the top of the throne platform and turned. He did not speak, but scrutinized every face, as though cataloguing events and conversations in a new light. Presently, the general with the deeply scarred face came in, followed by ten men, all of whom bore a steady gaze. The last two soldiers to enter shut the wide doors behind them and took position as though to prevent anyone from leaving.

"Is this an inquest?" Thalia said sharply. "I hardly think you need to place a guard in your own keep. No one will enter a closed door without a summons."

"Nor will anyone *leave* until I have answers," Relothian added. "You are accused, Thalia. But you ask me to dismiss the Far's account, since she's a foreigner and we have no cause to trust her."

"What else makes sense?" Thalia raised her hands in question.

The king locked his gaze on his sister. "But the testimony of your own stable hand. How do you answer *his* account?"

Thalia laughed. "Is it a surprise that a stable hand living in a city that prides itself on combat and who, no doubt, finds himself underpaid, would lie to condemn me? My king, please, he rakes stable filth. He's half mad. I hired him out of kindness. Otherwise he would surely foul our streets with piss and become a menace. He was raving. Nothing more."

Relothian let out a long breath, his face cast in thought. "And the boy?"

Thalia shook her head. "As I said before, brother, he's a child. He's lonely. Some of the children are fortunate enough to be adopted, but others perish from disease. He's created stories in his mind to avoid dealing with their deaths or his own abandonment. If you would have it, I'll make it my personal responsibility to set a new standard for our fatherless. We'll increase their care and attention. But, Jaales, matters of the court shouldn't be decided on the witness of a madman or a lonely child."

Relothian looked over at Sutter, then back to his sister.

Thalia noted the exchange. "Nor the words of foreigners, however well-intentioned. If the Far stole onto the private grounds of House Relothian and overheard a conversation, then let us acknowledge first that she broke the law. Beyond that, she would have heard bits of a longer conversation your general and I were having about the war. Nothing more. I beg you, brother, be sensible. You're always cheerless when the men return. So am I. It's hard to look at the lines where fallen men no longer march. But don't let your melancholy become a hunt for traitors. The enemy is in the north and west, not here among us." Her face became earnest, imploring. "I swear it."

Relothian looked next at the man to Thalia's right. "What would you say, Jespan? You stand accused with my sister."

"I've risked everything for you many times, sire. I hope that speaks for itself." The general's tone never rose or became defensive. "And I think our time is better used considering how we'll defeat this latest Nallan army that marches south."

The king then turned toward Sutter, whose patience had begun to wear thin. There were lies here, and this politeness with which they came angered him. Before the king could put new questions to him, he pulled his sundered Sedagin blade from its sheath, and walked directly to the foot of the throne platform. He shot a callous look at the king's family and advisors, then turned his attention on Jaales.

He didn't know what more he could say to convince the king that his court had been corrupted, or that he must join himself to Convocation's purpose. He wanted to ask the king why the evidence and testimonies he'd already heard weren't enough. But he didn't. Instead, he stared at the man, and thought about his own childhood. About the many roads that had taken him from the Hollows to Recityv to the Saeculorum and now here. As he did, he also recalled Thalia's last words on the parade yard: *Remember who sent them.* It made him think about the king's words when they'd first arrived here at Ir-Caul: *Only a fool uses the name Vendanj to beseech this throne. . . . But I wouldn't call him a friend.*

Sutter touched the Draethmorte pendant in his pocket, and found he had a question after all. "What has Vendanj done to make you distrust us?"

A bitter frown drew Relothian's face into an awful look, as though he were remembering something he would like to have forgotten.

"Your Sheason served here some years ago," the king said, his words coming like those of a reluctant storyteller. "A hundred kings have had Sheason as counselors. In my ignorance, I thought I needed one, too. I agreed to have Estem Salo appoint one to my court. So came Vendanj to Ir-Caul. . . ."

Relothian took a few steps backward, his eyes still distant with the look of remembrance.

"He's not a man of compromise," the king continued. "I respect that about him. But his constant objections challenged my authority. Raised doubt in my other counselors about my choices." Relothian pointed southward. "So I sent him away."

The king paused, looking now at the throne directly on his right. He reached out a hand and caressed the chair of woven bones. Sutter had thought the seat gruesome when he'd first seen it; but now he believed he understood. Any king seated there would recall the blood of generations lost to preserve the kingdom it represented. And yet, Sutter realized, he'd not yet seen Relothian sit there.

"But that isn't really the reason, is it?" the king said, quietly questioning himself. "I would be no king if I couldn't suffer some dissent."

Still touching the assemblage of bones, Relothian raised his eyes again to Sutter. "Did Vendanj tell you how I came to wear the crown of Alon'Itol? How any man comes to wear it?"

Sutter shook his head.

"We pay no respect to bloodlines," the king announced loudly. "The right to rule from this throne is won on the battlefield. One king dies. Another is chosen from among the ranks. One who is believed to possess skill in combat and cunning in politics. The right choice is usually obvious. Each generation breeds its own heir. But the origin of that heir . . . it isn't manors with stable hands, or families who can afford tutors and trainers. No, more often our kings come from the small places of Alon'Itol, villages that have little more to offer their children than a place in the king's army." He paused. "I was a company smith."

Sutter looked over at Thalia, and understood the worry he now saw on her face. Relothian wasn't an old family name or bloodline. It had been established with the smith king's rise to the throne through the realm's military. Any plot she had for her brother's successor would have carefully laid plans that Sutter and Mira threatened to upset.

"That's why I prefer the cold air and hard stone of my rooftop to a feather mattress," he said, reminding Sutter of their predawn meeting. "I wear a king's crown, but I came by it from the scratch of a straw bed—the best a smith could afford." He smiled fondly. "That and many years with nothing but a footman's wool wrap, as I lay amidst rock and scrub."

Then the king's expression darkened. "If there's a contagion in my court, it won't be the first time." Relothian straightened, and came menacingly toward Sutter, stepping down with one foot on the first stair of the throne platform. "In the north of Alon'Itol, near where the rivers Tolin and Cantle separate, there was a town, Telamon. Not an important place. It grew no great crop, quarried no useful stone. There was no particular reason that anyone should want to go there. It had a dock for river trade; but it was used mostly as a place to moor when the sun went down. Rivermen rarely left their barges, and pushed back into the current before light.

"But for the most part Telamon was filled with good people. People who never complained about the weather or passed an unkind word that wasn't deserved. A place of heavy coats and heavy beards to ward off the chill. A place where strong drink didn't make men mean."

Again the king stopped, his eyes glassy with memory and regret. What did this have to do with Vendanj? The feeling grew inside Sutter that maybe he didn't want to know.

"Telamon," Relothian said with languor, "was the home of my father, and mother, and sisters. It was *my* home until I stepped onto a barge and floated south into the ranks of the army." The king lifted his arms to his sides, palms up. "This is where I landed after so many years."

Sutter nodded, and pushed forward despite the dread in his gut. "And Vendanj?"

Relothian's face went slack. "A year after he came here, the Sheason disappeared from my court for several days. He said he had things to tend to. I thought nothing of it. Even enjoyed his absence; I breathed easier when he wasn't around." Again the king's eyes took a glassy, faraway look. "When he returned, he told me that the Quiet had infested a town in the north. He said they'd been using it to transport women and children upriver to their own dark purpose. He said that the Quiet had taken root there. That there was no way to save the town. He said he'd burned it down, all of it, killing everyone. He told me he was sorry. . . ."

"Telamon," Sutter said with reverence, his gut tightening.

Then the king's face changed, as though he'd drawn some connection between then and now. He looked past Sutter to Yenola. "Come," he said, motioning her forward.

Relothian's younger sister approached the throne.

"Did you see any of what the boy claims?" The king's voice sounded strangely hopeful.

"No," she replied. "But I don't believe the boy is lying, or deceived by his own fancies."

Sutter leaned forward, and spoke softly. "A friend of mine was attacked by Bar'dyn. They took her unborn child. Later, she and a small boy were captured by a highwayman who tried to sell them to Quietgiven." He paused to let that much settle in. "The orphan's story you heard today isn't a delusion. It's not even an isolated example of what's going on. Whatever you feel toward Vendanj—and I'm no great admirer, myself—don't let it cloud your thinking. He burned Telamon to try and stop what's happening. Do you really need more evidence? Your army and your city's children are being sent into the hands of your enemies by people close to you. How many empty beds will it take before you see the truth?"

"Careful, boy, I am yet the king." Relothian's threat sounded hollow, as his thoughts seemed still far away.

"Then act like a king!" Sutter demanded. "You told me we didn't really know why Vendanj sent us here. You said he knew you would never take your seat at Convocation. I'll go farther. I'll say he doesn't *want* you to take your seat there! You would infect it as surely as your own court and kingdom are infected. Why did he send us, then? Tell us. Then we will hate him together! Or are you still a fool in the dark, as you were when he murdered your parents?"

Relothian dropped down another step and grasped Sutter's neck in an iron grip. "I should crush your throat."

The man had a smith's clench. Sutter couldn't breathe, but returned the king's violent glare, daring Relothian to kill him.

Behind him, the ring of a blade being drawn rose in his ears. "Take your hand off him or you're going to lose it." Mira was suddenly beside them.

Around the room, countless scabbards were emptied. The sound of steel being drawn filling the air like sibilant applause.

"The 'boy' and I might both die," she said. "But not before you go to your own earth."

Relothian held on for several more moments, then let him go. Sutter wasted no time. He climbed past the king to stand in front of the Throne of Bones. "You are *all* guilty," he cried out, sweeping his arm in accusation. "You connive in chicken coops. You fail to question the poor judgment of your generals. You barter with the lives of the fatherless!"

Sutter looked around the room, feeling a bounty of indignation. "Even if this boy Mikel is lying, you're guilty. Because what else do you fight for if not to preserve his childhood? You march to battle but have forgotten the *reason* for war. It's not the glory of your parade yard, or the manors you live in, or even the reverence you show for dead kings." Sutter slammed a fist down on the arm of the throne, rattling the bones.

Relothian spun around toward him. "You disrespect our fathers!" He pointed at the throne. "And what are *you,* boy? Messenger? Sedagin? . . . Rootdigger. And bearing the mark of the Draethmorte!" The king's gaze narrowed, questioning.

"He's Quietgiven," Thalia broke in, her voice shrill and accusing. "It makes sense now. The plot is his. How clever to turn it on us, and make us believe that House Relothian would betray its king. Take him!"

More than a dozen men moved fast on Sutter, their weapons drawn. Mira took a few quick steps to get to his side.

The king's narrow, confused stare remained fixed on Sutter as the leaders of his army flowed around him toward the throne. In the last seconds before their swords met, Yenola slipped between Sutter and the encroaching mob.

"It's true!" she screamed. "Thalia and General Marston have conspired to dethrone my brother. Most of Marston's generals are part of their scheme. Even I . . ." She shifted to look at Sutter. "I came to you at their bidding, to learn who you were, what you were here for." She lowered her eyes. "I'm sorry, Sutter. But the children . . . I didn't know about that."

Distaste and anger filled him. He'd shared her bed. Been duped by her artful lovemaking.

Yenola didn't linger on the revelation, and turned back to the men poised to seize them. "They told me that we could have peace with Nallan. But they said the king was too mired in his war. Too enamored of his gearsmiths to see new ways. And so they prepared to replace him."

Through the sword-bearing soldiers, the king slowly made his way toward his youngest sister. The look in his eyes spoke of a broken heart, and of sorrow for the deaths of countless footmen and children that his trusted friends and family had caused.

The heavy silence in the room fell over them all, until Thalia spoke again, her voice almost conciliatory. "Brother, you're no longer fit to be king. I don't think you really even want to be king anymore. Your perceptions of Nallan are misguided. Step down. Leave the throne to another. We can sue for peace. And your smiths can still be useful."

The king turned. He held a pose of dignified wrath, glaring. When he spoke, he spoke not to Thalia, but to the whole room.

"Those here who would side with my sister and her bastard lover stand with her now. Those who are true to me stand close." They were the words of a king, and Sutter's skin tingled when he heard them.

One by one, men either turned and fell in beside Thalia and Marston or came to the steps of the throne. The sound of boots on the polished granite floor struck Sutter as far too polite for the decisions of fealty that were being made. And when silence retook the room, the imbalance clearly disappointed the king. The general with the ruined face stood near the throne, him and the men he'd brought with him. Beside them, there also stood a short, wiry man who wore a leather toolbelt. Sutter guessed this was Gear Master Mick that Mira had told him about. The gearsmith lifted a hammer and used it to salute Sutter, then winked at him while wearing a lopsided grin.

Still, they were severely outnumbered, Thalia with forty swords at her command. A dark, thin smile spread on her lips.

"Yenola, you always did choose the wrong man. But no matter, your overused box has served its purpose." She gave a dismissive laugh as one might over the antics of a mindless bitch in heat. "Caldwell, I could have guessed you and your little band would choose to die defending some vague sense of honor. If that's your choice, so be it." Then her tone became softer, more earnest. She looked directly at Relothian, her brother. "I give you one last chance to save the lives still sworn to you. Have you any wisdom left?"

The king, instead of answering, turned to Sutter, looking intently from one eye to the other. "Why did you come here?" he whispered.

Sutter looked back, having no good answer. He understood better now that Relothian would never have joined Convocation at Vendanj's entreaty; it was an insult to even ask. Yet the Sheason had sent them here. Why? Had he known of the conspiracies in the court? Could he have known how dire the conflict with Nallan had become? What of the children?

The questions spun in his head as he sought to answer the king before the man committed his friends to a hopeless fight. He looked at Yenola, whose eyes were wet with tears—a sister who'd now betrayed both her siblings in their effort to rule. Sutter then looked at the Throne of Bones. It occurred to him again that he'd never seen the king seated in the gruesome chair. Sutter had come to view it as nothing more than a symbol. Part of him even imagined that sitting there would be a crime of disrespect.

He then remembered something about Tahn's pendant he carried. *It's a glyph. . . . It stands for fraternity. Family . . . connection and familial bonds that cannot be undone or unwritten.*

Sutter looked back at the king. "I think this is why."

He pulled the pendant from his pocket and took two steps to the throne. Before any could protest, he sat carefully into the midst of bones fitted together from hundreds of dead kings.

The people there have forgotten who they are. Make them remember. The glyph will help. Sutter remembered Vendanj's words, almost like a prayer, and placed the sigil directly on the arm of the chair.

The moment he did, the throne began to thrum beneath and around him. The old bones twisted and wove. Yenola and the dozen men still loyal to the king backed away, awe and terror in their faces. Only Relothian did not move, his face beaming with a strange glint of hope. Sutter put his hand over the glyph to keep it from slipping to the floor, and braced himself in the throne.

Then the entire floor and room began to thrum, as if it were a vibrating string. Sutter could see doubt spreading on Thalia's face; her coconspirator, General Marston, looked like a man who'd seen a god and was desperate to repent.

A soft white light began to emanate from the bones, and Sutter could hear distant voices, as though they spoke across a great gulf. The sounds rushed in and around his ears, causing a wind that licked at his hair then passed out to touch all those in the chamber. Men and women shielded their eyes and ears, raising their hands against the flurry.

Feeling the throne move and change beneath him, Sutter tried to see what was happening. The light made it all but impossible. The thrum grew louder, like two great trees being ground against each other to produce a deep vibratory note.

Then in an instant, the light and sound vanished. Men and women lowered their arms and stared toward Sutter, marveling. He now sat not on countless individual bones, but on a single, unified bone mass. A smooth white throne fit for a king.

Far from ornate, the changed seat showed a simple elegance. Gently curving lines gave it a royal quality it had lacked before.

When Sutter looked up again, almost everyone had gone to one knee, heads bowed toward him. Some few yet stood, wearing expressions of fear and surprise and wonder.

In the long silence, Yenola asked with an unsettled voice, "What happened?"

It was the king who answered. "You've made us one with our past. It is . . . remarkable, my young friend."

When Sutter considered the throne of woven bones, and looked at the Draethmorte sigil, he saw the pole-star—the star in the night sky that never moved. Every set of eyes in the wide world looked up to see that star in the same place, every day. He sensed a single, unbroken unity was the meaning and *power* of the glyph.

The throne had been how this people had tried to stay connected to their past, but it had become only a rickety, ghoulish seat. A tradition without conviction or direction.

The king gave a faraway-looking smile. "Thalia says I'm unfit because I'm always looking back. But there's much worth remembering . . ." Then Relothian drew his sword and held it out to Sutter. "To replace the Sedagin blade I ruined."

Shouts and rushing footsteps filled the hall beyond the throne room. A moment later, the doors crashed inward, and men bearing swords and pikes swept in. Their arrival snapped Thalia from her state of shock, and a look of grave certainty stole back into her face.

"Brother, peace is more expensive than war," Thalia declared, "and requires more strength."

"Strength?" Relothian said, incredulous.

"Before I stepped in, your forges annealed ordinary blades. I brought you palontite to make Alon steel." She paused a moment, pointing at the sword in his hands. "But that rock can only be bought one way, from one place."

"You forsook your people—"

"No," she said. "I'm simply willing to trade the lives of a few to save the lives of thousands. I'm the one who has been building your army, Jaales. With greater strength we can broker peace with Nallan. And stop this endless war!"

"Nallan won't negotiate for peace—"

"You're wrong. I've already met with King Solomy. He assures me they are weary, too." She gave a smug smile. "But I'm no fool. I'll only sign the truce once our own army is able to enforce it."

"*You* will sign a truce?" Relothian's voice cut throughout the throne room.

Thalia stepped defiantly forward. "They're not savages, Jaales. They're like us. Do you even remember why we're at war? Do you know how it started?" She waved a dismissive hand. "Of course you don't. No one does. It's madness."

Relothian said nothing for several moments. Everyone seemed to be waiting for him to deny Thalia's claim, explain how the war had begun. With a look of admission, he nodded. "You're right, Thalia. I don't know how it began."

She smiled in vindication.

"But," said Relothian, "I know how it's been in *my* life. Years ago I was weary, too. I sent word to my generals to ask for a meeting on the field. To bargain for peace. They met with Nallan. They were seized. Over the next several days, eight of our best men were kept alive by Levate hands, as their arms and legs were carefully removed. Each night they were forced to sit and watch Nallan field captains sup on the braised flesh of those taken limbs."

Sutter shivered, and looked to Mira, whose expression had become hard.

The king finished softly, "They returned those men to us, armless, legless, strapped to the backs of asses. Most of them soon took their own lives with the help of friends. Those who didn't are broken men you'd no longer recognize." Relothian looked up at Thalia. "You're being used against me."

"You tell lies," she said. "Why are we hearing about this now? Why would you keep this from us?"

"To remove its sting," he explained. "Nallan's purpose was to paralyze us with fear. Instead, we kept it secret, and declared those men fallen heroes."

Thalia began shaking her head. "That won't happen again. We'll negotiate from a position of strength."

"They won't negotiate, Thalia," repeated the king, "and neither will we."

"This is why you must step down, Jaales. This war has become about your pride and glory. Don't you see?"

Relothian offered a soft laugh. "I agree with you on one point, this war has become too much about glory"—he settled a firm look on her—"and not enough about honor." He glanced at Sutter and then the throne. "That will change."

She raised her arms to indicate those soldiers beside and behind her. "And it will change with the army I've been building now for years while you've been watching men march the parade yard." There was earnestness and excitement in her eyes. "It will change with Alon steel. It will change with gearsmiths building better gears. Peace through strength, Jaales."

Relothian showed his sister a tender look. "Thalia . . . they're children."

The woman said nothing, her expression unreadable, and somehow more awful for that.

"And why do they want them?" The way the king asked it, Sutter didn't think the man wanted the answer.

Thalia simply shook her head. "You're a good man, Jaales. But you're not a good king. Step down. Please. I ask you this one last time."

"My dear Thalia, you don't understand war. It is not a game. And Nallan is not a bedfellow." Relothian's hard glare swept across all the well-dressed, well-fed generals and advisors who stood with her. "And even if you could do what you say, every citizen of the land I call home would rather die than buy peace with a child's life."

Sutter thought he saw regret in her eyes when she said, "Kill them all."

The scar-faced general barked and his men formed a line between the king and Thalia. The fray broke out immediately. Men wearing the same Ir-Caul uniforms fought one another, their swords clashing and filling the throne room with the noise of battle.

"Follow me," Yenola said, and rushed to the rear of the room.

The king didn't move. Instead, he gently but firmly pushed his sword and sheath into Sutter's hands. "Go with her. Protect her."

"We should help you—"

Relothian offered a gracious smile. "You and one Far?"

Sutter spared a look at Mira, remembering her disappearing Far gifts.

"My sister and your friend need you more. And this here." He pointed at the brawl behind them. "It'll be a hard fight, but we won't lose." Relothian then glanced at the throne, his eyes still holding some awe at the sight of it. "We lost the meaning of the bones." He looked back at Sutter. "Now we remember *why* we fight. I cannot go to Convocation, especially now, but my best man will leave this hour for Recityv to announce our allegiance to its cause. You have my word."

"I'm sure Convocation is over," Sutter observed.

The king grinned. "Nonsense. Convocation isn't an event. It's a promise. They'll take our support when we show up to give it."

"Thank you." Sutter ducked as something sailed past his head.

The king took him in a handgrip only a smith could possibly have. And only a rootdigger could possibly bear. The two shared a kinship Sutter wouldn't have imagined when he first arrived.

He then quickly strapped on the king's sword near his Sedagin blade. He and Mira hurried to catch up with Yenola. In the far corner of the throne room, the king's sister pressed a small stone in the wall. An unseen door swung inward, revealing a dark corridor.

"Wait," Sutter said.

Yenola looked up at him as he drew his sword. "Where are you going?"

Sutter gave her a quick look. "I can't leave like this. I'm going to help your brother."

"Don't be a hero. We need to get you two out of Ir-Caul." She nodded toward the dark hallway.

"I'm no hero. But I don't let friends fight alone."

Yenola's face hardened. "Then let's all go."

Mira handed the king's sister one of her blades and they started back toward the fight.

"Bet you expect me to stop you," he said, striding beside Yenola.

"You could try." She tapped his knee with the flat of her sword.

Sutter jumped to Relothian's side. Together they fought at the center of the line. Yenola was to his left; she'd found her sister, Thalia—the two locked in their own fight.

A blade came hard at Sutter's chest. He parried the blow and thrust his blade into the man's gut, dropping him.

The king shook his head. Smiled. "You're a fool. But it's good to have you at my side." He lowered a crushing blow on his own assailant.

Two men rushed Sutter next. Before they got to him, the king stepped in and brought a huge forge hammer down on one man's wrist. Bone cracked. The man screamed and dropped his weapon. Sutter lowered his center, bending his knees, and ducked under the second attacker's strike, stabbing up hard into the man's gut.

A few of the king's men had fallen, but they gave better than they got. The clamor had dimmed by half, men fallen or fleeing, when General Marston stepped toward the king. By silent agreement, men gave the two opponents room.

"You should have been satisfied bedding my sister, and left the throne alone." The smith king spun his hammer in his hand.

"She's a shrew. But she had her uses." Marston raised his sword and shield.

As the two circled, Sutter spied one of Marston's men against the far wall, crossbow cocked. The man was waiting for his general to draw the king around for a clear shot. Sooner or later the king would be exposed.

Sutter looked around quickly, and saw a fallen short ax. *Like splitting wood,* he thought. He scooped up the ax and came up throwing. He imagined a tree at the far side of their stock pen and let the ax fly. Concentrating on his aim, the general's man didn't see the ax coming. The blade buried itself deep in his side, and he dropped his crossbow.

A flurry of battle followed. The king took several cuts, one particularly deep in the forearm. But the gleam in his eye never wavered. And a few moments later, he blocked a thrust, spun the general's weapon out of his hand, and shoved his hammer into the man's throat, crushing his larynx. The general fell, flopped, clutched at his neck, then went still.

A scream rose, and Sutter turned to see Yenola with her blade buried in her sister's belly.

"You whore!" Thalia cried. "You've no idea what you've done!"

Yenola remained silent while her sister dropped first to her knees, then to her ass, and finally lay down, heaving. "Wrong. I know exactly what I've done." The words were quiet, but clear.

An instant later, Sutter saw Mira take a knife in the side. She'd been a half moment too slow to evade it. She returned her attacker a death blow in the throat.

A few more men fell. A few more ran. In the end, the smith king had lost eight. Thalia and her betraying general were both dead and had lost nineteen of their own. No telling how many had abandoned their would-be queen.

"They'll bring support," Sutter suggested.

"Maybe. But when they see the head has been cut off, they'll lose their enthusiasm." He flipped his hammer up; it spun three times before he caught it again by its bloody grip. "I'll see to that. Now, you," he turned to Sutter, "will you be on your way. A king could begin to think he can't get along without you."

They shared a last smith grip over weary smiles before Yenola led Sutter back to the corridor. He helped Mira, who struggled a little to walk.

Their eyes adjusted to the dark as they navigated by the light of the room behind them. Moments later, that light flickered, then went out. Quickly after came hurried footfalls. *Chasing* footfalls.

Yenola grabbed his hand and pulled. "Thalia's supporters. Come from an adjoining corridor. Run!"

"This is getting ridiculous," Sutter said, looking back.

"Hurry," she said, and yanked him deeper into the corridor. They moved more swiftly, guiding themselves with their hands against the walls. They turned several times, moving for what seemed like half a league.

With the rushing steps of their pursuers echoing toward

them, they came to a set of stairs that led down to a door with a small window that admitted faint light. They went down quickly, Mira missing a few steps and nearly pitching forward. At the bottom, Sutter looked back and saw the three men halfway down the stair, gaining fast.

As Yenola fumbled for a keystone, Sutter raised his sword, his lungs burning from exertion. Mira clung tightly to him. She'd never cried out, though her body had tensed often as she bit back pain.

Boots descending on the stairs produced a maddening mix of echoes. Sutter prepared to climb a few steps to block their pursuers, when Yenola pulled the heavy door open, revealing the light of stars over an open plain. They'd gotten to the city's edge.

Once outside, Sutter let go of Mira, thinking he'd help brace the door. The Far dropped to her knees, her eyes shut tight in discomfort.

From the dark corridor shouts rose up. He had just started toward Yenola, who'd begun to close the door, when a dagger flashed through the thin opening and buried itself in the girl's shoulder.

Yenola flew back, hitting the ground hard. Sutter launched himself at the door. Before he could get it shut, a man wearing the Relothian lion slipped through, brandishing a sword as he rushed for Yenola.

Sutter finished closing the door, turned, and drew his blade. As he did, he watched his lover get to her feet, pull the dagger from her shoulder, and circle on the man. The solider made a quick sword-lunge at her. With expert grace, she deflected the attack and stepped in close, burying his own dagger in his belly. He groaned and dropped to his knees. A look of hard determination lit Yenola's face as she pulled the dagger out and put it into the side of the man's neck. His eyes closed and he slumped to the ground.

Before Sutter could get there, she dropped and rolled over on her back.

Sutter rushed to her side and knelt, breathless. "I'll get help."

Yenola grabbed his sleeve. "You don't have time for that.

I'll be fine." She swallowed, the look of it difficult. "Is it possible to fall in love so fast? Or is that just me wanting to think I was not a—"

"It's possible," Sutter said, and smiled to share his own feelings. "But you might have wanted to die. Save yourself from a life beside a rootdigger."

She smiled back, blood now over part of her lips.

Guilt seemed still to linger in her face. "I'm sorry," she said. "I was a fool."

"I think you turned that around," Sutter replied, nodding.

Then her expression became determined again. "I won't let this court forget what you've shown us. You've reminded us of who we are. Our honor. I'll be sure it's carried through."

Looking at her, Sutter had no doubt of it.

Through the quiet, the sound of hooves approached. None of them rose when the rider stopped nearby. If this stranger meant them harm, they'd be little help to themselves. The man jumped to the ground and walked directly to Sutter and Yenola, leading two mounts. He handed Sutter the reins to their horses. "The lady told me to meet you here," he said, looking at Yenola. "Your mounts are fed and rested, and your saddlebags are ready with food and water. There are ointments, too." He glanced at Mira. "But you should go quickly. It's likely I was followed."

Sutter looked back at Yenola. "You've thought of everything."

"Well, clearly not everything." She reached up to the wound in her shoulder.

The rider went around and helped her up. "My lady, we should go."

Yenola nodded, and stepped close to Sutter, wrapping him in a one-arm embrace. "You come back. I've no idea how to plant a garden."

Sutter laughed, and kissed her. Then the rider helped her into his saddle, and they started off in the other direction at a canter.

He'd only known her a few days, though it seemed longer. She'd meant more to him than he realized. And he instinctively knew it wasn't simply that she'd been the first woman he'd lain down with. He wasn't such a fool as that. A different kind of fool, sure.

He helped Mira into his saddle, and climbed up behind her. He spared a look down at Relothian's sword on his hip. It reminded him that he shouldn't show his Sedagin gifts. He removed his glove and once again adopted the persona of his friend. He would play the part of Tahn now until they reached the Randeur. Taking hold of the reins, he led them southwest, moving at as brisk a pace as he dared, given Mira's condition.

With a new kind of determination, he looked into the darkened horizon toward Estem Salo. Dear absent gods, but he missed his roots.

• CHAPTER NINETY-TWO •

Echoes of a Song

What you need to understand, what you'll learn, is that we don't sing Suffering for ourselves.

—Final instruction offered to Leiholan before
their first day of Suffering

WENDRA RACED THROUGH the corridors of Descant, rushing toward the Chamber of Anthems, toward Suffering. Something now sounded . . . wrong. Strained.
Wine-colored moon.

She turned down a final hall, stirring candles as she ran. Her own shadow leapt in the light of the silent flames, coursing up vaulted halls and down the corridor ahead. Besides the low hum of Suffering, only her feet made any sound, marking a desperate rhythm in the silence.

A moment later she was at the Anthem door, and pushed through. Inside, she came to an abrupt stop.

The great domed hall appeared to have no walls. Instead, at the center of a vast plain stood a lone singer, head tilted slightly back, intoning what at that moment sounded like a plea. The woman raised her arms in a kind of supplication. Her song lifted softly but certainly into a vast sky and out against faraway peaks that Wendra thought were themselves alive, listening. The power of Suffering had virtually transported this Leiholan woman, who took no note of Wendra as she stood watching in amazement.

The song grew more agitated, more staccato. The horizon darkened with the shapes of countless flying things moving against the far range of mountains. The air charged as it does in a lightning storm, growing musty and warm and pregnant with the imminence of a strike.

Then came rain. Real rain. Falling hard from a cloud-darkened sky above, pelting down on the Leiholan and Wendra and the floor, which appeared like a hardened, varied terrain, and not smooth Descant stone.

Into the storm, a crack of lightning sizzled. A thunderous roar followed, rumbling not up the walls of the Chamber of Anthems, which Wendra could no longer see, but out across the land.

The song grew strident and loud and challenging, tearing through the wind and rain. At that moment, Wendra heard the *wrongness* again. And the Leiholan faltered. Fell. She struggled to keep singing, but she'd landed on her face. Her nose and lips were bleeding. And she was out of breath besides. The dark shapes grew larger, more clear. They filled the sky. They came by foot, too. And they pushed ahead of them a feeling of sorrow like a wave you could feel pressing on your skin.

The Leiholan gasped and choked out what song she could.

From the other side of the chamber, a door seemed to open in midair, and a young man stepped into the scene. He crossed toward to the fallen young woman, his own lips beginning to move, picking up the lyric and melody and rhythm in perfect unison. But stronger. Then he was at the first singer's side as she stopped singing altogether. Wendra rushed forward on instinct, helping support the young woman as the young man focused his attention on the Song, his commanding voice rising into the coming gloom.

Wendra had only gotten a few steps back toward the door, when she heard the crack of bones on stone. She turned to see the new singer fallen, clutching at his throat, fighting hard to keep the song alive. He looked over at her, panicked and pleading. Wendra gave him a firm look. *Sing hard!*

He turned back into the scene, the greys and silvers and blacks, and pushed. He did well for a few moments, but then his tones grew strangled, and he went forward onto his hands, barely able to utter a note.

What's happening? What do I do?

She thought of Soluna. She thought of the Quiet army on the Soliel plain. She thought of broken instruments, and breed stock traders, and shotal, and singing to the inside of someone, and a dysphonic Suffering.

She let go the Leiholan she was carrying, and rushed not to the young man but to the music stand. She glanced down at countless pages written in music notation. Notation she could read. She picked up the top sheet, feeling its waxen surface—to protect it from the elements—and scanned. She did the same with three pages, taking them not note for note, but in general. Movements. Key changes. Feel. Tempo. The words. The meaning.

Then the young man ceased to sing. There was a deafening silence that lay under the wind and rain and roll of thunder over the hard ground. A deafening silence that came ahead of whatever raced toward them out of the deep places brought to life by Suffering.

Pray the deafened gods I don't get this wrong.

She started to sing. The words were what she'd read. The notes were the same. She caught the meter and sound of it all. But the feeling. The shotal. The intention. These things she changed. Or perhaps she sang them the only way *she* knew how.

She started low, soft, getting the music underneath her, using those first passages to warm her throat.

In those moments, the young man struggled to his feet. She caught his eye, seeing gratitude and some worry, too. She nodded toward the woman lying a few strides away. *Get her out of here.*

He nodded back and went to the other Leiholan, lifted her up, and carried her out. Wendra was alone in the Chamber of Anthems. Singing Suffering. The vision around her was a place and time she didn't know. But it was more than a vision. There were no chamber walls. The sky was filled with dark clouds dropping rain. The air hung with the smell of old dry earth struck by that rain. The wind pulled at her hair. And the Quiet came. She saw them. But more than that, she could feel them. She could feel their long bitterness, and indifference to the sufferings of men. This was not simple remembrance. This was war. It was real. And paralyzing.

Not today, she thought. *Come Quiet or chorus, not today!* And she let go.

Her voice rose in a crushing crescendo of dysphonic staccato. It echoed like a great torn bell out over the darkened plain. Up into the grey skies. It shrieked toward whatever was shrieking toward her. Defiance. A warning. It was Suffering. But it wasn't simply a recounting of what had been. Or even a reenactment. This was new. It was the voice of pain in every way she'd ever known it.

She hit a great, high note. And began to find a cadence. Everything on the page she'd read, she sang an octave up. And roughened. And voiced in clipped, harsh beats like the strike of a hammer against stone.

And as her song gave Suffering life, it connected to that wave of sorrow. Connected to the Quiet that descended toward this chamber, as though it were a great Telling that had opened a way into this place. This time. And while she took in a new ache, connected to all this, she also made sure they felt what *she* had to share. She made use of that connection to be sure they knew what *her* song had done. Could do. Made damn sure they knew that, in these next few pages of song, she was willing to die if she had to, if they came.

Your song finds the darkness, doesn't it, my girl.

She had no idea if this was what always happened when singing this passage of Suffering. But it was all she could think to do. And it felt right.

The Quiet did not slow.

And somehow she thought the song *had* changed. Not because she sang it her own way. But because this attack was different from the way the story of Desolation had actually occurred when the world broke. And from the way it had been sung for ages ever since.

From the sky above, over broken stone, and from inside her own fractured memory, Wendra endured the assault. Suffering had grown beyond a relation of events. Or a song. It had become this moment. It was all these things, and her own brokenness besides.

She raised her chin and began to sing-shout the next set of phrases, calling the Quiet out. Challenging them to come at her. And they did. It was too dark to know exactly what descended from the sky, or rushed over land. But each one that came she shouted down. Her body was soaked with rain. The ground around her slippery. Weapons were raised. Massive arms swept toward her from high, from low.

But as each came, she drew up from inside her resonances she felt would touch them. And she found those same resonances inside the song, inside these creatures out of history. *I am attuned. Attuned to them.* And they fell. One after the other. They fell.

She knew she'd taken a step closer to absolute sound.

Before her now rushed an army, a legion of Quiet memories come here to tear away the barrier between them and this place. Between then and now.

The dark flying shapes fell heavily around her, crashing and crushing the soil and rock. Figures large and immense dove toward her. Wendra shouted a note or two at each. And they, too, fell. The bodies stacking.

She thought she might tire. But in some way, the song strengthened her. Each passage made her feel she could sing longer. Louder.

And soon, the shapes stopped running and rushing. They slowed. Walked. They were regarding her from far away, aware that she was singing the Song differently. They watched, waited, measured.

It infuriated her. She leapt up on top of the largest downed

Quiet and renewed Suffering. She focused on the resonance she could feel inside them, on that connection she'd known before. But it became everything now. And she made her song travel that connection, unseen, but direct and into the bodies and minds of her enemy.

As Belamae did when he was a young man fighting in his own war . . .

More Quiet fell. Their thoughtful, placid faces slackened, their eyelids closed, and they fell. Scores of them. Her song swept outward like a wind coursing across a field of wheat, undulating like a wave. And the roll of it was Quiet deaths, races unknown to her falling as a resonant note inside them rang too loud. A suffering note that grew too much for them to bear.

Then something in the air changed. She was like the charge in summer air before a lightning storm. A moment later, they came at her again. Not rushing, but with a steady march they came. And not all at once, but individually.

She turned her song on each of them as they approached. But the sound didn't find them, didn't slow them. *Why isn't it working now?* No glee or wicked indignation shone in their faces. They simply came, staring at her with awful indifference. Some looked like Bar'dyn. Some winged gracefully down as if coasting on great thermals. There came Maeres, like those that chased her from the Hollows. Creatures on four legs. On six. Others looked very much like men. And women. None growled or gnashed. They simply came.

Inside this very performance of Suffering, the need of the Song had changed. How it must be sung had changed. *Or had they adapted? Is that even possible?* Perhaps she just hadn't found the signature of these Quiet.

Looking into the slowly advancing faces, she began to worry. They were close. And she didn't know how to resonate with them. She couldn't find the right Suffering.

Then a thought. *Maybe some songs can move only one. Some Sufferings individual.*

In those moments, she found the center of her intention, shotal, the current of life in these Quiet. In each. One by one. *You both are changed.*

She faced the closest one of them, a creature with limbs as thick as trunks, hide like old elm. It came hard, eager and indifferent, to strike her down with its one arm. She sang to it alone.

An image of it working in a camp filled with humans. Of one man grown tired, falling in a dredging field, and this Quiet reaching to stop his fall.

Later, a saw-blade had removed its arm for doing so. To make an example.

She saw the lost limb. *It* saw the lost limb. It was not stirred. It came on, carrying an impossibly long sword. It brought it around to cleave her in two. She shout-sang, finding the resonant note inside what was left of it.

Its eyes fluttered and it crashed down hard before her.

She shifted fast to a Quiet flier descending on her now in a rush. This creature had the features of one of the sculpted stone beasts that stood watch over burial grounds and churches.

Images rose of family, parents that were too old to be useful. Their old wings were clipped, and their scrabbling bodies tossed into open-air gardens on the side of a great mountain where younger of their kind ate them.

This child-creature had starved, because it would not eat.

The flier dove at her, remembering, and struck loud notes inside Wendra. But she embraced them and lifted Suffering to it, stilling its wings. She had to jump out of the way as it nearly fell on top of her.

Next came a creature with a heavily corded neck and the scars of brands over its entire body. Hollow cheeks set in a narrow face. Sinewy muscles in a tall frame. And a placid expression. Wendra sang to it alone.

Images of forced copulation. The get of those unions being deemed inadequate and silenced. If they came at all.

The creature's eyes widened slightly, and it began to rush her. Still no anger, but some urgency. It raised a long hammer.

Wendra shifted her song to a stabbing shout and gave his resonant notes all their awful sound. His body went limp, his face fell to peace, and he crashed down at her feet.

One by one, she faced them, modulating Suffering to strike the notes of their hearts. And the things she saw, witnessed . . . lived, they remade her. A little, anyways. Her own sound and song changed. The vibrations of her life were altered. Wendra's own anguish deepened.

And as she sang these moments of Suffering, this movement of the song known simply as "War," she noted something more: a measure of control. It *was* her song. It was filled with her shotal sound. But it wasn't random or blind. She'd taken Suffering and sung it the way it needed today to be sung.

And over the next several passages, the attack ended. The army that she could see and hear and feel—those that remained—simply stood, looking at her. In the connection she shared with them she sensed no anger. No shame.

The rain subsided. The movement of music that followed was a different kind of singing. Mournful. Resigned. Like endings. It was called "Self-slaughter." Wendra sang it at the dark shapes as they retreated back into the far mountains and night skies. And even that song changed in the singing. Somewhere along its sad passages, she stopped singing it *at* them. And started singing it *for* them.

She didn't know how long she'd been at it when she realized she stood alone on the darkened plain, singing about one taking her own life. Or the life of someone who wants to die but cannot do it for herself. That song wasn't rough and loud. It was low tones. It was a barrow weeper's broken cant.

And she wept as she sang it. Wept because she understood the song's meaning. Understood that many of those sent into the Bourne chose to end their life rather than be bound there. Failing to win their war meant more than failing to earn the right to live with men in the east. For many it would have a final meaning.

Then a sound interrupted her song. Or rather joined it. Much as the young man had joined the first Leiholan's song, another voice now picked up Wendra's melody in perfect unison. She turned to see another man, this one considerably older, step gently toward her. He put a hand on her shoulder as together they offered a lament over those who would take their own lives. Or who *had* taken their own lives, since Suffering described events from the Craven Season.

Except this was real. This happened today. Just now.

Then, this Leiholan man nudged her in the direction where she'd find the door, though she seemed still in a different, real place. Wendra nodded and began to move away, continuing to sing. She finally let Suffering go as her outstretched hands found a wall she couldn't see, and she pushed out into the corridor.

As she went, the Song tugged at her to return. *Not today.*

Across the hall, Wendra saw the young Leiholan woman who'd fallen. She sat wrapped in a large blanket on a cushioned bench. She shivered there as one long in the cold. The Leiholan who'd helped her leave the chamber knelt before her, briskly rubbing her hands and arms.

The woman said nothing, her lips trembling. Her wet hair hung down in front of her face, and quivered with the shudders of her body. Something wasn't right. The girl then raised her eyes, aware of herself, it seemed, for the first time in several minutes. "Thank you," she managed.

Wendra studied her face. "The Song is changing, isn't it?"

The young woman stared back, unspeaking. Her silence, Wendra thought, wasn't because she was reluctant to tell the truth, but because she couldn't put it into words. Finally, she just nodded.

"The words, the melodies, they're the same." The young Leiholan slumped further forward. "But the way they must be sung is different. To combat the visions, to make them real. And the images that are returned from Suffering are more . . . insistent. Even the historical sections. It's as if the events of the past want to be rewritten . . . *are* being rewritten."

Wendra listened intently, phrases of Suffering still playing in her mind. Heavier now. They tugged at her again to return and sing. "How do you know how to adapt the song?"

The girl rubbed warmth into herself, and slowly stopped shivering. "You're the new Leiholan."

Wendra nodded.

The girl offered a weak smile. "There's a lesson. Comes much, much later. Inola, it's called. Closest way to explain it is *intuition*. Has to do with attunement. And it's something . . ."

"Yes?" Wendra gently urged.

". . . you don't always get it right." She offered Wendra an apologetic smile. "I heard what you did. I've never heard Suffering sung that way. Today, you got it right. Though I have no idea how you managed it. Unless it was inola."

Today, you got it right. It felt like the kind of thing that once you'd learned it, you were somehow accountable for it, too. Like when a child finally has the courage to talk about what happens when a father comes into the room late at night with bitter on his breath.

In the hall outside the Chamber of Anthems, the young woman offered a terrible insight.

"This kind of singing"—she nodded as though to affirm her own words—"it's more than just resonance." Her voice became distant-sounding. "Some songs can't be unsung."

A chill raced across Wendra's skin. What about the songs she'd sung since learning of her gift? What resonances had she taken into herself, what echoes had she begun? A new burden settled over her as she thought about the next time she'd have to sing.

The sound of Suffering grew inside her. The weight of the Song got into her flesh. She now burned with fever.

Moments later, footfalls came in a running rhythm. Soon Belamae and two attendants rushed into view, bearing handlamps.

Belamae's two companions helped the two Leiholan up, and escorted them away, gently supporting the young woman on each side. The glow of their lamps receded, leaving him staring at Wendra over the top of his own lamp. His face took a warm cast from the small flame. She had the sense that he knew her education had just been enlarged in a way he could never have taught.

"What you did tonight, Wendra . . ." His eyes were distant, as though seeing possibilities he'd rather not consider. "Thank you. We might have lost another Leiholan, as we lost Soluna . . ."

He cleared his throat, emotionally resetting himself.

She told him then about the bloodred moon she'd seen on the Soliel. And she told him she thought Soluna's death had corresponded to that moon, and to the Quiet breaching the Veil and attacking Naltus. His eyes showed understanding.

"We have an eclipse tonight," she finished. "But with Ardua."

"Telaya has been researching these things for us." He pulled at his chin with his thumb and forefinger. "We're starting to see patterns for when and why Leiholan fall ill." He paused. Shook his head. "A lunar eclipse of both moons. Our good fortune. Damn."

With her fingers, Wendra brushed back her wet hair. She couldn't stop thinking about the Chamber of Anthems, and how it had *changed*. "Tell me again how the Song affects the Veil from so far away?"

He offered a gentle smile. "It's absolute sound, Wendra."

She nodded, struggling to concentrate. Her body felt like cast iron slowly being heated on forge coals, but it was the heat in her mind that worried her. She had the sensation that at any moment, her mind would tear free of her flesh and she'd be nothing more than an echo of song.

It changed me. I changed when I sang it.

"Sound carries on indefinitely?" This idea worried her deeply.

"Vibrations carry on indefinitely," he clarified. "Or touch things infinitely. I'm no scientist, but somehow the vibrations of our song touch the Veil."

Or reach backward to the Placing itself.

"And there," Belamae continued, "they are enough to strengthen the Veil, modifying its composition in the smallest of ways. But that's not so hard to understand, is it? In small ways, many things are made strong."

She suddenly recalled something Telaya had said: *There was a time, Wendra, when thought and sound were taught as the same thing.*

"And when we begin to view song this way, we see the

power of absolute sound, don't we? Some songs needn't be heard to have effect." He smiled as though delighted at the opportunity to begin tying their discussions together. "You also learned that every song has a place. A time. And that every song is different with every rendering. That's important knowledge to have."

"Suffering is changing," she said, looking at the door, beyond which the Song was still being sung.

"Of course it's changing," Belamae agreed.

"No, not as each rendering of a song is different." She struggled with the right words to make it clear, her head now filled with a pounding rhythm and melody—a Suffering kind. "This isn't the color of a vowel or the brightness of a pitch. Or even inola."

His brows went up in surprise that she'd heard of this concept. *Yes, a mere minute ago.*

She shook her head. "The way it needs to be sung is changing, Belamae." She looked back at him, expecting to see disbelief, needing him to understand.

The elder Maesteri was nodding. "I know, my girl. And we're learning how to do so. You taught us quite a lot about that tonight. But," he raised a finger, "despite your success, I won't send you back into Anthems to sing Suffering again until your training is complete. I'm grateful. But what you did was damn risky. Much as I wish you were, you're just not ready to sustain it."

Wendra thought about the Quiet races that had descended on her, and knew she'd come very close to dying.

"Damn risky for *you*," Belamae added, ". . . and for the Song, too."

She collapsed to her knees, feeling sick inside. The pain of her bones striking Descant stone was a faraway sensation. It seemed everything lay muted beneath the Song filling her mind. And in the cacophony of echoes and choruses that only she seemed to hear, she began to forget who she was. She felt a moment of gratitude for the forgetting, until she could no longer remember why she was grateful.

The weight of Song grew inside her. Sweat flowed freely

from her skin. Her vision swam as she fell over, her head bouncing once on the stone.

There was blackness. But no end to the Song.

It was that way a long time.

Then a new sound came to her. A low, droning note. It silenced all other notes. It demanded complete attention. She listened. Followed. And light returned to her eyes. Color. She could hear again with her ears, not just her mind.

She had a sudden errant thought about absolute sound. *It's the signature of a thing that can be touched at any distance . . . with a song.*

A few moments later, the low, droning voice became soft words. "Each of us is a song. A changing song. But one worth singing, no matter how old or broken."

Wendra lay a long time, staring up at Belamae. She heard only her breathing as it slowed. She sighed deeply. "Thank you."

Belamae put a hand on her forehead, smiled, and nodded. "You'll be fine. But you won't be singing Suffering again anytime soon."

She heard more in his words than their simple meaning. "What are you saying?"

"You and I are ill-fated to never finish anything we begin, aren't we?" he answered.

Wendra looked back at Belamae, more confused.

The Maesteri let out a breath. "As much as I wish we had time to talk about what just happened, or even just continue your training, an envoy is leaving tonight, headed for Y'Tilat Mor. It's an old land. One which mostly keeps to itself. Has for centuries."

"Then why is someone going there now?" A dull dread began to spread inside her.

"The Mor nations have a distinctive culture, one you'll appreciate more than most: They create with song. And much of it is dysphonic song."

She remembered then Belamae's refashioning of Suffering, which he took into his homeland, the Mor nations, as a younger man, for war.

His expression turned serious. "You already know the Quiet are pushing at their bonds. You felt it this very hour." Belamae pointed at the door to the Chamber of Anthems. "We'll need help against them if the Veil falls. And the Mor nations have a set of refrains—songs imbued with a kind of power. They create an aural storm—" The Maesteri cut himself short.

"Why are you telling me this?" She could guess the reason, and was preparing to argue the point.

Belamae offered his paternal smile. "Because, my child, you must go with the envoy to the Mor nations."

She looked back, her feeling of dread answered, but with a seed of understanding. "Because of my own song."

The Maesteri nodded. "That's right. I can't afford to send any of the fully trained Leiholan. They're needed to sing Suffering."

"Send another student," Wendra suggested. "One with more training. Telaya—"

He shook his head. "No, you're the right one to go. You've only had a few lessons, but your understanding and ability are that of a three-year student." His smile deepened in the lines of his cheeks. "Despite your having brayed your dark song at me, I consider you my abaretteli, my labraetates."

Wendra shook her head in confusion and shrugged.

"My protégé. But that's rather a weak way to say it. It's a designation that will, by itself, mean something to the Mors."

She shrugged again. "How will my songs help?"

Belamae's smile faltered, his gaze instantly looking past her toward some image he must have held in his mind. His next words came slowly, carefully. "The Mor Nation Refrains are very old songs. They arise from a place of pure and extreme brutality, though some are likewise as simple and beautiful as a flower opening itself to morning sun. Both airs," Belamae explained, his eyes again focusing on her, "are . . . exacting. They're not unlike the harsh songs you've found on your own. Except that by comparison, Wendra, their severity is the difference between light . . . and the absence of light."

Worse than my own song?

"The refrains will be needed if Suffering fails and the Veil falls." Belamae looked again at the door to the Chamber of Anthems. "And in you they'll sense a kindred ability. The amplitude of your gift will convince them that song hasn't gone out of man. There's hope in that. But you need to remember control. You've learned a great deal, but you're at a delicate place in your training . . . control the darker songs if they come."

I have *learned some control.*

Belamae's eyes showed some impatience then, something Wendra had rarely seen in the man. "There isn't much time. You must gather your things and get to Solath Mahnus within the hour. Recityv needs to be far behind you when the sun rises."

Staring back at him, Wendra considered the request. She admitted part of her liked the idea of a place where her songs would be accepted. Most of all, she wanted to learn anything that could help her against those who had taken Penit, taken her own child . . . against those who sold men and women and children into the Bourne. Those were songs she wanted to hear, to sing. They might help her if she meant to go to the Bourne, to free as many captives taken there as she could. Maybe she'd put an end to the stock trade altogether.

Thinking of the Bourne and those traded into Quiet hands, she nodded and stood, ready to go. Belamae rose himself, taking hold of her hands. "Be careful, my child."

Then he hugged her close. She felt the warmth of the man, smelled the mild musk of his robes. She couldn't help but feel like she was hugging her own father, and understood it was the love and concern the old man had for her that made the difference.

Then he stepped back and gave her a reassuring nod. Wendra offered a slight smile and rushed to her room. She gathered her things quickly and quietly, wrapped herself in her traveling cloak, and soon found herself striding from the Descant steps into the dark hours of a Recityv evening.

She might well return to Descant, finish her training, and

sing Suffering again. She might also go to the Mor nations. But not today. And probably not soon. Before anything else, she would be led by a different need. A feeling that she must do something about all those being taken into the Bourne. People caught and sold by highwaymen like the one who'd taken her. And she now had more musical tools to help her do it.

Once out of sight of the cathedral, she turned left, not in the direction of Solath Mahnus, but in the direction of the river. In the direction, she hoped, of Jastail. And eventually, the Bourne.

She stopped only once, thinking about how her mother had also walked away from Descant and Suffering. She wondered if Vocencia had also been changed by Suffering, as Wendra had. Because despite Belamae's restorative song, something inside her was not the same.

Singing resonance changes both the singer and the thing resonated with.

Suffering was now inside her. Part of who she was. *How* she was.

For now, though, she was able to relax as a mild evening wind flowed around her. She let the songs of things wash over her. She eased through the streets, drawn by a powerful, low-pitched song she felt rather than heard. The song of the river. It gave her a kind of companionship that suggested she might never be alone.

Epilogue

*The heavens make music. And if you watch the stars close
enough, you'll hear it.*

—Spoken to Tahn, age seven, by Mother Polaema, on his first
night away from the Scar, hours after another of his friends
had chosen to take his own life

TAHN STARED UP from his chair at the night sky. Around
him Polaema, Rithy, his Succession team, Martin, and
Shaylas—holding her baby—passed out cups for a toast.
They were in the rear open-air portion of a quiet mealhouse
at the east end of Aubade Grove. Cornhusks, it was called.
It was a place that let Martin hold court for his friends, and it
served the best hot drinks, besides. Martin liked to play out
skits and rhea-fols here. Tahn had seen dozens of them when
he'd been here as a boy.

"Here you go, Gnomon," Martin said, handing him the
warm drink with a bit of flair. "With my own hint of concern added."

Tahn arched a questioning brow.

"It's chocolate blended into cream milk," Rithy said fac-
tually.

"With some mint leaves and a capful of something to
sharpen it up," Martin added, romancing the drink some.

"Brandy," Rithy said, adding the last fact.

"Never cared much for mathematicians," Martin observed.
"But this one's got a sense of humor. I like her." He took a
sip of his chocolate. "Now then, our toast. Polaema?"

Mother Polaema raised her cup. "Gladly. First, I'll remind
you all that we've only had one argument so far. And opinions vary on whether it's the easiest or hardest in Succession
to win." She glanced at Rithy with a good-natured grin on her
face. "But it's worth celebrating. We're now in the College of

Physics ledger as having shown a possible explanation for Continuity."

"Resonance," Martin supplied. "My dear dead gods, what a thought. I can't wait to watch what happens with the College of Mathematics." He slapped his forehead. "Ho, and after that: the philosophers. I may sell admission to that one, Gnomon!"

Polaema lifted her cup and drank, signaling for them to join her. They all did. Martin had indeed sharpened the chocolate. But only a little. Mostly it tasted of mint and cocoa, and reminded Tahn of so many chill nights taking measurements of stars. He'd almost never done so without one of Martin's capped mugs of steaming chocolate. He looked back up at the sky, as he'd been doing when they brought him his drink.

"You're wondering about the chalkboard, aren't you?" Martin asked.

Tahn dropped his gaze again. "Scalinou was right, wasn't he?" Tahn wiped his lips, remembering the night he'd spent in the cosmology dome, just before he'd had to leave the Grove.

"He's one fine astronomer for a cosmologist." Martin laughed and slapped Tahn's shoulder. "But it sure looks that way. Pliny Soray is off her course." It was Martin's turn to look up. "The grand clock is telling a funny time."

"The math says more than that," Rithy interjected.

Both Tahn and Martin looked over at her with questioning eyes.

She shrugged. "I don't know what yet. But I don't think it's just a planet that's found a different way around the sun. Something made her go astray."

Martin rubbed his hands together. "I love a mystery. It's the only thing that got me to quit the pageant wagons. These high-heaven secrets need our attention."

"But why do you hide it on the chalkboard?" Tahn asked. "I'm sure there are plenty in the Grove who've seen Soray off her course."

His old friend pointed at Rithy. "It's like your friend says, the math tells more than that. And the math on that board belongs to Lour."

My skies, Lour Nail. Lour used to be a member of the Grove. A philosopher. But he'd been run out. Lived north of the city. He'd become one of Tahn's best friends while he was here.

"How is he?" Tahn asked.

"Foul as ever," Martin said, smiling wide. "But I don't know a better philosopher . . . or star man."

Tahn wanted to see his old friend. But it would have to wait until after the argument with the College of Mathematics. Then, perhaps, Lour might even be of help to him. Especially in preparation for his Succession argument with Darius.

Shaylas' babe uttered a weak cry, and settled back into her mother's arms. Tahn wondered what dreams the child had that would cause its momentary distress. *And who cradled me the way Shaylas cradles her child?* He'd learned Grant was his father. But his earliest memories were of the Scar, and no wife or mother had lived with them there. Only later did Vocencia begin taking care of him in the Hollows. And as much as she'd loved him, she'd not been the one who would have soothed him as a babe.

The unanswerable question gave way to images of his father. The thought of Grant, and the Scarred Lands, and the babies left in the hollow of a tree for his da to try and place in a home . . . it reminded him of the wards of the Scar. Tahn's friends. It reminded him that some of those friends had given up and taken their own lives in the wastes of that desolate place. *Thirty-seven.*

But the darker memories didn't claim him tonight. He was comfortable. And happy. Perhaps never so happy. He was in the company of friends, and doing something he was good at. And for a damned good reason.

There was a lot of work ahead. A lot of reading and researching and arguing. They'd have to prepare to face the College of Mathematics, the College of Philosophy, the College of Cosmology, his own College of Astronomy. He was eager for every test. He nearly wanted to leave their celebration now and get started. It had been a long time since he'd felt so useful, so needed. So able and ready. He couldn't help his sense of urgency and excitement.

There were large questions to answer. Perhaps one of them was the math on Martin's hidden chalkboard. Tahn guessed it had something to do with his reason for being here. But for now, they needed to focus on the College of Mathematics.

"Rithy?"

She turned, sipping her chocolate.

"I was serious, you know." He smiled, taking another healthy draught off his own cup.

"About me singing?" she said, not missing a beat. She really did know him in an uncanny sort of way.

He nodded. Laughed.

"I know what you meant," she said. "We'll have a look. But not tonight. Tonight we should be happy the physicists didn't have their way with us."

"I couldn't agree more."

Tahn finished his cup and made his way to every person there, to thank them: Mother Polaema, Rithy—who he very nearly kissed—and the rest of his Succession team, Martin, and lastly Shaylas. She hadn't been part of the argument. Nor even part of the discussion about Pliny Soray, their stray planet. But he went to her and thanked her anyway. Thanked her for a different reason. Thanked her on behalf of her child . . . who would never know a Scar. Not if he could help it.

· GLOSSARY ·

Abandonment, the: The cessation of Creation at the hands of the Framers, and their subsequent abandonment and absence from the lives of men.

Aeshau: From the Language of the Covenant, meaning "gathered."

Age: A reckoning of time roughly equivalent to a thousand years.

Anais (Ah-NAY): An honorific used for women, derived from Anais Layosah Reyal.

Ars and Arsa (AHRS and AHRS-ah): Alternate terms from the Covenant Language for "body" and "spirit," denoting also the beauty and elegance of both sides of Creation individually and as a unified whole.

Artificer: See Quietus.

Ayron (EYE-rahn): A Far drink made of plain yogurt and water.

Baenel (Bay-NELL): Covenant Language term meaning "eternally left behind."

Bar'dyn: Creatures created at the hands of Quietus to balance the efforts of the Council of Creation, and consigned to the Bourne at the Abandonment. Three heads taller than a tall man, they have a thick, fibrous skin as resilient as most armor. Due to its roughness, the skin often appears to move independent of the muscle and bone beneath. They have protruding cheekbones and long arms ending in hands with a thumb on each side of three taloned fingers. Still, they make use of weapons, and possess an unsettling intelligence belied by their brutish appearance. Their strength is expressed in a common folk myth that with their bare hands they could crush stone.

Blade of Seasons: A blade forged from a block of metal

folded a thousand times. It is said to have the power of remembering.

boards, the: A term referring to the platforms where the human auctions take place.

Bourne, the: The great area north and west of the Eastlands where the races given life by Quietus were sent and sealed behind the Veil.

Castigation, the: When Regent Corihehn of Recityv sent the Sedagin people to almost certain death, the Randeur of the Sheason sent his Order into the court and council of every nation and caused them, upon threat of death, to reassemble in Recityv to honor Corihehn's lie and go to help the Sedagin.

Chamber of Anthems: A great round hall in Descant Cathedral, where the Leiholan sing the Song of Suffering.

Change, the: See Standing.

Charter, the: A legendary code of principles and dictums, said to have been authored in the Language of the Covenant by the Council at Creation, it sets forth the fundamental covenants of life, the model for joyful living, and the universal laws that govern all Forda I'Forza. It is said to be the mind of the Great Fathers, the hope of man. Yet it remains largely a myth, with but a few of its tenets still uttered on the lips of men, and these known only by oral tradition too old to be reliable. Still, invoking the very name of this treatise inspires silence and reflection.

Children of Soliel: See Far.

Civilization Order: Order authored by the League of Civility that makes rendering the Will, or asking a Sheason to do so, a crime punishable by death.

Convocation of Seats: A council called first by King Sechen Baellor to answer the threat of the Bourne in the war of the First Promise. The convocation seated rulers from almost every nation known to Baellor. Its unified efforts helped bring the war of the First Promise to an end.

court wastery: Sewage area of a big city or palace.

Covenant Tongue (or Language of the Covenant): A language used by the Framers to put the world in place.

Cradle of the Scar: A dead, white tree not far inside the Scarred Lands. The tree bears a hollow at a height just above the head of an average-sized man.

Craven Season: The age that followed the High Season. Known as craven because the designs of the First Ones seemingly came to naught, leaving the land in a state of debility. During this period, the Veil weakened and gradually let slip those hidden up in the Bourne, resulting in the Convocation of Seats and the War of the First Promise.

crest of Mira Far: White banner with two red swords described in vertical lines, one pointing up, the other down.

crest of the Sodality: A quill dancing on the flat edge of a horizontal sword, typically rendered in white and black.

crest of Vohnce: A tree with as many roots as branches, typically white upon a crimson field.

collough (Kul-LAW): A term defining the standard military complement of the Bar'dyn; typically numbering about a thousand.

dark hour: Midnight.

Dissent: A legal term for a case or issue brought before a court.

Dissenter: A legal term for one who brings a Dissent or dispute before the court.

Draethmorte: Those first Adherents to the cause of Quietus, given the right and privilege to direct the Will by Maldea himself. Some believe they were created when the Artificer knew he would not be allowed to finish his work and at great personal cost formed from his belly and mind these sacred few to aid him in the ages that would follow.

Drum of Nicholae: A mythic instrument that, when played, it is said, causes the hearts of all those fighting beneath its drummer's banner to beat in unison, effectively creating one great heart to thrust upon the enemy. The legend tells that the drum is an inelegant thing, with a dark origin.

dust gone up: A phrase used by traders and highwaymen to refer to the auctions held to sell human stock. It is derived from the chalk put to the feet of those to be auctioned.

Alternately, the phrase refers to mortality, dust being the reduced Forda of mortal flesh, life.

earthsky: A common term, meaning horizon.

Emerit (EM-ehrit): A warrior with sworn fealty to men and women of station. His feats of prowess might only be surpassed by his keen intellect. It is a title bequeathed on only the greatest fighter by only the highest office of government.

Estem Salo (EH-stehm SA-low): The seat of Sheason leadership, inhabited primarily by those of the Order and their families. It is said to be a small city of energetic thought and applied principle.

Far: A race that lives in the Soliel Stretches and is known for exceptional speed and weapons handling. Legend holds that they live a shortened life, having been given a commission by the First Ones ages ago. Little is known about them, to the point that distant nations consider the Far nothing more than an authors' story. Few have ever seen a Far, as they remain a reclusive and well-protected race in the harsh terrain of the Soliel.

final earth: Euphemism for either death or a grave.

First Fathers: See Framers.

First Ones: See Framers.

First Promise, the: A covenant to answer every injustice with an equal measure of justice. The First Promise was entered into by nearly every nation, kingdom, principality, throne, and dominion with a government to be represented at the Convocation of Seats. It was the beginning of the end of all things craven, and gave men hope again after the Abandonment. Fealty and honor meant something between friends and countrymen. Equity and fairness were the highest law, and scarcely anything needed to be codified or written, one's word being as certain a thing as the dawning of another day.

First Steward: The honorific given to one who stands as witness to a melura's Change.

Fleetfoot: See Far.

Forda (FOHR-dah): From the Covenant Language, meaning "matter" or "body," and sometimes "earth."

Forda I'Forza (FOHR-dah ee-FOHR-zah): The union of matter and energy, body and spirit, earth and sky, that makes up life. Even the First Ones are bound by the laws of this governing dynamic. One without the other collapses, and is brought to unhappiness or stasis. It is a delicate balance, upset by Maldea during the creation of the world and for which he was Whited and bound.

Forgotten Cradle: See Cradle of the Scar.

Forza (FOHR-zah): From the Covenant Language, meaning "spirit" or "energy," and sometimes "sky."

Framers: The gods who created the world of Aeshau Vaal.

gave me the crawls: A colloquial phrase meaning "it was creepy."

handcoin: Worth ten jots or plugs. Sometimes called simply "a coin."

Hargrove (HAR-grohv): A renowned poet, whose work often took historical themes.

High Council: A body of select representatives empowered to enact change and provision for Recityv in particular and the nation of Vohnce in general.

Hollows, the: A small town in the Hollows Forest. It's name changed over time, as it was once known as "The Hallows," consecrated to protect those residing therein from the Quiet, should they come into the land.

hostaugh (Hoh-STAW): A poisonous serpent from the Mal.

Inner Resonance: See Sheason.

Inveterae (In-VEHT-er-eye): If the stories are to be believed, the Inveterae are those creatures given life at the hands of the First Ones (not Maldea, but the others of the Creation Council), yet still consigned to the Bourne alongside the Quiet. Most Eastland folk consider this folklore created to keep children in line.

jaybird: A euphemism for the male genitalia.

Je'holta (Jeh-HOHLT-ah): A gathering of thought and feeling from things tangible—even if inanimate—and given form in a dark fog that coaxes those enveloped within it to experience their own fears. It carries voices that belong to souls lost while serving Maldea, tainted and languid because there is no redemption for them. They cry, their hollow voices audible within Je'holta, like a touchstone of awful remembrance. It is a unique instrument of the Quiet. It may be called spontaneously anywhere, having no imprisonment behind the Veil. See also Male'Siriptus.

Jo'ha'nel (JOE-hah-nell): Legend holds him to be the presiding member of Quietus's servants. Rumors abound of diaries held deep in the libraries of Estem Salo that bear the handwriting of this Quietgiven. It is said that he was the first to follow Maldea. There are old stories about his first fight with Palamon for the lives of men.

Jurshah (JER-shaw): A complement of four Leaguemen in which each of the four League disciplines is represented. Originally, each branch of the League represented simply the four directions on a map. Now, these disciplines pursue separate fundamental skills deemed needful by His Leadership: politics, justice and defense, history, and finance and commerce. Just as the directions on a map combine to indicate middling courses, so too are their factions with covert purposes unspoken of by His Leadership.

Kaemen Sire (KAY-men SIGH-er): The second organized entrance into the Eastlands by the Bourne was led by a creature of unknown origin. Some believed Kaemen Sire to be one of Maldea's first creations, others a Draethmorte, and still others are sure it was Inveterae. Whatever the truth, its madness and rage was said to blind men for merely looking upon it. The defeat of the Quiet during the War of the Second Promise did not claim this creature, which escaped back beyond the Veil.

King Sechen Baellor (SEH-shen BAY-lohr) the Swift: The king of Vohnce—which later moved to a more representative government—at the beginning of the War of the First Promise. Baellor called the first Convocation of Seats.

Latae: Used with "dance" or "stance" to describe a series of battle motions learned by the Far for battle.

Layosah (LAY-oh-saw), the Great Defense of: Referring to one of the Wombs of War who shamed King Baellor into calling the First Convocation of Seats.

Leadership, His: Euphemism for the leader of League of Civility, currently Roth Staned.

League of Civility: An association of presumably civic-minded militants who believe that enlightenment trumps all. Self-appointed administrators of the law, they are dedicated to the quelling of insurgency that runs counter to their described goals: peace, equality, and prosperity. In the interest of their creed, they have made strict enemies of the Sheason by forcing ratification of a "Civilization" order (death) executable upon evidence of a Sheason's exercise of the Will. The League holds that rendering the Will is at best an arcane practice with unnatural and unholy origins, smacking of stories that assume the reality of the Great Fathers, and ultimately becomes nothing more than a cover for deception and manipulation of the working class. With four branches—politics, justice and defense, history, and finance and commerce—the League has evolved to have political representation in almost every nation. Their sigil is four arms in a circle, each gripping the wrist of the next, now extolled as a metaphor for unity of the people, though originally a symbol of its four branches, each branch coming to emphasize particular goals in the interest of the League.

Leiholan (LAY-ih-HOLE-uhn): From the Language of the Covenant, meaning "Wrought by Song." An inborn ability to exercise the Will through song. It is a gift of Resonance. The term is also used to refer to one who possesses the gift.

Lesher Roon (LESH-uhr ROON): A race run at Recityv by children ages twelve and below. The winner occupies a seat at the regent's High Table as the Child's Voice, and is thus a member of the High Council, able to cast a vote in all decisions that relate to Recityv and the nation of Vohnce.

Levate (LEH-vuht): One who practices the healing arts.

Library of Common Understanding: A repository of laws and codified principles by which all residents of Recityv, and to a larger extent Vohnce, may be reasonably expected to be held. It is also the immense library that serves the nation of Vohnce.

light storm: Also sometimes known as a Forza storm, this phenomenon appears as a series of light bursts with no apparent source.

Loneot: A renowned architect from the flourishing years of the Dispensation of Hope.

longblades: Euphemistic name for Sedagin. See also Sedagin.

Low Ones: A disparaging term applied to those born with abnormalities. Also sometimes used to refer to any not highborn.

Lul'Masi (Lull-mah-SEE): A race of Inveterae escaped from the Bourne during the War of the First Promise. Similar to the Bar'dyn in stature, they stand three full strides tall, and have broad, flat features. Most notable is the sheer size of their legs, which cause them to move in more of a gallop than a run, swinging each leg out around the muscled bulk of their thighs. Known for their stoic natures and generally reclusive tendencies.

Lyren (LEER-uhn): Music students at Descant Cathedral. Typically describes students early in their studies and those without Leiholan abilities.

Maesteri (My-STAIR-ee): Instructors of music at Descant Cathedral.

Mal i'mente (MAHL ee-MEHNT): An imprecatory prayer offered in battle by Maere Quietgiven that holds the power to alter the substance and fabric of its adversary's life. It is an unhallowed phrase of the Covenant Language.

Mal Wars: A series of wars focused west of the Divide in the Mal lands during the Age of Disdain, giving evidence to the thinning of the Veil along the Rim. The failure of the Second Promise left the Sedagin unwilling to commit itself. And most rulers had no desire to see the Convocation of Seats re-called.

Male'Siriptus (Mahl-eh-Sih-RIP-toos): Most often referred to as "the caress of Male'Siriptus," it is sometimes used in place of Je'holta. Though it is a singular term, giving a single, unending voice and hand to a host of shadows and dark fates. Male'Siriptus is what Je'holta can do, by surfacing darkness of fear to the individual.

Maere (MAYR): A servant of Quietus, these are wraithlike creatures. It is believed that the Maere are the final state of those who've lost their physical lives in service to Maldea, living a fate they wish to extend to those still alive in the flesh.

melura (Meh-LOOR-ah): The term used to describe someone who has not yet reached the age of eighteen and undergone the Change.

meridian: Midday, noontime.

Mor Nation Refrains: A mythic set of songs held safe by the Mor Nations. Said to bear more power even than Suffering.

Noble Ones: See Great Fathers.

Northsun: A festival now largely observed only in rural communities where the League has yet to exert any real control. It is a celebration of the sun's northernmost passage through the sky, and a time of reckoning one's age. It is likewise often attended by a Reader, who brings news and recites histories and stories to entertain and remind.

Ogea (OH-gee-uh): A Reader who comes to the Hollows at Northsun to relate the stories of ages past.

Opawn, Hambley (oh-PAWN, HAM-blee): Proprietor of the Fieldstone Inn located in the Hollows.

Ophal're'Donn: The bridge crossing the Lesule River into Stonemount.

order, the: See Sheason.

pageant wagon: A large traveling wagon on which a troupe plays rhea-fols (plays) for communities large and small.

Palamon (PAL-uh-mahn): Often regarded as the first Sheason, he is a hero to those who oppose the Bourne.

Passat (Puh-SAHT): A reverent festival held at Midwinter in the Hollows to commemorate the spark of life and light within, and the hope for a return from the long nights of winter to the long days of summer. Hollowed gourds are fitted with candles emblematic of both observations.

Pauper's Drum: See Drum of Nicholae.

penaebra (Peh-NAY-brah): A ghost of the dead.

pinchcomb: A kind of barrette used for a woman's hair.

Placing, the: Thought to refer to the consignment of Inveterae in the Bourne. Alternately meaning the dire days when all things were sealed behind the Veil. Some believe it refers to secrets even Quietus does not know that are held at the farthest reaches beyond the Rim.

Preserved Will, law of: A law understood as existing in the Charter, in which any action that might be shown to harmonize with the design of the Will cannot be prosecuted as unlawful.

Quiet, the: The name, singular or plural, given to those who follow Quietus.

Quietus: One from the Council of Creation, known then as Maldea, given responsibility for establishing balance in the world. His vaulting ambition and exceeding ability toppled the delicate scales of harmony as he brought forth unimaginable darkness and creatures out of madness to harrow the races given life in the land. For his crime, the Council Whited him, binding him in a far place where there would be little opportunity to stretch forth his hand to exercise the Will.

Qum'rahm'se (Coom-rahm-SAY): A library established ages ago to gather and study any and all available documents relating to the Language of the Covenant.

Randeur (RAN-djeeoohr): A title given to the leader of the Order of Sheason. In the Language of the Covenant, it is thought to mean "descended below them all."

Reader: A branch of the Scola given entirely to the study of history and books for the purpose of relating the stories to others. Readers are often considered to be seers and scryers, as well as historians and fanciful storytellers.

Resonance: A principle that underlies a Sheason's ability to render the Will, just as it also underlies a Leiholan's ability to render song with power and influence.

Reyal, Layosah (LAY-oh-saw Ray-AL): One of the Wombs of War during the War of the First Promise, and the one who stood on the palace steps in Recityv and called for a council to do something more concerted to combat the Quietgiven, resulting in the Convocation of Seats.

rhea-fol (RAY-fohl): A dramatic presentation with actors typically inspired by a historical event.

Right Arm of the Promise: Name given to the people later known as the Sedagin for the zeal and loyalty of their service in the War of the First Promise. See Sedagin.

Rudierd Tillinghast (ROOD-yahrd TILL-eeng-ghast): From the Language of the Covenant, meaning "return of all things."

Scar, the: Abbreviated term for the Scarred Lands.

Scarred Lands: An area east and slightly north of Recityv where the last battle of the War of the Second Promise took place. That battle is also known sometimes as the Battle of the Scar or the Battle of the Round. The Scarred Lands have lost their vitality due to being raped by the Velle, who drew their essence and life to darkly render the Will during that great last stage of the war.

scriveners: A highly literate association whose purpose is to assist in the collection of ancient documents and genealogy, with emphasis on studying the Covenant Language and its applications.

Season of Rumors: Name some have given to the current age.

Second Promise: An attempt to renew of the First Promise, added upon by a spoken commitment to end, once and for all, the shedding of blood by emissaries of Quietus. It was forsaken by some governments, either because they never attended the Second Convocation of Seats, or because they did and simply didn't keep their word.

Sedagin (Sehd-ah-gin): Name of the people living in the High Plains whose mastery with a greatsword is legendary. They live by the principles of the First Promise.

SeFeery, Denolan (she-FEER-ee): See also Grant.

Sento, Belamae (BELL-ah-may SENT-oh): Chief Maesteri at Descant Cathedral.

Sheason (SHAY-son): From the Language of the Covenant, meaning "servant." Members of this Order possess the ability to render the Will—influence Forda I'Forza. When the First Ones abandoned their work in Aeshau Vaal, they conferred the authority to direct the Will in the interest of men to Palamon. The right and privilege to render has since been passed down only after vigorous training. Though the Order was conceived on the principle of service and sacrifice, they are often disliked or distrusted. Much of this has grown under the influence of the League of Civility. The Sheason are also sometimes known as "three-ring" for the emblem that signifies their order: three rings inside of each other, and all meeting at one point. This same symbol also describes another name the Sheason bear: Inner Resonance.

Shenflear: An acclaimed writer of the early years of the Craven Season.

Sky, the: The overreaching, never-ending constant of life. Often used interchangeably with the word "life," it connotes assurance, stability. The sky holds the sure patterns and procession of the stars, and the unvarying, necessary return of the sun and daylight. It represents that which is known without being touched or proven. "The Sky" is also the shortened term for "Tabernacle of the Sky."

Slope Nyne: Tenendra word for Bar'dyn. See Bar'dyn.

sodalist: A member of the Sodality, and one given to the study of the Authors as well as the crafts of war. Ancient diaries define the sodalist as both Author and Finisher, though the meaning of the phrase is unclear. See also Sodality. By virtue of a sodalist's study, he or she often serves in a community as teacher, Levate, and counselor.

Sodality: A brotherhood of men and women aligned to protect the integrity of Authors' words, and to bring them to bear in conjunction with the bite of steel. The Sodality's highest call is as protectorate to the Order of Sheason, to which it holds a solemn oath.

Solath Mahnus: The buildings and castle constructed on a risen hill in the center of Recityv, where governing activities are held.

Song of Suffering (also called just "Suffering"): The musical rendering of the Tract of Desolation, performed in the Chamber of Anthems of Descant Cathedral. Sung entirely in the Language of the Covenant, a single performance has but one refrain and lasts seven hours.

song of the feathered, the: Colloquial phrase referring to morning time.

spine-root: A low-lying plant which grows barbs and needles.

Standing (or to Stand): A rite of passage which takes place at the first full moon after a melura's eighteenth birthday. The ceremony is witnessed by a First Steward, typically the child's father or mother. Beyond this time, the child becomes an adult, and is considered responsible thereafter for his or her actions.

Staned, Roth (STAN-ed, ROTH): Defender of Civility himself, Roth is the Ascendant of the League of Civility, its ranking officer, and often referred to as "His Leadership."

Stem: A paper rolled with tobacco inside to be smoked.

Stipple toes: A common cooking root similar to rhubarb.

Stonemount: An abandoned city near the Valley of Lesule almost entirely constructed of stone: granite, marble, and other indigenous rock. Legend holds that the inhabitants simply vanished, no war or disease accounting for their disappearance.

Storalaith, Helaina (Hel-AY-nah Stohr-uh-LAY-eth): Regent of the nation of Vohnce, who wields discretionary power of the High Council and all other governmental powers of Vohnce and Recityv alike.

Stranger: See Quietus.

straw-drift: Backstreet folk; moneygrubbers, informants, thieves, etc.

Strong-wagon: A large, heavy wagon with thick walls used to convey important cargo.

sword and quill: Emblem of the Sodality. See Sodality.

Ta'Opin (Tah-oh-PIHN): One of the Mor races. Rumor and myth surrounds their origins. Some believe them to be a lost race escaped from the Bourne, one of the Inveterae. A race unusually strong with song, they are generally unwelcome around others, though their outward geniality and fierce loyalty belies this social estrangement.

Tabernacle of the Sky: A set of great, tall buildings and theaters in the heart of the Divide where it is believed the First Ones worked to bring about Creation.

Table of Blades: The ruling body of the Sedagin people.

Teheale (Te-HEEL): From the Language of the Covenant, meaning "earned in blood." It is the High Plain risen by the power of the Order of Sheason as a gift and home for the Sedagin.

Telling, a: Written by an Author, a specialized document used to travel from one place to another through a kind of portal. Most Tellings are made usable by the gifts of the Leiholan.

tenendra (Tuh-NEHN-drah): A large traveling carnival where feats of strength, acrobatics, strange sights, merriment, games, and exotic foods can be had for a price.

tent folk: Euphemism for those who work the tenendra.

Therus (THEER-uhs): The Quietgiven name for a Sodalist.

three-ring: Euphemism for a Sheason, due to the sigil they bear of three rings—one inside the next—all touching on one side.

Tillinghast: A place on the far side of the Saeculorum Mountains, where the earth falls away into clouds, and it is said one has all their choices returned to them.

tongue-money: Common term referring to money used to buy someone's silence.

Tracker: A Quietgiven that moves upon the land with ease, possessing an unearthly skill to follow anything that lives. Some believe the tracker's capability is to see or smell the passage of Forza, the residue of which remains in a place much longer than physical—Forda—traces. Their skin is hairless and translucent, showing striated lines over jutting bone, and their eyes protrude like a dead, bloated animal's.

Tract of Desolation: The written account of what transpired when Maldea was Whited and all those given life by his hand were sent into the Bourne.

upright dust: See walking earth.

Veil, the: The boundary between the Bourne and the races of the Eastlands of Aeshau Vaal, maintained (it is thought) by the Song of Suffering.

Velle (VEHL-uh): These renderers of the Will serve Quietus. Some came to their dark path through the baser, self-gratifying motivations of avarice and vanity. They sully the authority to direct the Will by transferring the personal cost to other living things. By so doing, they cheat death a long time, their own Forda hardly depleting. In every age since the Abandonment, there have been Sheason impatient and wanton enough for their own gain and comfort to reject their covenant and embrace the reward of the Quiet. Most, though, are descended from other Velle inside the Bourne who grant the power—usually too soon—to others to grow their ranks. From the Covenant Language, meaning, "my wish, my desire, or my will."

Walkers: When the Abandonment took place, there remained a few Inveterae "untabernacled"—without a physical form in which to live or experience joy and adversity. Forgotten by the First Ones, they were not herded into the Bourne with the rest. Thus twice forgotten, these lonely children of Forza seek a suit of flesh to wear. With no authority to command living things, they attempt to claim the lost bodies of others to make themselves finally whole. Over time, their bitterness and their own dark arts have grown.

walking earth: Used to refer to one who is alive, but doomed.

Wall of Remembrance: The wall surrounding the Halls of Solath Mahnus to provide privacy and protection, but more importantly to chronicle the history of Recityv and its place in the events of the family of man.

War of the First Promise: During the Craven Season, the Veil weakened and Quietgiven escaped the Bourne. The war to press them back to their confinement lasted four hundred years and brought into existence the First Promise and the Convocations of Seats.

War of the Second Promise: The Quiet again descended into the Eastlands. From several points beyond the Veil, they came, more purposeful and more studied in their use of the Will. Individual nations could not alone fight back the threat to their people, so the Convocation of Seats was re-called. The Right Arm of the Promise, the Sedagin longblades, was called to march into the breach.

Responding promptly, they did so, losing every man when the Army of the Second Promise—supposedly comprised of battalions from every nation in the Second Convocation—never arrived to relieve them. This Second war lasted two hundred and sixty years before the Quiet were pushed back.

we are made: A colloquial expression meaning "it's a deal."

went to his earth: Euphemism for death.

Whited One: See Quietus.

Whiting, the: The marking and punishment of Maldea for his overreaching ambition. This describes the event where the Creation Council stripped all color from Maldea and gave him his new name: Quietus.

Widows' Village: A dreary settlement where surviving spouses of Sheason reside, having been robbed of the Undying Vow of their marriages by the Velle—and some by other means.

Will, the: The power whereby all things are created, and without which there can be no growth or progression. Rendering the Will, causing change in Forda I'Forza, has a price, which is nothing less than the same, Forda I'Forza. For matter and energy cannot be created or destroyed, only changed, transubstantiated, rendered. Balance can be maintained if the renderer offers his own matter and energy, body and spirit, to the exchange. Transference of the personal cost to a secondary source of Forda I'Forza deepens the wound of disharmony between the two sides of Creation—matter and energy.

winter's pen: The writing an Author completes during the winter.

womb: Derogatory term used to refer to human females by the Bar'dyn.

Wombs of War: A term the women of the First War of Promise gave themselves, when wives and mothers gave up their children to the army ranks to defeat the Quiet. It resulted from generation after generation of women giving birth to yet another generation of children who went to war.

• FROM BOOK THREE OF •

The Vault of Heaven

PETER ORULLIAN

Coming in Fall 2017
from Tom Doherty Associates

A TOR BOOK

• CHAPTER TWENTY THREE •

The Might of Few Words

Through the backstreets of Reinyard, the poets skulked with the kind of stealth Sutter would have attributed to a flimflam man, or an alley clipper. They crept through the shadows, their cloaks pulled around them, hoods drawn far forward, little more than shadows themselves. He only hoped that, beneath the folds of those cloaks, these poets carried more than rhyme.

At the edge of the city they moved swiftly toward *the hole*—a compound dug into the face of the hill. As they strode through the chill air, V'Saunche handed Sutter a short sword.

Sutter took the blade and used it to point. "In and to the right. About five cells down on the left."

V'Saunche nodded. "Stay behind us. If the League discovers we're here, don't get in the way. Watch our back. Let us know if anyone tries to come in from behind."

"I'm not exactly new to swordplay," Sutter began to argue. "I—"

"We've no time for your qualifications. Do as I say." She spoke with playful condescension, a thin smile on her lips.

If they weren't able to get in and out without being noticed, Sutter couldn't imagine what six poets were going to do against so many trained leaguemen. But he raised his hands in a surrendering motion. "Fine. But my friend is in there, too. So if this begins to go badly—"

"Of course," the poetess said, with no hint of dispute or sarcasm.

Then the circle of poets began to cross the compound, bent low and moving with quiet, hurried steps. Sutter followed, sword in hand, looking back and forth across the several buildings for any sign of movement.

They'd nearly reached the entrance when a band of leaguemen filed out of the arch that led into *the hole*. They formed themselves into two lines, blocking the entrance. There must have been at least twenty of them.

"You were right," one of the men said, elbowing his mate. "He went for help. And look what he's brought. More scribblers."

His friend laughed. "Some help. Mush mouths. Spend their time on fancy words."

Another leagueman added, "He killed the captain. He'll have to stand trial."

"His trial will be conducted here at the end of my blade," said the second man.

V'Saunche motioned for her friends to spread out into a line. When they'd taken position, as though choreographed, they all threw their cloaks back off their shoulders with a theatrical flair. Sutter stood behind them, and couldn't see what made the leaguemen's faces draw tight in concentration and concern.

Then the poetess spoke, her voice easy and conversational. "This goes one of two ways, gentlemen. Either you set our friends free, or we will. If we must fight, a warning first"— she seemed to delight in offering it—"we don't fight in half measures. If we begin, it's once and for all."

One of the leaguemen stepped forward. "Poems against steel? Don't be fools. I'll give you one chance to surrender. We've more cause to throw *you* in the hole than your mother. Either way, Reinyard will be rid of your rabble-rousing."

"It's sad," V'Saunche replied, "that the noble root of your order is so far removed from its current flowering weed."

In response, several leaguemen drew their blades, some also pulling knives. One man hurled a spear at V'Saunche. The poetess easily sidestepped the long weapon, and, in a blur, tossed several small, vicious-looking daggers into the air—not at the leaguemen, but straight up. The other poets did the same.

She and her friends then uttered words soft and quick. Sutter didn't catch every syllable, but the *feel* of what he heard left him cold. At the sound, the arrow-like knives leapt upon the air and shot with impossible speed at the leaguemen. But it wasn't merely the command of the weapons that gave him chills. It was the way they moved. The daggers found their marks with an eerie prescience.

Guided by words uttered on the lips of their masters, the daggers pierced necks and eyes, and broke past teeth to pierce the backs of throats. Several men fell immediately. Cries rose up: some of pain, some of outrage. Those not hurt charged toward them, and again the poets tossed their daggers into the air. More commands followed, and, this time, he heard a snippet:

> Slip upon the air and cut
> From here to there, the bastard's throat

More knives shot through the shadows, dropping several more leaguemen as they crossed toward the poets' line. The words didn't just describe the attack, or even direct it. It seemed to Sutter like the words, the way they were spoken, prepared a path. As kids, he and Tahn would dig shallow dirt trenches in which to roll rounded river rocks in a game they called *stones*. Watching the daggers, it was like the words were carving an unseen trench in the air for the knives to follow.

But that wasn't exactly right either. It was more like a thin line of space between the dagger and its target was *emptied*. The knives were pulled at an impossible speed to their endpoint by a hard slipping void.

The leaguemen who still stood came on. Sutter raised his sword, preparing for the fray, when he heard something move behind him. He swung around to see three men running fast at their flank. He shouted a warning and ran to meet them. Before any of the poets could respond, one of the sneaking leaguemen heaved a short spear.

Sutter reached the closest man, parried an ax blow, and stuck him in the gut. The man dropped his ax and scurried away.

The sound of a scream rose up behind him.

Sutter turned to see the spear had buried itself in one of the poetess' backs. Caught in pain and surprise, the woman threw out her arms and fell to her knees. She knelt there only a moment before toppling sideways. She lay still on the cold yard. A howl of satisfaction rose from the killer, who drew two long knives and rushed at Sutter.

A battle-ax wasn't the same as a wood ax, but they weren't altogether different either, and Sutter knew how to handle and throw a wood ax well enough. He swept up the abandoned weapon and launched it at the advancing leagueman. The ax punched its way into the man's chest, dropping him, his knives skittering over the hard ground. Sutter snatched them up and turned on the third flank-man, who'd remained tentatively at the edge of the fight.

"Go home!" Sutter screamed. "Or you will join your brothers!"

The man backed away and soon raced into the darkness.

Sutter swung around to help the poets, and saw that another of them had fallen. But so had twelve leaguemen. Some lay motionless. Others grasped at wounds in futile attempts to staunch the flow of blood. The four remaining poets stood like statues before the remaining leaguemen. These eight appeared more seasoned. Their shields bore poet knives like quills. They stared a long moment, eyes and mouths in grim lines. Then they began to come forward.

V'Saunche gave a mirthless laugh. A bitter sound. She set her feet, not at all like an orator or reader or pageant-wagon buffoon, but like a woman getting ready to take a hard fist in the belly. She widened her stance, tucked her chin a bit, grinned devilishly with one corner of her mouth . . . and did the damnedest thing Sutter had ever seen. All in a swift streak of clipped poetry, she talked down the line at each leagueman.

> *Your own sword*
> *Should like your foot*

The leagueman on the far left lost control of his blade, and, like a dowsing rod, he turned it earthward, spearing through the top of his boot and pinning himself to the ground. He cried out as the heavy steel broke skin and sinew and bone.

And your own lord
Should burn like soot

The leagueman next to him began to scream as the heavy chainmail coat he wore began to smoke beneath the emblem of the League Ascendant.

And your own sword
Should like your lord

The next man in the League line lost control of his sword, which flew up and struck the man next to him—the brigade leader (their local lord)—in the neck where he wore a League tattoo.

And your own foot
Should rise like soot

The leagueman who'd just sliced open his headman's throat found his left foot beginning to rise of its own volition. It swept him up off his feet in a sudden jerk that brought the back of his head down hard on the cold-packed ground. An audible crunch sounded around the yard.

The four remaining leagueman stared a moment at what V'Saunche had done to their brothers. Instead of taking to their heels, they dashed straight for her. Sutter tried to jump between them, but she slammed her forearm across his chest, driving him back.

The other poets began short quick utterances, driving rocks up off the ground to batter the faces and necks of the rushing men.

V'Saunche pivoted a half turn, not giving a jot of ground. She glanced down at her fallen friends, and became visibly enraged, not wildly, but *solemnly*. Her jaw flexed, and she turned back toward the men. When she did, she had something in her hand. With her thumb, she flicked a heavy handcoin into the air. The men were now just a few strides away. Quickly, but with deliberateness, she seethed another verse through clenched teeth:

Yours are teeth that need to move
And yours are loins you must reprove
For you this poet's art's a waste
For you hard coin's the only taste

While the coin turned end over end, high in the gleam of torchlight, the first man's mouth exploded in a bloody mess. A few of his teeth ripped through his cheeks. The second man took a thick knife and involuntarily stabbed himself in his manhood. *Reproof.* Then a thin slip of air popped, like a tube opened fast, and the third leagueman grabbed his ears, screaming at the sudden pain and deafening silence. The last man was smiling when the large gleaming coin V'Saunche had tossed zipped into his mouth, shattering a few front teeth and lodging deep and hard in his throat. He dropped his sword and began trying to reach inside to tear it free.

The anger in the poetess ebbed, seeming to fall off as each of the leaguemen stopped moving. She and her circle of poets surveyed the many dead. Their lips moved, though they did not vocalize their words. Two of the six poets had fallen.

A long moment later, as they stood in the midst of the carnage, he did hear one of them softly reciting a poem. The sound of it was like shouldering a yolk with two heavy buckets of coal you know you have to carry up a long hill.

As blood for blood
Is given here
To nourish cold, hard ground we trod
And sere the hearts
Of those who fought
With words that curse unmindful gods.
Damn us, then.
Damn us. And we will dance
In the black pit of circumstance.

The words struck Sutter like a barrow prayer. One that might be offered at an altar made of broken stone.

He paused a moment more for the fallen, but soon realized he couldn't afford to linger. He retrieved his sword and moved past the poets, who quietly followed. They hurried into *the hole* and came fast to the cell where Mira and the authors were held. When he opened the door, A'Lissem looked up with worry in her face—Mira still lay in her lap, her eyes now shut.

They had to get her help. Fast.